Dedication

For Paul, real love.

and for all those living with Parkinson's and their carers.

Special thanks to my editor, Jane Lake.

Thanks also to Dr. Wyn Cudlip, my helpful and ever patient brother-in-law and to my old friend Nina, who was the first person to read Chapter One and encourage me with my writing.

Thank you to all those incredible people in my life who have Parkinson's who have taught me so much about living with courage and good humour, despite their daily battle – the late and much missed Harry Wright, Garth Taylor, Doreen Fenner and Geoff Mackenzie, who has just been brave enough to go through DBS.

Thanks to Matt Eagles, diagnosed at 8 years old, for his encouragement and his assurance that I had the emotional turmoil of having Parkinson's right - and to Vikki Claflin, a writer with Parkinson's, who wrote me a very kind email after reading Chapter One.

Special thanks to Paul, for everything, and to all my lovely family, especially my one in a million mum, who always made life so much fun.

Everlasting thanks to my extraordinary, wonderful and unforgettable dad, who is behind everything I do and everything I am.

But one man loved the pilgrim soul in you
And loved the sorrows of your changing face

William Butler Yeats

Preface

The February night air was ferocious and bit at my cheeks. Not that I cared. I now had a sneaky, creeping, heartless disease called Parkinson's that would, no doubt, rob me of my sense of self and make me invisible. The last few days had seen a gentle snowfall on London and standing on my patio there was an evocative white light given off by the smattering of snowflakes.

That night though it was clear and I tilted my head towards the midnight blue sky. It was littered with stars, just about seen beyond the vast city's light pollution. Why I had wandered out there I had no idea, except that I felt imprisoned by my diagnosis and needed to breathe. One star, much bigger than the rest and lower than the others, was brighter, more effervescent with its dazzling, silver pointed edges. It seemed to draw me in and I longed to touch it, feel its brilliance and bathe in its natural beauty. I raised my tremulous arms.

'Heal me,' I whispered, 'please, heal me.'

A voice, not really a voice, but almost recognised by me from somewhere in the distant past, replied out of the inky blackness.

'I will send you what you need to be healed.'

Chapter 1

Hunched and defeated like a beggar in a doorway, head drooping down like a snowdrop in a storm. Looking at his back I could tell he was a haunted man. The air was fresh and as clear as ice and a callous wind was nipping at my heels as I ran past the bandstand towards the duck pond where I first spotted him. It was a raw, bitter-blue tinged February day with a milky sun making the snow glisten like jewels. I had been jogging and my ears and nose were tingling. As I sat down beside him I noticed his hand, holding a half-smoked cigarette and shaking. I took off my trainer and shook a tiny stone out of it.

'I've given this up,' he muttered, waving the cigarette in my direction. His voice was cultured, rich and unusual like running molasses and being closer to him, he now appeared graceful, with a diffident charm and quintessentially English.

'I should think so too,' I replied, glancing at him. He had fair, silvery hair and a square, craggy face, a lived in face, with deep lines on his forehead. His eyes twinkled with mischief, even though they were almost hidden by thick, dark-framed glasses. 'It's bloody freezing, isn't it?' I added.

'It certainly is,' he said, instinctively touching the navy-blue scarf wound round his neck. 'I have no idea why I'm sitting out here when I could be drinking hot coffee somewhere warm, but this place makes me feel somewhat alive; the air biting at your face and the little ducks … you know, nature and all that.'

I felt an instant affinity with him. 'Yes, I know what you mean,' I smiled.

He glanced at my trainers. 'Isn't running about in winter terribly bad for you?' he asked, straight faced, but the humour was there again.

'No, of course it isn't; the opposite in fact.'

'Oh,' he mumbled, scrutinizing the cigarette, whose ash was drifting slowly towards the ground like the snowflakes.

'*That's* bad for you – you can't dispute that,' I told him.

The corner of his mouth turned up and the lines around his eyes formed into tiny creases, just like a crumpled piece of cloth. 'I know it is; that's why I've given it up. The doc said it had to go, so it has.'

I had to smile. 'Well, pardon me for saying, but you appear to be still smoking.'

He stared at the cigarette with surprise and indignation. 'Am I? How extraordinary. I don't know how that happened. A habit of a lifetime I'm afraid.'

The sudden, unexpected exchange amused me and the sophisticated expression on his face made me laugh out loud. And when I say out loud, I mean very loud. He gave a little jump as if shocked.

'Madam, you have the most glorious laugh.'

'Do you think so? Thanks, it just kind of comes out and there's not much I can do about it,' I explained, quite used to apologising for it.

He turned to look at me, his movements rather stiff and he seemed to be perplexed.

'Don't do anything about it,' he told me, before turning back to look at the cigarette again as if he'd never set eyes on it before.

He was wearing a black overcoat, the navy scarf, smart black trousers and impossibly shiny black leather shoes; expensive shoes most definitely, but totally unsuitable for the weather conditions. I could just see a flash of his bright red socks and they complemented the rest of his outfit perfectly. I imagined he was a bank manager, stockbroker, maybe even the Dean of the local university. This was an educated man, a gentleman with impeccable manners and speech. I didn't come across many of them in my mostly unremarkable life.

'Gotta go, have a good day,' I said, jumping up because I could feel my temperature dropping rapidly and having been sweating I didn't want to get chilled.

'A good day ...' he repeated, under his breath without looking up.

'See you then,' I added.

'Yes, yes,' he said, as if suddenly coming out of a trance and he stood up slowly. 'See you ...'

For some completely unknown reason I felt uneasy about leaving him there on his own. I didn't know the man so the feeling was inexplicable, but the haunted expression was plainly there on his crumpled face and it troubled me. I hesitated, jogging gently on the spot to keep warm.

'You'll wear yourself out doing that,' he commented, 'terribly hard on the joints.'

'I've got lots of energy, don't worry about *my* joints, 'I laughed, thinking to myself, worry about your own, at your age, sitting in the hostile and bitter cold. 'Don't sit there too long, will you?'

'I won't, I'll just watch the little ducks for a few more minutes.'

I sped away, towards the bandstand and a few flakes of snow blew across my face like confetti. Minutes later I turned and looked towards the bench, but he had already gone.

&

The day before I met her for the first time I was told I had Parkinson's disease. I didn't object so much to the Parkinson's, but I objected greatly to the 'disease' part. I had my suspicions of course because I simply couldn't ignore my symptoms; the tiny tremors, the dreadful fatigue, the muscles in my face feeling rigid, the stumbling over some words because my mouth refused to move and the occasional loss of balance. I had also noticed that typing on the keyboard had become hit and miss – mostly miss. It was all extremely tiresome and that's exactly what I told the impossibly young doctor with the soft voice and twitching eyes who blurted out my diagnosis.

'I'm sorry, Mr Marshall, but the tests have confirmed what I feared. You have Parkinson's disease.'

I let the dreaded name hang in the air for a moment before taking a deep breath.

'I knew there was something wrong. Will I end up a doddering old fool who dribbles and wets himself? Well, more of a doddering old fool than I am already?'

He had given me a wan smile that didn't exactly give me much confidence, but his words heartened me a little. 'Not if I have anything to do with it,' he declared. 'The tablet regime works very well these days.'

'It's progressive though, isn't it? I mean, you don't cure it, do you?' I asked, though God knows why because I knew the answer.

'Well, no it isn't curable, but as I said, the tablets work very well. There are four stages to Parkinson's, but you may be in the first stage for a very long time. You need to live as healthily as you can: gentle exercise, no smoking, cut down on alcohol, good nutrition; you know the drill,' he said, tapping his computer keyboard, twitching both eyes again and printing out a prescription.

'Christ,' I spat out. 'The words 'gentle exercise' are a contradiction in terms, aren't they? What kind of exercise can you do when you stumble over nothing every few steps?'

He merely twitched and gave his wan smile again. 'Start taking the tablets straight away. I promise they will help you. There will be some side effects, but that's to be expected. If for some reason they don't suit you, we'll try others, but they should really help. Give them time to get into your system though. Any problems in the meantime see your GP and if she's worried she can always send you back to me. I can also assign you a Parkinson's nurse to help you.'

And that was it. I walked out of the clinic in a dream - with a disease, and ended up in my local pub. I hadn't planned to go there, but its twinkling lights in the winter's afternoon gloom were so inviting. Three Scotches later, standing at the bar watching my hand shaking as I held my last cigarette, I realised my life had now changed forever and I hadn't even asked the doc one sensible question. I should have asked, was the low mood I had been battling for the past year to do with the disease? What about the unusual lack of interest in the opposite sex that I had put down to age, and the frantic searching for the right word in the middle of a sentence when having a conversation? Beth had phoned from America, one of her numerous calls to her dear old dad, and accused me of being drunk before lunchtime because I was apparently slurring my words.

I watched as a cold, misty darkness fell suddenly over the river and the lights in the new apartments across the black water began to sparkle. Families eating together, couples chatting, cooking their evening meal, people arriving home from work and relaxing within the warmth of their complex relationships; it all compounded my isolation and my diagnosis. The lounge bar was slowly filling up with snatches of conversation, chinking glasses and laughter. I could smell the steak cooking and I was tempted to stay, simply for the comforting sound of human voices, but my feelings of isolation were a weight across my back I could bear no longer and I shuffled out.

I didn't share my news with anyone that evening. I simply fell asleep in front of the television because of the alcohol, and when I awoke at four in the morning I still had the disease plus a stiff neck and shoulders from slumping on the sofa in an awkward position. I stumbled to bed and slept until the early, gritty February dawn filtered through the curtains. I could tell immediately by the quality of the unusual light flooding in that it had snowed heavily.

I should have stayed in and drunk copious amounts of coffee, but I had to get out. I had always loved the park and luckily for me it was literally on my doorstep. I had spent so many happy hours with Beth there, every inch of it held a memory worth smiling at: teaching her to ride her purple bike, feeding nuts to the squirrels, falling out of a rowing boat on the boating pond, pushing her on the swings and, her favourite pastime, throwing stale bread to the ducks. Many of those moments had been recorded in her story book at school.

'My Daddy stood up in the rowing boat when the man told him not to and he fell out and got wet.'

'My Daddy says squirrels are bloody pests.'

'My Daddy is the only person in the world who understands what ducks are saying when they quack.'

'My Daddy had to sleep in the car because he was so drunk at my uncle's party Mummy wouldn't let him sleep in the house.'

It made me ponder – was my fondness for anything alcoholic all these years the cause of the disease? Was my falling out of the rowing boat all that time ago the insidious painful beginning of my brain being invaded by tiny Parkinson's-shaped missiles? Those were my useless tortuous thoughts as I sat staring at the ducks where I had made up countless stories and conversations out of their incessant quacking, to amuse my three-year-old daughter.

It was frighteningly cold, I remember that and I had taken one drag of my last, well and truly last, honestly last, cigarette. As I drew the smoke slowly into my mouth it was as if it poisoned me, burning and scratching at my mouth and I coughed it up without inhaling. And I knew that was that! But I hung on to it as if it was the last thin link to a life without a disease. I had brushed a large wedge of snow off the park bench before sitting down to watch the docile, sleeping ducks with their heads buried in their feathers and I was suddenly aware of a young woman appearing from behind me, silently. She sat down and pulled off her shoe giving it a good shake. She glanced at me I think. I said, 'I've given this up,' before my Parkinson's-addled brain engaged with my frayed-at-the-edges mouth and I immediately regretted it. Sitting with a lighted cigarette between my fingers and telling a stranger I no longer smoked wasn't my best moment.

'I should think so to,' she replied, looking disgustingly healthy with cheeks blooming like new summer roses and dark hair falling across her eyes. 'It's bloody freezing, isn't it?' she added, not looking cold at all but wonderfully warm and alive.

'It is.'

That was all I could think of to say because she was full of vibrancy and glowing with health and she made me feel old and full of diseased cells. I think I babbled on about the ducks and nature while thinking that she had the most unusual eyes, grey and shaped like almonds. When I spoke she answered quickly, no hint of shyness, just straight and honest. She commented on the cigarette again and then threw her head back and laughed at my reply. I had to congratulate her on its raw power because it made me tingle inside, despite the temperature. She appeared pleased at my commenting on it because her face broke into a broad grin which completely transformed her face. I had never seen such a smile in my entire life. And on such a day; the day when my disease had become a horrible, eternal, stark reality. How could anyone have such a life-affirming smile when my body was decaying slowly?

Then she wished me a good day, which seemed terribly ironic at the time, and I mumbled something back or perhaps was ungracious and I struggled to my feet to show that really I was a terminally polite man. And then she was gone, in an instant, and within a minute it had started to snow and I shuffled away from the duck pond.

That evening I attempted to call Beth; well, a half-hearted attempt because my nerve failed me and four times I picked up the phone only to replace it a moment later. Eventually I changed my mind and sank into the sofa with a whisky. Sidney knocked on the wall three times, meaning his wife was out and, as the coast was clear, could he come in and join me for a few? Normally I would have jumped at the chance of a drink and his banter, which perfectly suited my sense of humour and knocked back three times in the affirmative. But that night I wanted to wallow in my diagnosis and so I knocked back twice – which denoted thanks, but no thanks, and I spent the evening watching my hand tremble as I raised my glass countless times. I thought about how my rake-thin body would find it almost impossible to fight the illness and how I had once been young and energetic, full of enthusiasm, sexual energy and ambition. Now, I had very little of that, but a disease instead.

I dozed in front of the expensive coal-effect fire I had bought on an impulse to remind me of the open fire in my childhood home in Sussex and crawled up to bed early, because I could no longer bear the nagging ache in my upper back and neck. Sleep was what I craved, to put another day between me and my diagnosis.

&

I awoke to a light smattering of snow on the ground and I almost took a mug of tea back to bed, but running made me feel so free and I missed that feeling if I didn't do it every day.

He was there again, on the bench, on his own, but this time he had a red woolly hat pulled low over his forehead. I knew it was him though from the way he was sitting, slightly hunched, casually elegant and watching the ducks.

'No cigarette today?' I asked, still breathing hard from my run.

'Oh, hello, no ... I've given it up, honestly,' he replied, his eyes lighting up with that look of mischief again.

'I'm really pleased to hear it.'

'All that getting out of breath isn't very good for you, you know,' he murmured, with a little smile, 'especially in this weather.'

'Actually, it's very good for me, I'll have you know. Doesn't the park look stunning like this,' I added, perching next to him.

'Yes,' he muttered, glancing around him at the trees with their branches hanging low with snow over the pond. 'Actually I hadn't really noticed, how awful.'

'Do you think the ducks feel the cold?' I asked him, because they were strangely still and silent. He gave a little chuckle.

'My daughter used to ask me that.'

'What did you tell her?'

'Well, I would pretend I could understand them ... you know, when they quacked, and I explained that their feathers were like a warm blanket and they were lovely and cosy even in the snow.'

I gave him a warm smile because I thought his explanation endearing and I imagined him as a younger man, holding his little girl's hand and reassuring her.

'I like that,' I told him.

'Do you?' he asked, looking surprised. 'She believed every word I said in those days.'

'I'm sure she still does.'

He turned towards me, his movements slow and stiff. 'That's very kind of you ... to say that. Do you run every day?'

'Most days,' I admitted, 'unless I don't feel all that.'

'Say that again.'

'Not well, feeling not well.'

'Ah, yes.'

'But I'm usually here. Not sure I've ever seen you before though.'

'I don't normally walk in the winter, I'm a fair-weather walker I'm afraid, but the last couple of days I felt like coming to see the ducks again.'

There was something in the way he spoke, the way he looked, the way he was sitting, that unsettled me.

'Because it makes you feel close to your daughter?'

'How very perceptive of you,' he said, looking wistful.

I smiled and held out my hand. 'Thanks. I'm Helen, but call me Nell.'

He took my hand in his. 'I'm Benedict Marshall, but call me Mr Marshall.'

I laughed loudly, my usual raucous, embarrassing laugh that just sprang out of me before I could stop it.

'I'm very pleased to meet you, Mr Marshall.'

'I'm only kidding, call me Benedict, please.'

'No, you said Mr Marshall, so Mr Marshall it is. I'd better keep moving. Don't get cold.'

He went to stand up, but his legs seemed to buckle and he sat down again and swore under his breath. 'I'm going in a minute – places to go, people to see. Sorry, cramp ... old age creeping up on me and the years passing with ever-increasing rapidity.'

'Did you swallow a dictionary earlier?' I laughed.

'No, I talk like this all the time,' he replied, 'I just can't help it.'

'You're funny,' I added, because he had a light in his eyes, shining with mischief and amusement.

'Why, thank you...I think.'

'You ought to come running with me one morning.'

'My dear girl, I need nourishment not punishment.'

'Bye, Mr Marshall,' I called, already on my way.

I sprinted off and briefly looked back. He was sitting with his head down and I stopped abruptly, again feeling awkward about leaving him there and, for the rest of that day, he was firmly on my mind.

&

Heavy snow fell again that night. I had woken early with cramp in my calves and an unearthly light flooded the bedroom. When Beth was a toddler I had eagerly watched the evening weather forecast in the hope she would wake to a winter wonderland, just to see the excitement on her little face. Consequently, any heavy fall would have my mind coursing backwards to building wonky snowmen, sledging in the park and snowball fights. But now, being older and having the disease, my mood plummeted because of the fear of falling and being unable to get up without a stranger's help. And I minded not feeling excited about it; I minded greatly.

I wondered fleetingly if Nell would run that day. I had an idea she would and I smiled at the thought of her – brave, hardy, free-spirited woman. The sky was a sombre rock grey and the trees in the park transformed by the fresh fall of snow. A lone robin was standing in my front garden on spindly legs, pecking for food and something in his frantic repeated movements touched me. I grabbed my coat, scarf and hat and made my way carefully downstairs. If he was that determined in his solitary quest then surely I could summon up the courage to step out into compact snow with my shaky limbs and take a walk to perhaps get a glimpse of a young woman's smile. That was my hasty, foolhardy and somewhat pathetic plan. The icy, crisp air felt like a slap round the face as I ventured towards the duck pond.

The park was almost deserted, except for a couple of intrepid dog walkers and it had a rare, desolate beauty. The pond was completely frozen over and the ducks were huddled together on the bank with their heads bowed. The snow had silenced any normal everyday sound and it was eerily tranquil. In my haste I had forgotten my gloves and my already stiffening fingers felt even worse than normal. The bed of heather behind me, usually different shades of gentle mauve and pink, was covered in a pure sparkling white blanket. There were snowdrops, exquisite in their fragility, still and graceful, dropping their heads with the cold. I glanced around me, expecting, hoping to see the figure of a runner with dark hair flying behind her, but there was no-one and my isolation and increasing fear of becoming an elderly, immobile, sick man flew up into my throat from my chest and I shuddered. What was I doing out there, for God's sake? I had to be careful now, sensible, do as I was told for once in my ridiculous life.

I had to tell Beth about my wretched diagnosis. That thought made me shudder again and I pictured her face crumpling and her singsong voice breaking on the other end of the phone. I imagined her first words – 'I'm coming home, Dad.'

And I cursed myself and all the years I had taken risks with my body and health. Those thoughts must have had an immediate impact on my limbs because I jerked violently. I then stumbled and staggered and putting one foot in front of the other became the hardest task in the world. I gritted my teeth and imagined standing there for hours with ice hanging from my hair. Hopelessness and self-pity swept over me and I imagined being found by a park keeper flat on my back, stiff with the cold. To my horror hot tears swam in my eyes and I felt completely and endlessly alone.

'Hello, Mr Marshall.'

Her voice caught me so unawares I grabbed the fence around the pond and looked up, despite hardly being able to move my stiff neck. I hoped to God she hadn't seen me stagger. 'Oh, good morning,'...

'What an earth are you doing out here in this weather?'

Her face was pink and glowing like the light around the moon and she had a multi-coloured striped hat pulled over her head and matching gloves.

'I have absolutely no idea,' I said, as an attempt at humour, but my words sounded hollow and ridiculous in the face of her honest, open manner. I decided to say what I was feeling, pure and simple – a first for me. 'No, I do know. I was hoping to get a glimpse of your lovely smile. It cheers me, makes me remember that life has a meaning ... you know?' She looked touched because her eyes softened immediately and she hung her head momentarily as if remembering something upsetting.

'That's so sweet of you, but you look frozen. Not good at your age,' she chided, trying to look serious.

'What a nerve, young woman.'

She looked down at my gnarled, white hands. 'You haven't even got any gloves on.'

'I didn't think ... I was watching this little robin ...'

She took off her own and gave them to me. 'Here, take mine.'

'No, I couldn't possibly ...'

'Take them, otherwise I'll give you an almighty shove and you'll end up face down in the snow,' she told me, pretending to be fierce. What could I say?

'Fair enough, but they'll be too small.'

She helped me put them on. 'I've got quite big hands and they will stretch. There you go, not too bad.'

'Thank you,' I muttered, feeling quite overcome by her small act of kindness.

'Isn't it magical out here?' she continued, her eyes alight with enthusiasm. 'I'm not surprised you wanted to take a walk, it all looks so wonderful in the snow. It takes my breath away.'

Listening to her, watching her animated face, it made me wonder how on earth I had missed the wonder of my surroundings. Then I realised, of course, I had been looking at the ground to make sure of my footing. But looking at the ground I had missed its vivid beauty. 'You aren't running in this, I hope,' I told her, sounding a little like Methuselah.

'No,' she shrugged, 'just walking.'

'I'm glad; it could be dangerous, even for you.'

I watched as her eyes took in my posture and manner in a split second and the look on her face was one of sympathy. Normally I would have detested anyone feeling pity for me, especially a young, attractive woman or in fact any woman at any age, but for some unearthly reason I didn't mind the pity coming from her. And, of course, I could do that quite easily myself now. Feeling sorry for myself was my new hobby. But I had the strangest notion that she and I were going to be great friends and I had no wish to hide anything from her. I had never experienced that feeling before and I had no idea where it came from. Perhaps it was age or experience, but more likely it was the disease doing something odd and unknown to my brain.

'Which way are you going?' she asked. 'I'll walk with you, shall I?'

'Well, I live in that direction, just by the gate over there.'

'Come on then,' she urged, 'lean on me, Mr Marshall.'

'Yes ... thank you ... that's very kind ...'

I was shuffling slightly, I knew that and I tried desperately hard not to, but it came so easily to me now, as easily as breathing. She didn't comment but I knew she was watching me, taking it all in. Her question didn't come as a surprise.

'What's wrong with your legs? Is it the cold? Have you got arthritis?'

'No ...'

'Sorry, sorry for asking,' she gasped, 'I shouldn't have, forgive me.'

'Ask me anything you like,' I said, leaning heavily on her arm.

'No, I should mind my own business. I've always been nosey. Lean on me a bit more otherwise you'll go arse over apex.'

I leant more heavily on her.

'Say that again. Arse over apex,' I repeated, 'what a very interesting phrase. I like it.'

13

'Do you?' she asked, looking bemused. 'And you - such a cultured man.'

'I'm not so much cultured as posh, I'll have you know.'

She looked up at me with laughing eyes. 'You can be cultured *and* posh, can't you?'

'Yes, yes, okay then, I have to admit I'm cultured and posh, but don't hold that against me.'

I wanted our slow, ambling walk to last an hour because being near her seemed to rejuvenate me, give me life, as if I had been plugged into her source of energy. We all too quickly reached the gate.

'That's my house there ... the one with the attic windows ...'

She took a sharp intake of breath. 'Not that one - I don't believe it! Bloody hell, that's my favourite house. You *are* posh, it's fabulous.'

'You think so? How kind,' I said, knowing that all my thoughts about my three-storey, red-brick, Georgian property in the last few months had been - how many stairs there were to climb, how vast it was, the size of the garden and how on earth was I going to manage?

'I've always wondered who lived here. All my life I've walked by and dreamt about what it looks like inside. I've always wanted to meet the owner of this house. You are *so* lucky,' she cried, full of enthusiasm and bubbling with energy. 'Didn't it used to be the Rectory?'

'Yes, it did. But no prayers have been said inside since I've lived there, I assure you. Come in for a coffee,' I added, hoping she would.

'That's really nice of you, but I have to get to work.'

'Yes, yes, of course; Saturday then or Sunday?' I suggested, trying not to sound too pushy and surprised at the undisguised neediness of my voice.

She gave me one of those smiles. 'Saturday would be good. Are you sure?'

'I'm more than sure.'

'Saturday it is then,' she agreed, 'and I won't be running tomorrow, so save yourself a walk in these conditions. Stay inside and keep warm.'

'Right, yes, I will, thank you,' I replied, not feeling at all embarrassed and wondering why I didn't.

'I hope your legs feel better later.'

'Fingers crossed,' I said, hanging on like grim death to my front garden fence.

'Bye, Mr Marshall.'

'Goodbye, Nell.'

His house exceeded my expectations, with its long windows, spacious Georgian rooms and huge adventurous garden. He looked better, more alert, not quite so fragile and he opened the door with gusto. He was dressed beautifully, in a dark-grey suit, open-necked blue shirt and what looked like black and white spats on his feet.

'Nell, do come in.'

'Wow, great shoes,' I gasped.

'Thank you,' he replied, surprised I had noticed. 'These were my mid-life-crisis shoes.'

'This is a dream come true for me. I've always wanted to see inside this house. I can't believe I'm actually doing this.'

'Well, I hope it doesn't disappoint you.'

'How could it?' I cried, buzzing with excitement like a mobile phone on vibrate. 'Are you going out?'

'No, why do you say that?'

'You're dressed so perfectly.'

'Well, don't tell anyone but I always dress like this,' he whispered. 'I can't stand leisure wear.'

'You look wonderful.'

He looked highly delighted with my compliment and that surprised me because I had already decided he was the kind of man who had been on the receiving end of many in his life. He was so sophisticated, elegant and charming.

'Thank you for that. This is the hall as you can see, through here the dining room and here the lounge that stretches from the front right through to the back. This is the conservatory, which is new obviously … and this side of the hall is a study and through there another dining room …'

'It's fantastic,' I gasped, walking in front of him into a spacious, octagonal, glass extension overlooking the garden. 'You must sit in here and think you're in heaven.'

'Well …'

'You must be *so* happy here.'

He shrugged his shoulders carelessly. 'I have been,' he started to say, but then his eyes glazed over as if someone had turned a light off. 'To be honest …'

'Aren't you happy here now?' I continued, butting in and he looked a little shocked.

'Your question … it's rather hard to answer. All I think about at the moment is how many stairs there are and how long it takes me to move from one large wretched room to the other. And how will I manage if I … I'm getting older and …'

I stepped forward before he had finished speaking and stood just a few inches away from his tall, impossibly thin frame.

'Why are you worried?' I asked, looking up at him, pressing him for some kind of honest answer, but he faltered and his eyelids flickered as if he was about to blink back unexpected tears. 'Sorry,' I added, jumping in again before he could open his mouth, 'there I go again, being nosey. Ignore me, pretend I'm not here. Pretend I'm on holiday.'

He smiled and his craggy features softened considerably. 'What an interesting expression. I have no intention of pretending you're not here and on holiday because I'm very glad you're here. And your questions, with your unusual, inquiring eyes and your open, honest face make me want to answer you as directly as I'm able to, but the truth is, I often haven't a clue how I feel lately. Please sit down, Nell.'

I made myself comfortable and gazed around me taking everything in: the paintings and prints on the walls, the dozens of photographs, the many bursting bookshelves, expensive furniture and curtains and lumpy old walls. 'You should be the happiest man alive living here in this old house - with its history, creaking floorboards and ghosts. All these books, have you read them all?'

'I'm afraid I have,' he admitted, rather shyly.

'It must be like living in a library,' I laughed, knowing my eyes were shining with enthusiasm. 'No wonder you talk as if you've swallowed a dictionary. You've probably even read the dictionary from cover to cover.'

'I probably have,' he said. 'I'll put the kettle on, the kitchen is through here. Do you want to see the bedrooms because they're on the next floor? I'll leave you to go up on your own, if you don't mind.'

I let out a burst of my usual laughter. 'I don't have to see the bedrooms, this will do. I get the picture. I'm very envious, Mr Marshall. I've often wondered what the park looked like from one of these windows and now I know. It's stupendous, thank you.'

'Don't be envious,' he muttered, looking at the floor.

'And the little rooms, right at the top...are they bedrooms too? They look so quaint from outside.'

'One is a tiny guest bedroom and the other is a small bathroom.'

I picked up one of the many photographs of the same young girl at various ages. 'Is this your daughter?'

'Yes, that's Beth.'

'How old is she?'

'That's the latest one of her, she's almost thirty. I'm hoping she'll come home for her birthday,' he said, walking into the kitchen. 'She's in New York.'

'She's lovely,' I called, 'and very like you.'

'Poor kid,' he called back.

'Don't be daft you have a very distinguished face.'

He appeared at the kitchen door. 'My dear young woman, when was the last time you had your eyes looked at professionally? My face is one of those easily missed in a crowd, but thank you. That's the second compliment you've paid me and I haven't had any in twenty years.'

'I don't believe that. You have something very rare.'

He looked perplexed. 'What on earth could that be?'

'Class,' I told him, 'gravitas and charisma.'

'I don't know what to say,' he replied, looking bemused, 'except that I'm grateful for your kind words.'

'Oh and lack of ego, which is quite something considering all these,' I added, looking at his numerous awards.

He gave me a small smile. 'You don't have to be particularly bright to win those, just lucky.'

I shook my head. 'No, luck may come into it, but you have to be pretty clever to win all these. Are you a writer then?'

He appeared slightly uncomfortable. 'I'm afraid so, *used* to be anyway.'

'Why used to be and no longer?'

'Because that's how I feel,' he shrugged. 'The man who wrote those plays is a stranger to me now. I look back at him with some amusement, some warmth and some shame.'

I put my head on one side, trying to make him out. 'Do you write now?'

'No. I'll make the coffee,' he said.

I expected her to ask me why I felt shame, but she didn't. I just about managed to carry the two mugs of coffee in without spilling any, although my hands were trembling. She was sitting by my fire, watching me intently and frowning.

'What are your plays about?' she suddenly asked.

'They're comedies.'

'That doesn't surprise me.'

'It doesn't? What makes you say that?'

'Because you're funny – you don't think you are, but you are, even when you don't mean to be. There's something in your eyes, your manner of speaking, I don't know ... I can't explain it, but I find you funny.'

'Well, thank you ... I think that's a compliment.'

She sat opposite me sipping her coffee, her eyes shining like headlights over the top of her cup. 'Why don't you write now?'

'I have nothing to say,' I replied, candidly.

'Of course you have.'

'No, really, that part of my life is over,' I told her, hoping I didn't sound too pathetic and self-absorbed.

She frowned. 'How can it be? You're still alive; write about your life now. There must be something ...'

'Not really.'

'Mr Marshall, I don't believe you can't write now. I'm sure you could if you wanted to.'

I sighed. 'Is persistence or stubbornness your greatest virtue?'

'Both! Well, one of those anyway, now answer me please.'

'I'm not sure I can answer because I don't know how I feel.'

She appeared slightly exasperated. 'Are we going to be friends? Would you like us to be friends?'

Her straightforward approach caught me off guard and I swallowed hard, my words falling away like a crumbling cliff.

'That would be lovely, to be your friend.'

She gave me that life-affirming smile again. 'I'd like that too, but let's start off by confiding in each other, shall we? You have something wrong with you. I could guess, but I won't. So that's the first thing you can get off your chest if you like, but maybe you don't want to. Then tell me why you can't write, I'd be interested.'

I had to smile. Her way of speaking was amusing and entertaining. I could have sat there quite happily and listened to her for hours. She was moving constantly, full of life, vivacious. I felt she deserved an answer for her boldness. 'I can't write at the moment because I don't find anything particularly humorous. In fact I don't feel much about anything. My emotions appear to be asleep. I feel frozen. I have this disease.'

Her face fell. 'Parkinson's,' she muttered.

'Yes; that obvious, is it? The only part I think about is the disease bit.'

'That's only a word.'

'There's power in that word, Nell.'

'So, if your emotions are asleep you won't have any feelings about having Parkinson's then.'

I smiled at her. 'That's a good point-clever girl.'

She sat back in her chair, her head on one side. 'How does it make you feel to have it then?'

That was an easy question to answer. 'I'm terrified.'

'Terrified of living with it?'

I thought for a moment before replying. 'Of getting incapacitated, dribbling, not being able to articulate, falling, shaking and being dependent, being assigned a nurse. All of that, you know?'

'I bet,' she said, under her breath, 'and telling Beth.'

'Yes, telling Beth.'

She looked thoughtful for a moment and then a slow smile spread across her face. 'I think, every time we meet we should have fun. You need fun, Mr Marshall.'

'You think so? And you?'

'Oh, I could *always* do with fun.'

'Fun sounds wonderful,' I declared, 'not sure how we're going to achieve it though.'

She suddenly looked playful. 'Have you got a piece of scrap paper?'

'By the computer there,' I told her, pointing across the room.

She picked up the piece of paper and rolled it into a ball. 'Right, best of three - see how many you can get into the waste paper bin over there.' She took aim and threw the ball of paper, missing every time and swearing loudly. 'Okay, your turn.'

I took aim, as much as I could with my slight tremor and I missed twice, but the third time it dropped into the bin. We turned to each other, laughing. 'Pure brilliance,' I told her, shrugging.

'I don't bloody believe that. And you with the disease too,' she added, with the cheeky grin I was beginning to be slightly addicted to.

'How dare you,' I cried, pretending to be hurt.

'My turn ...'

We played the daft game for about fifteen minutes and I beat her every time. 'I'm bloody useless at this, aren't I?' she laughed.

'Yes, my dear, I'm afraid you are.'

'How come you're so good, even with the shakes?'

From anyone else that term would have made me flinch, but from her it sounded sweet and amiable. 'I should let you into a secret. I've played this before, whenever I had writer's block, before I learnt how to use a computer. I would screw up my paper and throw it or kick it into the bin.'

Her eyes lit up. 'Have a go at kicking it now,' she cried, looking like an excited child.

'I can't possibly ...'

'Oh, go on, please.'

'I haven't the co-ordination now and I can't balance on one leg.'

Her eyes were glinting. 'Bet you could. Go on, I dare you.'

She picked up the ball of paper and placed it in my hand. There was no skill in what I did next. I simply tossed it in the air and aimed my foot at it. Balancing, even for a split second, was out of the question and I staggered, but quickly regained my composure with her help. Within that couple of seconds the ball hit the ceiling and bounced off at great speed before landing in the bin. It seemed to happen in slow motion and Nell turned to me with her mouth open.

'I don't believe you,' she cried and I laughed, despite myself because her face was a picture of indignation and joy.

'It's just a question of skill ...'

'You are bloody brilliant.'

I bowed. 'I have been told that once or twice in my life.'

'Is modesty your greatest virtue?'

'Touché,' I smiled.

'Well, was that fun?'

'I have to admit it was.'

She was standing beside me and her face suddenly fell and she unexpectedly took my hand in hers, squeezing it gently. 'Don't you dare give up,' she urged me.

Her eyes were serious for a split second. I tried to smile and I wanted to be able to promise her I wouldn't give up, but my mouth froze. 'Nell ...'

'Now, must be off,' she said, her expression changing instantly and dropping my hand. 'Thanks for the coffee. I'm not running tomorrow, visiting my mum. See you in the week maybe, but don't come out if it's too cold.'

'I'll see you out and please visit any time, I'm here most days, on and off.'

'No, don't move, stay here. Thank you for letting me see inside your beautiful home, Mr Marshall.'

'It's been my pleasure, Nell.'

I shuffled quickly to the window to watch her as she crossed the road and disappeared into the white night. I then sat motionless on the sofa and thought about her animated face and *that* smile, like a high-voltage beam of light. I felt as if I'd been struck by lightning. Without me realising it she had wormed out of me my most intimate secret – the disease. And that was done deftly, with honesty and without giving away anything about her life. All I knew about her was her name and that she loved to run. But her secrets could wait for another time. The promise of her friendship shone like dark jewels in my ocean of self-pity. I now couldn't give up. Nell had asked me not to.

Snow fell later that afternoon and I sat in my conservatory watching its softness with different eyes. The day before I had cursed its presence because of my faltering legs, but a young woman had stood under my glass roof with her eyes shining and called me a lucky man.

Sidney was standing outside on his patio, his face up to the sky as if catching the sun's rays; but then he was completely mad, in a pleasant, humorous way. Sidney Walpole was a law unto himself and always had been and he took the view that if he couldn't do exactly what he pleased at nearly seventy, when could he? He glanced over to me and made the sign of having a few drinks together. He and his long-suffering, saintly wife lived in the annexe of the Rectory that I had sold many years before because I felt the house was much too big for me at that time and I needed money to get Mary off my back. We had got to know each other over cards and whisky in my house on long, gloomy winter afternoons and the occasional evening propping up the bar and making an utter hash of the quizzes in the Fox and Hounds round the corner. I had been constantly astounded and amused at his ability to delve into the far reaches of his alcohol-sodden brain to come up with all the correct answers to the football questions. He expected me to know everything about politics, literature, classical music, history, any subject *other* than football. He would prop up the bar and I would be beside him like a lanky coat stand, often staring in wonder at him because of his ability to make me laugh with his childlike simplicity and the way he looked at the world. He and I were so wonderfully different and yet we understood each other perfectly. Often, just by a look or a raised eyebrow, Sidney and I could communicate across a room full of people without any of them knowing. I understood he was a walking disaster area and he understood I was a supposedly intelligent, rather ridiculous and deeply flawed man who admired him and needed his friendship to keep me grounded. And I now knew, with my diagnosis, I would also need him in the future to keep me sane. I beckoned to him and opened the conservatory door.

'Are you trying to catch your death, Sidney?'

'It's not cold, just a bit fresh. I believe the sun's over the yardarm, Benedict.'

'It certainly is. I take it Sheila is out.'

'Visiting the old girl,' he said, referring to his mother-in-law who was ninety-eight not out.

'Let yourself in.'

I instinctively went to my drinks cabinet and took out an old malt. 'Put the kettle on,' I told him, as he appeared.

'A coffee with a bit of Scotch in it?' he asked.

'Most certainly,' I replied.

He had only just put one foot in the lounge before his curiosity got the better of him. 'A friend of Beth's visiting earlier?'

'Is your nose permanently against the window pane or do you occasionally give it a break?'

'Pretty girl,' he murmured as he sat opposite me. 'If she isn't a friend of Beth's there's life in the old dog yet.'

'Not much, Sidney, not much,' I assured him, handing him a drink. 'My legs are frozen, I can't seem to warm them up today.'

'Aren't you having one?' he asked, looking surprised, as well he might.

I glanced at the empty glass on the bureau and my mouth felt dry. One wouldn't hurt of course and I had only just started my regime of tablets so now was the time to have a few before going on the wagon. There was nothing better on a bleak, snowy February afternoon than having a drink by the burning flames of my fire with a good friend, putting the world to rights. Hell, you were a long time dead and I already had the disease. I poured myself a large one. The smooth feel of it flowing down my throat was heavenly and I stretched my legs out and leant back.

'So, when are you coming to see my back passage then?' he suddenly asked, grinning.

'Could you please rephrase that, Sidney?'

'Okay, when are you coming to see my *fully tiled* back passage?'

'Well, as it's fully tiled that's different. Just make sure you only ever speak about your fully tiled back passage when you're at my house.'

'Oh, I don't talk bollocks when I'm with anyone else, only you mate.'

'I'm quietly flattered, Sidney,' I said, shaking my head.

We both sipped our drinks in a mutually comfortable silence for a minute sitting directly opposite each other as usual. I liked having him opposite me because his flushed face was entertaining to watch with all its varied, comical expressions. Watching Sidney was so much more interesting than anything I could ever watch on television. I sensed something was brewing in him and threatening to come out of his mouth at full speed. I had an uncanny knack of being able to read him perfectly because to me he was an open book. Sidney Walpole did not have a devious or untrue bone in his body and could only ever tell the truth, however unsavoury that truth may be.

'So, what's occurring then, Benedict?' he asked, astute as usual.

'Nothing much, Sidney, as you can see.'

'Don't give me that,' he said, eyeing me from under his bushy white eyebrows and over his glasses. 'You've got something up your sleeve.'

'You think so? I really have no idea what you mean.'

'I know so; you've been rather distracted recently, not yourself. Now, either you've been having clandestine meetings with that young woman ...'

I had to laugh. 'What clandestine meetings! Hardly clandestine when she's coming to my house.'

'Well, something or someone is making you look tired ...'

'I've got a disease,' I blurted out.

There was a moment's silence as he took in what I had said, but then a small smile crept across his mouth. 'Is that a joke?'

'I only wish it were, Sidney.'

He screwed his nose up in distaste. 'What kind of disease?'

'Parkinson's disease.'

'That's not a disease,' he declared, looking heartily relieved. 'I thought you meant malaria or AIDS.'

'That makes me feel much better I must say.'

'That's bad luck, mate.'

'It is.'

'How can I help?' he asked, now looking more concerned.

'You can help by just being yourself – speaking before you think, treating me with as little respect as you normally do ... in other words we carry on as if I don't have it.'

'That's fine by me, but Benedict, if there's anything you need ...'

'Thank you.'

His lined, world-weary, sympathetic face was full of concern. 'Will you have to take a load of tablets? You won't die, will you?'

'Not straight away, here and now,' I told him, trying to make light of it for him. 'I'll be taking tablets every day and that's about all I know.'

'Didn't you ask the quack about drinking and leading a normal life? You know, all of that nonsense.'

'I have to admit ... no. I was a little distracted by his twitching eyes. A neurologist who twitches badly is rather unfortunate.'

Sidney frowned. 'He had twitching eyes?'

'He did, yes.'

'How did they twitch then?'

I laughed. 'If you think I'm going to sit here and mimic his twitching eyes, you've got another think coming,' I declared, knowing Sidney wouldn't leave it there.

'You've got enough of your own,' he remarked.

'That is cruel, Sidney.'

'Someone should tell him. He might not realise he's doing it, poor sod. I'd tell you.'

'I'm quite aware of that.'

'Fancy sitting there all day telling patients, who have twitches, they've got Parkinson's and the like, when you're twitching more than they are. Some people might think he's taking the piss.'

'I doubt that, but it's just one of the many absurdities of life, Sidney.'

'I used to have some nervous twitches when I was a little boy ... do you want to see some of them?'

I put my hands up. 'I absolutely do not.'

He ignored me, as he always did. 'One was to do with my eyes. I'd open them as wide as I could, like this ... kind of stretching them, you know? Then one was to do with my mouth and I'd open that as wide as I could like this ...' He opened his mouth like a floundering fish and kept it open for what seemed like an eternity. It looked faintly bizarre and wholly ridiculous.

'Yes, I get the picture, Sidney ...'

'But when I did the two together ...'

'Will you please stop it? That is grotesque!'

'Then I did another one where I made a double chin then jutted it out, but I didn't do that very often because it hurt.'

'Priceless,' I muttered. 'And the point to all this is?'

'The point is ...'

'Ah, there is a point then?'

'The point is you know you're doing it. The doc will be aware of it, I'm sure. Did you have any twitches when you were little?'

'No, but as you kindly remarked, I'm more than making up for it now.'

He frowned. 'I wouldn't say you twitched, more like shake and jerk.'

'How very comforting ...'

His face then broke into a sheepish grin. 'Meanwhile, back at the ranch, the sun is still over the yardarm.'

'It is, Sidney,' I agreed, aware of the fact that he wanted, needed, everything to be as it had been for the last few years; us being mates, drinking together, chatting, laughing, playing cards for money and cheating each other-that sort of thing.

He held out his glass. 'Oh, are you allowed? No, you didn't ask the quack, so ...'

'I don't think a couple on our usual Saturday afternoons, to warm the soul in the depths of winter, is going to make much difference to my precarious state,' I said, taking hold of the bottle. I saw his eyes watching my hand.

'Is that what's giving you those shakes? I had noticed them, but ... well, I thought it was age to be honest.'

'I'm not as old as you, remember.'

'Fuck me,' he cried, almost waking up from a dream, 'that would be awful if you couldn't have the occasional drink.'

'You know me too well.'

'What will happen ... in the future I mean?' he asked, his concern quite touching.

'Let's not mention the future; it's a place I'm fearful of.'

'I'm sure it can be controlled.'

'I'm sure it can. Now Sydney, what have you been doing this week?'

He chuckled. 'Changing the subject are we? Okay, fair enough. I've been finishing my fully tiled back passage and making a bloody mess of it to be honest, but I like to keep active.'

'I hadn't noticed ...'

'I like to keep active and feel I can still do things. I haven't got anything better to do. I banged on the walls a couple of times because I felt like pestering you, but you must have been out.'

'Or asleep...'

'Do you want to come to lunch tomorrow?'

'What's on the menu?'

'Oh, please yourself then. Beef as it happens.'

'As Sheila's beef is the best this side of the Thames, I'll grace you with my presence.'

'I've bought a beautiful bottle of red too,' he almost whispered, his eyes playful.

'Sidney, stop encouraging me.'

'A couple of glasses won't hurt you.'

'How do you know? Are you an expert on my disease?'

He shuffled about in his seat a little and looked over his glasses at me, like a schoolmaster. 'I'll get Sheila to look it all up on the internet, shall I?'

'No! I'd rather not know to be perfectly honest.'

'So, who was she then?'

'Who was who?' I asked, knowing full well that he would return to Nell's visit sooner or later.

He sighed. 'Who was the pretty young thing with dark hair?'

'I don't know to be honest.'

'You don't know? So you just picked her up, you old reprobate? I don't know how you do it, Benedict.'

'I don't know how I do it either, because I don't any more. I met her by the duck pond, her name is Nell and she runs – that's all I know. She took pity on me because I could hardly stand up straight in the snow and she helped me back here. She couldn't believe I lived here; it's always been her favourite house. We had a coffee together and that was it.'

He looked at me rather sternly, which was unusual for him. Then he appeared thoughtful. 'Watch out, she'll be after your money.'

'Sidney, don't be such a cynic.'

'Well, if she's after anything else she'd choose a younger man, surely,' he commented, blunt as usual.

'I'm glad you're taking me at my word and not thinking before you speak. Anything else meaning ... '

He gave a ridiculous wink. 'You know.'

'I assure you I don't.'

'Yes, you do.'

'For your information,' I started to explain, 'I'm not the slightest bit interested in anything remotely physical because I couldn't actually take part in anything remotely physical. I have very few of those feelings now. My joie de vivre has gone and the worrying thing is, I don't really care.'

Sidney chucked the rest of his whisky down his throat. 'Fuck me, Benedict, that's not like you.'

I sat forward in my chair. 'But that's what I'm trying to explain, Sidney. I'm not me anymore, I'm someone else.'

He looked confused. 'What someone is that?'

'I haven't the faintest idea. That's what I've got to find out, because that's who I'll be for the rest of my life and I'd like to get to know him.'

Sidney gave me a fond smile. 'You think too much, you always have. Academics analyse too much. It's much easier being a twat like me. You aren't so different.'

'Maybe not on the outside, but on the inside I feel very different.'

He looked bemused. 'Who the hell are you on the inside then?'

'Sidney, I don't know. That's what I'm trying to explain to you.'

'Is it the Parkinson's that's made you feel like that then?'

The chill winter darkness was beginning to settle outside and I felt tired, drained and bereft of words to explain. Sidney wasn't as stupid as he liked to make out, but he was a simple soul who never searched his heart for any deep answers in life. Deep philosophical discussions weren't his forte, but he did try for my sake. I tried to explain.

'Not only the *disease*; these are feelings I've had for a couple of years now. I haven't grown into myself very well. I've been hanging on to both the young man and the middle-aged man I was. Now, I'm someone different.'

Sydney looked perplexed. 'I think I know what you mean, I remember having a major depression when I realised I wasn't young anymore; wanted to colour my hair, buy a sports car, the lot. But I actually quite like being nearly seventy now. It's a relief not worrying about my belly and my bald patch … and women. It's all rather liberating in a funny sort of way.'

'I hope to eventually feel like that and I had noticed you weren't bothered about your belly anymore.'

Sidney ignored my rude comment and smiled. 'I hope you find out who you are, Benedict, so you can describe yourself to me.'

I had to laugh at him. 'Thank you.'

He then looked slightly worried. 'I hope whoever you are you won't change much. I hope we'll still be friends. I like you as you are.'

His vulnerability where I was concerned was always deeply touching and if I'd believed in a God I would have said a silent prayer for his friendship. 'Thank you again and of course we'll stay friends.'

'Now, let's have a top up and drink to age.'

'Sidney, you're a bad influence on me.'

'Fuck off - it's the other way round, mate.'

We spent a pleasant couple of hours putting the world to rights and talking about inconsequential things as we normally did. The whisky had warmed me from the inside and the fire had brought colour to my cheeks. Sidney and I had an easy intimacy based on mutual respect for our differences. I couldn't have cared less that he wasn't an academic and he forgave the fact that I was; or he thought I was. Eventually Sheila arrived home and banged once on the wall; the sign for Sidney to put down his glass and go home for his afternoon tea.

'Tea and cake, Benedict?' he asked, standing up.

'No, thank you, Sheila feeds me enough. What time is lunch tomorrow?'

'Half past one and don't be late.'

'Well, it all depends on the traffic …'

'You'll upset the wife,' he warned, wagging his finger.

'The wife … the chair … the table, Sidney? She isn't a piece of furniture. *My* wife, *my* wife, not *the* wife. That's how you should refer to the saintly woman who puts up with you.'

'I don't give a flying fuck about how I should say it. I can't change the habits of a lifetime.'

'I've just had a thought.'

'You don't want to do too much of that.'

'I'm going to call my disease 'The Walpole'. Shall I tell you why?'

'I know why – because you'll never get rid of either of us!' he laughed.

'Sydney, you're not as daft as you look. Now bugger off and leave me in peace.'

'Bye, mate, thanks for the drink, lovely.'

I gave him a dismissive but friendly wave and watched as his head disappeared behind his fence. On my own again I contemplated calling Beth to tell her the dreaded news, but once again I chickened out.

The following day it was ice bright, sunny and clear. I spent the morning cooking myself some porridge with fresh fruit, drinking tea, catching up on emails and reading the papers. Sidney banged on the wall three times, at about half twelve, to signal he had uncorked the wine and I sauntered in just afterwards.

I drank too much of the wine and felt dull and listless when I returned home. My head throbbed and my legs felt like lead. I wondered momentarily what Nell was doing and I pictured her with friends, talking and laughing that unique laugh of hers, being warm-hearted and vibrant. I sat by my fire and leant my head back as the light faded to blackness outside. I wanted to doze but my head felt full of cotton wool and I couldn't relax enough. I was sitting alone at that time, on a Sunday, when if you have nobody to be with the day seems too long, too quiet and the darkness stretches before you endlessly. The shadows on the walls appear unfriendly and the ticking clock deafening. Sidney had urged me to stay and play cards, but I suddenly felt anti-social and I knew my mood was heading in a downward direction and I had no intention of inflicting that on him or Sheila.

Just as I felt my eyes closing, I heard a muffled thud against the front window. There it was again and again. Someone was throwing snowballs and, with some effort, I managed to stumble across the room to find out who it was. The sight of Nell in her striped hat made me spring alive immediately. She was waving and gesticulating for me to open the door, which I did, slowly.

'Hello, Nell,' I said, standing aside to let her in, my heart pounding in an unusual manner.

She was glowing and radiant. 'Hello, Mr Marshall. You said to pop in any time, so I've come for afternoon tea.'

'You are very welcome; after you. Do go in, please.'

I followed her into the living room and she turned to me wrinkling her nose in distaste. 'It's so gloomy in here.'

'The fire gives off quite a bit of light.'

She looked up at me. 'Are you hard up?'

'No,' I replied, bemused.

'Put a light on then.'

'Yes, madam.'

'Can I sit by the fire here? It's perishing outside.'

'Of course, have my chair.'

'No, I'll sit here, you should never take an elderly person's chair,' she replied, laughing. 'Get the kettle on, I'm frozen.'

I had to smile, she was such a breath of fresh air filtering, or rather, rushing through my house; it was so refreshing. I made us tea in my best china and attempted to pick up the tray, but my useless hands would not allow me to because of the tremors. My initial thought was to try and hide this fact but then my second thought was, this is Nell. I put my head round the kitchen door. 'Do you think you could carry the tray in please?' I asked her and she jumped up and took hold of it. She placed it on the glass table in front of the fire. I envied her strength, her steadiness.

'Are you okay to pour it, Mr Marshall?'

'Yes, yes, fine ... I think,' I assured her, wishing I felt as sure as I was pretending.

'So, what have you been doing today?' she asked, her eyes shining with her usual enthusiasm and her expressions changing constantly.

'Eating, reading, writing ...'

'Writing?' she gasped.

'Only emails, unfortunately. I told you, I have nothing to say ... well, nothing funny to say and I can't write any other type of script.'

She sipped her hot tea. 'I don't believe that.'

'Did you visit your mum? How is she?'

'Full of life, as usual.'

I raised my slightly shaking cup to my mouth. I noticed she was watching me intently. 'It's lovely to see you, thank you so much for coming round. What made you come round?'

She frowned at me. 'What were you doing sitting in the dark just now?'

'I was feeling sorry for myself.'

'That's why I came round. My mum lives just round the corner - not in a house like this I hasten to add,' she laughed.

'I'm sorry to be so predictable.'

She put her head on one side. 'Tell me about your life, Mr Marshall.'

'My life?'

'Yes, your life. You know, the one you've been living since you were born.'

'I'm not sure where to start.'

'Start at the beginning!'

'I'm not sure what to leave out,' I muttered.

'I heard that,' she said, laughing again – the sound of that laughter seemed to reverberate around the room before seeping into the walls.

'Would you find it interesting?'

She gave a deep sigh. 'You know, I'm drawn to you, Mr Marshall – I don't know why, but I am. I'd like to get to know you – again I don't know why – and I'd love us to be friends. And friends know about each other. I've often been cautious where friendship is concerned, but with you I don't want to be so cautious. There must be something in you I find too interesting to pass by. Maybe it's your finely tuned mind, your humour, or your mesmerising voice. I really have no idea, but I do have a feeling we need each other and that's something I don't want to miss out on because I rarely feel that.'

She paused, obviously waiting for my response but, for once in my life, I was quite literally lost for words. I seemed to be struck dumb as my addled brain tried to form some sensible thoughts and my lips wouldn't move in the way I wanted them to. Eventually she smiled and raised her eyebrows in what looked like an expression of surprise.

'Say something then,' she added after a few moments of heavy silence. Eventually I managed to make my mouth surround the words and I took a deep breath and concentrated hard.

'My dear girl, I have no idea why you would need me, but I am honoured you feel that way and I would consider it my great fortune to have you as my friend. However, I must warn you, I am infuriating, irascible ...'

'Oh, I don't care about all that,' she interrupted, 'in fact I don't even know what that last word means. Now, tell me about your life and pour me another cup.'

My hands were feeling feeble. 'Could you pour it, please?'

'Why, are your hands useless already?'

'They seem to be shaking a little more than they were.'

'But you must keep using them, go on, try,' she urged.

I did as she asked and the tremor was noticeable, but I managed to pour us both a cup.

'Not easy,' I muttered, 'bloody tremors.'

'There you go, you did it. Not bad! Thank you. Now ... back to your life.'

'I was born in Sussex,' I started.

'What were your parents like? What did they do?'

'My father was a teacher, my mother a dressmaker, an excellent one I might add, people came from miles around ... and he loved being a schoolmaster.'

'How wonderfully old-fashioned,' she laughed, clapping her hands together in delight, 'a schoolmaster!'

'That's what he always called himself. However, he came from a wealthy family of business people and they wanted him to follow in that business, but he was a man of principle and longed to teach and that is exactly what he did all his life. I have an older brother, two younger sisters, one of whom Beth is named after. I went to Oxford ...'

'No! You're a clever old bugger.'

'You think so? Thank you, I never think of myself as being particularly clever. I simply have a phenomenal memory. Where did I get to? Oh yes, Oxford. I read English Literature and taught it for a while and then took further qualifications.'

She leant forward, her grey eyes narrowing. 'What further qualifications?'

I felt a little embarrassed. 'Well, I'm actually a Professor of English.'

'Professor Marshall,' she whispered, in reverential tones.

'I'm afraid so.'

'Me being here is a bit like Educating Rita,' she laughed.

'I think there is very little I could teach you, Nell.'

'Go on,' she urged.

'I then started to write in my spare time. I met my wife and we had Beth. We divorced when Beth was ten ...'

'That didn't last long then.'

'Yes ... I mean no, it didn't; mainly because of my drinking and partying and getting drunk at all the university and literary functions. Eventually I had some success with my plays and um ... that's about it I believe.'

She had been listening intently as I spoke, but her face was full of life, alert in every way and there seemed to be a light shimmering around her, like the outer edges of a star in a dark sky.

'You must love literature then.'

'I have to say I do.'

Her eyes were shining with enthusiasm. 'So do I. What's your favourite book?'

'That's a tough question. I'd have to think about that, Nell.'

'Mine is *Testament of Youth*. All those vivid descriptions of all those young men Vera Britten knew and loved going off to war to get slaughtered. It's simply unforgettable.'

'An unusual choice ...'

'I *am* unusual,' she grinned.

'I don't doubt it.'

She suddenly looked amused. 'Do you think it's an unusual choice because I'm a girl and it's about war?'

'Ah, you think because I'm over sixty I'm a dinosaur,' I remarked.

'Are you?'

'I do hope not, but I would imagine Jane Austen or the Brontë sisters would be more your type of thing ... not because you're female, but because I have you marked down as someone with a romantic soul.'

'I am a romantic soul at heart and I love *Jane Eyre* and *Pride and Prejudice*, but *Testament of Youth* made the most lasting impression.'

'I can understand that, Nell. It's a book of alarming imagery and profound sadness. It is unforgettable, I agree with you.'

'I remember being at a party somewhere and looking at all the young men and thinking, my God, if this was 1914 they would all just disappear into the army, get sent to the trenches in France and never come home again. It really affected me – still does,' she added, looking into her tea. 'I've never forgotten it.'

'The power of the written word, eh?'

'I assume you like poetry?'

'I certainly do.'

'What poetry do you like?'

'Anything that rhymes...'

'You're taking the piss,' she laughed. 'Who's your favourite author?'

'I feel like I'm back at my interview for Oxford University.'

She opened her eyes wide. 'Is that what they asked you? Oh, I'd love someone to ask me stuff like that in an interview. I could talk for hours about books and poetry. So, carry on, who's your favourite author?'

'Well ... I like Somerset Maugham, Joseph Conrad ...'

'No,' she cried, 'don't tell me, you like *The Secret Agent*! I had to do that for A Level and it was deadly dull. My teacher kept on and on about how it was his favourite book and I just couldn't see it. I didn't understand one word of it.'

I smiled fondly at her. She was so honest. She was constantly moving, her face, her hands, her whole body.

'Don't tell anyone, but I didn't understand a word of it either. However, I understand enough of words to know that it was brilliantly written.'

'Yes,' she said, wagging her finger at me, 'and that's because you're an academic.'

'Well, don't tell anyone this, but I'm a *pseudo* academic. I spent my life pretending to be one and being terrified of getting found out. Believe me, I've worked with true academics and they are a breed apart. I simply have a phenomenal memory, honestly.'

She narrowed her eyes at me. 'I'm not so sure - you seem bloody clever to me, especially with that voice of yours.'

'Can I ask you a question now? Is that allowed?'

She sat back in her chair. 'Depends what it is.'

'Why didn't you study English Literature? I mean, I'm guessing you didn't. You appear to be so enamoured ...'

'You can love something without wanting to study it. Why are you ashamed?' she added, staring straight at me and deflecting the conversation from herself.

'I beg your pardon?'

'The other day you said you were ashamed.'

'Oh that,' I shrugged, 'well, of my drinking and being more interested in socialising than coming home to my wife. I feel quite a lot of guilt about that.'

'Are you a good father?'

'My God, Nell, you ask some probing questions of someone you've only just met.'

'But I don't feel as if we've only just met,' she replied, her eyes softening.

'No, I have to agree with you on that, neither do I.'

'Odd isn't it?'

'Yes, it certainly is.'

'Why do you think that is?'

'Reincarnation,' I said flippantly.

'I'm open to that idea,' she gasped, moving forward in her chair towards me.

I was surprised by her admission. 'Are you?'

'Yes. Why not? I'm open to most things, except Eve being made out of Adam's rib and the existence of Heaven and Hell. Anyway, you didn't answer my question.'

I paused for a moment. Talking about my role as a father was hard for me because although I had tried my hardest to be the best father to Beth I could possibly be, given my inadequacies as a man, I doubted I had been home enough to have blossomed adequately in the role.

'All I can say is, I hope so. You'd have to ask Beth. I suspect I could have given her more of my time. I know my wife thought that.'

Nell put her head on one side. 'I think you are.'

I was so touched by her words I could feel unwanted tears pricking at the back of my eyes. 'Dear girl, how can you possibly tell that?'

'Because, Mr Marshall, I had a good father so I know what one looks like and you look like one to me.'

'But,' I interrupted, 'I could have been a better one.'

'How?' she asked, inquisitive as ever.

I don't know why I said the next thing that came out of my mouth, except, perhaps, because just being near Nell made me a more honest man. 'By loving her mother more.'

She tilted her head to the other side. 'Didn't you love her then?'

I looked down at my trembling hands - the trembling hands that were perhaps my punishment for being a selfish man. It was difficult to admit, even to myself, that I had not loved Mary, but here I was just about to voice it out loud to this young woman I had met only days ago. 'No,' I muttered, 'I thought I did at the beginning, but when I look back now I know I didn't. And that makes me ashamed, guilty and sorry.'

Nell didn't appear shocked or even surprised. 'Who did you love then?'

'Myself.'

'And Beth...'

'Yes, yes, only Beth.'

'And anyone else?'

I hesitated. There had been many women; too many to actually remember, but love had eluded me and that was hard to admit. The words stuck rigidly to the back of my throat before frothing at the corners of my useless mouth.

'No,' I whispered, as if by saying it quietly it would change the fact.

Nell's eyes looked troubled - almost sorry for me. 'Why?'

'I often ask myself that question, but I don't know the answer.'

'I'm surprised.'

'You are?'

'Yes.'

I was going to ask her why she was surprised, but I didn't. 'And you?' I inquired instead, 'have you ever been in love?'

'Yes, when I was seventeen, eighteen, but not since.'

'I'm glad you've loved someone,' I told her, because I felt instinctively that someone like her should be in love and be loved. 'I would have liked to have been in love,' I blurted out, without thinking. 'I would have stayed home then, but I wasn't you see. So I was searching, without knowing what I was searching for.'

She said nothing for a moment and looked deep in thought. But then her face lit up. 'Was teaching English Literature exciting?'

'Yes, some of the time, but I regret ...'

'You shouldn't have regrets if you were a teacher; it's the noblest of professions.'

'Nell, you could be right, but you're only ... how old are you?'

'I'm thirty-five.'

'Oh to be thirty-five again and know what I know now!'

'My mum says that,' she laughed.

'Yes, well, thirty-five is a time to be living your life, not looking back. You won't understand this yet, but when you're sixty-two, you'll spend a hell of a lot of time looking back.'

'Don't look back, look forward,' she urged.

'Into a void and into the disease...'

She frowned at me as if I was a young child. 'No, you're looking at uncertainty maybe, but not a void. You have no idea what's going to happen tomorrow.'

I gave her a wry smile. 'Oh I do, I'll still have the disease.'

'A few days ago, did you think you'd be sitting here having tea with me?'

'Not in my wildest dreams.'

'Well, there you go.'

'I see your point.'

She glanced briefly at her watch and my mood plummeted because I knew she would have to be going.

'Look at the time. Gotta go, Mr Marshall - don't get up.'

'Do you have to go just yet?' I asked, trying my best not to sound needy or pathetic.

She gave me a sympathetic smile. 'Yes, but I'll see you Wednesday.'

'You will?'

'Yes, because you and I are going for a healthy walk.'

'God forbid!'

'A walk followed by bread pudding and hot chocolate in the park café. Or, coffee and banana cake, whichever we prefer. We have to have fun, remember?'

'Fun is exactly what I need, Nell.'

'So I'll see you then, I'll pick you up at ten.'

'It's been lovely chatting with you.'

'Ditto,' she replied, the life-affirming smile lighting up her whole face, my living room, Greenwich and the whole of London - no doubt.

'You know all about me now, but I know nothing about you.'

'Oh, that can keep till next time,' she said dismissively, 'not that there's much to know.'

'I'd be interested.'

She smiled at me. 'All I'll tell you for now is that I'm an often out of work actress and, in those long weeks where I don't get a sniff of a part, I teach dance classes and work in my sister's café. There you have it,' she shrugged, 'it's not nearly as fascinating as your life.'

'I don't agree,' I replied as sincerely as I could. 'There must be more to tell about your past. If you ask me, you seem to be a vast, deep ocean of inspiring, complex emotions.'

She opened her eyes wide in surprise. 'That's very poetic of you, Mr Marshall.'

'I thought so!'

'No, really, it was lovely.'

I preened slightly for effect and stuck my nose in the air. 'I have awards you know.'

She gave me a dazzling, high-voltage beam of a smile and took my hand again as she had done before. She squeezed it gently and watched its tremors with large eyes that seemed to turn darker with emotion. The instant switch of expressions was impressive and in my mind I pictured her on a stage in front of a large audience.

'What I will tell you is,' she began - her voice barely above a whisper, 'the person I adored most in this world had this disease and all my love couldn't save him from himself and his dark thoughts, or stop him giving up and leaving me, so I'm going to save you.'

I hardly knew what to say. 'That's terrible, Nell. I'm so, so sorry. Do I need saving then?'

'You certainly do,' she declared, with a sudden twinkle in her eye. 'And remember,' she added, her expression changing in a flash from mischievous to serious, 'one day very soon, a brilliant neurologist who is working away night and day in a lab somewhere, will come up with a cure for Parkinson's and your life will be transformed.' Her eyes filled with tears suddenly. 'Don't forget, Mr Marshall, don't give up. See you.'

I tried to get up, but my legs felt like two large, immovable tree trunks hacked down in their prime and I simply sat there like an old man waiting for a commode. 'Nell, thank you very much for coming, I appreciate it.'

She gave me a little wave. 'When I'm gone don't sit here with your complex thoughts. Promise me?'

'I promise.'

Then, with a turn of her head and her hair swishing across her shoulders with a certain flourish, she was gone. I heard the door close quietly and I sat quite still, as if struck by a thunderbolt. Within one week I had been given a life-changing diagnosis and by chance stumbled across the astonishing, incomparable Nell. I had the distinct feeling she would seep into my bloodstream and invade my cells as vigorously as my disease.

Chapter 2

I was ready by nine, waiting eagerly like an expectant child, with my red woolly hat in my hand and my overcoat and scarf on. I had eaten my breakfast early in the conservatory, mesmerised by soft snowflakes drifting by the windows. Sidney had tottered outside with his mug of tea and a piece of toast in his hand, with his protruding stomach resembling a large pudding. He started mouthing something at me and pointed to his watch. I shook my head and shrugged to signal that I hadn't a clue what he meant.

'Cards,' he yelled, 'at coffee time?'

'I can't, I'm going out,' I yelled back.

'Oh,' he sneered, pretending to be hurt. 'I see ... better fish to fry; later on then?'

I was well aware that he had a need for things in his life to stay more or less the same. He did not want change now – at nearly seventy.

'Yes, later then, at about four.'

Touchingly, he appeared relieved. 'Four it is then,' he called, putting his thumb up.

The time seemed to drag like a wet Sunday afternoon until Nell arrived. Every tick of the clock reverberated around the room and settled on me heavily. At one point I wondered if she might forget, but I quickly dismissed that thought as absurd. This was Nell – reliable, honest and kind. Eventually, at two minutes to ten a snowball hit the window with a heavy thud. My heart sang like a daft schoolboy's and I made my way gingerly into the hall and opened the door to find her resplendent in a deep purple cloche hat pulled so low over her eyes she had to peer out from under it. Her beautifully animated face was pink with the fresh, snowy air.

'Hello, Mr Marshall.'

I knew I was smiling foolishly. 'Hello, Nell.'

'Are you ready?'

'I am. Is it very slippery out there?' I asked, peering round her. 'I'm not very steady on my feet at the best of times.'

'Not really, they've cleared the roads more or less, but hold on to my arm and you'll be fine.'

'Which way are we going?'

'Up the hill to the café of course,' she replied, succinctly.

My heart sank to my knees. 'I'm not sure ...'

'Yes you can,' she interrupted, knowing full well that I was going to complain about not being able to make it up the steep part of the park towards General Wolfe's statue.

'Hush my mouth,' I muttered.

'We're doing two laps and then we'll give ourselves a treat,' she told me determinedly – brooking no argument from the likes of me.

'Are you quite sure about this?' I asked her, in a small voice that sounded slightly hoarse and blurred around the edges. She simply laughed and ignored my mounting anxiety which gave me courage. This was enough to turn my anxiety into excitement.

'Don't look down at your feet,' she ordered, as we slowly made our way up the snow-covered path, through the bare horse chestnut trees with their bony branches, 'or you'll miss all the beauty around you.'

'I'm trying hard not to.'

'But not hard enough, obviously because you're still looking down.'

'You're extremely hard on me,' I told her, leaning heavily on her arm for support.

'You need it,' she replied, looking up at me from under her sublimely understated hat, 'otherwise you'll sink into a pit of despair quite easily. I can tell.'

'Can you now?'

'Then what would your daughter think?' she added, for good measure.

The keen, white, icy air was making my legs feel quite numb and I was suddenly light headed. The mere mention of Beth caused me to stumble slightly and I grabbed at Nell's arm as if my life depended on it.

'She doesn't know yet,' I whispered, almost sheepishly, 'and I'm not sure when I'll summon up the courage to tell her. I may well not tell her at all ...'

'Mr Marshall ... '

'Nell, please don't tell me off for being a coward. I already know I'm a coward.'

She stopped abruptly, aware no doubt of my heavy breaths.

'Take a rest,' she said gently, 'and just listen to me before you start calling yourself names.' She peered up at me from under the purple felt of her hat. 'I was going to say, you know your daughter best, so you must do what you think is right for her.'

I was quite taken aback. 'Oh ... were you?'

'Yes! And you aren't a coward at all, so please don't say you are.'

My breathing had settled down a little and I looked down at this young woman who was bursting with health. She had a sense of timelessness about her; timelessness in the sense that she lived right in the moment. For her, every second was filled with enthusiasm for whatever she was doing or experiencing at that particular time and her expressions changed constantly. Being near her was life enhancing and if I'd been strong and healthy I would have felt moved to scoop her up in my arms and swing her round in my delight at knowing her and having her friendship. But there it was – her friendship, sweet and warming as it was, would not have been enough if I had been younger and stronger. I would have seen friendship with a lovely young woman as some sort of failure – a lessening of my not so discreet masculine powers. But now, with my wretched, unwanted disease, it was a gift.

We had begun walking again and London was stretching out behind us under the cold winter sun. 'Thank you for your words of support, Nell, but I'm afraid I am a coward in so many ways, too many to admit to.'

She stopped abruptly and looked up at me again, her expression a mixture of exasperation and resignation. 'But that's in the past and you need to let it go. Every single human being on this planet has made mistakes, including me. Do you know what your problem is?'

'Well ... no, but I bet you're going to tell me.'

She laughed out loud 'You're right, I am. You're at a stage in your life where you've been given a life-changing diagnosis and it's rocked your world and made you question everything. You're wondering whether you got Parkinson's because you did this or that – or didn't do this or that. Who the hell knows what causes it? It's still a mystery, but it's definitely not because you may or may not have done something you wish you hadn't. So, please don't call yourself a coward any more. I don't believe anyone is a coward, we all just have different ways of dealing with life.'

I watched her as she spoke; her unusual grey eyes that seemed to see right inside you, even when you wanted to hide something. Her perfect, expressive mouth, and the vast array of facial expressions that changed second by second, had me spellbound.

'Nell, how did you get to be so wise by the age of thirty-five?'

She shrugged and had a glint in her eye. 'Pure brilliance I suppose.'

I had to laugh and my breath floated upwards in the icy, February air. She was so refreshing and I was in desperate need of being refreshed.

pose it must be.'

ow come on, stop hanging the time out. We're off!'

ay that again.'

'Why are you always asking me to say things again? Aren't I speaking English?'

'Hanging the time out,' I repeated slowly, examining the words as I said them. She put her hand in the small of my back and pushed me gently forward. 'What a curious expression.'

'Haven't you ever heard that before? Where have you been all your life?'

'I've been in my ivory tower.'

'That's obvious.'

When we reached the top of the hill we paused and looked across the river at the mix of buildings, all huddled together – their different sizes and shapes stretching out as far as the eye could see. London was eternally majestic, still and silent, yet throbbing with life. The gherkin, which I had always considered a ridiculous piece of architecture inspired by someone slightly unhinged, was clearly visible with its windows sparkling in the white winter sun. The windows of the buildings at Canary Wharf shone like jewels, intimidating yet oddly attractive, with their tops skimming the marble sky. We moved on past the snow-covered tennis courts where I had often played with Beth, in the days when my legs did what I wanted them to do. That thought filled me with a quiet, momentary despair. How Nell picked up on those thoughts I have no idea. Perhaps I had stumbled, paused or let out a sigh, but she squeezed my arm and steered me quickly and expertly towards the café.

'Oh, you've taken pity on me,' I murmured, remembering her threat of walking up the hill twice.

'We can build up your stamina slowly, there's no rush. I don't want to knacker you.'

'How kind,' I muttered, in my best sarcastic tone.

'Shut your face, otherwise I'll make you walk more,' she said. 'I'm warning you, Mr Marshall, not another word.' I clamped my lips together firmly for effect. 'Yeah, yeah,' she added, 'that'll be the day when you do as you're told.'

I felt carefree and happy as I smiled down at her. They were two emotions I had felt so seldom in the last few years, I hardly recognised them and yet there they were. I was pondering the reasons for life's rich pattern while Nell opened the café door and helped me negotiate the many tables and chairs. We sat in the corner overlooking the deserted, frozen rose garden and I reached automatically into my overcoat pocket for my wallet.

'What are you doing?' she asked, frowning slightly.

'Getting some money out ...'

'You're not paying,' she declared.

'Why on earth not?'

She pursed her lips. 'I bet everywhere you go, you always end up paying, be it with friends, women, family ...'

'Well, yes, usually.'

'Why should you?' she asked, her eyes open wide in indignation.

I wasn't sure what to say. 'I suppose it's because I have a lot of money and people presume ...'

'Exactly and that's not fair. Someone should treat you, so I'm going to treat you.'

'You don't have to, Nell – really, I don't mind.'

Her eyes softened and she looked at me as if I was her favourite uncle who was being sweet and silly. 'I know you don't mind and that's my point. I want to treat you – please.'

I gave a little shrug. 'If that's what you want, thank you, but only if I can repay the treat at some other time.'

She waved her hand dismissively. 'We'll see about that. Take a seat before you fall over,' she grinned. 'Would you like coffee and cake?'

'Lovely.'

'They do wonderful bread pudding, but the banana cake is to die for and it's my favourite. I know the owner and it's his speciality.'

'Let's go for that then.'

I watched as she approached the counter and spoke animatedly with the young man who was serving. He leant forward eagerly as they chatted and his unlined, fresh face gave away how pleased he was to see her and how obviously attracted he was to her. She laughed back at him and I felt a sharp, stabbing pang of envy at the man's youth and obvious vigour. I knew instinctively that he had rippling muscles under his black short-sleeved shirt and a stomach as hard as a brick wall, damn him. I had no doubt he could do back-flips and full press-ups with someone standing on his back for good measure. My ridiculous envy sent my premature carefree and happy mood heading south, not because I begrudged Nell her relationships and multi-faceted life, but because I realised, in that instant-how old, infirm and careworn I felt. I experienced a sudden and intense longing to be youthful, with an unlined face, full of optimism and testosterone again. I felt a surge of great sadness and regret that I had been made to wait nearly all my life for a woman like Nell to appear to make me a better man. I knew that I was foolish to imagine, even in my deepest subconscious, that she might be even slightly attracted to me in some bizarre way or even come to love me.

I forced myself to look away and my eyes wandered around the café at the few people sitting quietly drinking their coffee, reading newspapers or simply deep in thought. One man appeared lost and grave as he gazed out of the window at the frozen, bare roses. He was slightly hunched and repeatedly put his head in his hand. I was wondering what battle he was fighting with himself and I suddenly realised that was how I had been feeling a few days earlier, before meeting Nell.

'Here we go.' Nell was sparkling opposite me with a tray of mugs, cake and napkins. 'Are you feeling okay, Mr Marshall?'

'Yes, I'm fine. Why do you ask?' I stuttered.

'You look a bit sad.'

'Do I?' I was going to deny it, as I usually did with my deepest feelings, but I simply couldn't when her vibrant, inquiring eyes were searching my soul. 'Well, I suppose I am. I mean, I don't want to be, but sometimes, you know, it comes over me.'

She gave a little laugh and it sounded to me strangely like the bells on Santa Claus's sleigh. 'What on earth are you babbling on about?'

'I have no idea.'

'Go on, tell me,' she urged.

'You'll think me pathetic, stupid ... and I am, of course.'

'Come on, Mr Marshall,' she cried, 'spit it out.'

I took a deep breath. 'I was wondering, why on earth you wanted to spend time with a decrepit old bugger like me, when you could be sitting chatting to anyone you choose.'

She looked bemused. 'There's an easy answer to that question; because I like you and I want to be here.'

'Ah,' I muttered, not convinced.

She turned her head to glance at the young man who had served her and then smiled at me fondly. 'I understand. You think I should be spending my spare time with men nearer my own age who are ruled by their testosterone, rather than their intellect. Is that *really* what you think I should be doing?'

'Well, yes,' I admitted, in my smallest mouse like voice because I already wished I had kept my ridiculous thoughts to myself.

Her face looked pained, as if she was trying desperately hard to get a point through to someone with very little understanding of the world, of emotions, of anything much. And someone who had spent his entire life being led and motivated by his would-be sexual conquests.

'You know what?' she eventually said.

'No.' I replied, expecting something profound that might help my complex emotions.

'You're as nutty as a wagon-load of blue monkeys!'

'Say that again.'

'It means you're a silly arse!'

I gave a nervous smile. 'I'm well aware of that.'

She leant across the table and put her hand over mine. 'Listen very carefully to what I'm going to say and take that off.' She pointed to my head. 'I can't take anything you say seriously when you're sitting there wearing that woolly, pork pie excuse for a hat. In any case, it's hiding most of your gorgeous face and with that and the glasses I can only really see your mouth.'

I smiled and removed my hat. She reached over and flattened down my wayward hair. 'My gorgeous face, eh? My dear girl, you flatter me. I really think *you* need to wear glasses. It's a lived-in face, a crumpled face, like a screwed up paper bag; a face with deeply etched lines, but gorgeous? I think not.'

She cast her eyes heavenward. 'Will you shut up a minute and listen?'

'I will, sorry.'

'To me, you're interesting, clever, funny and great company. You are wise, intellectual, kind and charismatic. Those are characteristics I find entertaining and wonderful. Younger men are more self-centred, more egotistical. I like to hear you talk. The way you form your sentences is endlessly fascinating and your voice is rich and mesmerising. I could just sit and listen to you for hours. For an actor, voices are vitally important. You should be doing voice-overs, you know. I want to learn from you, listen to you and laugh with you. But mostly, I like who I am through your eyes.'

I grew visibly with each sentence she uttered and the soft feel of her hand on mine made my heart swell with gratitude. 'What can I say, except thank you?'

She gave me her mega-wattage smile. 'Now, eat your cake and stop worrying about who I should or shouldn't be spending my time with. I choose to spend some of it with you. So, let's put all that to one side and have some fun. What do you say?'

'I agree.'

'And, for your information, I do wear glasses – at least I should, but I often leave them at home. Vanity you see.'

'I'm sure you look delightful in them,' I told her.

'I don't, I look like a prim librarian ... Why are librarians always prim? Right, come on; let's guess the names and professions of all the people in here.'

'All five of them ...'

'You start, Mr Marshall,' she urged, her eyes glinting with mischief.

I glanced over to the solitary, miserable-looking man on his own who was staring blankly into his coffee. 'Henry,' I whispered. 'He's a Henry and he's a recently redundant civil servant.'

'What makes you say that?' she whispered back, conspiratorially.

'His coat is quite expensive, denoting he has had a reasonably well-paid job and his shoes are Clarks – comfortable, but smart for the office. He loved his job, lived for it and it was a safe job until this recent economic downturn. He is shattered by his redundancy. I can tell that by the despair on his face.'

'Wow,' she muttered, for my ears only. 'What department in the civil service?'

'Ministry of Defence I would guess, because he looks reliable and honest – the type who would sign the Official Secrets Act and slit his wrists rather than give anything away.'

'Yes, you could be right. Now, see that old woman over there?'

'Who is possibly the same age as me?'

'No, you're older,' she grinned.

'I'm only too aware of that.'

'The truth always hurts. I think she's a retired schoolteacher.'

'And what makes you say that, pray?'

'An air of superiority, whether warranted or not.'

I smiled at her. 'I take it you don't like school teachers.'

'Not much,' she replied, wrinkling her nose. 'I never met one who inspired me. Maybe I was unlucky, I don't know, but I found them too strict, harsh and domineering and she looks like she could be like that.'

At that moment, the woman in question, who had been flicking through a magazine, looked up – and slightly down her nose – as she glanced briefly around the café. Nell raised her eyebrows at me.

I smiled. 'I see what you mean. What do you think her name is?'

She paused before saying, 'Anne or Janet, maybe Rosemary – something a bit old-fashioned and boring.'

'She's probably a very nice woman,' I declared.

'Right, it's your turn now. Who are you going to choose?'

I looked slightly behind me at a young girl, barely past her teens with a child on her lap. 'I'll go for her with the unfortunate-looking baby.'

'Don't be so cruel,' she whispered, spitting out some of the cake she was eating as she laughed.

'She got pregnant at seventeen, a mistake, or maybe not,' I added, because she appeared quite aware of her pretty face and full mouth as she flicked her hair away from her eyes and glanced at the man with hidden muscles behind the counter. 'No, she wanted a baby.'

'Why would she at that age?' Nell frowned, the concept completely beyond her comprehension.

'Something to love and to love her, I can tell. She's called Ruby and the baby is called Jade or perhaps Tiffany.'

'Right, I'm having another turn,' she said, looking across the room to a young woman who had her nose resolutely stuck in a paperback book. 'Her name is Abigail. She could be like me: a performer between jobs; and she's trying to keep her mind occupied rather than think about how few acting or singing roles she's been offered in the past few years. Her world is superficial, challenging and competitive, with few true, close friends. Her mobile is on the table beside her and she's hoping her agent will call with that one part she's been waiting for; the part that will send her career into the stratosphere and make all the rejections worthwhile. She's quite shy in her personal life, not as confident as people think she is, but when she inhabits a character she comes alive, freely and completely. She isn't in a relationship at the moment because men find her quite difficult to deal with, mostly because of her independent nature and the need to put her career first. She would drop everything for any role and most men find that hard. They want to be put first, but she can't do it - she just *can't* anymore. She did once, a long time ago, but he let her down.'

I watched her intently as she spoke. My eyes didn't leave her face for one second. She talked freely, eloquently, without pausing. There was silence for a moment while she continued to look at the young woman she was describing and in those few seconds I saw everything around Nell fall away, leaving her alone and dazzling in a difficult and demanding world. And that world, although the one she had chosen, was so tough it was often heartbreaking and possibly friendless. She turned and smiled at me.

'And I thought she was an accountant,' I said, in my best sardonic tone, breaking the spell for her sake. She let out her glorious, raucous laugh and the redundant civil servant jumped out of his skin as if he'd been electrocuted and looked towards us with a frown.

'You're funny, Mr Marshall. How's your banana cake? Delicious, isn't it!'

'It certainly is, if I can get it from my trembling hand into my mouth without it going via Camden.'

She leant forward and gently wiped a crumb from my chin.

'There you go - that's better.'

'How on earth did it get there?' I said, laughing despite myself and curious as to why I didn't feel embarrassed.

'It's just a gift you have.'

'It's a gift I could do without.'

'Are you warmer now? Let's go and talk to General Wolfe.'

My heart sank. 'I could sit here for hours.'

She wagged her finger at me. 'I know you could, but we have to walk and then I have an audition ...'

'Oh Nell, my dear girl, I'm sorry – I'm taking up your time. Of course you have places to go, people to see. How selfish of me. I'm sorry.'

'Don't be silly, I have another hour or two. Put your hat on.'

We rested on the bench under General Wolfe and she sat close to me. I could feel her warmth and it seemed to seep into my veins. We chatted about inconsequential things and she was constantly interested in whatever I had to say. She had such a love of life, grabbing at it with both hands; it was beginning to rub off on me. Her infectious enthusiasm for every sentence I uttered often rendered me speechless. Simply sharing a coffee with her, walking through the park, talking, playing silly games, learning about her, witnessing that laugh of hers from close quarters, were what I wanted to focus on now. I needed to focus on that instead of my illness and that was an enormous relief.

Sitting by the statue, looking out over the grandeur of the city before us and watching the sombre skies with a winter sun sparkling on the river was like seeing it all for the first time for me. There was a feeling of urgency and renewal that seemed to rejuvenate me.

'How many buildings can you name, Mr Marshall?' Nell suddenly asked.

'More than you, that's for sure.'

'That's because you've been alive so much longer than me,' she retorted.

'*That* I can't deny.'

'What's your favourite building?'

'I'd have to say the Queen's House.'

'Mine's the Dome. It's so futuristic; it looks like a space ship.'

'I rather like the old power station over there.'

She grinned. 'That's because it comes from another time – like you.'

'Ah yes, time's winged chariot and all that. The ravages of time are certainly showing on my face, that's for sure.'

'You aren't so bad.'

'How very kind of you, dear Nell, but I think you're being a stranger to the truth.'

'Stop speaking like a bloody dictionary, for God's sake!'

'But I speak like this all the time,' I protested, 'that's what I do.'

She frowned. 'Are your plays like that?'

'I'm afraid so.'

'Blimey!'

'How dare you. Have some respect for my craft.'

'I would have loved to have seen one of them.'

'You can read a script if you like.'

She opened her eyes wide. 'Can I really?'

'Of course, I'll dig one out for you.'

'I'd love to act in one of them. I think I'd be good at comedy, although I say it myself.'

'You need perfect timing more than anything else and a knack of getting humour from the flimsiest of lines. Many people think of comedy as lightweight, but it isn't. It's often harder than tragedy.'

'Are they romantic comedies?' she asked, her inquisitiveness quite touching.

'A couple of them are,' I smiled, almost wistfully, because writing them came from an easier and more fruitful time for me, 'although not romantic in the normal sense of the word. More like banter between the sexes and misunderstandings that are eventually resolved.'

'Like Noel Coward?'

'Oh, Nell, I can't confess to being as clever as him.'

'But that kind of thing?'

'I suppose so.'

'Michael Frayn, maybe?' she suggested.

'Something like that, but again, I don't think I'm in the same league.'

'Can you teach someone to write a play?'

'Possibly ...'

'I tell you what,' she said, sitting upright and grabbing my arm, 'you teach me to write and I'll teach you how to dance.'

'Dance!' I almost screeched. 'Dancing is out of the question now as well you know. I can't even walk properly let alone dance.'

She looked indignant. 'Of course you can still dance.'

'And, you're presupposing that I *want* to learn how to dance.'

'I'm not asking you to do a grand jeté across the living room,' she laughed.

I turned my nose up. 'I'm not even sure what that is.'

She put her face very near mine. 'A little Fred Astaire would be right up your street.'

'I can't imagine anything worse.'

'Don't start being a grumpy old man.'

'But I *am* a grumpy old man,' I replied, 'and I can no longer dance I tell you.'

'So you could then?' she asked, her face full of mischief like a naughty Spaniel puppy.

'Very clever ...'

'I'm telling you, you can still dance. Tap dancing isn't hard.'

I put on my best sneer. 'Let's not go into the realms of fantasy now.'

'Watch, you can do this.'

She jumped up and stood in front of me. She began by tapping one foot, then with both feet and she turned quickly with a slight flourish and began again. Her movements were light and fluid and had just the right amount of natural flair without being too theatrical. A few hardy dog walkers and a handful of tourists with their back packs and cameras were watching from afar and I noticed some admiring glances from them. I found I was smiling and clapping, entranced by the graceful, athletic way she used her body and in those few moments, watching her, I completely forgot to focus on my disease for the first time since my diagnosis. It was as if my head suddenly cleared and I saw only her moving. She laughed and gave a little bow at the end and I cheered, along with some of the foreign students who had gathered and we all made eye contact fleetingly in admiration.

'Now you try,' she urged.

I sat back and folded my arms across my chest. 'If you think for one minute I'm going to stand here and make an utter fool of myself, with my stumbling legs, in these conditions, you're very much mistaken.'

'Get up, you silly old bugger,' she ordered, pulling me gently to my feet.

'Nell, there's ice ...'

'Right, follow me.'

'Nell ...'

'Don't stand there with a face like a wet weekend in a fortnight, Mr Marshall.'

'Say that again.'

'Tap, tap, tap, tap, step ball change.'

'What the hell is a step ball change?'

She laughed out loud. 'I knew you were going to ask that, just follow me.'

I reluctantly cast aside my inhibitions and fear of failure and followed what she was doing as best I could, but my brain didn't seem to want to send any messages down to my useless legs and my left side especially was doing its own thing rather deftly. But with Nell grasping my hand and laughing up at me, I quickly forgot my embarrassment and my hopeless, uncoordinated limbs and just enjoyed the moment. In fact, it suddenly dawned on me, it was the first time in my life I had ever just enjoyed a moment for its own sake and pleasure. All my life I had been nostalgic for things never experienced, chasing the next challenge, racing full speed at anything and everything which I thought might give me a mental or physical thrill and then, for some reason now incomprehensible to me, dulling my senses with alcohol.

This moment, this one exhilarating moment, I was free from imagining what was coming next, anticipating where my next fix of excitement might come from and simply enjoying the present. I no longer wanted to live in an expectant future because that future was uncertain and a blank canvas onto which my disease would spread like a stain. Living one frame at a time, as if looking at life as separate photographs, felt more secure, interesting, satisfying and playful. And I longed to be playful – I wanted to live in my world with a child's expectancy and find joy in the smallest things, like dancing with Nell.

I realised she was looking up at me. 'You did it, Mr Marshall,' she whispered.

'I suppose I did, but as to whether I did it *well*, that's another story.'

'It doesn't matter with dance. You just have to do what you feel. Who cares if you get it wrong?'

'I suppose you're right, but some semblance of an art form would be better than none at all.'

She let out her glorious laugh again. 'What are you on about?'

'I have absolutely no idea. I feel quite light headed and almost boyish,' I declared, pretending to flick my hair back with a flourish, to amuse her.

'That's really funny,' she said, her laugh bellowing out like a blast from a cannon. 'Come on,' she urged, taking my arm and leading me back towards the tennis courts, 'I think that's enough excitement for one day, don't you?'

'At my advanced years, yes it is. I enjoyed it though.'

'Well, that just proves my point doesn't it, Mr Marshall?'

'And what point is that, Nell?'

'That you can do anything you set your mind to, with or without Parkinson's. Remember that.'

I felt ridiculously grateful to know her as she scrutinised my face.

'I will remember that.'

She looked up at me from under the rim of her hat again and her eyes were large and solemn. 'Do you promise?'

'Yes, I promise.'

She left me at my front door after steering me successfully around some hideously icy patches and deep compact snow that had been shovelled to the edges of the road and piled up like mini mountains.

'Sorry I have to dash. I can't be late, it looks so unprofessional. And it looks a bit grey over Bill's mother's.'

'Say that again.'

'It's just one of my sayings. I must go ...'

'Where exactly are you going?'

'Only up to town for an audition, but I won't say too much about it because it could jinx it and I'm ever so superstitious.'

'Fair enough, good luck, Nell.'

She grinned. 'Thanks! See you soon, Mr Marshall. Take care of yourself. And remember this! I'm going to teach you how to dance. It'll be so good for you. Bye.'

Then she was gone before I could form a reply and I watched the Nell shaped space where she had been for a long time. I fell asleep almost immediately after sitting down in the conservatory and when I awoke I felt groggy and listless. I put some of it down to being outside in the fresh, freezing February air, but I knew part of how I felt were the tablets kicking in to my system. I imagined them settling into my blood stream, seeping into my cells, my nerve endings and changing the way my brain worked. That thought frightened the life out of me and I felt peculiar, as if I was floating just a few inches above the ground.

Sidney suddenly appeared at the door, all flushed face and belly to the fore and I beckoned him in with my trembling hand. 'It can't be four,' I spluttered.

'It is, almost,' he replied. 'Did I wake you up?'

'No, don't worry.'

'So, what's occurring then, Benedict? Are you okay, matey? Your face looks a bit rigid.'

'The pills,' I slurred and I felt some saliva slide down my chin.

He sat down opposite me. 'Aren't they supposed to help you?'

I nodded feeling drained and lethargic as if my blood had seeped out of my veins and across the floor. 'I'm sure they will poison me, but what can I do? Fuck, I'm starting to dribble now.'

'Well, all these bloody things have side effects. Bet they make you impotent too.'

I found myself frowning. 'Least of my worries ... can't imagine ever bothering with that again.'

Sidney opened his eyes wide in surprise. 'Blimey!'

'I can't quite believe I'm saying this, but there are pleasures in life other than sex, Sidney. You must know that. Your marriage must have changed over the years.'

'Yes, it has,' he said, leaning back and making himself comfortable.

'Well then ...'

'But that's a natural thing that takes place when you've been married a lifetime. I thought you would always be an old reprobate.'

'Is that a compliment?'

'Yes.'

'It didn't feel like one.'

'Sheila said, do you want dinner tonight?'

I blinked hard to focus my eyes better, but my head was actually clearing and the conversation had livened up my sleeping brain. 'What's on the menu?'

'You've got a bloody nerve!'

'I'm joking. That would be lovely.'

'Fish and chips, as it happens, as it's a Friday.'

'I didn't know you were religious.'

'If dinner's at six,' he continued, ignoring my comment, 'I think a couple of hours of cards till then is required.'

I struggled to sit up. 'Don't think you're going to take advantage of me because I'm doped up on tablets.'

'As if,' he replied, smiling and shuffling the cards that had been sitting snugly in his pocket. 'So, have a nice walk, did we?'

I shook my head. 'You'll turn to stone sitting by that window and nosing all the time.'

'Lovely looking girl ...'

'I think so.'

'Very young,' he added.

'Not so young, older than Beth.'

'I should bloody well hope so!'

'It's not like that ...'

'What does she do?'

'She's an actress,' I replied, waiting for the next comment.

'Oh yeah,' he sneered.

'What does that mean?'

'What's actress a euphemism for?'

'Sidney, I didn't know you knew long words like that.'

'I don't usually. That one just popped into my head for some reason. I must have heard it somewhere. Oh yeah, on Radio Four. I listen to Radio Four sometimes so I can be as intelligent as you, but it's not really working because I can't understand half of what they're on about.'

'Don't keep putting yourself down, Sidney.'

'So, she's obviously at a loose end at the moment.'

'Who is?'

He gave a heavy sigh, 'Nell, you twat.'

'Yes, resting I think they call it.'

'Oh yeah ...'

'Will you stop saying that? Deal the cards.'

He was shaking his head. 'Fuck me! I don't know how you do it.'

'I don't ...'

'You used to,' he laughed.

'Cruel, Sidney...'

'Not got a lot of money then,' he said, sniffing for effect. 'Nell, I mean.'

'I have no idea, but I wouldn't have thought so.'

'Where did you meet her?'

'In the park, we just kind of started talking. I told you all this, didn't I? She couldn't believe I lived here, it's always been her favourite house.'

'Oh yeah ...'

'Sidney!'

He looked over his glasses at me. 'She'll be after your money, mate.'

'Don't be such a cynic,' I snapped and immediately regretted it because his cheerful face dropped to the floor and he looked like a child who had been rebuked.

'Sorry, Benedict, I didn't mean to be cynical, but just be careful. You'd be a good catch.'

'Don't be ridiculous, a good catch! I'm hardly that now,' I cried. 'I know I now look daft and I'm dribbling like an idiot and the illness and pills will no doubt affect my brain in the long term, but I'm not daft yet I'll have you know and I'd be fully aware of anyone materialistic, believe me. I can spot it from a hundred yards. I was married to Mary remember. Now,' I added, 'let's change the subject, shall we?'

'What shall we play?' he asked, the cards resting in his right hand. I went to answer him, but my speech slurred badly and I couldn't remember what the hell I was going to say. 'Benedict, what shall we play?' he repeated.

'Sidney,' I muttered and my voice was small and insignificant, 'I think I'll pass, do you mind? I need to have a rest before dinner, if that's ...'

'Sure, fine with me,' he butted in, looking concerned. 'Have a kip and I'll see you about six.'

'Thanks. I think the fresh air has tired me out.'

'No problem, no problem, see you later, mate.'

He wandered out, glancing back briefly and as he left I put my head back and closed my eyes. They felt heavy, gritty and sore. Colours swirled around inside my head and I could hear soft voices, conversations in the distance, but I couldn't quite make out the words being said. I thought I recognised my mother's voice and my father's laugh, but it had been so long since I had heard either in this life I wasn't sure. I almost felt as if I was moving around the room, a few inches above the carpet with my head being thrown back, like on a ride at a fairground. It was an oddly pleasant experience and I was tempted to stay in that position and relish the feeling. But then a voice, deeply resonant and familiar called my name.

'Benedict, come along and help your mother.'

'I will,' I replied, straining to open my leaden eyes.

He was sitting on my piano stool, his face as distinguished and handsome as ever. His good looks and charming manner were what had attracted my mother initially, but his kind, sunny and generous nature were what had made her love him from the moment she first heard him speak. He was dressed in his best, dark Sunday suit and I smiled inwardly at his moustache. As children my siblings and I were fascinated by it because it was dark brown, a few shades lighter than his golden brown hair.

'Papa,' I stuttered, struggling to sit up, 'what on earth are you doing here? I thought you were dead.'

'I am, my darling boy, but it doesn't mean I can't drop in on you.'

His eyes were soft and welcoming. I remembered those eyes. They were unusually blue, like the shallow sea surrounding a Mediterranean island. They would crease up when he smiled and almost disappear. Seeing him there suddenly, I recalled how deeply I had loved him and how missed he was still. In the late gloomy afternoon twilight, it hit me again as it had when he died, that the death of someone very much loved meant never not missing them, but simply accepting your life wasn't ever going to be the same again and having to learn to live in a world where they no longer existed, however hard you searched for them.

'I'm so pleased to see you, Papa,' I told him, blinking hard. 'Why are you here now, after all this time? Look at me. I'm almost an old man now.'

'I needed to see you, Benedict. You've been upset by your illness. But you must live your life and make the most of every day.'

'Yes, yes, I know. I was upset, very upset. It was a bolt out of the blue, but I'm better now, honestly. You don't need to worry.' I had something pressing to tell him and it was weighing me down. I had to explain, ask forgiveness for how I had lived my life. 'Papa, I've not always been the son you knew. I lost my way a little after you died. I haven't always been honest, mostly with women, and I'm not the man you were I'm afraid...I'm so sorry...but you should see Beth now...she's lovely and...I'm proud of her.'

'Are you kind, Benedict? Have you always been kind?' he asked, his dear face becoming a little blurred. 'Are you a good man now? That is all that matters.'

'I hope so ... I think so. I think I've been a good father to Beth.'

'Good boy,' he whispered, smiling. 'That's the most important thing. Just be true to yourself. We love you.'

I smiled back relieved to have finally been able to declare my anxieties and feelings of guilt to him. 'And I love you. Papa, I'm so happy to see you again. So, so happy, I've missed you so much, we all miss you.'

He gave me one of his fond looks that I had forgotten in the intervening years since he had left us. 'Benedict, let her go and she'll come back to you,' he whispered.

I found myself staring at an empty space by the piano as my clock in the corner chimed six times prettily. Then, in sharp contrast to the delicate chiming, I heard a heavy thumping on the wall. It agitated me and I was disturbingly confused. What year was it? Was Beth still a child? Something had been making me feel happy in the last few days, but I struggled to remember what that something was.

The intrusive thumping continued and suddenly it was as if a cloud of dense, moist fog lifted and I was left clear-headed after the crashing confusion. It was Sidney knocking! After a few more moments he appeared outside the conservatory, his face strained.

'Why didn't you answer, for Christ's sake? Benedict, why didn't you answer?'

'Give me a chance. I can't move as quickly as I could,' I told him, deeply touched by his worried expression.

'Have you been sitting there since I left?' he asked, eyeing my crumpled clothes no doubt.

'I fell asleep again. I'm coming, Sidney.'

'I'll tell Sheila.'

'Get a grip, Benedict,' I hissed, annoyed at myself for worrying him and wondering what the hell had happened.

I was subdued at Sidney's because I was fixated on my father's face. His laughing eyes and elegant, gentlemanly manner were what I had longed to emulate all my adult life, failing miserably most of the time in my own estimation. It had all been there, in front of me, inches away after all these years. What on earth was happening to me? At least I had managed to confess to him my regrets, my lack of honesty, my failings as a man. His answer to me after all these lonely years without his guidance and affection comforted me greatly. But what had he meant about letting her go? Letting who go? Beth, presumably, but I had, reluctantly, encouraged her to go to America.

I made my excuses to Sidney and Sheila as soon as I could without being impolite. They both picked up on my unusual lack of wit and sarcasm and imagined I was tired, letting me go without any fuss or reluctance. As I wearily climbed my stairs at about seven the phone was ringing. I hoped it was Beth.

'Hello, Mr Marshall,' Nell's cheerful voice said.

'I don't remember giving you my number,' I muttered, my voice flat and uninteresting and worrying that my memory was flying away to a faraway place where I wouldn't be able to retrieve it.

'I looked it up in the phone book,' she said. 'I can be very resourceful. Was that OK? I didn't think you'd mind.'

'Yes, of course, dear girl,' I stuttered, knowing I had snapped at her and wondering what on earth possessed me.

'What's wrong?' she asked, picking up my mood immediately.

'I feel a little strange, Nell. It must be the tablets.'

'I'm coming round.'

She must have run all the way. When I opened the door her face was flushed and she was puffing hard, her long dark hair swimming around and falling into her eyes.

'Did you run all the way?'

'Yes, because you didn't sound right. Come and sit down. You look a little grey, Mr Marshall.'

I gave her a weak smile. 'I *feel* a little grey.'

'You were fine when I left you.'

We made our way slowly to the conservatory and my legs felt as if the blood was flooding back into them. 'To be honest I think the tablets are suddenly reaching the parts other tablets haven't reached before ... like my brain.'

She was staring intently at my face. 'Shall I make some tea? Have you eaten?'

'Yes, I had dinner with Sidney and Sheila. But a cup of tea would be wonderful, thank you. Nell, whatever did I do to deserve you in my life?'

She shook her head and gave me a stunning smile. 'Shut your face, you daft apath.'

'Delightful, I must say.'

'That sounds more like you,' she said, looking highly relieved. 'I'll make the tea.'

Hearing her pottering about in my kitchen flooded my body with warmth and I could feel my anxiety retreating slowly like little waves over sand. I thought to myself, I don't need tablets, I just need Nell.

'Do you want biscuits?' she called.

'Say it a bit louder. Sidney next door didn't quite hear you.'

'Very funny,' she replied, appearing with the tray of tea. 'Sidney must be a good friend of yours.'

'Yes, he is.'

'What's he like?' she asked.

'He speaks before he thinks, has no respect for my finely tuned intellect ...'

'Hark at you!' she said, laughing, flicking her hair out of her eyes. 'But he's kind to you.'

'Yes, Nell, he's kind to me and so are you. Thank you for coming.'

She waved her hand as if brushing away a fly. 'It's nothing ...'

'You say it's nothing, but it is to me.'

'Do you feel any better?'

'Yes, I do. Too much time to sit and think about my symptoms,' I told her.

My first instinct was always to make light of how I felt, but then I looked over at her sweet, open face, radiant with life and yet caring about an ageing, infirm man she had only just met and I sighed. She picked up on the sigh of course.

'What's wrong, Mr Marshall? Something is, so tell me.'

'No, it's nothing ... really ...'

She pursed her lips in exasperation. 'You speak the words, but your eyes tell me something completely different so just spit it out, for goodness sake. I feel terrible about dragging you out in the cold and making you walk all that way ...'

'And dance, don't forget about the dancing.'

'Are you sure it isn't my fault you feel odd?'

'Nell, I'm not even going to answer that question. You do me good, you always do me good, so stop worrying.'

'You did sound peculiar on the phone though,' she said, still scanning my face.

'Look, I'm going to tell you something that might make you think I'm going a bit ... you know, losing it a bit.'

She leant towards me. 'Just tell me,' she urged.

'I fell asleep as soon you as you had left,' I started, encouraged by her openness, 'the fresh air and exercise no doubt and coming into the warm and when I woke up I felt groggy, as if my head was full of cotton wool.'

'You probably went into a deep sleep.'

'Yes, yes, I'm sure I did, but I had the strangest sensation too as if I was floating just above the ground and I thought I heard my mother's voice ...'

Her eyes opened wide in surprise. 'That's lovely.'

'Hold on, I haven't finished. And this wasn't a dream, I was awake ... I saw my father sitting by the piano and he died in 1984.'

She instinctively glanced over towards my piano. 'Blimey,' she mumbled. 'What did he look like? Was he wishy-washy or solid and did he appear to be young or as old as he was when he died?'

'You believe me then?'

She appeared even more surprised. 'Of course I bloody well believe you! Why wouldn't I?'

'Thank you, Nell.'

'Well, go on,' she urged, enthralled, 'what happened next? Did he speak? Did you ask him what it's like on the other side?'

'Yes, he spoke ...'

'Oh, my God,' she gasped.

'He appeared young, well ... no, middle aged, as he was when we were growing up. He was an attractive man, well mannered, charismatic ...'

'Just like you.'

'No, much more than me, but thank you for that. He was a true gentleman, courteous and kindly ...'

'Just like you,' she said, again.

'I don't think I'm anything like him,' I admitted, my tone of voice revealing my sense of regret. 'He had such an elegant way about him and it was all there as he spoke.'

'This is wonderful,' she whispered. 'Imagine how many people would love to see their loved ones again.'

'Yes,' I muttered, knowing she was right. 'But it is rather a shock and I'm convinced it has something to do with the inner workings of my muddled, decaying brain rather than anything else.'

'Maybe, but who cares? I'd sell my soul to the devil to see my dad again. What did he actually say?'

'That he loved me,' I replied because at that moment, sitting opposite her, it was all I could remember.

Her eyes filled with tears in an instant. 'How lovely for you,' she gasped, wiping them away as they fell down her face. 'I wish ... sorry, go on.'

'And he said something about Beth, I think.'

'What was it?'

'Something about letting her go and she'll come back to me, I think it was that. I don't know what it meant because I let her go quite happily to America. Not that I don't worry about her, of course I do, but it was never an issue between us. I'm not that kind of father. I only ever want her to be happy. I don't care about myself in relation to her and her life.'

'I know,' she said, 'I can tell.'

'And then he was gone and I was staring at an empty space and Sidney was banging on the wall and then he rushed round because he was worried about me ...'

'I bet he was.'

'I ate my tea with them, pretty subdued and in shock and I made my excuses early and left. I think I fell asleep again and then you rang, dear girl, checking in on me I suppose.'

'Good job,' she remarked, 'what with you talking to the long departed.'

'Nell, he was real.'

She gave me a little smile. 'I believe you, Mr Marshall.'

'Thank you. It's probably the tablets, but even so, he was as real as you are.'

'I'll look it up on the internet for you – the side effects of tablets for Parkinson's. What are they called?'

'They're in the kitchen, go take a look.' She jumped up and went to the kitchen. 'By the bread bin,' I called.

'Got them,' she called back.

'There's a pen and notebook in there by the phone, write them down.'

'Gotcha,' she replied, reappearing with a piece of paper in her hand.

'Nell, you are an angel.'

She let out a blast of her wondrous laugh. 'I don't know about that, but you look better now, thank God. The colour has flooded back into your cheeks.'

'Dear God,' I gasped, 'how was your audition?'

She shrugged carelessly, but her eyes gave away the fact that she had encountered another disappointment. 'I won't get it, I could tell by the way they spoke to me. Thanks, but no thanks kind of thing; but onwards and upwards as they say. I did my best, but it wasn't a singing part and it's my voice that gives me the edge I reckon.'

'I'm so sorry.'

'Something will come up,' she said, trying to convey positivity when she felt anything but. 'It obviously wasn't right for me.'

'No,' I mumbled, not knowing what else to say.

'Look, I won't see you for a few days because I'm working in my sister's café, but I'll call you and we'll walk again, as long as you don't think it's too much for you.'

'It's not too much for me,' I declared, desperate for her company and even if it had half killed me I wouldn't have let her know.

She looked at me sternly. 'Be honest, Mr Marshall.'

'I am always honest with you, Nell.'

'Do you feel it will do you good?'

'Oh … yes,' I stuttered, thinking to myself that her company was the best medicine I could possibly have.

'Are you sure?' Then she grinned. 'I never know if you're taking the piss.'

I gave her a small smile. 'Nell, as if I'd do that.'

'And the dance lessons? Don't forget I'm going to teach you to dance.'

'I'd hardly forget that!'

She got up to leave. 'Bye, see you soon.'

I tried not to look too forlorn. Our easy intimacy was something I was beginning to cherish and I knew if I saw her every day it wouldn't be enough.

'Bye, Nell.'

Her light footsteps away from me seemed to echo gravely around the whole house and I heard the front door close quietly, leaving me alone in the black shadows with my jumbled, half crazy thoughts and the memory of my father's face. What was happening to me? My heart and head had been hijacked; my heart by a lovely young woman and my head by Parkinson's.

For some reason, the next morning my legs felt leaden and determined to do whatever they wanted, irrespective of the signals my brain was sending them. I decided, probably foolishly, to get in some provisions and made my precarious way to the local supermarket. Getting there was relatively easy and I leant on a trolley all the way round, but carrying two heavy bags back again turned into a nightmare. My spindly legs began to buckle, misbehave and become rather floppy. At one point I felt my walking resembled someone under the influence of quite a bit of alcohol. I remembered how hopeless it had been attempting to walk in a straight line when I had been drinking all night and how trying to do just that, to fool my eagle-eyed wife, had resulted in me studiously staring at the ground and smiling inanely at anything and everything. Drunks trying to hide they are drunk were the most ridiculous sight and fooled nobody except perhaps themselves. Now my Parkinson's was hurling me back to those ludicrous moments, whether I wanted to go there or not because the illness didn't care. I imagined it as an actual entity who was laughing at my predicament and teasing me mercilessly. I could almost hear it saying, 'So, what are you going to do about *this*? I control you now! You have no choice but to give in and be my slave!'

My thoughts had an immediate effect on my legs and I tripped slightly and fell across the pavement, dropping my bags to steady myself against a wall. It didn't help that I had just passed the pub on the corner, so to anyone glancing at me, it must have looked as if I had stumbled out of the saloon bar. I heard someone sigh loudly and as I glanced up an older woman with an unfortunate blue rinse was glaring at me from over her glasses, with a face like thunder. I seemed to shrivel up like a dry leaf under her disapproving look.

I steadied myself and went to pick up my shopping slowly when I stumbled again and alarmed at my uselessness I leant against the wall and simply blinked repeatedly at the chasm between myself and the bags, which was all of ten yards but might just as well have been a hundred.

'I'm not drunk,' I muttered at anyone who might be listening, when a young man appeared out of nowhere like an angel without any wings. He was gangly yet energetic and he knelt down easily and put some of the items, which had ended up sprawled across the pavement, back where they belonged. He looked up at me.

'Is this your shopping, mate?' I noticed his extreme youth first, his freckles and his open, friendly manner. His eyes took in my demeanour immediately and his expression turned to one of sincere sympathy. 'Are you OK?'

'I'm not drunk,' I said again, rather too loudly and forcefully, in the hope that she with the blue hair and sour face was still within earshot. Alas she had moved on, no doubt concerned about the type of person hanging around her neighbourhood.

The young man picked up my bags effortlessly as if they were as light as a feather and brought them over. 'I know, mate,' he replied, 'and I wouldn't care if you were. Would you like me to carry your shopping home for you?' He reminded me of a young fawn, skinny legs and arms, large brown eyes and quite beautiful, especially in his manner which was immensely compassionate and gentle. 'Where do you live?' he asked.

'Not too far, just up the hill a bit, by the park, but please don't worry...'

I felt truly grateful that he ignored my protestations and walked by my side carrying my bags and I told him as much. I also told him I detected an Aussie twang in his speech.

'That obvious is it?' he said, smiling. 'My mum is English, so when I was at school in Melbourne the other kids made fun of my accent.'

'Are you here on holiday?' I asked as we neared my house.

'Nah, I'm studying at Greenwich University and loving every minute of it.'

'Wonderful,' I said, envying his enthusiasm and his muscular arms. 'This is my house, thank you for your help.'

His eyes opened wide in surprise and he whistled through his teeth. 'Wow! Cool house, man.'

I thought of Nell. 'Yes, so I'm told.'

He put out his hand. 'Well, great to meet you. I'd better get going.'

I took his hand and shook it firmly. 'Thank you...'

'I'm Hugh by the way.'

'Benedict.'

His eyes lit up. 'That's a classy English name. My mum had an uncle called Benedict. He was almost a Lord.'

'Almost a Lord, eh?'

'Yeah, bloody rich too. But hey, hope you feel better soon, man.'

'Ah,' I said, 'getting better is not an option. I have Parkinson's.'

His face fell. 'I'm sorry to hear that, Benedict. But you can live with that, right?'

His sunny disposition, his youthful positivity and obvious love of life seemed to shine from him like a golden aura of sizzling summer heat. 'Yes,' I replied, 'you can live with it. *I* can live with it.'

'Well, good luck, mate. Good to meet you.' He bounded off like a young puppy eager to catch up with its owner.

I stood watching him speed away with an easy athleticism that I could only envy. Stinging tears streamed down my face. They had been brewing since the undignified sprawling across the pavement. The young man with his strength, his smooth, unlined face and clear complexion, his casual grace, his kindness and his clear eyes that held no fear of the future, all reminded me of what I had lost. And yet his words, 'But you can live with that, right?' they resonated deeply.

I had to stop feeling sorry for myself. I had to focus on what I *could* do, not what I couldn't. I would have to wage war on my Parkinson's. And if I declared war, I had to be prepared to fight with all I had.

Chapter 3

'Benedict, you look quietly content,' Sidney said, as he sipped his afternoon tea in my conservatory.

A warm winter sun was drenching us as it streamed through my glass roof and despite the vicious, snowy conditions, it gave the illusion that warmer weather had arrived early. I had slipped a little whisky in both our mugs and it brought a burning red to Sidney's already flushed cheeks.

'Do I?' I replied, not giving anything away because I wasn't sure in which direction he wanted the conversation to head.

He narrowed his pale blue eyes. 'Is it that young girl putting a twinkle in your eye?'

I pretended to look shocked. 'I wasn't aware I had a twinkle in my eye, Sidney. And what actually *is* a twinkle anyway?' I asked, leaning back on my sofa and stretching my cramped legs.

'You know, a sparkle, a kind of mischievous look, like you're up to something you shouldn't be.'

I had to smile because he looked almost envious. 'I assure you I'm not up to anything. I haven't the will or the energy, but I agree that I feel oddly contented although I really shouldn't with this illness.'

Sidney pointed his finger at me. 'Exactly, that's what I mean and you didn't answer my question.'

'What was the question again?' I asked, knowing full well.

'Stop taking the rise.'

'Sidney, she's just a friend – honestly – and I have nothing else to tell you other than that I feel incredibly lucky to have met her. Getting to know her has been truly wonderful and given me something other than my symptoms to focus on.'

He appeared suitably indignant. 'Why does she want to be friends with you?'

'Well, I hate to point this out to you, but you're a friend of mine.'

'Yeah,' he mumbled, 'but that's different.'

'Aha, I see.'

'She's after something,' he added, in his usual blunt way, pointing his finger at me rather accusingly.

'Look, she doesn't want anything from me and anyway I have nothing to offer her. I'm sixty two and I have a chronic illness ...'

'Money!' he declared. 'You have money and lots of it. She probably has sod all if she's an out of work actress.'

'I'm so glad you're continuing with your lifelong habit of speaking before you think and embarrassing yourself,' I told him, shaking my head and putting my hand over my eyes as a way of escaping his accusatory look. 'Drink your tea, eat your fruit cake and shut up.'

'I'm just saying,' he continued, ignoring me as usual, 'be careful, keep your eyes open and don't be swayed by her pretty face. There's many an old fool been swayed by a pretty face.'

I laughed loudly. 'I thought you were going to say, there's many a good tune played on an old fiddle. But I'm an old fool now, am I?'

'All men are fools,' he remarked.

I sighed. 'I know this disease may turn my brain to mush, but I'm not an idiot yet.'

'Your disease may not turn your brain to mush, but she will.'

My heart had inexplicably begun to jump around wildly and I felt suddenly irritated with him for making Nell out to be something I knew instinctively she wasn't. 'Sidney, we've been good friends for more years than I can remember and I care deeply for you and Sheila, but I have to tell you, I won't have a word said against Nell, so please ...'

He didn't let me finish before he began apologising. 'I know, I know, I'm sorry. I shouldn't have said anything, but you have to agree there's a huge age difference.'

'For romance, yes,' I sighed, beginning to feel exasperated with him, 'but who made the rule that you can't have friends of all ages? Now, let's discuss politics or religion, something mundane like that. Anything other than why Nell likes me.'

Sidney's face was beginning to look a little too flushed. 'I'm not saying it's surprising she likes you. *I* like you, you're a great bloke.'

'Thank you,' I said, feigning surprise.

'But Benedict, be careful. I'm just watching out for you.'

'You don't have to. I'm capable of being quite sensible you know.'

'Not where women are concerned,' he muttered into his tea cup.

'I heard that.'

'Sorry.'

'Just change the subject.'

He peered at me over his glasses. 'Does Beth know?'

'Does she know about the Parkinson's? No.'

'No, you twat, I mean about Nell.'

I paused for a moment before answering. 'No, she doesn't know about either.'

'I see,' he said, in a certain way.

'There's nothing to tell,' I insisted, sounding rather indignant. 'We have fun, we laugh, we play silly games ...'

'Oh yeah ...'

'Sidney, shut up.'

There was a moment's uneasy silence while he chomped on his cake, but I knew something else was brewing – something equally as blunt – by the blank expression on his face. It indicated that something would jump out of his mouth without engaging in his brain first.

'Fuck me! You don't love her, do you?'

And there it was. I sat dumb. The white sunshine sparkled across the table between us and I wrestled with my answer. I felt as if I was pinned down, stark naked under the spotlight of his searching questions. Denying the emotions that had bubbled up quickly and constantly since I first heard Nell speak would be akin to denying what I felt for Beth. But, if I had admitted it, Sidney would turn it into something less than delightful and pure.

'Look...'

'Oh, mate, you poor bastard!'

'Why do you say that?'

'Because if you love her she'll probably disappoint you and you'll be hurt and you don't need that at your time of your life,' he cried with a genuine softness in his eyes, 'especially with the illness. Stress won't do it any good at all.'

'You only think she'll disappoint me because you think she's after my money and she isn't,' I protested, wearily.

'Benedict, you're sixty-two, you have Parkinson's ...'

'Thanks for reminding me.'

'Are you ready for disappointment?'

I finished my tea and wrestled with his question. I knew he had a point and I understood that without meeting Nell he would continue to wonder. 'I'm ready for whatever comes my way connected to her because she is kind, caring and thoughtful and honest. If she disappoints me I'll forgive her. She's a beautiful person and talented and she has a depth of feeling I haven't come across in any other woman, irrespective of age. If everyone else in my life turned against me, but I still had Nell, I could stand it.'

He stared at me, his mouth slightly open like a hungry fish. 'Fuck me!'

'What, Sidney?'

'She's really made an impact on you in a short space of time, hasn't she?'

'Yes,' I admitted, without embarrassment, 'she has.'

'What are you going to do about it?'

I shrugged because I hadn't thought deeply about what I felt for her or how she felt about me – none of it. I had simply been relishing her company and enjoying the moment.

'Live with it,' I replied, eventually.

He rolled his eyes dramatically. 'You are a silly old sod.'

'I quite agree that I can stand in the ranks of all the silly old sods who ever lived,' I declared.

'You aren't supposed to agree ...'

'T'was ever thus ...'

'For fuck's sake, why can't you talk like normal people do?' He rolled his eyes yet again as if I was a hopeless being.

'Sidney, I'm not normal people. You must know that by now.'

He laughed out loud and his belly began wobbling up and down alarmingly. 'Don't I just! You sound as if you're in one of your posh plays.'

'That's because I wrote them you idiot.'

He appeared thoughtful for a moment. 'So, what's she after then?'

'Are we back to Nell again?'

'I mean, there won't be much how's your father with you, will there?' he asked, smirking.

I shook my head in despair at him. '*How's your father*? What an awful expression. Sidney, where's your sense of decorum?'

'It's gone up the pictures with your common sense! Why don't clever people have any common sense? Answer me that.'

I was confused. '*Gone up the pictures*? I take it that means disappeared, gone away somewhere...'

He laughed again. 'Sometimes I wonder where you were brought up. Did everyone speak like you?'

'It was only Sussex, Sidney, not some far-flung colonial outpost and no, not everyone spoke like me – only my brother and father.'

He looked a little wistful suddenly. 'I'd like to speak like you,

Benedict.'

'Why on earth would you?'

'Because people listen when you speak and...'

'That's extremely kind of you, Sidney, but I fear my disease will eat away at my vocal dexterity.'

'There you go again. What does that actually mean?'

'It means, I'm beginning to splutter and slur and I've noticed my voice falling away at the end of sentences. Some days I sound drunk.'

'I had noticed.'

'Thank you.'

He crossed his arms over his protruding belly. 'So, what were we talking about? Oh yeah, Nell. Just keep your wits about you, Benedict,' he warned, his face resembling a bloodhound, all doleful eyes and saggy chins.

'Look, enough about Nell. Let's talk about how much weight you're putting on around your middle, shall we?'

He laughed loudly. 'I don't give a flying fuck about my stomach anymore,' he said, proudly.

'You have a wonderful command of the English language, Sidney. I've never heard anyone use that word as an adjective, a noun *and* a verb.'

Obviously determined to have the last word, Sidney ignored my comments, sighed and shook his head. 'Well, I can see she has cast her spell on you already, so I won't say any more.'

He stayed until six –his dinner time – and we chatted together about mundane matters, as usual. I didn't ask Sidney to speak of deep, life-altering subjects because he didn't know any. He had a one-track mind about most subjects: his track, which he had been meandering down all his life.

I remembered once having had a short and comical conversation with him about religion. I had always been an atheist, despite being a confirmed member of the Church of England and having been dragged, unwillingly, to Sunday school as a young child. But Sidney had been baptised a Catholic and, despite the fact he had never set foot in a Catholic Church since he came of age, when I had laughed at miracles being performed at Lourdes, he had at once become a zealot and crossed himself four times.

'What on earth are you doing?' I had asked, perplexed. 'You don't believe in all that codswallop, do you?'

'Codswallop! You'll be struck down,' he'd gasped, 'mocking like that.'

'I'm not mocking. I was just expressing an opinion and my opinion is, you can't possibly call yourself a Catholic when the last time you went to church you were just out of short trousers!'

'It never leaves you, Benedict,' he'd replied, his eyes serious and almost sorrowful. 'Miracles, small miracles, happen every day.'

'You're only hedging your bets, Sidney,' I'd chuckled, 'just in case. All that sackcloth and ashes, and crossing yourself, what on earth do you get out of it?'

He had looked at me in disbelief. 'I get a sense of belonging.'

'Belonging to what?' I'd derided, 'you never go anywhere to belong to anything. Oh no, sorry, the pub, you belong to the local pub. That's the only place you go regularly, apart from my house. It's all just hogwash, Sidney - and you know it really. You just don't dare say it because you were made to feel afraid as a young child. Try thinking for yourself for once.'

He had then crossed himself again. 'I hope you never have reason to regret saying that, Benedict. I'll say a prayer for you later.'

'Don't bother,' I'd replied, knowing the conversation was going straight into a dead end.

A couple of hours after Sidney had gone home for his dinner it crossed my mind that he probably secretly thought my disease had been brought on by my sacrilegious words in that previous conversation. I fleetingly envied him his beliefs because, if I believed too, I could ask for a miracle to release me from my symptoms and have some small hope that my prayers would be answered. But it *was* fleeting and I quickly returned to my view that I was simply unlucky and that no miracle was going to rescue me. But he was a good man, a simple soul who forgave my many faults and accepted me as I was, trying his best to look out for me because he knew women had always been my weakness.

Darkness had fallen softly and unknowingly and I switched on the two lamps in the conservatory which gave out a soft, comforting golden light. I shifted my rambling thoughts to Nell and wondered when I would see her again. A few days seemed an eternity to me. Being with her automatically lightened my mood when it was careering towards sombre and I had never before felt such an affinity with a woman at any stage of my life. I switched on the television and dozed through a couple of lightweight programmes until the telephone woke me with a jolt. My heart leapt when I heard her voice on the other end.

'Did I wake you up?' she asked, in her sunny, joyful way.

'No, I was watching a gardening programme even though I never do any gardening myself, so I'm overjoyed to hear your voice. Is everything okay with you, Nell?'

'Yes, fine, I've been on the internet on a medical site,' she replied. 'I clicked on a link about your tablets.'

'Oh dear, am I going mad?'

'Far from it,' she went on, 'there are people with your illness on a regime of tablets who are – wait for it – seeing dead relatives.'

I reflected before answering. 'So, they are doing something peculiar to my brain cells and it was simply a hallucination and not my dear father popping in to comfort me. I'm almost sorry.'

She gasped, 'Oh no, I was hoping to make you feel better by knowing you weren't going loopy. Bugger, you feel worse now. Sorry, Mr Marshall. Why don't I keep my big mouth shut?'

'No, no, Nell, you misunderstand me,' I hurriedly assured her, kicking myself for seeming ungrateful for her kindness. 'That was said in jest. I'm really thankful that you took the trouble to look for me. I don't deserve such friendship.'

'Yes you do and I was thinking, well, it seems a bit odd to me that he would say something ...'

Her words trailed off as if she had quickly changed her mind about what she was going to add.

'Go on, what were you going to say?' I urged her.

'It doesn't matter. It's just me being daft.'

'Tell me, Nell,' I said.

She hesitated, obviously not sure that I would want to hear what she had been thinking, and then asked, 'Well, why would he say something you didn't understand?'

'I'm not sure I follow you.'

'Hallucinations normally originate in your own mind, so you may see something that isn't really there, but it's because your mind has conjured it up for a reason. My mum sees snakes when she's had morphine after an operation because she's terrified of them, so her brain conjures them up out of her subconscious mind because they mean something to her, albeit something horrible and frightening. So, for instance, you wouldn't see the Duke of Wellington or Elvis Presley or King Henry the Eighth because they mean nothing to you. But your father does.'

'Right, I think I follow you.'

'So your mind conjures up the hallucination of your father because deep in your subconscious mind it's exactly who you long to see but – and this is the bit I'm trying to get over to you – why would he say something you didn't understand if your own mind had conjured him up?'

Her words hung lightly in the space between us for a few moments while I concentrated hard on the point she was trying to convey. In the silence I could hear her gentle breathing and the beautiful, rhythmic sound of it not only made me feel happy to be alive, but ecstatic that she had quite literally run into my humdrum, past-its-sell-by-date life and turned it upside down with the force of her personality.

'Mr Marshall, do you get what I mean?' she asked, urgently. I didn't answer immediately, so she bellowed down the phone. 'Get your arse in gear and tell me what you think.'

I laughed out loud. 'My arse is fine where it is, thank you very much and I didn't reply straight away because I was wondering what on earth I had done so right in my pathetic existence to deserve you waltzing into it at this late stage?'

'Don't say you had a pathetic existence,' she ordered, sounding quite cross, 'being a teacher is never a pathetic existence and anyway, it's the other way round. I'm lucky to have met you. Now, do you understand what I just said?'

'I do Nell and I can't make it out either.'

'Maybe, just maybe, he did come to see you to comfort you. I prefer that idea, don't you? But it's nice to know it's happened to other people, so that must be a comfort too. You aren't going bonkers.'

'That's a comfort, thank you. I appreciate you researching it for me, I honestly do. I wouldn't have done it myself.'

'You're very welcome and I wanted to speak to you anyway.'

'You did?'

'Yes, I love hearing your voice.'

'Say that again,' I stuttered, not sure whether I heard her correctly.

'Bye Mr Marshall, see you soon.'

'Bye Nell and thank you again.'

The line went dead and I sat with the receiver in my hand for a long time. Had I heard correctly? Did this gorgeous, immensely kind and generous free spirit say that she loved to hear my voice? I repeated the question over and over again in my head until I doubted that she had said those words. Had I conjured them up in my subconscious mind because I longed to hear her say them? I then leant back in the low light, put my feet up on the coffee table in front of me and wondered whether I should believe in the Almighty after all.

&

Hearing his perfect pronunciation, his quintessentially English way of speaking, the deep, cultured timbre of his voice and the ever-present touch of humour made me feel all would be right with the world. This was the kind of old-fashioned gentleman, with impeccable manners, who could use his intellect to clear a room of ignorant fools if he so wished and be friends with anyone he chose. But, for some reason I couldn't fathom, he seemed to enjoy being with me and I blossomed under his wise and tender gaze. Even when I made a fool of myself by babbling on using slang and phrases he had never come across, he simply found me amusing, interesting and funny, without patronising or correcting me. When I was with him I felt equally intelligent in my own way and yet I knew I could learn so much from simply being with him. The elegant way he walked and moved his hands, despite the stumbling and tremors, the slow, deliberate turn of his head when I spoke and the wry smile that always reached his eyes, made me sparkle and grow in his presence.

Sitting together in the park after I'd urged him to climb the steep path to General Wolfe's statue and the Meridian Line, with the fierce February air seeping into every muscle fibre, I hadn't actually felt cold at all. His warmth, the light humour in every sentence he uttered and the desperate longing on his face not to give in to his illness was inspiring. I had days where I felt like giving up my quest for a decent part because the constant rejection was slowly and insidiously eating away at my fragile confidence. But how could I give up when he was so willing to fight? Fighting for a good role in a play or musical was nowhere near as hard or soul-destroying as fighting a chronic disease like his. Meeting Mr Marshall had given me a reason to keep waging my own personal battle and helping him was my way of remembering the man I had lost.

&

Two days dragged by like a dreary church service without seeing Nell. Sidney immediately picked up on my mood and he tried to engage me in some card playing and the taking of mind-altering substances like alcohol and tobacco, which I strenuously declined. To be fair he actually only offered me one cigar and a couple of glasses of wine, but I knew if I had just the slightest puff I would be lost and I was too frightened to drink because my tablets were causing me some concern. I felt decidedly odd for those couple of days and at one point I wondered if I was having an out-of-body experience when I dozed off in my chair and found myself floating about near the ceiling. But having shaken my head violently, I realised I had been dreaming and not swinging from the chandeliers.

I really did not need alcohol to add to my weird and wonderful experiences, so Sidney looked particularly hurt one evening when I asked him, quite distinctly not to offer me anything but a cup of tea.

'Point taken,' he muttered, 'if that's how you feel about it.'

'I do, Sidney.'

'You know what? I reckon you should go and see your GP and get all these things cleared up,' he declared.

'What things?' I asked.

'Being able to drink a bit and having the occasional cigar ...'

'I know what she'll say so I won't bother.'

'She's a good GP, isn't she?'

'She is, Sidney, which is why she won't encourage me to smoke or drink. We were having a chat the last time I saw her and she told me that her father was a black cab driver.'

Sidney frowned. 'I saw her in Sainsbury's once when we were buying some red wine.'

'And your point is?'

'She wasn't mixed race.'

I was completely bemused. 'What on earth are you talking about?'

Sidney appeared equally bemused. 'What are *you* talking about? You just said her father was a black cab driver, didn't you?'

I had to laugh at him. 'No, you bloody idiot, I meant her father *drove* a black cab.'

He looked even more bemused. 'What's that got to do with the price of fish?'

'Sidney, are you deliberately being dense?'

'No, it just comes naturally. Now, what were we talking about?'

I gave a deep sigh. 'It matters not. Maybe it's me who is losing the thread of our conversations.'

He raised his eyebrows. 'Stop speaking like Shakespeare.'

'How would you know what Shakespeare spoke like?'

'I don't, but I reckon it was like you. Nobody normal can understand Shakespeare and nobody normal can understand you. It's amazing we ever have a conversation at all.'

'We don't. I speak and you get the wrong end of the stick.'

He gazed out of my conservatory window before saying suddenly, 'I wish I knew more.'

'Sidney, you know more about life than I do because you've lived in the real world. I've been closeted in academia.'

'Yeah, and that's why you know everything, Benedict,' he said, pensively.

'I assure you I don't. You know how to build walls, how to tile your back passage...'

'That's no big deal.'

'Maybe, but it's more useful than knowing what Shakespeare was on about ...'

'No, it isn't and you know it. I want to be educated. I want to be inside your head for *one* day.'

'What, even with this disease?'

'You know what I mean ...'

'Sorry, Sidney, I was being facetious.'

He looked smug. 'There you go. I can't be facetious because I don't really know what it means.'

'But, it's better not to be facetious because it's not very kind.'

'Well, you make it sound like an art form.'

I put my hand over my eyes. 'Good grief! I must sound like a pompous idiot to you.'

'You can be a pompous idiot and I can be a twat. That's why we get on, mate,' he declared, laughing. 'If you hadn't been a teacher, what other job would you have done?' he added, frowning.

I was starting to lose the thread of our conversation again and my face was feeling rigid and stuck. 'Oh, I don't know, maybe something romantic – like an artist.'

'You think art is romantic then?' he asked, turning his nose up.

'I do.'

'I think most of it is cobblers.'

I could feel my tremors quickening and my thoughts were becoming jumbled.

'Sidney, I'm getting rather tired.'

His eyes lit up. 'Shall I pour us a drink, mate?'

'No! I told you we were only going to drink tea from now on. I'm getting tired,' I repeated, hoping he would get the message.

He appeared deflated. 'I'd better go then.'

'You don't have to.'

'No, it's fine. I know you've had enough of the bollocks I talk – I can tell. You've had a knock back, no doubt.'

'A knock back,' I echoed, 'in what sense?'

'You know in what sense, a knock back from a pretty, dark-haired young woman.'

'What are you talking about?'

He peered at me over his glasses. 'You know.'

'Sidney, don't be ridiculous. Now go home and leave me to my dark moods.'

'Right,' he replied, 'see you tomorrow then?'

'No doubt,' I muttered, suddenly and inexplicably not caring much.

He went to leave, but hovered. 'Give you a knock in the morning.'

I had gone to speak, but my face became stuck, just as if I'd been slapped. I slurred badly and then could not be bothered to try again so I waved my hand dismissively and I just caught sight of his concerned, forlorn expression before he left. I felt a little guilty, but only fleetingly because he could be extremely insensitive, routinely blunt and hard work when he wanted to be, so I dismissed him from my mind and slept.

Nell rang the next day and sunshine flooded into my life again. I knew when the telephone rang that it was her by the way the sound swept away the dust and cobwebs from my body.

'Hello, Mr Marshall, feel like coming out to play?'

'Ready when you are,' I told her, feeling bold.

'I'll be there in half an hour. It's bloody taters in the mould, so put your hat on.'

'Say that again.'

'Are you going deaf in your old age? It's cold, bloody cold,' she repeated, 'so wear your hat.'

'Yes, madam,' I said, my smile stretching from ear to ear.

Within half an hour she was standing on my doorstep once again, this time in a dark blue jacket with the hood pulled up tight around her chin.

The sight of her kick-started my sleeping, redundant engine of a body and I felt the life energy surge through me once again. I couldn't care less about the effect my tablets were having when her face was smiling up at me.

'Seen any more dead relatives?' she asked, grinning.

'Alas, no...'

'Shame, I wanted to hear about it.'

'Sorry to disappoint you, Nell.'

'Lean on me, Mr Marshall, it's a bit slippery out here,' she urged me and I took her arm. It felt the most natural thing in the world, to be strolling next to her, talking to her, holding onto her for support and wishing the rest of the world away. 'Your neighbour is watching us,' she added, looking up at Sidney's window.

'He's rather unhappy with me because I won't drink with him.'

'Does he need you to drink with him? Can't he drink on his own?'

'Well, it's not the drink, it's the cards and the chat; you know, that sort of thing – two old codgers together.'

Her face fell. 'So, he misses you.'

'That's perceptive of you, dear girl.'

She turned and glanced up at where Sidney had his face pressed against the glass. Then she gave him one of her best, most glorious smiles and waved happily at him. He looked surprised and appeared not sure how to react, but he recovered quickly and gave a little wave back. At this she beckoned him down and my heart sank like a stone, but luckily he declined with a shake of his head.

'Thank God for that,' I muttered, with a wry smile.

'Don't be so rotten,' she cried. 'He just feels insecure. He doesn't want you to change. He doesn't want his life to change.'

'I know, but he's grown up and he has got Sheila,' I told her, defending my petulance.

'But you're his old mate, it's different. Be kind to him please, will you?' she pleaded, her thoughtfulness quite overwhelming.

My guilt hit me in the solar plexus and made me breathless. 'Yes, yes, I will,' I stuttered, 'I was going to apologise to him, but he's like an old woman sometimes. Don't think badly of me, Nell, I'm not an unkind man. I just get a little impatient with him. Blame it on the tablets.'

'I know you're not unkind,' she smiled, 'so stop defending yourself, you daft apath.'

'Apath,' I repeated, 'you called me that before.'

She put her hand in the small of my back and pushed me gently forward.

'Shut your face and come on.'

It was a crystal-clear day with a smoky grey sky and I could smell more snow in the air. We climbed slowly up the steep path once more and this time my breathing appeared a little easier, which she commented on immediately.

'I'll have you running the marathon yet,' she told me, her words making little clouds of icy breath before my eyes.

'Fantasy, Nell, fantasy,' I replied, clinging to her for dear life as we reached the top.

The café was deserted except for two young student types with heavy rucksacks on the chairs beside them and small, round glasses on the end of their noses. I didn't even bother offering to pay as she had already approached the counter and I watched as she chatted with the same attractive, dark-haired man again who looked even more muscular and disgustingly fit than the last time I had set eyes on him. As she came back with the tray full of coffee and cake and a pile of napkins, which were no doubt for my dribbling and spluttering mouth, she had a small smile on her lips. 'That's hilarious,' she muttered, placing my mug in front of me.

'What is?' I asked, feigning interest, but desperate to know what he had said to her.

'He asked if you were my father,' she said, adding with a straight face, 'and I said no, you were my grandfather.'

I thought her words would make me feel embarrassed or slightly miffed, but they didn't. I had no intention of spoiling the pleasant, carefree mood we had created between us just because of some misguided egotistical thoughts on my part. 'How dare you! I am certainly not old enough to be your grandfather. Mind you, I *feel* old enough to be your grandfather. Nell, please assure me I don't look that old.'

She grinned. 'You don't.'

'Thank God for that. I'm thankful for small mercies.'

She leant towards me. 'He's a nice enough bloke, but he's ever so vain,' she whispered. 'Never read a book in his life and hasn't even heard of Lord Byron, can you believe it? Spends all his spare time in the gym, what a bore, eh?'

'Aha,' I whispered back, 'that must be where he tones all those bulging muscles.'

'Yeah, I bet he's got muscles in his spit.'

'Say that again.'

'So,' she started, ignoring my puzzled expression, 'what you been up to?'

'Nothing much, chatting to Sidney, listening to music, resting my weary limbs, staring into space, floating around the ceiling ... that kind of thing.'

'Floating around the ceiling, eh? Lucky you! Was it fun?'

'Not really. It was a bit scary to be honest.'

'You could always go back and tell your doc you feel a bit weird,' she suggested, thoughtful as ever.

'If I'm not better in a couple of months then I will. But I'll let the pills settle into my system for a while and see what happens. Heavy-duty drugs are always going to have strong side effects and they have to do something extreme to my brain and nerve endings to stop the tremors and the stumbling.'

'You know best.'

'I could bloody well murder a cigarette when I drink coffee though,' I grumbled, as I instinctively felt my pockets.

'Tough, you aren't having one.'

I sighed. 'It's hard sometimes.'

She was sitting with her chin in her hands and her eyes looked inquisitive. 'Tell me about the women in your life.'

I was quite shocked for a moment and could think of absolutely nothing to say. 'I wasn't expecting you to ask me that. Um, well ...'

'Took your mind off the fags though, didn't it? Come on, there must have been loads,' she urged, a mischievous glint in her eyes.

'I can't remember most of them.'

'That's charming!'

'Well, I am sixty-two, for goodness sake!'

'Yeah, I suppose we *are* going back to the dark ages.'

'I really only remember four of them with any clarity.'

She appeared intensely interested, 'Why do you only remember *that* four?'

'Length of the relationship I suppose,' I shrugged, finding it hard to concentrate on my past life with her expressive face inches from mine. Those women seemed like shadowy figures now, unwanted and unloved, like a dose of 'flu. 'Mary, my wife – Beth's mother; Angie, who I lived with for about a year after my divorce; Joanna, my first steady girlfriend who my family wanted me to marry and Fi, my last long-term thing who did everything in her power to get me up the aisle.'

She didn't speak for a moment and put her head on one side, as if trying to get inside my head and heart and find some honest, genuine deep feeling there. It was on the tip of my tongue to say that I hadn't even liked my wife, but I felt that may be one admission too far at this stage in our friendship. That would have made me appear callous, hard-hearted, uncaring and unforgiving in nature. I had no intention of letting Nell think badly of me and yet I had been all those things at some point in my dissolute past. But I had always believed that somewhere in between all my damaged relationships there was a good man trying desperately to struggle to the surface; a good man, like my father.

She sighed and covered my hand with hers. 'I bet none of them were worthy of you.'

Her words shook me to the core, not only because they were kind – I expected that from Nell now – but because I suspected part of it was true. I had behaved badly, I knew that, but if I had chosen a woman who had Nell's qualities I would have gone home more. In between my drunken episodes of loneliness and isolation in my relationships, I had always known I had picked women who were totally wrong for me. This was because I was a visual man, my head completely turned by an attractive face and figure and not once did I take the time to find out who they were as people. 'Thank you for that,' I muttered, feeling humbled, 'I'm not sure I deserve your flattery. There were others of course, but they were so fleeting I can't recall their names or what the hell they looked like.'

She laughed hard, 'You old rascal.'

'I know, and at the time I thought I was having fun. But looking back now with these blurred, unfocused Parkinson's eyes, I don't know why the hell I thought it was fun.'

'That's just age and experience talking,' she remarked.

A strong blast of deep winter wind suddenly shook the windows and somehow it seemed to mimic the bleakness of my memories at that moment. 'But it all seems so soulless and empty now, Nell. What was I playing at? Who were those women? How did they feel about uncomplicated sex? Did I promise to call? How did they feel when I didn't? Would I want Beth to be treated like that? What on earth made Mary and me marry? Why didn't I see that her materialistic and self-centred nature would eventually be like poison to me? I can't even defend my actions by saying I was blinded by love.'

'What about lust?' Nell asked, seemingly riveted by my explanations and not taking her eyes off my face for one second.

'Oh well, yes there was quite a bit of that between us, which is probably why it lasted thirteen years and of course we had Beth. I spent most of the time inebriated and somewhere else, anywhere else other than at home.'

'Beth probably doesn't see it like that.'

'I hope to God not and if I'm honest I did try to make the time we spent together exciting and meaningful: going to the swings, the circus, the cinema and theatre ...'

'And the duck pond.'

'Yes, the dear little duck pond, she loved that so much. She thought the ducks were actually hers,' I said, remembering Beth getting cross with someone who was throwing *her* ducks huge chunks of bread. 'But if you ask her if she can remember being with both of us, she'd more than likely say no.'

Nell ate her banana cake and looked thoughtful. 'Which one of them was best suited to you then?' she asked.

My eyes probably reflected my sadness. 'None of them were, Nell.'

She looked surprised. 'Not one? There must have been one, Mr Marshall. I hope there was one, for your sake.'

'Really and truly,' I insisted, 'not one. That's hard to admit, but it's the truth. There was always this underlying feeling of having my wings clipped in some way. Not one of them wanted me to be myself. Sad isn't it? They wouldn't let me out of their sight. They wanted to clip my wings instead of letting me fly.'

She gave me one of her rare smiles. 'That's because you're so gorgeous they were terrified of losing you.'

I felt myself flush slightly at her compliment, which for a man my age was quite ludicrous and unsettling. 'Well, I'm not sure about that, but if you put chains around someone, they automatically want to break free.' I longed to add, that I would welcome her chains around me and those heavy chains could bind me to her for the rest of my life and I would never complain. 'And thanks for the gorgeous, by the way.'

'And anyway,' she began.

'And anyway...'

She crossed her arms across her chest. 'Who said they were waiting for you to call at all? Why wouldn't it be the other way round? I hate this notion that all women are sitting indoors hoping for their knight in shining armour to pick up the phone and make their life complete! That's a load of old nonsense put about by men to make them feel wanted.'

'Is that my subconscious sexist nature surfacing?' I asked her, amused at her indignation.

'Probably, but I know what you meant, don't worry,' she said, smiling warmly. 'I've not come across a man who truly wanted me to fly yet. But I'm still hoping. Shall we walk back?' she asked. 'We won't go so far this time because I knackered you last time.'

My heart felt as if it was falling towards my stomach at the thought of her leaving me at home and flying off somewhere. 'But Nell, if we go back will you stay and chat awhile?'

She gave me her fondest most perfectly beguiling smile. 'If that's what you want.'

'It is.'

We sauntered back to my house as if it was a warm and pleasant morning because my legs had stiffened up cruelly and the cramp in my calves was excruciating. Nell was so patient and walked at my snail's pace with her arm through mine. Once at home I all but collapsed on the sofa, groaning loudly.

'Oh my God,' she gasped, 'give it a rest. You look like two penneth of Gawd help us.'

'Say that again.'

'You heard.'

'Yes, I heard, but I haven't a clue what it meant.'

'Let's have some fun. That piano,' she said, pointing to it standing at the other end of my lounge, 'can you actually play it or is it for decoration purposes only?'

'How dare you! I'll have you know I *used* to play it.'

'Why used to?'

'This disease ... my left hand won't behave.'

She looked playful. 'Teach me then.'

'I'm not sure ...'

'Please, Mr Marshall, let's just have a go.'

'What would you like to play?'

She thought for a moment. 'Chopin.'

I laughed at her, making my way to the piano and lowering myself slowly onto the stool. 'Go for the best, why don't you? Come and sit down.'

'I'm kidding,' she said, squeezing next to me on the stool, 'just play me anything.'

'What about the *Moonlight Sonata*?'

She gasped and her hands flew to her mouth. 'I *love* the *Moonlight Sonata*,' she cried.

'Right, I'll play most of it and then when I want you to play a note I'll nod my head towards the said note. Are you ready?'

'I'm ready,' she grinned, looking like an excited child anticipating a birthday present.

I began to play, my right hand moving easily, my left as if it had been stuck in icy water for an hour and occasionally nodded my head purposefully. She roared with laughter and simply guessed which note to play, sometimes guessing correctly and often not. She laughed so loudly, all the way through – rocking slightly forward and back – that I felt sure Sidney would appear to find out what on earth was going on. I was completely transfixed by her ability to live so completely in the moment and was finding it hard to concentrate on my playing.

'Nell, do you laugh at everything?'

'Yeah, I do, mostly.'

'I thought so.'

She turned her head to look at me with sparkling eyes. 'But especially when I'm with you.'

'Thank you ... I think.'

'You just looked so funny nodding like that. You looked like you were having a fit.'

'How delightful,' I muttered and she laughed out loud again, right in my ear. 'My God, that laugh could shatter a glass at a hundred yards.'

'I know, sorry. But you just make me laugh. It's the way you speak: ever so slightly sarcastic all the time. I just love it.'

'I've always spoken like this and my wife didn't find it quite so funny I assure you.'

'Well, I do so don't ever change, Mr Marshall,' she said. 'Do you know any jazz or rock?'

'You hum it, I'll play it. I can play anything you like.'

She looked bewildered. 'How do you mean?'

'I actually play by ear, mostly.'

She gasped. 'No! Aren't you a clever old dog? How did you get to be so flipping talented? Don't tell me you can paint as well.'

I preened impressively. 'I have to admit I sketched a bit.'

'I knew it.'

'Don't hold it against me,' I said. 'However, I'm a master of absolutely nothing.'

She leaned nearer. 'Don't give me that, you've got awards.'

I could smell her faint, musky perfume and it was sweet and fresh. I hadn't been as close to any woman who wasn't my daughter in at least three years and it was a strange sensation; strange because it was like a long-forgotten dream, almost remembered, but just out of reach. 'But I can't sing, Nell. You can sing.'

She smiled. 'Yes, I can, I admit it.'

'Sing to me.'

Like most performers she didn't need to be asked twice and she immediately started to sing. I hadn't ever heard the song before, but her voice was pure and immensely strong and clear. It completely filled the room and I pictured her alone on a stage, her voice reaching the rafters, soaring away and escaping into the night sky.

I was almost speechless, not only at her talent, but at her proximity to my ageing, useless body that at one time in my life would have reacted in a rage of hormones. But at that moment I simply felt hugely grateful just to have her there, when she could have been anywhere else she chose. When she finished she turned to me, and she appeared intensely vulnerable.

'How was that?' she asked, frowning and unsure.

'Spectacular,' I replied.

'Glad you liked it,' she grinned, looking relieved. 'It's a Ray Charles song. Now, let's play something lively.'

'How about ...'

'Traditional jazz,' she suggested, jumping in.

'Your wish is my command.' The speed of the piece I chose, however, was too much for me and my left hand missed the notes repeatedly. To my ears it sounded outrageous and only compounded the fact that my Parkinson's was affecting every part of me. 'Sorry, that's enough of my pathetic playing.'

She picked up on my mood. 'Let's talk then,' she suggested, taking my hand and leading me gently towards the sofa.

'Talking I can do – just,' I said, easing myself down and sitting back.

'What would you like to talk about?'

'How devastatingly attractive I am?'

She burst out laughing, 'In your dreams, mate.'

'I know.'

'Poetry,' she cried.

'Right, poetry,' I replied. 'What's your favourite poem? No, don't tell me, something by Lord Byron?'

'Nah, he's too flowery. I like Keats and Shakespeare's sonnets. But one of Yeats poems moves me to tears.'

'Does it really? Which one moves you to tears?'

'I'm not telling you, you can find out,' she declared, with a look of pure mischief on her face.

'I actually have a book of his poetry,' I told her, glancing over to my bookcase, 'so I'll read them all and see if I can detect which one moves you to tears. It will be like a quest.'

She suddenly frowned. 'Do you think love transcends death?'

Her question threw me for a moment. Who was I, an ageing, shallow and terminal flirt, to give her an honest answer? 'I'm not sure asking me that question is a good idea.'

'You can give an opinion.'

I thought for a moment and my mother's anguished face came strongly into my mind. Years after my father's death she would cry silently and confide in me about how she could never remarry because she was still in love with him. 'I think *if* you're lucky enough to find the right person and you adore them unconditionally and the love is real, then yes, love will transcend death.'

'*Real* love,' she whispered. 'Anything other than *real* love isn't worth having, is it?'

'No, Nell, in my opinion it isn't worth having,' I replied, knowing I was well qualified to answer *that* question.

She sat with her elbows on her knees and her chin in her hands, looking into my eyes. I noticed she always did that. It made me feel as if she was hanging on my every word and perhaps trying to find sincere feelings somewhere hidden inside me.

'And do you think there are different layers to love? No,' she added, shaking her head, 'I mean different kinds.'

'Yes, I think so. There's the love of friendship, of family members ...'

'But love is still love.'

I felt quite out of my depth. 'I wish I was an expert, Nell, so I could answer your questions with first-hand experience.'

Her eyes were searching mine. 'But *romantic* love,' she continued, 'it's different, isn't it?'

'You mean from friendship?' I asked. 'Well, yes I suppose so.'

'Sex is the missing ingredient.'

'Well, yes, sex is an important ingredient, but...'

I had no idea how to finish my sentence. Sex had been such a huge part of most of my life and yet love had eluded me. Now, sitting there opposite a woman who was quickly becoming everything to me, without one tiny sexual urge coursing through my body, how could I say romantic love was different from friendship? I knew I would gladly take anything she offered me. Even half an hour of her company every fortnight I would have grabbed with both my frail, shaking hands.

She said nothing more for a few moments and I felt an indescribable longing somewhere in my guts; a longing to be younger, fitter, more worthy of her. But hard on the heels of that longing was a mounting anxiety that she was asking these questions of me, someone supposedly wiser because she had fallen for a man and didn't know how to handle the situation. Yes, of course, my lovely Nell had a secret affection for some young stud she had come across. Why wouldn't she? They were obviously lining up at her door waiting to be picked off one by one. She assumed, quite wrongly of course, that I could give her sensible, man-of-the-world advice. But the only world I had inhabited was a selfish, puerile, senseless one.

'But what if sex is off the menu? Can't you love someone in a romantic way then?' she asked, frowning hard.

'I don't know. What *is* romantic love anyway?' I said, not knowing what else to say because the conversation had taken such an unexpected turn.

'Being *in* love,' she replied, 'rather than loving them as a friend.'

'Ah I see, well,' I paused, considering my answer carefully because if she was speaking of a young, potential lover I wanted my precious Nell to get it right, despite the fact that my envy of the man in question would probably tear me apart, 'I think you just know if you love someone and you know if you don't.'

She smiled at my simple explanation. 'Yes, of course.'

I decided to be bold. 'Who was the man you loved more than anyone else with this disease.'

Her face fell in an instant and I wished to God I had kept my stupid, spluttering mouth shut. 'Joshua,' she muttered, almost wincing as if saying his name caused her physical pain.

'He was a lucky man.'

'In some ways, yes, but he was so young when he was diagnosed with Parkinson's, he didn't consider himself lucky.'

I could have cut my tongue out. 'No, of course, I'm sorry, that was a crass thing to say.'

She smiled fondly at me. 'That's okay, Mr Marshall, I know what you meant.'

'What happened to him, Nell?'

She turned her head slightly and gazed out of the window, as if hoping to summon up a little courage from the beauty of my snowy garden. The pure, white light shone across her face making it look paler than usual. Twice she attempted to speak, but swallowed hard instead. I was trying to imagine what a man who Nell loved looked like, but no vision came to mind, just an empty space.

'I was so young, so headstrong, so opinionated ...'

'*Determined* is what I'd call it, Nell.'

'Determined is a kinder word,' she said, 'but you would say that.'

'Yes, I would where you're concerned.'

She gave a tiny, almost imperceptible shrug. 'I just fell headlong for him and pursued him until he gave in. One week we decided we could get married and the following week he was diagnosed with Parkinson's.'

'He must have been older than you.'

'I was seventeen when I met him, he was forty and after two years of telling me I had a crush on him and to go away and find someone my own age, he caved in when I reached nineteen. And then his diagnosis changed everything. He gave up; quite simply, he gave up.'

'He gave up even though he had you?' I asked, astounded by the man's stupidity.

'Yes, even though he had me. The circumstances of his going are too painful to go into.'

'Yes, of course; you don't have to tell me...'

'He left a note with one word scrawled across it: freedom.'

'Nell, I'm so sorry.'

'The hard part is I'll never know whether he meant freedom for him or for me and if he meant freedom for me it was all such a bloody waste because I didn't want to be free. I wanted to care for him, for the rest of his life. I was young and I just took it in my stride. But looking back I know I didn't really understand the seriousness of it. I just knew I wanted to look after him.'

I loved her most at that moment; her strength, her deeply caring, fearless nature and her optimism in the face of such heartache. But there it was; I *loved* her. What on earth was I going to do with that love? Admit it and embarrass her? Admit it and spoil this burgeoning friendship? Admit it and make her feel obliged to stay friends and visit for an hour on a Sunday? Admit it and watch the sickening sadness in her eyes when she had to tell me she didn't feel the same? No. As I told Sidney, I would simply live with it. But what kind of man could leave Nell? A fool no doubt and yet perhaps a noble one. Yes, a noble fool and a better man than I.

'I can't pretend to know what his feelings were when he made his decision, but I understand his despair about having Parkinson's,' I told her, 'and it's a fearful place to be.'

Her face softened. 'Yes, it must be.'

'Thank you for telling me about Joshua and I promise you I won't give up. I'll fight it with everything I have for you and our friendship.'

She beamed at me then. 'Thank you, Mr Marshall, I know you will. You still had a light in your eyes when I met you by the duck pond, a light and a hell of a lot of mischief.'

'Mischief,' I repeated, 'ah yes, I remember that. I used to get up to quite a bit of mischief.'

'The problem with Joshua was, he had lost his wife years before in a terrible accident and when I asked him to fight it he said he had nothing left to fight it with. All his emotional courage and fortitude had been used up when he lost her. Put quite simply, he had nothing left. He became like a shell, an empty shell. It was just as if someone had reached into his brain and turned a light off.'

'That's awful.'

She gazed out of the window again. 'You know, snow always makes me feel hopeful.'

'That's an interesting concept,' I remarked.

'It makes everything pure and new,' she explained. 'All the dull, grey concrete disappears and it's renewed by a fresh cleanliness. All the humdrum sounds of suburbia become hushed and calmed. There's something about the tranquillity that gives me hope.' She suddenly grinned. 'Daft, aren't I?'

'As a brush,' I said, smiling back at her.

'I'm not explaining myself very well. I think it's to do with feeling wistful and nostalgic, remembering the joy of waking up as a child to that incredible light that floods through the curtains after a heavy fall of snow.'

'You explain it perfectly,' I told her. 'I cursed this recent snow, but now it will forever be connected to meeting you in the park.'

She flashed her wonderful smile at me. 'That's so lovely. Now,' she cried, jumping up suddenly, 'let's cheer ourselves up by dancing.'

'Do we have to?' I asked, forlornly.

'Do you feel like dancing?'

'Well, I...'

'It would be good for you, you know.'

'Good in what way?' I asked her, my scepticism quite obvious.

'Good for your strength, your balance and your posture,' she declared.

'I believe you, but forgive me if I look rather doubtful about my ability to balance or give the impression of having anything remotely related to good posture because I fear it would all be quite random.'

She was laughing at me now. 'What are you on about?'

I laughed back. 'I have absolutely no idea.'

'You must have danced in your youth!' What was it then, the Charleston?'

'Sometimes I feel that old, Nell. No, the men just kind of stood there and felt foolish, swaying a bit and tapping our feet while the girls looked free from any crippling insecurity or feelings of self doubt.'

'I bet you looked great,' Nell declared.

'I assure you I didn't. I was too lanky...' I stopped mid sentence as Nell took hold of my hands.

'You, Mr Marshall, are going to learn how to hold yourself properly.'

'Would you like to rephrase that?'

She looked sternly at me. 'You *need* to dance. You need it for your health and well- being. So, dance!' She took hold of my hands and pulled me up gently. Her strength surprised me. 'Hold in your core...'

'Hold in my what?'

She was smiling now. 'You know... your abdominals.'

'I have none!'

She went over to my CD and vinyl collection and whistled through her teeth as she rifled through them. 'There's some heavy classical stuff here.'

'Well, I'm posh you know.'

'Aha, here we go, Swan Lake.'

'The Dying Swan, how very appropriate for me.'

She turned the music up loud and it blasted from the speakers. I knew Sidney would hear it and wonder what on earth was going on and that thought made me smile. 'Now,' Nell was saying, standing right in front of me, 'hold in your core, I mean abdominals, feet apart, soft knees and neutral spine.'

'I don't understand a word...'

'Stop talking and do as I say!'

'I'm trying, honestly.'

'Bring your arms out, like this. Now, bend your legs and extend your arms more and now, stand on one leg and extend the other one forward...'

'Good grief,' I muttered, as every muscle in my body complained violently about the position I was in. But I did as she asked. I felt self conscious and exposed, but I managed to move in an understated way.

'Bend again and follow through with expression,' she cried, 'and bend again, Mr Marshall...and again.'

'I am,' I told her, 'I think!' She began to laugh and ordered me to keep going while she went back to my stereo and looked through my record collection again. 'Something a little easier to move to would be good,' I said, breathlessly. Suddenly the Kinks were blaring out and I stood there like a limp rag, unsure and in my eyes undignified. I was twitching slightly, desperate to free myself from the ghastly symptoms that made me feel such a prisoner in my own body. 'What do you want me to do now, Nell?' I asked her.

'Dance, Mr Marshall,' she yelled above the distorted guitar, her body swaying like a tree in a gentle breeze and her eyes sparkling. 'Dance for your life!'

Her choice of words seemed to ignite my sleeping subconscious and I began to move without self-consciousness. If I was going to dance for my life, I would put up a good fight. Nell was twirling and jumping around without any inhibition. She appeared fluid, like a fast flowing river that knew not where it was headed and I followed and swam after her as best I could. I lost myself in the music completely and it was only at the end of the song that I felt my tremors quicken slightly and I almost lost my balance. Nell flung her arms around me to hold me up and commented that the neighbours would wonder what I was doing. I clung to her and replied that I knew Sidney would have a glass against the wall, at which she flung her head back and roared with laughter. Holding on to her, I could feel her warmth and her vibrancy and it made me feel achingly alive. But I did not want her to feel embarrassed about the nearness of my stick thin, ageing body, so I let go as if I had been electrocuted. I stepped back, breathless, standing before her like a shy, insecure sixteen year old.

'How did that make you feel?' she asked after a few moments of awkward silence.

'Free,' I replied, 'it made me feel free.'

She gave me the most beautiful, encouraging smile. 'I have to go. I'll see you soon and don't come to the door, stay there.' She went to leave and I sat down heavily, struggling to make my mouth work properly.

'Nell ...'

She turned and her face, with the silver snowy light shining across it, was even more beautiful. 'Yes, Mr Marshall?'

'Thank you.'

'Don't forget,' she told me, 'Yeats poem.'

'I'll find it.'

She gave a little wave and left me there, comfortable, yet stuck on my sofa. I heard the front door close quietly. I sat and mused about our conversation before my horrendous attempt at dancing. I replayed all her words over and over again in my head until they became confused and faint. What lucky bastard was going to be the recipient of her affections? My God, he wouldn't know what had hit him if Nell turned the full force of her personality in his direction. He wouldn't be worthy of her of course, but then nobody human would be. I just hoped she would want to continue our friendship when she was in the throes of an all-consuming love affair. What the hell would I do with my torrent of feelings if she didn't? What would I do with my *life*? She had completely invaded every part of it and I knew I would never be the same man again. I was patently aware, deep down, that everyone would imagine I had fallen for a younger woman as a pathetic attempt at recapturing my youth or to flatter my crumbling ego. But my feelings had nothing to do with her youth or beauty. It was her kindness I craved. If she had been older than me with deep lines of experience cut into her face, I would still have longed for her company, her conversation and her depth of feeling. It made me realise that kindness was what had been missing in my relationships. Kindness was what had been sorely lacking. Kindness was what I had been subconsciously searching for and craving all my life without knowing it. But Nell loved someone else, someone younger and more worthy, with no chronic illness to hang over them like a gloomy, haunting shadow. I could still feel the touch of her hands as she pulled me up to dance. I could feel her comforting, steady arms around me as we laughed together. I felt exhausted by the dancing, but strangely at peace. I turned my head slowly and narrowed my eyes. Where was my book of Yeats poetry?

&

I wandered home in the chill, snowy air with the muffled sound of traffic in the near distance. I felt deliriously happy that I had managed to make Benedict dance, but I also felt empty and yet relieved to have shared my past with him. The memory of Joshua loomed over me still, as if he walked silently beside me. He was there in every conversation I had with Benedict, watching, listening and hovering. From my first meeting with Benedict I had recognised the dark hand of Parkinson's on him, pressing him downward towards the edge of despair and sapping his energy and life force. It stood rigidly in his way and was slowly invading every cell in his body, urging him to give in. I had seen him stagger, stumble and shake, and my heart had leapt to his defence. He had such an elegant way with him, a casual elegance, almost as graceful and fluid as a trained dancer. He tried desperately hard to hide his symptoms by using little mannerisms and movements that were comical and endearing and I'm sure most people would have been fooled. But I wasn't most people. Unfortunately I was a reluctant expert. At times he would turn the tremors into a tapping, as if he was playing an invisible piano. The occasional jerk would become a shake of the head, as if he had a ringing in his ears. The slurring would be turned into a cough or the quiet humming of a tune. But he couldn't hide the strain on his face however hard he tried and he often looked distracted and haunted. It was the haunted look that worried me most. A strong wind blew up from the river and whispering voices crowded in on me.

'He is the one! He is the one!'

'I know,' I answered them, 'and I won't desert him, but I can't do it again. I just can't.'

I turned into the narrow, cobbled street where I lived with the flat faces of the houses staring blankly at me with unblinking eyes and I started to cry.

Chapter 4

February seemed to come to an abrupt end and March blew in with moody skies and warmer temperatures that melted most of the snow within a couple of days. The evenings were becoming noticeably lighter and my hitherto precarious mood continued to lift because of Nell's presence, despite the Parkinson's causing me to doubt my sanity. I had the strangest notion that I wasn't alone, as if there was a *presence* with me at all times – a *presence* that made itself felt without me actually seeing it. Often on waking I imagined my father was leaning over me, but the notion was so brief, so momentary, that I put it down to sleep clinging to my eyes. Beth had telephoned twice and on one occasion I had called her Nell.

'Who's Nell, Dad?'

'Oh sorry, darling,' I had spluttered, 'just a friend.'

I had changed the subject quickly; bitterly disappointed that I had used the phrase *'just a friend,'* when it didn't come anywhere near describing what she meant to me. I admitted as much to Nell on our next walk when she had forced me to brave a strong, gusting northerly wind despite my arguing that it would send me flying on my back. 'I'm so sorry, Nell,' I stuttered, breathing hard. 'I just didn't know what to say at that moment.'

She appeared surprised. 'It's no big deal, why are you always so tough on yourself? I know you didn't mean it.'

'You're too kind. I'm tough on myself because it was like denying what your friendship means to me.'

'Stop worrying ...'

'Forgive me,' I whispered, with the wind blowing my hair all over the place.

'There's nothing to forgive,' she insisted, smiling, 'and I can't take you seriously with your hair like that. Be careful, your syrup might come off.'

I was bemused as usual by her use of words. 'Say that again.'

'Syrup means wig, syrup of figs rhymes with wig,' she said, laughing. 'Well, it nearly rhymes. Where have you been all your life?'

'In academia, unfortunately, and in no way does it prepare you for life. But I understand the fig connotation now – I think.' Glancing askance at her, I pointed at my hair and added, 'and I'll have you know, it's all my own.'

She let out a blast of her laugh. 'You are a nut case!'

'But seriously, Nell, I'll tell Beth about you next time she calls.'

'She'll automatically think there's more to it. Don't tell her on the phone, wait till she comes home,' she suggested, moving towards me and flattening my hair into place as best she could. 'These things are best said face to face, don't you reckon?'

'Yes, you're right, of course,' I mumbled, heartily relieved and wishing the wind would gust even more and send my hair in an upwards direction so she would touch it again and pat it into place. We sat in our usual seat in the café and continual blasts of wind rattled around our heads. It made a faint moaning sound. Nell let out her wonderful raucous laugh yet again.

'It's just like camping.'

'I've never been camping,' I remarked.

'That doesn't surprise me.'

'What makes you say that?'

Her eyes sparkled. 'Because, Mr Marshall, you're posh.'

'This is true,' I admitted and she laughed even more.

'Fantastic sound though, isn't it?' she enthused. 'Imagine being in an old house and hearing that howling outside. I used to love going camping as a child, tucked up snugly in my sleeping bag and hearing a storm raging outside, especially the rain tapping on the canvas. Magical! We were camping in Devon once when I was little and there was such a terrible storm my mum was convinced the tent was going to blow away. So she sent my poor dad out in his pyjamas. You know the old fashioned striped ones all men used to wear? He had to fasten the ropes more tightly and when he came back in and took his pyjama top off he had striped skin where the dye had run. My God, did we laugh?'

I watched her eyes dancing with delight as she reminisced and for me it was like being plugged into an energy source. My aches and pains and muddled thoughts melted away and I had an idea that Nell ought to be routinely prescribed to me by my doctor.

'You sound like a happy family,' I commented.

Her eyes softened. 'Yes, we were. Well, we are still except Dad isn't with us now. I couldn't imagine at the time how we were all going to survive without him. We thought the despair would last forever, but we soldiered on and we're a happy family to this day. That's what he'd want, that's what he gave us.'

As she spoke about her father she had a transparent vulnerability that I found endearing and mesmerising. I had known all along that Nell had been brought up in an atmosphere of love and fun and a closeness that had given her an inner confidence and enormous self-esteem. Her words only compounded the fact that I hadn't created that for Beth.

'Nell,' I ventured, 'I don't even know how many brothers and sisters you have.'

'I've got an older brother, James and an older sister, Abigail. We're all very alike, except they aren't dramatic like me. I'm the show-off in the family; that's what my Mum says anyway.'

'Talented, Nell, that's what I'd call it.'

'Thank you, Mr Marshall,' she said. 'That's a lovely word.'

We finished our snack and sauntered, or in my case stumbled, towards our bench under General Wolfe even though the weather was taking a turn for the worse. Sitting there watching an approaching storm fly across the sprawling skyline of London felt exhilarating and I longed to be young again, join hands with Nell and run for our lives, keeping ahead of the rain by inches before sheltering under the spreading branches of an enormous oak tree. We would then laugh together with the joy and excitement of being healthy and carefree, knowing nothing could touch us.

'What was that sigh for?' she asked, turning towards me with her large inquiring eyes.

'Did I sigh out loud? Well, I just had this intense longing to be young again and I never will be. That's hard, dear girl.'

She frowned. 'But if you were young again you wouldn't be sitting here with me.'

I had to smile at her simplicity. 'How very true, I didn't think of it like that. I'll shut up, shall I?'

'I know what you mean though,' she added, thoughtfully. 'But don't look back, Mr Marshall, not with your grave and regretful disposition. You're too analytical for your own good.'

'I do try not to be analytical,' I assured her, 'but it isn't easy, especially when you've made such a hash of things. But no, you're right as usual. From this moment on, I will always look forward.'

'Do you promise?'

'I promise.'

'I think you've promised me that before.'

'I think I have.'

'Talking of looking forward, I have yet another audition today.'

'Yet another one? Your agent is working hard on your behalf, Nell.'

'Yes, he does. It's just up to me to get the part,' she remarked, taking a sharp intake of breath as if about to climb a mountain. 'Keep your fingers crossed for me, Mr Marshall.'

'Always, Nell, if I can actually cross the stiff, wretched things. What's it for?'

She ran her hands through her tumbling hair because it had flopped forward into her eyes in the wind. Off her face it made her look older, more sophisticated, even more beautiful, if that was possible.

'Only an ensemble part, but it's also first cover for a main.'

'You're too good for the ensemble surely,' I suggested, biased of course.

'Thanks, but there are people with loads more talent than me in the ensemble. It's such a competitive business.'

I put my hand gently on her arm in a gesture of support. 'I know.'

She pursed her lips in exasperation. 'I just want to work; to perform. I'm lucky, it's a laugh serving in the café where I work, but I'm a crap waitress. I tripped once and spilt custard all down this bloke's back. It was highly embarrassing. And I enjoy teaching dance to kids, but it's not what I was born to do. I really come alive on stage.'

I opened my eyes in astonishment. 'Even more alive than you are normally? I find that hard to imagine.'

She grinned. 'That's because you're an old codger. Everyone seems alive to you.'

'I'm painfully aware of that.'

'I'm kidding you, Mr Marshall. You aren't so bad.' I still had my hand resting on her arm and she frowned. 'I can feel all the little tremors under the surface. Isn't it a strange and complicated illness?'

I tried to smile. 'I'm afraid to say it is.'

We sat in silence for a few minutes watching some American tourists in colourful clothes and overstated hats taking photographs of the Meridian line and the large, twenty-four-hour clock. It was on the tip of my tongue to ask Nell if she had embarked on the love affair she had been considering, but I thought better of it, telling myself firmly it was none of my business. She hadn't mentioned it again so I entertained the vain hope she may have realised he wasn't worthy of her.

'Look at that marble sky, isn't it magical?' she was saying. 'It should be painted by someone.'

'We'd better take refuge in the doorway of the Observatory,' I suggested, worrying about my frail body.

'You go,' she urged, 'I'm going to dance in the puddles. Go on, I'll see you after it has passed. You can watch me.'

'I'd love to stay out here with you, but ...'

'You could, rain won't hurt you.'

'Well ...'

She gave me a firm, but gentle push. 'Go, go, quick.'

I walked as quickly as I could and took shelter with the noisy tourists, some of whom blocked my view of Nell and I became irritated and short-tempered with them wishing them miles away. 'Excuse me, excuse me,' I stuttered, 'can I just get there, please?'

They were friendly, smiley and amenable and I immediately felt guilty about my bad manners. But they didn't seem to notice and were full of warmth and a certain kind of optimistic cheerfulness as Americans in Britain always are. I could just see Nell, splashing about and kicking her feet through the puddles. She appeared weightless, like the rain itself, yet graceful and strong. There was a wildness about her that was inspiring to someone like me who felt trapped in his own body. As the cloud burst was in full force she lifted her face to the sky and allowed it to drench her. She looked vibrant and animated and her expressions changed second by second. It was as if a spell had been cast and I stood motionless, transfixed and speechless. My legs were chilled and I was painfully aware that my face felt rigid and stuck, but I couldn't have been happier at that moment. I wondered about life's rich and ever-changing patterns and how I had been struck, as if by lightening, by my diagnosis, alone and anxious and in grave danger of giving in, but now simply watching Nell dancing in a rainstorm made me feel thankful to be alive. If only, I thought, if only I could splash about in the puddles with her, my life would be complete.

A shaft of dazzling sunlight that resembled a spotlight followed the cloud burst, and the pavement outside the Observatory sparkled like tiny jewels. The tourists began to wander outside aimlessly and I made my tortuous way towards Nell.

'That was fun,' she called, her eyes wild.

'It looked it,' I replied.

'I always think to myself,' she began, looking up into my face, 'that I'm still young and healthy and fit and people who aren't can't do this anymore and I can, so I do. Do you understand?'

'I do, Nell. I understand perfectly.'

She reached up and kissed my cheek softly. 'I knew you would.'

'I only wish I could have joined you.'

'What, at your advanced years?' she laughed and I laughed back at her, my head reeling from the soft kiss. 'One day you will, you'll see. Come on, Mr Marshall, I should get back.'

'You shoot off, Nell. I'll take a wander to the duck pond before I go home.'

'Are you sure? No getting sentimental now,' she warned me. 'You're looking forward from now on.'

'I am,' I told her, my voice firm. 'Good luck, dear girl. I'll be thinking of you. Call me, let me know.'

'I will.'

I kept my eyes firmly on her until she disappeared.

I sat by the duck pond for a while, watching small children throw breadcrumbs with enormous excitement and no skill until cramp invaded the lower part of my legs. One little girl had short blonde hair just like Beth's had been and I was about to sink into my usual rambling reminiscing that started with fond memories of her and always ended with me wondering how on earth Mary and I had stayed married all those years, when I remembered my promise and forced myself to turn my mind to positive thoughts. I smiled as I thought of Nell splashing in puddles, her wet hair plastered against her animated face. I shook my head slowly in wonder that in all the years I had been sitting there watching those hardy ducks, one snowy morning she had just happened to run by and shake a tiny stone from her shoe and our lives had collided. How long had I known her now? A few short weeks, but in that time her incomparable personality had hit me like a tidal wave and swept me off my shaking, unsteady feet.

My musings were interrupted by the *presence* again, which appeared to hover so near me I could almost smell it. For a moment I imagined it was Nell come to find me, but despite looking everywhere I could see no-one. I pushed myself up against the fence, my neck and shoulders aching and tight, struggled to find my balance and then staggered towards home feeling the wretched *presence* constantly.

&

The audition was running late, but that was quite normal. Dozens of us sat side by side, huddled together in a small, overheated basement room with no natural light. Some were warming up their voices with scales, but I was straining to hear what was going on in the next room. It sounded pretty rough to me, like someone was thumping an old pub piano. The girl sitting opposite me, who had put her make-up on with a trowel, was pulling the most peculiar faces as she practised her piece under her breath. I was struggling to concentrate and praying that I would remember the words of the song I had chosen.

'Helen Jackson.'

I jumped up and was ushered into a dingy hall where three faceless people sat behind a table shuffling papers and looking imperious and important. I glanced towards the young male pianist who looked as if he was spending his nights under Waterloo Bridge, to see if I recognised him. I did vaguely know him as someone who had played in the band for a show I had been in a year ago. He had been sacked for being unreliable and drunk most of the time. One evening, playing in front of the stalls, he had started vomiting up blood all over the violinist in front of him and an ambulance had to be called. He had been smuggled out without the paying public being any the wiser and the rest of the band had to think on their feet and play their instruments where the piano should have been.

I told him what I was going to sing and he nodded at me, his face deathly pale and his eyes sunken and dark. There was a moment of recognition on his face, as if he remembered me, but it was fleeting.

A woman with thick-rimmed glasses called over to me. 'OK, when you're ready, Helen.'

'Are you ready?' I whispered to him.

'Sure,' he muttered. 'I'll play the normal intro.'

'Thanks.'

I gave it everything I had, but his timing was ever so slightly out and he was varying the speed. I was constantly trying to catch up with him and so it ended up a mess in my eyes. Another woman behind the table with silver, cropped hair and a tanned face smiled at me. 'Helen, can you wait outside and come back in for the dance?'

I smiled and glanced at the pianist. He mouthed 'sorry' at me and I shrugged. An hour later ten of us were called in again and shown the steps to a modern dance, again thumped out on the same piano. We had to learn it on the spot and then perform it. The poser to my left who had white blonde hair piled so high on the top of her head it resembled a tall haystack, danced with her elbows sticking out and as she spun round she collided with me twice, knocking me slightly off balance. I had an overpowering urge to give her a quick swipe, but thought better of it and we all ended the routine more or less together, more by luck than talent.

'Cheers everyone, we'll be in touch.'

And that was that!

I escaped quickly, up the steep stairs and out into the daylight and heavy traffic of Charing Cross road, with my rucksack slung over one shoulder. My face was burning with embarrassment and unexpressed rage at the soul-destroying nature of auditions. I walked purposefully towards my favourite café where they played jazz at all times of the day and night because the music automatically lifted my spirits.

The small band was in full flow as I queued for a drink and students were working on laptops, huddled close together, spilling coffee on their notes and deep in discussion. I thought of Mr Marshall with his faltering hands as he played and our shared laughter and I immediately felt happier. Over the sea of heads I noticed the thick, golden-brown hair of Frankie, a fellow out-of-work performer who had become a friend while touring in the same show. I negotiated the narrow spaces between the wooden tables with my hot chocolate and planted a kiss firmly on his cheek causing him to jump.

'For God's sake, Hells, I wondered who it was,' he gasped in his usual theatrical way.

'You aren't on stage now you know. How you doing? Are you working?'

'Fuck-all out there,' he replied, his face falling. 'I've done some voiceovers and a bit of radio; it keeps the wolf from the door. What about you?'

'Teaching dance to kids, being a crap waitress, that sort of thing. I've just had the most horrendous audition. Don't know why I bother, Frankie.'

'You bother because you're good. Can I get you something to eat?' he asked, generous as ever despite having very little money.

'No, I'm fine. Good to see you, even if you haven't shaved.'

He laughed and scratched his stubble. He had a sweet face and enviable green eyes. 'I can't be bothered most of the time. I thought it made me look more interesting.'

'More rough,' I told him.

'Cheers. So, what's been happening with you?'

'I've had quite a few auditions, but nothing doing. I haven't had a part for the last four months and I'm getting a bit twitchy to be honest.'

'It's kind of draining, isn't it?' he said, turning up his nose.

He was dressed in a dark sweatshirt which accentuated the brightness of his eyes. It was a relief to talk to someone who understood perfectly what it was like to be constantly rejected.

'Yes, draining is exactly what it is.'

'Anyone on the scene?' he asked suddenly.

'No.'

'Nor me.'

'I have met the most extraordinary man though,' I added, eager to talk about Benedict, and Frankie was ideal because although he wasn't gay, he reacted like a woman whenever he was told anything personal. It was endearing and a quality I loved him for.

'Fabulous! Tell all.'

'He's just a friend, but we get on so well.'

He leant forward, reacting as I had imagined. 'Where did you meet him? Is he in the business?'

'I befriended him really,' I started, unsure how to describe our initial meeting and what happened between Benedict and myself. 'I just came across him in the park and we began chatting. Our chemistry was instantaneous ... non-sexual chemistry,' I added quickly. 'It was as if we'd been friends for years. He's an award-winning playwright.'

'What's his name? I'll Google him.'

'Benedict Marshall. You should hear him speak, Frankie. He has this beautiful, cultured voice. I hang on his every word because I just love hearing him talk. And his dry sense of humour, it just creases me up.'

'Marry him,' he remarked. 'Or someone else will snap him up.'

I laughed nervously. 'No, it's not like that. He's actually sixty-two, so ...'

He looked shocked. 'Another older man, eh! I see.'

'It's not like that, honestly,' I insisted, my voice sounding thin.

'He's a father figure then?'

'I had a lovely father. I don't need or want another one.'

The music had been taken up a notch and two people came to share our table so Frankie and I had to lean closer to each other. He smelt of stale cigarettes mixed with strong espresso coffee.

'But you need a replacement for Joshua,' he remarked. The mention of Joshua's name unexpectedly caused my stomach to turn over. Frankie picked up on it. 'I mean that in the best possible way, Hells. He was much older than you, wasn't he?'

'Yes, but ...'

'You like older men then, obviously.'

I paused before I answered him, only because I had not linked my admiration and affection for Benedict with Joshua in any way, despite the Parkinson's. It hadn't even occurred to me they were both many years my senior. It was as if a veil had fallen away from my face because of his remark.

'Obviously,' I replied, so quietly he couldn't hear me above the loud music.

'What was that?' he shouted.

'Joshua and I were in love. This is just friendship – honestly.'

He gave me a kind smile. 'Okay, Hells, if you say so. Is he like Joshua in any way? Are there any similarities?'

'No,' I snapped. 'They are very different men.'

He reached over and put his hand under my chin, scrutinising my face and turning it from side to side. 'There's something, come on, tell me.'

'I'm not telling you anything because you'll only judge ...'

'Just tell me!'

'There's nothing,' I insisted, my voice rising.

He frowned. 'He hasn't got some terrible illness, has he? Sorry, that's my black sense of humour, Hells.'

I avoided his eyes. 'Let's talk about something else ...'

'Oh bloody hell, he bloody well has,' he gasped.

'We're just friends, so it doesn't matter. To be honest he is rather gorgeous for his age; well, for any age actually. If he was younger it might be a different story.'

I hoped he would drop the subject of chronic illnesses. But no such luck. Frankie was relentless in his quest for gossip. He sighed heavily. I couldn't hear the sigh because of the loud music, but he lifted his shoulders up and down.

'What's wrong with him? He's not in a bloody wheelchair, is he?'

I laughed loudly causing the people who were sharing our table to glance curiously at us. 'No!'

'Had a stroke?'

'I wish you'd stop it!'

'Paraplegic then,' he added, starting to shake with laughter.

'Stop now! That's so cruel.'

'I can be even crueller...Parkinson's?'

I felt my face stiffen. 'Do you want another espresso?'

'Fuck!'

'I'm not taking him on,' I insisted, 'I've just kind of ...'

'Taken him under your wing? You collect waifs and strays, Hells.'

'He isn't a stray. He's so bright and funny and kind ...'

'Oh fucking hell.' He put his hands over his face. 'I don't believe you.'

'Let's change the subject, shall we?'

He took my right hand in his. 'Helen, do you remember what you said in Manchester when we were touring? When we both got pissed after the show that night because the audience were so slow to react? You told me you would never do it again and you'd rather be alone for the rest of your life than go through that pain again. Yes? Remember that?'

'I'm not going to. I'm very fond of him, he's fantastic company and a lovely person, but I'm really not taking him on.'

'You're a rescuer, Hells, good and proper. Do you know that?' he said, putting my hand to his lips and kissing it. I was surprised by this sudden gesture of affection and my face must have reflected that surprise because he dropped my hand and appeared to be embarrassed. 'Sorry, I just felt moved to do that. You've been through so much, I worry about you.'

'Thanks, but there's no need. He doesn't need rescuing. He has a daughter and friends and a stunning house. I just ... like him,' I shrugged, 'that's all.'

'Is he loaded then?'

'He's got quite a bit of money, yes.'

'That's a plus,' he remarked buoyantly. 'Look,' he added suddenly, 'have you finished your drink? Shall we go? I can't shout at you anymore.'

I nodded and we extricated ourselves from the crowded table and made our way out into the cool, gritty, pollution-filled afternoon air. We continued our conversation despite the noise from the heavy traffic.

'I'd still like him if he lived in a council house,' I told him, thinking to myself that I was probably protesting too much. 'It's his mind I love.'

Frankie burst out laughing. 'I've heard that one before. What a cliché.'

'It's true.'

'Be honest, Hells. Part of his attraction is that he's cultured and a successful playwright. I don't know anyone like that who lives in a council house, do you? If you've been that successful and made some money, the first thing you'd do is move.'

'I know, but ...'

'There you go. The beautiful house goes with the territory. Successful, intelligent, cultured *and* loaded. That's all I'm saying.'

'But I don't ever think about his wealth. I just like him, Frankie.'

'You did mention he lived in a stunning house.'

'Yes, well it is stunning. It's been my favourite house for as long as I can remember. I've always wondered who lived there. It has three floors, right next to a church and it used to be the Rectory. If I lived there I'd think I was in heaven.'

We had just turned the corner by the National Gallery. Frankie turned to me and smiled knowingly. 'I rest my case, Your Honour.'

'Frankie, don't be such a cynic.'

'I'm not; I'm just telling you that it's all part of his appeal, that's all.'

He stopped to look at some of the colourful chalk drawings on the pavement. The street artists had covered a large area just by the side of the gallery and tourists constantly gathered there to admire them.

'Look, I'm not going to *marry* him,' I continued, eager to make my point. 'We're just friends. I value his friendship highly.'

'I believe you, Hells,' he said, as we arrived in Trafalgar Square. 'You wouldn't be daft enough to do it again. Don't mind me, I just care about you.'

'Well, it's my life.'

'True enough *and* your mistakes,' he remarked. 'Are you coming to Charing Cross?'

'No,' I replied, rather rattled at the way our conversation had become so personal so quickly. 'I'm going in the Gallery.'

'Culture vulture,' he laughed. 'Not my scene at all. Look, do you want come to Jay's on Sunday for lunch? There's a few of us going from the tour.'

'I don't know ...'

He gave me a quick peck on the cheek. 'Go on, it'll be a laugh.'

'OK, why not? Ring me to confirm, yeah?'

He turned to go, but then paused. 'Hells, I hope he hasn't got designs on you, this bloke.'

'Shut up. It's nothing to do with you. And I am over twenty-one.'

'There won't be much of...you know,' he said, winking at me, his face half serious, half amused, 'what with all the tablets and stuff. But then you know all about that already, don't you?'

'Don't be so personal. I don't believe you!'

'He's not a dirty old man is he?'

'Frankie!' I gasped, unable to imagine anyone less like a dirty old man than Benedict.

'You have to think of things like that,' he insisted, but beginning to laugh.

'Only in a romance and it isn't ... we aren't ...'

'Not yet!'

'It's about time you stopped poking your nose in.'

'Oh by the way,' he added, reaching into his pocket for something and pulling out a crumpled piece of paper. 'Get your agent to put you up for this. It's a revue going to be on in Soho, ideal for you.' I took it from him.

'Are you going for it?'

'Not sure. I can't sing, can I?'

'Cheers mate.'

He gave me a wave and a smile. 'No problem. See you soon.'

I watched as his thick hair got blown about in the blustery March wind until he disappeared into the crowds. I sat on the edge of one of the fountains feeling slightly unsettled by Frankie referring to Benedict, who was such a gentleman with impeccable manners, in that way. Frankie had always been delightfully blunt, but he was such great company on tour and quite caring underneath all the black humour. Talking to him, I had completely forgotten the awful audition already and I was grateful to him for that.

Dark clouds were bubbling up and the wind was changing direction and cooling considerably. I knew I hadn't explained my relationship with Benedict very well to Frankie and my continuous denials had obviously sounded hollow to his ears. I took out my mobile as large spots of rain began to fall. I pictured Benedict struggling to find the phone and cursing his useless legs. When he eventually answered just hearing his voice made me smile and I felt curiously happy.

'Hello.'

'Hello, Mr Marshall. Are you having a kip?'

'How dare you,' he replied, with that usual hint of dry humour. 'Only silly old fools sleep in the afternoon and although I'm heading that way, I'm not quite there yet.'

'What were you doing then?'

'Preparing some lunch and awaiting Sidney's knock on the wall. His wife went out a little while ago so I'm giving him another few minutes before boredom gets the better of him and he comes in here to pester me. Nell, I'm forgetting myself. How did it go?'

'It was a disaster.'

There was a moment's silence. 'I'm so sorry, dear girl.' His voice was full of sincerity and compassion. 'What a shame,' he added. 'But you never can tell ...'

'I won't get it. Not a chance.'

'Fools,' he said.

'There was this pianist who I knew vaguely and I reckon he was drunk because his timing was right out and then I was dancing next to this Tittyfalalelou ...'

I heard him laugh. 'Say that again.'

'You know, fancied herself rotten, up her own arse. She was white as a sheet and had white blonde hair piled high on her head. She reminded me of Frankenstein's monster without the bolts.'

'Priceless,' he muttered.

'She was all over the place and collided with me a couple of times, but what the hell.'

'Are you terribly disappointed?'

'You know what? I don't get that disappointed any more, not for most things, because I don't expect to succeed.'

'Nell, I'm sorry for that. But something will come up, I know it will.'

His supportive words were just what I needed to hear. 'I did meet up with an old friend, so that was good. I'm just going into the National Gallery. I haven't been in there for years and I fancied a bit of culture after that fiasco.'

'I wish I could be there with you.'

'Ah, it would be brilliant to see all the paintings through your eyes. I bet you know about all of the artists, being an intellectual.'

'You flatter me.'

'It's just starting to rain here. What are you having for lunch?'

'Pasta and some grilled chicken.'

'Save me some.'

'Are you coming over?'

'No, I'm only joking, it just sounded so tasty the way you said it. I'll see you soon, Mr Marshall.'

'See you soon, Nell.'

I sat there in the light rain imagining him pottering around slowly in his kitchen in that elegant way of his, his shirt open at the neck and the sleeves rolled up and the thought of him warmed my soul. He had such a charming way about him and a kind of grace I had never seen before in a man. A sudden voice to my left made me jump.

'Hi, I'm sorry about my playing.'

The rough-looking pianist with the sunken eyes was perching beside me on the edge of the fountain. That close up he looked even worse than in the audition room.

'Oh ... hello ...'

'I cocked it right up for you, but if it makes you feel any better, I did the same for everyone else.'

His light-brown curly hair was matted and resembled a bird's nest, but he appeared so genuinely upset about his performance my heart went out to him. 'Forget about it, if they want me, your playing won't change that. I thought it was quite funny actually.' His pale face lit up making him look quite boyish.

'Did you really? Thanks for that. I detest playing for auditions, but I need the money.'

'How's your stomach? Weren't you coughing up blood in a show?'

'You heard about that then?' He looked suitably embarrassed.

'I was on stage at the time.'

'I thought I recognised you. I've got an ulcer.'

'Aren't you a bit young for an ulcer?'

'Drinking,' he muttered.

I warmed to him considerably. 'That's very honest of you.'

'I'm trying to get into another orchestra, but it's very hard.' He stared at the ground and his eyes were downcast. 'Musicians all drink and really I need to be around people who don't.'

'Yes, you do.'

The sky was turning darker and rain began to pelt down. I stood up, indicating I had to go, but he suddenly appeared rather desperate and his eyes held a wildness that worried me.

'I don't suppose you know anyone who would give me a go. It's not *what* you know but ...'

'I might actually, give me your number.'

'Oh cheers,' he gasped, his face breaking into a nervous smile. 'I'm Matt by the way.'

'Helen.'

He fumbled in his pocket and produced a pen and an old train ticket and scribbled his number on it. 'Cheers, Helen. I just need another chance in a band, you know? I'm broke to be honest.'

'I'll ask around for you. I'd better go, I'm getting drenched.'

'Sorry again, I hope you get the part despite me.'

I smiled at him and left him there standing in the cloud burst. I ran to the Gallery and looked back again and he was still there, as if he had nowhere to go.

&

Sidney duly knocked and I knocked back. He appeared five minutes later as I was finishing my pasta. He was wearing his usual retirement garb of casual light-coloured trousers, a darker shirt and an unfortunate bright-yellow tank top circa 1970. He had absolutely no dress sense whatsoever.

'What's occurring, Benedict?' he asked as ever.

'Very little, Sidney, as you can see. You are your usual sartorially elegant self though.'

'Is that meant to be a joke?'

'Well, it is said with a little wry humour.'

'I wish you'd speak like a normal person sometimes.'

'I'm not a normal person. I thought you knew that.'

'All those long words you use ...' He stopped mid sentence, suddenly folded his arms across his chest and, standing directly in front of where I sat on the sofa, fixed me with a smug smile.

'Why are you looking like that?' I asked, although heaven only knows why because I knew I probably wouldn't understand his answer.

'Vexatious.'

I was right, I didn't understand and sighing softly I said, 'I'm sorry?'

'Vexatious,' he repeated.

'Yes, I heard what you said, but I have no idea why you said it.'

'It's just a long word. I wanted to prove I do know some.'

I laughed out loud. 'Right, it's like that, is it? Try this one for size: egregious.'

'That's not a bloody word,' he cried indignantly. 'You've just made that up. What the hell does it mean?'

'I haven't a clue.'

'It doesn't count then.'

'Right then, try this one for size: propensity.'

'Oh fuck off! What does that mean then?'

'It means you have a propensity to say fuck off.'

'Okay, you win.'

'I wasn't aware it was a competition.'

Changing the subject instantly he said, 'Sheila's off spending all my money in town so I'm let off the leash for a couple of hours.' He finally sat down in front of me and stretched his legs out.

I let out a derisory laugh. 'You've never been on a leash in all your married life, so don't give me that.'

His eyebrows shot up. 'I assure you I have,' he insisted.

'I've never known anyone as easy-going as your wife, but then she has to be.' He leant back in his chair, accentuating his large belly and sighed loudly. I picked up on it because I knew he wanted me to. 'Were you going to speak?'

'Moi?'

'Well, you are the only other person in this room.'

'No, not really,' he answered, rather vaguely, but then his inquisitive nature for all things to do with my life got the better of him. 'What were you laughing at the other day?'

'What was I laughing at?' I repeated, just as vaguely to tease him, 'I have no idea, maybe the television.'

He looked at me rather accusingly. 'You don't watch television.'

'How would you know? Actually you're right, I don't. I think I was laughing with Nell.'

'Oh yeah ...'

'Sidney! Don't start all that. I was playing the piano and she was laughing. She laughs all the time, it's such a tonic. Then I laughed at her laughing,' I explained, and as I did it all sounded so innocent and lovely and yet his face was indignant for some reason.

'I haven't ever heard you laugh like that.'

'You know, you're right,' I admitted, 'I can't remember the last time I did. They say laughter is the best medicine and I have to say I agree. It seems to relax all the muscles in your body.'

'So ...'

'So?' I countered, unsure of what his next comment would be.

'Anything you want to tell me?' he inquired, peering over his glasses.

'No,' I replied, looking at him over mine, 'I don't believe so.'

Silence from both of us. He shuffled in his chair a little. 'Is Beth coming home for her birthday?'

'I do hope so. I'm expecting her to call any day. I miss her terribly at the moment, probably because I haven't spoken to her for a few weeks. I *do* get emails, but emails aren't the same as hearing someone's voice, are they?'

'Don't ask me, I hate the bloody computer.'

'I thought you might.'

'Will you have a party for her?'

'I'll have a gathering, not a party, but yes.'

He suddenly looked highly amused. 'You can invite Nell.'

'I intend to.'

As the words came out of my mouth it was the first time I had even given it any thought. However, it took the smug look off Sidney's face.

'Oh,' he cried, 'well, we can all meet her then.'

'Do I take that to mean you have invited yourself to this gathering then?' I asked. He had the grace to look a little embarrassed.

'That's if me and the wife are invited.'

'*The* wife,' I repeated. '*The* chair; *the* table; it's *my* wife, Sidney.'

'She's not your wife!'

'Very funny ...'

'I thought so.'

'Of course you're both invited. You're my closest friends.'

'Thanks, matey. So, how are you feeling? You look a bit haggard today.'

I had to smile, he was so blunt. 'Do you ever really think before you speak? I'm not convinced you haven't got a form of Asperger's Syndrome.'

'What's that when it's at home?'

'It's a form of autism.'

'That's charming. I was only saying because your face looks a bit ...'

'Stiff?'

'Stuck, I'd call it.'

I smiled at him. 'Do you remember years ago, if you pulled a face at your parents you'd be told, the wind will change and you'll stay like that forever?'

'No.'

'My mother used to say it to me and that's how I feel sometimes with this disease, that my face is stuck in one expression.'

'Good job you're not ugly then,' Sidney commented.

'Indeed and thanks for the compliment.'

He frowned. 'What compliment?'

'Never mind ...'

'You never answered my question,' he said, eyeing me curiously, 'how are you feeling?'

'Physically I feel quite odd, as if I'm in a permanent state of decay. Emotionally, never better.'

'Oh yeah ...'

'I'll ignore that, Sidney,' I sighed. 'Physically I feel shaky, lethargic and my hands and legs often won't obey my brain's signals. I go to speak and it comes out as a slur and mentally, some very strange things are going on.'

His face was quite blank. 'How do you mean?'

'I have the feeling I'm being watched, that somebody is standing behind me, near me, or over me. I saw my father sitting by the piano one day and he died in 1984.'

Sidney's face was a picture. 'Fuck me!'

'Quite.'

'Have you spoken to the quack?'

'What do you think?'

He looked concerned. 'I think you should.'

'Maybe,' I muttered. 'But all in all, I'm not so bad.'

'You splutter when you speak sometimes.'

'I'm well aware of that and I can do absolutely nothing about it,' I replied, wondering how on earth his wife put up with him.

He laughed suddenly. 'It's better than pissing yourself though.'

I laughed back at him. I had to otherwise I might very well have cried. 'I'm grateful for small mercies at this stage in the proceedings.'

There was an uneasy silence for a moment in which I hoped Sidney was regretting some of his observations. But no such luck. 'Well, I've been here ten minutes and not been offered a drink.'

'I'm sorry, I'm forgetting myself. Parkinson's or no Parkinson's, I must not forget my manners.'

I struggled up and went into the kitchen to make some tea. Filling the kettle, I noticed my right hand was trembling badly, but I simply swore under my breath and it made me feel infinitely better.

'I expect you're dreading telling Beth,' Sidney called out.

I put my head round the door. 'I may not tell her at all.' He looked aghast at me, as well he might. 'What, Sidney?'

'Don't be stupid, she'll know something is wrong.'

'Do I look that bad, that different?'

'Not always, but sometimes ...'

'It's fine, Sidney. I know I do.'

I made a pot of tea and carried it in carefully on a tray with two china cups. Sidney liked my best china. He said drinking from it made him feel cultured. He took the tray from me.

'Well, if you ask me, I think she deserves to know, Benedict.'

'That may be your most sensible comment to date, my friend,' I told him, smiling. 'I'll probably just blurt it out.'

He laughed. 'Or I will.'

'You most certainly will not.'

'You tell her then,' he insisted, 'as soon as she comes home or I'll be thinking, oh Christ I hope I don't slip up and say something I shouldn't.'

'Yes, that's probably best. Can you pour the tea, please?' He poured and handed my cup to me without as much as a rattle. I silently envied his steadiness. 'Thank you, my friend.'

'I love this china. I know I'm a heathen normally, but I do love it. I bet the Queen has china like this. What did he look like?'

Sidney's change of subject with barely a breath drawn flustered me. 'Who are we talking about *now*?'

'Your father, and did he speak?'

'He looked as he did when we were growing up; it was extraordinary, and he spoke as he always had. You forget; you think you remember, but over the years you actually forget their mannerisms, the tiny nuances of their facial expressions and their voice. He used words he always had, except one phrase which baffled me and then he vanished.'

Sidney's face was a picture. 'Sounds like a scary business.'

'No, it was all rather lovely actually.'

'If my old man came back I'd shit myself.'

'Thanks for that eloquent comment, Sidney.'

'Well I would! It's all a bit bloody barmy if you ask me.'

I opened my mouth to reply, but the phone rang. Endearingly Sidney jumped up and passed it to me. Beth's voice on the other end unexpectedly, made me smile from ear to ear.

'Hello, Dad.' I went to speak, but I slurred badly and no actual sound came out. 'Dad, are you there?'

'Darling,' I spluttered.

'How are you?'

'Fine, how are you?'

'Great. Have you had a beer or two with Sidney? Your voice sounds a bit funny.'

'Yes, a couple,' I lied. 'He's here with me now. What's happening with you?'

'I'm coming home next Friday if that's OK?' she said, her voice excited and full of life with an ever so slight American twang.

'Sweetheart, that's wonderful. Sidney and I were just talking about that. Hang on, do you mean this Friday or next Friday?'

'Sorry, I meant this Friday.'

'I'll send a cab for you, shall I?'

'Yes, please, that would be great. I'll email the time of the flight and everything. What have you been doing?'

'Not much, walking a bit, trying to get fitter ...' I heard Sidney snigger and I glared at him.

'You're kidding me,' she gasped, knowing her father of old. 'Don't lose any weight, you can't afford to. Look, I'll stay a few days at yours and then go to Mum's if that's cool with you.'

'Yes, of course, darling, everything is *cool* with me where you're concerned,' I replied, laughing inwardly at my repetition of her words which sounded bizarre from my frayed lips. 'I'll have a few of the family over on the Sunday lunchtime for your birthday.'

'Fantastic, but don't go to too much trouble.'

'Just a select few who would love to see you.'

'That's brilliant. Make sure Aunty Bethan comes. I'll email you then, okay? Take care, Dad ...'

'How's work?' I asked quickly, wanting to keep her on the phone just for a little longer.

'Fantastic, thanks. But I'll fill you in when I get home. See you soon.'

'Bye, darling, bye.'

I handed Sidney the phone and he placed it back on the bureau. He was smiling broadly. 'Coming home then?'

I felt a warm contentment spreading through me, despite my knowing I would have to burst her bubble of happiness and excitement by explaining about my disease. 'She is. I'm so pleased. I miss her terribly.'

Sidney looked decidedly smug. 'It's going to be an interesting visit; telling her about the Parkinson's *and* Nell.'

'Are you enjoying this, Sidney?'

'The bit about Nell, yes,' he declared.

'Hopefully not the bit about telling Beth ...' I stopped myself when I saw his hurt expression, regretting my words instantly.

'Benedict, that's unfair. I don't want to see Beth upset, you know that.'

'I'm sorry.'

'I'm very fond of her,' he added.

'Forgive me, my friend. Truly, forgive me. My brain isn't what it was.'

'You're forgiven,' he said. 'You could ask Nell to the party and introduce her to everyone at the same time.'

'I might just do that.'

'Can you imagine? Benedict's gone and got himself a bit of fluff,' he laughed, his belly wobbling up and down alarmingly.

'A bit of fluff is an awful expression.'

'That will set the cat amongst the pigeons. Everyone will think you've turned into a dirty old man.'

'I have, I dribble sometimes,' I said.

'Not a dirty old man like that.'

'I know what you mean and I'm not.'

'I know you're not,' he said eventually, after much sniggering.

'She will be introduced as my friend and that's exactly what she is. End of story.'

'So, the bash will be next Sunday,' he continued, enjoying himself immensely. 'Shall I bring some booze?'

'You don't need to, but if you want to, that would be lovely.'

He rubbed his hands together. 'I can't wait to meet the firecracker.'

'Sidney,' I sighed, 'if you call her anything but her name to her or anyone else I will cease our friendship.'

His face fell a mile. 'Fucking hell, Benedict, you don't mean that.'

'I assure you I do,' I lied; but his expression was so sorrowful I backtracked immediately. 'No, I don't mean it, but please, think before you speak. That's all I ask of you.'

'OK, I apologise,' he said. 'I know you're tetchy because you're dreading telling Beth about your illness, but it's not cancer.'

'I'm her dear old dad; she'd worry about me having a bad bout of flu!'

'She's strong, Benedict, and young. We all take stuff in our stride in our youth, don't you remember?'

'Alas, no.'

'I wonder what everyone will think of your young friend. I can't wait.'

'So I see by your demeanour. Of course Nell may not come.

His face dropped instantly. 'Don't say that!'

'Well, despite your intimations and knowing looks, we are not romantically involved. Nevertheless, she may find meeting all my family, and others she doesn't know,' I said, looking pointedly at Sidney, 'all a bit too much.'

'That's true,' he muttered, obviously disappointed. 'Shall I rig something up?'

'Something as in one of your disasters you mean?'

'Yeah, lights or fireworks,' he said, his face lighting up like a young boy's.

'I seem to remember your firework display last November was an utter catastrophe.'

'It was brilliant, it just went slightly wrong,' he protested.

Just going slightly wrong was an understatement in the extreme. He had rigged up a contraption whereby he should have been able to light the first firework which would then ignite the next one and the next one and it was meant to be a wonderful spectacular for his grandchildren. Unfortunately, and typically for Sidney, it all went horribly wrong and the only spectacular happening was the one huge bang when everything exploded at once; all over in ten seconds. That was Sidney though, great inventive ideas, a sweet flamboyancy and not much luck with almost everything he touched, but it was his most endearing quality.

Looking at his animated face now, I had to smile, 'Yes, slightly wrong,' I agreed, 'like the idea of painting every brick on your patio a different colour.'

'I thought that was a stroke of genius.'

'It was until you knocked over the yellow paint pot.'

'That was just unfortunate.'

'It certainly was.'

'I do have wonderful ideas though. Remember when I fell off the roof?'

'I'm afraid I do. Remind me again why you were on the roof?'

'A tile had fallen off. I could have killed myself doing that.'

'I'm well aware of that and you nearly did. Sheila really should be canonised.'

'So what if I just rig up some lights,' he suggested.

'I'm losing the will to live.'

'And balloons,' he added for good measure.

'I need a drink,' I muttered.

'Oh let me do something for Beth!' When I didn't answer him immediately, he wheedled, 'Benedict?'

I gave in, 'Oh all right, fine. But let's have something understated and not too ridiculous.'

'I don't do understated.'

'That's the understatement of the year.'

'I'll give it some thought.'

'And run it by me first!'

'Fancy some cards?' he asked, changing the subject before I changed my mind.

'You know, I quite fancy having a snooze. Do you mind, Sidney?'

'No, no, of course, I'll leave you to it. Thanks for the tea. I'll let myself out.'

'Please do.'

Hauling himself out of his chair, his parting shot was: 'Can't wait for next Sunday.'

'Bugger off!'

Allowing the sofa back to cradle my head, I listened to the gentle sound of early spring rain tapping on the conservatory roof. My body ached with tension, especially my neck and shoulders and I attempted to relax them by concentrating on the soft sounds around me: the rhythmical ticking of the clock at the other end of the lounge, an imperceptible whispering of the wind through the tall trees at the end of my garden and a slow, deep breathing near me. The *presence* was hovering a few inches from my side, distracting me with its shadowy colours on the wall. I closed my eyes, longing for that pleasant feeling between sleep and waking where all reality is far away in some other distant place.

'Benedict.'

The voice came from inside my head at first, but struggling to open my eyes it appeared to be at the other end of the room. 'Papa, is that you?' He was sitting on the piano stool again. 'Is that really you, Papa, or are you a dream?'

'I'm here, Benedict.'

'This is a wretched hallucination, isn't it? I know you're not really here, but it's comforting to see you. You look so substantial though.' His eyes were twinkling with that old mischief that his children had loved because it meant there was fun to be had.

'I am here,' he said. 'I'm always here. You must take good care of yourself. People need you, Benedict. They need your constancy, your kindness and your love.'

Hot tears were pricking the back of my eyes. 'But I'm not like you, Papa. I haven't been as constant as you. You're such a hard act to follow. Have you any idea how much you were missed? I have this illness now ... this *disease*. It will slowly eat away at me ...'

'No, it will only do that if you allow it to. Be strong, be brave and be true to yourself. It will define the kind of man you are in the end: one who gives up or one who fights.' He smiled at me encouragingly. '*And,*' he added, 'when the time comes, let her go and she will come back to you.' His words became slightly jumbled after that, as if I were hearing them on a bad telephone line.

'What did you say? Let who go? I support Beth in everything she does. Oh Papa, she would have loved you so much had she known you, but I have spoken about you to her. I'm a good father, I'm sure of that. But I wasn't a good husband and I feel so much guilt about that. I'm sorry; I'm truly sorry.'

He gave a little shrug of his shoulders and touched his moustache, a mannerism I remembered well. 'Did you have a good wife?' he asked. I opened my mouth to speak, but when no sound came out, I simply shook my head and he went on, 'Then I'm sorry for that. And Benedict, I know you ... you would have done your very best. Don't live with guilt, don't live with regrets. It's too heavy a burden to carry around and you need your strength. Don't forget, I loved you very much and I love you still.'

Tears streamed out of my eyes and into my mouth. My nose began to run and I had no tissues near me so I simply wiped my face with the back of my hand. A yellow light flickered somewhere and shadows danced on the wall, shadows of scenes long ago, almost recognised and remembered and far away laughter that was commonplace. I hugged myself tightly, hanging on hard to my shirt sleeves and I began to shake violently. I strained to hear a conversation between a group of people that I knew, but the voices merged together and became one and he was then gone.

I sobbed loudly, not caring who heard me, until I felt exhausted and limp and hollow. It was as if all my deepest emotions about my disease flooded out of me. Childhood memories of long sun-drenched days running through fields with my brother and sisters came to me thick and fast. I concentrated as hard as I could on the memory of my father's face until the shaking became less and less dramatic and turned into small, manageable but still unwanted spasms. I continued to focus on the comforting memory of how it felt to be loved by him and the spasms slowly reverted back to the known tremors.

The man I had been all my adult life, who felt alone, lost and desperate much of the time, who was often floundering and grasping for the support of alcohol and unsuitable, shallow women, suddenly vanished and the man I wanted to become, who I'd always longed to be, was left in his wake, gently swaying and profoundly changed. I felt free of the old Benedict. I felt I could move on and perhaps, in my own way, resemble the wonderful, honourable man my father had been.

I sank into the sofa, exhausted. I tried to focus my aching and reddened eyes on the piano stool where he had sat, so lifelike, so incredibly substantial; everything about him perfectly the same as it had always been: his soft silver-blonde hair swept over his ears and the small, darker-blonde moustache we his children had been fascinated by and used to tug at mercilessly until he could stand it no longer; the kindly, Mediterranean-blue eyes, his tall, slim figure that I had been blessed with also, and the gentle, elegant sweep of his hands as he spoke.

I had seen the deep lines on his forehead and at the side of his mouth and the square chin that my older brother and I had both inherited, and I delighted in his courteous, reserved manner and genteel way of speaking. Good manners were everything to him and all he asked of us, his children, was that we were polite at all times to each other and to strangers. But more than that, he had such a charismatic air about him, women of all ages flocked to him for his warmth, his kind nature and his gentle, self-mocking humour.

It was all there, as he spoke to me; all of it. But beyond all of that, what shone from him most was his constant, deep love.

I sat quietly and motionless for almost an hour. My mind drifted onto certain moments of my past and I watched them float away into the distance. I no longer recognised that man. He was someone else completely with a different nature and understanding of the world. It was as if all those moments in all those years had happened to another person.

I didn't even feel I was a writer any more. Who was that man whose writing had flowed effortlessly from his pen; the man who had made the most of every tiny opportunity with a woman because his ego was the size of the cricket pitch? The man who often felt so isolated in his own life he drank to drown the loneliness. I had even walked aimlessly into a church in the City one morning and sat mute at the back watching an elderly woman arrange flowers prettily near the altar. I had no idea why I was sitting there, but I had the most intense longing to belong to something – someone – and find a purpose to my shabby life. However, unlike Sidney with *his* sense of belonging to the Catholic religion that I had mocked, I had found no solace in the chilled atmosphere of that church, only echoes of past worship and beautiful stained-glass windows.

But now, having met Nell, I felt different. I imagined stepping out of my old body and into a new one. The new one had a disease, but he was a better man. And Beth would be back in four days. I knew I would need some strength of character to explain about my illness without putting the fear of God into her. But telling her would come from the new Benedict who would now try and look forward without dwelling constantly on his past mistakes. I would attempt to be the man my father knew I could be from this moment on. He believed in me and so did Nell. I couldn't let them down.

Chapter 5

Nell and I went walking two days before Beth's arrival. It was a breezy spring day with strong white sunlight and clouds that resembled soap suds. We were wrapped up in anticipation of an easterly wind that had been forecast, but the sun was gathering its strength and held the promise of an elusive early summer. After we had negotiated the steep path to the tennis courts she spoke briefly about her audition.

'I met an old friend afterwards; we toured together once and had a real laugh. He's a very talented guy, brilliant actor.'

'Does he get the parts?' I asked, breathing hard.

'Sometimes, but they've been a bit thin on the ground lately. It's such a shame, he's great on stage.'

'Lots of talented people and not enough jobs,' I remarked, wanting to empathise.

'No, you're right, there aren't,' she replied. 'He's great company – a black sense of humour. I know I shouldn't laugh at some of the things he says, but I can't help it.'

She gazed out over the city spreading its greyness beneath us, her face glowing with health and vitality and her shining dark hair ensnared by a colourful scarf wound tightly round her neck. Was this the man Nell was enamoured of? Was this the man who would bring out the raging monster of jealousy in me that had been sleeping and dormant for most of my life? 'Is he good looking?' I ventured, despite trying desperately to stop myself from asking.

'Yes, lovely face, cute, incredible green eyes like a cat's.'

'How I envy him.'

She looked up at me, frowning. 'But you've got a lovely face. I bet there wasn't anyone to touch you ...'

'In my day,' I laughed, finishing the sentence for her.

'I happen to think you're still a good-looking man, Mr Marshall,' she declared.

My heart began thumping wildly. 'Nell, you do me a power of good.'

'I mean it,' she insisted, her eyes sparkling with sincerity.

'Bless you.'

'Beauty is only skin deep anyway. It's the person inside who counts, don't you think?'

'I do, Nell.'

'Come on, let's get going to the café, you'll get chilled otherwise,' she urged, taking my arm gently. 'I was speaking about you to Frankie. Were your ears burning?'

'Were you really? That must have been fascinating for him.'

She picked up on my sarcasm. 'But you *are* fascinating.'

'What did you tell him about me?' I asked, not wanting to, but my vanity got the better of me.

'That you were cultured, intelligent, funny ...'

'That I dribbled and slurred ...'

'Hardly,' she laughed.

'What about my being devastatingly attractive?'

She grinned at me. 'Shut your face.'

'Delightful.'

We arrived at the cafe which was nearly full and two rather large women were in our seats so Nell steered me over to the other side and we ended up sitting next to an elderly man with the shakes sipping his tea carefully. As usual I put my hand in my pocket for some change, but she had already disappeared up to the counter and was chatting animatedly to he of the washboard stomach and line-free face. When she carefully placed the tray of coffees and cake before me she carried on with her conversation where we had left off.

'I told Frankie you were a writer and he's going to Google you.'

'Will it hurt?'

'That's very funny, Mr Marshall! You know what I mean.'

'I wonder what he'll find. And did you mention the disease?'

Her face dropped a little. 'I wasn't going to, I never would, but we spoke about Joshua and one thing led to another.'

My stomach sank to my knees at the thought of Nell's cute, green eyed actor friend looking aghast at her. 'I imagine he was shocked.'

'Not shocked exactly,' she said hurriedly, 'because I explained we were just friends.'

'Just friends, yes,' I muttered.

'He's a great guy; you'd like him.'

'If you like him, Nell, I'm sure I would too.'

My attention was diverted suddenly by the elderly man to my right taking a sip of his tea but missing his mouth and slurping badly. Nell and I exchanged a quick look of sympathy and I could tell by her face she could read my thoughts. She shook her head and frowned at me as if to say, no, you won't end up like that and I ended up smiling back at her despite myself.

'Anyway,' she started, 'I'm going to some lunch-time party with him on Sunday. I'm quite looking forward to it, I haven't been out in ages, haven't felt that sociable to be honest, but I thought, do I want to go? Yes I do.'

I found I was trembling slightly. I imagined Nell working her magic at the party, smiling her perfect smile, dazzling everyone, especially the good looking, talented Frankie who would have so much in common with her, being in the same business. He would say something humorous and she would let out a burst of her wonderful laugh, showering everyone with her effervescence. But I could not and would not appear churlish in the face of her enthusiasm and I wanted her to have fun. She was born to have fun and deserved it after the many rejections she had faced in her professional life. Her personal life was absolutely nothing to do with me. After all, as she had told the impossibly cute, black humoured Frankie, we were just friends.

'Nell, I do hope you have a wonderful time at the party,' I said, with as much sincerity as I could muster, 'it will do you good.'

She beamed at me. 'Ah thank you, Mr Marshall. I'll tell you all about it.' She suddenly looked carefree and excited. 'There should be quite a few people there I know through work. Not friends, but people you come across, you know?'

'Yes, of course.'

'It will be interesting to hear what others are up to you. My God, this banana cake is to die for. It's my favourite by far.'

'I used to go to quite a few parties when I was writing. Mind you, I left most of them in rather an inebriated state. I came across quite a few extraordinary characters: other writers, directors, publishers, musicians. God, could the musicians drink? They left me standing.'

'I know,' she gasped, 'it seems to be a requirement of the job. Your life sounds fascinating.'

'Not so Fascinating, Nell and I don't see any of them now, of course. But that's my fault as much as theirs. I remember making a bit of a fool of myself once ... well, many times actually, with the sister of one of my directors. She cornered me, in the study I think it was, of this huge palatial house and wouldn't take no for an answer despite her husband being in the next room, literally yards away.'

Nell's face was a picture. 'No!'

'I promise you.'

'How awful, what happened?'

'It *was* awful, but she was a very attractive woman and to my eternal shame I took advantage of the situation. But then that was how I behaved in those days.' Nell's face immediately betrayed her disappointment in me, plain and simple. 'Are you ashamed of me?' I asked her.

'Ashamed of you?' she replied, frowning, as if the idea of it was anathema to her. 'I could never be ashamed of you, Mr Marshall. We all have situations that occurred in our past that we regret and would do differently now. Flattery is a powerful motivator. Did she stay with her husband?'

'No, they separated months later – not because of me I hasten to add. She found out he'd been having an affair for the past six months with a girl in make-up, so that was that. I do regret it though. Looking back I thought I was having fun, but it all feels a little sordid and vacuous now. I can't remember why I acted as I did. I can't even recall my feelings at the time. I should have acted honourably and I would now. Maybe the disease was festering in me even then and invading my brain cells and turning them to dust.'

'I hope not,' Nell said, wrinkling her nose. 'You seem lucid now, very sharp.'

'Thank you, dear girl. You do me so much good.'

She leant towards me. 'Can we talk about your writing?'

'It's a dim and distant memory.'

'But I'm interested.'

'Then ask me anything you like.'

'How long ago did you write your award-winning plays?'

'In the late eighties – a lifetime ago,' I remarked.

'What made you stop?'

I found her inquisitiveness touching and wanted to answer as honestly as I could. 'I had said everything I needed to say, truly. I wanted to change my life; retire from all that.'

'I find that hard to believe with your sharp wit. Don't writers continually find subjects to write about?' she asked, appearing genuinely interested.

'Not this one,' I replied. 'I think most creative people have one great book in them, one great album, one great play, with a few exceptional exceptions. And if you continue you become a little less of what you were.'

She appeared thoughtful. 'So you only wrote one great play?'

'I believe so, yes.'

'But all those awards!'

I shrugged. 'They are all for two of my plays only, but I honestly didn't think the second one was worth any award. I actually went to see the play I thought should have won that year; a brutally frank, clever and fascinating piece of work, but the powers that be overlooked it and gave the accolade to me. I intended to refuse it, but my then wife wouldn't hear of it. She loved all the kudos involved, you see. I should have insisted but ...'

'You feel guilty now.'

'I do, yes and ashamed.'

Nell looked perplexed. 'But there's nothing you can do about it now and anyway, who's to say yours wasn't the best? I bet it was.'

'For some reason, Nell, I have guilt about so many aspects of my life and it's hard living with it constantly. It's as if it's written in my DNA now, but I wasn't like that before this disease. I don't know whether it actually changes how your brain cells work, but I am now much more introspective and introverted. I seem to always look inward, not outward. Does that make sense?'

She nodded and gave a little smile. 'Yes and I suspect it may be the Parkinson's. Joshua was the same. Maybe, just maybe that's why he ... perhaps there were things he couldn't live with. But, Mr Marshall ...' She hesitated, appearing troubled. Her eyes grew larger and she swallowed hard. 'You wouldn't ever, you know ...just disappear from my life.'

'My God,' I muttered, when I realised what she meant, 'I could never do that to you.' She smiled instantly and looked highly relieved.

'No, I know that really. I just get a bit anxious sometimes when I hear you speak of regrets and guilt.'

'No need, Nell, I assure you. I've stopped all that from right here and now.'

'Good.'

'Did Joshua have any specific regrets or guilt that he spoke about?' I ventured, hoping my question would not upset her too much.

'Oh yes,' she said, 'he was riding a motorbike with his fiancée on the back and he crashed. He survived, but tragically she died. They were two weeks away from their wedding, can you imagine? That's what he meant when he told me he had no fight left in him. All his emotional strength had been used up getting over her death. Well ...' she paused, her almond-shaped eyes full of tears, 'I say getting *over* it, but really he hadn't, not even by the time he met me, which was years later. He even felt guilty about our relationship, not only because of her, but because I was so much younger than him and he had Parkinson's.'

'I see,' I mumbled, understanding the emotional pain he must have been going through perfectly after her vivid explanation. 'I sympathise with him. He not only had the physical problems to deal with, but the mental and emotional too. The physical part is quite enough for anyone.'

She gazed out of the window at the newly sprouting roses, her face wistful and pensive. I detected a deep, still-raw emotional pain in her eyes too. I knew only too well how selfish actions caused ripples for years to come for those we loved. Nell was obviously still suffering with regards to her lost love and probably always would. I knew I had caused her mood to drop and I intended to bring the smile back to her face.

'Would you like to come to a gathering on Sunday at my house? It's Beth's birthday and I've invited a few of my family, Sidney and Sheila and …'

'That's a quaint word, gathering. Oh I can meet Beth,' she gasped, but her face fell immediately. 'Oh bugger, I'm going out this Sunday, aren't I?'

'Yes, yes of course. Don't worry,' I told her hastily, 'all my family may be too much for you anyway …'

'No, they wouldn't, I'd love to meet everyone, but I promised Frankie.'

'Ah yes, Frankie with the green eyes.'

She visibly brightened. 'I could come on after.'

My heart leapt. 'Would you?'

She grinned at me, 'Yeah, why not?'

'Fabulous.'

'I'll try to get to you by four, half past at the latest.'

'It will still be in full swing,' I assured her, my heart rate picking up apace with excitement. 'Won't Frankie mind?' I added as an afterthought because in reality I didn't give a damn about Frankie.

'No, of course not, why would he? I can't wait to meet everyone,' she enthused, her eyes shining and I loved her for that. 'Now, did you find my favourite poem, Mr Marshall?'

'Aha, yes the poem. I'm not convinced I've found the right one, but I may have.'

'Let's stride back and have a look.'

'*Stride* is not a word in my vocabulary any more. Shuffle maybe, stumble, stagger, all of those fit now.'

'Not when you're with me!' she declared, jumping up. 'Now come on, let's stride together.'

I laughed at her. 'I'll do my best, Nell, just for you.'

We actually partly strolled and partly strode back to my house although I shuffled a little of the way when I lost my balance. I detested my shuffling action, it made me feel like a puppet with someone unhinged pulling my strings, but Nell simply took my arm and guided me carefully and I took such pleasure from her gentle grip I could have trekked to Scotland and back.

Once back safely in my lounge I immediately collapsed on the sofa to catch my breath and my equilibrium and Nell automatically went into the kitchen to put the kettle on. I allowed myself a fleeting dream of how, if she lived with me, she would potter about in my huge, lonely house as she pleased and I would sit happily and hear her light footsteps and glorious laugh everywhere. But I shook my head and tried to focus on Yeats and his soulful poetry because dreaming like that would do me no good at all. I glanced over to the bookcase where I knew the volume of poetry was nestling, intending to retrieve it when a little rested, as Nell placed a pot of tea between us.

'I can only stay another half hour,' she said, 'I have a shift in a little while.'

'How selfish of me, Nell...'

'What is?'

'I never think about your life and how busy you must be. I only think about how I love having you here. Let me show you the poem I believe to be your favourite.'

I stood up too quickly and stumbled forward across the low coffee table. I must have looked pathetic and ridiculous in my attempt to get my balance. Nell sprung up as quick as lightening and grabbed me.

'Did you hurt yourself?' she gasped.

'No, no, I'm fine, I think. I'm so sorry.'

'Don't be daft, nothing to be sorry about.'

'I made you jump, I do apologise.'

'It's fine, really,' she insisted, still holding me fast.

'Balance is a little bit of a problem sometimes.'

Her eyes scanned my face fleetingly. 'You just jumped up too fast, that's all. You should take your time.'

I looked down at her, steadfast and sturdy as she was. 'You'll be on at me to get a stick.'

'Sticks are in this year,' she replied, laughing and I laughed with her, despite my initial embarrassment. 'Everyone seems to have them.'

'But only silly old men have sticks.'

She didn't answer immediately and her eyes scanned my face once again. 'You have the loveliest eyes, Mr Marshall. Has anyone ever told you that?'

'Actually, yes,' I said smugly, to make her laugh, despite the joy I was feeling that she had noticed my eyes or even commented on them; and laugh she did, loudly.

'Shut your face, you.'

'Delightful.'

'Can you walk now?'

'Yes, I can,' I told her, touched by the concern on her face, 'and I'll get the book for you. It's just here. Now, I'm not entirely sure I have this right, but I chose this one because there was one line I felt described ... well, you have a look.'

She glanced at the poem, but her face did not betray whether I was correct or not. In fact, I could hardly see her face because it was tilted down, almost as if in prayer or reverence for the Yeats collected poetry. 'Why exactly did you choose this?' she asked. 'You didn't finish what you were going to say.'

I wanted to explain that some of the lines described exactly what I felt for her, but I struggled with my conscience and my speech. She didn't need to know that a silly old fool with a chronic disease loved her utterly and completely and would until the day he died. That would embarrass her and make her feel obliged to be my friend and if I ever considered she felt obliged to me in any way, it would have killed me, finished me off swiftly and deftly.

'Because,' I started, searching for the right words, 'there are words here that I believe fit how you wish a man to love you. And this is how I believe you deserve to be loved. I see you as a pilgrim soul, Nell.'

She appeared moved and bit her lip. 'You are completely right, Mr Marshall,' she declared, 'but I knew you'd pick it out. This poem is about *real* love, not physical attraction or obsession or lust or a passing fancy that drags on. Real love knows no boundaries of age or disease or ...' She hesitated for a moment. 'It has nothing to do with what a person looks like; it's about loving the person inside. I've had many men think they were in love with me, but they weren't. They didn't know me and it wouldn't have lasted. The words, "but one man loved the pilgrim soul in you and loved the sorrows of your changing face," are a wonderful description of the nature of *real* love. It's exquisite, don't you think?'

I couldn't answer her because up until then I had not known the true nature of real love in my life, except for Beth and that was entirely different. And yet, as she recited those few words it was as if every day of my paltry existence, every experience great or small, every mistake, every false triumph and emotion had all happened for one reason only: to ultimately meet, get to know and love her.

I could see that meagre existence tagging along behind me; chart its course, its meanderings and setbacks, including my empty relationships, and ultimately the wretched diagnosis. But then, on that fateful day when I could no longer stand being in my decaying body, desperate to breathe properly, I sat out in the snowy February air to at least try to feel somewhat alive, Nell happened to run by.

A few months earlier, Yeats' words would have either flown over my head or made me shrug with indifference. Now it was as if he had written them just for me. She continued to look at me with that inquisitive expression of hers, expecting me to answer intelligently.

'I think,' I started, 'Yeats understood perfectly the nature of real love.' I knew I could say nothing more, for fear of giving too much away, but I saw the relief spread across her delicate features.

'I'm so glad you understand; I knew you would and it means a lot to me.' She smiled self-consciously for a moment, but suddenly her eyes sparkled and she added, 'Now, let's have fun.'

'What shall we do?' I asked, wanting to please her.

'What would you like to do?'

'Nothing too strenuous, thank you very much.'

'We could dance together or shall we just chat? I think the walking has been enough today.'

'Chatting sounds just fine with me.'

'Let's talk about your family. Tell me about them.'

'Would you like to know more about my parents?'

'No, tell me about your brothers and sisters. If I'm going to meet them I need some background information, don't you think?'

'Ah, well … my brother William is the eldest at sixty-five and just retired from being a GP. He's a widower, but he has a partner, Lily. She's a very friendly, sociable type, extremely attractive.' Nell was pouring the tea for both of us.

'What's he like? Does he look like you?'

'I'm afraid he does.'

'Great. What's his personality like?'

'He's quieter than me, more studious and reserved I suppose. But a steady, reliable type, as doctors should be.'

'He sounds lovely.'

'He's a good man, always has been, unlike myself,' I remarked.

'Don't be daft,' she laughed, leaning towards me with her chin in her hands. 'So you're next and then who?'

'No, I'm not next, my elder sister Sarah is next; she's sixty-three and a retired headmistress of a small school in Sussex. She's married to Rich who is an accountant. They are Beth's God-parents.'

'What are they like as people?'

'Sarah is a little bossy, but she would be being a headmistress. She bosses Rich constantly and he never answers back. He is solid – a little boring if I'm brutally honest. My wife used to beg me not to leave her with him at any social event because she said he could bore for England, which wasn't terribly kind, but that was Mary.'

'Ah poor bloke,' Nell commented. 'Boring is just an unkind way of saying someone's reliable. There's nothing wrong with being reliable. I think it's an underrated quality to have, don't you?'

I had to smile at her. That comment was pure Nell. 'Yes, yes, I do.'

'Perhaps doing figures all day he doesn't have the need to converse much so he's out of practice.'

'You could be right there. But they are both kind and have always been very supportive of Beth so ...'

'And then there's your youngest sister?' she asked.

'Yes, Bethan,' I replied, wondering how to describe my sister without putting Nell off appearing at the party. 'She is fifty-seven, divorced and on her own at the moment. She's a barrister ...'

'Tough then,' Nell interrupted, pulling a face.

'You could say that,' I laughed. 'She can argue a point to the death and beat you every time, has the memory of an elephant and is passionate about justice – or the lack of it. We are very close, even though we're so different, always have been. She has always said I have terrible judgement where women are concerned and of course she has been right most of the time.'

'I expect she looks out for you. Sisters do that.'

'You're probably right; she is fiercely protective of me. She doesn't think I can look out for myself and I suspect, deep down inside, she probably thinks I'm weak. Not many men like to be told how many mistakes they have made,' I muttered, remembering many occasions where Bethan had hauled me over the coals for my errors in judgement.

Nell finished her tea and looked thoughtful. 'Have you told them ... about the Parkinson's I mean?'

I glanced down at my visibly shaking hands. 'No.'

She frowned. 'Why haven't you told them?'

I sighed. 'I don't know, Nell. That's the honest answer.'

'You don't want to upset them.'

'Perhaps,' I admitted, 'but I also feel the need to keep it to myself. The more people I tell the more real it becomes. Does that make any sense to you?'

She gave me a fond smile. 'It does, but I think they would want to know. In my experience most people only want to help, especially those that love you.'

'You have a lovely, naïve and sweet view of the world.'

'I know,' she said. 'So, what's Beth like? Her personality I mean.'

'I thought for a moment. 'She's quite outgoing, bright, hard working, has a dry sense of humour ...'

'Is she more like you or her mum?'

'I would say she looks more like me, although her voice is almost identical to her mum's. I think she's more sociable than me and she can be a little blunt, which is like her mother *and* my sister Bethan. She doesn't suffer fools, but has a great sense of the ridiculous ...'

'Like you.'

'Yes, she loves a bit of mischief.'

'And her faults,' she asked, tilting her head to one side with interest.

'Well, I'm her besotted father so I don't see many,' I replied, 'but I do know she can be stubborn and a little materialistic, but she works very hard for her money so why not enjoy it? American banks are hard taskmasters, so I'm told.'

'I bet,' she remarked, 'I couldn't work in a bank, I'd die of boredom.'

'That's because you have to perform, Nell. It's in your blood and you'll never be happy or satisfied doing anything other than that.'

She gave a deep sigh and tucked her thick, dark hair behind her ears neatly.

'It's a tough life though … if you're struggling to get the parts,' she said earnestly. Then, her mood changing once more, she suddenly clapped her hands together and leapt to her feet, 'Let's dance together, shall we?'

'Do we have to?' I asked forlornly.

'Yes, I believe we do! Up you get, no complaining now.' She took hold of my hands and pulled gently. 'Feet apart, turned out a bit, like this…'

'Good grief! I feel like a rag doll…'

'You *look* like a rag doll, Mr Marshall.'

'How kind…'

She suddenly jumped forward and grabbed hold of me. Her left arm went behind my back and her right hand took mine. She pulled me closer, looking up at me playfully. Despite her nearness making me slightly breathless and even shakier than I was already, I decided to act the fool to save her and myself from any embarrassment. So I tossed my head as if shaking my hair from my eyes and pulled an imperious face that I knew would make her laugh. And laugh she did, throwing her head back and sparkling like polished jewels.

'Hang on, this calls for proper music,' she told me and she rifled quickly through my CD collection once again. 'This will do nicely,' she added as Strauss blasted out from my speakers.

'Good God alive! Strauss is too fast for me, Nell. I'll end up flat on my face!'

'Not with me holding you,' she replied and she began to move me around the room expertly and firmly. 'Hold in your core…'

'Don't start all that nonsense about cores and abominable muscles…'

'Abdominals! Abdominals! Keep upright, don't look down, balance…balance…feel the music,' she commanded as I did my utmost to be the partner she deserved.

'I am feeling the music,' I declared, 'the bass is so loud I can feel it through my backside.'

Nell began to laugh again and because of the shuddering as the laughter rippled through her whole body, she clung on to me like a limpet and gave up. Looking into my eyes she whispered, 'I *love* being with you.' There was a moments silence as I internalised what she had just said and more to the point *how* she had said it and I instinctively went to hug her as tightly as my tremulous arms would allow, but she sprung back and said, 'I've gotta go.'

'Must you?' I asked, rather pathetically for a man of my years.

'Yes, I must, Mr Marshall. I'll see you Sunday … I can't wait.'

'Good, I'm glad you're looking forward to it.'

'Can I bring anything?'

'No, just bring yourself, dear girl.'

'See you then,' she said, with a little wave and I listened intently to her light footsteps walking away from me and out of the front door.

Later that day I made myself some pasta and thought about what I would buy Beth for her birthday. In the last couple of years I had run out of ideas, she had so much so I settled on perhaps giving her a cheque to spend on whatever she liked.

After I'd eaten I telephoned my family but had to leave messages on various answer phones because none of them were at home. I had begun to detest answer phones more than I ever did because as I went to speak I stumbled over the words, sounding like a demented fool. Attempting to have a snooze was my next bright idea, but that too was thwarted when Sidney began to knock. I knocked back and when he appeared by the conservatory door five minutes later, I beckoned him in. He was looking pretty pleased with himself.

'What's occurring then, Benedict?'

'Not much, Sidney, as you can see. I feel slightly odd as usual.'

'Lovely day here at Lords,' he added, which was one of his favourite sayings.

'It is and why are you looking like that?'

'Like what?' he asked, innocence personified.

'Like *that*! You're up to something and I'm not sure I want to hear about it because it's bound to end in tears.'

'I don't know what you mean.'

'Fair enough,' I muttered, knowing my indifference would make him spill the beans.

'Well, actually I've rigged something up for Beth's party ...'

I cast my eyes heavenward. 'Oh God, no ...'

'Don't be like that,' he replied, looking suitably hurt.

'It will be a disaster.'

'Where's your sense of fun?'

'It's up the...what was it now? Oh yes, gone up the pictures with your sense of decorum.'

'There you go with your posh words again – decorum!'

'Sidney, don't tell me what you have rigged up, just check with Sheila first that it's suitable, please.'

He put his hands up and pulled a typical Sidney face which was an almost blank expression with the merest hint of haughtiness, masquerading as innocence. How anyone managed all of this on one face I have no idea, but Sidney did.

'You have my word, Benedict. Now, the sun is just over the yard-arm.'

'It's too early,' I protested, 'even for me.'

He frowned. 'Early in what sense?'

'There's only one sense of the word early, my friend.'

'You aren't becoming boring, are you? I couldn't stand that,' he said, shaking his head.

'I hope never to become boring, Sidney. But think about your weight,' I told him. 'Your stomach appears through the door five seconds before you do these days.'

'I don't give a flying fuck,' he grumbled.

'You speak with such eloquence.'

'Oh I can't speak like you and I never will,' he replied, dismissively.

'I actually like the way you speak.'

He looked quite shocked. 'Do you?'

'Yes, I do, it has a certain native earthiness.' He laughed out loud, his belly wobbling up and down and his chest wheezing noticeably and I joined in.

'What the fuck are you on about?'

'That's precisely what I'm on about.'

'Hang on, hang on … prestidigitation!' he declared, looking smug.

'Now that *is* a long word. What does it mean?'

'No idea …'

'Antidisestablishmentarianism,' I offered.

'Oh fuck off!'

'Quite.'

'And I bet you know what it means too,' he sneered.

'I'm afraid I do,' I replied, 'and I also know what prestidigitation means, but it doesn't mean I know more than you about life or love or that I'm a nicer person than you because I know I'm not.'

'But you had an education, Benedict and that's what I wanted and what I missed out on. His sudden forlorn face was deeply touching. 'I want to be educated.'

'I know, Sidney and I do understand, I really do.'

He looked vulnerable. 'That's why I like being with you; you educate me.'

I instantly felt tears prick at the back of my eyes at his painful honesty and his longing for what he thought he had missed out on. He had what I had always wanted: a happy, relaxed, mutually supportive marriage and I had what he felt he had missed: an education. The complex nature of all our hopes and desires in life and how my kindly, generous and blindly supportive friend Sidney obviously envied my upbringing always made me feel humble and undeserving of his unconditional friendship.

'Sidney, don't say that. I can't teach you anything.'

'It's true, you do. I feel more intelligent just sitting opposite you.'

I had to smile at his simplicity. 'You flatter me and I don't deserve it.'

'Yeah, you do deserve it. So break out the whisky,' he urged, grinning. 'What do you say?'

'Your flattery has got you everywhere, my man.'

I poured him a large one and myself a thimbleful, feeling quite self-righteous as I did so and when I felt the smooth, silky liquid slide down my throat it felt like well remembered bliss. I sat back and felt my muscles relax immediately.

'I feel back in the land of the living,' I sighed.

Sidney was resting his glass on the part of his large stomach that resembled a ledge sticking out and looking thoughtful. 'Did the quack actually say you couldn't have alcohol?'

'The consultant said not too much.'

'What's too much?'

'I think we both know the answer to that, Sidney.'

'Whisky may actually be medicinal.'

'Ah, I wish.'

'Sheila's old man, he had his veins stripped once because of all his smoking and when we visited him in hospital he was sitting propped up, grinning like a Cheshire cat.'

'And the point of this story is?'

'He had pure whisky going in his veins through a drip,' he laughed. 'Can you imagine it?'

'Intravenous Scotch,' I declared, 'what an idea.'

'It's true, as true as I'm riding this bike. No, seriously, ask Sheila.'

'I don't believe a word you are saying, but I never do where alcohol is involved. I have to say though this does knock the edges of a cruel, harsh world.'

'I'd check with the quack,' he continued. 'I can't see a few would harm you. I think it could do you a power of good. You body looks so stiff sometimes, I'm sure it would relax all your muscles.'

'That,' I remarked, 'I'm not contesting, but it may interfere with the tablets.'

Sidney nodded sagely and sipped his Scotch before asking again, 'So, what's occurring then?'

'Very little, Sidney as you can see,' I repeated patiently.

'I meant with Nell,' he added, with a knowing look.

'I know what you meant and I say again, very little.'

'She left a while ago.'

'She did and we had been for a short walk. We then had a pot of tea and relaxed.'

'Oh yeah ...'

'Sidney!'

'Relaxing in what sense then?' he asked, peering over the top of his glasses.

'We were discussing poetry, if you must know.'

'Fuck me, you *must* be ill,' he chortled. 'Can you imagine the old Benedict having a beautiful woman in here and talking about poetry?' I thought his observation quite poignant. 'I can't quite believe it.'

'Well, as I've been trying to explain to you lately, I'm not the old Benedict, I'm someone else.'

Sidney frowned. 'Who are you then?'

'I recall going through this with you a little while ago. Someone older, frailer, more vulnerable,' I replied. 'And someone who no longer wants to be predatory, or egotistical or macho in any way, shape or form. In fact,' I added emphatically, 'I'd quite like to be a woman.'

'Fucking hell,' Sidney declared. 'I'm not going to walk in one day and find you dressed up, am I? You know, in women's clothes.'

'I think I'd look utterly ridiculous in tights, don't you?'

'With your thin legs, yeah,' he laughed. 'Not a pretty sight. That happened to a cousin of Sheila's once.'

'What did?' I asked, losing the thread slightly.

'She'd been married to this bloke for twenty-five years and she came home early from work unexpectedly one day and found him wearing some of her clothes.' Sidney's face was a picture of shock and indignation as he added, 'Can you imagine it? Quite a big burly bloke he was, built like a brick shit house.'

'Did she divorce him?' I asked, picturing the man in a floating summer dress with rugby player's legs sticking out from underneath like two heavy tree trunks.

'Yeah, course,' he said, 'wouldn't you?'

'Well, it's never happened to me, obviously, but I wouldn't have said that alone was grounds for divorce.'

Sidney appeared outraged. 'Well, if that isn't I don't know what is.'

'But it's not the dressing up itself that's the problem, is it?'

'What are you on about?'

'He was a transvestite, yes, and probably always had been, but he could have told her before they married,' I explained. 'Now, if he'd told her then, she would have been able to make the choice as to whether to go ahead and marry him or not.'

'*And ...*' Sidney prompted, wanting more of an explanation.

'It was the hiding of his secret that was the crime. She married him having no idea. That was the deceitful part, not the transvestite part. Do you understand what I'm getting at?' I asked him, because his face was a blank canvas at that point.

'No.'

'It wasn't the dressing up part that was the ...'

'What the fuck would you know about how a woman would feel if she came home and found her husband dressed up like a tart?'

'Shall we discuss poetry instead, Sidney?'

'Stop taking the piss.'

'Sorry.'

'I might just have another one before I go,' he said, getting up and pouring another large one into his glass.

'You'll sleep all afternoon.'

'I'll be in the garden,' he told me, 'mowing the lawn and doing a bit of weeding. Boring, but somebody's got to do it. Lovely day for it though.'

'If you say so,' I said, yawning.

'So, Benedict ...'

'Yes, Sidney,' I replied, eyeing him coolly because I felt his hesitation meant a personal question was about to be aimed at me.

'When are you going to tell her?'

'Tell who, what? Tell Beth about my disease?'

He rolled his eyes at me. 'No, tell Nell that you love her.'

I blanched visibly. 'I have no intention of doing anything of the sort.'

He looked aghast. 'Why?'

'And embarrass her? Make her feel obliged in any way? I'd rather die,' I muttered, my voice slurring badly on the last part.

'You do though, don't you? Love her, I mean. You're completely hooked, you silly old fool.'

'As you see, Sidney, I may well be an educated man, but I'm also a silly old fool. I can be as silly and as much of a fool as anyone else,' I sighed. 'You may not regard yourself as an educated man, but at least you're not a silly old fool like me.'

'Oh I am,' he replied, kindly, 'but just in different ways. I'd never fall for a young woman though.'

'That's because you're happily married,' I observed.

'I've known a few of my men friends over the years be happily married and still fall hook, line and sinker for a pretty face. You haven't got exclusive rights for that.'

'But was it love or was it lust?'

'Lust probably.'

'I have no lust left.'

'She might feel the same.'

I shook my head, feeling weary and every one of my sixty-two years, and my body, although relaxed from the whisky, felt rigid and tiny tremors were coursing through every inch of me. I also found my thoughts were slightly scrambled and the *presence* was hovering near me. I glanced across the room looking for my father.

'She doesn't,' I mumbled, finding my voice. 'I'm her friend, her confidante. She relies on me for pearls of wisdom, advice, that sort of thing, although in reality she has more wisdom in her little finger than I have. I learn from her.'

'Has she ever spoken about any men in her life?'

'Ah yes,' I sighed, 'the cute, green-eyed Frankie; a handsome actor who understands the business, the rejections, the heartache, the wretched auditions.'

'He sounds perfect for her.'

'My point exactly, my friend.'

'Plus lots of you know what,' he winked.

'Sidney, will you ever think before you speak?'

'Sorry, but it's important when you're young, you know that.'

'You don't need to tell me, I've spent my whole life chasing it and now ... it's gone.'

'I don't believe it when you say that,' he scoffed.

'I promise you.' Sidney appeared not to believe me, as well he might. 'Cross my heart.'

'What, completely gone?'

'Yes, completely and utterly gone.'

'Fuck me,' he muttered.

'Or not, as the case may be and in my case: not!'

He wrinkled his nose. 'It must be the illness.'

'Yes, but I've felt like this for the last couple of years, long before my symptoms developed.'

'Might have been the illness coming on though,' he suggested, with a sudden un-Sydney like insight.

'You may be right. My body now needs all its energy to fight my symptoms and fighting them is my sole purpose now. At first I was ready to give in I'm ashamed to say, but not now. I met Nell and life started afresh.'

He crossed his arms over his belly. 'If you ask me ...'

'Sidney,' I cut in, 'just think before you speak, please.' He appeared wounded by my comment. 'I'm sorry, you were going to say?'

'I was going to say,' he said deliberately, 'if you ask me she does feel the same.'

I was perplexed by his words. 'But you've never actually met her.'

'I've seen you out of the window and ...'

'Ah yes, that nose of yours pressed against the glass.'

'It was something in the way she looked up at you, she was so ...

'So?' I urged, desperate to hear what he had observed.

'What's the word?'

'I have no idea.'

He shrugged. 'Neither have I, but I know what I meant.'

I had to laugh at him. He was funny without meaning to be and there was no harm in him at all. He didn't have a bad bone in that ageing, tubby body of his. 'Well, there you have it. She was so – whatever you meant.'

'Oh you know, Benedict, you're the man with all the big words. It was her body language that said it all.'

'Do you mean, she was so solicitous of me?' I asked, attempting to guess what the hell he was trying to say.

'Yeah, that's about it, I think.'

'Sidney, Nell is kind to everyone. She's *always* like that.'

'Nah, it was more than that.'

'Let's imagine for a moment she does feel the same, although in truth that's laughable. Wouldn't it just be the most selfish act of my life to expect her to take me on … like this?' I waved my hand up and down my body to emphasise the point. He was silent for a moment, but then he gave a little smile.

'Yes, it probably would be.'

'There we are then,' I muttered, my mood dropping like a high-speed lift.

'What are you going to do then?' he asked me.

'Let her live her life and love her from afar,' I replied. 'It isn't about me, Sidney, it's about *her*. As long as she stays in my life as my friend, I can let her go to the cute, green-eyed actors of this world. I'll always be behind her, watching from the shadows, to catch her if she falls. That will be my role in life and I'd be thankful for that.'

Sidney drowned the last drop of Scotch from his glass, making a satisfied sound as he did so. 'It seems a shame for you, but I understand. I may be just a simple man with simple pleasures and not educated to a high standard, but I do understand.'

'I'm grateful you do and that was eloquent, my friend.'

'If it was me I wouldn't give a flying fuck. I'd tell her.'

'And that not quite so eloquent …'

'Life's too short, Benedict,' he said, with an almost pious expression on his face.

'I'm well aware of that,' I slurred, glancing over his shoulder where I felt the *presence* hovering.

'You look a bit knackered, mate,' he observed, his expression one of concern and sympathy, 'I'll leave you to have a rest, shall I?'

'I do nothing *but* these days, it seems.'

'You're always out walking with the firecracker,' he declared with a wink.

'*Nell*, Sidney,' I sighed, 'her name is Nell and on Sunday you call her by her name only otherwise you'll be *persona non grata* with me.'

'Well, whatever that means I'm quaking in my boots.'

'It means …' I started, but my head was swimming slightly and I forgot completely what I was going to tell him. 'It doesn't matter, Sidney.

Goodbye.'

'Bye then, matey. Cheers for the whisky, lovely stuff,' he said and the last thing I saw before I fell asleep was his smiling, chubby face.

I slept for over an hour and when I woke the light was fading because of a sudden spring squall. The rain was beating hard against my glass roof and I immediately thought of Nell and her delight at camping in high winds and raging thunderstorms. The heavy drumming was strangely comforting and the lashing of the rain against the windows filled me with a sense of calm. My eyes were a little out of focus and I felt relaxed and at ease for once.

My daughter would be back under my roof within two days and that gave me a feeling of deep contentment. Nell was cutting short her time with the cute actor and rushing to my house to be at my side. What on earth had I done in my restless, sometimes quietly desperate existence to deserve that?

My mind shot backwards suddenly, inexplicably to a social evening at my agent's house. At first I couldn't understand why that particular moment in time came back to me so vividly, but slowly, painfully, I recalled what had happened there and my subsequent feelings. Mary and I had rowed in the car because of my insistence that I was intending to refuse my second award on the grounds that I simply did not deserve it.

'Don't be so bloody high and mighty,' she had shouted at me, her face pale and contorted with anger, 'who on earth refuses an award for God's sake?'

'Please don't shout,' I had responded calmly. 'It's not a case of being high and mighty. I think Goddard's play is completely brilliant and I feel such a blasted fraud.'

'Don't be such a prig,' she'd said, through gritted teeth.

My suppressed anger had shot up into my throat threatening to cut off my air supply and my distaste at her choice of words and obvious longing for some kind of kudos, brought a bitter taste to my mouth, which had made my tongue feel like it was on fire.

'It's not a case of my being a prig,' I'd replied coolly, trying to keep my voice and emotions steady. 'I just don't think it's fair.'

'Who gives a toss about fairness when awards are being dished out? And why the hell don't you ever speak like everyone else instead of talking as if you're in one of your stupid plays?' she'd cried, her voice rising enough to shatter the windscreen.

'If you think my plays are so stupid, why are you insisting I take an award for this one?' I had asked, knowing my clever comment would make her explode – and I had been right. Her face was almost purple with rage and obvious hatred for me.

'Oh shut the fuck up, just shut the fuck up. You make me sick with your intelligent arguments. Why can't you just argue like everyone else?'

'I'm not everyone else, Mary. I'm me.'

'Yes, unfortunately!' she almost spat at me. 'But you aren't refusing it, Benedict, believe me, you aren't!'

Her final words had left me in no doubt that she would make my life unbearable if I did; so that was that. I gave in and accepted an award I knew I did not warrant and my sense of fair play caused me such anguish for years afterwards I wished with every cell in my body that I had stood by my principles.

Later at my agent's party I had stood in the corner alone and miserable. I looked over at my wife and wondered about her swiftly changing moods that were becoming unbearable; she could be sweetness and light one moment and spitting blood and foul language the next. At that moment the charm was being turned on as she stood with a drink in her hand chatting to someone she did not know, pretending to be interested in them because she was aware they had quite a bit of money.

Others had been huddled in corners laughing loudly, interrupting each other, posing, networking, finding out who could advance their careers and I'd felt the loneliest, most desperately isolated, abandoned man in the world. I was quite used to feeling sorry for myself, in fact I was extremely adept at it, but that evening it became like a dark, unrelenting nightmare playing continually in my mind: Mary's gritted teeth, her blazing eyes, her lack of warmth, my sarcastic comments, my lack of consideration for her feelings, our loveless marriage, my drinking, my continual worry that Beth would be affected by our rows. But that had been long ago, in another life and now I had Parkinson's, no wife and Nell's friendship. I knew which scenario I preferred, despite the illness.

The rain continued to hammer down above me and the sky had turned to black ink. I pictured Nell with her inquiring mind, dancing eyes and inquisitive face, interested in everything I had to say. Her gentleness and kindness were what I had longed for throughout my bleak marriage and yet I had not realised it then. I knew instinctively something was missing, but it was difficult to pinpoint what that something was.

Nell was my equal and I had continually longed for an equal, even in my youth. All I hoped was that she would stay in my life somehow, because to lose her after waiting so long to find a person with her qualities would be cruel and damaging. The difference in our ages and what other people thought did not matter to me. Whatever she wanted me to be, I would be. Her mentor, her friend, her soul mate, her advisor, any of those would suit me. But to be loved by Nell, in any way possible, was what I yearned for, and as the drumming of the rain beat out a loud rhythmical tune over my head, I closed my eyes and imagined her sitting near, gazing at me fondly and whispering my name.

Chapter 6

I met Frankie outside the Slug and Lettuce at half twelve. He was dressed in his usual ripped jeans and long black T-shirt, which someone had once told him accentuated his eyes and it certainly did. I had made more of an effort knowing I was going on to another, probably more formal party and I had dug out a white blouse that hung loosely over my tightest black trousers.

'You look like you're going to an interview,' Frankie commented, looking at me as if he detected I wanted to impress someone.

'I am,' I muttered.

'What did you say?'

'Nothing, come on, let's go.'

We strolled through the park together towards Jay's house in west Greenwich, but knowing we were passing the tennis courts, I felt an irresistible urge to make a slight detour to point out Benedict's house to him from a distance.

'Bloody hell!' Frankie gasped, 'he *is* loaded.'

'Isn't it stunning?'

He whistled through his teeth. 'I'd call it *palatial*. Full of history no doubt.'

'It was the old Rectory so yes, must be.'

'He's a lucky man.'

'That annexe on the side was built later and his friend lives there with his wife. He's having a party for his daughter's thirtieth today so I'm going to pop in later.'

'Can I come then, just to be nosey?'

I laughed at him. 'No, you bloody well can't.' He turned to me, his face serious. 'What's that face for?' I asked, trying to keep the atmosphere light.

'Are you ashamed of me?'

'Don't be ridiculous.'

'Why can't I come then?'

'He doesn't know you,' I protested.

'That hardly matters. I'm always going to parties where I don't know the host. You hardly know Jay. That's how it is in our game.'

'This is different. It's his daughter's bash.'

'Please yourself,' he shrugged, almost petulantly.

'Frankie, I'm sorry, but ...'

He waved his hand theatrically. 'No, I understand.'

I smiled at him. 'Do you?'

'Not really.'

I was at a loss as to how to explain. I was sure Benedict would have welcomed him, but he was my friend, my Mr Marshall, *mine*. 'Look, it's just ...' I didn't finish my sentence because he had leant forward and kissed the side of my mouth. 'What was that for?' I said, shocked.

'I don't know,' he shrugged. 'I just felt like doing it, you looked so troubled. Look, Nell, are you in love with this old geezer?'

I felt uncomfortable. 'Why are you so fixated on him?'

'I don't know,' he said, scrutinising my face, 'it's just something in your eyes when you mention him. You get a bit possessive over him, a bit rattled, that's all.'

'I don't know what you mean,' I declared, in such a standoffish way I knew it sounded insincere. He stood in front of me with his hands on his hips.

'You didn't answer the question,' he said.

'I'm not in love with him,' I answered, and my voice sounded thin and not as definite as I had intended it to and I felt irritated and unsettled.

'Great,' he cried, his eyes glinting, 'I've got a chance then.'

I laughed out loud, thankful that the tense atmosphere had lifted slightly. 'You've got a nerve, Frankie.'

'You have to take your chances when you can,' he told me, wagging his finger in my face. 'I was going to make a clumsy drunken pass on the tour in Manchester, but we were too drunk.' I decided to tease him. He was so easy to tease.

'I wanted you to then.'

He looked crestfallen. 'Did you? Fuck it! What about now?'

'No, not now.'

'So, what's changed?'

'I don't know,' I replied, 'maybe it was because we were away, a bit drunk, you know. I'm sorry. Moments happen and then they pass...'

'I know what's changed ... the old geezer in that bloody beautiful house.'

I was now beginning to feel he was getting too near the truth for my liking and I felt my face flush up. 'You're wrong. I'm sorry I brought you here now.'

'I'm not wrong,' he murmured, looking at me out of the corner of his eye. 'I'm rarely wrong about these things.'

'Come on, let's go,' I urged, even more unsettled and wishing I hadn't shown him Benedict's house.

We sauntered along the river side in the company of cyclists, walkers with heavy back packs and parents with noisy, excited children on a Sunday stroll before lunch. Both the Trafalgar pub and the Cutty Sark were heaving with tourists and the smell of the roast dinners and steak and fries wafting from them smelt delicious. I made a mental note to perhaps ask Benedict to join me for lunch at one of them after Beth had returned to America. I imagined us sitting in early spring sunshine by the water and talking together over a glass of white wine.

'What are you smiling at?' Frankie asked suddenly.

'Nothing much,' I replied dismissively. 'I always smile.'

'If you say so,' he mumbled. 'You look to me as if you're keeping some kind of secret.'

I shook my head. 'I have no idea what you mean.'

Jay's house was a stone's throw from the edge of the Thames and as we approached, live music was thumping from inside; guitars, fiddles, a viola and a piano could be heard and my mood lifted immediately. People were crowding in his tiny lounge and rammed in the kitchen and dining room, holding drinks and plates of barbecued food. A few people I knew called my name and I waved and acknowledged them, but it was impossible to have a conversation because of the noise. The musicians were jamming and I tugged at Frankie's T-shirt. 'I hope they've invited the neighbours,' I shouted and he laughed and looked more his usual carefree self and motioned that he would get us a drink.

There was the sweet heavy smell of incense burning mixed with tobacco and the musicians were chucking alcohol down their throats and playing wildly and I suddenly felt the intense desire to be younger and throw myself into the party atmosphere fully as I used to. I wanted to be able to get drunk without having a hangover for three days and blot out my memories for just a little while; forget my love and longing for Joshua and my dreams that he was still in this world somewhere. But I knew those days were gone forever and I felt stubbornly stuck between extreme youth and sensible middle age. I was living in nowhere land, making precious little headway in either my career or personal life, often feeling lost, confused and frustrated.

I glanced over towards the kitchen where Frankie was pushing himself towards the drinks table, when the music stopped abruptly, except for the piano. I immediately recognised the messy, brown curls of Matt and his playing, left to amble freely, was accomplished, cheeky and note perfect. His pale face, so sorrowful and melancholy at the audition was playful, expressive and cheerful. He looked a completely different person. Simply watching his face change as he thumped the notes out made me smile. He was moving his head in time with his hands as if nodding in appreciation of every note played. It was captivating and I could have become completely lost in his performance. It made me long to dance, be at one with the music, forget everything around me, float above the ground and fly, but the others joined in and the spell was broken. He took a quick gulp of the drink standing on the top of the piano and ran his hands through his thick curls. I made my way over to him.

'That was brilliant, Matt.'

His face lit up. 'Hi, Helen, how are you? Did you get in to the show?' he asked immediately.

'No.'

His face dropped instantly. 'It was my fault, I'm so sorry.'

'It's never the pianist's fault,' I remarked. 'It's no loss, honestly.'

'It was *definitely* my fault.'

I laughed to make him feel better. 'I don't think so. If they had wanted me they would have ignored your playing. But I have to say hearing you play here bears no resemblance to your playing at the audition.'

'That's because I have to play to order at auditions and I find that really hard to do. It's just for a bit of pin money,' he shrugged, 'here I can be myself.' I put my hand on his shoulder in a gesture of support.

'You're completely brilliant.'

He gave a little shy smile. 'Cheers, Helen.'

I glanced at the glass on the piano. 'Should you be drinking?'

'No,' he admitted, 'but you're a long time dead.'

I understood his sentiment completely, but I felt slightly uneasy at his relaxed attitude to his health. 'Yes, you are, I agree, but take it steady.' His wild eyes sparkled as I spoke.

'*Steady* isn't a word you can ever apply to me.'

'Do you play classical stuff too?'

'I was classically trained, but I play everything – music is music. But jazz is my favourite.'

'Have you any jobs coming up?' I asked, although I knew what his answer would be.

'A couple ...'

'I haven't seen anyone to pass your number on to, but I will,' I told him, feeling slightly awkward and not wanting him to think I had forgotten. He gave me a beautiful smile that transformed his whole face to someone carefree, boyish and full of optimism – none of which he seemed to be normally – and said, 'Don't worry, whenever.'

Appearing next to me, Frankie handed me a glass of wine and nodded to Matt who acknowledged him by opening his eyes wider and nodding back. Frankie looked back at me and was about to say something but, because all the musicians were now in full swing again, he leant forwards and yelled in my ear, 'I've just spoken to Jay and there are some auditions coming up for a new cast to join a show in America.'

'Do they need a pianist?' Matt cut in.

'Yeah, actually they do. There's a pianist on stage for much of the show,' Frankie replied.

'Ask Jay,' I told Matt, 'if you can find him in here.'

'I will ... thanks.'

Frankie took my arm. 'I was thinking of us, Hells.'

'Might as well have a go,' I shrugged, feeling battered by my recent rejections.

'You should,' Matt urged, 'your voice is sublime.'

'Sublime!' I gasped. 'Thank you for that.'

'I mean it ...'

'I've told her that,' Frankie said, looking petulant again.

'I don't think you've ever used *that* word,' I said. 'I would have remembered.'

Frankie appeared rather possessive suddenly, moving closer to me and taking hold of my hand. 'Did Logan send you for that other one I told you about?'

'Yes, I'm waiting to hear if they want to see me.'

'What's that for?' Matt asked me, genuinely interested.

'It's only a small revue, a tiny theatre, but intimate. The audience can touch you they're so close.'

'How fantastic,' Matt remarked. 'I know the one you mean, in Soho.'

Frankie had gone rather quiet so I put my mouth close to his ear and asked him if he had heard Matt play. He shook his head and appeared uninterested and I immediately felt irritated with him and pulled my hand away. The viola player called Matt's name and motioned for him to join in which he did, picking up the piece instantly and running with it. His hands flowed over the keys like trickling water and made my heart flip over with pleasure. When in full flow there was an electrifying aura of danger about him that was undeniably attractive. Frankie was making a big deal of pretending not to listen and I thought of Mr Marshall because I knew he would never have behaved like that. He would have been polite, considerate and appreciative even if it had been of no interest to him, because that was his nature. Other people had started to crowd round the piano and clapped along and the encouragement made Matt appear even more light-hearted and carefree. I felt Frankie move my hair from my face gently.

'Shall we go outside for a bit?' he asked, looking uncomfortable for some reason.

'Why? Are you feeling ill?'

'No, it's just so noisy in here.'

'I love the music; it makes me feel like singing.'

'Probably because you're a singer,' he remarked, grabbing my hand. 'Come on, Hells, we can't talk in here.'

His persistence exasperated me and I snapped at him. 'Okay, in a minute.' He said no more, but I could feel the tension coming from him and it unsettled me. 'Come on then,' I sighed and we squeezed ourselves past everyone and escaped into the garden.

The wind had picked up a little and the small patio area smelt of barbecued chicken and smoke. Once outside Frankie seemed to relax a little and leant forward and kissed me again, his lips just brushing the side of my mouth as before.

'Will you stop that?' I gasped.

He shrugged. 'Sorry, just got the urge to kiss you today.'

His green eyes were glinting like a cat's about to pounce on its prey and he touched my hair again. I had the suspicion he was going to make a fumbled pass at me because he appeared embarrassed and a little harassed. I instantly rehearsed a reply in my head because although I found him attractive and we had quite a bit in common, a relationship with him was not something I had ever considered, apart from the drunken episode on the tour.

'I wanted to come outside because ... well, you must know how I feel about you.'

'No,' I spluttered, 'I don't actually.'

'Oh come on, Hells, I've been in love with you since the tour.'

I was expecting some form of declaration of his feelings, but love was not something I had anticipated and it knocked me back for a moment. I swallowed hard and tried to find the right words to form a reply without hurting his feelings.

'You're in love with me? I would never have known Frankie and I don't believe you are. You're attracted to me physically, we laugh together and understand each other's insecurities and ... I don't know. But love me? I don't think so.'

He looked bemused. 'Why do you say that?'

'Because if you loved me I think I would feel it.'

He sighed dramatically. 'You don't feel it because I don't get to spend any bloody time with you; you're always doing shifts, teaching the kiddies, flying about to auditions. The one time I spent six weeks with you, I fell hopelessly in love. You must have realised.'

'I didn't, honestly!'

'Where were we on that night we got so pissed?' he asked, pausing and frowning hard, trying to recall every detail to hammer his point home before answering his own question. 'Manchester I think, bloody terrible crowd and we were seriously fed up so we had a few and you opened up about Joshua ...'

'I know, you've told me this before and things have changed. I must have been drunk.' There were few people I spoke to about Joshua because of the pain it caused. But alcohol had obviously loosened my tongue. 'I'm sorry, but that's the truth.'

'I felt there was a real connection between us and we did nearly ...and you said in the park you had actually wanted to. I wish we had now ...'

I wrinkled my nose. 'I'm so sorry, but it's just as well we didn't otherwise it would have been totally embarrassing.'

He looked a little hurt. 'Don't look like that.'

'Sorry, I didn't mean ... that was cruel. I meant that it would be embarrassing because we run into each other so often.'

'So, what do you reckon?'

I looked at his handsome face; it was a face that you could easily stare at all day, not only because of the incredible colour of his eyes, but also because of its perfect shape. His features were soft and expressive, dramatically so, and he possessed a slim, athletic figure; all the kind of looks a camera adores. Added to that, I couldn't help but love his black sense of humour, which often made me laugh till I cried, particularly when he used it in his observations of other people. We lived the same life he and I, understood the pressures and unfathomable rejections and we both lived to perform. I was tempted, sorely tempted, imagining being held and supported by his muscular arms; I could almost feel his taut body next to mine and see his unique, feline eyes inches from my face. It would be lovely to relax in his company for a few weeks and enjoy his physicality, but there had always been a tiny part of him I found difficult. He could be impatient and moody, sometimes not as kind as he should be in certain situations and I suspected he could be guilty of possessiveness, which I could not bear in any shape or form. But nobody was perfect, least of all me and yet I knew two creative personalities would more than likely clash often.

'Say something, Hells,' he urged, his eyes intense.

'I don't know. I'm not ready.'

He sighed with disappointment. 'You've been on your own a while now and you need a bit of fun.'

'I don't need a man to have fun.'

'You know what I mean. What's stopping you?'

My mood had begun to plummet. 'I don't know. I want a man to love the pilgrim soul in me.'

He looked perplexed. 'What? Is that something the old geezer wrote?'

'No, it doesn't matter. Look, I'll have to have a think about it.'

He pulled a face. 'Ooh,' he sneered, as if I was being supercilious. 'Don't think too long, will you? The moment might pass. There's a time for everything.'

'Not for love,' I murmured. 'Love has no time limit.'

'I know, I know,' he added quickly, wanting to please me rather than agreeing with what I said.

A couple of people stumbled out of the kitchen, a little the worse for drink and the smoke from the barbecue was wafting in my eyes. It was already clinging to my hair and clothes and I had no intention of arriving at the next party stinking of burnt chicken.

Frankie gave me a small, conciliatory smile, knowing he had overstepped the mark and I didn't want to fall out with him, he was good company and, more than that, I was very fond of him. 'Frankie, I'm sorry,' I started, 'I don't mean to knock you back, really I don't, but something just isn't right between us and I think it would all end in tears.'

'I don't agree,' he frowned, 'why not just give it a go. Life is short.'

'Life is *very* short,' I said, 'but let me ask you something. If I was ever in an accident and hideously burned or scarred, would you feel the same?'

'Hideously scarred?' he asked. 'Hells, what are you on about now? You take life too seriously.'

'Yes, hideously scarred, unrecognisably so,' I added dramatically, for good measure. 'Would you feel the same?' He looked totally blank, as if I had lost my marbles.

'I don't see the point of this conversation.'

'Just humour me, will you?'

'I don't know, it's a difficult question to answer.'

'What if I got a terrible disease,' I continued, 'and slurred my words or dribbled and changed from being a fit, healthy performer to a shadow, a ghost of who I had been; what about if I was totally different ... an invalid even?'

He put his hands up in defence. 'Okay, I get the picture.'

'I don't doubt you love me now as I am, but there's more to love than that and one day you'll find that out for yourself.'

He suddenly grinned. 'I wasn't asking you to marry me, just a fling, a summer fling, a bit of fun ...'

'I know,' I said, laughing, 'but ... I need time to think and I'm not entirely sure a fling is what I need.'

'It's that old geezer,' he muttered.

'It is not!'

He winked. 'You aren't ...he's not getting his leg over, is he?'

'No!'

'Only asked, only asked,' he replied, looking amused at my response. I was beginning to laugh because of his pious face.

'Well, don't!'

'And what about him in there, the piano player with the obvious drink problem? He's got danger and catastrophe written all over him.'

'Just shut up, will you?'

'You'd do better with the pianist than the old git. There would be more sex with the pianist.'

'I'll ignore that remark and don't call him an old geezer; he isn't old, just older than us. He has more intelligence and wit *and*,' I paused, searching for the right words, but nothing came to mind.

'*And* ...' he urged.

'Just everything,' I added, 'than anyone I've ever met.'

'Ooh, has he now?' he smirked.

'Yes and I'll thank you not to speak about him like that.'

He sniffed. 'I'm only jealous.'

'Why the hell are you jealous? You're both just friends of mine.'

'Not jealous like that,' he answered, 'I suppose a better word for it is envious. Envious of his money, his brain, his success, this fantastically cultured voice he supposedly has. I want a voice like that.'

'But you can do accents, you idiot. You *can* speak like him.'

'I mean naturally. It would give me more gravitas on stage.'

'You're brilliant on stage. Why are you so lacking in confidence?'

'You're the same,' he remarked.

'Yes, I know, it's just our insecurities from all the knockbacks, isn't it?'

I glanced at my watch. Frankie picked up on it. 'Am I boring you?'

'Don't be daft.'

'Desperate to get to the old git's,' he muttered.

'Not desperate, just watching the time. And he's *not* an old git!'

'His daughter's going to get a shock on her birthday.'

'Frankie, give it a rest.'

'She'll think you're after his money, Hells. She'll have a face as long as a wet weekend in a fortnight when she sees you,' he said, laughing hard and throwing his head back. 'She'll think her old dad's become a dirty old man.' I took a swipe at him, but he ducked and I missed.

'Why would she think I'm after his money? We are just friends,' I insisted.

'Don't be naïve,' he replied curtly. 'And you're not, are you?'

I paused for a moment because he had insisted before that part of

Benedict's charm was his stunning house, his awards, his cultured voice which all together made him more interesting and I had reluctantly agreed that it was all part of his overall charm.

'Of course I'm not after his money.'

He pointed his finger in my face. 'You hesitated - you bloody well hesitated!'

'No, I didn't.'

'You bloody well did.'

'It was only because you said it was part of his charm and I thought about that seriously, but it's *him* I like, not his house.'

His eyes were glinting again. 'You *love* his house; you said it had always been your favourite house.'

'What's this, the Spanish Inquisition?' I cried. 'I'm not defending myself any more. I have nothing to hide and it's none of your business anyway. Now, let's go in, I'm getting chilly.'

Frankie followed me saying, 'Fine, but let me just warn you ...' I frowned at him as he paused, expecting a gem of wisdom suddenly or at least hoping for that, but he smirked and whispered 'Me or Matt will have better hard-ons!'

I took a swipe at him again and this time caught him right where I wanted to.

At about half past three I said my goodbye's and escaped into the chilly afternoon air. I walked purposefully along the river and it looked dark grey, deep and choppy because of a strong breeze that had picked up. It was whipping up the water and causing tiny waves to roll in on the shingle near the Trafalgar. There were some enthusiasts searching for long hidden treasure with metal detectors and a couple of fearless children were paddling. When I reached the park it was busy with joggers and dog walkers and I felt a sudden urge to dash home, pull on my trainers and run with the wind in my hair. Frankie had unsettled me with his sudden declaration of love and Matt had unsettled me with his remarkable playing and laughing eyes. My nerves felt frayed, frazzled and unusually disturbed and I longed to pound the paths and grass and run freely, catching my breath and feel the sweat trickling down my face.

Benedict's house came into sight and I could see lights twinkling in the windows. He would be there, elegant and casually dressed, full of warmth, his sea-blue eyes sparkling with mischief. I stood outside and glanced up, hoping to see his face because for a moment before ringing the bell, I hesitated. For some inexplicable reason I felt as if I had reached a crossroads. If I walked up those stairs I had an inkling I would be lost forever; lost to my old life, lost to Frankie and Matt and any man like them and hurtling towards something infinitely less carefree, but ultimately more fulfilling. I knew if I rang his doorbell certain challenges would face me. I went to walk away, I tried my best to, but it was as if an invisible hand pushed me back. I rang the bell quickly and imagined my old life slipping away like a morning tide. The door was pulled open by a woman in her fifties with shoulder length, dyed brown hair and a strangely attractive, serious, inscrutable face. I knew instantly this was one of Benedict's family because she resembled him slightly. But her eyes were cold and held no mischief or sparkle of any kind.

'Hello,' I ventured, 'I'm Nell.'

She was heavily made up and slightly supercilious. I knew immediately that this was a woman you didn't mess with. 'And I'm Bethan,' she replied.

My heart began to thump with sudden, unexpected nerves and I had a feeling this woman was already trying to size me up before I had even put a foot over the threshold. I realised I would have to act my socks off to hide the fact I was nervous.

'I'm a friend of Benedict's,' I added, wondering whether she was actually going to allow me in. She was eyeing me coolly.

'Are you now?'

The challenge had begun.

&

Sidney had rigged up an array of fairy lights, all quite tasteful for him for a change, until he switched them on. They flashed intermittently, but not all at the same time. It was unusually mesmerising because you couldn't tell which one was going to flash next. He had also placed a few around my large oval mirror above the fireplace which spelled Beth's name. He had the enthusiasm of a young child at Christmas while erecting them all, so I didn't have the heart to tell him it was all rather trashy.

'What do you think then, mate?' he asked, teetering on the edge of a small ladder.

I stood by the kitchen door, with a pinafore on, where I had been cooking frozen sausage rolls. 'Well, I … it's all quite … yes, lovely, Sidney. A trifle tacky in places, but why the hell not?'

'You can't stand there in that pinafore and seriously tell me my lights are tacky,' he said and he had a point as the pinafore was bright pink with mauve and yellow flowers on it. 'You'd better not wear that when Nell's here, she'll go off you like a shot.'

'I do believe you're right, Sidney,' I murmured.

When Beth had come downstairs from trying to sleep off a little jet lag her face was a picture. 'Oh Sidney,' she cried, 'you've surpassed yourself this time.'

I knew she was humouring him, but he had no idea; his face lit up in an instant and, giving me a told-you-so look, he said, 'Cheers, Beth.'

Watching Sidney and Beth talking animatedly, I thought back to when she had arrived on the Friday evening. I had been watching for the taxi and as the driver took her cases out of the boot I'd hurried to open the door. She had looked tired and a little pale from travelling but had called out cheerily, 'Hi, Dad.'

I had flung my arms around her with as much strength as I could muster, which wasn't a great deal. 'Darling, so lovely to have you home,' I'd mumbled, trying my best not to slur and hoping my increasingly rigid face was betraying some emotion.

'It's lovely to *be* home.'

'Let me carry one of those,' I'd suggested, taking her biggest case, as I always had in the past, but my lack of stamina and tiny tremors told on me instantly and I more or less dragged it in behind me.

'You okay with that?' she'd asked.

'Yes, of course, just getting on a bit these days. I'm fine, go on in, darling.'

We had chatted long into the night, about her work mostly and her friends and the life she was leading. It had all sounded pretty frenetic to me, but she appeared to be revelling in it. I did detect a slight change in her features. She appeared older, a little tougher, more mature and a little more ambivalent to many things she used to be interested in. Her sweet, childlike, oval face had turned into a woman's and her temperament appeared radically altered. She was a little more short-tempered, more independent, and a little aloof. I had mentioned it to her immediately.

'It's just the stress of the job, Dad, that's all. And living in New York is very different from London. Everyone is a bit short with each other and it's hard to wind down from that.' She had smiled, 'It's quite normal.'

'But I'm your old Dad.'

'I know, just give me a few days to relax and switch off. It's me underneath, honestly.'

'But in a few days you'll be at your mum's and then away again,' I had told her forlornly, but her face had dropped instantly and I felt terrible criticising her in any way so I'd given her an encouraging smile. 'Don't mind me, I'm just so happy to see you and I miss you so badly. I'm sure stress has a big part to play in it. You need your holiday so I'll just shut up.'

'I understand, Dad. I miss you too *and* Mum, but I'm happy there, really. I love it. I wouldn't be anywhere else at this point in my life. It's tough, but it's exciting.'

'Good,' I'd muttered, 'that's good, sweetheart.'

She had then changed the subject and spoken about her salary and the perks of the job and how all her American friends had huge expense accounts, fast cars, exotic holidays and fabulous apartments. My heart sank a little and I thought of Mary and her insistence that she should always be the first of her friends and wider circle to have anything new. It worried me that she would become increasingly materialistic like her mother, but my disappointment gave way to delight whenever Beth smiled at me.

Although we had gone to bed late, I had slept fitfully, often staring at a silver moon and asking for the courage to tell her about my disease. The next morning I had risen early, but Beth had slept in and when I heard her moving about and singing in the shower my heart swelled with contentment and gratitude that she was under my roof again. The evening before she had asked to borrow my car to visit some old friends in Bromley for the day and therefore I had made pancakes so that we could enjoy breakfast together in the conservatory before she went. My heart had danced wildly because as we had sat opposite each other in the early sunlight, I knew the time had come to tell her about the Parkinson's.

It had been a bright, blowy day and white clouds like soap suds were hurrying across a pale blue sky. Two days before, I had felt upbeat, contented and enthusiastic about the immediate future; 'immediate' meaning the next few days with Beth near me once again, and I had been looking forward to my gentle walks with Nell, in all weathers, talking together, having fun and simply watching the many expressions flitting across her incomparable face. I asked for nothing more than that and my long-term future I would leave where it was and hope for the best. But that morning, I was preparing to shatter my daughter's world and I would have preferred to rip my tongue out than do that to her. While I had been busy with my thoughts, Beth had reached across the table, touched my arm and spoken softly.

'Dad, you look a bit strange today.' Her words had pulled me together sharply and I shuddered.

'Do I really, darling, in what way strange?'

She had leant towards me and scrutinised my face, touching my cheek and ruffling my hair before shrugging, 'I don't know. You're still the best looking Dad in the world though.'

'Thank you for that,' I'd murmured, tears pricking at the back of my eyes because she had always told me that; she had even written it in her news book at school, much to my amusement. Mary had teased me mercilessly about it for years afterwards.

'How have you been anyway?' she'd asked, as if she suspected something.

'Fine ...' I had hesitated because a voice in my head was screaming at me: you must tell her! You must tell her! And I'd given in to that voice, 'Beth, I need to tell you something.'

She had immediately given me her full attention. 'You okay, Dad? You look a bit ...'

I'm fine, I'm fine ... well ... actually I'm not that fine.'

She had looked perplexed. 'What do you mean?'

'I've had a few strange symptoms ...'

'Like what?'

'Some trembling in my left hand and a couple of other things...'

'Did you see Dr Cameron?' she had interrupted.

'Yes.'

'And what happened?'

'I had some tests and had to see a consultant.'

I had immediately seen the fear on her face and my whole body began to tremble quite violently. She had picked up on it straight away and murmured, 'Dad, you're shaking. Don't shake, please.'

'Beth, I have Parkinson's.'

Her stare of bewilderment had made her look five years old again, vulnerable, and she'd whispered, 'Dad? Dad; my God, I can't believe it.'

'But look, darling, I'm fine, you can see I'm fine,' I'd stuttered, my voice slurring.

She had put her hands over her mouth. 'I thought your face looked a bit odd, to be honest, a bit blank sometimes. And you slurred on the phone once or twice. Oh Dad, I'm so upset for you,' she'd cried, tears springing into her eyes.

'Please don't be, darling. My life has gone on as usual. The pills are fantastic ...'

'But what will happen to you? You're not going to ...'

'Certainly not! As I said, the tablets are wonderful and stop the tremors in their tracks more or less. You live a normal lifespan; it's just certain things happen to your body.'

Her tears spilled over onto her burning cheeks and I'd felt wretched. A searing pain shot through my chest as if I had been shot with an arrow and my stomach was churning with distress at seeing my daughter cry.

'But what about when you're older? Will you need looking after?'

'I certainly hope not. No, I could stay the same for years.'

'Why didn't you tell me on the phone?'

'I've been putting it off.'

'You should have shared it with me. Does Mum know?'

'No.' I had tried not to show on my face that her mother was the last person I wanted to tell. 'I wasn't going to tell your mother.'

'Aunty Bethan?'

'None of them know yet, Beth.'

'Did you keep it completely to yourself?'

'Well, no ...'

'Who did you tell?'

'I told Sidney and ... and Nell, a friend of mine.'

She had looked at me blankly. 'Why did you tell your friend before me, Dad?'

'I didn't actually tell her, she guessed. Her partner had Parkinson's and she recognised the symptoms.'

'Right ...'

'Don't be hurt by it, Beth. You are the only person I wanted to tell, that I dreaded telling.'

'I'm not hurt, just surprised!' she had replied a little sulkily, her mouth turned down slightly. 'Is there anything else you want to tell me?'

'About?'

'This Nell and you...'

'I don't think so.'

'Are you going to marry her?' she'd asked bluntly, staring intently at me with widened eyes. 'I always thought you would marry again.'

'Marriage isn't for me, I'm not very accomplished at being a husband,' I'd told her, with a wry smile.

'That's not true.'

'Sweetheart, I'm afraid it is.'

Indignation had crossed her tear-stained face, 'I don't remember you not being good at it. Mum was happy enough.'

I had been about to say, yes well, your mum was happy as long as she had her hand in my wallet, but how could I? That would have been cruel and unnecessary and my reply had been simple, 'I'm glad that was your perception of it.' She had sniffed and looked utterly miserable.

'Did you love Mum?'

That question stunned me and I tried to form the appropriate words, but I mumbled and slurred badly. 'Of course, why do you ask?'

'I don't know,' she'd shrugged, 'I always knew you loved me by how you were with me, but you seemed a bit aloof with Mum at times and she used to get so angry with you and I could never work out why.'

'That was me being not very good at marriage,' I'd remarked. 'Your Mum was right to be angry with me sometimes.'

Her eyes had grown larger again, and questioning. 'You can tell me if you didn't love her. I'd rather know.'

'Beth, why would you rather know?'

'Because,' she'd begun, 'I used to think you didn't love each other and I want to know if I was right.'

'Darling, I don't want to upset you ...'

'Please, Dad, just tell me.'

'I think, if I'm completely honest, at the beginning, we were besotted with each other in a way and there were deep feelings on both sides when you were born but ...'

'You weren't in love with her.'

'Beth ...'

'Look, it's fine, Dad, honestly,' she'd said, suddenly appearing older and much harder. 'I'm grown up now.'

I had taken a deep breath. 'I wasn't in love with your Mum, no.'

'And this Nell?' she'd asked, sounding rather put out.

'*This* Nell,' I repeated, because the inference had offended me, even out of my daughter's mouth.

'Do you love her?'

I had laughed nervously. 'Why are you asking all these questions, darling?'

'I just want to know about your life.'

'I've told you everything there is to know. I wanted to get it off my chest about the illness.'

'Don't call it that,' she pleaded.

'But it *is* an illness, a *disease* ...'

'That word is even worse.'

'I know, but if I call it that, it's part of me fighting it.'

'How do you actually feel?'

'I ache sometimes and I get cramp in my legs. My left hand won't behave as it used to and my brain and body often don't engage with each other. I slur and stumble over some words and my walking can be affected, but all in all I don't feel ill. I am a little worried that I slur and have been known to dribble ...'

'Yuck, Dad!'

I had laughed. 'I agree.'

Her face had softened. 'I'm kidding you.'

'I can't drink like I used to which is a crashing bore, but I was a crashing bore when I did drink so ... I'm not too bad, honestly.'

'Honestly?' she'd repeated, fixing her eyes on mine for the truth.

'Honestly, darling.'

I thought we had got over the worst of the crying and I had silently congratulated myself that it had gone better than expected, but suddenly her face crumpled and she began to sob loudly. 'Dad, I don't know what I'd do if you ...' I had staggered to my feet and crouched beside her, despite the severe cramping in my legs as I did so.

'Beth, don't cry, please. I'm not going anywhere yet, I promise you.'

She had put her arms around me and hugged me with all her strength. I attempted to hug her back, but my arms hung loosely somewhere around her shoulders.

'It's just that you and Mum are always behind me, you know? Always, always in the background ... especially you ...'

'I know, darling.' I'd tried to sooth her. 'But you have my word I'm going to be around for a very long time. By the time I give up the ghost you will be married and perhaps have children of your own and you'll have support from a wonderful husband and he will supersede your dear old Pa.

Now please stop sobbing, it upsets me greatly. Dry your tears, we are all still here and happy so let's make the most of it.'

'Sorry, it was a bit of delayed shock, I'm OK now,' she'd snivelled loudly and attempted a smile.

'Good. Now let's get you off to your friends and look forward to the family coming tomorrow.' I had patted her hair into place as if she was tiny again and kissed her forehead. 'I love you, Beth and that will never change. We are lucky, darling, that we have each other.' Kissing my nose playfully as she had all her life, she had wiped her nose with a tissue.

'I love you too, Dad.'

Within an hour she had driven off to her friends quite happily, but I had sat motionless in the conservatory for some time, driven mad by voices in my head that told me I could have handled the situation better. Seeing her sob had floored me and I felt exhausted. I thought back to when I had to tell her that her beloved guinea pig had died and she had been distraught and cried for five days until I could stand it no more and bought her a Labrador puppy. Those days had gone though when I could easily replace something she loved, and I felt mentally comatose for the rest of that day.

The morning of her birthday arrived without us discussing it again and Beth seemed calm and happy and was upstairs getting ready for her party when William and Lily arrived. He looked suave and sophisticated with a yellow cravat and dark sports jacket and Lily, who had apparently been a seasoned party-goer all her life, was dressed in a long purple dress. Her pure white hair was swept back in a pony tail and she appeared many years younger than her sixty-five.

'How lovely to see you both,' I declared, 'Lily, you look ravishing as usual.'

'Benedict, the Marshall charm is alive and well in you. When I'm old I'll wear purple!' she said.

'I love that poem too,' I told her, giving her a gentle hug. 'You really are a most attractive woman. My brother struck oil when he met you in his later years.'

'Bless you for that.'

William shook my hand firmly. 'How are you, old son?' he asked, scrutinising my face and frowning.

'Not so bad, brother, thank you. Come in, Beth is here somewhere.'

Beth flew at her uncle William and covered him in kisses. He had always been her favourite because he resembled me so closely and because he had endless patience with children and had spent hours playing pickup sticks with her when she had been obsessed with the game.

'I'm so pleased to see you, Uncle William. How's Thomas? It's such a shame he couldn't be here.'

'I know, I told him that, but New Zealand is a long way to come for a party, Beth,' he replied.

'Lily, you look fabulous,' she gasped, kissing her. 'I hope to God I look like you at sixty-five. Some women your age seem old, but you look like a model.'

'Darling, you do me a power of good,' Lily laughed.

'Doesn't she though, Dad?'

'I've already told her she looks ravishing but she thought it was flannel,' I remarked.

'Well, you always did have more flannel than an army blanket,' William commented.

'I don't know what you mean,' I declared, noticing Sidney and Sheila arriving by the conservatory door carrying two large glass bowls full of a rich and delicious looking trifle.

'Are you using the tradesman's entrance as usual, Sidney?'

'You haven't switched the lights on, Benedict,' he complained, looking hurt.

'Sidney, do shut up about the lights,' his sensible wife told him before smiling at me. 'He's been going on and on about them all bloody week.'

I kissed her cheek. 'Sheila, you restore my faith in human nature. Just when I think I'm cracking up by spending so much of my time with your beloved husband, one sentence from you and I realise it is he who is stark raving bonkers and not me.'

'Doesn't he get on your nerves,' she sighed and it was a declaration not a question. 'For God's sake let him switch them on or we'll get no peace. Sidney, take these in the kitchen,' she ordered.

'Right, love,' he replied, used to obeying her immediately. 'Then I'm switching on the lights.'

Beth was laughing. 'You switch them on, Sidney. Don't take any notice of the grumpy old man.'

'He never does,' I muttered.

'The others are here, Dad. Aunty Bethan is just parking and Aunty Sarah and Uncle Rich are just about to ring the doorbell ...'

'You go then, darling.'

Having taken up enough space for two cars to have parked, Bethan swept in, carrying a suitcase and a small wrapped parcel under her arm, air kissing everyone, except me who she grabbed by the arm and swung round to face her. I staggered slightly and lost my balance, but recovered sufficiently before anyone noticed. She put a hand either side of my face.

'What's the matter with you lately?' she demanded, scrutinising me as if I was one of her criminals.

'You're looking at me as if I've done something unspeakable.'

'You sounded odd on the answering machine.'

'That's because I *am* odd and I detest the wretched things.'

She frowned even harder and narrowed her eyes. 'Mmm, we'll see ... you aren't telling the truth. I know instantly when someone is telling lies.'

'Yes, Your Honour, now go and get a drink.'

'I intend to have quite a few as I'm staying the night.'

I hastily transferred my attention to the other arrivals. 'Rich, how lovely of you to come, and Sarah, glad you could make it.'

'Traffic was heavy on the M11,' Rich answered, as traffic and directions were his favourite topic. He could name and describe all the service stations from London to Carlisle and recount every meal he had eaten in all of them. 'Unusual for a Sunday really, but you can never tell.'

'Indeed,' I mumbled, steering him towards the kitchen. 'Have a large one, Sarah can drive home.'

'Cheers, Benedict, I will.'

'Did he say I'm driving home?' Sarah asked as she gave me a hug. 'Nice of him,' she added. 'How are you, darling?'

'I'm fine and you?'

'So, so,' she answered mournfully, as she always did when it came to her health because she had acquired the hypochondriac gene from our mother.

'You look well.'

'I'm not bad, not really. Just a few aches and pains.'

'Beth, take Aunty Sarah's coat, would you?'

'Yes, Dad,' she called from the kitchen. 'Sidney, where are my lights?'

'Beth, don't encourage him, please,' Sheila called back, rolling her eyes.

'Coming up,' he declared, bending down behind the sofa and flicking the switch.

The flashing lights came on in all their glory and the ones around the mirror spelling Beth's name looked especially spectacular because they flashed once and that was it.

'The usual disaster,' Sheila muttered in my ear.

'Bugger,' Sidney spat out. 'Never fear everyone, I'll get them going.'

I turned to Lily who was enjoying every moment. 'Priceless,' I commented. 'And if he doesn't fuse the whole house I'll eat my hat!'

She squeezed my arm. 'I get the feeling, by your face and his wife's that this is a common occurrence.'

'Let's just say he means well, shall we? And leave it at that!'

She laughed. 'Bless him.'

The party was in full swing within half an hour. Plenty of laughter, catching up on news, soft music in the background, eating and drinking and just the right atmosphere for a family get together. Beth was a little disappointed none of her seven cousins could make it, but we were a far-flung family in that generation and I tried to explain to her that I had only decided on a small party at the last minute after she had called me. She enjoyed being the centre of attention with her doting aunts and uncles around her. She even resembled the young daughter I had always known, which heartened me because before they had all arrived I was beginning to wonder where the old Beth had gone. Apart from her tears at my announcement she had altered in so many small ways. But I reassured myself that it was simply New York and the fast, hectic and stressful lifestyle there.

I glanced at my watch just before four and wondered whether Nell was on her way. My stomach fluttered slightly with a mixture of nerves and excitement. I was making a hash of getting the jacket potatoes out of the oven when Sidney sidled over.

'She is coming, isn't she?' he whispered loudly, as if he were on stage.

'Patience, Sidney, patience!' I whispered back through gritted teeth.

'She's not I bet and I've so been looking forward to this.'

'She said she was.'

'She might chicken out,' he suggested.

'She'll be here, Sidney.'

'Give that tray to me, you'll drop the whole lot on the bloody floor knowing you,' he scolded, grabbing a tea towel and taking the scalding tray out of my shaking hands.

'You're nothing but an old woman,' I told him and as I said those words the doorbell rang and we stared at each other conspiratorially.

'Fucking hell, she's here,' he cried, a little too loudly, his face flushed.

'Keep calm,' I told him, like a doting schoolboy with a crush on his teacher.

'I'm calm, *you* keep calm.'

'I *am* calm ... I think.'

'I'll go,' Bethan called.

'Christ,' I muttered, knowing my straight-faced sister was the worst person to open the door to Nell.

They appeared a few seconds later. Nell was resplendent in a crisp, sparkling white blouse over impossibly tight black trousers that accentuated her slim legs. Her long dark hair was shining like coal and fell over her shoulders. She literally took my breath away with her simple, understated beauty. Bethan had a smile on her face that you would imagine a tiger to have when it had caught sight of its prey.

'A friend of yours I believe, Benedict.'

'Hello, Mr Marshall,' Nell said, with absolutely no side, seemingly unaware of the sudden silence in the room. 'Am I in time for some food? I'm starving.'

'It's perfect timing, Nell. Thank you so much for coming. How's the dashing Frankie?' I muttered in her ear.

'He's fine,' she muttered back, 'but not so dashing, not in the least. Not like you.'

'I'm so pleased to hear it.'

'He is quite gorgeous though,' she added cheekily, her voice so low nobody could hear her except me and that's just what we both intended.

'I hate him.'

'Shut your face,' she replied, a little louder and then she let out a blast of her wondrous laugh.

'Was it fun?'

'Great music ...'

'And now into the lion's den.'

'Don't worry I'll pretend I'm on stage.'

'Everyone, this is Nell, my friend.'

Sidney's face was a picture. He quite literally beamed from ear to ear with delight. Sheila caught him and put her elbow in his ribs. My eldest brother gave Nell a small wave of welcome and Lily smiled warmly because she knew what it was like being introduced as a newcomer to my family.

'Hello, dear,' Sarah said, nudging Rich who was studying a CD cover intently, 'pleased to meet you.'

Nell appeared completely at ease with herself and the situation. 'Hello, everyone, it's great to be here.'

I glanced over to where Beth and Bethan were sitting together and their faces were a mixture of surprise, interest and dismay. Bethan was not so surreptitiously looking Nell up and down as if she was a suspect in the dock. Beth stood open-mouthed, her eyes large and questioning. Sidney came over and put his rotund stomach between myself and Nell so I had no choice but to introduce him formally.

'Nell, this is Sidney from next door.'

She grabbed his hand and shook it warmly. 'Sidney, I've heard so much about you ... all good I have to say.'

Sidney flushed. 'Have you?'

'I know your wife is a fantastic cook.'

Sheila laughed. 'That's why he's so tubby.'

Nell turned her smile on to Sheila. 'And I know your beef is famous this side of the Thames.'

'Yes, it is,' Sheila agreed, 'but thank you.'

I took Nell to where Beth was sitting. 'Darling, this is Nell who I told you about.'

Nell immediately put her hand out. 'Hello, Beth. I'm so pleased to meet you and thank you for allowing me to come to your birthday party. My God, aren't you like your father?'

Beth gave a shy, almost force smile. 'I know, but I'm like Mum too.'

'And this is my little sister, Bethan.'

Nell turned her incomparable smile Bethan's way. 'Now, you are a barrister, I know that much.'

Bethan's eyes were as cold as a dead fish. 'I am and I can spot a fraud or a criminal a mile off. They only have to speak and I can tell whether they are telling the truth or not,' she replied, with a knowing smile that made me wince because it looked so false. Nell merely laughed.

'I'd better keep my mouth shut then.'

Bethan wasn't expecting such an upfront reply and appeared disappointed. I felt strangely proud because most people were intimidated by my sister, but not my Nell. She didn't need to be intimidated by anyone; she had nothing to hide.

'Nell, would you like a drink?' I asked her.

'A glass of white would be lovely, thank you.'

Sidney followed me into the kitchen as I knew he would. 'Fuck me, what a cracker!'

'I would have laid money on you following me in here.'

'She's bloody lovely.'

'I think so.'

'I can see why you're nuts about her.'

'Keep your voice down,' I hissed.

'Not sure what she sees in an old fuck like you,' he declared.

'Very true, but do you have to keep reminding me what an old fuck I am, Sidney.'

'Except you've got money of course ...'

I had hold of a corkscrew and I put it in his face. 'Sidney, if you say that one more time, I'll stick this right up your fully tiled back passage and turn it as many times as my hands will allow, until you beg for mercy. Do I make myself clear?' He completely ignored me, as I fully expected.

'No, she's *really* lovely and I mean a few years ago there was no bugger to touch you. You were suave, elegant, bloody good looking, but now ...'

'Times winged chariot and all that ...'

'If that means the years have caught up with you, you're dead right,' he whispered, peering into my lounge again where Nell was talking animatedly to Lily. 'What a cracker though.'

'Sidney, will you stop staring?'

'I don't know how you do it. Even now, with your craggy face and silver hair, you're still pulling them. I'm so bloody envious.'

'I'm not pulling anything these days except rigid faces,' I whispered back, pouring Nell's drink carefully because my tremors appeared to be getting worse as the day went on. 'And you don't need to envy anyone, you have Saint Sheila. Nobody else would put up with you.'

'When I die I'm coming back as you.'

'What, even with this disease? And don't be ridiculous, how can you come back as me if I'm dead too? And why am I even taking part in this ridiculous conversation?' I asked, looking up to the heavens for divine intervention.

'I tell you, I'm coming back as you,' he repeated, obviously not listening.

'Try dribbling for a day and see how it feels.'

'Beth's not pleased though,' he added.

'I expected that and I'll deal with it. Now, will you please remove your protruding stomach from my kitchen?'

As I approached with her drink, Nell said, 'Now I know where you get your brains and beauty,' and she smiled warmly at William who appeared rather pleased at her paying him a compliment.

'Don't tell him that, I'll never hear the last of it.'

'The only difference is the glasses,' she added. 'If you wore dark-rimmed glasses, William, well … it would be hard to tell you apart.'

'He's actually the clever one,' William said generously.

'I don't know about that,' I protested.

'Oh he's dead clever, isn't he?' Nell gasped. 'But he hasn't heard of half the sayings I come out with.'

'That doesn't surprise me,' William replied.

They are rather … colloquial,' I said, in my defence.

'Wonderful,' Lily said. 'I'm not surprised you don't know them, Benedict. He's not exactly streetwise, Nell.'

'That's why we get on,' Nell said, smiling at me.

'Opposites do attract,' William added.

Nell looked up at me without embarrassment. 'We're just good friends, aren't we, Mr Marshall?'

'We are, Nell,' I replied.

The afternoon gave way to an evening with a red-streaked sky. I sat down by the fireplace at one point because my legs felt shaky and watched Nell weave her magic. She held almost everyone captive within an hour of being there; enslaved and entranced. Even Rich, who normally wouldn't join in any of the conversations unless it was something to do with traffic, motorways or diversions, was smiling in appreciation when Nell spoke with him about the Dartford Bridge. She appeared fascinated by what everyone had to say and even tried to help Sidney work out why the lights over the fireplace had not worked. Her head would tilt and turn and she would lean closer and open her eyes wide with interest. Her sparkling face lit up the whole room and when she let out a blast of her canon-fire laugh at one of Sidney's unintentional jokes I noticed Lily and William smile almost fondly at her in appreciation. Sarah appeared to be enjoying her conversation and Rich gave her a sneaky glance occasionally, which meant he was more interested in Nell than he usually was about anything else. Everyone laughed with her, except my daughter, and Bethan merely appeared slightly amused yet somehow distant. Sheila's glass was empty, so I took it from her and went into the kitchen to fill it up, but my left hand suddenly twitched violently and I dropped it.

'Shit ...'

Nell appeared by my side instantly. 'Why are you throwing stuff about in here?' she asked. 'And good stuff too by the look of it.'

'Sorry ...'

She took my hand in hers for a moment and squeezed it. Feeling her skin next to mine made me deliriously happy. 'Leave it, I'll do it.' She mopped up the wine and swept up the pieces of shattered glass in the dustpan. I watched her every move. 'There you go. Are you OK, Mr Marshall?' she asked, gazing at my face with her almond eyes.

'I've just got a few tremors, Nell.'

'Have you told anyone yet?'

'Only Beth ...'

Her face grew solemn. 'How did she take it?'

'She cried.'

'Oh no,' she gasped, her hands flying to her mouth. 'That must have been so hard for you.' She took my hand again in a gesture of support and empathy and curled her fingers around mine. Looking down at her lovely face I felt my heart lurch with unspoken love and despair; despair because of the unspoken love. I bent down and kissed the top of her head in a fatherly way.

'Thank you, Nell ...'

'What for?' she asked, completely bemused.

'For caring how she felt.' She gave a little shrug and placed her hand gently on my arm.

'She's your daughter.'

She carried the wine in for Sheila and I looked up to find Bethan had been watching us. She shook her head imperceptibly, as if I was a young boy doing something I ought not to, but at that moment I simply did not care. I loved her, that's all I knew and if I had been younger and free of the Parkinson's I would have pursued her with every ounce of adoration I could muster and make her love me back. I would have offered her everything: my life, my money, my house and bombarded her with gifts and showered her with all the power of my deepest feelings. I would have sworn to love her, to hold her and keep her from harm for the rest of my life. But that was all a dream, a wonderful, fleeting dream because I was no longer young, no longer powerful or strong and I had a chronic illness that was slowly robbing me of many things, but it had also given me something back: I no longer had surging desires. They had been replaced by a gentle and calm longing to love and be loved for the man I had become. I had let go of the old Benedict and settled into the Benedict I wanted to be until I died.

This new Benedict craved affection instead of desperate, joyless sex; kindness, gentleness and humour instead of sparks flying. This Benedict longed for intelligent conversation and humorous exchanges rather than being out in a rowdy crowd. I wanted to be loving in a tactile way instead of being at the mercy of my uninhibited desires. I just wanted to live quietly with an equal, sit in comfortable silence with them without any emotional roller coasters or shallow encounters. I had within me the intense longing to live for someone else instead of for myself and I had been lucky enough to find the one woman who could be all those things for me, but unlucky enough to be twenty-seven years older than her with a chronic disease.

I had no thoughts about Nell feeling the same because I had no intention of ever telling her how I felt. I feared rejection of course, but more importantly I would not put her in the unenviable position of having to inform me she simply didn't feel the same. And so, I would adore her silently from afar, and simply be thankful that this unique young woman was my friend and enjoyed spending time with me.

I had been standing in the kitchen doorway watching Nell speaking, tossing her silky hair over her shoulder and out of her eyes. She was constantly smiling and gracious and even attempted a light-hearted chat with Bethan, who eyed her coolly and appeared icy and aloof. My heart sank because I knew Bethan would grill me about her later and I would have to defend Nell and it all struck me as rather tedious when all my sister had to do was accept her as a friend of mine. But she had always been a suspicious person, it came with the territory of being a successful barrister and she would take nothing in life at face value.

'Benedict,' Sidney said, appearing beside me, 'you're standing there like a limp lettuce.'

'That's because I *am* a limp lettuce, hadn't you noticed?'

He grinned. 'I'm having fun.'

I smiled at him. 'Are you now and at whose expense?'

'Yours, of course...'

'How kind and you seemed to have swallowed quite a bit of my best Beaujolais.'

'Well, *I'm* not on any tablets,' he declared without thinking first, which was his usual style.

'That's inordinately cruel, Sidney.'

He stood behind me looking over my shoulder. 'She's undeniably lovely. But you're not the first man to lose his marbles over a young firecracker and you won't be the last.'

'What are you trying to say, Sidney?'

'That despite all the awards, you're a silly old bugger.'

'Thank you. It's such a relief to know I'm just another silly old bugger. It's a comforting thought that I appear in the ranks of all the silly old buggers that ever lived.'

'You may be an academic, but just another silly old bugger. When all's said and done you're just a man,' he sighed, as if it was all beyond my control.

'Just a man, yes and a silly old bugger to boot.'

'Yes.'

'Thank you so much.'

'You're very welcome,' he replied, in a self-satisfied way. 'Now, I'm going to fix those bloody lights if it kills me.'

'And it probably will, knowing how good you are with electrical matters! But I am insured.'

I lit Beth's candles and carried her cake through, with my hands shaking noticeably. Bethan had her eyes on me and was watching my every move. I felt a little like one of her prisoners in the dock awaiting her cross examination.

'Did you make that, Sheila?' Sarah asked.

'No, not this time, love. Benedict bought it.'

'Cool cake,' Beth drooled, draping her arm around my shoulders and planting a kiss on my nose. It was made entirely of profiteroles and stood tall, a mountain of melted chocolate.

'It's actually from Fortnum's.'

'It bloody well would be,' Sidney called from behind the sofa where he was supposedly mending a fuse. 'What a poser.'

'I agree,' Sarah chipped in.

'Always have been, always will be,' I commented, 'only the best for my one and only daughter.'

'It must have cost a flipping fortune,' Nell added, her eyes shining with delight and surprise. 'I've never, ever seen a cake like that.'

Suddenly the lights around the mirror spelling Beth's name flickered on. They were alternately silver and blue and quite eye catching, for a Sidney effort.

'Aha,' he cried. 'Lift off.'

'Let there be light,' William said.

'And there was light,' I added.

'Oh ye of little faith,' Sheila laughed. 'Now don't touch anything else, Sidney.'

'I won't. I know you don't trust me.'

'Raise your glasses please,' I told everyone, 'to my darling Beth on her thirtieth birthday.'

'To Beth...'

'To Beth...'

'Lovely to see you...'

'Happy birthday...'

'Thanks for coming so far everyone,' Beth said, after blowing out her thirty candles.

'That's our pleasure,' Sidney laughed.

'Ha bloody ha,' I added and as I did all the fairy lights went out.

'Oh fuck,' Sidney muttered.

'Sidney,' Sheila scolded, 'please don't swear in mixed company.'

'Sorry everyone, I never bloody swear.'

Lily nudged me. 'I love coming here, Benedict. It's always such a hoot.'

The party came to its natural end at about eight when Sheila took hold of Sidney's arm and told him, quite firmly, that he had drunk enough and they were going home.

'Thanks, Benedict,' she called over to me. 'You and Beth come to lunch tomorrow.'

'I'm going to Mum's,' Beth told her, 'sorry, Sheila.'

'I'll still be here,' Bethan said, never one to stand back.

'Then you and Benedict come,' Sheila told her. 'And you, Nell,' she added, warmly.

'Yes, you come too, Nell,' Sidney insisted, his eyes lighting up.

'I'll be at work, but thank you for asking me.'

Sheila guided Sidney through the conservatory, out into the back garden and through the adjoining gate, where he promptly tripped over something on his patio and went flying. I could hear her telling him off for drinking so much and he was complaining his knees hurt, which she told him quite firmly was his own fault. Their warm marital repartee always amused me and I was constantly grateful to have them next door.

I spoke at length to Sarah and mentally wished I saw more of her because she had the same dry sense of humour as I did and we sparked off each other. I noticed she appeared quite pale and drawn, but I didn't dare tell her because her hypochondria would have taken immediate hold of her tongue and she would have had herself dead and buried within six weeks. But I gave her a special hug when she commented that my face appeared a trifle different in some way, but she couldn't quite put her finger on how.

'I'll ring you in a couple of days,' I told her, when they were leaving. 'I have a couple of things to tell you.'

She looked concerned. 'What's wrong?'

'Nothing to worry about, I just want to have a chat, that's all.'

'Tell me now,' she urged, scrutinising my face for some kind of truth.

'I'll ring you, I promise.'

'You'd better,' she warned in her best schoolmistress tone of voice. 'Rich, come on,' she ordered. 'If I'm driving, hurry up.'

Rich did as he was told as always. 'Lovely do, Benedict,' he said, shaking my hand. 'Traffic might be heavy on the M25 and you know what the M11 is like. Cones, road works, and lorries, you get the picture.'

'I know, Rich,' I nodded in sympathy. 'But thanks for braving all that and coming. Beth was very pleased to see everyone.'

'Bye, darling,' Sarah said, kissing me on both cheeks. 'Call me.'

Having seen William and Lily off, with a smacker of a kiss from her right on my mouth, I sat heavily on the sofa. Beth and Bethan were chatting in the kitchen and clearing up and Nell was watching me carefully so I gave her a tired smile. She came over, leant down and gave me a soft kiss on my right cheek.

'Don't get up, Mr Marshall.'

'Nell, don't go ...'

'I'm going to leave you with your sister and Beth. Well done, you did her proud.'

'Thank you and thank you for braving it,' I whispered.

'Anything for you,' she whispered back. 'I'll see you in a couple of days.'

'Looking forward to it,' I replied, gazing at her loveliness.

I wished she could stay, curl up on the sofa beside me and rest her head on my shoulder. I wanted to talk with her, hear her comments on my family, laugh and relax in her company. I wanted to hear her moving about my house as if it was her own, singing her scales in the toilet, tripping down the stairs like a fairy and dancing around the furniture. But it was not to be and I watched her swaying gently as she walked out of the room. I listened intently to the sound of her footsteps on my wooden floor as she went away from me. I felt deliriously happy that she had braved the lion's den for me. I looked down at my tremulous right hand that she had held so gently and curled her fingers around and I let out a contented sigh. All was right with my world now because I knew Nell, and I considered myself the luckiest man alive, even with the disease.

Bethan carried a tray of tea in and placed it in front of me. I could feel a little tension in the air so I smiled up at her. 'Thank you.'

'Has she gone then?' she asked, straight faced.

'Nell you mean?'

'Yes, of course,' she replied briskly. 'Beth, come in here a moment.'

Beth sauntered in and they both stood in front of me with their arms folded against their chests. My daughter appeared a little tense too for some reason and I was about to open my mouth to ask what the problem was, but I didn't get a chance.

'So, Benedict,' Bethan started, her eyes full of mischief. 'Beth and I want to know who she is exactly and are you getting married again?'

Chapter 7

'I feel as if I'm in front of a firing squad,' I remarked.

'Don't be silly, Dad,' Beth declared. 'We're just concerned about you, that's all.'

'I have no intention of ever getting married again. I wouldn't inflict myself on anyone at this point in my life. Once was enough for someone like me, so please don't worry on my account. There's no need, I assure you.'

'There's every reason to worry on your account,' Bethan laughed, a little derisively. 'You've always been a fool where women are concerned.'

'Bethan, please,' I said, my voice firm, 'Beth is standing right beside you and I won't have you counting her mum amongst any foolish, rash decisions on my part with regard to my relationships with women.' She had the decency to look a little ashamed.

'Sorry, Beth, I'm not including your mother.'

Beth shrugged. 'I'm a big girl now; you don't have to worry about what you say in front of me.'

'Nell is a friend, that's all. Is it so difficult to understand?' I asked, wearily.

My sister scoffed. 'Benedict, she'll have her feet under your table within a year, I'm telling you. And before that, she'll be in your bed, if she isn't already and then you'll be even more besotted than you are now.'
I glanced at Beth who had turned her nose up in distaste at the thought of her father being in bed with anyone and I wished with all my heart that my sister wasn't so blunt and thoughtless.

'I'm going in the kitchen if you're going to be *that* personal, Aunty Bethan,' she declared, taking herself off.

I shook my head in despair. 'You always were too forthright. And I repeat, I don't intend to marry again.'

'That sounds pretty lame to me. "Oh sorry, Your Honour, I didn't *intend* to punch my neighbour on the nose, it just kind of happened".

'We aren't in one of your courts now. This is my life we're talking about.' Bethan sat down opposite me and tried the softer approach.

'Look, I know she's beautiful and she has an engaging, dynamic personality, full of fun, but she's artful too.'

I frowned. 'Artful?'

'Yes.'

'In what way is she artful?'

'Well, firstly she knows how to work a room, but that's the actress in her. Sidney told me she's an out of work, *very* out of work, actress ...'

'Oh, did he now? I'll have words with him.'

'Don't blame him, I wheedled it out of him without him really being aware of what I was doing. You know what I'm like. Secondly,' she continued, the softer approach having fled instantly and her face as hard as flint, 'she's patently aware of how people are drawn to her and she plays on that. She knows exactly how you feel about her and she knows how to play you.'

My heart had begun to jump around in my chest and was thumping against my temples. 'Play me?' I repeated, astonished, 'in what way?'

Bethan looked exasperated. 'Because she knows how you feel about her, she'll take advantage of your adoration, believe me. She is quite aware that if she gives you one of her wide-eyed looks you will give her the world. And at some point in the future she will ask you for precisely that and as you're not materialistic in any way, you won't even be aware of any of this. Beware, Benedict.'

I could hear Beth loading the dishwasher and I wished she and I were on our own so I could talk freely about Nell without Bethan's cynical stance on everything. I was certain I could talk my daughter round eventually.

'Bethan,' I whispered quite calmly, despite beginning to feel enraged, 'I don't even recognise the woman you're describing.'

She threw her back and laughed, but it was a harsh laugh and didn't sound like my sister. 'Listen to yourself,' she replied, 'that's because you're in love with her. What a fool. Apart from anything else, she's so young ...'

'Not *so* young.'

'How old is she then?' she demanded.

'Thirty-five ...'

'Oh for God's sake!'

I sat opposite her feeling like the limp lettuce Sydney had described me as. 'Bethan, please don't try to make it something it isn't, and stop looking at me in that way.'

She was scathing. 'I'm not looking like you in any way?'

'Yes you are, you're looking at me as if I'm a dirty old man.'

'I can't help my face,' she said. 'And don't try and tell me it's her mind you're interested in. What could someone as clever as you find to talk about with her?'

'Everything,' I mumbled, but she wasn't listening, more intent on voicing her opinions.

'And of course there's the element of control when an older man wants a young woman, which I'm surprised at.'

I was completely at a loss. 'Do I look as if I could control anyone or anything?'

'Then help me here ...'

'Help you with what?'

'Help me understand what's going on. Is it a pathetic attempt to recapture your youth?'

I was flummoxed and hurt by her bluntness. 'My God, Bethan, where did all your human decency and understanding go?'
She let out her loud, harsh laugh once more and it sounded and felt like the crack of a whip. It made me shudder to hear my younger sister laugh like that. I wondered what on earth had happened in her later life to turn her into the tough, hard hearted woman she had become.

'Oh don't start all that nonsense. Just because I'm the only one who will ever be completely and utterly straight with you, I get accused of being too hard. And you didn't answer my question?' I was beginning to feel battered by her brittleness.

'Which was?'

'Recapturing your youth?'

'I think you said my "pathetic *attempt*" at recapturing my youth!'

'Don't try to be facetious, Benedict.'

'I don't want to recapture my youth! I'd prefer to forget my youth. I prefer the man I am now.'

'Then what is it you want from her?'

'For crying out loud, I don't want anything *from* her. I just want her in my life.'

She merely raised her eyes heavenward in exasperation. 'You know what I mean.'

'No, I don't. I just want ... her kindness, her funny sayings, her laughter, her inner beauty, the way she is, the way we talk together, the way we *are* together ...'

'I get the picture. Just remember this conversation in the future. I still say she's artful.'
I put my hand over my eyes. The tremors were noticeable and I felt slightly breathless with anger. I tried to compose myself but I found it very difficult

under my sister's barrage of criticism.

'No, I know her. She isn't artful at all. She's the most honest woman I've ever met.'

'Oh, Benedict,' she sighed, as if I was a hopeless case. 'I realise there's nothing more I can say.'

'I think you've said enough.'

'You need to stop being defensive. I just hate you being a cliché, that's all. Older man, plenty of spare cash to spend on a young woman who has none...'

'Please...'

'Mark my words, it will end in tears,' she warned.

'Hopefully mine and not hers...'

'You're a complete idiot, do you know that?' Her eyes had softened a little.

'Always have been,' I replied, my anger dissipating.

She looked me straight in the eye, with a look that had been honed and practised in many a courtroom, I had no doubt. 'But especially where she's concerned.'

'You're wrong about her.' I was smiling weakly.

She was frowning hard at me. 'Didn't I warn you about Mary?'

'Ah, I wondered when we would get on to that.' I leant towards her and said softly, 'Please remember Beth is in the kitchen.'

'We ought to ask Beth what she thinks about the young actress then.'

'No,' I hissed, 'don't bring her into this.'

But it was too late. Beth ambled in with a tea towel in her hand, looking embarrassed and tense. I knew she must have been able to hear some of our conversation from the kitchen and I regretted that deeply.

'Beth, tell your father what you think of Nell.'

'You don't have to say anything Beth,' I told her, wanting to save her from being caught in the middle, but I also hoped she would take my side against her aunt and tell me it was *my* life, I could be friends with whoever I chose.

'She's much too young for you, Dad,' she began, 'it's a bit embarrassing to be honest. I mean, why would she ... Oh hell, what I'm trying to say is that it's like me going after a man your age. You wouldn't like that, would you? And it's a bit weird, especially with the ... you know.'

Bethan looked perplexed because she had no idea to what Beth was referring. 'I'm sorry if it's embarrassing, Beth,' I murmured, a little disappointed with her response. 'I would never want to be an embarrassment to you.' She immediately joined me on the sofa, put her arms around me, kissed my cheek and hugged me tightly.

'I didn't mean it like that. You're not an embarrassment, it's the situation that could be embarrassing, that's what I meant.'

Bethan attempted to soften her features a little by giving me a warm smile, but it was difficult for her; her smiles had always been a little contrived. She had always been blunt to the point of being hurtful, even as a young child. I had often secretly admired her honesty because she never appeared bothered by the consequences of her actions or her brutal tongue and I always thought it would be so much easier to be like her instead of feeling guilty about every single sentence that came out of my mouth. But now, with her acid tongue directed against my lovely Nell, it merely sounded twisted, mean and bitter. Any softness she had held in her heart when a young girl growing up with me had completely disappeared.

'Sorry, Benedict, but it had to be said. I like to tell you the truth. I love you, but look at yourself. You're how much older than her? I know lots of older men go for young women, normally to recapture their youth and you're still gorgeous, always have been, but – mark my words – there's something artful about her. I can spot it a mile off.'

I was speechless and my addled brain tried desperately to send signals to my mouth, but nothing happened and the messages stayed as tortuous thoughts. I felt let down, hurt by and disappointed in my sister; for her to be so vile in the face of my deep affection for Nell was staggering. And, if truth be known, I was disappointed in my daughter too. All her life Beth had defended me at every turn, even against her own mother when I had often been in the wrong and yet in this she was strangely acquiescent.

Beth gave me another hug. 'Just keep your eyes open, Dad. You're a little vulnerable at the moment. Keep your wits about you. That's all we're asking,' she whispered and I had the distinct feeling she was already regretting her part in the unwanted, uncalled for, conversation. Bethan leant over and squeezed my hand.

'Now I've hurt you and I'm sorry.'

I found my voice at last albeit a small, slurring voice. 'I know I've been foolish in the past where women are concerned, but I've never been a fool. There's a difference.'

Laughing out loud again, Bethan said, 'Only in the spelling.'

Beth looked into my eyes, her face serious and a little forlorn and my stomach turned over with guilt. 'Just take a step back, Dad, catch your breath and look at the situation from a distance. Please will you do that, for me?'

'For you, my darling, I will,' I told her, because I would have given her the moon, the stars and anything else she wanted from me. However, even saying those words caused me anguish because I was implying Nell could not be trusted and that left a nasty taste in my mouth.

Bethan sighed. 'Well, I suppose that's all we can hope for. But if she mentions marriage or borrowing money ...'

'That's enough, *please*. I repeat, I am not marrying anyone!'

'Dad, as we're all being so honest, this could be a good time to tell Aunty Bethan about... you know,' Beth urged, 'as we're talking so frankly.'

'Tell me about what?' Bethan demanded and her face was instantly alert.

'I have Parkinson's,' I said, without any preamble or softening of the news because I didn't feel she deserved any at that point.

Her face fell. 'My God,' she gasped, 'I'm so sorry, Benedict. I thought something was different about you, but I couldn't put my finger on what it was.'

'I'm surprised you didn't notice the shakes.'

'I did and I was going to ask you about it. You walk differently too.'

'Yes, I do.'

'He feels fine though,' Beth interrupted. 'Don't you, Dad?'

'Yes, I feel fine, the tablets are working and apart from a few annoying symptoms, I am the same old me ... I think.' I saw my sister narrow her eyes and I knew what was coming next, so I mentally braced myself.

'Does Nell know?'

'How did I know you were going to ask me that? And why is that relevant?'

'Does she know?' she asked again, more insistently.

'Yes, she does,' Beth answered.

Bethan let out a loud dramatic sigh. 'Even more reason to wonder why on earth ...'

'I don't want to hear any more about it,' I protested. 'I mean it. Nell is my friend, end of story, now, no more!'

Bethan could tell by my voice that I meant it and she appeared instantly deflated. She picked up the brandy bottle and poured herself a large one, offering me the bottle. I shook my head.

'Benedict, I'm really sorry to hear about the Parkinson's. If there is ever anything I can do at any time, just call me. Will you do that?'

'Yes, of course, but I'm fine.'

She shook her head at me. 'I knew there was something ...'

'The slurring probably...'

'No, I just have this unerring knack of knowing when something isn't quite right. Don't ask me how, I've always had it and it comes in pretty handy in court. That's why I picked up on something that isn't kosher about your young friend.' She paused for a moment, deep in thought. 'Look, I truly am sorry,' she added and at last her hard, work-weary expression changed to one of concern. 'My poor brother; you don't deserve it.'

I gave a little shrug. 'Nobody does.'

'Oh some do, believe me. Are you happy with your doctor? Do you want a second opinion?'

That question immediately made me jump down her throat, 'No! I don't need a second opinion.' But I regretted it immediately and felt my usual shot of guilt. 'Sorry, thank you, no, no second opinion required ... it's most definitely Parkinson's.'

She took a swig of her brandy, watching me as she did so. 'Are you on many pills?'

'Not so many,' I answered, not particularly wanting to share every piece of information about my disease with her. 'I just have to pace myself a little more than I did, live a healthy, stress-free existence, exercise gently – all of which I've been doing like a good boy.'

'And alcohol?' she inquired, knowing me of old.

'I seldom drink now, believe it or not.' I said, shrugging my shoulders slightly as if alcohol had been easy to give up. 'My body, my health and my time have become extremely precious and although at first I reacted in a negative, self-destructive way, feeling sorry for myself and wondering what the hell I had done to deserve it, all those ludicrous thoughts, now I just get on with it, think positively and try to have fun.'

'I'm surprised,' my sister muttered, 'knowing you as I do with your introspection and complexities.'

'Ah well,' I replied, knowing that my next words would ignite our previous debate again, but simply longing to let them both know how huge a part Nell had played in my transformation, 'I have Nell to thank for all of that, which is why I intend to keep her as my friend and defend her until my last breath.' There was an uneasy silence while Beth and Bethan exchanged surprised glances.

'Even more ammunition for her,' Bethan commented unkindly. 'You really won't be able to live without her, will you?'

I did not reply, but at last Beth leapt to my support. 'Well, if she's helped Dad that's great. I hope she continues to help you and doesn't let you down otherwise you're going to get hurt.'

I put my arm around my daughter. 'She won't hurt me, darling,' I told her. 'Believe me, she won't hurt me.'

&

I wandered home through the park a little dazed and unsettled by my first encounter with Benedict's family. I felt I had made quite an impression on most of them, especially the sweet-natured William and Sarah. Lily, I knew I could make a close friend of if I saw enough of her. She was attractive, intelligent, good humoured and trustworthy and in her eyes I could see experience and loyalty and an understated sense of fun and kindness. Rich was a simple man with simple pleasures, but he lacked social graces and gave the term 'small talk' a whole new meaning. And Sidney and Sheila were the type of couple everyone should have living next door. I sensed Sidney's closeness to and love for Benedict despite their differences and standing next to each other with their heads together they had a unique bond that was obvious and touching.But Beth and her aunt were a different matter and that worried me. I had so wanted to like Beth and had hoped for an immediate rapport with her, but she had treated me with a subtle indifference; so subtle it was probably only picked up by me. Physically she resembled her father in many ways, tall, slim, fair hair and a square face, but she didn't have his sense of mischief or playfulness. Bethan's ice cold eyes and haughty behaviour almost made me turn on my heel at the door and leave them all to it. But I could not have let Benedict down for all the tea in China, despite her behaviour and seeing his face light up when he caught sight of me was worth every cool, disdainful look from her and Beth.

The wind was picking up again and the river looked deep and mysterious. The pubs were still full of noisy tourists, all with their cameras slung around their necks, and maps and guide books spread out in front of them on the tables in the beer gardens. Greenwich was always teeming with different nationalities throughout the spring and summer and I often made a game of trying to place all the different accents and languages.

I paused by the Cutty Sark pub and leant on the wall outside gazing across the dark water to the new apartments on the Isle of Dogs that resembled Lego of varying bright colours, shapes and sizes. A few small boats sailed by and some old, weather-beaten barges were tied up together underneath where I stood, knocking against each other periodically. The pub sign flew about in the strong wind and sounded like the creaking door of an old, ruined house. This part of the river had always held a certain fascination for me, although I could never quite put my finger on why. It almost seemed haunted, desolate and timeless.

My thoughts were racing through my head at top speed: Beth's slightly open mouth when she first saw me; Bethan narrowing her eyes and watching me carefully as I moved around the room to speak with everyone; Sidney's beaming smile of delight when I shook his hand; William, Lily, Sarah and Rich, all warm and welcoming albeit a little surprised, probably because of my age; and my Mr Marshall with the mischievous twinkle in his eyes, his stumbling walk that he was desperately attempting to hide from his family and his obvious pride in me. It was that pride that made hot, stinging tears, unwanted and unasked for, pour down my face in a torrent. The sudden surge of emotion was stemmed in an instant by my mobile ringing and when I saw my agent's name flashing on it my stomach turned over with anticipation.

'Hello, Logan.'

His broad Scottish accent cut into my tortuous, jumbled thoughts and dispelled them instantly. 'Can you speak, darling?' he asked.

'Yeah, I'm sitting outside the Cutty Sark pub.'

'You have an audition for the show in New York this Wednesday at the rehearsal rooms in Soho and one for the revue is on Tuesday in the same place. I've emailed you all the details so go home and bloody practise when you read it. I need to earn some money off you soon otherwise I'll be in the poor house,' he declared, his sarcastic humour somehow perfectly matched by his hard, Glaswegian vowels.

'Brilliant! Thanks,' I replied, immediately feeling excited and yet apprehensive in case I faced more rejection.

'The revue is only small mind,' he added, 'and runs for six weeks, but it would be fabulous experience and the New York one is for six months, possibly a year and I've had word they're looking for someone just like you for one of the four leads.'

I screeched, 'A lead?' not caring who was listening. 'Oh my God, did I hear you right?'

'You did, darling. There's the main man and woman and then four other leads with solos and I expect you to get this, Helen. It's right up your street. The Yanks need a fresh team over there and they want Brits.'

'I can't get too excited,' I murmured, 'in case they don't want me.'

'You get as excited as you bloody well like and then you can rev yourself up like an engine and blast them with that turbo-charged voice of yours, so bugger off home and read my email.'

'I will, I will,' I promised. 'I'm going now.'

'Good. Oh and Helen, didn't you say you know a fabulous pianist?'

'Yes, yes I do.'

'Get his agent on to the New York one and quick. Jobs like this don't come around that often. I'll see you,' he said and the phone went dead.

My head was spinning as I ran along the riverside walk towards east Greenwich, past the old, deserted wharves and the flat faces of the tiny pre-war houses. I intended to call Matt straight away. It would be a wonderful opportunity for him too. This was to be my time, my chance, and as the wind blew through my hair and into my face, my only thought was that if I was successful I would be paying a price: it would mean separation from Benedict and I would have to tell him.

&

The next day Beth went to her mother's after breakfast and I waved her off as she drove away in my car. When I rejoined Bethan she was sitting in the conservatory with her coffee and the newspaper and, without her make up on, she appeared to have aged quite a bit. Deep lines cut into her forehead and at the sides of her mouth, and her white roots were showing clearly on top of her head. She had always been so particular about her roots showing so it surprised me that she had let it all go so long. When I mentioned it she gave a hard laugh.

'There are times when I can't be bothered anymore,' she told me. 'I have so little time to get to the hairdresser because I'm always so busy.'

'We should always bother,' I commented, 'otherwise what's the point of it all?'

'I might let it go grey, it would show my wealth of experience in court and that's important. There's a young guy in my office who told me he thinks white hair and dark eyes are pretty sexy.'

'I'm a little surprised you take any note of what a young man in your office says.' She didn't answer, but merely raised her eyebrows slightly. 'But if dark eyes and white hair are sexy, no chance for me with eyes as blue as mine.'

'You aren't so bad,' she said, smiling. 'You are just as irresistible to women now as you were at thirty. As we all saw yesterday, Benedict.'

I pottered about in the kitchen, wondering what Nell was doing and what she had thought of everyone. I couldn't wait to be alone with her and hear her views on them all. Bethan was making calls on her mobile and discussing cases and clients and it all sounded such a horribly violent, verbally aggressive and complicated life, no wonder she looked as tough as old boot leather. I knew she would leave as soon as she could because she was addicted to the thrill of it all and sitting with her laid-back, slightly wound-down brother would not be enough for her. It made me feel a little wistful because as children and young adults we had been virtually inseparable.

'Aren't you coming to Sidney's for lunch then?' I asked her between her quick-fire calls.

'No, I'll have to shoot. I'm in the middle of a long drawn-out trial and I have so much reading to do. I did intend to. I'm sorry, I'd love to sit and chat, but I can't.'

I was quietly amused. Her eyes did not betray any sense of sorrow because sitting and chatting about non-consequential subjects did not rock her boat one little bit.

'That's fine,' I said, a little relieved because it meant I could call Nell.

'So,' she added, putting her mobile in her handbag as a sign she was leaving in the next ten minutes. 'What are we going to do about you?'

'What are *we* going to do in what sense?' I asked, as if I didn't know. 'If you mean my disease, there's nothing anyone can do. It's a case of accepting it and living with it. And I intend to do just that. I've had a self-indulgent few days of feeling sorry for myself, but that's no longer the case. I am embracing my future now.'

She set her lips and rolled her eyes. 'I meant about you and Nell.'

I sighed. 'Ah, I see. Well, as with my disease, there's really nothing to be done. You can accept it and live with it.'

'Very funny, Benedict,' she said. 'Look, you're still gorgeous, despite the lines on your face and the greying hair, you always were and women have always thrown themselves at you, we all know that. It's been like that since you hit puberty, but the Parkinson's, for God's sake! Why would someone as young and beautiful as her hook up with a man much older and infirm? Take a step back and look at the situation from a distance. Why would she want you when she could have someone young and vibrant?'

'Could it be my devastating good looks and engaging personality?' I quipped, but Bethan merely shook her head. 'She's just my friend,' I added, my voice sounding weary to my ears.

She waved dismissively. 'I know, I know, so you keep saying. I'll tell you what,' she said, her eyes glinting, 'offer her some money and see if she takes it.'

I was horrified. 'I will do no such thing.'

'Fine, have it your way. I'll say no more, but just beware and keep your hand on your wallet. Don't forget I come across people who aren't what they seem every day of my life and I can spot them a mile off ...'

'Yes; so you said last night. You know, your life and your job have made you cynical and mistrustful.'

'Maybe,' she shrugged. 'But I'd rather be like this than act like a fool.'

As soon as she had said those words I could see she regretted them because she saw my expression change and I said, 'Aha, now I know how you see your big brother these days; your *beloved* big brother, who spent his life looking out for you and defending you, is now just a fool.' She had the grace to appear genuinely sorry.

'Now I've hurt you again and I'm sorry. I didn't intend to.'

'I didn't *intend* to punch my neighbour on the nose,' I replied, mimicking her words the day before.

'Yes, yes, very shrewd. But tell me, do you remember the morning of your wedding?'

'I'm afraid I do,' I admitted. 'You told me Mary was materialistic in the extreme and I was making the worst mistake of my life. But it's because of my experiences with Mary that I recognise the honesty and integrity of Nell.'

She slung her handbag over her shoulder. 'Listen to yourself, you hopeless being,' she cried, laughing. 'But you can't say I didn't warn you and I'm sorry it has to be me who always tells you the truth, but it's always been the same.' She jumped up, leant over me and kissed my cheek roughly. 'I love you, brother. Take care of yourself and just don't act like a silly old sod.'

'I'll see you out.'

'No, stay there,' she urged, picking up her overnight bag. 'I'll see myself out. I'll be in touch.'

'Good to see you,' I mumbled, because despite upsetting me greatly, she and I had been so close as children, inseparable and I cared for her greatly. Her love for me had never been in doubt. I just wished she was a little softer and less brittle.

She paused and for the first time on this visit she resembled the little sister I had known. 'I mean it, take care. There's only one like you.'

And then she was gone.

I sat motionless for a long time as I tried once more to come to terms with Bethan's cruel attitude to my precious relationship with Nell. It was as if I had been slapped hard across the face by her and I was literally reeling. I was aware of every single tiny tremor in every cell at that moment and my whole body felt ice cold and rigid. All I could think about was my dear Nell and how she would be shattered by my sister's unkind words. Bethan had become someone I did not know when she had spoken about Nell. She had always been open, highly intelligent, yet blunt, but the cynical side she'd laid bare to me was extreme. Those barbed accusations: artful, playing me and wide-eyed looks? That wasn't Nell at all. Offer her money to lay a trap for her? The thought made me feel physically sick.

Finally my scrambled thoughts were interrupted by Sidney banging on the wall. I struggled to my feet and knocked back and a couple of minutes later he walked in the back door.

'Morning, Benedict. What's occurring then?' His rosy cheeks and playful manner made me feel a little better. He was a lovely antidote to my sister.

'Not much, Sidney, as you can see, but then not much does these days.'

'Where's your sister?'

'She's gone,' I muttered.

He whistled through his teeth. 'She's a ball breaker if ever I met one.'

'Sidney, you're very astute underneath it all.'

'She's not coming to lunch then after all?'

'I'm afraid not, and Sidney ...' I started, but my mouth misbehaved and I slurred.

'What's up, matey? You look a bit peaky,' he commented, staring in to my face as if examining something.

'I am a little drained. My sister can be exhausting.'

He smiled. 'It's all that excitement yesterday.'

'Perhaps, but do you mind if *I* skip lunch too? I need to be on my own for a while, regroup and have a siesta, you know the sort of thing.'

'No problem, all the more for me,' he grinned. 'Is it time for a couple of jars?'

'No, it is not, it's too early, even for you.'

'It's never too early for me especially in here where I know Sheila can't see me.'

'Sheila is aware of all your foibles.'

'So, what are we going to do about you and the stunner?'

'What do you mean? I replied, perplexed and awaiting more rude unwanted comments about my age and disease and her youth and beauty.

'You're a silly old sod,' he sighed, looking fondly at me.

'Thanks so much for that. I've just been told that by my ball breaker of a sister and she didn't say it as kindly as you or with as much grace.'

'I liked her,' he said.

'Who are you talking about, Bethan?'

'No, I didn't particularly like your hard faced sister. I liked Nell, you silly twat.'

I felt tears well up instantly. 'Sidney, do you mean that?'

'Of course!' he declared. 'I really liked her and I had a good time yesterday. I enjoyed myself, so did Sheila.'

'I'm glad you enjoyed yourselves.' He looked a little sheepish suddenly. I knew that look of his, it was when he regretted something he had said or done. 'Why are you looking sheepish, Sidney?'

'I'm sorry I said what I did about her ... you know.'

'You mean about her being after my money?'

'Yeah, that. It was hurtful of me.'

'You don't think she's artful?' I asked him.

He turned his nose up. 'Artful? No, I don't, not in the least. What you see is what you get with her, I reckon.'

'Sidney, thank you.'

'And she thinks the world of you.'

I could have cried. 'Bless you.'

He frowned at me. 'Who thinks she's artful?'

'My sister...'

'Nell's probably a bit too ...'

'Theatrical for her...

'Yeah, maybe, I don't know.'

'And maybe a bit too young...'

'Probably,' he said, shrugging. 'She can't see why she'd bother with you, but I can.'

I felt the tears spill over onto my cheeks, but I didn't bother to hide them in front of my old friend and he didn't comment on them.

'Can you?'

'Well, you're bloody clever for a start and although she's bright she knows she can learn quite a bit from you – like I do.'

I was scornful. 'You learn from *me*? What can I teach a wily old rascal like you? You've made more of a success of your life than I have.'

'Bollocks,' he spat out, 'you've got awards. I just built walls.'

'Awards,' I muttered, 'yes of course, those.'

'And you're kind, interesting and bloody good company. You probably make her laugh too.'

'Sidney, I don't know what to say.'

'And Sheila said ...' he started, wagging his finger.

'Go on,' I urged.

'Sheila said, when she walked in the room she could feel the electricity crackle between you. She reckoned if anyone had walked in between you they would have got electrocuted. What do you think about that then, you old rogue?'

'I'm flabbergasted,' I told him, 'but thank you. I was feeling pretty miserable before you came in, but now I've perked up considerably and if you pop in tonight when the sun has gone down, I think we'll sink a few together. What do you say?'

He grinned. 'You're on.'

He looked so delighted by my invitation it humbled me. I had always been aware of how much my friendship meant to him, but at that moment it hit me like a tidal wave how much he meant to me.

'Sidney, I want to thank you for being my friend.

He looked shocked. 'I should thank *you*.'

'Oh I don't think so.'

'No, I should,' he assured me, looking choked. 'You never turn me away; even when I'm getting on your nerves you never turn me away ...'

'You don't get on my nerves ...'

'Let me finish.'

'Sorry, go on.'

'You're the only real friend I've got, apart from Sheila, but that don't count,' he said. 'But if any of your family don't like Nell, well, quite frankly it's none of their business.'

'But Beth ...'

'Even Beth,' he declared. 'She wouldn't want you poking your nose in her life, so what's good for the goose and all that. So, fuck everybody!'

'I quite agree.'

'And especially the ball breaker!'

I laughed out loud. 'I'd love you to say that in her hearing.'

'I would,' he assured me. 'But I'll see you tonight; you look a bit tired now. Have a kip and I'll see you about ...'

'Seven,' I told him.

'Cheers, matey, see you later.'

I sat in the warm sunlight that was filtering through the tall trees in my garden and tried to relax my rigid limbs. I wanted to knock the edges off a cruel world that evening and allow the alcohol to relax those aching, stiff muscles and experience the sense of ease and calm it gave me. I smiled to myself at Sidney's kind words. He was never any different whatever the season, the occasion, the time or anything else that mattered. But lately I had been engrossed in my disease and its effects on my life and I knew at times I had been irritable with him when he hadn't deserved it. And yet he had never forsaken me and continued to be the same old Sidney: reliable, solid, endlessly chirpy and unwittingly funny. Now I had an ally in him too, someone who understood and appreciated my friendship with Nell.

I read the morning paper and made a sandwich for my lunch. I missed the sound of Beth's footsteps already and imagined her at her mother's chatting non-stop. When the phone rang later that afternoon I knew it was Nell by the way it jumped off the cradle and I grabbed hold of it quickly. My heart leapt at the sound of her voice.

'Hello, Mr Marshall, what are you doing?'

'I knew it was you, Nell. I'm doing this and that, you know, not much at all which is how I live my life now.'

'I expect you're a bit tired after yesterday, aren't you? It was a lovely party.'

'Thank you; yes I'm a little tired,' I admitted, 'but I'm taking it easy today. It's good to hear your voice.'

'Did Beth enjoy it?'

'Yes, she did, very much. It was lovely for her to see all the family, but she was disappointed none of her cousins could come. They're scattered all over the world now.'

There was a slight pause and I knew instinctively what question was coming next. 'Did she mention me?'

I hesitated. 'Yes,' I replied, slurring with nerves.

'Bethan didn't take to me,' she murmured, her voice full of unspoken regret.

'Nell, it's not a case of disliking you – she actually actively *likes* very few people, but she did describe you as beautiful and dynamic ...'

'But she can't understand why we are friends ... or rather why I am friends with you.'

'You are very astute and I can't lie to you,' I told her, 'but that was about it, yes. Please don't be upset, Nell. It says more about her than it does about you.'

'I'm not upset,' she assured me, 'it's what I expected. I would like to be friends with Beth though. Did she say anything about our friendship?'

'Well ...'

'You can tell me. Come on, no secrets.'

'I think she felt the same as Bethan: you're young, healthy and full of life, so what would you see in me, that sort of thing ...'

'I understand.'

'Nell, I don't know whether it's right to tell you this, but Beth has always imagined I would marry again. She didn't ever see me as the villain of the piece in my relationship with her mum, she always took my side and therefore she imagined I would tie the knot again at some point ...'

'Ah, that makes more sense,' she said, interrupting my flow, 'she sees me as a possible wife for you and *that* she can't understand, given our ages and everything. I get that,' she added, laughing. 'I couldn't understand why anyone would be against our friendship, but your sister and Beth ... yes, I get it now.'

'I'm sorry, it's embarrassing and I don't want you to be embarrassed.'

'I'm not embarrassed,' she declared, 'not at all, why would I be?'

'Well, the thought of someone like you marrying someone like me,' I spluttered, sounding rather pathetic. 'It's ridiculous!'

She said nothing for a moment and I longed for the ground to open up and swallow me. I wished I hadn't expressed Beth and my sister's views because said out loud, by me, they certainly did sound ridiculous.

'Mr Marshall,' she said gently, 'why on earth wouldn't anyone want to marry you? You with your fine brain, your mesmerising voice and cultured, gentlemanly ways; your kindness, dry sense of humour and mischievous eyes; your interesting conversation and gift of listening and your lack of ego, arrogance and condescension. Why is that embarrassing?'

I went to answer her, but my mouth wouldn't move and seemed to have a life of its own. Her words were comforting, kind in the extreme and perplexing because I didn't see myself like that at all, so I merely mumbled back. 'Thank you, Nell.'

'You're very welcome,' she replied, 'now, what are you doing tomorrow? Is Beth still there?'

'No, she's at her mum's for a few days and then she comes back for one night and then she'll be gone.'

'Right, we'll go walking tomorrow then; ten sharp.'

'I'll be ready, Nell.'

'And I think a bit of dancing is in order, to help your balance.'

'Fine with me...'

'And I'll tell you about my two auditions,' she added, sounding excited suddenly.

'Wonderful.'

'Bye for now.'

'Bye, Nell.'

'Oh and thank you for being so honest,' she added, and the line went dead before I could answer.

I sat back on the sofa with my head resting on a cushion and my feet up on the low coffee table. I was dazed by her description of me. I no longer saw myself as marriage material and although I knew she wouldn't ever make fun or laugh at what was on my sister's and daughter's minds, I hadn't dreamt it would provoke her to say all those lovely, thoughtful words. I closed my eyes and allowed the bright sun to shine on my face and its warmth immediately made me feel sleepy. Closing my heavy eyes and relaxing my aching muscles was a wonderful feeling and I imagined Nell's beautiful, expressive face in front of me.

I have no idea how long I slept for, but on stirring I felt the *presence* hovering somewhere in the room. I narrowed my eyes and tried to focus, but they were watery and tired. I sat up and looked around me and something touched my shoulder briefly. 'Who is it?' I asked, despite feeling rather stupid, because there didn't appear to be anyone there.

There was an unearthly silence except for the clock ticking and my breathing. Normally I was surrounded constantly by birdsong, the distant sound of lawn mowers and light traffic and Sidney singing loudly in his garden, but not at that moment. That moment was chillingly quiet. Something moved at the other end of the room, a fleeting shadow, half seen. The *presence* was extremely strong, almost touchable, but invisible.

'Is that you, Papa?' I asked, squinting towards the piano, but nobody answered and I felt immediately agitated and disappointed.

The light was fading quickly and dark clouds like distant mountains were forming in the sky. Light rain began to patter against the conservatory windows and hearing it comforted me because the silence had gone. I heard Sidney knock and I couldn't believe a couple of hours had raced by. I struggled to stand and made my way gingerly towards the other side of the room. I knocked back and poured both of us a Scotch. Seeing his cheerful face appear a few minutes later was a wonderful heart-warming sight.

'What's occurring then?' he asked, breezing in. I pointed to his whisky on the table. 'Lovely,' he added, picking it up and sipping it. 'Fuck me, Benedict, are you ill?'

'What?' I asked.

Sidney's face was one of surprised concern. 'Bloody hell, you look white as a sheet, mate. Can I get you something?'

'I don't feel white as a sheet, just a little tired. I've been asleep. I normally look pale when I've been asleep. It's just my colouring.'

'Are you sure?'

'Yes, I'm fine ... I think.'

'What do you mean, you *think*? Are you or aren't you?'

I poured some whiskey down my throat. 'This will do the trick, Sidney, don't worry.'

He was peering at me, 'If you're sure about that.'

'I'm sure.'

'Christ, you gave me a turn then. You looked as if you were going to pass out,' he remarked.

'I'm not going to pass out. I had a bit of a funny turn just before you walked in.'

'What kind of funny turn?' he asked, frowning.

'Oh, I've had them before so please don't worry, like when I've seen my father ...'

'Fucking hell,' he cried, 'don't start on about that again, it gives me the bloody creeps.

'It's the disease, but I'm going to have a few of these tonight because I deserve it.'

'Too right,' he replied. 'And I'll join you.'

I know I shouldn't have, but I did sink quite a few with Sidney that evening. We chatted more freely than we had since my diagnosis, which had been my fault not his because I had been so engrossed in my illness and symptoms and worrying about the effect it would have on my life. We settled comfortably into each other's company and, as dusk fell, we played a game or two of cards as we used to until Sheila knocked, signalling he was wanted.

'The wife,' he shrugged.

'*My* wife, Sidney, *my* wife, not *the* wife as in the table, the chair, the sideboard ...'

'Yeah, yeah, so you always say. Thanks for the English lesson, Professor.'

'Don't mention it.'

'Thanks for the Scotch too; lovely evening, mate. Good to see you relaxing and having a few.'

'You're very welcome, as always. Look, Sidney, I want to say ...'

'Benedict,' he interrupted, his eyes troubled, 'I need to tell you something.'

'Go ahead.'

He looked moved. 'It's hard to say it.'

'Sidney, just say it.'

'I was jealous you see,' he began, 'that's why I warned you off Nell. I was jealous. I saw you both when I was nosing out of the window one morning and I could tell she genuinely liked you by her manner, but I was jealous of your friendship. I thought she'd take you away from me. You were *my* friend and I thought because you had her you wouldn't need me.' His simple and strangely eloquent declaration made me admire and love him even more and I smiled at him.

'You are a silly bugger.'

'I know, but it's true.'

I stood up slowly and put out my hand and he took it. 'We are still friends, Sidney, always will be.'

'I know, I know. I'll be off then. What were you going to say?'

'I can't remember, but it was something along the lines of being sorry about being a bit morose since my diagnosis.'

He looked perplexed. 'I hadn't noticed.'

'See you tomorrow,' I said, so grateful the silly bugger was *my* friend and next door neighbour.

'Yeah and thanks again for the drink, lovely,' he repeated.

I spent the rest of the evening listening to sudden and heavy rain hammering against the roof and thinking of Nell's grey, dancing eyes. The endearing way she seemed to live in the moment and get the utmost from every experience, however fleeting, was inspiring to me. I found her an extraordinary life force that had swept into my life like the storm raging outside at that moment.

The analogy of Nell with strong, spring squalls and exciting, unpredictable March weather made me smile. She was so changeable, in her expressions, her movements, her blasts of laughter and the sudden looks of concern when I stumbled or slurred. The way she had walked boldly up to me at Beth's party, unabashed, without any hint of shyness despite knowing all eyes were on her, made my heart lurch with pride. The way she'd whispered in my ear, not caring what anyone thought, knowing full well they would all be wondering about us, was amusing and, as I had been sitting on my own then, I knew she had done it on purpose. Was that why Bethan had labelled her artful?

It occurred to me that Beth might tell her mother all about Nell and Mary would laugh when Beth told her of Nell's age and sneer and agree that she must be after my money. Mary being materialistic in the extreme herself wouldn't be able to imagine anyone liking me for myself. When we were separating she had called me all manner of names, simply to inflict as much hurt as possible and I had tried my best to dismiss them from my mind, but it hadn't been easy. After all, I was the master of introspection and complexity mixed with guilt and regret. If there had been a Nobel Prize for all of those emotions I would win it every time.

I remembered her raging at me one evening during one of our disagreements, 'You're hopeless, bloody hopeless. You haven't even the got the guts to stand up to your sister when she's having a go at you.'

'That's because she isn't having a go at me, she's simply being blunt, that's all. I'm quite used to her and I don't see the point of arguing.'

'You never stand up for *me* though,' she had spat out. 'When she gives me one of her withering looks and talks to me as if I'm a bloody fool, you don't say anything! You should stand up to her and defend me, but no, not you.'

'I have defended you in the past,' I'd replied, sighing. 'But just not in your hearing.'

She looked at me with utter contempt. 'So *you* say.'

I shook my head slightly to rid myself of the image of her face because it did me no good at all to allow my mind to wander into my past, especially the last couple of years of my marriage when it was in its death throes. It was a painful, difficult landscape to negotiate easily. So I focused on Nell, my muscles relaxed and I ended up smiling. The steady drumming of torrential rain sent me into a gentle sleep and there I stayed for the next few hours until the clock striking midnight woke me and I sensed the *presence* and heard my mother's laugh in the far distance.

Chapter 8

'Hello, Mr Marshall.'

Nell was looking up at me with her grey eyes shining like headlights on a dull day and her face radiant with health and vitality. She had a long cream scarf wound round her neck a few times and her hair pulled back in a ponytail.

'Good morning, Nell. Lovely day for it after last night's rain.'

She was grinning. 'Did you hear it? Just fancy being in a tent on a night like that.'

'I knew you'd say that.'

'It was so wild and stormy, it ignites something in me, makes me want to dash out and run with the rain lashing on my face,' she cried, looking as wild as the weather she was describing to me.

'I would join you if I could run.'

'Next time ... next time we'll run together.'

'I can't promise ...'

'We will, you wait and see.' I must have looked doubtful because she modified her words. 'Well, we can walk together in it, can't we?'

'Yes, we can,' I replied, wanting that more than anything else in the world.

'And dance,' she added, mischievously.

'Let's not go into the realms of fantasy, Nell.'

'You know you can dance. You've danced with me in the snow and in your living room.'

'After a fashion ...'

She linked her arm through mine. 'Right, come on, are you ready?'

'I'm ready and willing.'

We walked through the gate, up the steep grassy path and past the tennis courts with Nell chatting non-stop all the way, hardly pausing for breath. I listened eagerly to the news of her two imminent auditions and exactly how she would have to perform to impress the selection panel.

Rows and rows of bright daffodils were hanging their usually jaunty heads against a cruel northerly wind that was blowing harder and colder than it had in weeks and halted all hopes of early spring warmth. A quickly blackening sky was promising rain and I pulled my scarf tighter around my neck because I was feeling chilled, but Nell's blooming skin and enthusiasm made me forget my discomfort instantly. I felt almost carefree listening to her.

'Logan says I have to belt them out, like I've never done before,' she was telling me as she opened the café door. 'I have to make the hairs on the back of their necks stand up, really nail it, you know?'

I looked down at her eager face. 'You will, I know you will.'

'Do you really think so?' she asked; her usual confidence not in evidence.

I was suddenly aware of a vision of her, inside my head and somewhere else that I could not name, singing on a stage surrounded by others, under a spotlight, in front of hundreds of people. Those people were faceless, nameless, hushed and still as her voice soared to the rooftops.

'Nell,' I told her, 'I don't think so, I *know* so.' She peered at me, scrutinising my face as if she had never set eyes on it before.

'Why do you say that?'

'I don't know, I just do, believe me. It's your time, definitely your time.'

'My time,' she muttered, unsure. We sat down at our usual table.

'Listen to me. I may not have learnt much in my sixty-two years, but I know two things. The first one is that everyone has a time to shine and this may well be yours. We all have a gift and at some point in our lives we can use that gift. That is our moment, when all our struggles seem to disappear and we can fly, fulfil our destiny. It's time for you to fulfil your destiny, Nell.' With every word I uttered, her eyes appeared to grow larger and almost filled her whole face.

'There's always been a reason why I couldn't fulfil my destiny; lack of money, luck – or lack of it – relationships ... grief.' I placed my hand gently over hers.

'You can fulfil your destiny now. There is absolutely nothing to stop you.'

'I hope so,' she replied, obviously unconvinced. 'I'll really need to keep my wits about me though. There are loads of talented people out there.' She looked down at my hand and, smiling gratefully, slowly eased hers out from underneath it, 'Let me get the coffee.'

I was unused to her being pessimistic and unsure and I guessed it was for self-preservation. She obviously wanted these two parts desperately and I longed for her to be successful. I imagined her face, alight with happiness and joy when she told me she had the parts. And I would be quietly delighted and grab her hands and squeeze them in support. She sat down, placing the tray between us and I observed, 'It's unlike you not to be optimistic.'

'I want this *so* badly,' she admitted, with a small smile that didn't reach her eyes.

'I understand.'

She frowned suddenly. 'What was the other thing?'

'Sorry?'

'You said you knew two things for sure, what was the other one?'

What could I say? What could I tell her? If I'd spoken at all, my slurring, unstable voice would have betrayed my emotions. I longed to explain how she had enriched my life beyond my wildest imagination and that her vibrant, dynamic personality had quite literally swept me off my unsteady feet. I wanted to describe to her what her friendship had meant to me in these few weeks. That she had transformed every part of my life and that I would now be lost without her. I wanted to explode with unspoken love and longing for her and beg her to stay by my side for the rest of my days, but I could never do that. It wouldn't have been fair. If I had been younger, full of strength and vitality and with all my former faculties I would have said, 'Nell, the only other thing I know in life is that I love you with all my heart and will for the rest of my life. I want to surround you with that love, hold you, comfort you, look after you and support you through your disappointments and in every other aspect of your life.' But in the end I simply hoped my eyes conveyed some of that truth and shrugged my shoulders with a faint smile.

'Say something then,' she urged.

'The other thing I know is ... I know I am an inadequate man who has made so many mistakes ...'

But she waved her hand dismissively. 'Don't start all that, I won't listen. You are *not* an inadequate man! You're a deep - thinking, analytical man, which is why you keep harping on about your mistakes. Well,' she sighed, looking into my eyes, 'I thought you might say something about our friendship, to be honest. Because this is what I know for sure: our friendship is something unique and wonderful, something I cherish and always will. I don't really understand our connection, I just know it exists and I'm so thankful for it, it makes me want to sing and dance and shout out loud. I feel incredibly grateful to know you and lucky ... lucky that you're my friend.'

And there it was – her bravery in declaring her feelings and my weakness in not declaring mine was so typical of her and me, it made my heart sink with embarrassment. Even Sidney was a braver man than I, admitting his jealousy over Nell.

There was a moment of intense intimacy between us that you could almost grab hold of. It was there, in a bright colour in front of my eyes, shining and dazzling.

'Nell,' I started, but my mouth wouldn't form the words. 'Sorry ... I can't ...'

'Just nod if you feel the same,' she said. I nodded emphatically and her eyes softened. 'Thank you.'

'Nothing to thank me for, dear girl,' I eventually managed to splutter.

'Oh there is. I just wish your daughter and sister understood. I know you would love Beth to approve.'

I found my voice at last. 'Of course, but if she doesn't it won't change anything.'

She nodded knowingly. 'A friendship like ours is quite hard to understand. I mean, on the face of it what have we got in common? But we don't need to understand it; we can just allow it to evolve. I find you fascinating and you make me laugh. Others need to make sense of it, don't they?'

'Obviously,' I said, 'and thanks for the fascinating bit.'

'You're welcome.' She then appeared a little melancholy. 'You'd think they'd be happy for you.'

'It's just human nature. And human nature is often beyond me.'

She frowned suddenly. 'You weren't cross with Beth, were you? I can't imagine you ever being cross with her.'

'No, a little disappointed perhaps,' I replied. 'I think she may be a little jealous if I'm absolutely honest, but I don't like to admit that even to myself. I've been somewhat worried because she appears to have changed since being in New York. Nobody else would notice, except me.'

'In what way?' she asked me, eager to hear.

'She's a tiny bit ... oh, I don't know ... harder. It's barely perceptible, but enough for her old Dad to notice the subtle change.'

'It's probably the job. Acting can do that for you too; especially musical theatre.'

'That's what she said.'

'Don't be disappointed in her, Mr Marshall' she urged, kindness personified as usual. 'She's wary because she loves you...that's all.'

'Yes, of course, but Nell, they both seem to be of the mistaken opinion that you couldn't possibly like me for myself, with this ageing, infirm body, but that you must be after my money. Ridiculous I know.'

She blanched visibly and I immediately regretted the awful, stupid, despicable words escaping from my frayed mouth. Her shining, ever-dancing eyes changed from being full of life to sorrowful in an instant. Silence hung between us like a dirty, faded veil and she swallowed hard twice. The atmosphere had changed in a split second.

'Beth thinks that?' she mumbled.

'Well ...'

'And does your sister?'

'Well, she's always ...'

'Do you think it too?' she added, her voice croaking with emotion.

I took a deep breath. 'No! I absolutely don't.'

'Then why are you repeating it?' she asked, in a way that indicated hurt rather than anger.

I struggled to conjure up a response from a mind that was well past its sell-by date but, unsurprisingly, I drew a blank. 'I don't know, I just wanted to explain ... I wanted to excuse Beth's obvious lack of warmth because she isn't usually like that. My sister often is, but not Beth, not normally.' Her eyes widened.

'Did you *ever* think it?'

My heart began to pound in my temples. 'No ... never ...'

Her face had begun to crumple like a scrunched-up paper bag. 'Does Sidney think the same?'

I stuttered, falling over the words. 'No, he doesn't think that, not now.'

'What does that mean?'

'Not now he's met you ...'

'But he did *before*?' she gasped, her hands flying to her mouth.

I tried to make light of it. 'He couldn't understand how someone like you could be friends with someone like me? He knows me very well don't forget and given my age, my illness and all my faults and you with your vibrancy and zest for life.' Her eyes swam with sudden tears and I clutched at her hand over the table. 'Nell, I'm such an idiot, I shouldn't have mentioned any of this. Please, please don't be upset.' She withdrew her hand slowly.

'No, I'm glad you did. Honesty is the best policy, always.'

'Not always,' I muttered, staring at her hand.

'How could they think such a thing though? I mean, I can understand why they wonder about the nature of our friendship. I can also understand them being wary on your behalf because of our ages, but...' Her eyes were darting from my face to her hands and she appeared extremely uncomfortable. 'To think I'd be after your *money*. It never occurred to me...no wonder Beth is worried. My God, she must think I'm going to make you fall in love with me, reel you in, get you to the altar and...'

'Bump me off,' I added, desperate to inject some humour into the conversation. But as usual, I said the wrong thing and the colour appeared to drain from her face right in front of my eyes. 'Look, as you just said, people don't understand friendship like ours.'

'Neither do I,' she mumbled. 'It just happens.'

'Can we forget I said anything?' I implored her, my voice betraying how I longed to wind the clock back to the intimate moment between us when she declared what our friendship meant to her.

She didn't reply, but appeared deep in thought and those thoughts were troubled. A strong blast of wind rattled the café doors and I expected her to smile that beautiful smile, look excited and comment on it as she usually did, but she didn't appear to even hear it. My heart by now was thumping hard and jumping about in my chest and I was appalled at my stupidity and her obvious discomfort.

'Nell, forgive my ... I shouldn't have said anything, I didn't think ...' She didn't look at me, but merely shook her head slowly in disbelief and went to stand up.

'Look, I have to go, the auditions, you know.'

I tried to speak, but slurred badly. 'Don't go ...'

'I have to,' she replied. 'I can't sit here any longer when I know the two people closest to you think like that about us. I'm *so* embarrassed that I came to your party and they were sitting there imagining all sorts about me. I burst into your lounge like an over-excited puppy, so eager to meet everyone, now I feel ... *mortified*.'

I felt desperate and sweat was trickling down my face. I wiped it away and ran my hand across my mouth, just in case I was dribbling.

'Don't, Nell! Please, stay ...'

'Can you walk back on your own?' she asked, a huge tear rolling out of her eye.

'You're crying ...'

'Yes,' she said, still avoiding my eyes, 'I'm crying.'

'Nell ...'

She leant over the table and kissed my cheek softly. 'I'm not angry with you,' she whispered. 'Wish me luck at the auditions, Mr Marshall. I really need it.'

I struggled to my feet as she rushed out of the café and away from me leaving me gasping for my breath.

'Nell ...' I slurred, 'Nell ... Nell ... Nell ...'

&

The punishing wind blasted into my face as I ran down the slope and away from him. Tears stung behind my eyes and my face was burning with indignation and embarrassment. Was that how I had come across to them? I thought about how I had rushed confidently in behind his stony-faced sister, so sure of his reception and looking forward to seeing the expression of pride on his face as he introduced me to everyone. There had been warm smiles, handshakes, short introductions, small talk, the usual at a party, but I was sure I had made a good impression, until I faced Beth and her unbending aunt. Their cool indifference had been obvious, but with his unspoken support and mischievous eyes following me around the room I had felt above and beyond their hostility. It hadn't touched me because I knew I had his unswerving loyalty and friendship. What had they said about me that had forced him to admit they doubted my sincerity? And had *he* ever doubted me? Were their words merely a thinly disguised version of his thoughts? I had played the room; I knew that, as if playing a part on stage, but only because I wanted to make a lasting impression. Acting that way was in my blood and I often did it if I was uncertain of how a situation would play out. All actors did that. Had I come across as insincere? If I had then I wasn't as good an actress as I thought because one or both of them had rumbled me.

I had run all the way to the river's edge and I felt breathless and uncomfortable. Tears had streamed down my face and into my mouth. I had left him sitting there ashen-faced and trembling and I knew he would stumble home and berate himself for admitting the two people closest to him had serious doubts about my honesty. But a tiny voice inside my head began to nag at me. Had Frankie been right all along? Was it possible that his wealth, his magnificent house that I had always envied from afar and his cultured manners, all part of his appeal? Would I have continued the friendship had he been an out-of-work English teacher who lived in a semi-detached or terraced house nearby and spoke like I did? Had they picked up on how impressed I was by his beautiful, historic and unusual house? Had he told them all, before I arrived, how I had always longed to see inside it and meet its owner since I was a child? Did they notice my thinly disguised, almost reverential adoration for the way he spoke? Could they tell I was in awe of him and everything about him? Did that awe and adoration come across as materialistic in any way instead of being almost like hero worship? If it had, I had let him down and if I was, I had let him down even more.

'Mr Marshall,' I whispered into my hands, 'I'm so, *so* sorry.'

&

I had stayed in the café for what seemed like an age, frozen with shock at my stupidity and her reaction. Rain began to lash at the windows and the scene outside simply mirrored my feelings: desolate and miserable. The bony branches of the huge horse chestnut trees were swaying violently as if clutching ruthlessly at the wind and I could stand my sense of loneliness no longer. Sitting there without her smiling face looking across at me was unbearably poignant and I staggered to my feet and left.

The wind was gusting so badly I had to steady myself a couple of times and stand completely still. The old, wide-bottomed oaks appeared malevolent suddenly as if they were spreading their arms and drawing me in, creaking and moving slowly towards me. Their branches were stark against the sky, as if drawn with charcoal on cream paper. The rain beat down and swept across the city as I stumbled down the steep slope towards the gate near my house. At one point I lost my balance and slipped, my legs crumbling beneath me. Ending up flat on my back I swore vociferously and loudly and I knew I must have looked pathetic and ungainly. Luckily there was nobody to laugh at me, but unluckily nobody to help me to my feet either. I put all my weight on my right hand and managed to get to my knees. The grass was slippery and wet and I knelt for a few moments as if praying for deliverance, eventually staggering to my feet. Once inside my house I shed my coat and scarf and slumped on the sofa with the wet patches on my trousers soaking through to my skin and chilling me, but I felt too exhausted to climb the stairs and change them.

I was still dumbfounded at how quickly the atmosphere between us had changed. One minute the gentle intimacy had been almost touchable, the next the tension had crackled like a fire. I knew she had an emotional, dramatic personality, but the swift change had been quite astounding. My words must have hurt her so deeply.

'You bloody fool, Benedict,' I yelled out loud to the ceiling, 'you stupid, ignorant, despicable fool.'

Why on earth had I voiced my sister's opinions when I doubted them so much? Was it a subconscious desire to hear Nell proclaim them rubbish and untrue and hurtful in the extreme? How could I have possibly let her know about Beth's worries? Why hadn't I kept my mouth firmly closed instead of being blunt and rude? Wasn't that just what I had accused my sister of? Our father had instilled in us all consideration and courtesy at all times for others, even in the face of adversity or provocation. William, Sarah and I had lived by his words, but Bethan had always been a law unto herself and her profession had compounded her hard nature.

I made myself some hot coffee because the rain was beginning to seep into my bones and I sat in Nell's favourite chair listening to the wind gush through the trees in my garden. It sounded like the swelling ocean crashing over rocks, but every sound reminded me of her and how she loved nature's voice in all its forms and that thought caused me physical pain somewhere in my chest and lower down in my gut. I repeatedly put my head in my hands in despair and at one point the ticking of the clock seemed so loud and jarring I stuffed my fingers hard in my ears. Each interminable moment passing reminded me that I had hurt Nell and she was somewhere feeling that hurt and indignation. Why couldn't I simply have said nothing? Mary had always accused me of never knowing when to keep my mouth shut and letting a moment pass without a clever comment. Why couldn't I simply have put Beth and my sister's concerns to the back of my mind and trusted her? Did I mistrust her? Subconsciously did I think the same? Was I fooling myself by believing that this lovely, caring, lively, talented young woman, who breathed life and laughter into everything she touched, really wanted to spend time with me?

I sank deeper into Nell's chair and clearly heard my sister berating me for being a fool. Finally summoning the strength to push myself out of the chair, I went to my bureau and sifted through a few papers to find where Nell had scrawled her mobile number in a hurry one day when I asked for it. I rummaged through all the pieces of scrap paper because I knew it was there somewhere, but it wasn't evident and I ended up throwing the paper on the floor in a desperate, impatient fury.

The day dragged on endlessly, the rain becoming heavier by the hour. I ate no lunch because I didn't have any appetite and at one point I actually kicked the sofa hard which was an inane and nonsensical thing to do because it hurt and didn't even relieve my feelings of rage. And rage was exactly what I did for the whole of that day. Rage against myself and my past. Rage against my stupidity and thoughtlessness. Rage against my foolishness. Rage against my disease. Rage against my guilt. Eventually I sat down and the heavy beating of the rain sent me into a light doze, but my twitching legs and the tremors in my hands woke me soon after. Immediately I felt the *presence* very near me, almost by my shoulder and in the near distance my mother's voice.

'Benedict, cheer up, there's no real harm done,' she was saying.

'But I shouldn't have done it, Mother,' I replied.

'I know, but you're sorry for it and that's the main thing. I know you didn't mean any harm; it's just you being you. Now forget about it and cheer up.'

'I'm trying, but I feel so guilty.'

'You do guilt so well,' she said. 'Life is for living, not for feeling guilty. It all goes by so quickly, believe me. Let her go and she'll come back to you.'

'Let who go? I don't understand. I let Beth go gladly, with a few reservations. I'm sorry. I'm so sorry. Forgive me,' I muttered and for some reason I repeated those words over and over again until my mouth felt stiff and wouldn't move. 'Forgive me. Forgive me. Forgive me. I'm not the man Papa was.'

'I do forgive you,' my mother said. 'I always forgive you because I'm your mother and *she* will forgive you.'

The phone started ringing and, still feeling confused, I rushed across to answer it, 'Nell?'

'It's me, Dad,' Beth said, sounding irritated. 'Not Nell.'

'Sorry, darling, forgive me.'

'What's wrong? You sound weird. Have you taken your tablets?'

'Yes, of course and I'm fine. I was dozing and couldn't work out where I was for a moment.'

'Are you sure?'

'I'm sure.'

'Look, I'm staying at Mum's an extra day, so I'll see you the day after tomorrow.'

'That's fine,' I told her, my heart thumping and sweat breaking out on my top lip. I was beginning to feel light headed and unwell, but I was trying to keep my voice as light as possible.

'It means we'll only have one day before I go back, but Mum has arranged a theatre trip for us both and I want to go.'

'Wonderful,' I slurred. 'Have a lovely time the both of you.'

'Thanks, Dad,' she said, her voice softer at last.

'Beth,' I started, 'did you tell your mother about my illness? I mean, if you have I don't mind.'

'No, I haven't, I wouldn't. I didn't think you'd want me to.'

'Thank you, darling. See you soon.'

My disappointment at it not being Nell made me feel immediately guilty and I was about to call Beth back and apologise, but I had no desire to speak to Mary in my current mood; she would have noticed the difference in my voice straight away and questioned me until I caved in and told her all the details. I tried again to find Nell's number, but it was nowhere to be seen and I sank into the sofa in despair. The light was fading quickly because of the dark storm clouds and I tried desperately to cheer myself by thinking that Nell would want to tell me in minute detail about her two auditions. That would break the spell of our unfortunate, ludicrous misunderstanding and we would be back on track immediately. Yes, I would wait to hear from her about how it all panned out and whether she had secured one or both parts. Then I would be able to convey to her my delight and happiness at her success and this hiatus would all be forgotten in our mutual joy.

Sidney knocking on the wall made me jump and I didn't have the energy to leave the sofa and knock back so I leant forward, picked up two apples from the fruit bowl and threw them both with great force at the wall. It worked because his cheerful, flushed face appeared a few minutes later.

'Afternoon, Benedict. What ho! And all that posh talk you use,' he cried.

'Sidney, I have never used "posh talk" like that in my life, as well you know,' I replied, 'especially that expression!'

'Your knocks sounded a bit odd,' Sidney went on, already bored with the 'posh talk'.

'That's because I threw those apples at the wall.'

'That's exactly what it sounded like. So, what's occurring then?'

'As always, nothing much, Sidney, as you can see.'

'You look a bit odd, matey,' he said, peering closely at my face over his glasses, 'if you don't mind me saying.'

'You always look odd, but do I comment on it? Actually I *feel* a bit odd. No, I'll rephrase that ... I *am* a bit odd.'

'What's up then?'

'I hear voices, I see things, I feel this *presence* hovering by me ... as if I'm never alone, you name it, I have experienced it.'

'Fuck me backwards,' he declared.

'That is so eloquent as usual.'

'Not your old Pa by the piano again?'

'Not this time.'

'Thank God for that.'

'It was my mother this time.'

'Jesus Christ ...'

'No, it wasn't Jesus Christ, it was my *mother!* There's a big difference.'

He looked perplexed. 'What did she say?'

'What she always used to say, that I should be cheerful, stop feeling guilty about everything, live my life, all the usual.'

'I think you should see the quack again,' he remarked. 'Anyway, enough of your nutty problems, fancy a game of cards? Or a trip to the pub with me for a change?' he added, looking hopeful. 'We haven't been to the pub for ages, mate.'

'If there's a quiz on I refuse to stand next to you while you expect me to know the answer to every single question.'

He looked bemused. 'But you do know the answer to every question, so why shouldn't I expect you to?'

'I really don't...'

'I remember you knowing the answer to one about Shakespeare once. Everyone stared at you in wonder. I was so proud.'

'Thank you, Sidney, but I was an English teacher.'

'The bloke behind the bar said he wasn't surprised you knew the answer because you *spoke* like bloody Shakespeare.'

'I most certainly do not!'

'You bloody well do. I should know, I talk to you every day.'

'You jest, my liege,' I said, with a straight face. 'What news on the Rialto?'

'I rest my case.'

'Sidney, I'm not sure I feel up to it.'

'What, a quiz?'

'Yes – no – I mean just going to the pub.'

'Fine, fine,' he jumped in, 'no problem, we'll sink a few in here instead.'

Suddenly the thought of sitting on my sofa staring at the ceiling or hearing voices or feeling the *presence* all evening made me shudder. I needed distraction; something different to take my mind off Nell crying and a pub full of laughing people was probably just the thing.

'No, you're right,' I told him, 'we haven't been out in ages, so let's do it!' His dear, flushed face lighting up made me feel humbled.

'Do you mean it?'

'I do, but no quiz.'

'Cheers, matey,' I'll be back about half six, shall I?'

'Lovely.'

'I feel the need for a few beers coming on,' he cried, patting his large stomach.

'Don't drink too many, Sidney, because I'm unable to help you home these days and that stomach of yours is fast resembling the Alps.'

'We can't all be as thin as you. It makes me sick. You eat what you like, drink what you like and still look like a bean pole.'

'That's so kind of you.'

'Why can't you be like normal people who get fat?'

'It's probably because I'm unique.'

'I know that.'

'And so are you, which is why we get on despite our differences.'

'I'll give you the knock and meet you out the front,' he said, ignoring my comment and hurrying out to no doubt eat the dinner that would be put in front of him by the redoubtable Sheila.

I made a last-ditch attempt to find Nell's number to no avail, swearing to myself for not putting it somewhere safe, and then climbed the stairs for a hot shower. Getting drenched on my lonely walk back from the park had done me no good at all and I felt shivery and chilled. Standing under the silky water and glancing down at my unbelievably thin legs I swore once more because I couldn't imagine ever again showing them to a woman. Sidney was right, I was impossibly thin.

I changed into the dark grey suit I normally wore when out in public, but chose a dark blue shirt instead of my usual light blue because it had been the shirt I had been wearing the day I first set eyes on Nell. Sidney and I walked purposefully, if not a little slowly, to the Trafalgar and all the way there he was chatty, full of beans, like an excited eight-year-old child on a day's outing. I felt terrible because I knew I was being monosyllabic and distracted because of Nell.

The heavy storm had cleared and a soft rain was falling. It made me think of summer rain and soggy family holidays by the seaside. The sky across the river was a threatening marble-grey and Nell would have commented on it, lifting her face up in delight. She may even have danced or splashed in the puddles because she could and I would have watched, adoringly.

The lounge bar smelt of stale beer and frying steak and I immediately felt hungry because I had eaten hardly anything all day. It was busy and noisy and lifted my spirits a little. It was better than sitting alone with my random thoughts and waiting for bedtime like an old pensioner.

'Bitter, mate?' Sidney asked, 'or maybe a whisky?'

'Beer for a change I think. Let me ...'

He already had his hand in his pocket. 'No, I'll get the first one. Two pints of bitter, love,' he told the young barmaid who had a stud in her nose, the idea of which always made me wince slightly.

'Shall we stay here or do you want to sit by the window?' I asked, longing to sit down.

'We can sit if you like,' he shrugged. 'I'll bag those two seats. Shall I carry the drinks or can you manage them?'

'I think so ... I hope so.'

Sidney looked concerned. 'I'll carry them if you like.'

'No, let me ... I should ... I need to.' I made my way to the bar.

'Here you go, sir,' the barmaid said, winking at me. 'How you been? Not seen you lately?'

'I'm fine, thank you. No, I haven't been in for a few months,' I told her vaguely, not wanting to give too much away. Her eyes quickly scanned my whole body.

'Have you lost weight?'

'My God, I hope not.'

She laughed and shook her hair playfully. 'You're the only person who says that! Good to see you.'

'And you,' I replied. I slopped the beer a little as I carried it over to where Sidney was sitting, but most of it stayed in the jugs. He had a suitably smug grin on his flushed face. 'What's that face for, Sidney?'

'Oh yeah ...'

'What on earth are you sneering at?'

'I don't know how you do it, I really don't.'

'Well, I *don't* do it – whatever it is to which you're referring.'

'Flirting, that's what I'm referring to.'

'I was not *flirting*,' I declared.

'I wasn't talking about you, you twat ... her! She was flirting with you, you silly bugger. Fuck me, I don't know what you've got, but I wish I'd had a bit of it when I was younger, I really do.'

'She wasn't flirting, she was simply doing her job and being nice to a customer,' I replied indignantly. 'For some reason you think every woman this side of the Thames wants to sleep with me and I assure you they don't because these days it's more a case of feeling sorry for me like they would their old grandfather.'

'She had a twinkle in her eye, I'm telling you,' he warned.

I leant towards him. 'Well, if she did fancy me in any way shape or form, which I seriously doubt, she would be barking up the wrong tree. I have no urges, no desires, no hormones racing around my limp body ... in fact *everything* is limp and will be staying that way forever and ever, amen.'

'Fuck me,' Sidney said, his face resembling a bloodhound's.

'Or not, as the case may be and, in my case, most definitely not...'

'And on that note,' Sidney interrupted, 'how's the firecracker? I saw you go out walking yesterday, but you came back on your own, which is unusual,' he said, gulping at his beer as if he hadn't drunk any for years.

I shook my head. 'Ah, was your nose against the window again, Sidney? You'll turn to stone standing there for hours. Get a life man!'

'My life is finding out what you're doing with yours! And I don't stand there for hours because she normally turns up at roughly the same time,' he said, succinctly. 'And when you're retired there's nothing much else to do except nose at what your neighbours are up to.'

'But as you well know, this neighbour is up to precisely nothing.'

He scoffed. 'I wouldn't say that.'

'I assure you ...'

'So, why did you come back on your own?'

I went to answer, but my voice slurred with emotion and I felt some saliva trickle down my chin. 'Fuck it,' I mumbled, reaching for my handkerchief, but because I had changed suits it was nowhere to be found.

Sidney put his hand in his pocket and produced a tissue and handed it over.

'Here you go.'

'Thank you,' I muttered, hoping nobody had seen. 'You see, Sidney, the barmaid wouldn't find that very attractive, would she?'

'I suppose not,' he replied and his eyes looked full of sorrow at my predicament. 'You've done it,' he added, referring to the saliva, 'it's all gone.'

I smiled at him, gratefully. 'Thanks very much.' His eyes were playful suddenly and I knew something was brewing.

'This will make you laugh ...'

'Go on,' I urged, 'I need cheering up.'

'Imagine ... no, I shouldn't, sorry.'

'Being in bed with a young woman like her and suddenly dribbling?' I asked. 'Don't think that hadn't crossed my mind, but as I have no intention of inflicting this revolting, disease-ridden body on anyone ever again, it's all hypothetical.'

'Well, we're both getting past a bit of how's your father now anyway,' he declared. 'The old body starts to creak and groan and it all looks faintly ridiculous if you ask me.'

'I agree and "a bit of how's your father" is a most interesting, but inexplicable expression. What exactly has it got to do with anyone's father?'

'Don't ask me, you're the one with all the brains. So, where was she then?'

I sighed. 'What are we discussing now?'

'You know what we're discussing: Nell.'

The mention of her name made my stomach sink to my knees and I had no way of hiding my feelings from Sidney because he knew me too well. 'What's happened, Benedict? Come on, tell me.'

I glanced out of the window which looked directly out over the Thames. It's deep, greyish-brown water was lapping against the old barges moored beneath us and I could hear the faint sound of chains chinking and the wooden hulls of the boats knocking together. Lights were twinkling across the river on the Isle of Dogs in the new apartments and I remembered looking at them on the day of my diagnosis and feeling such a crushing sense of loneliness and isolation, it had been almost too much to bear. But that had been before I knew Nell existed somewhere in the world and luckily, that somewhere happened to be in the same area as me and since then I had not experienced that desolation again ... until that awful moment in the café.

'Benedict,' Sidney said, clicking his fingers in front of my face. 'For fuck's sake, tell me what's happened. You look bloody awful.'

'I don't know what happened ...'

'You must know.'

'Well, yes I do know. I upset her.' He looked bemused, as well he might.

'You upset her? How the fuck did you do that? You adore her. Oh Christ, you didn't make a ridiculous pass at her, did you?'

I looked suitably indignant. 'I most certainly did not! You know me better than that.'

'You would have done, a few years back.'

'I'm not that man now. That was the old Benedict. I wouldn't do that to her in case it upset her.'

He appeared confused. 'But you just admitted you upset her.'

I took a deep breath and blurted it all out. 'I told her that Beth and my sister thought she must be after my money.' He put his head in his hands. 'I know, Sydney, I know...'

'What a stupid thing to do,' Sidney cried, interrupting my protestations, 'I mean, even *I* know that was a stupid thing to do.'

'Quite. And thanks for pointing that out.'

He looked perplexed. 'Why on earth did you do that?'

'It was simply honesty; wanting to be upfront with her as she is with me. I don't know, Sidney, it just kind of came out. She was aware that my sister didn't take to her and she asked me what Beth had said after meeting her at the party and I skirted round the issue and then it just came out. I suppose, thinking back, I was trying to excuse Beth's obvious indifference, but it all came out wrong and she was so upset and embarrassed she got up and left the café.'

'Blimey,' he whispered. 'Didn't you try to stop her?'

'Stop her with these legs? I just about managed to stagger home afterwards, I was reeling. She cried, Sidney, she actually cried. How do you think that makes me feel? I was in such as state on the way home I slipped on the wet grass and went flying, ended up flat on my back. For a few seconds I didn't think I was going to be able to get up. I can't believe I told her what they said. I can't believe it. Although I have to say I'm rather flummoxed she took it so badly.'

'Ring her and apologise,' he suggested cheerily, as if it was all so simple.

'I would if I could find her number. She scribbled it down one day in

214

a hurry and do you think I can find it? But what would I say?'

'I don't know,' he almost screeched.

'Well, thanks for that great advice!' I snapped before throwing him an apologetic look, 'After all, I can't take back what I said about their opinion of her because it's been said.'

'Your bloody ball-breaker of a sister is a pain,' he declared.

'I know,' I agreed, 'but she just cares about me and she knows I've made such a cock up of my relationships with women she doesn't trust me to make any sensible decisions as far as matters of the heart are concerned, especially now. And she always goes with her instincts on people.'

'I'm sure that helps in her job, but nobody is always right. She must make mistakes sometimes.'

'She says she doesn't.'

'She's wrong about Nell,' he added.

I wanted to lean forward and hug him. 'Thank you.'

We both sipped our beer in silence for a few moments and the bar was filling up rapidly. Groups of people were crowding in and surrounding us, all talking and laughing loudly. Their happy, smiling and animated faces seemed to compound my sense of despair at my stupidity.

'Oh, Christ,' I muttered, putting my head in my hands.

'What you going to do then?' Sidney asked, reaching in his pocket for some money.

'Bleed,' I replied.

'Talk normally,' he sighed, rolling his eyes heavenward.

'My ex-wife used to say that.'

'What are you *really* going to do?'

'Wait for her to call or come round. Hope that she does.'

'Don't you know where she lives?'

'Somewhere in east Greenwich, that's all I know.'

'What do you two talk about? You don't even know where she lives.'

'We talk about everything,' I said, forlornly.

'I bet you talk about daft stuff and nonsense knowing you; academic stuff.'

'Yes, knowing me. But she's incredibly bright and holds her own with me.'

He laughed loudly. 'Not like me then.'

'Sidney, I love your company as you well know.'

He held up his empty glass, 'I'll get another round.'

'I shouldn't ...'

'Shut up. You need it.'

'I always need it.'

Sidney pushed his way to the bar and I gazed out of the window where a few hardy people were sitting outside in the fresh evening air blowing up from the river. I had often imagined Nell and me sitting there one balmy evening in summer drinking a cool glass of white wine, chatting continually, laughing together, having fun as we normally did; but the thought of it now caused my heart to flutter wildly with anxiety because I realised that might never happen because of my thoughtlessness. The noisy laughter from a group beside me suddenly caused my nerves to jangle and my tremors became unbearably noticeable. I felt my mouth and the muscles in my face stiffen as Sidney placed a pint of bitter in front of me.

'All right, mate?' he asked, looking straight at me.

'Sidney, don't make a big thing of it, but am I dribbling?' His eyes earnestly scanned my face.

'No, you're not.'

'Thank God for that.'

'Your face looks a bit stiff, that's all.'

I allowed myself a little smile; well it felt like a smile, but I'm not sure anything actually moved. 'I can't help thinking about how my mother would tell us off if we pulled faces and say the wind would change and we'd stay like that. It's come true in my case.'

'You're not that bad.'

'Do I actually have any expressions left? Or does my face stay the same all the time?'

'What the fuck you on about?' he said. 'You look exactly the same as you always did – pig ugly.'

Dear old Sidney, always truthful, always constant, faithful and funny, sometimes unwittingly so. 'You're so kind. A minute ago you were telling me how you didn't understand how any woman could still be attracted to me and now I'm pig ugly to boot.'

'It's not that you're good looking,' he frowned, 'I've never thought that. It's just something you've got that most men haven't, especially me. I was bloody lucky the wife took me on, I can tell you.'

'Stop calling Sheila the wife? It's *my* wife, *my* wife, Sidney. Stop referring to her like the furniture.'

'Yeah, okay Prof!' He smiled tolerantly before asking again, 'So, what you going to do about Nell? You have to do something, you know that.'

'All I can do is try to find her phone number. Without that I can do nothing until she turns up on my doorstep with her beautiful smile.'

'Drink up,' he suddenly said, 'I'll help you look for it. I can't stand looking at your Bambi-like eyes for much longer, I really can't.'

'Sidney, what would I do without you?'

'No idea.'

We downed our beers and hastily made our way back to my house. We got caught in a sudden spring downpour that caught us unawares with huge raindrops bouncing off the pavements and trickling down the back of my neck. Its coolness actually refreshed me after the heat of the lounge bar and again I thought of Nell and how she would have lifted her face to the sky. Once inside I put the kettle on.

'Look through all those papers on my bureau,' I called to Sidney, 'I know it's there somewhere.'

'Everyone says that. I say that about my car keys, "I put them there on the table, I know I did," then Sheila finds them in my coat pocket.'

'Well, if it's not there I have no idea where it is and I must have thrown it away.'

'I'm looking now,' he called back. 'Fuck me, what a load of toot on here. You need to tidy up, Benedict.'

'I'm quite aware of that, Sidney. I don't need you to tell me. She wrote it in black pen at the top of a page ...'

'What was on the page?'

'I can't remember.'

He was rummaging around frantically. 'Well, that's no bloody good.'

'I'm well aware of that too.'

'Is that the Parkinson's?

'Is what the Parkinson's?'

'Not remembering things.'

'I hope to God not! I think I've always been a bit of a dreamer.'

'I'd have thought you would have put it somewhere safe,' he scolded, still rummaging.

'I thought I had.'

'Well, it's not here you bloody idiot. Have you looked in the wastepaper bin?'

'I have to say I haven't.'

He sighed. 'Does that mean *no*?'

'Yes it means no, if you see what I mean.'

He wiped his forehead. 'You talk as if you're in one of your flipping plays, but you lose an important phone number. Academics are always pretty useless in real life. I mean you couldn't tile your back passage, could you, matey?'

'I agree!'

I watched as he continued to look everywhere, including through all my scraps of paper in the bins and as he did so I was overcome with a sudden swell of emotion and profound gratitude again at having him as my friend. He cared about me and my sorrow and my dribbling and shaking almost as much as I did and his flushed, anxious face was as dear to me as a member of my close family. I took him for granted, I knew that and I had always been aware how much I meant to him and often that irritated me because he needed me so badly. My shame at that admission compounded my guilt and regrets and I needed to explain my feelings to him before I sunk under their weight.

'Sidney, come and sit down, you look a bit red in the face.'

'Probably my blood pressure,' he answered, laughing.

'No, really, come and sit down. You shouldn't be worrying about me and my lost piece of paper ...'

'But, Benedict,' he declared, looking straight at me, 'it means the world to you. *She* means the world to you.'

'Then *I* have to put it right,' I replied. 'And, I feel strongly that if our friendship means as much to her as it does to me and I believe it does, that she'll get in touch when she feels less bruised.'

He sat opposite me, perspiring a little. 'I suppose you're right.'

'I am right, now relax and I'll make us a coffee.'

'Put a dash of brandy in it,' he suggested. 'Have one yourself, you need it.'

'You are a terrible influence on me, Sidney Walpole. I would behave like a saint if it weren't for you,' I called from the kitchen. 'Are you aware of that?'

'You, behaving like a saint? Don't make me laugh. When is Beth back?'

I took our coffee in, hideously aware of my tremors. 'My blessed hands, I wish I could keep them still.'

'The tablets will help, won't they?'

'You are ever the optimist, Sidney.'

'Shouldn't they be kicking in by now?'

'They have kicked in, I believe, but there's only so much they can do. I try not to think about any of it if I can help it. Beth is here tomorrow and we'll probably have dinner somewhere and hopefully some quality time and then she's back off to New York.'

'Flying visit then,' he commented.

'I'm afraid so.'

He sat back in his chair. 'You must miss her.'

'More than I can say.'

Sidney appeared wistful suddenly. 'I wish I'd had a daughter.'

'You have three wonderful sons; all of whom thankfully take after Sheila, I hasten to add.'

'I know, I know, but every man should have a daughter. Don't get me wrong, I know my boys love me, but a daughter shows it more. None of mine would dream of hugging me. They hug their mother, but not me and I'd like a hug sometimes, you know?'

'I'll give you a hug if you like.'

'Fuck off! No, I'd like the boys to be a bit more ...'

'Demonstrative?'

'Yeah, that's the right word.'

'I know, but you have a lovely wife who dotes on you and worships the ground you walk on, so ...'

'I know; I should shut up, but I was just saying, that's all. When Kevin was born I was desperate for him to be a girl, knowing Sheila didn't want any more and having two boys already, it was my last chance, but it wasn't to be.'

He looked thoughtful for a moment and stared at the carpet and I realised I rarely asked him about *his* regrets in life, *his* moments of shame or guilt, *his* secret longings; I only ever spoke about my own.

'I didn't know you felt like that. But that's because I've never asked you. I'm sorry I never asked you; I should have.'

His face broke into a grin. 'Don't be daft, why should you have asked me? Blokes don't share stuff like that normally.'

'But we aren't blokes,' I remarked.

'Well, you aren't, that's for sure. But I reckon I am.'

'What am I then?'

'Clever,' he declared, 'dead clever!'

I sighed deeply. 'What use is that? I mean *really* what use is that?'

'You know so many things,' he insisted. 'Of course it's useful. Benedict, I'd give my right arm for your education, your brain, you know that.'

'Why do we have to end up talking about my wretched education? If you were me you'd have to have my shakes, my stumbling, my dribbling ...'

'I only want your brain, thanks very much, you can keep the rest.'

We both laughed and then a knock was heard. It was a Sheila knock for sure, short and sharp. Sidney finished his coffee and brandy.

'That sounded like a Sheila-type knock,' I told him.

'Yes, the wife has summoned me.'

'Sidney, it's *my* wife, *my* wife, not *the* wife.'

'So you keep saying, but I can't change the habits of a lifetime just to suit your tastes.'

'I don't blame you.'

He went to leave, but stopped and said, 'Benedict ...'

When nothing more was forthcoming, I prompted, 'Yes, Sidney?'

'If I had my life again, I'd listen at school. Why didn't I listen?'

I felt such an affinity with him then and an overpowering admiration for his continual honesty. 'Because you were young and you probably didn't realise then that you *should* be listening.'

'Maybe not,' he shrugged.

'You have so many qualities, Sidney; please don't berate yourself over your supposed lack of education. I know long words, but so what? If I was at school again I'd listen in French.'

His face was a picture. 'Listen in French? Why would you listen in French? What's wrong with listening in English?'

I shook my head at him. 'I mean I'd love to speak another language ...'

'You do; you speak bollocks!'

'Very amusing, I must say.'

'Oh and ...'

'Yes?'

'Fuck, I forgot it. I read an incredibly long word yesterday in the paper and I thought, that'll get the clever bastard, but I can't remember it.'

'Goodnight, Sidney.'

'Goodnight, Benedict, lovely evening, mate. And I hope she calls.'

He left me there, smiling, and I realised I was often smiling when Sidney left my house and I was grateful for that. I then searched yet again for

Nell's number. I tried to do it systematically, but I ended up swearing and collapsing on the sofa in a frustrated heap. I must have fallen asleep instantly because I was woken by heavy rain hammering against the conservatory roof and windows. My eyes were so heavy I couldn't keep them open so I gave in to my exhaustion and slept again. The clock striking four woke me and I instantly felt the *presence* hovering in the darkness. I ignored it though, as four in the morning was not the time to be trying to find something you know is only there as a feeling and not a reality. I staggered upstairs and, without undressing, fell on the bed, rolled onto my side and sank into oblivion until eight.

Half an hour later when I looked in the mirror, a gaunt, unshaven face stared back at me and my first thought was of Nell and what she would say if she set eyes on me in that state. A couple of beers and a brandy had made me bleary-eyed and as pale as parchment and I had no recollection of taking my regime of tablets the previous day because my mind had been so preoccupied by Nell's tears. I had no idea what time Beth was arriving and I knew she would be horrified to see me this unkempt and I therefore had a shower and changed. I attempted to shave, but my hand was unsteady, making me fear for my life, and I gave up. I had no intention of letting Beth return to America worrying about her old Dad; it wasn't necessary and it wasn't fair on her, I wanted her to feel free to live her own life without a care in the world.

I spent the day answering a few emails that had been in my inbox for a week including one from Sarah reminding me I had promised to call. I couldn't remember ever saying that to her, but I picked up the phone immediately knowing I had to tell her about my disease.

She answered immediately. I tried not to stutter. 'Hello, Sarah, it's me.'

'About time too; don't you check your emails every day?'

'I most certainly do not.'

She laughed, 'You're such a dinosaur, Benedict; you really are.'

'I'm quite aware of that and actually I'm immensely proud that I am.'

'Oh, do shut up. How do you communicate with Beth then?'

'We speak, as normal people should.'

'I bet you'll never have a mobile.'

'The idea of a mobile makes me feel quite ill.'

'Anyway ...'

'Anyway ...'

'How are you, dear brother?' she asked.

'I feel fine, but I have some news to break to you that ...'

'Oh my God, you're not well,' she cried, her voice breaking, 'I knew you weren't, I said to Rich on the way home, there's something wrong with Benedict and he said, no he always looks that thin ...'

'Sarah, hold on a moment, please,' I cut in, because her voice was rising higher and higher with every word.

'Don't tell me,' she begged, suddenly sounding intensely vulnerable. 'I don't want to hear it. You know what I'm like with illness.'

'Sarah, calm down and listen because if I don't tell you then Bethan will and I'd rather you heard it from me.'

'What is it?' she gasped.

'I've got Parkinson's.'

She let out an anguished cry, 'Oh darling, you poor, poor thing. I can't believe it.'

'Sarah, I'm fine honestly and I don't want you to worry. I have a few tremors and fatigue, but I could stay like this for years.' She was crying quietly. She had always been the emotional, sensitive one of the family.

'I can't believe it,' she repeated, sniffing. 'What can I do for you? Should you be living alone? If only you were married to someone solid and faithful, someone kind...'

'I'm fine living on my own, so don't worry on that account, please.'

'Does Beth know?'

'Yes.'

'She must have been so upset. I knew there was something, but I couldn't put my finger on what it was. Life is so cruel; you've never done any harm to anybody your whole life ...'

'I don't know about that. I feel at the moment as if that's *all* I've ever done in my entire life,' I muttered.

'What do you mean?'

'I don't know, but I have a feeling that it's all part of the disease.'

'You aren't making sense, Benedict.'

'I think it does something to your mental processes because Parkinson's is all to do with the brain after all and I spend most of my time looking backwards and inwards and having regrets.'

'You listen to me,' she said, her schoolteacher voice firmly in place, 'you've been the loveliest, kindest, most generous brother anyone could ever have and I won't hear a word against you.'

'I wasn't a good husband, Sarah ...'

'I beg your pardon,' she jumped in, 'you most certainly were, but you happened to pick an unloving, ungrateful wife.'

'Please don't ever say that in Beth's hearing.'

'Don't be daft, of course I wouldn't. But it's the truth. I saw enough of you and Mary together to know what your marriage was all about, so don't waste time beating yourself up about anything. Beth adores you and that's because you have always been such a super father, so not another word, I warn you.'

'Well, thank you for that, but you are my sister.'

'Oh Benedict, I'm so upset this has happened to you. You don't deserve it,' she cried.

'Nobody does.'

I heard her blow her nose. 'I'm distraught for you, really I am.'

'Sarah, listen to me. I'm simply experiencing a few slight symptoms and I could stay this way for years, but if I don't, all the symptoms are eased by the tablets so it's not as if I have cancer or something like that. I honestly feel ... well, I feel the same as I always did except for some fatigue and that could just be part of the ageing process. Does that make you feel better?'

'I suppose so,' she mumbled. 'Who else knows about this?'

'Bethan knows, Sidney, Sheila and Nell.'

'Nell,' she repeated blankly.

'My friend at Beth's party...'

'Oh yes, she's a stunning young woman.'

My heart sank. 'Yes, she is a stunning young woman, in every way.'

'She's quite a sweetie, isn't she?'

'Yes, she is.'

'Very theatrical though,' she added, although not in a critical way. 'Quite aware of needing to make the right impression, I think. Bethan had a face like thunder when she saw her, God knows why. Mind you, she's often like that.'

'I'm afraid both Beth and Bethan think she has an ulterior motive for being friends with me,' I reluctantly told her. There was a moment's silence before Sarah spoke, as if she was weighing up what to say for the best.

'Well, it did cross my mind that she may be attracted to your lifestyle, but women have always fallen for you, Benedict, so...'

'I don't know about that.'

'You know they have and you have such a great sense of humour, I can understand why she's friends with you. If it was a romance I'd be a little more surprised, but only because of the age difference. Mind you, what am I saying? Lots of people of different ages fall in love.'

'Yes, they do.'

'Are you in love with her, Benedict?' she suddenly asked, perceptive as always. 'I did notice your face light up when she arrived and there was a kind of frisson between the two of you.'

I paused, not knowing whether to admit it and face more ridicule like Bethan had heaped upon me. But Sarah had always been softer and more understanding of human nature and I finally murmured, 'We're just friends ...'

'Are you in love with her?' she reiterated.

'I'm afraid ... yes, I am,' I replied, waiting for the derisive laugh and scornful words.

She sighed deeply. 'Then do you care?'

'Do I care?'

'Yes, do you care what it is she's attracted to? I should imagine you didn't ever think in your wildest dreams you would fall in love at your time of life, so do you care what it is she likes about you? Just make the most of it, especially now you have Parkinson's. Make the most of every minute ... I would.'

'Our sister assumes she's just attracted to my wallet.'

'Our sister is such a cynical bitch,' she said, almost spitting the words out, 'but that's the world she inhabits and, I repeat, do you care? If she's attracted to your money, does it matter? You've plenty of it, spend a bit on her and spoil her, if you think she's worth it. Is she worth it?'

'Most certainly,' I replied wistfully.

She sighed. 'Bless you, you soft bugger. Look, I must go. I'm so sorry about the Parkinson's, Benedict, I truly am. Please take care of yourself. I only have one brother like you.'

'You have two actually.'

'I know I have, but you were my favourite, always have been, you know that. Bye, darling and take care. Speak soon.'

'Love to Rich,' I spluttered as the line went dead.

Speaking to Sarah about my disease and Nell had been such a relief; her words had heartened me, given me hope. Hope of what I wasn't sure, but I certainly felt better for having discussed both Beth and Bethan's fears with her.

I searched again in vain for Nell's scribbled number, wondering all the time why she hadn't called and how the auditions had gone. I was now longing to hear her voice, see her face and hear that unique laugh, and that longing was beginning to cause me physical pain and anguish. I was gulping in air at times, my legs felt as heavy and cumbersome as enormous tree trunks and anxiety rippled through my whole body in tiny shudders. My neck and upper back ached so much it was as if I was carrying a heavy rucksack. Often I didn't feel as if I was inhabiting my own body at all, but hovering near it and watching myself from afar; all very odd and troubling.

I sat in the conservatory and stared aimlessly out of the window at the tall, swaying silver birches between my garden and Sidney's. I thought I saw wounded sorrowful faces between the branches and whispering voices in the gentle wind. I remembered Nell holding my arm with that light touch of hers: 'Lean on me, Mr Marshall,' she had said, looking up at me with a smile that would light up a stadium. Her absence was beginning to feel like bereavement and I wasn't entirely sure how much more of it I could stand when I fell into a light doze.

Beth arrived at about four that afternoon and woke me gently before sitting opposite me, leaning towards me and asking, 'How's things, Dad?'

Seeing her sweet face banished my low mood immediately because I couldn't ever have her close to me and not feel contented. 'Oh you know, darling ... all is fine with me as usual.'

'You look a bit white if I'm honest.'

'I'm always white as a sheet when I wake up. Your mother used to shake me sometimes to make sure I was still alive.'

'Oh don't say that.'

'I'm kidding you, darling, but my face does go like a piece of old parchment. But,' I added, sitting up, 'I'm full of life, as you see, and I'm taking you out to dinner. Where would you like to go?'

Her face lit up. 'Great! Can we go to the Italian by the theatre? I love it in there, especially the waiters.'

'That's settled then; half seven about right?'

'Yeah, that's brilliant.'

'How was your mother?' I inquired, as I felt I should, because in truth I rarely thought about Mary.

'Full of life, as usual,' she said. 'She's got quite a good social life where she's living now. We did a bit of shopping, went to the theatre, that sort of thing. You know Mum, she likes to get out.'

'Yes,' I muttered, remembering how she would jump at the chance of attending any literary gatherings I was invited to because she was a snob and loved to impress all her friends by name dropping artfully.

'She looks quite a bit older though,' Beth added, '*suddenly* looks older, you know?'

'Well, we are all getting older, darling.'

'But you look so great for your age, Dad.'

'Do I, even with the disease*?*'

'Yeah and don't keep calling it a disease, please, it sounds awful.'

'I'm sorry.'

'Let's call it a blip,' she urged.

'Well, I hate to correct you, but a blip is something that doesn't last, a mistake, something sudden and short ... this is none of those things, but ...'

Her eyes looked just as they did when she was a child, if she was frightened and needed reassurance. 'Can't we pretend?' she asked.

'Of course, darling, we can pretend,' I assured her, wondering where the self-confident thirty-year-old who had a high-powered job in New York had suddenly gone. 'You're right, positive thinking is the best way forward.'

'I agree.'

'Now, I feel awful that I haven't asked you if there's a man on the scene at the moment. Is there anyone special?'

She screwed her nose up. 'No, not really; well, yes and no.'

I laughed. 'I'm not entirely sure I understand that answer, but I would hazard a guess that there *is* a man, but you're not convinced he's special.'

'How do you know so much, Dad?' she asked, tucking her feet up under her.

'It's just age, sweetheart.'

'He's a nice enough guy, American, works with me, but we both work such long hours ...'

'I know, I understand and there's plenty of time, don't rush things, Beth.'

'I won't,' she said. 'I've got the chance for promotion,' she began to say, but the phone ringing made me visibly jump and I struggled quickly to my feet in the hope it was Nell. Beth jumped up too.

'I'll get it, Dad, sit down.'

My heart was doing somersaults, 'No, I'll get it,' I told her, trying not to sound anxious and, thankfully, I beat her to the phone, 'Hello?'

'Benedict, what's this I hear?' It was William's voice, not Nell's, and he sounded subdued as he went on, 'Sarah says you've got Parkinson's.'

'Yes, I ...'

'Why didn't you say anything?'

'Well, it was Beth's party and to be honest I didn't know how to broach the subject, but I'm fine, really.'

'What bad luck, old son,' he muttered. 'I'm so sorry.' His sympathy was heartfelt but I knew it would only be moments before his doctor's instincts kicked in, and I was right. 'What stage are you in?' he asked and then answered his own question, 'the first probably. What are your symptoms like? Are they troubling you?'

'They aren't too bad, honestly. I have a few tremors, a bit of a problem with balance sometimes, but on the whole I'm lucky. I could stay this way for years, you know that,' I told him, aware that Beth was watching my face intently, scrutinising it for any half truths.

'I did say to Lily your voice had altered, but I couldn't quite put my finger on how. I must be losing my touch in retirement because I didn't spot it. I thought you looked tired, that's all.

'How is Lily? You're a lucky blighter to have met such a charming woman,' I remarked, wanting to change the topic of conversation to something a little lighter.

'I'm well aware of that. She's very well, thank you. We're off on a cruise in a couple of weeks, Mediterranean, should be lovely. But getting back to you; is there anything we can do for you? How do you actually feel?'

'I'm quite well enough, William, honestly. I feel awful at having to tell everyone and worrying all the family, especially Beth. I get a little fatigued, but that might just be age. I mean, I don't know how tired you get at sixty-two because I've never been sixty-two before.'

He laughed quietly. 'True enough. Any side effects from the tablets yet? They are pretty heavy duty; have to be.'

'Yes, they are,' I replied, longing to tell him about seeing our old Pa and hearing our mother's voice, but glancing at Beth's anxious face I thought it better left unsaid at that moment. Besides, he would probably have heard of Parkinson's related hallucinations from patients. 'A few unpleasant side effects and a couple of pleasant ones, funnily enough, but I'll tell you more when I see you. Beth is here now and we're just having a chat before going out to dinner.'

'Enough said, Benedict,' he said, knowing exactly what I meant. 'By the way, it was lovely to meet your young friend the other day ... anything in it?'

'By which you mean?'

'Ah yes, Beth's listening still, eh? Well, are you just friends, or is there more to it? Oh God, that's hard to answer too. I'll ask the question and you say yay or nay,' he urged. 'Are you just good friends, as the old adage goes?'

'Yes,' I replied, as firmly as I could.

'Nothing more to it...'

'No.'

'Right, good, I mean, well ... that's your business, but she's very young.'

'Yes.'

'Mind you, nothing to say you can't have a younger woman, many do, many have, but she'd be taking quite a bit on, what with you ...'

'I agree!'

'Beautiful face though,' he added, 'quite beautiful, and she's extremely friendly, not fazed by any of us. Mind you, Bethan wasn't enamoured, but she's not enamoured of anyone these days ... the job I think.'

'You are spot on, brother.'

'And Beth appeared a little concerned, but if you're just friends there's nothing for her to be concerned about.'

'Correct again.'

'Had any hallucinations?' he suddenly asked. 'Answer without letting on to Beth.'

'You could say that, William.'

'I thought so.'

'Is that common?'

'Not uncommon,' he replied, with the typical reserve of his profession.

'That makes me feel a little better, I think.'

'And have you had any obsessive thoughts?'

'That's a hard one; but um, yes, but probably different from what you would expect.'

'Look, when is Beth going?'

'Tomorrow,' I replied, turning to smile at her.

'I'm going to call you tomorrow evening, chat about a few things because knowing you, you won't have told your GP anything. I bet you've not been back since the diagnosis, have you?'

'You know me too well.'

'Right, I'll speak to you tomorrow, old son.'

'Thank you,' I muttered, my voice cracking slightly with emotion as I realised how much I needed to talk with him.

'What was all that about?' Beth asked as I put the phone down.

'It was Uncle William, doing what doctors do, that's all.'

'I love Uncle William, he's so like you.'

'Poor unfortunate man.'

'Shut up, Dad, you know you're the best.'

I looked over at her delightful face that I knew better than my own and that I knew closely resembled mine. 'Am I really, Beth?'

'What, the best?'

'Yes.'

'Yes, you are, you always were.' She smiled adoringly at me, 'Always loving, always patient, never cross, never moody. I've never heard you raise your voice in my whole life, Dad. You must know what a great person you are to be around, don't you?'

'I may have once, but not now. When I look back I see only mistakes, darling.'

She came over and sat next to me, draping her arm around my shoulders and putting her cheek next to mine. 'You look a bit frail, don't be frail. Stay well and live forever, Dad,' she urged and there was urgency in her voice, 'I couldn't do without you.'

'For you, I will live forever,' I declared.

We sat together for a few minutes longer in silence and I was making the most of having her near me because she was so far away most of the time. I wished with all my heart I could hold that moment, with her cheek next to mine and her small hand resting against my shaking one, and recreate it at any time to comfort me when I was missing her physical presence.

'Right, I'll pop in the shower and get myself changed,' she said suddenly and the moment passed.

'Okay darling. Don't rush.'

She went to walk up the stairs, but paused and looked over her shoulder at me, her face quite sombre. 'Dad ...'

'Yes, darling...'

'Are you happy?' she asked.

'Do you mean at this moment? Very happy, because I have you, sweetheart.'

'I mean generally.'

If she had asked me the question a few days earlier I would have answered easily. I had met Nell. Nell and I were close friends. I was luxuriating in Nell's friendship, despite my disease. Nell was helping me see my world with fresh, optimistic eyes. I had found love for the first time in my life, at my advanced years, albeit an unspoken, probably unrequited, secret love. And yet, even though Nell and I had experienced a hiatus in our relationship and a misunderstanding, due to my insensitivity and lack of understanding as to what might upset her, I could not say I was unhappy because she existed and I now knew she existed. That was cause for celebration in itself and if I never saw her again, although it would cause me intense mental and emotional turmoil, I would always remember her and be grateful for the short time we had together.

'Yes, darling,' I replied, smiling at her. 'I'm very happy.'

Chapter 9

I was running annoyingly late for the audition. My train had been cancelled, much to my horror and, although I had jumped on the next one, it meant I had to fork out the money for a black cab at Charing Cross. I could have run faster than the taxi because of the heavy traffic in the Strand and we inched nearer to the back streets of Covent Garden at a snail's pace. I had to warm my voice up and the cab seemed to be the ideal place.

'I'm just going to sing, if that's OK with you?' I told the weary looking cab driver.

'Go ahead, love,' he replied. 'Seen and heard it all before.'

As I stepped out of the cab in Soho, the London air seemed gritty and grainy. I flew into the rehearsal rooms with only a few minutes to spare, flushed and perspiring. I gave my name to an important-looking man with a clipboard and he told me to wait in the coffee bar next door and I would be called in due course.

The coffee bar was heaving, but there was an anxious, tense silence. I was the only one not concentrating hard on a score sheet, script or piece of paper and I didn't appear to be as jittery as all the others either. The young woman opposite me was so white and drained of any normal colour I feared for her life and her sanity as she twitched her eyes and flicked them from side to side constantly. I attempted an encouraging smile her way, but she didn't even appear to be aware I was there. My lack of nerves was not due to any particular ill-founded confidence on my part; I was just so used to rejection I couldn't find it inside me to even begin to get excited any more. And although a part in the revue would add to my experience, it was the part in New York I coveted.

'Helen Jackson.'

'Yes.'

The man with the clipboard beckoned to me, 'This way, love.'

I was ushered into the large, bare rehearsal room where three people sat behind a desk. It was a scene I was quite used to, but it constantly reminded me of my interview for grammar school. That little episode in my life had gone spectacularly badly because I had always had a tendency to be dramatic and the headmistress, who resembled a pantomime dame, had no intention of encouraging that. However, my older sister was already ensconced in the third year there and was a model pupil, so they reluctantly allowed me in.

I nodded to the pianist who was an older man with a long, bony face. I could tell he had been round the block a few times and would probably follow me rather than the other way round. A woman in her fifties with dark-rimmed glasses like Benedict's, who I vaguely recognised, smiled warmly at me.

'Hello Helen; when you're ready, darling.'

I went over and whispered to the pianist which one from the revue I had chosen to sing. He smelt of women's perfume, overpoweringly so, and had delicate, thin fingers.

'OK, darling,' he whispered back, 'I'm with you all the way. Good luck.'

I did my best, belted it out and hit all the right notes, but even I felt something was missing from my performance. I went to slink out, but the woman wearing Benedict's glasses called me back.

'Do you want to try another one?' she asked.

'Yes, please.'

'Try something you love,' she urged, 'with or without the piano.'

'Right, OK, thank you, without piano if you don't mind.'

'Go ahead.'

I sang the Ray Charles song I had sung for Benedict, which had been Joshua's favourite and without a musical accompaniment I could hear a raw power in my voice that I hadn't heard in a long time. It sounded clear and pure and at one point I noticed all three of them whispering to each other.

'Well done, Helen,' the woman with glasses called, 'can you come over for a second?' I approached the table that was strewn with papers and coffee cups and lists of names, some crossed out with black pen and some with a star next to them. 'Are you coming to the audition at Marshall Street tomorrow?' she asked.

'Marshall Street? I thought it was Wardour Street?'

'No, there's been a last minute change. We let all the agents know earlier.'

'Oh, I haven't checked my messages. Yes, I'll be there.'

'Great, see you there then,' she said, smiling warmly.

The other two were busy scribbling as I left and I had a feeling the outcome would be come to Marshall Street because you won't be getting this! I made my way out, giving the pianist a little wave before I left and he smiled and executed a perfect theatrical wink in my direction.

Marshall Street. It seemed to be a sign for me. He had been so supportive in every way; maybe this was an omen. I walked through the tiny maze of streets to Covent Garden, with him firmly on my mind. I longed to call him, to hear his distinctive voice and describe everything about the audition, especially the pianist and his perfume, but embarrassment stopped me every time. I wandered into a café and ordered some tea and a piece of cake and listened to my messages. I expected to hear his voice, with the occasional slur and stumble, perhaps telling me he was so sorry for upsetting me and could I forgive him? But there was only Logan with his hard, thick Scottish accent informing me of the change of venue for the audition and then one from Matt telling me the same. My disappointment caused me to lose my appetite instantly and I pushed the cake away and abruptly left to make my way home.

Later that evening I soaked in a hot bath and practised some scales to warm my voice up and then sang the two songs I was singing in the morning. They were two solos and I knew them back to front and inside out. I was trying to think of some unique way to impress them, to allow me to stand out from everyone else. One of the songs was about lost love and although I had first-hand experience of that in the worst possible way, it was still too painful to dig into my own private agony to enable me to convey that kind of desolation in my voice. Normally I dressed smartly for auditions, to show I had made an effort, but something told me this time to change tack, to dress down by scraping my hair back, and wearing no make up, like someone in the throes of their own private battle with grief; someone who didn't give a damn about the rest of the world and life slipping by because they weren't engaged with it. Even then I wasn't entirely sure I would be able to picture Joshua's face when singing and yet that was probably what it would take for my voice to reflect the depths of despair a lost love could bring about.

The following morning I made my way to Marshall Street and allowed myself a little smile at the name. I wondered why Benedict hadn't called. Subconsciously, did he suspect my motives too? Was he waiting for Beth to return to New York? He worshipped his daughter; that was quite obvious in the tone of his voice whenever he said her name. Perhaps she had actually expressed even more hostility towards me than he had let on. I had been so sure of his friendship, but now his silence was insidiously eating away at my confidence in his affection for me. I missed him more than I ever imagined I would.

In the waiting area there were about a dozen of us, but I caught sight of Matt immediately, not only because of his unusual hair that resembled a ransacked bird's nest on that morning more than any other day, but also because he was quite literally hopping about on the spot with pent up tension and nerves.

'You could have brushed your hair,' I told him.

'I did,' he replied, his hands automatically trying to flatten it. 'I'm so nervous, I can't tell you.'

'I can see that.'

'I really need this, Helen.' My heart went out to him as he looked more wild and desperate, like a trapped baby animal, by the minute.

'I know you do. But do try and calm down a little. It's fine to be a bit nervous, the adrenaline will help you, but if you're shit scared you'll cock it up.'

'I know ... I know.'

'You know the pieces back to front I expect.'

He gave a little smile. 'Yes.'

'Well then ...' I was about to try to be more reassuring but my mobile started to vibrate and as I pulled it out of my pocket Logan's name was flashing on it. I barely had time to answer it before he said cheerily, 'I'm glad I caught you. Good luck, girl.'

'Thanks, I need it.'

'Well, this might give you a lift – you got the revue.'

'Oh my God,' I gasped, my heart beginning to thump with excitement.

'Now go in and let them have it, both barrels, and you'll be in work for the next eight months.'

'Thanks for letting me know.'

'I thought it would boost your confidence,' he said, his brittle voice now a little softer.

'It has; thanks so much.'

Matt was staring at me, his eyes wide. 'What?'

'I got the revue.'

His face broke into the broadest grin and it totally transformed him into someone infinitely more handsome and approachable from the slightly scary, unwashed, young drunk he usually resembled.

'That's fucking brilliant, Helen, well done.'

I looked up at him and my heart melted because of the sincerity in his eyes. 'Thank you. I hope you have something to celebrate soon. I really hope you get this.'

'I'm *praying* I get this.'

'What exactly does the pianist play in the show?'

'The intro to the whole thing, a solo piece before the band comes in and then I'd be on stage nearly all the time. If you get one of the lead parts I'd be accompanying you and the others. I've practised and practised ... you've no idea. I didn't even have a drink last night,' he declared, in all innocence.

'Blimey.'

'I know! It's never been known.'

'But you have to play freely, Matt, like you did at Jay's party. If you play to order there will be something missing. You just have to play from your heart, as if there's nobody listening. Imagine you're just playing for me. Imagine me just standing behind the door.'

'I will,' he replied, beginning to look excited now more than terrified, 'but you'll have to wait around because I'm after all you singers.'

'That's fine, I don't mind.'

A woman came out of the rehearsal room and called somebody's name and everyone flinched slightly. A girl at the back of the room swept by us with an air of confidence I could only envy.

'You always get someone like that, don't you?' Matt almost sneered.

'She's probably shitting herself, but she's an actress so she's hiding it.'

'How many songs are you doing today?'

'Two.'

He bent down and kissed my cheek. 'Good luck, Helen ... really, I mean it, best of luck.'

'Same to you,' I said, grabbing both his hands in a gesture of support.

'Why do we do this?' he asked and his eyes were suddenly troubled.

'Just because we have to, it's in our blood.'

'Yeah, I know.'

'I've been trying to find an angle on this one, you know?'

'Do what you told me,' Matt urged, 'sing from your heart.'

'That's the problem.'

'Why?'

'Because both songs, especially the second one, is about losing someone you love and my partner died.'

Matt's face conveyed his horror at my words perfectly. 'God ... I had no idea ...'

'Of course you didn't, why would you? I can't go there otherwise I'll break down.'

He shrugged. 'Break down then; it might impress them.'

'Only a fellow performer could say that,' I remarked. 'I can't use his death to impress them, it doesn't feel right.'

'You aren't using his death to impress them, just the feelings.' The girl who had just auditioned came out, tears streaming down her face. She grabbed her sweatshirt and rushed out without a backwards glance. 'That went well then,' Matt muttered.

'Oh dear, she looks so upset. I've dressed down, no make up, hair pulled back, to convey someone heartbroken.'

'I noticed,' he laughed, 'and I've dressed up.'

'That's dressed up?'

'That's very funny, I'm sure. God, I'm nervous.'

'So am I.'

We stood side by side and I could feel him shaking. Again I thought of Benedict and his tremors and how he had to put up with them constantly from now on. Suddenly my name was called and my stomach turned over violently. Matt squeezed my hand tightly.

'Go girl,' he whispered.

Walking into the audition room was always a lonely and difficult experience. You were completely on your own. It was all down to you, nobody to help you in any way. There were so many pairs of eyes on you, looking you up and down. Were you the right height? The right weight and build? Did you match what was in their minds already? And that was before you even opened your mouth. This time there were four people behind the desk, including the woman with the dark-rimmed glasses who had been at the other audition. She gave me a lovely smile.

'Hello, Helen, congratulations on the revue.'

'Thank you, I'm thrilled.'

'Start when you're ready.'

This time I had been warned I would be singing to a backing track, so I waited to see which one came on first, as she hadn't told me and I hadn't asked due to nerves. I felt I sang it well, if a little hesitantly, but as the introduction to the second one started, Benedict's mischievous face and distinctive voice came sharply into my mind; 'This is your time,' he had told me. I pictured his sparkling, clear blue eyes and the mesmerising quality to his voice, his elegance, his humour, his forlorn expression when he slurred and his rock-steady support. Here I was in Marshall Street; Marshall Street no less on the most important day of my life. I began to sing. The words were, after all, not as significant to lost love as to lost friendship. All became clear as I sang, as if a faded veil fell away from in front of my eyes and gave me a clear view of my life. I had been in love with Joshua, but he hadn't been my friend. He hadn't wanted me to fly; he had somehow bound me to his side without ever actually asking me to be there. The song was about losing your second self and I could see clearly a hunched, haunted and lonely figure sitting by the duck pond thinking about his daughter many miles away. A figure losing his balance and staggering, or insisting on carrying a birthday cake in to a crowded room with his hands clearly troubling him and shaking badly. A figure attempting to tap dance in the snow because I had asked him to and kicking a scrap of paper into a bin, again because I had asked him to, despite being afraid of falling. A figure eating cake, constantly worrying that it was smeared across his face, and a figure whose heart must have been broken when Beth said what she did about me.

The impossibly high note near the end flowed effortlessly, but my voice then cracked with emotion on the very last note and I found I was staring at the floor completely lost in the moment. I heard someone talking in the distance.

'Lovely Helen, thank you.'

I think I smiled and then wandered aimlessly out to where Matt was standing right by the door, beaming.

'Bloody hell, you caned it,' he declared.

'You think so? I don't know what happened; it all seemed to go by in a dream. That's never happened to me before. I'm not sure I was even singing the right words.'

'Would you like some water?' he asked, leading me like a child to the filtered-water barrel.

'Yes, please.'

We sat in silence as four other singers went through their auditions. I felt exhausted with relief that it was over, knowing I couldn't do any more. Matt was still jittery, but he was now silent and continually flexed and stretched his fingers. Eventually his name was called.

'Oh, Christ ...'

'Look at me,' I ordered. He did as I asked, but his face was taut with tension. 'You can do this. Remember, play freely.'

He smiled and gave a little nod and then he was gone. I stood with my ear to the door, wondering momentarily why he was the only person I had ever done this for. Normally auditions were an isolating experience and I flew in and flew out. It wouldn't have occurred to me to be this supportive for Frankie or any other of my friends or acquaintances. But Matt was more vulnerable, less confident in his exceptional abilities than anyone I had ever known before and yet the most naturally talented. I felt as if I had left my child on their first day at primary school. He was now in the wolves' den, on his own, fending for himself and I just hoped he would do himself justice. They needed to hear him at his brilliant, carefree best to be able to judge him properly. Standing with my ear against the firmly-closed door, I could hear some muffled laughter, then a couple of minutes silence and then he began to play. Within seconds I knew he was playing at his best; his performance flowed perfectly and moved me to tears. Someone even clapped at the end, always a good sign and then he was at the door, his face composed, but very pale.

'Well?' he whispered, in anticipation of my opinion.

I flung my arms around him. 'You couldn't have played any better.'

His face relaxed and he beamed. 'Cheers, Helen. Thank God it's over.'

'I second that. Let's go and get a coffee.'

He shook his head slowly, stating categorically, 'I need a drink and nothing else will do.'

'OK, if you must.'

'I must, believe me, I must.' I followed him out into the street.

'Will anywhere be open?'

'I know just the place,' he grinned. He led me to a backstreet pub with low beams and dark corners. A few customers were already huddled together and Matt made straight for the bar and ordered himself vodka.

'Sorry, Helen, what do you want?'

'An orange juice, please.'

'One orange juice coming up,' he said. He then joined me by the window and before I had taken one sip of my drink, his had gone in a second. I was aghast at how quickly he had drunk it and he glanced over towards the barman, obviously wanting another. 'I could do with a beer ...'

'Hold on,' I told him, 'let that go down first. It's very early, Matt.'

'Yeah, sorry, I know.' He looked a little ashamed. 'It's the trauma of the audition. This is how I relax; otherwise I stay all hyper like a coiled spring.'

'Well, if you let that vodka touch the sides it will relax you.'

He shook his head. 'One won't relax me, Helen, believe me. I just have this incredible capacity for alcohol ... unfortunately for me.'

'Think of your ulcer!'

His legs were constantly moving and he was tapping on the table as if playing an imaginary keyboard. 'Yeah, course,' he said, 'wonder when we'll hear.'

'Soon I hope-this afternoon maybe. They know who they want I reckon, almost straight away. But there will be recalls I'm sure.'

'Oh Christ, can't imagine going through it all again. Maybe this lark isn't for me.'

'There's no way anyone could play better than you did, Matt.'

He smiled bashfully. 'Thanks, but there are plenty who play like me. You'd be surprised.'

'I really hope you get it.'

'And I hope you get it. Just imagine, the States together, what a blast!'

'We won't be that lucky surely.'

'We might be! Someone has to be that lucky, why not us?'

'That's true.'

'Is your mate Frankie going for it?'

'I thought he was, but he hasn't said. He's better at drama than musicals to be honest. He's a fantastic actor, really transforms himself into someone else entirely.'

Matt was jittery again, still drumming his fingers on the table and his left leg moving up and down rapidly. 'Helen,' he said, his face serious, 'I've got to have another one. Do you mind?'

I laughed out loud. 'It's your body and it's really nothing to do with me, but you'd better behave if you get this job. No being carted off with your stomach bleeding.'

'Talk about put a damper on things,' he sighed. 'You're right of course, but I'm not in New York yet. Can I get you another one?'

'No, I'm fine, thanks,' I said, my heart sinking because I knew by his face he couldn't have not ordered another vodka if his life had depended on it.

While he was at the bar I took out my mobile and the need to ring Benedict was so strong tears burned at the back of my eyes. I imagined giving him the news about the revue and how well this audition had gone and I could almost hear his cultured voice telling me how proud he was of me, how he knew I could do it and how I deserved it after all the rejections and heartache. 'Well done, Nell,' he would say, 'I couldn't be more pleased. I will come and see it and sit in the front row. I'll be so proud, so very proud.' Matt came back to the table and immediately picked up on my mood. He leant forward and frowned.

'You OK?'

'Yes, I'm just a little tired.'

'You looked as if you were going to burst into tears then.'

I gave him a small smile because it was endearing that he recognised heartache when faced with it. 'It's just the emotion of the day. Look, I'm going home and then I have to teach the kids.' I felt suddenly unable and unwilling to sit there and watch him chuck alcohol down his throat. I was becoming too fond of him to witness that. 'Are you coming?'

'No, you go,' he replied, avoiding my eyes.

'Call me when you hear?'

'Course and you call me or text me when you hear.'

'Course,' I said and I gave him a quick kiss on the cheek as I left.

I called my mum from the train and sent texts to my brother and sister, all of whom were delighted about the revue and keeping everything firmly crossed for a recall. I taught my class with my mind in many different places except there with the uncoordinated, all over the place but full of enthusiasm kids, and then changed and went for a run. There were a few dog walkers and ever-present tourists in the park and although it was decidedly chilly with a darkening sky and spots of rain, I sweated profusely. I felt as if all the nervous tension of the day was flowing out of me leaving me feeling free and cleansed. I had been determined to avoid running anywhere near Benedict's house, but the savage easterly wind seemed to blow me fiercely in that direction and I found myself staring longingly at it. The familiar red bricks and its attic windows made my heart swell because I remembered that for most of my life I had longed to know what it looked like inside. And now I knew and I knew its extraordinary owner too, or at least I had. It seemed suddenly as if it had all been a dream. A dream you knew you were going to experience at some point and a dream that could never be forgotten. For a split second I thought I saw him standing at the lounge window and I caught my breath, but it could have been a shadow or reflection.

I ran on through the masses of daffodils and crocuses past the tennis courts and towards General Wolfe, avoiding the duck pond. It would have been almost a betrayal to sit by the pond without him. Even gazing out at London's immense and spectacular skyline was difficult because I knew how he loved the view. For a moment I felt an exhilarating urge to just dash back to his house, knock on the door and throw away my embarrassment at his words in the cafe that day, but I still felt too bruised and I wasn't entirely sure I could face him. My scrambled thoughts were interrupted by my mobile and when I saw Logan's name flashing on it, my hand started to shake with anticipation of bad news.

'Hello, Logan.'

'You've got a recall tomorrow,' he said, hardly able to disguise his joy even though, because of his brutal Scottish brogue, his emotions were always difficult to interpret.

'Oh my God,' I gasped.

'Helen, no bullshit but I think you're going to get this one. They were glowing about you. I don't want to get your hopes up so I don't say that lightly, but there was something ... oh I don't know, I just have feelings about parts and I think this is yours.'

'I can't believe it.'

'Have an early night and don't balls it up, OK?'

'What time do I have to be there?'

'It's ten thirty, same place, Marshall Street, and best of luck.'

'Thank you so much, Logan.'

Marshall Street! Marshall Street! Marshall Street! I kept repeating it over and over to myself in my head. Lucky, lucky Marshall Street and here I was at *our* place and I had heard the news I had been waiting for practically all my life: a possible lead role, in New York. I glanced behind me towards the impressive, ancient oak trees that shielded his house from the statue. I imagined telling him again and his reaction. 'My dear, Nell, you deserve this so much. I'm ecstatic for you.

That voice, that perfectly beautiful, distinctive voice that I missed so much, saying those words, was filling my head wherever I went, causing a lump in my throat and an ache somewhere in my chest that I couldn't get rid of. I was going to call Matt, but if he hadn't heard I didn't want to worry him so I kept my news to myself in case I jinxed my recall by telling anyone.

That night I went to bed early and listened to the wonderful, earthy sound of spring rain hammering against my bedroom window. As always, it made me feel comforted and expansive; as if I could turn my face to the rain, feel the wind in my hair and take on the world. Again, it reminded me of my childhood camping holidays and I thought of the amusement in Benedict's eyes and his laughter when I'd described them to him. I felt so disheartened by his silence, this enforced separation from him and missing him. Every aspect of our friendship was beginning to make me feel unusually lonely and abandoned and those were two emotions I had only ever felt before when losing two of the most important people in my life: my father and Joshua.

I finally fell asleep and dreamt about the three of them, but it was a hazy, mixed-up dream where they were all standing together in a room and I was watching them through a window. I tried desperately to get to them but, as is often the case with dreams, my legs wouldn't move and I was crying and hammering on the window asking to be let in. They were so close and yet I couldn't reach any of them. I woke up gasping and throwing my arms about wildly. The wind was moaning softly and the rain was pouring from some broken guttering and although the dream had unsettled me, surprisingly I went back to sleep immediately.

The next morning, demonstrating the superstition of my profession, I repeated the previous day's routine for luck by jumping in a black cab again and asking the driver if he minded me warming my voice up in the back.

'You go ahead, love,' he said, flicking his eyes at me in his mirror. 'I've had them all in here, quoting Shakespeare, singing all sorts and practising lines. Can I make a request or does it have to be what you're going to be singing there?'

'No, you can make a request,' I told him, laughing inwardly because I had never had a cabbie ask that before. 'Not sure I'll do it justice.'

'My Mum used to sing, '*You made me love you,*' to my old Dad and he loved it.'

'What, the one Judy Garland sang to Clark Gable's picture?'

'Yeah, that's it I think. Sing it and I'll let you know.' I started the first line and he nodded and put his thumb up. I knew all the words, but I sang it through twice to make sure my voice was sounding strong. 'Good God,' he laughed, when I had finished, 'you can't half belt a song out. That was really lovely. I could listen to you all day. I wish my old Dad could have heard it.'

'Thank you. Now I'm just going to do some scales, not so lovely, but entirely necessary.'

'Go ahead, but be quick, we're almost there.'

He was right; I had only managed two scales when we pulled up outside the rehearsal rooms. He wished me the best of luck and told me if I didn't get the part they had no bloody idea what they were doing and had no taste, at which point I gave him a tip, a smile and a wave.

The recall was nerve-racking. The same four people were there, but there was a little less tension in the room. I was first in and had to sing the same two songs I'd sung the previous day and then read from the script. There was much whispering, a few glances at each other and an awkward silence before the lady with Benedict's glasses smiled at me.

'Thanks, Helen. I'm the producer and that sent shivers down my spine.' Nobody had ever said that to me before in an audition.

'Oh, thank you very much,' I stuttered, hoping she had meant in a good way.

'We'll be in touch and we won't keep you waiting in suspense. You should know by this afternoon.'

'Thank you.'

I left the room knowing I could do no more and waiting in the bar next door were three other girls. We exchanged sympathetic smiles and I escaped into the street and leant on a lamp post for support. I felt drained and yet exhilarated at the same time. I wandered about, going in some old bookshops and music shops and then I sat on a bench in Soho Square with my mobile in my hand. I couldn't settle my mind on anything except Benedict and how I missed his companionship and his humour. I decided to give it one more day and then I would swallow my pride and my embarrassment and contact him. It did cross my mind that he might be unwell and I felt a sudden stab of pain in my chest at the thought of him sitting alone with his thoughts and his symptoms and wondered whether a blast of my unbridled laugh would still bring light, life and relief to his face.

I thought about buying some lunch, but I knew I wouldn't be able to eat it with my stomach churning with nerves. I aimlessly watched the pigeons pecking at the grass for pieces of discarded food and listened to London's constant hum of traffic all around me. A man sitting beside me engrossed in his newspaper suddenly tut-tutted loudly and stalked off leaving the paper on the bench. I picked it up and smiled when I realised he must have been reading an article about the rights and wrongs of breast feeding in public, which held no interest for me whatsoever. I turned my attention to another piece about how Viagra could make you deaf, which I found quite hilarious. But my hilarity was stemmed instantly when my mobile buzzed and my stomach turned over so violently I thought I was going to be sick.

'Logan, break it to me gently ...'

'You only bloody well did it, girl,' he shouted down the phone.

I began to cry silently. 'No! No! Are you sure? It's not some kind of mistake, is it? You haven't got it wrong?'

'No, I bloody well haven't. One of the four leads, well actually one of the three leads, one of the leads isn't so much of a lead, if you see what I mean. I don't know which one yet. But that doesn't matter. It starts rehearsing here two weeks before the revue ends so you'll have your work cut out. Then you go to the States, you jammy bugger. Are you there?'

'I can't speak.'

'Go and celebrate, Helen. Thank God, I'll be earning some money off you at last.'

'Thank you, Logan, thank you.'

I sat shaking for a few minutes and put my head in my hands with relief. Then a feeling of such happiness flooded through me I wanted to jump around wildly, dance and shout at the top of my voice. I wanted everyone in Soho Square to know, everyone within spitting distance: the man with the expensive charcoal-grey suit and briefcase, the young woman with impossibly high heels, the young lad with his iPod headphones firmly in his ears, the middle-aged woman with the obvious weight problem; everyone and anyone. I wanted to dance with Benedict by my side, holding onto my hand. But typical British reserve got the better of me and I merely grinned from ear to ear and whispered to myself, 'I did it, Mr Marshall. You were right. I bloody well did it!'

When we had finished our meal we strolled along the riverside walk, with a decidedly chilly breeze blowing straight in our faces, to the Trafalgar pub which had long been Beth's favourite because of the galley bar. She loved to stare over the wooden balustrade at everyone below without being seen. As usual the whole place smelt of old wooden floorboards, stale beer and grilled food and was full of tourists and regulars mixing together, standing shoulder to shoulder. I approached the bar where my multi-pierced barmaid friend was flying around, attempting to serve every customer with a smile.

'Hello there,' she called from the pump at the other end of the bar. 'What would you like?' she asked, winking at me.

'An orange juice and a sweet white wine, please. When you're free, don't rush.'

'It'll be coming right up, sir.'

I watched as she deftly opened bottles, wiped the counter, pulled the beer handles and took money all at the same time. I envied her dexterity and energy greatly. When I handed over a ten pound note I saw her glance at my shaking left hand.

'Thank you,' I said, smiling down at her, as she placed some coins in my right hand which was somewhat steadier.

'Was that your daughter who went through to the galley?'

'Yes, Beth.'

'She's the image of you.'

'I'm afraid she is.'

'Has she got a lovely voice like you too?'

'Well ... I ... I don't know, she lives in New York so there's an imperceptible American twang now.'

'She doesn't talk like you then,' she commented, laughing. 'I adore your voice – just adore it; just wanted to tell you that.'

I felt curiously grateful to her for the unexpected compliment. 'Why, thank you,' I replied, thinking of Nell immediately.

She smiled rather shyly at me. 'You're very welcome.'

My mood began to plummet as Nell's expressive features sprang into my mind, so I thought of Sidney and his insinuations that the barmaid was attracted to me and flirting with me. It was so preposterous; I laughed to myself and managed to stave off my heartache. I managed to get the drinks to the table Beth had chosen without mishap and she smiled up at me.

'I can't believe this is my last evening. The time has flown,' she blurted out excitedly.

Beth was obviously looking forward to returning to America. She tried hard to hide this fact from me, but I was her father and knew almost every expression that flitted across her face. In contrast, *my* face, despite my feelings of emotion, felt stiff, impassive, but I forced some expression into my voice.

'Hasn't it just? I don't feel we've spent much quality time together. Sorry, darling.'

She took hold of my hand. '*This* is quality time.'

'Yes, of course it is.'

She stared at my hand. 'Dad, I can feel the tremors. It's as if they're all under the surface.'

'I know, strange feeling, isn't it? But it could be worse. Honestly, it could be far worse.' She gave me an encouraging smile back.

'Just take care of yourself when I'm gone, OK?'

'I will, I promise.'

'Have you seen Nell?' she suddenly asked, without looking at me, as if it was simply a passing comment.

'No, no, I haven't.'

She looked surprised. 'Oh, haven't you?'

'No, she's busy with auditions and teaching ...'

'Well, at least I get to have this time with you on my own. I thought perhaps you might have invited her along.'

'Darling, why did you think that?'

She gave a little shrug. 'I don't know, I thought you would maybe want us to get to know each other better. Hopefully get me to like her, you know, that sort of thing.'

I felt she was testing me. 'I wanted this time for us, Beth,' I stuttered.

Her face lit up. 'I'm so pleased you did,' she said. 'I thought perhaps ...'

'What did you think, darling?'

'It doesn't matter,' she replied, looking a little guilty for some reason.

'Tell me, Beth, please.'

She kicked her foot against the wooden slats in front of us. 'I don't know, I don't know what I thought. Well, maybe I thought we wouldn't have this ... this time together. I expected her to be around.'

'We aren't like that, Beth, I explained to you and Aunty Bethan after your party. It's just a lovely friendship and if I'm honest I think she probably took pity on me. We met just after I had my diagnosis given to me and I was in a bit of a sorry state. Nell is a very kind and caring person and she could probably tell I needed some help.'

'You needed help?' she asked, frowning. 'How do you mean?'

'The diagnosis was a terrible shock and it had rocked my world. I didn't feel able to share it with anybody, don't ask me why. It became like a burden and I wanted to off-load it and she happened to be there. Actually, she guessed what was wrong with me, I didn't tell her. I told you that already, didn't I? I tried to tell you about it. God knows I picked up the phone so many times and chickened out.'

'It was right to tell me to my face, Dad,' she smiled gently. 'It would have been really hard hearing it down the phone and not being able to see you.'

'Yes, I know.'

'But you're OK, aren't you?' she asked, putting her arm around me and giving me a hug. 'You would tell me if you weren't, wouldn't you?'

'Beth, I give you my word.'

'Super Dad,' she whispered, using the name she always had when a little girl.

'And Super Daughter,' I added, which had always made her giggle with embarrassment when said in front of anyone else. 'So, tell me more about the man who isn't particularly special.'

'His name's Steve,' she said, 'Steve O'Connor. Irish grandparents from County Cork I think or somewhere like that. His parents live in Dublin and he's been in New York since he left university.'

'How long have you been going out with him?'

She laughed. 'Only a couple of weeks...'

'Oh dear...'

'Why?'

'Because often it's in the first few weeks that Cupid's arrow hits us hardest and then as the relationship goes on and we get to know the other person better; well, the shine begins to wear off, so to speak. And I know I sound like a grumpy Methuselah and a cynic, but that's the truth of it where human nature is concerned. So, if he isn't particularly special now ...'

'But sometimes it's the other way round, isn't it?' she asked. 'You know, when you only *quite* take to someone and then as you get to know them inside out you begin to realise and appreciate all their qualities.'

'Yes, that can happen. But I think it's more often than not the other way round. But Beth, don't take romantic advice from your dear old Dad. You should ask someone who has been successful in their relationship, like Sidney or Sheila.'

'Those two are made for each other, aren't they?'

'Aren't they just?'

'Do you think that's luck?'

'Luck, good judgement, hard work and love,' I declared.

'And the most important of those?' she asked, looking intently at me and appearing impossibly young.

'I would put love at the top of the list, always. If you love someone you have a good chance, if you don't, life becomes impossible. Look at Sheila and Sidney,' I added, with a smile, 'you can see she loves him even when she's nagging him or laughing at his antics or when he's getting on her nerves. You can just see it in her eyes when she looks at him and he's the same. Sidney wouldn't last a month if something happened to Sheila. He worships the ground she walks on, always has, always will. They have everything because they have each other.'

Beth was watching me closely as I spoke. 'I'd like you to marry again,' she suddenly said, 'have someone here with you.' I must have appeared surprised because she qualified it immediately. 'I mean, you don't have to *marry*; just have someone to love and who loves you. I do want that for you, Dad.'

'Do you, sweetheart?'

'Yeah, someone classy like Lily, someone *your* age,' she urged. 'She's so lovely, isn't she? She'd be right up your street.'

'Perhaps, but Uncle William found her first,' I said teasingly, my thoughts still filled with Nell.

'She's your intellectual equal I reckon.'

'She's probably my intellectual superior,' I remarked. 'I'm not as clever as I sound.'

She put her hand on mine and squeezed it. 'You would enjoy being with someone like her, wouldn't you?'

'I'm sure I would, Beth,' I replied, even though I knew she was trying to sow a seed in my mind that Nell was entirely unsuitable for me and too young and not clever enough, and I hoped she would stop. But then, as was always her way, my daughter did something that made me realise how wonderful it was to have her by my side. She put her head on my shoulder and sighed.

'This is lovely sitting here together chatting.'

'Yes, it is and it's lovely that you want to spend time with your old Dad.'

'You'll never be old.'

'Darling, I *am* old.'

She sat up straight again. 'I wonder how she makes ends meet.'

'Who are you talking about? Lily?'

'No, Nell,' she replied, which completely gave away what her train of thought had been. 'If she's an out-of-work actress I mean.'

'Well, she's not always out of work as an actress and she teaches dance and works in a café ...'

'But that must pay peanuts.'

I felt uncomfortable and shrugged carelessly, 'Perhaps, I really don't know.'

'Maybe she's out of work because she doesn't cut the mustard as an actress and performer. Maybe she's not good enough.'

I leapt to Nell's defence trying not to sound as if I was. 'Oh I think she's good enough, but she says there are so many talented people out there and not enough parts. It's a very tough world.' Beth's comments were making the tremors worse and my left hand was shaking badly although I tried desperately to hide it. I knew Beth had noticed, but she did not comment.

'Dad, I'll get us another drink.'

I felt in my pocket for some money. 'Here, take this.'

'Thanks. I won't be a second.'

I watched as she went down the steps and made her way to the bar and then I turned, leaning forward to look over the rail, seeing if there was anyone I knew below me. There were so many people crammed into one fairly small space and yet I saw Nell immediately. She was in the far corner listening intently to a young man who was leaning towards her and talking in her ear. Her face was quite serious, which was unusual and she occasionally nodded or shook her head in response to whatever it was he was saying. He was good looking in a cute kind of way and I guessed this was the green-eyed Frankie. They were part of a small group of people who were all of a similar age to Nell and yet she stood out from the rest, not because of her beauty, but because of her aura and her poise. My heart was beating wildly with suppressed emotion. She was a few feet from me, within touching distance, calling distance, and as lovely as ever with her dark hair falling over her shoulders and her expressions changing constantly. She laughed a couple of times, but it was a very poor relation of her characteristic full-throttle laugh and she appeared distracted, staring aimlessly at the floor in a dream. If my resolve had been strong enough, I wouldn't have worried about my physical frailties, I would have gone down to her, asked to speak to her in private and inquired about the auditions, but I felt like a young, inexperienced teenager struck dumb by being in the presence suddenly and unexpectedly of his first love.

'Dad, here you go. Dad ... *Dad* ...'

Beth was waving her hand in front of my face wildly. 'Sorry, sorry, sweetheart, I was in a dream.'

'Here's your orange juice. The barmaid knew I was your daughter,' she laughed. 'Am I *that* like you? I thought I was more like Mum.'

'You are like both of us, as you should be,' I replied softly.

'She said you are a true gentleman,' she added, looking immensely proud, 'isn't that nice?'

I was still trying to watch what was going on as a rough-looking young man sprang in through the door and hugged Nell very hard. 'Very nice, darling,' I agreed, but I wasn't really listening and missed what she said next; my focus was still on the young man on the floor below. He was scruffy, hair all over the place, unshaven and dressed in tatty clothes. He appeared to be so excited about something he was quite literally jumping about on the spot like a six-year-old child. I envied him his close proximity to Nell. I envied them *all* their close proximity to Nell and their youth and health.

'Dad,' Beth said, waving her hand in front of my face again.

'Yes, darling?'

'I *said*, let's drink to the next time we see each other.' She held up her glass. 'Cheers!'

I felt immediately guilty. My child, my beloved daughter, was here with me, wanting to spend her last evening in London with her father and I wasn't even paying attention; I was too distracted and heart-heavy. Pulling myself together, I said jauntily, 'Yes, cheers my darling, here's to the next time and I hope it won't be too long.'

She shrugged. 'A few months, that's all.'

'Oh I think I can hold out that long,' I told her, glancing down towards Nell again, completely preoccupied by her presence once more.

The group seemed to be crowded around her, like a bee swarm possessively protecting its queen and I had to look away because my stomach was churning over at the fact that I was in the same place as Nell and didn't feel able to approach her. Beth was looking around the room, her wine clutched in both hands and, as I studied her profile, I realised she still looked like a child to me: the child who threw bread to the ducks and hung on my every word; the child I read to every night until she fell asleep, even if I was drunk; the child who flung herself into my arms every evening when I came though the front door; the child who started every sentence with, 'My Daddy says ...' When I realised she was gazing quizzically at me, I said 'Beth, I'm sorry.'

She looked perplexed. 'What on earth for?'

'I don't know ... everything I've ever done wrong. Every mistake, every row with your mother, not being able to make the marriage work and being preoccupied with my disease while you've been here ...'

'But you haven't, Dad, and I don't even remember you rowing with Mum.'

'And I'm sorry that you were shocked and worried about my friendship with Nell. My affection for her is ... pure and spiritual. There is nothing seedy about it in any way, nothing for you to be embarrassed about at all. I wouldn't do that to you, be an embarrassment I mean.'

She looked upset. 'I know that. You don't need to ...'

'My illness has made me question and analyse everything in my life. That's what happens when you ...' I paused and felt my face and mouth stiffen, but I was determined to explain what I felt before she left for America again. 'It makes you introspective and you think about everything very deeply. I have many regrets I'm sorry to say, but the one thing that is constant in my life is my love and devotion for you.'

Her eyes swam with tears. 'I know that, Dad. I've always known it. I know how hard this has hit you. You of all people, so clever, so articulate, elegant and fastidious, but you're still my Super Dad,' she said, clutching my hand. Feeling it quivering once more she spat out, 'And ... and as for these bloody tremors ...' as if she detested them.

'Yes, these bloody tremors.'

She leant towards me and kissed my nose. 'Come on, let's go home and have a coffee.'

I was content to take my daughter's hand and be led downstairs. I thought I would be reluctant to leave because of Nell, but I was happy to leave her with her friends, which is where I was beginning to believe she belonged. They understood her life, the ups and downs, her frustrations and the never-ending round of auditions, recalls and rejections. They knew what it was like to long to perform and have your talent recognised. They all spoke the same language and led similar lives. They belonged, I did not. And yet as we left, I felt she resembled a tiny, remote island: surrounded by a sea of people, but in reality alone and isolated. I also saw that it wasn't the cute green-eyed Frankie who was standing as close as he could to her. No, it was the scruffy-haired, unshaven, lively young man who couldn't take his eyes from her face and was obviously besotted with her.

Beth held my arm firmly all the way home. It had turned colder, that raw type of cold only a north easterly wind in March can bring; a sharp wind that settles in your bones and stays there for hours. My house felt deliciously warm when I opened the front door and with the lights on Beth had commented on how inviting it had looked from the end of the street. Again I thought of Nell and how she loved the old place: 'This has always been my favourite house, Mr Marshall.'

'Christ,' I spluttered.

Beth scrutinised my face. 'You OK, Dad?'

'Yes, I'm fine, darling.'

'Are you sure?'

'I'm absolutely sure, sweetheart.'

She helped me onto the sofa. 'You sit down. I'll make us a coffee.'

'Thank you.' I leant my head back and tried to relax my tense muscles.

'I will be glad to see Steve when I get home,' she called from the kitchen.

'And I'm sure he'll be glad to see you.'

She popped her head round the door. 'I've got a photo of him in my purse.'

'Aha, have you now?'

'Take a look.'

'Where's your purse?'

'In my bag,' she replied, her head disappearing.

I didn't really feel like moving, but I wanted to show an interest in all aspects of my daughter's life so I got up slowly and found the purse tucked snugly down the side of her handbag, bulging with coins and bits of paper. The photo was sitting between a scrap of paper with a torn-off edge and a credit card. He looked normal enough, clean cut, mousey-brown hair, blue eyes and enviable teeth. Although appearances can be deceptive he seemed to be the type of person you could trust your precious daughter with.

'Have you found it?'

'Yes, good-looking boy.'

I heard her laugh. 'He's not a boy, he's twenty-eight.'

'That's a boy to me.'

I placed the photo back exactly where I had found it, but something caught my eye and made me pause. The scrap of paper, ordinary enough, had some numbers written on it in black ink. It looked like the unusual, italic pen I had been given from my agent when I had been a writer. My heart began to somersault as I recognised Nell's writing where she had scribbled her name and her phone number. My hands began to shake uncontrollably as it slowly dawned on me that Beth had seen the scrap of paper and put it in her bag. I couldn't think clearly. I could hear her voice in the far distance talking to me, but I appeared to be in a long tunnel, many miles away. I had to clear my head and act normally. Beth had seen the name and number and hidden it. Beth, my lovely girl, my darling daughter had hidden it, no doubt intending to throw it away in the hope that perhaps, just perhaps, I might forget Nell. Instinctively I placed it back where I had found it. I could have put it in my pocket, but then she would have realised I had found her out in her deception and I loved her too much to allow that to happen. I had no intention of ruining her last night with me. I stumbled back to the sofa.

'Here you go.'

She placed my coffee on the table in front of me. I went to speak, but no words were forthcoming and my facial muscles began to twitch and feel stuck. I tried to avoid looking at my daughter's face, but she picked up on my sudden silence. She was sitting opposite me with her legs tucked up under her, just like she did as a three-year-old.

'Is everything OK?'

I nodded. 'I ... yes ... all OK,' I stuttered.

'Are you sure? The colour has drained from your face.'

I hoped to God my eyes weren't betraying my disappointment in her so I looked somewhere just over her head. 'Beth ...'

'Don't look so sad. You look so sad suddenly. I'll be back soon, you know that.'

'I know, I'm just sorry, that's all.'

A hint of impatience crept in to her voice, 'Please don't start all that again, Dad. You have nothing to feel sorry for, I told you that.'

'I think there is,' I muttered. 'I must have done many things wrong.'

'You didn't,' she declared, 'if anything you spoilt me.'

My face twitched again. 'Yes.'

She laughed at me. 'You aren't supposed to agree.'

'Sorry.'

'So, when do you think you'll see Nell again?'

I wasn't expecting the question so I spluttered badly. 'I ... I ... may not, who knows.'

She opened her eyes wide in surprise. 'Oh I thought ... well, never mind, that's life, isn't it?'

'Yes.'

Beth had suddenly become the young woman who had arrived a few days ago from New York; harder, older, a little aloof and businesslike. Very different from the daughter who had rested her head on my shoulder in the pub and felt my shaking hand.

'What time is the cab coming?' she asked, as if she now couldn't wait to leave.

'Half past nine.'

'Great.'

'Yes.'

'Right, bedtime for me I think. Thanks for dinner. See you in the morning.' She bent down and kissed my nose. 'Sleep well.'

'Yes, see you in the morning, darling.'

She paused at the stairs, frowning. I think she was aware something was bothering me because even though the disease could wipe the expression from my face, she was able to read it, but she was having trouble deciding what it was.

'I love you, Super Dad.'

'And I love you, Super Daughter.'

I stayed on the sofa hardly moving for the next couple of hours, simply staring at the ceiling. I tried in vain to find a way of excusing what she had done. In fact, I went round and round in circles so many times my head and neck throbbed and I ended up trying desperately to force my mind to stay blank. In the end the *presence* distracted me and hovered very near, almost brushing against my face at one point. I only had two lamps on, one on my bureau and the other at the other end of the room near the front windows. The low lighting cast shadows on the walls; shadows of haunted, sorrowful faces I could not decipher. I longed to hear Nell's voice and to talk with her, just talk, as we had, about anything and everything and to see that life-affirming smile. I recalled how she had said, 'Lean on me, Mr Marshall,' and I wished with all my heart I could do so now.

Another familiar and loved voice suddenly cut into my thoughts of Nell. 'Benedict ... *Benedict*, don't blame yourself. You always blame yourself.' My father was sitting by the piano, upright and elegant as always, his kindly face looking concerned.

Seeing him again after Beth's dishonesty caused me to cry out in anguish, 'Papa, what shall I do? Why did Beth ...'

'Benedict, take a step back. This will pass.'

'But Papa ... I'm *so* disappointed in her, you can't imagine. It hurts so much.'

'I understand, my boy. But that will pass, all will be well. Nobody is perfect, son. Let her go and she will come back to you.'

'Let who go? Beth is going tomorrow. I would never try to stop her, you know that.'

'You will find a way. I trust you; now rest, my boy, rest.'

I closed my eyes briefly because they were unbearably sore and when I opened them he was no longer there. The space where he had been seemed like a gaping hole and I felt restless and anxious, but the stairs to bed seemed insurmountable and I rested my head on the back of the sofa and gave in to my physical and emotional exhaustion.

Chapter 10

I was finding the pub airless, noisy and quite uncomfortable because it was so crowded. It had always had a strange, pungent smell which was a mixture of stale beer and strong wood polish. We were standing near the large windows that overlooked the river and that evening the water appeared dark, but unusually still. Frankie and two of his friends who I knew vaguely were laughing riotously at some anecdotes about a film shoot they had all been on in Wales where the weather had been so unpredictable the trailers were actually swaying and creaking from side to side like a ship on a heaving sea. I smiled and laughed in the right places, but most of their conversation was passing me by. My mind was on Benedict and however hard I tried to force myself from thinking about him, I simply couldn't help wondering how he was and how delighted he would be if he knew my news. It reminded me of how isolated I had felt just after Joshua's death, when for the first time in my young life I had understood how a person could feel lonely in a room full of people.

I glanced around me at the sea of laughing faces and it was as if I was caught in a tunnel, with the sides slowly creeping in on me and everyone's voices merged into one great cacophony of noise. At one point I even felt hideously claustrophobic and I peered over all the heads to the front door, where I would make my escape if I felt the walls begin to crush me. Frankie repeatedly glanced at me, frowning and narrowing his green eyes like a cat on the prowl at night. At one point he asked me directly, 'What's up with you? I thought you'd be on a high.' I assured him I was delighted, but oddly shocked and thoughtful about my good news. He wasn't to be fooled though. He was extremely intuitive and could hone in on people's moods very well.

'How's the old geezer?' he asked suddenly, after watching me carefully while his friends were telling tall stories. I shrugged and told him I had no idea. 'Oh,' he sneered, 'fallen out, have we? Did he try it on? Did you feel old age creeping up on you?'

I gave him a playful slap. 'It's none of your business, but no, he wouldn't ever do anything like that.'

'You aren't the actress you think you are,' he responded, 'you say the words, but your face tells another story.'

'I don't know what you mean,' I told him, but I knew that something in my eyes betrayed the fact that I although I was overjoyed about landing the part in New York, I couldn't share that joy with the one person I longed to.

Luckily we were distracted by Matt crashing through the door like a tornado with his hair literally standing on end as if he had been electrocuted. He spotted me immediately and barged through the crowds, not caring if he spilled their drinks and ignoring their annoyed and surprised faces, in his desperation to reach me.

'I've only bloody well got it,' he cried, grabbing me and squeezing me so hard he almost crushed my spine. He stank of alcohol and cigarettes mixed with sweat and I tried very hard not to recoil from his grasp. 'Can you believe it?'

'I'm so pleased for you, Matt, but I had a feeling you would. You must be over the moon.'

'I'm ecstatic!' he declared, his eyes full of tears. 'I'll have some money at last *and* I'm going to New York with you.'

'Lucky buggers,' Frankie muttered, just behind me. 'I'll get you both a drink.'

'No, I'll get them,' I told him, aware that he had been out of work for a long time.

'Don't be daft,' Frankie smiled, 'I can afford to get you both a drink to celebrate your news.'

Matt was fidgeting on the spot, full of pent up energy that he didn't know what to do with. 'Cheers, mate, I'll have a neat whiskey,' he told Frankie.

'I think you need a tranquilliser, mate,' Frankie remarked. 'You'll need to conserve your energy if you're going to be on stage for six months.'

Matt threw his head back and laughed. 'I've got plenty of energy when I've had a couple of drinks. I can play all night.'

'Until you start coughing up blood,' I found myself saying.

'Oh that was just a one-off,' he said, dismissively, 'it won't happen again. The doc gave me some pills and they healed it. Anyway, don't put a damper on my news, Helen,' he continued, his face falling, 'I thought you'd be pleased for me.'

'I am, I am,' I insisted, hugging him tightly, 'it's great we'll be together. We'll have a fantastic time.'

'We'll have a fucking blast,' he cried, hopping up and down on the spot continually. Frankie handed him his drink and we watched, open mouthed as he poured it down his throat. 'God, I needed that.'

'Fucking hell,' Frankie muttered in my ear, 'that didn't touch the sides. You'll have to watch him, Hells.'

'He won't be able to drink like that when he's in New York,' I muttered back, but my pleasure and happiness for Matt was sinking into my boots as I watched him immediately make his way to the bar for another drink.

'That's musicians for you,' Frankie shrugged, and he squeezed my arm in a gesture of support and a little sympathy. 'The old geezer would be a better bet than the nutcase after all,' he added, his eyes glinting.

'Shut up,' I snapped, 'please don't refer to him like that.'

Frankie was laughing now, 'Which one are you talking about?'

I had to smile. 'I'm not telling you.'

'I thought there'd be more you know what with this bloke,' he whispered in my ear, 'but brewers droop and all that...well, brewers droop or old age droop, take your pick.' He was laughing and enjoying himself immensely. 'You do pick them, Hells.'

'You're only jealous,' I told him, planting a little kiss on his cheek.

He nodded. 'You're right there.'

I managed to lift my spirits as the evening wore on and between Frankie and his friends, who made me laugh with their stories of hellish auditions, and Matt, who was as high as a kite set free in a stormy sky, I began to relax and imagine myself in a hot, bustling and exciting New York. Eventually I made my excuses and intended to take a stroll along the river with just my thoughts, but Matt stuck to me like glue and offered to wander back with me. I gave Frankie a quick kiss on the cheek and he winked at me and whispered, 'He's a disaster waiting to happen,' and I nodded in agreement.

We stepped out into the brisk night air. A blast of wind, sudden and sharp, whipped up from the river, caught us full in the face and I hurriedly pulled my coat on. Matt didn't feel it though because he was in a complete dream. The orange street lights were shining on wet cobbles and I noticed a man and woman walking arm in arm just ahead of us. Nothing extraordinary about that, but the languid way the man moved made me glance at them again. It was Benedict wrapped up in his long, dark overcoat and he was with his daughter. They were laughing together and Beth looked up at him constantly, supporting and guiding him. Their closeness was obvious and at one point he bent and kissed the top of her head. My heart was beating so quickly I had to take a couple of deep breaths. I longed to call his name, watch him turn with surprise and tell him my wonderful news. But I imagined her face, taught with jealousy, and his discomfort at that jealousy, so I let the moment go and watched them as they walked away and out of sight. Matt was talking to me and I was trying my best to listen.

'I've never felt this happy,' he was saying, 'here with you, going to America, money at last. Life is wonderful, you know?'

'Yes,' I murmured, unable to say more. He immediately picked up on my mood and turned abruptly to look at me.

'What's up? You looked bothered by something.'

I was going to deny it, but I didn't have the emotional energy to make anything up that sounded as if it was half true. 'I just caught sight of a friend of mine. I didn't expect to see him and we've had a bit of a...'

'Falling out?' he asked. 'It's only a guess, but by the look on your face it was a falling out.'

'Not exactly a falling out. I don't know what I'd call it.'

He appeared genuinely concerned. 'You look upset, Helen. Tell me about it while we walk. That's if you want to.'

'Yes, I'd like to talk about it, but...where to begin? Well, he's quite rich...'

'Good start,' Matt remarked.

'I knew you'd say that.'

'Sorry, go on.'

'He lives in this wonderful house overlooking the park, my favourite house and all my life I've wondered who lived there. I'd daydream about what it look like inside and imagined living there myself. Then I ran into him, quite literally and we became friends. He's cultured, was a successful playwright a few years back, but he's sixty-two now and he has Parkinson's.'

Matt looked suitably sorry. 'That's awful, poor guy.'

'His life has changed quite a bit recently, as you can imagine and I suppose I took pity on him at first. But then we got chatting and the pity vanished and we hit it off straight away.' Matt was listening intently, with his hands stuffed in his trouser pockets and his scarf wound loosely and carelessly round his neck. He looked every bit the scruffy, broke musician he was. 'He's charming,' I continued, 'and I'm fascinated by the way he speaks, his intelligence, his sense of humour, his elegance...'

'I get the picture,' Matt said, smiling.

'I find *everything* about him fascinating actually.' We passed by the Cutty Sark and found ourselves by the dark river, which now was choppy and being whipped up by an increasingly cutting wind. 'It's been a lovely few weeks getting to know him,' I added and talking about Benedict was so easy and emotionally liberating after days of pretending I wasn't as upset as I knew I was.

'He sounds quite something,' Matt commented.

'He is, Matt.'

We stopped for a while by the railings. The creaking of old boats jostling together on the lapping water below us could be heard and Matt looked at me curiously. 'So, what happened? I can't imagine you arguing with anyone.'

'He invited me to his daughter's birthday party and to put it bluntly, she didn't take to me and neither did his sister.' Matt gave a scornful laugh. 'Why are you laughing?'

'Didn't take to you?' he asked, looking bemused, 'what's wrong with them then? I can't imagine anyone not taking to you, Helen.'

'To be honest, I think his daughter is a tiny bit jealous.'

Matt appeared even more perplexed. 'But he's her dad,' he said, shaking his head, 'that's a concept I can't get my head round.'

'I know, but human nature is a complex thing. She's always been number one in his life and she obviously feels threatened...'

'Silly cow,' he declared, 'she should be pleased.'

'Well, I think she can't understand why I'd want to spend so much time with him and neither can his sister. They're suspicious of my motives, but my partner who died had Parkinson's and I suppose I'm kind of drawn to it.' Matt looked bewildered so I smiled and said, 'Sorry, I'm not explaining any of this very well, am I?'

'I think I still follow,' he said, smiling back.

I continued. 'I was having coffee with him a couple of days after the party and he let slip that they both suspect I'm after his money and it hurt me and I was so embarrassed, I just got up and left.'

Matt whistled through his teeth. 'I bet he's regretting telling you.'

'*I'm* regretting him telling me and I'm regretting taking it so badly.'

Matt was leaning on the railings and he looked deep in thought for a moment before asking, 'Why did you? Take it badly I mean. Why didn't you just laugh and shrug it off?'

'Because before this all happened, Frankie had said something to me that really hit home. He said, that Benedict's money, his beautiful, expensive house that I'd always loved from afar and all of that stuff was part of his appeal for me and...'

I didn't finish my sentence because, as I was explaining it to Matt, it felt even more obvious to me that I had indeed been attracted not only to Benedict, but also by his elegant lifestyle too. And that was probably what his eagle eyed, cynical sister of his had picked up on. Matt suddenly put a protective arm around my shoulders.

'I can't see you being so materialistic,' he said, kindly. 'I mean, I know I haven't known you long, but you don't strike me like that at all.'

I looked up at him. 'Would I have pursued our friendship had he been broke and living in a seedy flat somewhere like an eighteenth century poet in a Parisian garret?'

'Probably,' he replied, without pausing for thought. 'That sounds kind of romantic, although in reality there's absolutely no romance in being broke, as I know only too well. It's a horrendous way to live. You said he'd been a successful playwright, didn't you?'

'Yes, very successful; awards, the lot.'

'Then I reckon that was probably more appealing to you than his house or his money because of what you do.'

'Maybe, but the *house*,' I insisted, 'it was always my dream house and then there he was, showing me round and I was enthralled, totally enthralled by it and him and the awards and...'

'I get the picture,' he told me, his arm still draped around my shoulders, 'but I think you're being too hard on yourself.'

'You think so?'

'Yeah, definitely,' he replied, 'I mean look at us. We've hit it off mainly because we understand perfectly what the other one is going through and feeling.' He moved away from me slightly and stood with his back to the river, leaning carelessly against the railings. 'All the brutal auditions, giving it your all, then being told you aren't good enough over and over again until you doubt you were ever talented enough in the first place. He's a creative spirit, like we both are. It may be a while ago, but it's still there in him somewhere. It can't be a sexual thing at his age, if you don't mind me saying, what with the illness and everything. You must be fascinated by his mind.'

'Yes, yes I was, I am,' I gasped, so thankful to be speaking about Benedict to someone non-judgemental who understood. 'I'm fascinated by his intelligence, his manner, the way he moves, the way he speaks, the words he uses...all of that. But...'

Matt interrupted, 'But what, Helen?' If he lived in a run-down flat, but was still educated and an intellectual, would he still be as interesting?'

'Well, yes, but...'

He interrupted again, this time a little more forcefully. 'What *is* it about this guy's house?'

'For years, since I was a little girl, I've loved it. I would pass by the front door every day and imagine I lived there. I would try to picture what it was like inside and imagine spacious rooms with long, velvet curtains swishing on the deep pile carpets. I'd dream about having all these wild adventures in the huge garden, sleeping in the tiny attic rooms at the top, and seeing ghosts and hearing voices of the people who used to live there but by then long gone...'

'Sweet,' Matt muttered.

I continued, now in full swing, 'I wished more than anything that I knew the owner so we could somehow become friends one day and I could gaze out of the long front windows and watch the slowly changing seasons in the park.'

'Sounds pretty romantic,' Matt remarked.

'Matt, you can't begin to understand how I longed to sit and have tea and sandwiches with whoever lived there. I even thought up conversations and what they might look like.'

Matt appeared enthralled. 'And when you imagined what they looked like, did it look anything like him, your friend?'

'No, I could never have imagined anyone as unique as he is. That house has been part of my life for as long as I can remember and suddenly, out of the blue, I come face to face with the man who lives there. It was like my wildest dreams coming true, so...'

'Destiny,' Matt said, 'that's what I'd call it.'

'Destiny,' I repeated, 'yes, it felt like that.'

'OK, I get the full picture now. It's all part of his mystique and charm,' he suggested.

'Yes,' I admitted, 'it is.'

The wind had picked up as we were talking and unexpected, heavy rain began to fall. We ran across the cobbles, past the domineering Cutty Sark sailing ship to a shop doorway nearby.

'But that's different from being after his money, for Christ's sake,' Matt continued, running his hand through his thick hair that was now dripping all over his T shirt.

I was immensely grateful for his interest in my problem and at that moment as we faced each other, I felt a bond was struck between us. A bond that would take us all the way to America together, where we would support each other through the run and perhaps come home closer than ever.

'Is it though?' I asked, looking up at him. 'Is it *really* different?'

He wiped the rain from my face with his fingers. 'Of course it is, Helen. You're thinking about it too deeply. But that's the noble person you are.'

'Not so noble, I replied, 'I just care about him so much, I don't want to use him in any way.'

Matt smiled. 'You must really like him.'

The rain was lashing down, swept roughly by the quickening wind across the river and splashing about at our feet. I smiled to myself when I thought about how I had described to Benedict being in a tent with my family, listening to raindrops hammering against the canvas and how his eyes had sparkled with amusement and delight at everything I said. 'Say that again,' he would ask, scrutinising my face because he hadn't a clue what I was talking about most of the time. Turning my smile on Matt I said, 'I feel as if he's my second self, Matt. Even though we're so different, we're the same. It's hard to explain, but when I'm with him, I feel like I've come home.'

As Matt listened intently to my somewhat rambling account of what I felt for Benedict, I saw his eyes begin to flicker and dart about. 'I know exactly what you mean,' he muttered, 'I feel the same about you.'

I had no idea how to respond so I simply said, 'Do you, Matt? I had no idea.'

He shrugged carelessly. It was a gesture that didn't quite match the words he had just said. 'Yeah, I feel like I've met a soul mate in you. I knew it as soon as you walked into the audition that day when I cocked it up for you with my awful playing. You were so sweet about it. Everyone else looked daggers at me, but not you. But I suppose, if he's your soul mate, then we can't be soul mates, can we?' he shrugged again and attempted a laugh.

'No-one's ever had a third soul mate, have they?'

I smiled up at him. 'Not sure it works like that. Oh heck, I don't know what to say. This has never happened to me before and I...I'm not sure where that leaves us.'

After having wiped the rain from my face Matt had stuffed his hands deep in his pockets, which was his usual stance and he appeared unsure of himself and nervous. 'I guess it leaves us as best mates,' he declared, 'and that will do for me. I have to take life as it comes. I don't know any other way. These are good moments for me. The dark days will come quickly enough.'

'I understand taking life as it comes,' I told him, thinking of the tortuous days after Joshua died. 'I hope your dark days don't come too often.'

His face fell. 'They come all the time and there's not much I can do about them. My dad died when I was eight and life changed so much. It was never the same again for any of us, so...I don't plan. And,' he faltered, shaking himself as if he was a wet dog, 'that's why I drink. It numbs the pain I still feel and it works until the next morning, when I'm sober and he's still dead.'

I touched his dramatic hair affectionately, hoping it would comfort him. 'I'm so sorry, Matt, about your dad and the fact that...well, how things have to be between us. But thanks for listening; it's helped to tell someone about everything.'

He beamed. 'No problem, glad to help, Helen. But look,' he paused, searching for the words, 'your soul mate, call him or go round. He must be really suffering.'

'You're so sweet. I will, tomorrow.'

'And now,' he started, looking excited suddenly, 'I feel like singing.'

'Do you?' I asked, distracted by the thought of the man I was missing so much suffering because of me. 'What are you going to sing?'

He began to laugh and sang loudly, '*Start spreading the news,*' before stopping abruptly and admitting, 'I don't know the rest except for *New York, New York...*'

I laughed back at him. 'That's very apt!'

He grabbed my hands and his face was serious. I was beginning to realise his emotions could change in an instant. 'You're my guardian angel, Helen.'

'I'm no angel, believe me.'

'Yeah, you are, you just don't know it.'

I took his arm. 'Come on, it's getting late and I'm feeling cold now.'

'I'm not going to drink from now on, Helen. Honest, I'm not. I'm not going to cock this up.'

'Good for you,' I said, hopeful of his sincerity, but unsure.

'We're going to America,' he yelled at the top of his voice to the black sky and we laughed together and walked arm in arm splashing through the puddles without caring who heard us.

&

The grey early morning light woke me and I thought of Beth finding me there, crumpled and deathly white, so I made my way to bed and slept for another couple of hours. I could hear her moving about in the next room and I glanced at the clock. She would be gone in two hours. Gone back to her other, exciting life in New York, to the not-so-special Steve with the enviable teeth and all her other nameless, faceless friends who I would never know. My chest felt heavy with a kind of grief and heartache; grief for my lost friendship with Nell and heartache at what my daughter had done.

'You awake, Dad?' she called, her voice light and relaxed; she was obviously relieved at the thought of returning to New York.

'I am, darling;' I called back, 'just getting up.'

'I've packed, so I'll go down and make some tea, OK?'

'That's lovely, sweetheart.'

Her soft step went passed my room and on down the stairs and I hauled my angular, stick-like body out of bed. My legs were shaky and I felt some saliva trickle down my chin, much to my horror. I let the hot water from the shower shoot down my face to erase all traces of it and rested my head against the glass. I knew I had to shake myself out of my lethargy and feelings of loss and disappointment. There was no denying that Beth had done wrong and I would just have to deal with it once she had gone. But my stupidity at freezing with shock at her deception and going completely blank when I could easily have memorised Nell's number, made me spit out half a dozen profane words into the jets of water.

Breakfast was eaten almost in silence because of Beth's preoccupation with the cab arriving on time and my wrestling with the thoughts of loss churning around in my head: the loss of Beth to New York once more, and the loss of Nell to somewhere, anywhere, other than with me. The silent house and the idea of Nell living, breathing and laughing elsewhere almost suffocated me.

'I might go for promotion, Dad,' Beth was saying, and I looked across at her. 'Good,' I muttered.

'You think so? It will be longer hours; they really make you work for your money over there.'

'There's no such thing as a free lunch, Beth,' I said, at least I think that's what I said.

She chatted on about her job, all the while checking her watch, and a lump was forming in my throat, threatening me with suffocation for a second time. I couldn't help wondering what on earth Nell must be thinking about my continuing silence when I had so obviously upset her and that caused my mood to darken and my breathing to quicken. She most probably thought I wasn't the man she had imagined me to be, that I wasn't a man of deep feeling or kindness and that I cared little about her and agreed with my daughter and sister.

'Dad, what on earth is wrong?' Beth asked, almost impatiently. 'Your eyes are so ...'

'I'm fine, darling, honestly.'

'Don't be upset I'm going.'

'I'm your Dad, Beth, of course I'm a little sad, but I'm not upset. There is a difference. I accept your life is in America now, at least at the moment, and I'm proud of you. You'll understand when you're a parent. I expect your mother was a little tearful when you said goodbye, wasn't she?'

She laughed. 'Not much, you know Mum, she can hide it.'

'Yes.'

She frowned at me. 'Is there anything else wrong?' she asked, her eyes probing my face. 'Is it your illness?'

'No.'

She paused for a moment and pursed her lips. 'It's not Nell, is it?'

I was going to pretend to laugh, as if the idea was ridiculous, but I did not want to lie to my daughter and I longed to be able to confide in her instead of hiding my feelings. And I wanted to give her the chance to own up and take the scrap of paper out of her bag and place it in my hand.

'Yes, it's Nell,' I said, attempting a smile. 'I miss her.'

Beth appeared instantly uncomfortable. 'Oh well, I'm sure she'll turn up one day out of the blue.'

'Perhaps,' I shrugged. 'But perhaps not.'

'Well, if she doesn't she wasn't much of a friend,' she declared, a little indignantly.

I felt like she had stabbed me, 'She *was* a good friend, Beth, I assure you.'

Her eyes flitted about from my face to her watch, to the clock at the end of the room and out of the conservatory window. I knew that look. She had often done that as a child when she knew she had behaved badly. She was now on edge, jittery and distracted and I immediately felt terrible. The atmosphere was tense and strangely at odds with our close, loving relationship and I knew that once she was gone and I was staring at an empty chair, I would cringe with regret at having admitted I missed Nell.

'That sounds like the cab,' she said, jumping up and rushing to the front window. 'Yes, it's here, Dad.'

'It's right on time.'

She picked up her suitcase and slung her bag over her shoulder. 'Don't come out. I'd prefer to say goodbye here.'

'Are you sure?' I asked, my voice faltering.

'Yeah, I'm sure. I hate looking back and seeing you waving at the door.'

'OK, fine, darling.'

'So ...'

I looked her in the eyes, 'So?'

Those eyes were troubled and her words faltered, 'You ... you look after yourself, won't you?'

I straightened myself up. 'Don't you worry about me.'

She took a breath and regained her determined way. 'I mean it, Dad. I might be a long way away, but I think about you all the time.'

'It's the same for me, Beth.'

There was a moment's silence before she placed her bags down again and flung her arms around me, hugging me so tightly I thought my bones would crumble. I made the most of feeling her face against mine because I wanted to remember that when she had gone.

'Bye,' she whispered.

'Bye, sweetheart, safe journey.'

She let go of me, picked up the suitcase and handbag once more and turned to go without looking back. 'I can't look at you again,' she called, 'otherwise I might cry.'

'I understand, darling,' I stuttered, my chest feeling crushed. 'Just go. Speak soon, safe journey. Bye.'

I heard the door close and I was going to rush to the window and watch her climb into the cab, but my legs felt stuck and I wasn't sure I could bear seeing the cab pull away. My chest felt as if it was going to explode. 'Bye, Beth.'

I sat on my own for a long time, just staring at the carpet. I don't even know what my thoughts were, they were so jumbled and all I kept seeing was Beth's concerned face when she was trying to work out what was wrong with me. That quickly turned into Nell's forlorn and disappointed expression in the cafe when I had inadvertently upset her. I think I then dozed before making myself a cup of coffee and I attempted to read the newspaper, but I could not concentrate.

A couple of hours later, luckily for me, Sidney came to keep me company and attempted to cheer me up. He insisted I lace our coffee with spirits. 'Sidney, it's too early to put whisky in your coffee.'

'I don't give two fucks how early it is.'

I looked across at him sitting there with his mug almost balancing on his ever-increasing stomach. 'You have a wonderful command of the English language.'

'Oh you know I can't talk like you. I wish I could, but I can't. Anyway, it's up to the individual how early he or she drinks,' he declared pompously.

'I never could drink before lunch,' I remarked, 'but I have to say I made up for it by the end of the day.'

'It helps me sleep.'

'There is that.'

We were relaxing in my conservatory, our usual place for conversation, cards and drinking. It was a bright and blowy morning after the night's sudden deluge, with pure white clouds racing across the sky and I wondered why Nell had been in the pub and what she was doing this morning. The separation from her was now causing me so much anguish I felt as if I was bleeding internally.

'Heard from Nell?' Sidney inquired, as if he could read my thoughts.

'Alas... no.'

He looked perplexed. 'Isn't she in the phone book?'

'I don't know.'

'Shall I look?' he asked, going to get up.

'No, thank you.'

'Oh yeah,' he sneered, in his usual manner.

'And what does that mean?'

He chuckled. 'Playing hard to get, are we?'

'The idea of playing hard to get with anyone is a ridiculous one, Sidney, because if I did that, nobody would come and get me.'

'So you say,' he replied, with a knowing look. 'You've still got it, matey. You still have that twinkle in your eye, I'm telling you.'

'What is a *twinkle* for God's sake? Oh never mind; whatever it is, I assure you I no longer have it, if indeed I ever did.

'If you say so,' he shrugged, as if he didn't believe a word of it. 'That barmaid with the ridiculous piercings wouldn't agree with you.'

I rolled my eyes heavenward. 'I'm sure you think I lead this oddly wicked double life in which endless beautiful women throw themselves at me, discarding their clothes with wanton abandon because of my so-called twinkle. Don't forget I was married for thirteen years and now if a beautiful woman threw herself at me discarding her clothes I would simply ask whether she was cold and would she like a blanket over her?'

'Yeah and the rest,' he quipped. 'I know you've slowed up a bit, but you had your moments, Benedict, and probably too many for you to remember.'

'Slowed up a bit? You are the master of understatement. That's putting it kindly, Sidney.'

'So, are you going to slurp a bit of whisky in this coffee or not?'

'I thought you were on a diet.'

'What diet is that then?'

'The one you told me you were on.'

'Fell off that wagon after day two.' He paused, running his hands over his protruding belly, 'I don't need to diet, do I?'

I smiled. 'I'm not saying anything.'

'It's only a bit of middle-age spread, that's all.'

'Sheila's cooking!'

'Why don't you ever put on weight? It's not fair.'

'I haven't got a Sheila, have I?'

'You've just got that type of build where you never put on a pound. It makes me sick.'

'Skeletal you mean.'

'The quack said I have to lose three stone otherwise I could get diabetes.'

I looked over my glasses at him with the most serious, headmaster-like expression I could muster. 'You kept that quiet. But if that's what he said, then you must lose three stone.'

'I know, but I seem to lose weight and then it finds me again.'

'That's very funny, Sidney.'

'At least it brought a smile to your miserable face.'

'Do I look that miserable? Is it that obvious?'

'To me it is.'

'I'm sorry. I just miss her.'

'You are a silly old sod,' he declared, as if he only just realised the fact. 'Let's have a game of cards; that will cheer you up.'

'It will only cheer me up if I win.'

He suddenly sat up straight and his face went blank, 'Ostensibly!'

'I beg your pardon?'

'I heard it on Radio Four this morning – great word.'

'And it means?'

'No idea, but it sounded clever.'

I laughed. 'That's fair enough.'

'Benedict, what are you going to do then? About Nell, I mean. You're obviously very unhappy.'

'That's very intuitive of you, my friend. Do try not to say her name because every time I hear it I lose a few minutes off my life.'

'I've known you long enough to be able to read your face, even though it's looking a bit rigid these days.'

'It's so wonderful to know that some things in life will never change,' I remarked. 'Like Sidney, my dear friend, speaking before he thinks. I don't know what to do. I was hoping she would call. I was sure she would, but ...'

'Where did you first meet her?' he asked, interrupting me.

'I met her in the park, by the duck pond. She was just running by and stopped to shake a tiny stone out of her shoe.' I paused, seeing in my mind's eye her glowing face and long, dark hair streaming behind her. 'She told me off for smoking,' I added, my voice faltering.

'Does she run there every day?'

'Most days I believe, unless she's very busy.'

'Why not sit and wait for her in the hope that if she sees you she will stop and have a chat?'

I was astounded by his sudden bright idea. 'My dear, Sidney, that may well be one of your better ideas.'

He appeared pleased with himself. 'I do have the occasional brilliant brainwave ... *very* occasional.'

'Why didn't I think of that?'

'Because clever bastards like you never have any flipping common sense,' he declared.

'That's very true.'

'I mean, what's the point of being dead clever if you have no common sense?' His face was indignant and it cheered me greatly. Although I felt miserable, being in Sidney's presence always gave me a lift, because he often had no idea how amusing he was being.

'I agree, Sidney. Being a clever bastard has done me no good at all.'

'You'd do better being a twat like me.'

'I do believe you're right,' I told him, trying to keep a straight face, which wasn't difficult with my disease. 'I would have been much happier if I'd been a twat like you.'

He turned his nose up. 'No, you wouldn't. If you'd been a twat like me you wouldn't have appreciated all the things in life that you have. I'd love to have your mind, just for one day.'

'Even with this disease invading my brain...'

'Oh you know what I mean, Benedict. You know so much. The only time I could ever do sums in my head was when I was playing darts.'

'Sometimes I think I'd be happier if I didn't know so much,' I admitted to him. 'I think too deeply. I'm too analytical and complex. That doesn't make for an easy life, you know?'

'The wife says I'm a one-off,' he said, smiling proudly.

'It's *my* wife, Sidney! But as usual, your wife is right.'

'I know, bloody annoying, isn't it?'

'Women have that knack of always being right about most things,' I sighed. 'They are infinitely superior to us in every possible way. Why do they want equality when equality means stooping as low as men?' I asked him, but his face had gone completely blank, as if I was talking Mandarin.

'What are you on about?'

'Nothing of importance, Sidney...I was just trying to be humorous.'

'Then stop trying to be humorous and make another coffee, this one's gone a bit cold and break out the whisky,' he grinned.

'For you, my friend – I will.' I staggered to my feet with my legs feeling numb and went to the kitchen to make us both a fresh coffee.

'So you'll sit by the duck pond then?' Sidney called.

'I will.'

'And hope that Nell will do her daily run?'

'Yes, Sidney.'

'And then ...'

'And then, Sidney?' I repeated, carrying the coffee with my trembling hands into the conservatory.

'You grovel at her feet and apologise?'

I suddenly felt lighter and happier than I had in days. 'That's precisely what I intend to do. A bit of grovelling is good for the soul.'

'And let's just hope she forgives you, or at least forgives you your ball breaker of a sister.'

I gingerly poured a tot of whisky into both our mugs, painfully aware of the tiny tremors in my hands and knowing as I did so that I should not be drinking alcohol that early, if at all, just as the telephone rang.

'That could be her,' I gasped, stumbling to the phone. 'Hello?'

My brother's sensible, homely voice on the other end of the line was such a disappointment I could have sworn out loud. 'Benedict, it's me.'

Then I felt instantly ridden with guilt. 'How nice of you to call, William, there's really no need.'

'I knew you'd say that, but I couldn't get you out of my mind. Look, old son,' he went on, 'it could be worse. There will be bad days and good days and there's nothing you have done to bring it on, it's simply very bad luck; one of those unfortunate things.'

'You sound like a doctor, brother.'

'The tablets work very well and reduce the symptoms considerably, but you know they will have side effects, don't you?'

'Yes, I do, unfortunately.'

'Loss of libido ...'

'Oh that went a couple of years ago; I'm not bothered by that, believe it or not.'

'You may go blank sometimes ...'

'I do.'

'And lethargy, that sort of thing.'

'Yes.'

'Balance may become a problem, trembling and so on and so forth.'

'All of the above, William...'

'But there are other side effects that can be a bit disconcerting,' he continued, as if in his consulting rooms again. 'Hallucinations are one of the more worrying side effects for patients and ...'

'Seeing dead relatives?' I inquired. 'Feeling as if someone is in the room with me at all times when there isn't anyone here, that sort of thing?'

'Ah,' he sighed, 'I see. Well, once you know it's not just you and you aren't going mad ...'

'Yes, it helps a little.'

'What about obsessive and compulsive thoughts?' he asked.

'Plenty of them,' I replied, trying to keep my voice light and watching Sidney relishing every mouthful of his coffee and whiskey.

'Any compulsion to gamble?' he added.

'No, but compulsion to be introspective, full of regrets, guilt ridden ...'

'Ah yes,' he said, his voice clipped and professional, yet thoughtful. 'I see, that is known, I have heard of that. That's not very nice for you.'

'No.'

'Try and distract yourself when your thoughts go down that particular route,' he told me sharply, 'it will do your mental health no good at all to dwell on past mistakes. Try to look forward, Benedict. I know that's not easy with your diagnosis but it's the only way.'

'Nell told me to do that.'

'Sensible girl,' he remarked, 'and very friendly, likeable.'

'Very.'

'Well, I have to go, taking Lily to a friend's for lunch and then playing a bit of golf.'

'William, I'm very grateful for your call. Thank you very much for thinking about me and it was lovely to see you at Beth's party, lovely.'

'No problem, take care of yourself, old son. And if you want to ask me anything, just call me.'

'I will. Thank you again. Bye for now.'

Sidney smiled at me. 'Everything OK, mate?'

'Well, I'm not going mad after all.'

'Who says so?' he mocked.

'William *is* a doctor, Sidney.'

'He's a nice man, I like him. Very courteous and friendly, unlike your sister,' he added.

I sat down and finished my coffee. 'She's not so bad. You have to know her to love her.'

'A bit like me then,' he grinned.

'Quite.'

I felt a sudden restlessness come over me. I wasn't sure if it was caused by William mentioning Nell, the fair, spring weather or my longing to sit by the duck pond, but my heart began to race and I had to take two, long, deep breaths.

'Sidney, I think it's time I took a stroll in the park.'

He gave me a wink and jumped up. 'Say no more. Good luck. Let me know how it goes. In fact I'll give you a knock tonight after dinner.'

'Fine, but don't panic if I don't answer, I could be otherwise engaged,' I declared, meaning having a doze on the sofa or in the shower.

'Oh yeah ...'

'Don't start all that, Sidney. You know the kind of thing to which you are referring is redundant in me.'

'Why don't you just say you can't get it up any more, instead of all that posh malarkey?'

'How very unsavoury...'

'Unsavoury, my arse...'

'Goodbye, Sidney.'

'See you later, Benedict.'

The park was a carpet of bright colours: masses of daffodils with their golden heads nodding playfully at each other, and little deep purple and white crocuses lining the paths. The sense of renewal and hope in nature made me feel instantly energised and optimistic, even with my stumbling, puppet-like walk and rigid jaw. Leaves were appearing on the horse chestnut trees and the grass was a rich green with a hint of dew glistening on it. The whole picture before me seemed magical and mysterious, as if I had never seen it before in that way. My legs carried me instinctively towards my daughter's beloved duck pond.

All the way I whispered, 'I'm coming, Nell. Forgive me, forgive me ...'

Once at my spot, I sat down with a weary sigh and watched a tiny duckling trying desperately to follow and keep up with its mother as she searched for old soggy pieces of bread. The water looked muddy and deep from the recent heavy rainfall and the trees overhanging the pond were coming into bud. The air smelt sweet and full of the promise of blossom and the rhododendrons were very nearly in flower. I took a few deep breaths and filled my lungs, wanting the fresh oxygen to fill my aching, fragile body and seep into my cells. I imagined my disease slipping away from me leaving me as vibrant and as free as the new sprouting spring flowers. But the *presence* was hovering, just to my right, a little behind me, waiting, watching and mocking my thoughts of being a well man again. I tried to turn my aching neck to locate its shadowy, ghost-like form when I heard a soft, hesitant voice behind me.

'Hello, Mr Marshall.'

I almost didn't answer because I thought it a dream and I simply smiled, thankful at least that I was able to summon it up so easily in my imagination. But then a movement just behind my shoulder startled me and I slowly, stiffly turned to find the beautiful vision of Nell's lovely face inches from mine. The sound of her voice again after such a long silence caused me to catch my breath with joy.

'Nell,' I faltered, 'I'm so pleased to see you.'

'Are you?' she asked, her vulnerability heart breaking to me.

'How can you doubt it, dear girl?'

She said nothing, but sat down next to me, within touching distance and stared ahead of her. I could only gaze at her perfect profile and try to summon up some articulate words to express my pleasure at seeing her again without slurring.

'Say something,' she said, turning to me.

'Forgive me ... forgive me ... forgive me ...'

Her solemn eyes blinked back tears. 'There's nothing to forgive.'

'Oh I think there is ...'

'How have you been?' she interrupted me, moving slightly closer.

'Inconsolable.'

She gave a little laugh and relaxed visibly. 'You're funny,' she told me.

'I'm quite aware of that. But am I funny ha ha or funny peculiar?'

'I'd say a bit of both.'

Words were climbing up my throat, desperate to be said, but my disease was getting the upper hand and making me dumb; dumb, inarticulate and struggling to think clearly.

'Nell, I want you to know ...'

She put her finger against my lips. 'I don't need to know anything.'

'Yes, you do,' I insisted gently, taking hold of the hand that was gently touching my mouth, 'I want you to know I never doubted you; thoughts like that wouldn't ever enter my head. You are my dear girl, my friend, my confidante, my ...'

'Second self?' she added, her eyes serious.

I smiled with relief. 'Yes, yes, my second self. You put it so perfectly. I'm supposed to be the man with all the words.'

'It isn't difficult to put words to emotions, not if they're heartfelt.'

'Unless you have this disease,' I muttered. 'But I'm sorry I voiced others' opinions, even if they were from people I love dearly. I should have kept it all to myself. What was I thinking? Well, I *wasn't* thinking, that's obvious. I wouldn't hurt you for the world and I did hurt you ...'

'Please,' she implored, 'don't get upset by reliving it. I know you're going to feel guilty and go over and over it, like you do, but there's no need.'

'I'm just an old fool.'

'I agree,' she said, impishly.

'I knew you would.'

'So, Mr Marshall ...'

'So, Nell ...'

'How have you been? Really, how have you been?'

'My walking is a little unsteady sometimes.'

'Have you been dancing? Like I showed you?'

'You know the answer to that, Nell.'

'Well, you should have been.'

'I didn't feel like dancing.'

She sighed. 'It's just an attitude of mind, Mr Marshall. You know dancing is good for you, it'll help your balance and stop you going arse over tip.'

'What an interesting expression! I've always wanted to know, the tip of what?'

She thought about it for a second. 'I don't know.'

'It suits though,' I remarked.

'I think so,' she replied.

There was a moment's silence as we both took in the joy of being together again. A gentle tension crackled in the air and I longed to express my buttoned-up, unspoken adoration of her. I rehearsed in my head how one day I would summon up the courage to tell her she was the loveliest, kindest, most interesting creature it had been my good fortune to come across, but even though the words were only thoughts they went via Edinburgh and my lips felt rigid and frozen and as I went to speak I slurred badly. She noticed immediately and her dancing eyes softened.

'Do you know why I'm here?' she asked with a sincere playfulness.

Gaining control of my words again, I said, 'I have absolutely no idea.'

'I'm here because I've missed you more than I can say.'

'Oh,' I said simply, unable to believe that the radiant woman beside me would miss an ageing, infirm and complex man like me when she could have all the cute, green-eyed Frankie types and young, energetic men with wayward hair and nervous energy to spare, who obviously adored her, in the world.

'I missed talking to you,' she continued, 'I missed learning from you, listening to you. I missed your sense of humour and the way your eyes sparkle when you're up to mischief. I missed your voice most of all. I love hearing you speak, the unusual way you form your sentences, even with the slurring. I missed the way your eyes never leave my face and how you listen so carefully to me, even when I'm talking nonsense. I missed the way you frown slightly with concentration as if I'm reciting Shakespeare or revealing a Nobel Prize winning plan to cure Parkinson's, when in reality I'm using some phrase you've never ever heard before. I missed *us*, Mr Marshall,' she said, almost vehemently. 'Do you understand?'

I nodded, like a mute glove puppet, trying to force my mouth to synchronise with my racing thoughts. 'I do understand, Nell,' I eventually managed to say. 'And at this moment, when I need all the eloquence I used to have, it is just out of reach. If I could describe how you enrich my life in great detail, I certainly would, but I just can't!'

'Try,' she urged, 'for me. Or at least just say you feel the same about our friendship.'

I went to speak but slurred so badly again it was unintelligible. I swallowed and tried again. 'I feel the same. And one day, when my hands aren't trembling so much, the playwright in me will write down how I feel.'

Her eyes lit up. 'Would you really? I'd love that.'

'Then I will.'

She glanced at the duck pond. 'And we don't have to worry about what other people think or say?'

'Nell,' I started, my mouth suddenly behaving for once and yet hesitating because of her obvious vulnerability, 'I have reached a point in my life, for obvious reasons, where I have to do what *I* want. If I don't now, when will I? To be perfectly honest, whatever you did it wouldn't make the slightest bit of difference to me. I couldn't ever think any less of you because that just isn't possible. But I hope I know you well enough to be sure that you are the noblest of women and I'll shout that from the rooftops until my last breath.'

She smiled from ear to ear. 'Thank you.'

I longed to add that I loved her and lived for our times together. That she was my first thought in the morning and my last at night, but I didn't. I couldn't. I was an ageing man with a chronic illness and it might have embarrassed both of us. I would have loved to have told her that she was the woman I had been waiting for all my life, but I would have sounded and looked ridiculous, with my shaking hands and ludicrous walk. So I tried to tell her with my eyes and put my longing away in a place where it couldn't cause me any discomfort or shame.

'But what about Beth?' she asked, concerned. 'I know how much you love her, Mr Marshall and what about your sister?'

I gave her a little smile, as much as my failing facial muscles would allow. 'My sister can think what she likes. I love her dearly, but ...' I paused before continuing, 'often I don't like her very much – a difficult thing to admit, but there it is. And, as for Beth, well, I would have loved you two to have hit it off, but there wasn't enough time for you to get to know each other.'

'I did expect her to be a little jealous, if I'm honest,' she said, adding quickly, 'if that's OK to say that.'

'Yes, it's OK to say that.'

Her almond eyes grew large. 'Why didn't you call? I thought you would.'

I went to speak, but slurred badly again because I didn't want to betray my daughter. 'I lost your number.'

'I left it on your bureau ...'

'Nell, that's not the truth,' I muttered.

She looked perplexed, as well she might. 'What do you mean?'

I took a deep breath to steady my nerves. 'This is very hard for me to admit to you – to anyone – but Beth hid your number in her bag.'

Her troubled eyes betrayed her astonishment at my admission, but as usual she thought of my feelings before her own and took my trembling hand in hers.

'That must have been rotten for you, to realise what she'd done.'

'Yes, it was.'

'Did you tackle her about it?' she asked me, knowing the answer.

'No, I couldn't. I'm just her adoring father who is weak and foolish and who spoilt her.'

'You didn't want to ruin your precious time together. I understand that.'

The relief at having told her was so immense that my shoulders suddenly felt less tense. 'I knew you would, Nell.'

'I really wanted her to like me, but as you said there wasn't enough time.'

'No.'

She brightened a little. 'I saw you with Beth when you came out of the Trafalgar.'

'And I saw you.'

'Did you?'

'Yes, surrounded by men, one of whom had the most incredible hair.'

She laughed out loud. 'That was Matt, a brilliant pianist. His hair looks like a birch broom in a fit.'

'Say that again.'

'You know, it sticks up for fine weather,' she explained.

I shook my head and smiled lovingly at her. To hear all her unusual, unheard of expressions again was heart warming. 'And was one of them the cute, green-eyed Frankie?'

'Yeah, good looking bugger, isn't he?'

'Well, not my type actually, but I know what you mean.'

'The other two I only knew vaguely. Did you see the other two? They're musicians too.'

'I can't say I noticed, I was looking at you,' I mumbled.

'One of them has an amazing nose. Talk about behind the door when good looks were given out,' she laughed.

'Nell, say that again. I didn't quite catch it.'

'Oh you know, just like the old joke: he's got a Roman nose, roaming all over his face.' She let out a blast of her wondrous, raucous laugh. 'He's nice enough though. I'm only trying to make you laugh.'

I was revelling in her chatter, making the most of having her sitting so close to me. 'My God, Nell,' I gasped, 'your auditions! How did they go? I'm so sorry, I forgot to ask.'

I expected her face to fall, but she beamed. 'I got them both, Mr Marshall.'

I felt moved to put my arms around her and I engulfed her in a congratulatory hug, with no embarrassment. She squeezed me tightly, a little too tightly in a nervous, clinging embrace.

'I don't know what to say. I couldn't be more pleased. I knew you would succeed this time, I just knew it. I can't quite believe it, *two* shows. It's incredible. You'll be discovered at last.'

'Found out more like!'

'Say that again.'

'You know, not *discovered,* but found out,' she explained. 'Do I have to spell it out?'

'No, no, I get it ... I think. It's wonderful news, Nell.'

'I know, I can hardly believe it myself. It seems like a dream,' she almost whispered, as if saying it loudly might jinx it. 'It's what I've been hoping for all my life. And one of them is a lead. It's a very demanding role, dramatic and funny, just right for me really.'

'You deserve it, Nell. At last somebody with a bit of sense has recognised your unique talent. Where will they be on? I'll come to both.'

She immediately appeared uncomfortable. 'One is in Soho.'

'I think I can manage Soho.'

'The other one ...' she paused, watching my face closely.

I interrupted her. 'We must celebrate. I have some champagne at home.'

'Hang on, I haven't told you everything.'

'There's more? Go ahead.'

'The revue in Soho is a very short run and we start rehearsing soon. The other one is ... is on Broadway, well just *off* Broadway, but I call it Broadway.'

'Broadway,' I repeated vaguely, as though I had heard the word but couldn't recall when or why.

'Yes ... Broadway.'

My heart had begun to race. 'That's Broadway as in New York?'

She was watching me, waiting for my eyes to stop sparkling, for my speech to slur, but I wouldn't disappointment her. I was ready. I had been anticipating Nell's departure, whether it be for a man, a part or simply because she was too busy with her life to spend as much time with me. I reacted perfectly, without a hint of sadness, or any other negative emotion. My throat felt impossibly tight, my thoughts muddled, but for once I was grateful for my rigid facial muscles.

'Yes, as in New York,' she confirmed, and smiled apprehensively. 'Be pleased for me, Mr Marshall.'

'Nell, that's fabulous,' I told her, forcing my voice to ne upbeat. 'New York! That means my two favourite women will be in the same city.'

She scanned my face for the truth. 'You're really pleased?'

'I'm really pleased.'

She gave an enormous sigh. 'Thank you.'

'How long will you be there?' I asked casually, as if it was an afterthought.

'The actual run is six months. We'll do some rehearsing here and then go out there to rehearse, so probably all in all about seven months.'

'Seven months will fly,' I told her, my heart now pounding against my chest and my body going into slow, paralysing shock.

She stared ahead of her at the little ducks paddling gently and frowned hard; she appeared so troubled it didn't look like her at all. For me, the whole world felt as if it was frowning, even the normally happy ducks. 'I've always felt as if my wings were being clipped by circumstance,' she whispered, 'by bad luck, poor auditions, relationships, responsibilities ... and I want to fly ... I *have* to fly.'

I took her hand in mine. 'Then that's what you must do.'

She turned to me once more, still searching for the slightest hint of sadness or disappointment in my eyes.' And you *are* pleased?'

'I am pleased, delighted and proud,' I declared.

'It's only seven months,' she insisted.

'It will pass so quickly.'

'Yeah, it will,' she muttered, adding, 'and you won't forget me?'

'Forget you, Nell?' I gasped, my tremulous voice beginning to slowly lose its strength. 'I'd as soon forget Beth.'

She gave me that life-affirming smile. 'I knew that really ... just checking.'

My legs and arms had begun to feel chilled and I felt a shiver run down my back. 'Shall we go home for some tea?' I suggested.

She leant close to me. 'It's great seeing your craggy face again.'

'My craggy face,' I remarked, enjoying the moment, 'is merely age.'

'It is not,' she insisted, 'it's distinguished.'

'Why, thank you, dear girl.'

She now looked excited and happy. 'Yes, let's go home and have a laugh. What shall we talk about?'

'How I got to be so devastatingly attractive?'

She laughed out loud again. 'Shut your face you.'

'I will,' I said seriously, 'For you I most definitely will shut my face.'

She suddenly looked playful. 'What you got to eat at home, Mr

Marshall?'

'I have cake and lots of it.'

'What type of cake?'

'Oh, it matters does it?'

'Of course it matters.'

'As it happens, I have chocolate cake.'

'I'll have a big bit,' she declared.

'I thought you might.'

She gently pulled me to my feet. 'And after the delicious chocolate cake, we're going to dance.'

'God forbid,' I muttered, but just loud enough to make her laugh and laugh she duly did. The sound of her laughter was like an injection of adrenaline to me and I felt my whole body relax, yet come alive.

We strolled back to my house arm in arm mostly in silence, the comfortable, contented silence of two friends who were grateful to know each other. But then a slow, unwanted despair was creeping through my veins at the thought of her so far away, being my impulsive, dramatic, incomparable girl with nameless, faceless strangers.

Chapter 11

We were sitting in the conservatory enjoying hot, steaming tea and moist chocolate cake from the delicatessen at the end of my road and Nell had been describing in detail the painful, soul-destroying and deeply personal, but necessary process of auditioning and how the two parts she had secured meant no more of that particular torture for almost a year.

'Something else to celebrate,' I remarked. 'I'll find the champagne in a minute.'

'I don't need champagne, Mr Marshall,' she said, 'it's enough to be here with you. Tea and cake will do for me.'

'Are you sure, Nell?' I asked, quietly pleased because the thought of its sweet fizzing in my mouth that early in the day turned my stomach.

'I'm sure, thanks.'

A warm, white sunlight was shining across her expressive eyes. I was doing my utmost not to stare at her like a daft, lovesick sixteen-year-old boy, but watching her inquisitive, lively, ever-changing face coupled with being witness to her deeply kind and caring nature, continued to inspire me to be the best man I could be, not only in her presence, but every day.

'Are you happy, Nell?' I asked her, without knowing why.

Her eyes shone. 'Yes, at this moment I'm supremely happy, but it's a constantly changing state, don't you think?'

'Yes, I would agree with that.'

'Are *you* happy at this moment, Mr Marshall?'

'I am ecstatically happy!'

She grinned at me. 'Let's have a laugh.'

'Kicking scraps of paper in the bin or watching me dance?'

'No, come and play the piano.'

'*Play* the piano?' I echoed, 'not sure I'd call it playing any more, not with these hands. Thumping is a better word, ambling, rambling even.'

'Come on you silly old sod,' she said, laughing and taking my hand she lead me to the piano stool. 'Please play.'

'Oh, all right, if you insist; why not?' We sat side by side on the stool. Her shoulder touching mine made all sensible thought fly out of the window. 'What shall I play?'

'Reviens Mon Amour, by Chopin, my favourite piece in the world.'

'Tristesse,' I told her, with sham arrogance and condescension. 'Its proper name is Tristesse, my girl.'

'Yeah, whatever it's called.'

'Wonderful! Here we go.'

I began to play, my left hand actually behaving for a change, probably in honour of Nell's presence and out of the corner of my eye I could see her watching my face the whole time. And because I felt light-hearted and full of joy at seeing her again and being reconciled, I thought Tristesse a little unsuitable for the occasion, so I ran straight into the Sooty theme tune. Nell gave me an up close volley of her ear-splitting, glorious laugh and I involuntarily jumped out of my skin.

'That's Sooty, isn't it? A bit before my time, but I recognise it. I love Sooty and Sweep!' she cried. 'You're so funny.'

'Chopin interspersed with Sooty, not much difference really,' I said, my face full of mischief. 'I just thought it suited the occasion.'

'Brilliant, absolutely brilliant, please carry on playing it.'

'No; no repeat performances, Nell,' I told her, my face as serious as I could make it.

'Oh go on, please,' she pleaded, full of fun, 'just one more time.'

'OK, just for you then.'

I played the Chopin again and even though she knew what was coming she laughed even harder the second time. 'I must tell Matt about this,' she declared, 'and he can play it when we're in New York to remind me of you.'

I stopped abruptly. The nervous, excitable young man who was so obviously mad about Nell was going with her. I thought I would feel the brutal and immediate stab of jealousy, but for some unknown reason I didn't. I felt pleased, inexplicably pleased.

'Matt with the wild hair is going to New York too?'

'Yeah, he's so thrilled. He's the pianist for the entire show. He's on stage nearly the whole time, well, *all* the time I think. I hope he can hack it,' she added, 'he's a bit ...'

'Temperamental?'

'Not exactly temperamental ...'

'Unreliable?'

'He can be, but this is his big chance so I'm hoping he doesn't blow it.'

'Why would he?' I asked, not understanding.

'Well, I wouldn't normally talk about other people's ...' She hesitated and bit her lip before rushing on, 'He has a drink problem. But you will keep it to yourself, won't you, Mr Marshall?'

'Silly boy,' I muttered, knowing he would regret it later in life. 'But many creative people seem to find solace in drink.'

'As far as my experience goes, *all* musicians drink.'

'And not only musicians,' I replied, remembering my alcohol-fuelled youth.

She sighed. 'I'm going to have to keep an eye on him.'

'That's one hell of a responsibility, Nell. You have your own career to worry about. Drinkers have a way of dragging others down with them. Be careful.'

'I will,' she promised and there was a moment's silence before she sighed again. 'I need to speak to you about something else.'

I turned towards her. 'Go ahead, I'm listening. It sounds serious. You aren't now going to confess after Broadway you open in Singapore, then Sydney, then ...'

'No,' she hastily interrupted, laughing.

'I'm grateful for small mercies.'

All of a sudden her face became unusually troubled and it never ceased to amaze me how quickly her expressions changed. 'You were completely honest with me about Beth and I appreciate that, so I'm going to be completely honest with you.'

'Oh dear, must you?'

'I asked why you didn't call me, but I could easily have called you, couldn't I? You didn't ask me why I didn't.'

'I'm sure you had your reasons, one being how upset you must have been at my thoughtless words.'

'I didn't call you because ...'

'Nell, there's no need to explain, the whole episode was entirely my fault.'

She frowned. 'No, listen please.'

'Go ahead, sorry.'

'From the first moment I met you, you fascinated me,' she began.

'You may carry on in that vein ...'

'Will you be quiet, Mr Marshall?' she demanded with mock severity.

'I'm sorry...again.'

'I knew instantly we would get on, don't ask me how,' she continued, 'it was almost like meeting an old friend and I've only ever seen you as a man

I care for, who I love being with. I don't even think of you as being that much older than me because you have such an interesting, lively mind. You'll never be old even if you live to be a hundred. But – and this is the hard bit ...'

The *disease*, I thought, my wretched disease. The stumbling block being my ever-increasing dark thoughts and moods; constant introspection and regrets were difficult to be around for very long even with Nell's deeply caring nature, especially when she had been through it all before with the man she had loved.

'I understand, Nell.'

She looked surprised. 'You do? But I haven't finished ...'

'I realise my precarious moods can be wearing and I do try desperately not to be so analytical and complex but I'm sure it's part of the illness. William is a doctor and he told me ...'

She put her whole hand gently over my mouth. 'Don't you dare apologise for being unlucky enough to have Parkinson's. There is nothing about you I would change for my sake, only for yours. If you are analytical, introspective and full of senseless guilt it is *you* that suffers, not me.'

'Then if that wasn't what stopped you calling, what was?' I asked.

'Well,' she started, taking a deep breath, but her eyes playful, 'if you'd let me finish instead of interrupting! When your sister and Beth told you of their concerns about my motives for befriending you – about me obviously being after your money ...' She paused because she must have seen me wince, but she carried on. 'It made me look at myself with a little of your introspection.'

'Why, Nell, I don't understand.'

'Because of this house...'

'This house,' I repeated, blankly.

'I kept asking myself, was it the house that had initially attracted me? Was it this house I wanted to get to know? The house I had dreamt about living in, owning even, all my life. If you had lived in a run-down terraced house in the undesirable end of Greenwich near me, would I have pursued our friendship with such intensity? I had to examine my motives without being blinded by seeing your incomparable face every day.'

I interrupted her, 'My incomparable face? Good heavens.'

'Do you understand, Mr Marshall?' she asked, staring intently into my eyes. 'Do you understand my dilemma? I care about you too much to spend time with you for anything other than friendship.'

'And having examined your motives, what did you decide?' I asked, my mouth stiff and immovable and holding my breath in anticipation of her answer.

'That it *was* part of your initial appeal – as was your illness; the illness because it reminded me so much of Joshua. The unusual ever so slightly loping walk, the stumbling, the stiffness, the slight slurring of some words, the dark thoughts, all reminded me. The house, this beautiful, unique, fascinating house was a factor in my ...' she paused, as if she felt she had given too much away, 'but what I'm left with now,' she added, fixing me with her glass grey eyes, 'is seeing before me a man I ...' She faltered and looked away.

I put my hand over hers as it rested on the piano. 'Go on, Nell,' I urged. 'Don't stop. Tell me.'

'A man I find original and true in every way imaginable, who gives me hope and who I would much rather spend time with than anyone else. So ...'

'So,' I could only repeat the word softly, completely dumbfounded that she would rather spend time with me than anyone else. I was lost for words or any sensible thoughts initially, but then I felt mischievous and wanted to ease the mood for her. I took a chance on our closeness. 'So, you're *not* after my money then?' The tension was blown away immediately by her machine-gun-fire laughter. 'Laugh a little louder, Sidney didn't quite hear you.'

'We're fine then, Mr Marshall?' she asked, her eyes shining like headlamps in the rain.

'We're fine, Nell, more than fine.'

I took her hand and put it to my cheek for a split second, overwhelmed by the need for a moment of intimacy between us that wouldn't embarrass her. She instinctively moved closer to me and rested her head on my shoulder and I knew I would have to remember this scene and the emotional intensity, to recreate it in my imagination when she was gone from me; flying as she called it, flying as she deserved to. We stayed like that for a few minutes, the nearness of her making me feel grateful to be alive. Then I began to play Sooty again and she laughed loudly again.

'That laugh could shatter all the windows in this house,' I remarked.

'I could sit here for hours and listen to you playing that, but I have to go.'

'Yes, of course. Thank you.'

She looked bemused. 'What are you thanking me for?'

'I can't even begin to explain what for,' I told her. 'And Nell, well done, America will love you.'

She looked unsure. 'I hope so. I hope Matt can hack it. I feel a little responsible for him, I have no idea why. And you'll be OK, Mr Marshall?'

'I can't deny I'll miss you, but your triumphs will be mine too and I'll live every moment through you. And there's email and the telephone.'

'I'll Skype you.'

'Will it hurt?'

'That's very funny. Gotta go.'

'Yes.'

She jumped up. 'Stay there, I'll let myself out. A walk in the park is in order tomorrow I reckon.'

'That will be lovely.

'Three times round the park this time and some dancing.'

'Oh God ...'

'See you at ten-thirty.'

'Ten-thirty it is,' I agreed and just before she disappeared I called out to her. 'Nell, why do I give you hope?'

She turned and smiled shyly. 'I know you'll find this hard to understand, but I expect your illness has changed you far more than anyone will ever realise.'

'Yes, yes it has ...'

'That's what gives me hope,' she said, 'that everyone could find what you have inside yourself since the diagnosis.'

And with another faint smile she was gone.

I tried to make sense of her words as I heard the front door close, but I felt light-headed with joy at not only seeing her again and resuming our friendship where we had left it, but also building on that friendship and finding a closer, deeper level of intimacy that felt pure and just right for both of us. I sat on my sofa smiling and with such an often longed for contentment, I wanted to share it with everyone: my family, my daughter, my friends, everyone I knew. But that idea wiped the smile off my disease-ridden face because I could not share it with Beth or Bethan because of their displeasure at our relationship and the rest of my family had their own lives to live and would probably secretly think me foolish. As for my former friends I had lost touch with so many of them in the past three years, there was only really Sidney left to tell. Good old Sidney, reliable, funny Sidney, who cared about me whatever my mood and listened to my incessant ramblings about my disease with good humour and common sense. I staggered to my feet and knocked for his presence. His knock back came instantly; in fact I wasn't entirely sure he hadn't been listening with a glass to the wall.

His eternally cheerful, eager, flushed face appeared in my conservatory in less than two minutes. 'So, what's occurring then, Benedict?' he asked, excitement in his eyes. 'Did all go to plan?'

'I'm pleased to report it did, my friend,' I replied, 'and it's all thanks to you.'

He looked astonished. 'She turned up at the duck pond?'

'She did, as you well know because you must have had your nose glued to the window pane all morning, knowing you.'

'Well, I did,' he admitted, unabashed, 'but I had to take an unscheduled trip to the toilet at one point and I reckon I missed you coming in, but I heard her laughing and I thought, hello, she's back.'

'She is back and as lovely as ever.'

'How are you feeling then?' he asked, wiping sweat from his forehead.

'Ecstatic.'

'Good news, matey!'

'Sidney, why are you sweating like that? It's hardly warm in here, is it? I know I feel the cold lately. But ...'

'I'm always sweating these days, must be the weight I've put on.'

'You could be right,' I replied, feeling slightly concerned at the high colour in his cheeks. 'You should check with the quack if it carries on.'

'Hark at you!'

'Yes, quite.'

'So, normal service is resumed then. All's right with the world,' Sidney sighed, with a self-satisfied grin on his face.

'For now ...'

The grin fled immediately. 'What does that mean?'

'Nell will be going away in a couple of months, for work.'

'Going away?' he asked, as if it was a preposterous thought. 'Going away where?'

'America, New York to be precise.'

'What, for a holiday?'

'No, Sidney, I just told you, to work. She's one of the lead parts in a musical that's already on there. She's very happy about it and so am I,' I added, the last four words coming out very quietly and hideously slurred.

Sidney said nothing for a moment and then shook his head slowly as if he didn't believe a word I was saying. 'You silly old bugger, you must be gutted.'

'Thank you, Sidney. It's such a comfort to know I'm still a silly old bugger. It has such a marvellous ring to it.'

'How long will she be away for?'

'About seven months.'

He looked shocked. 'She might not come back.'

'It's also wonderful to know that some things in life never change; you always speak without thinking, Sidney.'

He was frowning hard. 'What are you going to do?'

'Bleed.'

'Speak normally,' he sighed.

'I *am* speaking normally, this is how I speak!' I declared. 'Look, it's what she's always wanted, dreamed of: recognition of her talent, steady work, travel. She deserves it. I can't and won't be selfish when it comes to Nell. I spent my entire marriage being selfish and it's an unhappy state to live in I can tell you. She will email and call and she's going to Skype me.'

Sidney's face was a picture. 'What the hell is that?'

'It's science fiction, Sidney.'

'Fucking hell, it sounds it.'

'Quite.'

'She'll probably meet some Yank ...'

I interrupted him quickly not wishing to hear my fear voiced and muttered, 'Why wouldn't she? She's the most beautiful, talented, kind-hearted, extraordinary woman and I expect them to be lining up at her door. If I was younger and didn't have this *disease* I'd be sleeping on her doorstep begging for a chance. I'd give her everything I have and surround her with love and affection and devote the rest of my life to making her happy.'

He gave me a fond look over his glasses. 'Silly old bugger.'

'I have to confess I think you're right.'

'But you're doing all of that anyway.'

'You've lost me.'

'Giving her everything, surrounding her with love and affection, devoting your life to her; she's all you think about, isn't she?' He suddenly opened his eyes wide and his glasses slipped down his nose. 'She's not in your will, is she?'

'Sidney, please!'

'Well, is she?'

'Have some decorum.'

'Well, I suppose this was always going to happen and she'll meet some young guy one day anyway so...'

'We aren't romantically involved, you know that. We're close friends, I never expected to...'

'You hoped.'

'No, I did not! Compare the two of us, Sidney. I am in my sixties, have an illness that isn't going to miraculously get better. Nell on the other hand is young and vibrant, full of life and has a fabulous future ahead of her. It's up to me if I love her. I ask nothing in return. Apart from my daughter it's the only selfless relationship I've ever had.'

'She'll be back, mate.'

'Yes, I'm sure.'

'Meanwhile, back at the ranch ...'

'The ranch feels a little like a prison suddenly,' I muttered.

'Christ.'

'I'll be fine, really; after all I have you and your friendship.'

He visibly preened. 'Thanks, Benedict.'

'It's true.'

'Do you want some lunch? The wife's just rustled up some shepherd's pie.'

'*The* wife, Sidney? *My* wife; it's *my* wife.'

'Yeah, yeah, whatever you say and she's not your wife!'

'I *should* have married the redoubtable Sheila. I would love some shepherd's pie, I feel like some company, unusual for me I know, but there it is.'

'Come on then, it's about to be dished up.'

I followed like a meek little lamb, grateful to know him.

I spent the afternoon sitting at Sidney and Sheila's table, listening to their easy-going, humorous chatter and drinking copious amounts of tea. Their home was comfortable, with obvious affection and warmth. The three of us had a couple of games of cards and then I made my excuses because I wanted to have a late afternoon doze after the large meal Sheila had heaped upon my plate.

That evening, an inspiring red sky could be seen from my conservatory window and I watched the ever-changing cloud formation until a gentle dusty pink dusk fell. The brilliant red sky had reminded me somehow of blood running slowly across a dark floor. I read for a while, listening to the comforting sound of birds singing before they fell asleep and then I made my weary way to bed for an early night for a change.

The next morning I thought of Nell as soon as I woke, even before I opened my eyes. A hazy sun was shining on my face through the bedroom window and I focused on a gorgeous mackerel sky before I stumbled to the shower. On waking I would forget about my disease momentarily because motionless in bed I was the man I had always been, but as soon as I sat up and put my feet to the floor I could feel the trembling in my nerves and muscles.

Ten-thirty could not come soon enough for me and I ate my cereal standing by the living room window staring at the masses of horse chestnut and oak trees that hid the path to the tennis courts. I was trying to imagine Nell being in New York, living her exciting life, surrounded by adoring men and full houses applauding her in the theatre. It made my heart ache to think of her being thousands of miles away and I didn't want to ruin the next few weeks with her by focusing on her absence, so I made a silent promise to myself and to her that I would be upbeat and positive about her impending move. How could I be anything else when I was so lucky to have her back in my life?

I opened the door dead on half-ten and there she was, dressed in a bright red sweatshirt and black trousers and, for a change, her long hair was hanging loose in front of her shoulders. Her face was radiant with happiness and she took my breath away.

'Hello, Mr Marshall,' she said brightly.

'Good morning, Nell. It's a lovely day for it?'

'It's not very sunny, but it's mild and a perfect day for a walk and a dance,' she replied.

'Your enthusiasm is almost infectious; almost, but not quite.'

'And your sarcasm is almost infectious,' she laughed. 'Come on, you know you enjoy it really.'

'I have to admit I do,' I told her, 'only because I'm with you.'

She beamed at me, 'Ditto.'

We walked side by side into the park, across the long sweep of grass that led to the steep path to the tennis courts and around the blooming and colourful flower garden near the duck pond. Some dogs were frolicking around the bandstand as we made our way to General Wolfe. The pace had slowed considerably because my legs were seizing up and when we sat under the statue in front of our favourite view, I heard Nell laugh.

'What's it like being sixty-two?' she asked, her eyes full of fun.

'Hard work,' I replied.

'No, really, isn't it great to be wise?'

'I should imagine so, but I have no idea. Wisdom comes from learning from your mistakes and I'm not convinced I have.'

'You must have, don't be daft.'

'Yes,' I agreed, with mischief in my eyes, 'I must stop being daft, it really isn't an attractive quality.'

'Why is a brush daft?' she asked.

'Good question, to which I'm not sure of the answer.'

'You must know, Professor of English.'

'Well, I think it comes from being as daft as a brush with no bristles.'

'I knew you'd know. You must have learnt a lot in sixty-two years.'

'Not as much as you may think.'

'My dad used to say that so much had gone into his brain something had to come out. That was when he couldn't remember something.'

'He sounds a pretty sensible man.'

Her eyes appeared wistful instantly. 'He was a lovely man.'

'I can only imagine.'

The air felt strangely warm despite the sun being hidden by low, wispy light-grey cloud and yet London appeared to be sparkling and effervescent below us because Nell was by my side.

'So go on, tell me what you've learnt,' she urged me.

'What, in life?'

'Yeah, of course, what have you learnt in life?'

'Let me see. Well, I've learnt that life isn't fair, that very clever people often have little common sense, that political correctness and the slow erosion of free speech makes me shudder, that having a sense of humour is vital to happiness and makes even the plainest man attractive to women and that men are in no way, shape or form equal to women. We are infinitely inferior in every single way.'

She looked perplexed. 'That's interesting, but what about love? What have you learnt about love?'

'Ah, love,' I sighed. 'Two things; both are famous quotations, but they explain my feelings about love perfectly.'

'I wouldn't expect anything different from an English teacher. Go on then, tell me them.'

'The first is by Shakespeare, although this is not an exact quote: love is not love if the feeling alters when the person you love changes. It's something else, anything else, but it isn't *real* love. Love does not ebb and flow, it's constant. And the second is Tennyson; the one about it being better to have loved and lost ...'

'Than never to have loved at all,' she finished for me.

'You may not agree, Nell,' I said hastily, thinking of Joshua.

'No,' she answered, her face quite solemn, 'I agree completely. Imagine never having been in love. It must seem like there's a gaping hole in your life. Mind you, if you haven't ever been in love perhaps you don't know what you're missing out on.'

'No, you know...'

'You think so?'

'Yes, I do. There's a kind of longing that won't go away, a searching, even if you're not always aware what you are searching for, it is always there. And then, on long, dark evenings when you're alone with your thoughts you begin to realise what is missing, but because you don't want to admit it to yourself, you focus your mind on other things and live your life in a distracted, frenzied way to ease the sense of loneliness.'

'You make it sound awful.'

'That's because it is, Nell.'

We both sat in a comfortable yet thoughtful silence for a few moments until she leant against me in an affectionate way. 'What do you like, Mr Marshall?' she asked.

'What do I like?'

'Is there an echo around here? Yeah, what do you like?'

I gave it some thought. 'Well, I like puffy white clouds that look similar to cotton wool, masses of bluebells in a wood, bright daffodils with their jaunty little heads swaying in the spring breezes, playing the piano, reading, listening to Puccini and Chopin ...'

'Playing the Sooty theme tune ...'

'Playing the Sooty theme tune,' I repeated, 'and hearing you laugh.'

'And what do you dislike?'

'Oh, well, bad manners, litter, crowded places, loud noise, rudeness, violence, convenience food, supermarkets and my disease most of all.'

'And now, what do you *love*?'

I smiled at her characteristic openness and nodded slowly. 'Hearing my daughter's voice, seeing her happy, Sussex where I grew up, all British countryside, watching cricket being played on a village green, my family, the smooth feel of whisky in my throat, chatting with Sidney about very little, literature, theatre, my country – sitting here like this with you.'

'That's lovely, she murmured.

I turned to look at her. 'And you, Nell?'

Her eyes were shining, pure and glass grey. 'I don't have many likes, I just *love*,' she replied.

'I could have guessed that.'

'I love the skyline of London, watching the ocean, rain beating against a tent or a window, the smell of wisteria, wild roses, the wildness of the Yorkshire moors, winding Devon lanes with high hedges, English meadows, singing, performing, trees, laughing fit to bust but, most of all, hearing you speak.'

I was stunned by her admission. 'What, even with the slurring and stuttering.'

'Even with the slurring and stuttering,' she said. 'I love the softness of your voice, the gentleness, the way you ask questions, your impeccable accent and pronunciation, even the slight stumbling over some words. I'm an actress so I'm addicted to wonderful voices. There is *nobody* who speaks like you, nobody in the world,' she declared.

'Nell, you flatter me. I don't know what to say. I think I sound like a newsreader from the 1950s.'

She grinned. 'Yeah, you do.'

'I don't know any other way to speak.'

'Of course you don't and neither do I.'

'I actually speak like my father.'

'Do you look like him too?'

'Yes, more so than any of the others do, I believe.'

'You and William are very alike.'

'Facially yes we are, but not as people. He's steadier, more reliable, always been dedicated to his profession.'

'And you weren't?'

'I wasn't steady and not always reliable when I was a young man and although I enjoyed my years of teaching I can't call myself dedicated.'

She sighed. 'That's just you being you. You're constantly putting yourself down. I have a feeling you were probably inspirational as a teacher.'

'I wish I could say I had been, Nell.'

'I would have listened to you even if you'd been reciting the dictionary.'

'How very kind of you, but Mary thought my voice affected and Sidney is amused by it.'

'I was in a television series once – it was a walk-on part; two lines that sort of thing, rubbish really – anyway it was with a famous actor who I won't name. He was such a snob and spoke with a plumb in his mouth; his voice had none of your natural flair.'

'Was he putting it on?'

'Yeah, he came from Peckham,' she continued, 'and when he got rattled he'd revert to his south-London accent – it was hilarious. Some of the lighting boys used to try and wind him up on purpose.'

'It never works to try and be someone you aren't.'

'I tell you,' she added, laughing, 'he thought his arse was studded with diamonds.'

I was completely bemused. 'Say that again.'

'He did, honestly.'

'How very painful to have your arse stuffed with diamonds,' I remarked.

'Not *stuffed* with, *studded* with diamonds.'

I wrinkled my nose with obvious distaste. 'Oh studded with, even worse.'

She looked at me affectionately. 'You're funny.'

'So I believe.'

'What else shall we talk about?'

'How I got to be so devastatingly attractive?'

'Shut your face you!'

'Delightful! Nell, I need ...' There was something I suddenly desperately wanted to tell her, but I hesitated not quite knowing how to continue or even if I should. Finally I blurted out, 'Nell, I need to confide in you.'

'Go on then, I'm listening. I love listening to you.'

'It's about my marriage; something I haven't ever told anybody.'

She frowned, looking surprised. 'Wow that's an unexpected change of subject! But are you sure you want to tell me? You don't have to.'

'I'm sure,' I replied. 'You see, my marriage was a tragedy because ... because I didn't like my wife.'

She didn't appear shocked. 'That's so sad, especially coming from a man like you.'

'Yes,' I admitted, 'it was profoundly sad. There was a vast emptiness where the closeness should have been. I'm sure she found me difficult and selfish, especially when I drank, but I found her shallow, materialistic, very much on one level with little depth, unkind ...'

Nell looked shocked. 'Unkind?'

'I'm afraid so.'

'How was she unkind?'

'Let me give you an example, and I could give you many.' I took a deep breath while I rallied my thoughts, 'This one sticks in my mind and still upsets me. Friends of ours, well friends of Mary's really from way back, had money problems. We had just had a brand-new kitchen put in, expensive and over the top as Mary wanted. I told her not to mention it to these friends because it would have been rather infra dig.'

'Say that again, Mr Marshall.'

'Touché, Nell.'

She grinned. 'Go on.'

'I felt to have rung them and asked them round to see our sparkling, grand kitchen and preposterous appliances and cupboards when they were struggling would have been like ...'

'Rubbing their noses in it?' she chipped in.

'Yes. So I told Mary firmly that if she had to boast about her new split-level oven, dishwasher and freezer, as I knew she would, she would have to boast to friends who were equally as well off. One evening I came home earlier than usual and Joanne, this friend, was on our sofa looking rather subdued and uncomfortable and Mary was in full flow about how expensive the wretched blinds were.'

'No!' Nell cried.

'I promise you. My unease and distaste couldn't be hidden and I offered to take Joanne home in the car. She was grateful to be able to make a quick exit and I apologised profusely throughout the ten-minute journey for my wife's insensitivity.'

'Did she accept your apology?'

'Oh yes, she was extremely gracious and forgiving and told me Mary had been like that since her teens. I'm not sure whether that made me feel better or not, I can't remember. When we arrived at Joanne's home, I went in with her and made her and her husband an offer, in the most sincere manner I could, to pay off their debt. A loan, you understand, just to help them.'

Nell squeezed my arm. 'That was very kind of you.'

'It wasn't really, Nell. The amount was nothing to me and everything to them and they were lovely people. But it was as I was driving home alone that I knew my marriage was over.'

'What do you mean?'

'I did want to help them out of kindness, I promise you, but the other reason for doing so was to teach Mary a lesson, to make her angry, to irritate her. I'm not proud of that, believe me. It saddened me because those feelings weren't what I wanted to feel about the woman who was my chosen life partner. Our marriage diminished me. I yearned for a wife who when I looked into her eyes I became more of who I am.' I glanced at Nell to see how she was reacting to my unsavoury tale, but she was suitably sympathetic.

'That's a sad story and awful for you.'

'Yes,' I replied softly, '*and* for her.'

'Did they take the money, your friends?'

'Yes and once they were back on their feet, which I knew they would be quite quickly, they paid it back. I told them it wasn't necessary, but he wanted to; male pride and all that.'

'And how did Mary react when you told her?'

'She called me condescending, arrogant, and said that I was being patronising to them and that the money was ours and she didn't agree to my lending it to them and that I should have discussed it with her. It was all very unpleasant especially as I knew she really didn't agree with the loan because she wanted to be able to spend the money herself on some rubbish we didn't need. She called me many other names that I don't care to repeat and as she was raging I told her I didn't want to be married to her anymore.'

Nell's eyes were huge and expressive. 'You told her there and then?'

'Yes and to say it took the wind out of her sails is an understatement! She visibly deflated and said I didn't mean it, I was being ridiculous, I needed her, what effect would it have on Beth? All of that and more.'

'But you stuck to your guns?' she asked, endlessly interested.

'I did, Nell, and it came as a real shock to her. At that moment I could see in her blazing eyes the realisation that she might, just might, have to live a simpler, less affluent, life without me. That understanding led to me being exposed to hours of emotional blackmail, although she wasn't upset or affected in any way about losing me as a man. But to be honest I don't blame her for that.'

'Has she remarried?'

'No.'

'And neither have you.'

'No and that may tell you what we both felt about our marriage. Don't get me wrong, I was no Eton choirboy. I was selfish and often thoughtless and it's taken me sixty-two years and a chronic disease to become the man I always yearned to be.'

'It doesn't sound like a match made in heaven,' she remarked, with a wry smile.

'No.'

'So, are you still looking for that match made in heaven or have you given up?' she asked, her almond-shaped eyes searching my soul.

I didn't know how to reply. I hadn't actively been looking for any kind of match at all until she had appeared at the duck pond with her wild hair and expressive face and then out of the blue I had found the woman I had unknowingly been searching for all my life. I was not about to admit to any of that though in case it embarrassed or shocked her and so I gave a wry smile.

'Even if I was, who in their right mind would take me on?'

'Somebody who loved you,' she answered, as if I was mad.

'Ah yes, love,' I muttered.

'Love that doesn't alter when people change, remember?' she said, her smile lighting up the sky, 'rock-steady, never-ending, never-changing ... *real* love.'

Hearing those words from her made my eyes fill with sudden tears, burning and unwanted. I had no intention of letting her witness such longing in me so I gazed out over London's steady skyline and gathered my thoughts before I spoke again.

'The problem with marrying again or with having any kind of romantic relationship is ...'

'Go on.'

I felt a little uncomfortable suddenly, even though I wanted to share with her my shortcomings. 'It's difficult to talk about it if I'm honest, Nell.'

She squeezed my arm. 'Be bold, be brave, it's only me listening.'

My normally white face coloured with an unaccustomed flush. 'I can offer no ...'

'No what?' she prompted.

'It doesn't matter.'

'It obviously does.'

'It's a little personal and I don't want to sound like ...'

'For God's sake stop starting sentences and not finishing them! It's enough to drive me nuts!'

'Sorry, sorry,' I spluttered, wishing I hadn't begun meandering down that particular path, but she and I were so close I felt I could share even my deepest concerns with her. I took a deep breath and plunged in. 'You can't have a celibate marriage, can you? The Parkinson's has taken away all my ...' I paused, searching for the right words to describe my predicament without subjecting Nell to any unnecessary descriptions. 'All my ...'

'Save yourself the embarrassment of having to explain, Mr Marshall,' she said, 'I get the picture. Don't forget I have first hand, close up and personal knowledge of your illness.'

'Yes, yes of course, I'm sorry, how silly of me. Forgive my lack of thought, Nell.'

'Nothing to forgive, as usual,' she said reassuringly before confiding, 'Joshua minded terribly about it, but he was younger than you.'

'Yes.'

She scrutinised my face. 'But do you mind? Really, do you? I don't know why, but I get the impression you have sown so many wild oats in the past, it may actually come as a relief not to be driven by your hormones any more.'

I was stunned by her insight. How could she read my innermost thoughts when my face was so often blank and stuck and devoid of much expression? 'Actually, no I don't really mind for myself and it is a relief in some ways, but I would mind for the unfortunate woman who decided to take me on.'

She frowned slightly. 'But what if she didn't mind either? I think there are probably more celibate relationships than we realise. I mean, who the hell is going to admit it? People don't admit it because they think everyone else is having loads of sex and will ridicule those who aren't, but I reckon it's all overhyped and over-exaggerated. Mind you, why should people talk about it anyway; it's a private thing and should remain so. Don't you think?' she asked.

'I do, Nell.'

'I think, for what it's worth, that if you met some woman and you both loved each other and neither was worried about that side of things then ... it could be perfect.'

I smiled at her. 'You make it all sound so lovely.'

She smiled back. 'Well, it could be.'

'Yes, perhaps.'

'I didn't mind with Joshua,' she added. 'Even at the age I was then.'

'Honestly?'

She looked into my eyes. 'Do you doubt me, Mr Marshall?'

'But you were so young.'

'But I would rather have been with him without any of that than with any other man *with* all of that. Does that make sense?'

'Perfect sense,' I replied, thinking to myself that the man must have been more than a little mad to have thrown Nell's love away.

'I know what you're thinking,' she said.

'Do you?'

'Yes and don't forget he was in the throes of a deep depression. Clarity of thought isn't available to you when you're severely depressed.'

'No.'

We were both silent for a few moments and I basked in the glow of our mutual intimacy. The kind of intimacy I had never experienced with a woman before, where I was able to be completely honest and not judged, especially where sex was concerned.

'And anyway,' she added with a cheeky smile, 'you could always hang it out the window and pray for a frost.'

I spluttered as I laughed. 'Say that again.'

'You heard.'

'You are priceless.'

'I know,' she said with her nose in the air.

'Nell, what do you think of me? I mean truly think of me?'

'I think you're wonderful,' she answered immediately without even thinking about it for a second.

'Thank you for that, but I'm not looking for compliments. I just doubt myself every day.'

'You promised you wouldn't be so introspective. You're supposed to be looking forward, not back,' she declared. 'And, I think you're analytical, kind, thoughtful, complex and smart.'

'I just wish ...'

She looked exasperated. 'Don't start all that again! Look, if you worry about the past then be the man you've always wanted to be from now on. It's never too late.'

'Yes, yes I'm trying, but often I feel haunted and I don't know why.'

'Perhaps you should go back to the GP or ask William about it because I can see it's beginning to eat away at you. I don't want that for you. Ultimately Beth loves you and that's all that matters, isn't it?'

'Yes, of course, but I could have ...'

'If you say you could have been a better father I'll crown you!' she cried. 'We could *all* do better, be better, but we're human and those mistakes make us better people. A little guilt might be a good thing because it teaches us not to act that way again, but guilt that eats away at you like yours is unhealthy and useless. It's such a waste of time and emotional energy, especially if it's unwarranted like yours is. Let yourself off the hook, Mr Marshall otherwise it will affect the illness, I'm sure.'

'You make life sound so wonderful, so simple.'

'I know,' she said, 'but I haven't got a chronic illness. I know it's a weight around your neck dragging you down. I do understand. Joshua was the same. He couldn't see past it, it was like a black cloud blocking out the sun. Every time he thought he'd got past it, another hurdle appeared.'

'Nell, did he ever talk about a *presence*?'

She looked intrigued. 'What do you mean?'

'Often I feel a *presence* hovering near me.'

'Do you mean your father?'

'No, it's a non-physical *presence*. I can't see it, but I can feel it. It's very hard to describe. It's a little like feeling you're never alone, as if someone or something is in the room with you.'

Nell looked thoughtful for a moment. 'He used to say he sensed his wife near him, but I thought that was wishful thinking. He did actually use the word *haunted* once. Is that what you mean?'

'Well, almost.'

'Just before he died he said he felt she was waiting for him somewhere, not in heaven, but somewhere he couldn't describe.'

'That makes sense to me.'

She gazed ahead of her. 'It was hard for me because I felt at times ...'

All of a sudden the tables had turned; now it was Nell who was unable to voice what she was feeling and I wanted to support and encourage her as she had me. 'Tell me, Nell, please.'

She nodded gratefully at me, 'Well, I felt that I was living with a ghost. She was always there between us. I didn't mind because he had adored her, but I was definitely second best.'

'I find that very hard to believe.'

'It's true and it's just the way it was. Nobody can predict human emotions, especially love.'

'No.'

'I'm glad I told you that,' she murmured, 'I've always wanted to tell someone, but I didn't want to admit it to myself.'

'It's lovely to be able to chat like this, Nell.'

'Yes,' she said, 'it is.'

'I don't want to burden you though.'

She gave me a winning smile. 'It's not a burden, it's a pleasure.'

'That's kind, Nell, thank you. You always have such a sympathetic ear for my problems and I should listen to you more; is there anything else you'd like to talk about?'

'Well, maybe you could give me a reason for my lack of interest in men.'

I glanced askance at her and spoke thoughtfully, 'I see; well, would that be *all* men or are we just talking about ones with cute faces and green eyes?'

'Are you talking about Frankie?' she asked.

'How many cute looking men with green eyes do you know?'

'I don't know many, and to answer your question, yes all men.'

'Ah! Well, that's a big subject; perhaps we should start with Frankie. Chemistry is a wondrous thing, but I'm guessing that chemistry is lacking and if it isn't there, it isn't there! Isn't that profound of me?'

'Oh yes, very profound. But he's attractive, funny, talented ...'

'And he has those incredible green eyes.'

'Yes and there are loads of women after him.'

'But he wants you.'

'He says he loves me.'

'But you doubt him?'

'Yes.'

'Why do you doubt him?'

'I doubt him because I don't *feel* it. Love is about actions and feelings, not words. Anyone can say he loves you, but it's the actual loving that's hard.'

'Or not as the case may be,' I remarked.

She said nothing in response, but looked intensely vulnerable. I longed to put my arms around her, but I knew it would be inappropriate and I had no intention of taking advantage of her sudden fragility.

'Were your parents happy together?' she asked suddenly.

'Yes, very.'

She gave a wistful smile. 'Mine too. Lucky, weren't they?'

'They were very lucky, Nell.'

'Then why hasn't it happened for us?'

I was perplexed by her question. 'What do you mean?'

'Oh you know; often the children of happy parents make happy relationships themselves because that's what they know and vice versa. Children of divorced parents often go on to get divorced themselves. But you and I, we aren't following in our parents footsteps.'

'Ah yes, but I'm the only failure here,' I told her with feeling. 'Your partner died, that wasn't anything to do with you. I'm the one who is a product of an intensely loving family and can't seem to reproduce the same in my life.'

'Failure!' she declared indignantly. 'Will you please stop using that term? You are not, have never been and will never be a failure. Who defines what a failure is anyway?'

'It's simply a feeling that won't go away ...'

'Well, *make* it go away,' she urged. 'I keep telling you, these feelings of guilt and failure will eat away at you and it won't help your health.'

I smiled at her indignant expression. 'Nell, you are right as usual.'

'About you and your tortured thoughts I am, that's for sure.'

We looked at each other in silence for a few moments and I was trying to read her face, but other than looking shockingly alive and brimming with vitality, I couldn't guess what her thoughts were. Suddenly her face broke into the broadest smile and my world sparkled with electricity and life and instead of merely sitting on that bench under a greyish sky, I was transported to a world of bright, swirling colours. The clarity of the air seemed almost unreal and I felt I was floating, weightless, inches from the ground. The intense and longed for happiness I had been chasing all my adult life was there beside me, inside me and hovering in front of me, as if it were a thing of substance and not simply an emotion. I put my trembling hand out and made a grasping movement hoping to actually hold it, but it eluded me until I touched Nell's face as softly as I could. I was lost, totally and helplessly in my love for her. Touching her wasn't something I had thought about, but it was instinctive at that moment. I drew my hand back immediately, embarrassed and concerned, as if I had touched fire.

'I'm so sorry, Nell,' I gasped, my heart racing, 'I was in a dream then.

I shouldn't have done that. It was only an affectionate ... it wasn't meant to be ... I'm sorry.'

'Don't be daft,' she murmured, 'I know it wasn't meant to be anything other than what it was. Relax, Mr Marshall.'

'Yes, sorry,' I stuttered, relief raging through me.

'What were you thinking then? When you touched my face?'

Although I felt relief at her calm response to my touch, I was still embarrassed and strove to lighten the atmosphere. 'I'm not telling you!' I declared, with an air of forced superiority that I knew would make her laugh and laugh she did.

'Oh go on, tell me.'

'I can't remember to be honest.'

'Yes you can.'

'I think you looked a little melancholy at one point when we were talking about happy relationships so I just wanted to ... I don't know ...' I shrugged and I thought, yes of course I can remember, but I can't tell you. But I had to give her an explanation and in my discomfort spoke a touch too loudly. 'I just wanted to offer a bit of comfort and...I don't know ...you looked...' I stammered, unable to continue.

'You mean I had a face like four pence?'

'Say that again.'

'A face like four pence,' she repeated, 'you must have heard that expression before in your ivory tower.'

'I most certainly have not! We never used expressions like that in leafy Sussex.'

She laughed. 'You are funny, Mr Marshall.'

'So you keep saying, but funny ha ha or funny peculiar?'

'You're definitely funny ha ha.'

'But let's return to the green-eyed Frankie.'

'OK,' she sighed, 'if we must.'

'Chemistry cannot be forced or called to order, that much I know. He may well love you in his own way, but if it isn't the way you want to be loved then that's up to you. I'm only going on appearances, but he doesn't strike me as someone who would love the pilgrim soul in you or love the sorrows of your changing face.'

She gave me a fond look. 'I knew you'd understand and you're right, but will I ever find that? What if I don't?'

'I ... I sincerely hope you do, Nell.'

Her face changed for a brief second and an expression of such longing came over her it made me catch my breath. 'I'd settle for your friendship any day,' she whispered.

I was stunned. What on earth did she mean? I felt my stiff facial muscles twitch with emotion. 'You will *always* have my friendship, Nell. You must know that. I give you my word, for what's it is worth.'

She beamed. 'Of course I know that and you have mine.' She held out her hand and I took it. We must have appeared, to anyone watching, like two people sealing a business deal. 'I am *so* glad I met you, Mr Marshall.'

'Thank you and I feel the same.'

She sat back and sighed. 'You remind me so much of Joshua.' I felt slightly uncomfortable at her words, but I couldn't work out why. I often lost clarity of thought when near her. 'Right' she continued, 'what shall we chat about now?'

'How I got to be so devastatingly attractive?'

'Shut your face, you.'

'I'm not sure I can actually shut my face. It may prove to be a little difficult. I can make it blank, rigid, twitchy, but shut it? I think not.'

'You're as daft as a lorry load of blue monkeys,' she declared.

I shook my head in disbelief. 'Say that again.'

'You heard.'

'I did and I agree,' I replied, succinctly.

Abruptly she inexplicably changed the subject, saying, 'I loved Lily.'

'Lily? Oh, yes, Lily is lovely.'

'What an attractive woman. She looks like she could have been a model. And she was so warm. So was William.'

'Unlike Bethan,' I added knowingly. 'Bethan doesn't mean to be so hard it's ...'

'It's her job,' Nell contributed.

'Maybe, but she's become so cynical and mistrustful, it taints her view of the world and everyone in it.'

'Yeah, but it would, wouldn't it?'

'I was cross with her.'

'She just loves you.'

'My generous Nell,' I muttered. 'I wish everyone was as generous as you.' I turned to smile at her, but she was gazing out at London's metal-grey skyline.

'Lily would be just the right type of woman for you.'

'Right for me?' I spluttered.

'Yeah, you know, attractive, mature, warm and intelligent.'

'Well ... I don't know.' My heart was sinking rapidly to my knees. 'I'm not sure...'

She turned to look at me. 'I'd love for you to meet someone like that.'

'Would you, Nell?' I mumbled and my voice sounded despicably forlorn.

'A woman like her would understand our relationship and not be threatened by it, you know?'

I didn't quite understand what she was getting at, but responded, 'Yes, I suppose so.'

'Same age, similar experiences in life, similar backgrounds, intellectuals together discussing academic stuff. Or should it be academics together discussing intellectual stuff? Oh you get what I mean.'

'Perhaps ...'

'And she's probably past wanting a brilliant sex life. No doubt she's been there, done it all.'

'Perhaps,' I muttered again, my mood fast following my sinking heart.

Nell peered into my face. 'Are you OK, Mr Marshall?'

'Yes ... fine ... a bit ... chilly ...'

My brain was bombarded with images of myself with a Lily-type woman, arm in arm, with Nell looking fondly on as she would her parents. The full and sudden realisation that my Nell was hoping I would meet someone perfect for me, instead of seeing herself in that role, caused all my muscles to seize up with tension. I could feel my face going rigid and blank. But why was I so affected by her words when I had been telling anyone who would listen that she and I were only friends and that I merely expected to worship her from afar and hopefully be the person she could turn to in times of trouble?

'My God, how selfish of me sitting here chatting on about a future partner for you and you're slowly freezing to death! Come on, let's go. You need to move about a bit I reckon. Take my arm.'

'Thank you.'

I staggered to my feet and took her arm gladly. I noticed a woman sitting nearby smiling in a way that told me she thought Nell was either my loving daughter or even worse, my carer. I shuddered at the thought and mentally kicked myself for having any other dreams about our relationship. What a fool! What a stupid, pathetic, stumbling fool to think that this beautiful, effervescent young woman, who could have any man she chose, would ever entertain the notion that she and I could be partners in that sense. Taunting voices echoed round my head.

'You are a silly old fool!'

'You're just being an idiot, Benedict.'

'She's too young, Dad.'

'It's such a cliché, Benedict! Older man with chronic disease, younger woman!

More and more whispering, chattering voices seemed to clamour for my attention, desperate to be heard, but it was only a fresh breeze picking up and starting to rustle through the horse-chestnut trees . Nell's sturdy walk helped to steady my progress on my shaking, spindly legs, but suddenly the *presence* hovered just in front of us making me uneasy, causing me to take a sharp intake of breath.

'What is it?' she asked, looking up at me.

'I'm being haunted,' I whispered.

She was immediately concerned. 'What do you mean? Being haunted by what, by whom?'

I couldn't answer her because I had but one thought racing through my head, tormenting me. I was being haunted by my own stupidity, believing I had a chance of being the man Nell could love and my longing for that. My head cleared in an instant; I was struck by the realisation that Joshua had ultimately been nobler than I could ever be; he had set her free. Now I had to find the strength to do the same by freeing her from the chains of our close friendship. To outsiders it would probably appear obvious that the intense and overpowering love she had felt for the man she lost, with his dark moods, introspection and Parkinson's symptoms was somehow being played out again in her desire to be friends with me. Yes, it was now becoming clear. She was attempting to recreate that relationship even though it had caused her so much pain. She still loved him. She still longed for him. She could no longer have him so she was recreating that closeness with someone who, every day, reminded her of him. And because she had strong feelings for me, she longed for me to have the same with a Lily type of woman. Someone she mistakenly thought was my intellectual equal because she revered my so called academic mind.

What a pathetic fool I was and I would have to make amends for all my useless dreams. I would set her free by distancing myself from her. Then she would be able to fly, as she had always longed to, without the men in her life hampering her longed for freedom.

Chapter 12

'You've gone ever so quiet suddenly, Mr Marshall.'

Nell's clear, expressive eyes were boring into my soul, trying to find out my deepest secrets. I knew I had to give an explanation for my sudden sombre mood and that if I made something up she would see right through me. We were making our slow descent of the path to the large expanse of gently undulating grass near my home. It caused me some intense aching in my knees which normally I would complain about, but my mind was so distracted by the thought of Nell finding me an ideal partner, I hardly felt the pain. I felt I had to stop though so I gasped, 'I'm sorry ...'

'What's wrong?'

'Can I rest for a second?'

'Of course you can. Shall we sit down here? I don't think it's damp.' She bent down and ran her fingers over the grass softly. 'No, dry enough.'

'I can sit down, but getting up may be harder.'

'I'll get you up, don't worry about that. You look exhausted.'

We sat side by side in the muted sunlight, my long, ridiculously thin legs reaching far beyond hers and I was attempting to bring some order to my dark, tortured and jumbled thoughts, 'Nell, give me a minute. I need to think.'

She appeared concerned. 'Take your time. I'm so sorry if I've knackered you. Take as long as you want.'

Her eyes never left my face as I struggled with my complex, incomprehensible emotions. What was I thinking? Well, yes there it was staring me in the face. I was a fool. Perhaps I had always been a fool. Maybe Mary had been more sinned against than sinning after all. Perhaps all my failed relationships had been due to my foolishness. Yes, it was plainly all down to me. I had an exaggerated idea of my own importance and thought every woman would ultimately find me fiendishly attractive and fall hopelessly in love with me. Even with the Parkinson's and the unrelenting battery of symptoms, they wouldn't be able to resist my charms. Nell included. Had I honestly thought that she, who could have anyone of her choosing, including all the cute, green-eyed, lusty, talented young men she came across every day, would prefer to be with someone old enough to be her father? What kind of choice would it be between youth, vigour, strength and a dynamic personality and an ageing, stumbling, dribbling man who was hurtling towards invalidity without a brake on? Ignorant, pathetic, idiotic fool!

The *presence* hovered near, mocking me and almost brushing against my shoulder and I waved my hand in front of my face to get rid of it. Nell continued to watch me closely and I could feel the tension coming from her body.

'Please tell me what's troubling you,' she urged me. 'It was something I said and I'm trying to work out what it was. Please tell me, Mr Marshall.'

My mouth went to move, but it was stuck and I made a mumbling sound that sounded like drivel. I took a deep breath of rage at my continual lack of eloquence. She put her hand under my chin and turned my head towards her. My glasses slipped down my nose and she gently pushed them up again. Her grave expression made me want to heave with guilt because it looked so unlike her. I tried to convey with my eyes how much she meant to me because God knows I couldn't say it out loud. I was searching for the courage to confront my feelings and express them without sounding like a dirty old man. Did I truly expect this rare, incomparable young woman to be my nursemaid? Did I really want her to wipe my chin, cook my meals, help me put on my socks? That would be my idea of hell – and probably hers too. Loving her and getting to know her had been delightfully natural and easy, but I had given so little genuine thought to the reality of my situation. No, I would have to set her free from any obligation; but how to do it without breaking my own heart and hurting her? How to explain without making her feel obliged in any way?

'Nell,' I began, 'I don't want...I don't want someone like Lily.'

Her face fell. 'Oh, I'm so sorry, I didn't mean to imply that you should ... how rude of me!' She looked crestfallen. 'How could I have been so thoughtless? It's nothing to do with me who you ... For God's sake, I'm so sorry, Mr Marshall.'

'Don't be.'

'I'd hate anyone to say that kind of thing to me. I'd tell them to mind their own bloody business and I didn't really want you to ... I mean, I just thought she was your type of woman. You know, sophisticated, super intelligent. I...'

'I don't know that she's super intelligent,' I interrupted, finding my voice at last.

'She seemed it to me.'

'Appearances can be deceptive and I'm not entirely sure I want to be intellectually stimulated with this *disease* attacking my brain cells because I have no idea for how much longer I can be intellectually stimulating back. I don't want any kind of rollercoaster. I would prefer a gentler, meandering ride with a few soft twists and turns and no sudden or abrupt beginnings or endings.' I took a deep breath and continued, wanting to get everything I was feeling off my chest once and for all. 'I've had enough shocks to last me a lifetime. I want stimulating, but easy, conversation that makes my heart sing. I don't need anyone to be clever, I need them to be kind and funny. I want to laugh with someone without the worry of being ridiculed when I stumble over my words and dribble. Lily is unquestionably a lovely, warm woman with a sharp mind who suits my brother because he still needs a challenge; someone who can be his equal and who wants to live the same kind of life, but he is a *well* man. He doesn't have Parkinson's and isn't staring into a bleak future of uncertainty. I am and I don't think it's fair to have anyone facing that uncertain future with me.'

She placed her warm hand on mine. 'But what would you do if you met a woman who wanted to face that uncertain future with you? You might you know.'

I gritted my teeth. 'I wouldn't let them. I'd set them free.'

Her grey eyes grew larger with sorrow. 'Like Joshua?'

I screwed my face up in frustration and despair at my thoughtless words. 'No, no, no, that's not what I meant to say. I'm sorry, Nell, I didn't mean to choose those words. To be perfectly frank, I'm not sure what I mean. I go to say something and then different words come out of this bloody useless mouth of mine.'

'Don't worry, I understand.'

'Nell, this much I know. I'm immensely grateful to have met you. Your friendship has been a lifeline for me. The mere thought of being with someone like Lily, no ... that you *wanted* someone like Lily for me ... Oh, I can't explain. I suppose what I'm trying desperately to say is ...'

She put her head on one side. 'Did you think that if you had a Lily in your life you couldn't be friends with me?'

I had no more sensible or coherent words to explain what I had been thinking because I didn't understand any of it myself. My mood had plummeted when I imagined she wanted me to find my ideal partner, when I knew full well that only *she* could fulfil that role. But then the mere idea of her administering to my every disease-ridden need was abhorrent to me so my thoughts instantly turned even darker and I toyed with the idea of letting her friendship go. She had even caught on to the fact that a future partner of mine might be jealous of our closeness, which hadn't even occurred to me because I knew there wasn't any future partner for me when only she could be that companion. My thoughts were scrambled, spinning in my head like clothes in a tumble dryer, but I knew I had to end the conversation before it drove me to insanity, 'Perhaps,' I mumbled. 'Yes, that might be it. I'm sorry.'

She gave me the most tender of smiles and squeezed my lifeless hand gently. 'Mr Marshall, if I'm perfectly honest, I can't see you with a Lily-type either. I don't know why I said it really. You see, we can all make mistakes.'

'Nell ...'

'I can't actually imagine who would take you on.'

I glanced at her and noticed the playfulness in her eyes. I decided to match it to release us both from a decidedly tricky conversation. 'I'll have you know, the barmaid in the Trafalgar has eyes only for me.'

She let out her wondrous, ear-splitting laugh and the tension melted away immediately. 'Has she now? You old devil! Who says so?'

I tried to look imperious. 'Sidney says so.'

'Does he now? Well, I think that wily old rascal could probably be right.'

'Maybe, but she's never seen me dribble.'

Her hands flew to her mouth. 'Oh, don't say that.'

'It's true though.'

'Even with the occasional slight dribble and a little slurring now and again, a stumble here and there, you are still a most attractive man.'

I feigned surprise. 'Why, thank you.'

'For your age,' she added, her eyes sparkling.

'Aha, I see.' There was silence for a few moments and then I sighed and took her hand. 'I'm frightened of being diminished, Nell.'

'Do you mean by the Parkinson's?' she asked, squeezing my trembling hand.

'Yes, I mean by the Parkinson's.'

'You will *never* be diminished, Mr Marshall, not in my eyes.'

'Thank you for that. Don't get me wrong, I'm not bothered about being invisible to women now. I don't want to be the man I was. But the future holds so many unknowns.'

'Yes, but it could also hold unlimited possibilities,' she urged, 'like gene therapy, stem cell therapy and deep brain stimulation...'

'Ah yes, drilling into your brain while you're awake!'

'But if it worked, it would be worth it, wouldn't it?'

'Of course,' I said, wanting to lighten the dark mood I had created. 'It's just that I imagined growing older with panache and flair, with dignity and eccentricity. I wanted to be one of those older men who everyone wanted to spend time with because they are fascinating.'

'But you are that *now*,' Nell cried, clutching both my hands, 'that's exactly who you are and Parkinson's can't diminish that.'

'I hope you're right, Nell.'

Her face suddenly lit up. 'And Parkinson's brought us together. I noticed you because of the way you were sitting.'

'How was I sitting?'

'Hunched, defeated, haunted and I found it hard to look away.'

'You mean you wouldn't have noticed me anyway? I'm cut to the quick, Nell. I thought I was hellishly attractive and irresistible.'

She laughed, throwing her head back. 'Well, I was approaching you from behind remember?'

'Ah yes, not my best side.'

'I'll say this only once, Mr Marshall,' she said, her face serious suddenly. 'You will never be invisible. You will never be diminished. Parkinson's will never make you less than you are now at this moment.'

'Thank you,' I muttered, so immensely grateful to know her I could have turned to any religion and give thanks for my luck.

'So, will you forgive me for mentioning a Lily type woman might be perfect for you?'

'Nothing to forgive, Nell...'

'Are we still friends?' she asked, in such an appealing manner I could have kicked myself for thinking of letting her friendship go.

'Always,' I told her.

Her face relaxed into a relieved smile. 'Your hand is cold. Shall we go home?'

Hearing her use the word 'home' made my stomach lurch-would that it *were* her home. No, it couldn't ever be. That would mean she would be looking after me. But what was I thinking? We were friends and that was all. Think, Benedict, think! I had to let go of any ridiculous dreams of her being anything but my dearest friend and before I could stop myself mumbled, 'It's not your home.' I hoped to God she hadn't heard me, but her face crumpled and she withdrew her hand.

'Sorry,' she gasped, 'I only meant ... sorry!'

I grabbed her hand back. 'No! You have to forgive *me*, Nell. I didn't mean anything by that remark. I apologise...this disease it ... Please, please, forgive me. I had been imagining someone, a future partner, living there – you know, what we were discussing – and it just came out as if ... What was I thinking?' I could feel my heart thumping in my temples and imagined the colour draining from my ridiculous face and spilling out onto the grass. 'Nell, I don't feel all that well ...'

'Hush, hush, Mr Marshall,' she whispered, placing one hand on my forehead and one around my shoulders, 'everything's OK, I understand. Let's get you back. Can you get up or shall I pull you?'

I could feel her steady hand on me and it gave me energy and courage, despite my whole body going into a kind of shock where everything felt as if it was grinding to a halt. I struggled, with her help, to my feet and guided by her gentle arms we walked back to my house. She said nothing, but was watching me constantly as I fumbled for my keys and unlocked the door. Once inside I slumped onto my sofa and closed my eyes, 'I just need to rest for a little while.'

'I'll put the kettle on. Don't move.'

'Thank you.'

The intense fatigue I felt at that moment had washed over me in an instant and every muscle seemed to ache and throb and I felt restless and listless at the same time. I knew my thought processes had been turned upside down and to not be in control of my brain was what terrified me most of all. What kind of future would it be not to be able to think clearly or have an intelligent, coherent conversation? I could hear Nell placing the tea cups on the tray and I could have cried.

'You know what I think, Mr Marshall?' she said as she carried our tea in.

'No, Nell, tell me what you think?'

'Well, remember I have some knowledge of this illness.'

'Yes, of course.'

'You haven't been back once to your GP since your diagnosis and I reckon he needs to look at your tablets,' she pronounced, pouring out the steaming tea.

'Do you now?'

'Yes, I do,' she said, succinctly. 'Often they have to try you on a couple before you find the ones that suit you. I've just got this feeling, instinct if you like, that you aren't on the best ones for you. Or, you're rushing things and need to give these ones time to settle into your system. It's something in the way you talk ...'

'Slur you mean.'

'No, it isn't the slurring or occasional stumble over your words. It's your thought processes that aren't right.'

'Are you trying to say I'm not making any sense today?' I asked, trying to smile.

'Well ...'

'Good grief!' I put my hand over my eyes for a moment. 'I can't bear the thought of not making sense.'

She passed my tea to me. 'You were and you weren't. I can't explain.'

'Don't worry, Nell, that's exactly how my thoughts were, sometimes making sense and sometimes not.'

'You look a little better now, thank goodness.'

'I feel a little better now – I think.'

'And you'll go and see your GP?'

'I will.'

She narrowed her eyes as if she didn't believe me. 'Promise me?'

'I promise you.'

There was a sudden knock on the wall, a Sidney knock. Nell laughed out loud. 'He's missing you.'

I didn't want her to leave. 'Ignore it, Nell.'

She looked a little concerned. 'Ah, dear Sidney, let him come in. He loves you and you need him more than you know.'

Her kind heart was enough to bring tears stinging into my eyes and I gave her a wan smile. 'Knock back three times then.'

She jumped up and knocked gently. 'I'll leave you two to it.'

My heart sank. 'You don't have to go.'

'I know that, but places to go, people to see.'

'Of course, I'm sorry.' There was a moments silence as we simply stared at each other. Me with what I imagined was a forlorn look and her with her sympathetic, constantly caring expression. I wondered what on earth she was thinking as she looked at my crumpled, decaying body. 'Go, Nell,' I urged. 'I'll be fine with Sydney.'

Her smile showed her sense of relief. 'Take it easy, Mr Marshall. I'll call you later to see how you feel.'

'Will you, Nell?' I asked, sounding like a pathetic old man, which of course I was.

'Don't get up,' she said, giving me her usual small wave and as she disappeared and I heard the front door close gently, Sidney walked in the conservatory door, all flushed cheeks and bushy eyebrows.

'So, what's occurring then, Benedict?' he asked, so cheerfully it made me feel exhausted.

'Very little, Sidney, as you can see.'

He peered at me and frowned. 'You look a bit pale, matey.'

'I *feel* a bit pale.'

'Are you all right?'

'Yes, I'm fine. I was walking with Nell and I became a little ...'

'Oh yeah ...'

I laughed, despite myself because he always said that in exactly the same knowing way, when in reality he knew very little. But at least he had made me laugh and I was grateful for that.

'Sidney, I fear I'm going slowly mad.'

'Huh! You're the sanest person I know, which isn't saying much of course.'

'I used to be sane, but not so much now. The Parkinson's is doing odd things to my brain.'

'It might be the tablets,' he commented, sitting himself down opposite me.

'That's what Nell said.'

'Go back and see the quack, eh?'

'Yes, I think I will. I made a fool of myself today.'

'Oh yeah ...'

'Not like that! God forbid!' I muttered, shuddering. 'If I ever sit here and confess to you that I've made a fool of myself in *that* way, I give you permission to call me all the silly buggers under the sun and put a pillow over my face.'

'I will.'

'Thank you. No, I just thought she was trying to suggest I find a nice mature woman to settle down with in my dotage and, I don't know, my mood altered dramatically and my body followed and went into a kind of shock.'

'What's wrong with finding a nice mature woman?' he asked, bemused.

'I don't want a nice mature woman; I want ... I want ...'

His fond smile told me he knew exactly what I wanted and he laughed, his belly wobbling up and down alarmingly. 'You are a silly old sod.'

'I am, Sidney, I agree.'

'An intellectual one maybe, but still a silly old sod...'

'If you say so, but I don't feel intellectual, I feel a fool.'

'All men are fools, aren't they?'

'Ultimately, yes they are.'

He looked thoughtful for a moment. 'I don't blame you for loving her, Benedict. She's very lovable and with that face, it's not surprising you can't take your eyes off her.'

'It's not her *face*,' I insisted.

'What?'

'I said, it's not her *face*. If she were hideously disfigured in an accident, do you think I could possibly love her less? It would make no difference to me. I would only mind because she would. It's just her: lovely, funny, kind, thoughtful her!'

Sidney sighed heavily and spoke deliberately, 'You – silly – old – sod; you're a hopeless case.'

'Yes.'

'Where's it all going to end?'

'With Nell falling in love with some man who will probably resent our friendship and I'll have to watch her walk away into the sunset with him.'

'Or she'll stay in America,' he suggested.

'Or she'll stay in America,' I repeated, 'and end up being a world-famous performer who once befriended a man who had lost his way in life.'

'Or, she may well just love you back.'

Sidney's well meaning remark made my heart begin to race with frustration and rage at my disease and the fact that I was no longer young enough to consider a relationship with Nell. 'Dream on,' I muttered.

'We all need dreams, Benedict.'

'Yes, Sidney, I agree, but that is one dream too far and if I long for it to come true I'll only end up making myself unhappy. Now, I promised Nell I would ring my GP and that's exactly what I'm going to do.'

I was lucky enough to get an appointment with Dr Cameron the next morning. I say lucky because Nell rang me later that evening to check I had done as she asked.

'I'm going in the morning,' I told her.

'That's great, I'm so pleased. I'm sure the doctor will sort you out. Something isn't right, Mr Marshall, believe me.'

'I do believe you, dear girl.'

'Let me know how you got on when I ring tomorrow evening.'

The next morning, Dr Cameron sat patiently and listened to my ramblings about my obsessive and jumbled thoughts, continual guilt, intense fatigue and all the other problems that had plagued me.

'It may be one of your tablets is not suited to you. Or you may need to give them a bit more time. I'm going to email your consultant later. Let's see what Mr Birch thinks, shall we? He's the expert after all. His secretary will ring you.'

I have no idea what Dr Cameron put in the email, but two days later I was in Mr Birch's pristine consulting rooms explaining in detail my tortuous thoughts. He was a no-nonsense kind of person, straight and to the point and obviously highly intelligent, with his fascinating twitching eyes and deep compassion.

'Is there anything else bothering you? Any strange feelings like ...'

I didn't let him finish his sentence. 'Yes, very strange feelings.' Immediately I had his full attention.

'Describe them to me in detail please.'

'I often feel as if someone is in the room with me when there is no-one. It's a kind of *presence* that I find hard to pinpoint, but it's most definitely there. It hovers around me, often when I feel unwell or I'm worrying unduly about something.'

He nodded slowly. 'It's well documented,' he commented, 'and just as you are describing it. So, it's just a feeling, no actual hallucinations?'

'Yes; I mean *no*,' I slurred, relieved to be telling him, 'it's not *just* a feeling; it's more than that, it's well, like I said, a *presence*. But there's also something else that's entirely different from the *presence:* I've also seen my father sitting by the piano. He died many years ago so it was quite a shock, but that's different from ... Sorry, I'm repeating myself and not making myself clear.'

He didn't appear surprised or bemused but simply asked, 'Did your father speak to you?'

'Yes.'

I anticipated some kind of reaction, but there was none. It was all in a day's work for him. He probably saw Parkinson's sufferers every day with the same tale. He tapped his fingers on the table and his face twitched. He was deep in thought for a few moments and I awaited his explanation eagerly.

'Well, Benedict,' he started, his eyebrows locked together in a firm frown. 'This must all have been very troubling for you. We do know the drugs work well on the more difficult aspects of this disease, but unfortunately they bring awful side effects for some people. I'm not going to change your tablets. You need to give them quite a bit longer to relieve you of any of this. However, I'm going to tweak the dosage. I don't know as yet whether it is the medication or the illness causing your guilty, obsessive thoughts or whether that's just you. Your hallucinations could well be caused by the tablets though. No, I'll rephrase that, they *are* caused by the tablets. Hallucinations can be exceedingly alarming; seeing your father must have been a great shock. But also I find that most people find the obsessive, guilty thoughts very difficult to live with on a daily basis. These thoughts may well be just the shock of the diagnosis; you know, looking back on your life, wondering what you did to deserve this, could you have lived a better life? All of that is common after a life-changing diagnosis so I don't want to change anything yet. The different dosage will help, I'm sure. We often have to tweak a bit to get things exactly right for the patient. You must allow the time to let the dust settle, but do avoid stressful situations, won't you?'

I felt immensely relieved that I might wake up one morning without the tortuous thoughts ruining my day. 'Yes, I'll do my best. Thank you.'

'What about the tremors and fatigue?'

'I can live with the tremors and the fatigue. I mean, I wish I didn't have to live with them but I can. The occasional dribbling is hard to accept though.'

His no-nonsense expression softened considerably. 'Yes, I can imagine, but keep a tissue with you at all times and if you feel a dribble is forming, swipe it before it gets a chance to do its worst. What about sexual function?'

I wanted to smirk and give a glib answer, but I checked myself in time and merely shrugged my shoulders. 'I have no sexual feelings at all and I can't say it's bothering me. I'm not married now and there is no significant other, so I have to admit it's the least of my worries.'

'Right then, give everything a little more time, don't be in a hurry and I hope you will feel less ...'

'Haunted?'

He gave an understanding smile, 'Yes, I can imagine that's exactly what it feels like.' He stood up and offered his hand. 'All the best and if you have any significant changes, call my secretary immediately. Otherwise I'll see you in a month.'

'Thank you,' I whispered, because my throat felt impossibly tight with tension and I shuffled out of his office.

When I recounted all of our conversation to Nell on the phone she gasped with delight. 'That's brilliant news, Mr Marshall.'

'Is it?'

'Of course it is! OK, so it's going to take a little time before you can hope to feel much better, but the consultant thinks you *will* and that's the important thing! And tweaking the dosage will help, I know it will.'

'Let's hope so, Nell.'

'I feel very positive for you.'

'That makes me feel better.' I felt we'd discussed my disease for long enough and asked her, 'What are you doing?'

'I'm learning my lines for this revue.' Her voice betrayed her excitement about performing again. 'The script is funny and lively and I think it's going to be a cracker, but we haven't got long so rehearsals are going to be full on. There won't be much time for our walks I'm afraid.'

My heart sank, but I summoned a cheerful voice, hoping I could fool her, 'Oh never mind about that, I can do that on my own.'

'Will you really? What about the dancing?'

'I'll dance every day,' I declared.

'Are you telling the truth?'

'Do you doubt me, Nell?'

'Yeah, I doubt you,' she laughed.

'Will you bring the script one day for me to read? I'd be very interested to see it.'

'Yes, of course I will. And you let me know how you feel, OK?'

'I will.'

'I'm going to be very busy these next few weeks so forgive me if I don't get round. It isn't because I've forgotten you.'

'Don't worry about me, please. Just live your life and have fun.'

'I'll speak to you soon, Mr Marshall.'

She was as good as her word and although she must have been horrendously busy, she called me every other day. But she had so little free time, many days went by without me being able to sit with her and watch the multitude of varying expressions flitting across her face. I had very little to report to her or Sidney at first regarding any changes or improvement to how I felt, but my mind felt immediately less jumbled. It was almost as if talking to the consultant had made me take the pressure off myself and I relaxed about my symptoms and the tablets side effects. I felt like I'd been given permission to sink into being myself and forget about my past without really saying very much at all. When and if my mind did stray in that direction, I was able to leave any guilt where it belonged and know that it was simply a part of growing up and making mistakes. The relief was enormous and I felt as if someone had tapped me on the shoulder and told me it had all been a big mistake, I didn't have Parkinson's after all. I felt immensely grateful to Mr Birch and thanked my lucky stars he was my consultant.

The *presence* continued to hover over me at times, however, mostly when I was dozing or just waking up from a nap. I had even begun to potter about in my garden again; nothing heavy duty, just snipping plants with my secateurs and attempting a much needed bit of weeding.

Sidney found this hilarious and was constantly peering over the fence and laughing at me. 'The speed you're going, it will be winter before you've pruned anything.'

'That's very funny, Sidney. The gardener is actually coming back next week now it is spring, but this is just a bit of rehabilitation for me. I'd forgotten how lovely it is to be out here.'

'On days like this,' he replied, looking up at a bright, turquoise sky.

'Yes, the air is so clear today, clear and fresh.'

'I've not seen Nell for a while.'

'She's rehearsing, very busy.'

'And I can tell you're missing her.'

I was surprised at his words. I thought I had been hiding the missing of her extremely well. 'Can you?'

'Yeah, you've got a face like a slapped arse all the time, matey.'

'I can't imagine what a face like a slapped arse looks like. Enlighten me, Sidney.'

'I've never actually seen a slapped arse so I can't, but you know what I mean. Fancy a beer?'

The thought of a cold beer made me feel quite boyish and carefree, as if I had no disease. The crushing fatigue had lessened a little and I felt more like my old self. 'Yes, I do. Come through in about ten minutes when I've finished this.'

And so my days went on. Doing little of any consequence, talking to Sidney, attempting to walk around the park on my own so Nell would be proud of me and longing for her to call round, even if only for half an hour. But she didn't call round; she was exhausted from the rehearsals and still trying to fit in teaching her dance classes and shifts in the café. She was very apologetic and telephoned often, but for me it was like a dull ache in my chest, as if somebody was tugging at my heart and trying to rip it out of my body. I told myself over and over again to get a grip, act like an adult and not a lovesick youth and to be grateful for her calls and her friendship, but it was no use and I was beginning to dread her trip to America more and more each day.

'You need distraction,' Sidney told me one evening when I was being typically monosyllabic.

'Yes.'

'Are you actually listening to me, Benedict?'

I shook my head. 'Sidney, how do you put up with me?'

'Fuck knows.'

'Neither do I.'

'Why don't you call up one of your old crowd, go out and about a bit like you used to. You were always out socialising.'

The idea appalled me. 'Perish the thought.'

'Why?'

'I don't know, I feel as if they are all strangers now and I'm a different person since, well, since my diagnosis. I'm not sure I have anything in common with that lot now.'

'Call Lance, he was a nice sort.'

'Yes, he was, that's true enough.' It was indeed true. Lance was an old-school publisher who believed in publishing a work because he felt it was worth reading, not just to make money out of it. I had enjoyed many an interesting discussion about literature with him, but my recalling those discussions was disturbed by Sidney's continued chatter.

'It's the only way to stop missing Nell and you'll need some kind of social life when she's in New York. You know I'm right.'

'You are, but I enjoy talking to *you*. That will do for me.'

He frowned. 'But I'm boring.'

'You most certainly are not! I love talking to you. You are unknowingly funny and great company.'

He beamed and appeared instantly taller. 'Thanks, matey.'

'It's true, Sidney. I'm not making it up just to compliment you.'

'So you'll call him?'

'I might,' I said, in a superior way that I knew would make him laugh and laugh he did.

'I know that face, it means you won't.'

'Leave it with me.'

'Yeah, all right,' he replied, not believing a word of it.

I didn't call Lance. After all this time I couldn't imagine what I would say to him, but everything else went on as before. I continued to rush, in my stumbling, puppet-like way, to the phone when I knew it was Nell, played cards and had a glass or two with Sidney and made the most of the unusually warm, sunny May weather by snipping at the plants here and there in my garden without knowing what the hell I was doing. I even put on some music and attempted an unusual, staggering type of dancing in my conservatory. I imagined Nell in front of me, telling me firmly to hold in my abdominals, soften my knees and stand up straight. I extended my arms like a tree stretching its branches towards the sun and then had to pretend I was swatting a fly because Sidney was watching me over the fence, but he wasn't fooled. The next day when he popped in he mentioned it and I couldn't be bothered to make up a story so I told him exactly what I had been doing.

'You looked like a real twat,' he remarked.

'I know, but I don't really care, Sidney. Nell says it's good for my balance.'

'Put some music on and show me...'

'I most certainly will not!'

'Oh go on,' he urged, looking excited.

'Only if you'll join me,' I pronounced.

'Well, it must be the spring air and the sap rising and all that malarkey because I think I will,' he declared. 'If it'll help your balance then I'm game.'

'Have you been drinking already?' I asked, putting on my Swan Lake CD.

'This music is terrible, I can't dance to this!' I changed the CD and replaced it with the Strauss waltzes that Nell loved. I turned it up as loud as I dared. Sidney had to shout at me. 'That's a bit better. What do we do to this?'

'We waltz of course. I'll be the man...'

'No, you won't! You'll be the woman!'

'That's fine with me.' We attempted a few stumbling steps. 'You have to push me around otherwise I can't do it, Sidney. Now, straight back, pull in your core...'

'What's a core?'

'It means your stomach muscles!'

'Do me a favour...'

'Now lift your head a little...'

'I feel like a twat!'

'You look like a twat...'

'Not as twattish as you, matey.'

And so it went on. We danced for about five minutes like the silly old fools we were and both laughed hard at our ridiculous, awkward bodies, until Sidney collapsed in a chair complaining he felt like Lionel Blair. I wasn't entirely sure who Lionel Blair was, but I sat down heavily opposite him quite breathless and thankful as ever that Sidney Walpole was my friend and that he was prepared to look a twat to help me improve my balance.

Nell was having the time of her life; I could tell that by her voice, which was full of enthusiasm and a love of life. During the short time I had known her she had been out of work, theatrical work, and if I thought she was lively and dynamic then, this was another thing entirely. She was bursting with news about the rehearsals, high as a kite, even more dramatic than usual in a lovely, carefree way. Hearing her babbling on was still the highlight of my day and I treasured every moment. She apologised profusely for not calling in on me, but I relieved her of the obligation by saying I had been walking and gardening and was extremely tired in the evenings and wouldn't be much company.

Towards the middle of May, with the vividly pretty pink and white pink blossom hanging heavily on the avenue of trees in the park which led to our resting place by the statue, I met Thea. She was taking photographs of the gentle mauve, bright yellow and deep red blooming rhododendrons and stepped back, not hearing me approaching because of my unsteady footsteps. We collided and she almost sent me flying backwards, but I managed to save my dignity by grabbing hold of the thick tree trunk beside me.

'Oh my God, I'm so sorry,' she gasped, clamping her hand over her mouth.

'It's quite all right,' I told her breathlessly, 'no harm done, honestly.'

'Are you sure? You look ...'

'I always look like this; slightly vexed and my hair all over the place. Nothing to do with you I assure you. And I'm wearing my best brothel creepers which is why you didn't hear me approaching.' She, on the other hand, looked disgustingly strong and healthy and had hold of me by the arm in a vice-like grip. 'I'm fine, honestly.'

She continued apologetically: 'I always knock into people because

I'm never concentrating properly. These flowers are so beautiful. I just had to get some photographs. I'm Dorothea, but that's a bloody ridiculous name so Thea will do. Thea Stephens.' She finally let go of my arm, much to my delight as I could feel the bruises forming already and offered her hand. 'Sorry to have knocked you flying.'

I took her hand. 'Benedict, Benedict Marshall, pleased to meet you, Thea.'

'Hello, Benedict.'

'Hello.'

'Beautiful day – had to get out.'

'I agree.'

I guessed she was in her early fifties, although it was hard to tell, with shoulder length, wavy chestnut hair and an attractive oval-shaped face with large dark-brown eyes and an extremely direct way of looking at you. I could tell instinctively by the way she had grabbed hold of me that this was a woman you didn't mess with, a woman of some substance and power. She was almost as tall as me, slim and athletic for her years and she spoke at a rate of knots.

'Do you live near?' she asked.

'I do, next to Our Lady Star of The Sea, just down by the gate at the bottom.'

She opened her eyes wide in surprise. 'I live near there. You aren't in the old Rectory are you, Benedict?'

'Yes, I am.'

She gasped. 'I've always wondered who lives in the Rectory.' Her words immediately made me think of Nell and her joy at meeting the owner of her favourite house and I felt my face stiffen and my heart sink. 'Is it OK to say that?' she asked cautiously.

'Of course, sorry ...'

'Only your face fell a mile then.'

I was surprised at her astuteness. 'That's very observant of you. I can't help what my face does these days I'm afraid, it kind of does its own thing.'

'Your garden has those beautiful, tall silver birches at the bottom. I live directly behind you. I'm your neighbour.'

'How lovely...'

'Funnily enough I think I saw the top of your head the other day,' she laughed.

'Oh, that's *not* so lovely for you!' I smiled ruefully and shifted my weight to maintain my balance.

Her eyes took in my awkward posture and she obviously took pity on me. 'Fancy a coffee?'

I glanced towards the café, Nell's and my café, where we had sat through the depths of winter and had begun to get to know each other through long conversations, with the wind howling outside and the rain beating against the windows. I wasn't sure I could go in there without her. 'I know I don't look as if I can walk another fifty yards, but I came out for a stroll so could we?'

'Yes, of course,' she said, with such a cheerful smile my heart warmed to her. 'I came out for a stroll too and to take photographs, but walking in this wonderful weather was my first thought.'

'Thank you.' We ambled towards the flower garden.

'So, Benedict, do you come here often?' she asked, laughing.

'I do, very often.'

'So do I. I absolutely love this park.'

'Yes, so do I.'

'What do you do?'

'Very little if I can help it.'

'Good for you.'

'And you?' I asked.

'I was a Clinical Psychologist.'

'Oh dear, I'm so sorry.'

She glanced sideways at me to see if I was serious or not and when she realised I wasn't she chuckled. 'I know, it sounds so grand. I'm retired now. Early retirement I'll have you know. I now work part time in the book shop in Trafalgar Passage. I love it, all the different customers coming in.'

'Do you try and analyse them all?'

'Sometimes I do, yes.'

'Do you agree with Freud?'

'That every human action comes down to sex or repressed sexuality?'

'Yes, something akin to that.'

She paused for a moment. 'Nah!'

I laughed. 'Thank God for that.'

'But I do think we are all the products of our early childhood.'

'Yes, I would agree. Not that I know anything about it.'

'Well, maybe not, professionally, but everyone has a right to their opinions. But tell me to shut up if I slip into Jung mode.'

'No, I think it's a fascinating subject. I just hope you can't see through me.'

'Well, I can, but don't worry, you pass my test.'

'Your test,' I said blankly, 'am I being tested then?'

'Yes. I can't stand snobs, bullies, arrogant or condescending people. You are none of the above.'

'Thank God for that too.'

'You have something on your mind though. I haven't quite worked out what it is yet and of course it's none of my business, so I'll keep it to myself.'

I was worried she might think my puppet-like walk and stumbling was down to alcohol so I hurriedly said, 'It's not a secret. I have Parkinson's.'

'I didn't mean that,' she replied, 'it's something else, but so sorry about the Parkinson's. Nobody would know though. Slight shaking under the skin when you shook my hand, but I assumed you found me so gorgeous I set you aquiver!' I wasn't sure how to take her, so I simply smiled. 'My daughter would find it very interesting though,' she continued, hardly pausing for breath. 'She's studying medicine in Scotland. Originally she wanted to be a neurologist, but now she's not so sure, she might be a GP instead.'

'That's wonderful.'

Her eyes misted over, 'Yes, but she's a long way away. I miss her.'

'My daughter is in New York, even further.'

'Well, depends if you get stuck on the motorway in bad weather and heavy traffic as I always seem to.'

'Perish the thought.'

Thea changed the subject abruptly, 'Isn't this flower garden kept beautifully?'

'It certainly is, but if I'm honest I prefer a less organised garden.'

'I do too.'

My legs had begun to feel like lead. 'Would you mind if I sit awhile?'

'Please do.'

'I sometimes think I might have to give in to a stick soon. I don't want to but ...'

'Well, if it helps, but don't give in too soon.' She shook her hair from her face in rather a dramatic way. 'Fight the blessed illness with everything you have and never give in to it.'

I thought of Nell and how she had grasped my hand when she barely knew me and urged me never to give up. My mood changed. Every footstep I took in the park reminded me of her, even though I was had an attractive, friendly woman by my side.

'You have a quiet sadness about you,' Thea suddenly said, staring right in my face, 'and I think you have something else on your mind – something other than the Parkinson's.

'Well, I...'

She was looking so deeply into my eyes, I felt almost naked in front of her. 'Are you missing someone?'

'My goodness, you *are* astute.'

'Is she married? Is that the problem?'

'No she's not.' I glanced askance at her, 'But you must have been very good at your job.'

'It's not difficult to work out.'

I suddenly felt the need to unburden myself. 'She's going away and she's much younger than me and ...'

'Does that bother you?'

'That she's young enough to be my daughter? A little, but the disease worries me more.'

We were sitting side by side on a bench. She continued to look directly at my face, her whole body turned towards me. It was unusual for someone you had just met. 'She has no idea how much you love her, does she?'

I raised my eyebrows. 'We've known each other less than ten minutes and not only are you unnervingly good at reading me, but I am also content to bare my soul to you.'

Her warm smile was encouraging. 'I am the keeper of many secrets and I've never heard one that I can't do something about.'

'Honestly?'

'Honestly.'

'Well, I'm not sure you can magic my illness away.'

'No, but I can help you look at it another way.'

'I'd be very interested to hear how.'

'Doe she love you?' she asked, steering the conversation back to Nell.

'I've no doubt she would say yes, but it would be a fond love, the love you would feel for your closest friend.'

'You would like it to be more?'

'Oh no, I'm just happy to have her in my life. I can offer her nothing.'

'But you would like to express your love for her?'

'I might want to sometimes, but I won't. I wouldn't put her in the position of having to tell me she didn't see me in that way. It would embarrass her and pulverise me. I never expected to be lucky enough to meet a person so downright bloody marvellous at my age and I'm not going to do anything to spoil our friendship.'

She nodded slowly. 'She's a lucky girl.'

I was somewhat bemused. 'Why lucky?'

'She's lucky to have someone love her in such an unselfish way.'

'Isn't that what real love is?'

'We hope so,' she shrugged.

I suddenly felt a little light-headed. 'Thea, I can't quite believe I have just told you all that.'

'Well, to make you feel better, here is some information about me. As I told you, I live in a huge house just behind you. Way too big for me, but my husband left me very comfortably off ...'

'Oh dear, I'm so sorry... when did he ...'

'Oh he's not dead,' she laughed, 'he buggered off with another woman; traded me in for a younger, silicone-enhanced model, the bastard! But he had the grace to feel guilty about it-his Catholic upbringing you know, so he left me with the house and quite a bit of money.'

'I did the same for my wife, not through guilt, but because I didn't have the guts for a fight over money, too sordid. She could have had the lot, as long as I had enough to live on, but don't tell her that.'

She laughed heartily, throwing her head back. A full, throaty laugh that sounded genuine and earthy. It wasn't a Nell-type blast, but it did make me smile.

'Marriage is a bloody silly idea, don't you think?' she suggested.

'I do. It might work for some people, like my friend and neighbour, Sidney, but not for many, including me.'

'How long have you had the Parkinson's?'

'I really don't know. I was diagnosed in February, but I would calculate a couple of years before that. It took me that long to summon up the courage to see my doctor.'

She rolled her eyes. 'You men, I don't know!'

'Yes, weak as dishwater.'

'It must have come as a shock.'

'Yes and no. I knew there was something wrong, but I didn't imagine it would be something like this.'

'I understand the side effects of the tablets aren't much fun.'

'They are a barrel of laughs.'

'What causes it?'

'They really don't know.'

Her eyes searched my face. 'What do *you* think?'

'What do *I* think?'

'Yes, deep in your heart what do you think? Tell me the first thought that springs into your head.'

'Frustration, regret, longing, stress ...'

'Aha, so in other words your mind and body were out of sync. I think that causes all disease.'

'But then a psychologist would.'

'I'm not your average psychologist.'

'I can tell.'

'Can you?' she asked, earnestly. 'That's good. I don't ever want to be average.'

'Nor me.'

'You couldn't ever be average with that voice.'

'Thank you.'

She was still scrutinising me. 'What were you longing for?' I went to speak but no words came out. She put her hand on my arm. 'You don't have to say.'

'For some unearthly reason I don't mind telling you.'

'That's good.'

'I'm not ashamed of my feelings any more. I would have been once, but not now.'

'And is that because of the disease?'

'Not only the disease ...'

'The young woman you love.'

'Yes.'

'So, tell me about the longing then?'

'At first it was indefinable and I didn't realise I had been longing for anything until I met the woman who made the longing go away.'

'How lovely.' she murmured.

'You think so?'

'But was the longing because you wanted someone to love you?'

'No; it was because I wanted to love someone with all my heart and live for them and not myself.'

Thea said nothing for a moment, but her eyes felt like lasers burning into the side of my face. Shaking her head, she finally said, 'Now, I must stop asking personal questions! Would you like to come to lunch tomorrow?'

'That's very kind of you.'

'Please say you'll come.'

I suddenly felt quite reckless. 'I'll come.'

'Fabulous! Do you like chicken?'

'I do.'

'We'll have chicken muck-up then.'

'Chicken muck-up sounds rather wonderful – I think.'

'It's just chicken and vegetables chucked in with a load of pasta.'

'My favourite, especially if somebody else is doing the cooking.'

She put out her hand and I took it. 'It's been so lovely chatting to you. I bet you feel like you've been hijacked. I'll leave you to your thoughts now. See you about half-twelve? It's number four by the way.'

'I'll take a short cut and hop over the wall.'

'I'd like to see that,' she laughed.

'Yes...me too.'

'Bye, Benedict.' She went to walk away and I watched her jaunty step with a quiet pleasure. She was one of life's cheerful, positive people, a whirlwind of chattiness and laughter. She was just about to disappear behind one of the tall rhododendrons when she turned and called out to me. 'Benedict.'

'Yes?'

'You're wrong if you think you have nothing to offer her. You have everything to offer.'

I was completely perplexed by her words. 'I don't ...'

'See you tomorrow,' she said quickly before I could finish the sentence.

I sat gazing at the space where she had been for quite a while. In the space of fifteen minutes I had come across a delightful, interesting woman who had probably been my neighbour for many years and yet we had never set eyes on each other. Not only that, I had confessed my love for Nell and told her my most intimate secrets. It was astonishing and remarkable and I felt as if I had been hit by a sudden thunderstorm and left reeling yet exhilarated. I would now have something to report to Nell when she phoned, other than telling her about my rather boring, amateurish gardening or dancing efforts or the money I had lost to Sidney through cards. And I was looking forward to having lunch with Thea and hopefully making a new friend who would help me stand the long lonely months when Nell was in New York.

Beth telephoned that evening, full of gossip and goings on in her office and she sounded relaxed and happy. When I managed to get a word in I told her about Thea. 'It's incredible. She lives behind us, darling.'

'What does she look like? I'm trying to get a picture of her in my head.'

'Oh I don't know, attractive, smiley, dark chestnut hair, tall; that kind of thing.'

'She sounds nice.'

'She literally knocked me over.'

'She sounds fun too.'

'Yes, that's the word I would use to describe her.'

'How old is she?'

'I'm not very good at being able to tell ages, but I'd say about fifty-two, fifty-three. I don't know really.'

'That's great,' she gasped, 'just right for you.'

'Beth,' I sighed, 'it's not going to be a ...'

'I'm assuming she's not married if she's asked you to lunch so could be the start of something, Dad.'

I knew what she was doing immediately. In fact it had crossed my mind before she rang that if I mentioned Thea to her she would be quietly pleased that she was more my age than Nell was. But could I blame her? It would be much easier and less embarrassing for her to tell any of her friends her father had a woman friend of about fifty, rather than thirty-five.

'I don't think one invitation to lunch is going to lead to ...'

'Don't close yourself off from it, Dad. She sounds like a lovely woman.'

'Nell is lovely too,' I said softly, unable to stop myself.

Beth ignored my comment as if she hadn't heard it. 'She sounds just your type.'

'OK, darling, if you say so,' I muttered.

'Email me how it goes, won't you?'

'Yes, if you want me to.'

'I do want you to.'

When I put the phone down I felt a wave of sadness wash over me because her attitude to Thea was so different from how she had been with Nell and Nell hadn't deserved that. But I reminded myself that this was my daughter and she loved me and only wanted the best for me; or what she *thought* was the best for me. Sidney, of course, was all ears when I mentioned meeting Thea that evening at about six when we were sitting in the soft early evening May sunlight in my conservatory with a bottle of light red wine between us.

'Which house does she live in?'

I turned and pointed to her tall chimneys, which were just bout visible between the trees. 'She lives in that one there.'

'Very nice too,' he commented. 'Not short of a bob or two then. And you collided with her?'

'Actually she stepped back and almost knocked me over. We introduced ourselves and had a little chat.'

'What did you chat about?'

'Oh, you know...'

'She's got a funny old name.'

'It's short for Dorothea.'

He turned his nose up. 'Bit posh, isn't it?'

'Is it?'

'Yeah, I reckon.'

'She's not particularly posh.'

He sneered. 'Well, you wouldn't notice if she was, would you? You're posh!'

'I most certainly am not.'

'Yeah, you are! So, does she live there with her old man?'

'No, she's divorced.'

'Oh yeah ...'

I pointed an accusing finger at him. 'Sidney!'

He looked mischievous suddenly. 'I bet she loved you.'

I frowned. 'Why would she?'

'Don't give me that. Women have always flocked round you, even when you were married.'

'That seems to be an urban myth.'

'I don't think so, matey.'

I just had to laugh. The way I saw myself, with the disease, the puppet-like walk, the dribbling, was obviously very different to how everyone else saw me, but I had no idea why that was. 'Well, anyway she was very nice, very chatty. I liked her. She's the type of person you take to straight away.'

'Oh yeah ...'

'Will you stop that?'

'Ask you round, did she?'

'Well, actually she did – for lunch tomorrow.'

His face was a picture. 'Fuck me, Benedict! How do you do it?'

'I don't! I assure you, I don't. She was only being friendly.'

He looked down his nose at me. 'I bet she was.'

'Shut up, Sidney.'

'What's Nell going to say?'

'What do you mean?'

'Are you going to tell her?'

'Yes, why on earth not? Sidney, I'm not actually in any kind of relationship with either of them. That's just not going to happen. Nell will be delighted.'

He appeared ridiculously smug. 'If you say so, mate.'

'I do say so.'

'Give me a knock when you get back tomorrow, won't you?' he said, looking decidedly excited. 'I want to hear all about it.'

'Yes, Sidney,' I sighed, because he was a hopeless case.

'And I bet you she asks you back again or asks you out somewhere.'

'I don't think so.'

'You mark my words!' he said definitely, before muttering once more, 'Fuck me, how do you do it?'

'I don't do anything,' I muttered back, but my mind was charging on to what I would say to Nell if Thea did indeed ask me back or suggest going out somewhere and how disappointed I would be if she didn't mind, but actively encouraged it.

'I'm not any kind of Casanova, Sidney,' I told him. 'I'm just a silly old sod.'

'I agree,' he replied succinctly.

And there we left it because it was the truth after all. But instead of looking forward to seeing Thea, as I should have, because she was so obviously a warm, funny and kind woman, I wished with all my heart it was Nell who had asked me to have lunch with her.

Chapter 13

'Benedict, do come in.'

Thea looked a little flustered and breathless, her hair bouncing, face a little flushed and a sharp knife in her hand. She was wearing a purple, figure-hugging dress that suited her.

'Is it safe to come in?' I asked, with my usual dry humour.

'Quite safe, chopping some carrots; as you do,' she laughed. 'Come through into the lounge, please.'

'Thank you.'

The rooms were similar to mine, spacious, airy and light with long windows, but there the similarity ended. There was a faint, musky aroma of joss sticks burning mixed with a delicious smell of chicken cooking coming from the kitchen. It was all rather bohemian and colourful and there were huge modern art pieces on every wall. They appeared to be just great splurges of colour, but they were oddly beguiling and Thea noticed me staring at them.

'What do you think?'

'I'm not sure actually – I think I like them.'

She laughed again. 'I painted them.'

'Then I like them even more knowing that.'

'You're very gallant. Look, you can just see your house from here nestling between the trees. I can't believe we've been such close neighbours and never met.'

'I know, but now we have.'

'What would you like to drink, Benedict?'

'I've cut down on alcohol, because of the tablets.'

'So, would you like non-alcoholic wine then?'

'Lovely.'

'Here, sit down,' she said, motioning to the sofa.

'Thanks.'

She sat directly opposite me and poured us both a drink, except hers was from a different bottle and, leaning forward, eagerly confided, 'I shouldn't really drink red wine at lunch it makes me rather uninhibited and talkative.'

'Oh dear ...'

'And then sleepy, but what the hell. I don't entertain that often now, so, cheers.'

'Good health.'

'It was great running into you like that, literally! I've been so looking forward to you coming over.'

'Yes, me too...'

'To be perfectly honest, Benedict, I could do with a companion for the theatre and you'll do very nicely,' she told me, winking.

My heart sank. The thought of struggling to get on a crowded train and being jostled about with masses of people made me feel drained and I didn't like feeling that way; in fact I resented it greatly because the theatre had always been my first love and I missed it. 'I'm afraid I'll be a bit of a disappointment to you. I have so little energy at the moment.'

She smiled sympathetically. 'Well, never mind, maybe an art exhibition now and again and lunch or afternoon tea occasionally.'

'That sounds perfect.'

I was strangely tongue-tied and nervous, ridiculous at my advanced years, but there it was. I wondered if it was Sidney's teasing about her asking me out and what Nell would think about it that sat heavily on my shoulders and perhaps it was. There was no denying that Thea was a bright, attractive woman, but it was my feelings – my love – for Nell that would keep Thea and me apart. I gave myself a mental nudge to stop acting like a teenager and tried to relax, knowing that with her intuitiveness she would pick up on it. I looked round for something to talk about and my eyes lighted upon an enormous photograph of a young girl of about twelve in close up that dominated the whole wall above the fireplace. Pointing at it I asked, 'Is that your daughter?'

'Yes, that's my Ellie. I miss her terribly. We have always been close so it's like losing a limb for me and I dare say for her too, but she wouldn't admit it. I try my damnedest to keep busy, distract myself, but it's not easy. Just something I have to get used to.'

'Has she changed much since she's been away, would you say?' I asked her, thinking of Beth.

She thought for a moment. 'A little perhaps – she's grown up obviously. Studying to be a doctor does tend to do that. When she first comes home I can see subtle changes, not all of them good if I'm honest, but by the time she returns to university she's back to being my Ellie again.'

I admired her frankness. 'I understand perfectly what you mean; you have just described exactly how Beth is when she comes home from New

York: a little more brittle each time and full of nervous energy and it can take the whole holiday for her to get back to being the daughter I used to feed the ducks with. Not that I'm expecting her to stay the same it's just that ...'

'I know,' she said, 'you don't have to explain.' She barely drew breath before switching to a new topic, 'How long have you been divorced? Oh, listen to me! I really should stop being a psychologist. I'm sorry; you don't have to answer my personal questions.'

'I don't mind, honestly,' I replied. 'But I can't actually answer that one because I can't remember although I know it's a long time. My memory seems to be affected by the illness or the tablets, I'm not being evasive.'

'Do you think Beth was badly affected by it?'

'At the time she seemed wholly *un*affected by it, but I was obviously being naïve or just didn't want to face it because, looking back, I can see she was. I regret that, of course. I remember her getting very defensive if her mother spoke about me in anything but glowing terms, which was very unfair. She idolises me and I don't deserve it I'm afraid.'

'I'm sure you do, in her eyes at least.'

'Thank you, but I'm an idol with feet of clay.'

'All idols have feet of clay. How's your drink?'

'Delightful.'

'What did you do? Your job I mean.'

'I taught English Literature at two universities.'

'Did you enjoy it?'

'I did mostly, yes.'

'You retired early though?'

'Yes, I did. You know when you've had enough of teaching I assure you.'

'I felt the same with my job. I'll just check the lunch.'

She jumped up and dashed into the kitchen from where delicious smells were wafting in and I was surprised at how hungry I was. I rarely felt hungry when I cooked for myself and only relished eating when Sheila put one of her excellent concoctions in front of me. I sat back and tried to ease the aching tension in my muscles. 'It's quieter here than in my front room,' I called to Thea, who sounded as if she was throwing pots around in the kitchen with gusto.

'Is it?' she called back. 'Yes, I suppose it would be, you have the road going right past your window. This is a side road so we don't get the through traffic. Sometimes I could do with something to nose at, if I'm honest,' she added, joining me again. 'It's almost ready. I hope you like it. I just throw everything in the pot and hope for the best.'

'It smells wonderful.'

'So, Benedict, what do you do with your spare time?' she inquired, leaning back in her chair and crossing her long legs.

'I do very little.'

'Do you get bored?'

I frowned. 'No, I don't believe I do.'

'Do you get lonely?' she asked, fixing me with her searching eyes.

'Um – I don't think so ...'

She threw up her hands. 'Sorry, another personal question. Don't answer it.'

'Thea, I don't mind, honestly. I don't call that a personal question. And no, I don't believe I've often felt lonely. I remember when I got my diagnosis, I went straight into the pub, God knows why, and I felt a – a sense of isolation rather than loneliness. I felt isolated in my own body. If you've ever been lonely in your marriage, well, that's the worst kind of loneliness and being on my own hasn't ever been as bad or as soul-destroying as that.'

'How interesting,' she murmured. 'And now of course you have your young woman.'

I smiled at the mention of Nell. I couldn't help it. 'Yes, I know Nell now and I don't think I'll ever feel lonely again.'

'But what if ... no, it doesn't matter,' she shook her head lightly.

I looked at her intently and surmised that the sudden severing of her sentence was because she was thinking there was a distinct possibility Nell and I might never be together. Taking that to be the case, I answered, 'It's OK, I've been through all the scenarios in my head and I have let go of any hope of Nell and me ...' I broke off myself, silenced by the notion of Nell never being by my side.

'But why let go of the hope?' she asked, peering directly into my eyes.

'Because it's not based in reality,' I replied.

'Dreams are rarely based in reality, but we can still dream, Benedict.'

'It's more complicated than what I want or desire. I may well think ...' I stopped abruptly, not wanting at this stage to reveal all my personal longings to a woman I had only just met, even if she was a trained psychologist. But she was scrutinising my face so intently I felt I had to continue, 'but do I really want or expect someone so young and full of life to have to take care of me?'

'Hang on, hang on,' she said, 'why think in those terms? Nobody knows what's going to happen tomorrow, do they? Next week, some brilliant doctor may win the Nobel Prize for finding a cure for Parkinson's; that's one scenario. Another is that you may not get much worse than you are now for a very long time. And another is ...' she paused, a half smile on her lips, 'maybe, just maybe, she loves you as much as you love her and she might actually *want* to care for you. You're a very attractive, intelligent man and I'm not just saying that. Forget about the age thing, who cares these days? Try to turn your negative thoughts around and see where it gets you. You might be surprised.'

'I do try – and thank you,' I said, my voice slurring badly.

'Well, try harder, Benedict and see where it gets you.' I gave her a weak smile and her face suddenly lit up. 'Aha,' she cried, wagging a finger at me, 'I know what's troubling you.'

I was aghast. 'I sincerely hope you don't.'

'It's as plain as the nose on your face! But that's because you are a man and you gauge everything by sexual prowess. But you men never think to actually ask a woman if it's *that* important to us do you?'

I felt my normally pale skin burning. 'Well ...I...' I was amazed by her perception once more, but I couldn't tell a woman I had just met the day before, who I did not truly know at all, that any thoughts of a physical relationship were pure fantasy and Nell deserved better than that, especially at such a young age. 'I don't really know what to say.'

She leant forward, squeezing my hand that was resting on my knee and giving me a delightfully understanding smile. 'Don't be embarrassed, Benedict. I've heard it all before I assure you.'

'Not from me.'

'Just ask her.'

I was mortified. 'I could never do that! I'd rather rip my tongue out than let her think I'm a dirty old man.'

'A dirty old man?' she laughed, looking delighted, but incredulous at the same time, 'let's give her some credit. She won't think that. Not if she knows you well. Why would she?'

'Much older men – young women – it's all a bit unsavoury, isn't it? I'm sure my daughter thinks it is.'

'What a prude you are,' she commented. 'Ah, bless you - so much intelligence and so little common sense, or confidence for that matter.'

'My dear friend Sidney would agree with that.'

'I told you yesterday, you have much to offer her.'

'I sincerely doubt that.'

'It all depends what she wants, what she needs. Have you ever asked her?'

'No! But I doubt she needs someone to nurse.'

Thea pursed her lips and shook her head at me as if I was hopeless. 'It also depends on what her experiences are. You are a mature man.'

I gave a wry smile. 'That's a kind way of putting it.'

'She may well prefer older men.'

'She does.'

'Well, there you are! That's a good start. You have maturity, experience, a dry sense of humour - some men have none of the above. You also have intelligence, a sense of fun, kindness, a good heart, I should imagine you are generous, have plenty of time to spend with her, and you are sincere.'

I felt a little uncomfortable. 'You make me sound much better than I am.'

'I'm a very good judge of character.'

'But the *disease* ...'

She ignored my comment and continued, 'She may well find men her own age immature. She may well need someone reliable, steady, but not boring ...'

'But the *disease* ...'

'Oh for heaven's sake, Benedict, *bugger* the disease! If she loves you it would make absolutely no difference at all to her.'

I found myself laughing. 'Say what you mean, why don't you?'

'But on the other hand,' she added, 'if she doesn't love you this is all immaterial. Shall we eat?'

She leapt to her feet and disappeared into the kitchen again. I felt as if I had been caught up in a whirlwind and was now left staggering around, breathless and flummoxed. She came back in with a stone pot and placed it on the table.

'That smells pretty good,' I commented.

'I hope it is. Sit here, Benedict,' she commanded. 'I'll just spoon it on your plate and you say when.'

She slapped it onto the large dinner plate in front of me in such a slapdash manner I found myself trying not to laugh. Everything she did, everything she said, was done with such gusto, flamboyancy, goodness and humour, it was heart-warming.

'When...' I cried.

'What?'

'When...'

'When what?' she asked, looking bemused.

'You said, say *when*, so I did,-but you didn't stop so I now have so much food on my plate.'

Her face creased up with laughter. 'Oh my God, I'm sorry. Here, I'll take it off.' She began to scoop bits of chicken up and put them back in the pot, spilling some on her clean, crisp white tablecloth and swearing loudly. 'Is that enough for you now?' she added.

'I should think so.'

'I told you I shouldn't drink at lunchtime. I'm quite squiffy.'

'That's an interesting word.'

'Well, pissed then.'

'Ah, I understand pissed.'

She put her hand on my arm and looked directly at me. 'Isn't this fun?'

'I have to say it is.'

'What do you think?' she asked, pointing at my plate with her fork.

'It's delicious.'

'Thank you, Benedict,' she said, looking relieved and my heart warmed to her that she cared what I thought.

'It's not often someone cooks for me, so this is a real treat, thank you, Thea.'

'You are welcome any time, really, any time.'

'You'll be sorry you said that.'

'Oh dear, that wine has gone straight to my head. My husband used to get so cross with me if I got even the slightest bit pissed because I get very vocal when I've had a few and if he'd been annoying me that day and we had friends round that evening, I'd always come out with something outrageous to embarrass him.'

'Accidentally on purpose,' I remarked.

'Exactly,' she laughed. 'One evening I said ... no, I can't repeat that, it's awful.'

'Oh go on,' I urged, laughing back at her, 'do tell.'

'Well,' she started, obviously desperate to relay the story and her eyes sparkling with fun, 'we had his boss and his wife over. He was pretty straight-laced and his wife was even worse and religious to boot! There were some of the boss's hangers-on here as well. They were all very la de da, or thought they were; you know the type. Anyway, Ed, my husband, was sitting in a rocking chair we used to have, smoking a cigar and pontificating about some rubbish and – I don't know what came over me, I really don't – but the way he was rocking in the chair just made me want to say ...'

'Don't stop now,' I urged, 'I'm intrigued; what did you say?'

'I said, Ed likes to sit in that chair and rock to and fro because he can pretend he's masturbating!'

I had just taken a mouthful of my non-alcoholic wine and I spat it out in an involuntary gasp. She had taken a gulp of hers after regaling the story and did the same and we were both so convulsed with laughter, neither of us could speak for at least two minutes. As the unsuppressed laughter shot through my body, I felt the tension evaporate instantly and a feeling of longed-for deep relaxation washed over me. It made me realise how rarely I felt like that.

'Thea,' I gasped eventually, 'I don't know what to say to that.'

She bit her lip. 'Are you ever so shocked?'

'No, well yes, but I'm nicely shocked. What was the assembled group's reaction?'

'Can you imagine? There was this stunned silence while everyone looked at each other and then pretended not to look at each other.'

'What did your husband say?'

'He went, "Dorothea *really*!" And then he apologised on my behalf. He never normally called me by that name, only when he was cross. But that's not the end of it. I then brought in the trifle and tripped on a bit of carpet sticking up and I did this amazing run with all these little steps as I tried to catch up with myself. I just about saved myself but the trifle ended up in his boss's lap, literally. I said... anyone for trifle? Ed looked daggers at me I can tell you.'

'I wish I'd seen that,' I remarked, my regard for her increasing all the time because of her risqué story. 'It must have been wonderful.'

'I thought so.'

The rain had begun to drum loudly outside suddenly and the room had grown dark in a few minutes. 'What's happened to the weather? When I arrived it was sunny.'

'It's very changeable at the moment, isn't it? Oh, listen to that thunder?' she said, just as a shaft of lightening lit up the sky and a deafening clap of thunder roared over the house.

I imagined Nell's delight if she could hear it. 'I didn't bring an umbrella,' I muttered.

'Oh dear, you'll have to stay the night,' she replied, with a grin. 'I'm only kidding. I've got loads of umbrellas.'

'Let it pour then,' I said, feeling quite carefree for a change.

'Would you like some tea or a coffee?'

'Tea would be lovely, thank you.'

She went into the kitchen and I walked over to the windows to watch the rain bouncing off the pavement outside. I wondered whether Nell could hear it wherever her rehearsal rooms were and hoped she could. The last hour spent with Thea had made me realise how insular I had become, apart from time spent with Sidney and Sheila, and Nell of course. I didn't socialise any more like this and that was remiss of me because I did enjoy good company, especially on a one-to-one basis. Parties weren't my scene, I had been to enough in the past where I would stand with a drink and wonder what the hell I was doing there, but this was different. This was an unexpected turn of events and all the more delightful because it was unexpected.

'Tea, Benedict,' Thea said, carrying a tray in.

'Thank you.'

'So, do you feel a little less tense about your relationship with Nell now? I mean, I know you didn't come here for a counselling session, but I like to help people look at the positives of their situation.'

'Yes, thank you. I think the best way forward is to let life unfold as it will and be thankful that I know her. I didn't expect to meet such a life force at my age and I have to go along with my gut feelings, which are ...'

'That she loves you, but sees you as her friend and mentor, that kind of thing,' Thea chipped in.

'Yes.'

She poured the tea and handed me a sweet, delicate little tea cup with red roses on it and said, 'Let's toast to friendship, whatever form it takes.'

'I second that.'

She looked a little bashful suddenly. 'And I include us in that toast.'

'Yes, of course.'

'I'm extremely pleased to have bumped into you, Benedict, and I hope this is the beginning of a firm and sincere friendship that will enhance both our lives.'

'That was very eloquent and I agree.'

'Do you know,' she added, 'I've hardly noticed any of your symptoms this afternoon. Just a slight shake of your hand and the occasional stumble over a word, but that's it!'

'I do have days like that; not often, but this is a good day.'

'Must be my influence.'

'It must be.'

There was a moment's silence while I sipped my tea, but I was aware Thea was looking at me and I had the distinct feeling she was going to blurt something out. That thought made my hand tremble suddenly.

'Oh dear, I spoke too soon,' she remarked, noticing instantly.

'It's just a slight blip.'

'Benedict ...'

'Yes?'

'I expect you've gathered that I'm quite outspoken.'

'Well, yes.'

'I really don't see the point in pussy-footing about, life's too short to pussy-foot about.'

'Quite.'

She leant towards me. 'I find you extremely attractive and ...'

'Thea, stop there, please.'

'No, let me say it. It's best to get these things out in the open,' she declared.

'I had a feeling you might like to get things out in the open.'

'I miss having a man's company. I feel as if you and I could become really close,' she shrugged, as if it was nothing at all to her to declare her feelings to a stranger. 'But, I know where I stand and how you feel about Nell, so you needn't worry on that account. Don't look so terrified.'

'I wasn't aware I was looking terrified. I thought my face was blank most of the time.'

'But if there's ever any change in your feelings for her or the situation as a whole, you know where I am.'

'Well, that's very kind of you. I didn't expect that, but thank you very much for the compliment.'

'You need to know you are still an attractive man,' she continued, 'it's important.'

'Well, I ... I don't think I am, I only see the parts that are going wrong, downhill, south; all of that. But I appreciate your honesty, Thea.'

'That's got all that out of the way then, hasn't it?'

'It certainly has.'

She bit her lip. 'You didn't mind me saying ...'

I interrupted her before she could go over it all again, 'No, not at all.'

'Great, so now we can become mates without any wondering on your part.'

I felt obliged to say something, anything about my feelings towards her and I was attempting to form the words, but my mouth stiffened. 'Sorry, that happens at times. I go to speak and...'

She waved her hand dismissively. 'Don't worry.'

'I do worry, I *detest* it. Thea, you are a lovely woman, undeniably lovely and if I didn't love Nell and if I was in the peak of health, I would be asking you out immediately, but life is as it is, I'm afraid. Friendship is vitally important to me though, especially now, so I will treasure your friendship always.'

Her face lit up. 'Thank you, that's so lovely of you. I hope Nell appreciates you.'

'She does, she does,' I declared, jumping to her defence, 'no question about it.'

'What does she do for a living?'

'She's an actress.'

Thea raised her eyebrows. 'That must be exciting!'

'Not as much as you may think. It's mostly auditions, rejections, long spells out of work trying to make some money to get by and then, if you're extremely lucky or talented, or both, rehearsals and then the actual work you are trained for: performing.'

'And then the whole process again.'

'Yes.'

'Is she working at the moment?'

'She is,' I replied, eager to speak of Nell's recent success. 'She's rehearsing for a small show in Soho, but soon she'll be heading off to America to act just off Broadway. She's so excited.'

'Wow! I can imagine. But how do you feel about that?' she asked, in her psychologist tone of voice which was completely different from the voice she had used when telling stories about embarrassing her ex-husband.

'It will be hard, I can't deny that, but how can I be churlish in any way when it's what she's been working towards all her adult life? And it's really not up to me to express an opinion on whether I want her to go or not. Her triumphs will be mine too. I'll relish her happiness as if it were my own, gladly.'

'You see, that's the difference between a more mature man and a younger one. A younger man would possibly mind terribly, feel a little jealous, envious and worried that she would be that far away surrounded by other men. A younger man would quite probably have a temper tantrum and beg her not to go. I applaud you, Benedict.'

I gave a wry smile. 'Thank you, but don't think for one minute I'm not dreading her departure. She once said to me that no man in her life ever wanted her to fly, but I want her to. I *want* her to fulfil her destiny, her talent and her dreams and if it means I am lonely without her, so be it. I'll suffer, but I'll suffer in silence.'

Thea was watching me speak with an expression on her face that I could only describe as one of sympathy, mixed with fondness. The wine had brought a pink blush to her face and she looked very appealing. She had an earthy sensuality and a few months earlier, before Nell, she would have been my first choice for a companion to laugh with and while away the afternoons. I imagined listening to her humorous stories, visiting art galleries, sitting together in my garden sipping wine on a summer's evening. It would all have been so lovely. But the clock could not be turned back and I didn't want it to be.

She sighed suddenly, 'We can still spend time together, can't we?' she asked as though she had been reading my mind. Her vulnerability shone out from her, 'I mean, when Nell is away. She wouldn't mind, would she? You're only friends after all.'

Her last comment was like a slap to my face because, foolishly, I had once more been thinking in terms of being in a relationship with Nell and I became flustered, 'Of course,' I said, 'Yes, of course, I'd be honoured to spend time with you.'

Her face lit up again. 'Fantastic! Let's make a date now.'

'Well ...'

'What about the weekend? Maybe Saturday, lunch at the wine bar. What do you say?'

I was flummoxed. She had surprised me with her insistence and although I knew I would enjoy a leisurely lunch with her, I was wavering. 'I don't know; I'm not sure what I'm doing Saturday.' Her face betrayed her disappointment immediately and I added somewhat hastily, 'That sounds awful, I'm sorry, Thea. It sounds like I'm giving you the brush off, I'm not. I'm in no position to give a beautiful woman, *any* woman, the brush off.'

'You're hesitating because you're hoping to see Nell,' she said.

'I haven't seen her in so long, so if she called and said she was coming round, I'd want to be there. It sounds pathetic, I know.'

'Not at all,' she said carelessly. 'I shouldn't be so bloody pushy. I'm always like that, so tell me to shut up, won't you? But I like to seize the moment and there's so much I'd like to chat to you about. We've only skimmed the surface. You look to me as if you've had a fascinating life.'

'No, my life really hasn't been that fascinating, not at all.'

'I don't believe that.'

'It's true, I assure you.' I suddenly had a change of heart and shrugging my shoulders said, 'Look, it's highly unlikely Nell will be free so ... Oh dear, that sounds as if you are second best. You aren't, I'm just losing the ability to express myself eloquently these days.'

'Don't worry. I tell you what; I'll leave Saturday free and if Nell hasn't made an appearance by midday, call me.'

I felt ridiculously guilty. 'That's fine by me; thank you for being so understanding.'

'No problem. We are both mature adults. Here's my number.' She wrote it hurriedly on a piece of paper. 'Don't lose it.'

'I won't.'

'Put it in your pocket now,' she demanded. 'Otherwise you'll drop it.'

I did as she asked. It had grown even darker due to the spring storm and I felt strangely on edge. 'Thea, I'll make a move, if you don't mind. I feel a little tired.'

'Yes, yes, of course. Thanks so much for coming over.'

'No, I should thank you for the chicken muck-up. I loved it.'

'Here, take this,' she said, finding a flowery umbrella in the kitchen. 'It's a bit girly.'

'I don't mind girly. I think girly is the best way to be.'

'I knew you wouldn't,' she laughed. She stood in front of me, her eyes shining and her hair slightly wayward. 'Well, Benedict, it's been lovely.'

I offered her my hand. She took it and squeezed it hard. She was a powerful, athletic woman, full of unbridled energy and too much for my now soft and quickly deteriorating physique. I imagined her flooring me in a rugby tackle and submitting me to her iron will. That thought made me tremble suddenly. 'It's been lovely,' I muttered, my voice quavering and dipping.

She was standing very close to me and the smell of her sweet perfume washed over me. There was a tension between us that made me sway gently on my feet. She leant forward suddenly and kissed me. I found myself trembling violently and I tried my utmost to disguise it, but my limbs would not behave and I looked everywhere but at her face.

'Saturday then – maybe,' she urged, her eyes now twinkling with anticipation and a blatant sensuality.

'Saturday – maybe,' I echoed and now eager to leave.

'Great. Bye, Benedict.'

'Goodbye and thank you again.'

I walked slowly away, thankful for the fresh, wet air that I knew would help revive me. The hand that was holding the blatantly feminine umbrella above my head was so shaky it didn't feel part of me. The rain was pelting about my feet, splashing up my trousers. The shock of feeling her kiss made me feel quite spaced out and the *presence* immediately hovered in front of me, unseen, but keenly felt. As I approached my front door, I looked up and saw Sidney looking down at me from the annexe front window. He waved frantically and I had to smile because I knew he was desperate to hear about my lunch date, so I beckoned to him and his face disappeared instantly. I was soaked through because the high wind had caused the heavy rain to fall at a slant and my back and legs were drenched. I unlocked the conservatory door just as Sidney appeared from his garden with a newspaper covering his head.

'What took you?' he panted. 'It's pissing down.'

'I'm well aware of that, Sidney. Give me time to get in,' I told him. 'I'm soaked to the skin. Put the kettle on while I get out of these clothes, would you?'

'OK, matey,' he said cheerfully looking over his glasses at me. 'Had a nice time, have we?'

I ignored him and made my way slowly up to my bedroom. I found a clean, pressed shirt and trousers and laid the wet ones over the hot radiator in the bathroom. I glanced in the mirror at my dishevelled hair and laughed at myself. I turned my head from side to side, scrutinising my rigid features, wondering what the hell any woman saw in me now. But there was no accounting for taste. Sidney had made a pot of tea and was waiting in the conservatory eagerly. Thunder still rumbled in the distance and it was so dark I turned on a lamp. He was perched on the edge of his seat in anticipation, his face flushed and a little sweaty despite the cool weather.

'That thunder has lasted ages,' I muttered.

'Never mind the bloody thunder!'

'What?'

'Well?' he demanded.

'Well what?' I replied, knowing full well what he meant.

'How did it go then?'

I took my time answering, just to tease him. 'Oh, you know ...'

'No, I don't!' he shrieked. 'So tell me.'

'She's...'

He sat forward eagerly as I faltered and urged, 'What? She's quite what?'

'Good fun, bright, sexy ...'

His face was a picture. 'Sexy! You've never said that about Nell. So, she's sexy, is she? I see!'

'I haven't said it about Nell because she is so much younger than me and it sounds a little ...'

'Like a dirty old man,' he commented.

'Yes.'

'Did she make a pass at you?'

'Not really ... well, a little.'

'Oh yeah...'

'Sidney, don't start that!'

He shook his head in disbelief. 'Fuck me, Benedict. How do you do it?

'I don't do anything, I promise you.'

'How did she make a pass?'

'She told me I was attractive.'

'Oh yeah...'

'That she'd like to see me again ...'

'Fuck me.'

'You know - that sort of thing.'

'And will you?' he asked, his eyes wide with surprise.

'See her again? Of course I will, as a friend.'

'That's not what she wants by the sound of it,' he remarked. 'I told you though, didn't I?'

'You did, Sidney.'

'I don't know what you've got, but I wish I'd had some of it when I was younger.'

'You would still have married Sheila. Nobody else would have put up with you.'

He looked bemused. 'I can't believe it. How old is she?'

'About fifty-two I should think, maybe a little older.'

'She's more your age then.'

'Do you mean more my age than Nell?'

'Yeah, of course I mean Nell.'

'Let's just say that Beth and my sister would find her much more acceptable than Nell. But it's not up to them.'

He was shaking his head in disbelief. 'Well, who'd have thought it?'

'Shut up and drink your tea, Sidney.'

'How come you find her sexy?'

'Well, she *is* a sexy woman.'

'But you said you didn't have any of those feelings now.'

'I know,' I replied, 'I didn't say *I* found her sexy, I said she *is* sexy, meaning most men would find her so.'

'Oh yeah...'

'You know what I mean.'

'I'm not sure that I do,' he said. 'Do *you* find her sexy then?'

I hesitated, not knowing what to say. 'I don't know; I haven't given it much thought.'

'Perhaps you better had,' he said, nodding gravely, which looked rather comical. 'If she's been that up front the first time you go round, imagine what she'll be like next time. Aha, got you there, matey.'

'She's not about to throw herself at me, Sidney.'

He sneered. 'Wanna bet!'

'Mind you, she did kiss me.' I thought Sidney was going to explode and I laughed out loud at his bewildered face. 'Aha, and that got *you*.'

'She kissed you? How did she kiss you?'

'Don't ask ridiculous questions. She just gave me a peck, that's all.'

'Where did she give you a peck?'

'She gave me a peck in her hall.'

He pursed his lips like an old woman. 'Oh, that's very funny, Benedict.'

'On the lips if you must know.'

'Fuck me!' he gasped, shaking his head. 'How the fuck do you do it?'

'Pure, irresistible charisma I suppose,' I shrugged and grinned at his dumbfounded expression, 'and if you believe that you'll believe anything!'

'So, what are you going to do? What's going to happen?'

'I like her,' I told him, 'she's forthright, funny, good company, great pair of legs.'

'Oh yeah...'

'I said that for your benefit.'

'Do you know what I reckon?'

I sighed, 'No, but you're going to tell me.'

'I reckon, you're in love with Nell, but because of the difference in age, you won't let yourself think of her in that way. But this lady – this *mature* lady – well, you can let your imagination run riot because you don't have to worry about whether anyone will think you're a dirty old man with regard to her. Bloody hell, Benedict! You've got the best of both worlds.'

'Sidney, I've told you, I have none of those feelings now and I stand by that. If I had, and I didn't love Nell, it might be different.'

He almost jumped out of his chair. 'I told you! I told you!'

'But that's life, isn't it? I love Nell with all my heart. I have this disease that has stripped me of any physical longing, so Thea will stay a good companion and that's the way it is.'

'I hope she sees it that way,' he muttered into his hand.

'She has to,' I replied.

Sidney stayed for half an hour, during which time he shook his head continually and tut-tutted in utter amazement at my predicament. It amused me greatly to watch him in that mood and all in all it had been an interesting and enjoyable day. All of a sudden Sheila hammered on the wall to signify his dinner was on the table getting cold. I could always tell what both Sidney and Sheila's knocks meant. He reluctantly got up to leave.

'I tell you, Benedict, I bloody love living next door to you, I really do.'

'Glad to be of service.'

'There's always something going on with you.'

I smiled benignly. 'I don't think there is, but if you feel that way, I'm quite happy to amuse you in any way I can.'

Sheila hammered again causing Sidney to scuttle towards the door, 'Whoops, better go. See you tomorrow, mate.'

'You will, Sidney.'

He left me there relaxing on my sofa, watching the incessant rain beating against my conservatory windows. The high winds were rocking the silver birches at the bottom of my garden and sweeping through the chestnut trees in Sidney's. I could just see Thea's house and I wondered if she had finished the bottle of wine on her own. She was a character that was for sure.

I was just beginning to doze when an ear-splitting roll of thunder roared over my house causing me to jump out of my skin. At exactly the same time my doorbell rang and I struggled to my feet. As I made my way towards the front door the thought that my caller might be Nell flickered across my mind, but I told myself that was a vain hope and I would be disappointed. When I opened the door to the sight of her with dripping hair and her collar turned up against the storm, I almost staggered with shock and delight.

'Hello, Mr Marshall, can I come in?' she asked, smiling up at me.

'Nell, my goodness, come in, come in.'

'Isn't this weather fantastic?' she cried, her eyes alight with excitement.

My heart was thumping wildly. 'I knew you were going to say that?'

'Did you hear that clap of thunder? It was right over my head! Brilliant!'

We were standing in the hall, face to face. I wanted to beam from ear to ear and clasp her to my chest and squeeze her until my arms ached. She shook her hair and wiped the rain from her face. I stood inches from her again, dumb with surprise and delight. I attempted to speak, but slurred so badly I ended up laughing at myself. I wouldn't normally laugh at any of my symptoms, but Nell was in my house again and all was right with the world.

'I ... I'm so pleased to see you ... I can't express ...'

'Are you going to stand there like a tit in a trance all night or are we going to go into the lounge?'

'Say that again.'

'You heard.'

'I ... I ... I'm sorry, my mouth is behaving very badly. Come in, dear girl. Let me take your coat.'

'I've got so much to tell you, Mr Marshall. I'm sorry I've been so absent, but it's been so full on, I've hardly had time to see anyone, not even my mum,' she told me, talking quickly and walking in front of me.

I was looking at the back of her head with her long, wet and shiny black hair cascading down her back. 'I'm sure,' I replied, 'but how wonderful to be so busy, Nell.'

'Oh it is; it's unbelievable to be working again. You know what? When I'm out of work for a while I forget how much I live for it and then when I'm performing again it's as if I come alive and I remember that this is what I live for.'

'You seem to be pretty alive all the time to me. But I do understand perfectly what you mean. Take a seat and I'll make you some tea.'

'No, you sit down, you're older than me,' she grinned. 'I'll make it. I know where everything is.'

'Thank you.'

'What have you been doing with yourself then?' she called from the kitchen.

'Not much really,' I called back. 'Usual stuff: talking to Sidney, playing cards, walking a little.'

'That's great,' she declared, positive as ever, putting her head round the door.

'Not without you, Nell.'

Her expression changed. 'Ah, you are sweet. I'm sorry I can't walk with you at the moment. I miss it too. Carry on, what else?'

'Nothing else really,' I shrugged.

She went back into the kitchen and I heard her pour the boiling water in the tea. The fact that Nell was in my kitchen again doing something humdrum like making tea made my heart sing. She placed the tray on the coffee table and smiled at me lovingly. I couldn't speak at that moment because all I wanted to do was stare at her.

'You OK, Mr Marshall?'

'Yes ... yes ... fine. Nell, there's chocolate cake in the tin there by the fridge. One of Sheila's, bring it in and a knife.'

'OK, will do.'

'Cut us both a piece,' I told her as she brought in the tin. 'I feel like celebrating.'

'Isn't it great to be together again?' she said, sitting down. 'I've missed you so much.'

'Ditto,' I whispered. 'And it's worse for me because I have so little else to occupy me. You are very busy so the time must fly.'

'It has, but that doesn't stop me missing you.'

Her words were unbelievable to my ears. 'I'm not worthy of your words, Nell.'

She let out a blast of her laugh. 'Don't be a silly arse, of course you are.'

'Thank you.' She handed me a slice of Sheila's cake and bit into her piece with gusto. 'It's going to be a lively show, lots of songs, funny songs, and sketches. It's a bit of a piss-take on musicals, you know. I have two solos and quite a bit of dancing. Loads to learn, but I'm getting there. It's surprising how much your brain can take in when it needs to. We have this leading lady who is a right pain, but so talented. She has an unbelievable voice, clear and deep and mellow – much better than mine.'

'I can't believe that!'

'It is, honestly, but she knows it too. I call her Nancy Pepperhole and all the stage hands think it's a brilliant name for her.'

I shook my head in wonder at her chattering on. 'Say that again; Nancy who?'

'Nancy Pepperhole,' she repeated, as if it were a name you heard every day. 'It suits her.'

'Why does it suit her?'

She wrinkled her nose. 'I don't know really, it just does. She's a bit up herself, you know?'

I smiled at her chattering on with her funny sayings and her expressions changing so often it was hard to keep up with them. Her face changed from excited, to eager, to knowing, to loving, all in an instant.

'You are wonderful,' I muttered, unable to subdue my feelings at that moment as I normally did.

She didn't react to my words, but simply poured the tea and passed me my cup. It was almost as if she was so used to being complimented by me, it simply passed her by. But that made me feel contented because it meant she felt at ease with my compliments and didn't object to them in any way.

'How have you been feeling in yourself, Mr Marshall?' she asked, changing the subject. 'I have to say you look really well.'

'Do you think so?'

'Yeah, you look really well. Your shakes aren't that bad at the moment. Maybe your tablets are working at last.'

'Perhaps, I don't know. I hope so though.'

'So do I,' she said, looking intently at me and frowning. 'You look absolutely gorgeous. I'd forgotten how gorgeous you are.'

'Carry on, Nell,' I laughed, 'you are doing me a power of good.'

She laughed with me, insisting, 'Well, you *are* gorgeous, and your voice is as wonderful as ever!' Smiling coyly she then sidestepped this conversation, 'How's Sidney?'

'He's still Sidney,' I replied, knowing I didn't need to say much more.

'Have you been playing cards today?'

'No, but he was here just now, swearing like a navvy and telling me he loved living next door to me.'

'What made him say that?'

'He says there's always something going on with me. I don't agree, but there you have it.'

'What did he actually mean by that? Did you ask him?' she asked, as interested as ever in me and my life.

'Well, I was going to tell you about my encounter with a woman when you had finished telling me all your news but ...'

'You had an encounter with a woman?' Her eyes danced wildly. 'Blimey, sounds interesting. Tell me more, go on.'

'We met in the park ...'

'Like us ...'

'Yes, dear girl, like us. She almost knocked me over and I had to cling to a nearby tree to stay on my feet.'

'I bet that looked funny.'

'I'm sure it did.'

'Were you OK though?'

'Yes, I was fine and we walked together for a while and had a chat about nothing in particular. And then she asked me to lunch, just like that. It surprised me, but I thought, why not? She's a very friendly person, talkative, bubbly ...'

'What's her name?' Nell asked.

'Thea, short for Dorothea, but that's a bit of a mouthful. But you'll never guess where she lives, Nell.'

She shook her head, 'Where?'

'Just at the end of my garden, look, you can see her roof and the tall chimneys, there.'

'Oh yeah, I can see them,' she said, 'that's amazing, Mr Marshall. How old is she? Is she married?'

'Divorced, early fifties I'd say, but that's just a guess. She's a lovely lady; very kind and warm.' Nell looked straight at me and I couldn't quite make out what she was thinking. 'I like her,' I added.

'And I bet she loved you,' she said, almost under her breath.

'Of course,' I replied, 'she probably thought me devastatingly attractive with my stuttering and shaking and the dribbling, don't forget the dribbling.'

'Don't be daft, Mr Marshall; nobody notices any of that when they're with you.'

'Thank you, Nell.'

'Are you going to see her again?'

'I have; I've been to lunch with her!'

She raised her eyebrows. 'Already?'

'Yes, today. I'd only just got back when Sidney came round and then you arrived. It's been a busy day for seeing people. I expect it will just be Sidney tomorrow,' I remarked.

Nell ignored my day's itinerary and astounded said, 'Blimey, she's really a quick worker! What happened?'

'What happened? What happened in what sense?' I asked, perplexed and feeling a little uncomfortable with her question.

'I mean, did you have a good time?' she laughed. 'Why, what did you think I meant?'

I felt my heart rate pick up and I suspected my face looked a little flushed. 'Nothing,' I replied, feigning ignorance.

Nell put her cup down and narrowed her eyes. 'What are you looking embarrassed about? Come on, spill the beans.'

'There's nothing to tell, Nell.'

'Mr Marshall, you're hiding something from me. Did she come on to you?'

'I ... well ...'

'She did!' she gasped, her hands flying to her mouth. 'I don't believe it! I mean, I do believe it because I've always said you were gorgeous. I'm not surprised she fancied you, but I'm shocked she came on to you so soon. My God, she's brave, isn't she? What did she say? Did she make a lunge at you? Don't look like that. You can tell me.'

I was obviously looking highly embarrassed because I *was* highly embarrassed. 'I feel a little like I'm being unfair to Thea if I disclose what she said or did; it's not very gentlemanly, is it?'

'How do you mean, unfair to Thea? But this is me you're telling, not a pub full of men. Did you tell Sidney?'

'Well...yes...'

'I'm your friend too, aren't I?' She appeared hurt suddenly. 'Why tell Sidney and not me? I'm just interested in your life, that's all.'

'Of course you are my friend,' I insisted, feeling decidedly uncomfortable, 'and I sincerely hope you always will be.'

'Then what's the difference telling me?' she asked, but before I could answer she continued, 'if you tell Sidney and not me it makes me feel as if you don't trust me.'

'Well, yes, I can understand that and that's not the case, I assure you.'

'So, are you attracted to her?'

'I...well...I don't know if I...' I knew I was floundering, but I wanted to be as honest as I could be and I hadn't expected the conversation to go in this direction.

She appeared subdued suddenly. 'Forget I said anything, please.'

'No, no, it's fine, Nell. I really don't mind, I just felt a little embarrassed, that's all, at my age.'

'At your age?' she said, bemused. 'What's age got to do with it? If you're attracted to someone age doesn't come into it. I never thought of Joshua as being too old for me. He was just Joshua and you are Mr Marshall.'

'Well, if I'm honest, I'm as surprised as you are at how quickly she voiced her feelings ...'

'She actually voiced her feelings for you?' Nell cried. 'Bloody hell, she must have been *instantly* attracted to you. I don't know,' she said, shaking her head and then she was silent for a few moments, as if she was trying to decide what to say next. Her face appeared intensely thoughtful, but also grave. Then suddenly she looked up at me and her eyes were full of mischief. 'I don't know. I leave you alone for a few weeks and some woman tries to get you into her bed.'

'It wasn't quite like that, Nell.'

'But she did say she was attracted to you?'

'Yes, she did.'

'Cheeky thing,' she commented, under her breath.

I was by now feeling seriously uncomfortable. Not because I felt I shouldn't tell Nell for Thea's sake, but because I wasn't entirely sure that Nell approved. Her demeanour had changed and so had her face and her eyes, and there had been something different in the tone of her voice. It was often hard to tell what she was thinking because she was an actress after all but, unusually, her voice had hardened imperceptibly. The only other time I had heard even the slightest change in how she spoke was when I had upset her in the café with my clumsy honesty about how Beth and my sister felt about her.

I tried to restore the closeness we'd had when she had turned up drenched such a short time ago. 'I think it was because she'd drunk a little too much wine and is possibly a little lonely. We seemed to just click, probably because we both have only daughters who live away. She's a very warm, generous person, Nell. I'm sure she will make a good friend, especially when you're away in America.'

Nell's eyes seemed to mist over and for one awful moment I thought she was going to cry. 'How quickly you forget me, Mr Marshall, and I've not even left yet,' she whispered.

My throat tightened and I felt the tremors quicken. 'Forget you! Forget you! Nell, I could never forget you. I didn't mean that, you must know you're my dearest friend.'

She brightened a little, 'I know, I'm sorry.'

'How little confidence you have in our friendship...' My voice slid away to nothing.

She gave a little smile. 'I'm not nearly as confident in any aspect of my life as people think.'

Certainly she now appeared intensely vulnerable and I could only say quietly, 'No ... obviously not ...' but her thoughts had drifted back to Thea.

'But she did fancy you, didn't she?'

'Fancy me? I'd hardly call it that.' I turned my nose up in distaste. 'I don't believe there is anything to fancy any more in this ageing, infirm body. She seemed to be a little attracted to me but, as I said, she was ever so slightly drunk.'

Her eyes were suddenly serious. 'Did she ... you know, make any other kind of move on you?'

My face felt rigid and stuck and my mouth wouldn't synchronise with my brain so I merely shrugged. This was not how I expected our conversation to be and I wished to God I hadn't mentioned Thea at all. I was confused and bewildered because I hadn't expected Nell to mind or disapprove of my lunch date with another, unknown woman. 'Did she make any other move on me?' I repeated. 'Not really ...'

Nell bit her lip. 'Did she kiss you?'

I avoided her eyes. 'Not really, just a peck goodbye, you know the sort of thing.'

'You're saying she *did* kiss you then?'

'Yes, she kissed me,' I admitted, like a beleaguered, unfaithful husband.

'So, she meets you in the park for the first time, asks you to lunch after a two minute chat, then, after that lunch, tells you she fancies you and kisses you. She must be some woman!'

'Put like that it does seem hard to understand, but she's quite forthright, rather pushy, but in a nice way and she's impulsive. I felt as if I'd been caught up in a whirlwind, buffeted about and then left staggering. Well, I stagger anyway on my own. I don't need any help with that.'

'When are you seeing her again?' Nell asked and her voice was flat.

'Oh I don't know, no idea,' I muttered. 'But let's talk about you, Nell. Is there any news of America?' I desperately wanted to change the subject. 'I'd love to hear.'

'We leave after the revue has finished, two days later in fact,' she muttered, her mind elsewhere. 'The time seems to be flying.'

'I won't think about that.'

'No,' she replied and I was desperate to lighten the atmosphere; an atmosphere I had created by my thoughtless chatter.

'Shall we dance, Nell?' I found myself saying.

Her eyes lit up instantly. 'Do you mean it? Have you been practising?'

'Oh, well...yes, I have a bit.'

'Let's dance together,' she suggested, and she took hold of my hands and pulled me gently to my feet. 'Let's do the waltz, I love it.'

'Aha, the waltz I can do. I've been practising with Sidney.'

'No! I bet that looked funny.'

'You could say that. I like the waltz because it's something I can actually do if I'm pushed around the floor a little.'

'Yeah, well you should be able to do it at your advanced years.' The lightness in her voice and the expression on her face told me she had briefly forgotten my encounter with Thea. 'You'll have to hold me close,' she continued, putting her hand on my back. 'No, hold me a bit closer than that! Now, straight back, remember?'

'I'm trying...'

'Hold you head up.'

'I'm trying...'

'Not hard enough though,' she laughed. She began to sing something that sounded like Strauss, but intelligent thought had fled to the stars with Nell so close to me. We moved around the room gingerly because of my legs and it resembled anything *but* a waltz in my eyes. 'You're doing brilliantly, Mr Marshall,' she whispered, looking up at my face.

Feeling her hand in the middle of my back made me feel breathless and light headed. 'I feel a little...'

'Slow?'

'No, a little...'

'Daft?'

'No, a little...'

'Limp?' she laughed.

I began to laugh then too. 'No, a little...'

'Well, whatever it is, who cares!' she declared.

'I agree,' I said and then I stumbled and she grabbed hold of me hard with both her arms tightly around my back. 'Sorry...sorry...'

'That's enough for now,' she told me, still holding me firmly, but looking up at my face.

'I wouldn't say that,' I muttered and she let me go and glanced at her watch.

'I'd better go.'

My stomach turned over. 'Do you have to?'

She seemed distant suddenly and the speed in which her mood had changed shocked me 'Yeah, I need to learn some lines and practise my songs.'

'Thanks so much for coming round, Nell.'

She gave a wan smile. 'Were you pleased to see me?'

I was stunned by her question. 'How can you doubt it?'

'I don't know,' she shrugged, 'I just feel as if ...'

'Go on...as if?'

'It doesn't matter, it's not important.'

'It is to me.'

She swallowed hard, as if summoning up courage. 'I feel as if I've lost you, Mr Marshall.'

I shook my head in disbelief. 'Lost me? Lost me? I can't believe you think that. How have you lost me? Am I not putting over how ecstatic I am to see you? If this stiff, blank face could only portray how much I ...' Anger with my face's impotence choked off the words in my throat.

'It's not your face,' she replied, with a small smile, 'it's a wonderful, distinguished face as it always is.'

'No, you misunderstand me...'

'It's your new companion,' she cried, interrupting me, 'who I know, by her impulsive actions, is already a little in love with you. And that scares me witless.'

'Why would it scare you?' I asked her, confused and perplexed by her words. 'And I don't believe for one minute she's even the slightest bit in love with me. Nell, I don't understand your concern. She is simply a neighbour who asked me to lunch out of kindness and had a bit too much red wine and made a sudden pass at me she'll probably regret.'

Her face was pinched. 'But she sounds extremely forward and full on.'

'Nell, what is it? Please tell me. What is it about Thea that bothers you so much?'

She sighed and shook her head at me. 'You may be sixty-two, but you haven't learnt very much about women in all that time, have you?'

'Oh I agree with you there, women continue to be a mystery to me. But I don't want *you* to be a mystery, so you'll have to spell it out for me.'

'No, I can't because it makes me look shallow and stupid and I'll seem less of a person in your eyes.'

'You most certainly will not! I promise you. That just isn't possible.'

She shook her head decisively and jumped up. 'No, I can't, work it out for yourself. I have to go.'

'When will I see you again? If you have an hour off sometime, do come and see me, won't you?'

She looked the most vulnerable I had ever seen her. 'Yes, of course I will, even though I have a rival now.'

I made a compulsive grab for her hand. 'You have no rival and no equal, I assure you.'

She glanced up at me with such an unhappy look on her face it took my breath away and I felt the tremors quicken under my skin. 'I'm really glad you'll have some female company when I'm away, truly I am but, if I'm honest ... Oh emotions are such a complex thing.'

'Nell, tell me what is bothering you about Thea, please,' I implored her, knowing that if she didn't our whole conversation would be on my mind constantly until I saw her again.

'If you must know, Mr Marshall, I'm jealous,' she told me, almost pitifully. 'I know it's ridiculous and stupid and childish because we're just friends, but I am. There, so now you know.'

I loved her most then, at her most open and sweet natured. I longed to hug her, kiss the top of her head and hold her there like that forever. I was desperate to express my searing love for her, to be as brave as she was.

Instead I stumbled on my words, slurred and staggered forward again.

'If you think anyone can replace you in my heart, as my friend, you are wrong. Nobody can and nobody will, as long as I live – apart from Beth and that's a wholly different relationship. Nell, I hope you believe that.'

Her face brightened a little, but I could still detect concern in her eyes. She squeezed my hand gently and then looked at it trembling in hers. 'Do you mean it, Mr Marshall?' she whispered, her voice suddenly breaking.

'I mean it,' I told her, 'with all my heart.'

Then she smiled her usual smile and it transformed her face. 'OK, if you say so. Now, I must go.'

We made our way to the door and she took her wet coat off the peg. I felt an anxiousness coming over me because we still weren't back to how we were. But she must have been feeling the same because as I reached by her and opened the door she flung her arms around me in a frantic, reckless way. I was dumbfounded and couldn't speak, but merely closed my eyes with the joy of having her so close to me. My weak arms hung loosely by my sides because she had pinned them to me in her embrace. She clung on for a few moments as if it was the last time she would ever do that and then walked away without saying another word. I stood paralysed until she disappeared from view and then made my way back to the conservatory where I sat transfixed by the memory of her touch and how she had trembled slightly with her head against my chest. And I didn't move until the darkness and the *presence* surrounded me and I leant sideways to turn on the lamp.

My father was sitting by the piano smiling, 'Let her go and she'll come back to you,' he said.

&

I left him on his doorstep and I knew he was watching me, but I didn't – couldn't – turn to look at him. I was oddly upset, surprised and rattled at the thought of a woman kissing him after only knowing him a few hours. I pictured her planting her impulsive kiss on his mouth and wondered if he had enjoyed their moment of intimacy. My emotions were all over the place; I felt strangely pleased for him and jealous of her at the same time. They were probably well suited, a perfect match and a relationship waiting to happen. She was of a similar age, attractive and well off, his intellectual equal perhaps, his class, his type. I thought he would no doubt show her his plays that he hadn't yet shown me, but perhaps he thought she would understand and appreciate them better.

Beth would be overjoyed of course and so would his hard-faced sister. Had he mentioned me to her? Did she wonder what I was after? Did she wonder about the nature of my relationship with him?

Why the hell was I so jealous? We weren't partners after all, but I *was* his friend. When I was in America he might get even closer to her. They would laugh together, talk incessantly, growing closer and closer by the day. She would replace me in his affections because she was more like him in every way than I was. I could see him in my mind's eye looking at her with that fond, affectionate expression he always had when he was watching me speak; when his blue eyes would narrow as he listened intently to every word and then soften gradually until they were twinkling like bright stars in a black sky. His voice, so unusual, distinctive and cultured without any hint of arrogance or imperiousness and the way he formed his sentences, so unlike anyone I had ever met. The Parkinson's made his voice rise and fall and those symptoms he despised made him even more dear to me.

I had arrived home, but I didn't remember getting there, I had been so deep in thought. As I fumbled for my keys and opened my front door I imagined him making a grab for her hand to steady himself, then apologising and looking down at her with his appealing face. I went to my bedroom and threw myself on the bed. It was dark and cool, with only the orange light from the street shining across the room. I had lost him I was sure. She would worm her way slowly into every part of his life and his gentle heart while I was away and be his closest companion in his latter years while I looked on with regret and sadness. I could picture them sitting in his conservatory together, chatting about politics, literature and the economic outlook for Great Britain. She wouldn't use silly sayings he had never heard of. She wouldn't laugh raucously at the way he spoke. She would be classy with a fine intellect, a Lily type who would accompany him to the theatre and they would discuss the script and compare it to his plays.

I couldn't be jealous, we were simply close friends. The problem was, I loved who I was through his eyes and that had given me a surge in confidence I knew had helped me secure the two roles I now had. He had done more for me in the few months I had known him than anyone else in my life.

'Oh Joshua,' I whispered into the blackness of my room, my throat aching. 'I'll lose him like I lost you.'

Chapter 14

'Benedict, sorry just to turn up, I know it's early, but you hadn't called and I wondered ...' Thea was standing on my doorstep, resplendent in a tight, bright red sweater and a smart pair of black trousers. Her dark chestnut hair was hanging around her shoulders and she had a white scarf thrown carelessly round her shoulders. 'Is everything...'

'That's fine; sorry, I've been rather preoccupied, do come in,' I replied, opening the door wider. 'Would you like some coffee?'

She looked thrilled at my invitation. 'I'd *love* some coffee, thank you.'

'Go through, I haven't had breakfast yet, would you care to join me?'

'I'd love to, if you're sure?'

'Very sure,' I smiled, surprisingly pleased to see her; but then any woman on my doorstep would be a pleasant surprise because it made a change from dear old Sidney and, before knowing Nell, it was an extremely rare occurrence.

'Thanks.'

'Sit here in the conservatory; it's lovely with the sun as it is today. I'll put some coffee on. What would you like for breakfast?'

'Oh I don't mind, whatever you're having.'

'Well, I don't eat that much this time in the morning, although I know that's not particularly good for me. Normally a little porridge or French toast, but I haven't had time to go to the delicatessen, so would a blueberry muffin be OK for you?'

'Muffins for breakfast, eh?' she commented, 'how very decadent of you! I try to be good and eat muesli, but I have to say that sometimes it tastes like sawdust in my mouth so having a blueberry muffin would make me feel incredibly naughty, as if I'm on holiday.'

I smiled at the vignette she drew, 'Well, let's pretend we're on holiday then, shall we?' I replied, rubbing my hands together in glee. I went into the kitchen and she followed me.

'Can I chat while you prepare breakfast?'

'Of course, chat away.'

'You don't mind me just turning up?' she asked, a little hesitantly.

'If you think I'd ever mind a lovely woman standing on my doorstep you're ...'

She butted in, 'I didn't want to presume.'

'You aren't, believe me,' I told her.

She looked somewhat relieved. 'Thank you. I know I'm pushy, but I don't know how to be any other way. I think we should all seize the moment because you never know if you'll get another chance.'

'No, that's true,' I replied, thinking of Nell and how one day, when she was far away, I might regret not telling her how much I loved her. Before my thoughts could carry *me* too far away, I heard Thea speaking again.

'So, how have you been these last few days? You look great!'

'I've not been too bad, thanks,' I told her, turning towards the fridge, not wanting to face her. In reality, I had been unsettled, deeply concerned and flummoxed by Nell suddenly flinging her arms around me, clinging on like a wounded child on her departure a few days before, and I knew Thea would probably pick up on my white lie. 'The tremors are actually behaving a little for once, which may be because the quack tweaked my tablets, but to be perfectly honest I haven't really been very active so maybe that's why.'

'I wondered if you'd like to take a stroll in the park later, if the weather holds. It's so beautiful this time of year with everything bursting with colour. Well, it's beautiful any time of year, but I adore spring.'

'Yes, so do I.'

'I like to share those kinds of moments with someone. That's the thing I find hardest about being divorced. Those moments, you know? We wouldn't have to walk too far, just around the flower garden, maybe sit by the duck pond.'

I involuntarily jerked a little at the mention of the duck pond; I associated it so deeply with Nell and couldn't bear visiting it without her, and was therefore grateful I had an excuse to say no. 'I can't, you see ...'

She raised her hands. 'Fine, fine, that's fine, I'm sorry, just me being pushy again. Ignore me.'

I leant on the work surface and smiled at her. 'You aren't being pushy. It's perfectly reasonable to ask me to go for a walk on a mild day with the smell of blossom in the air. But I can't go out because Sidney, my neighbour, is coming in to play cards while his wife is shopping and he relishes our time together so it wouldn't be fair if I were not here.'

'Of course, I understand. You have so many people wanting your company. Aren't you lucky?'

I gave her a wry smile. 'Not so many, I assure you.'

'More than me anyway,' she added, looking at the floor and it suddenly dawned on me that although she was very flamboyant, somewhat loud and full of fun, she was obviously rather lonely.

'Can we take a walk another day?' I asked impulsively.

Her smile told me quite clearly how she longed to spend some time with me and I was glad I had mentioned a walk on another day when I might not be so preoccupied by thoughts of Nell.

'That would be lovely; perhaps one day when I'm not in the book shop or you could meet me at the bookshop and we could take a stroll home via the flower garden.'

While she spoke I placed our breakfast things on a tray and murmured, 'Sounds wonderful,' before pointing at the tray. "Would you carry this through for me?'

'Sure,' she replied, picking it up with her rock-steady hands.

'Put it on the coffee table in the conservatory, just there.'

We sat and ate our muffins and washed them down with piping hot coffee. I tried desperately not to think of Nell while she was there, but it was second nature to me now and I wondered what she was doing, what she was thinking and who she was talking to that day, wishing it was me. Thea must have been born with an innate sense of when someone was troubled because she sat back in her chair, coffee cup in hand, crossed her long, athletic legs and smiled at me.

'How are things then?' she asked, her eyes probing my face.

'Fine, fine ...'

As my sentence petered out she turned the conversation to herself, 'I was mortified the other day after you had left that I'd told you that story about when I shocked everyone at our dinner party. What must have you thought of me? I'm not always so blunt and I really don't set out to shock; well, sometimes I do and I certainly did then, but not often.'

'I thought it a wonderful story. I wish I had the courage to say something like that. I wasn't shocked at all, just amused.'

'Well, I'd had quite a bit to drink and I can't take alcohol really, it makes me reckless.'

'I gathered that.'

'Have you seen your little friend since we met?' she suddenly asked, seemingly carelessly.

'Sorry, I'm not sure...'

'Nell,' she said, 'I think of her as Little Nell, you know as in Charles Dickens.'

'I sincerely hope she doesn't come to an end like Little Nell.'

'No, of course, it's just the name, it's quite unusual.'

'It's short for Helen,' I told her, 'and yes I've seen her, she popped in the other day. A flying visit, in the thunderstorm, soaking wet, but full of life as usual.'

'Oh she came round the day we had lunch?'

'Yes, she did.'

'Everything OK then, with her and you I mean?'

I was beginning to wonder if she could see right inside my brain. 'It was all rather lovely, just sitting and chatting to her, hearing about how her rehearsals are going, that sort of thing. Lovely, really lovely ...' I muttered, my voice trailing off to a whisper.

Thea sighed and put down her coffee cup quite firmly. 'What is it?' she asked, almost wearily.

It was quite useless to pretend to her. She had been watching people, listening to people and weighing people up professionally for so long, nothing escaped her beady eyes. But I wasn't sure I wanted to disclose all my inner emotions about Nell as they were private and mine alone.

'Oh nothing really,' I declared dismissively. 'She was just a little emotional when we said goodbye.'

Thea eyed me somewhat suspiciously. 'I suppose her emotions are pretty near the surface being an actress, but ...'

I resented the fact that she was implying Nell may be acting and cut in quickly. 'Just because she's an actress doesn't mean to say she doesn't feel things deeply. Creative people simply show their emotions a little more readily than the likes of me or indeed you, but it doesn't make them any less pertinent or real.'

She immediately picked up on my defence of Nell. 'Sorry, Benedict, it wasn't a criticism of her, simply a remark. I wouldn't dream of being critical of your young friend. I'm just a bit too honest and forthright for my own good.'

'I don't mind honesty,' I replied, 'but some people seem to think that being an actress means you aren't like others and of course you are. Actors are just people like you and I.'

'I agree, I agree, wholeheartedly,' she said hastily. There was silence for a moment and then she added, 'did you mention coming to my house for lunch?'

'Yes I did because she asked what I'd been doing and I told her about bumping into you and how you sent me flying and she thought that quite hilarious.'

Thea fixed me with an intense look. It was a look I was beginning to recognise as her interrogation expression. 'When you say she was emotional as she left, what exactly does that mean?'

'Well...'

'If you don't mind me asking...'

'I don't mind you asking,' I replied, although God knows why, when in fact I minded quite a lot. 'Simply that she hugged me so tightly, it was as if we were saying farewell forever and it shocked me. I wasn't expecting it and it threw me. It's been on my mind ever since, day and night. But let's not focus on me, how have you been?' I asked, trying to deflect the attention from Nell.

Thea gave a knowing smile. 'Stop changing the subject, Benedict. I think your young friend has truly deep feelings for you, deeper than you could imagine in your wildest dreams. I might even go so far as to say that I suspect she's in ...'

I put my hand up to silence her. 'No more about Nell, please. I don't feel comfortable talking about her when she isn't here and I'm not such a fool as to think she doesn't care deeply for me. I know she does, but it's foolish to pretend we are anything other than loving friends so ...'

My unusually eloquent and determined speech was interrupted by Sidney knocking on the wall and I struggled to my feet to knock back in the affirmative. Thea's face was a picture of bemusement.

'What on earth is all that about?'

'Sidney!' I shrugged, as if that was explanation enough.

'Shall I go?' she asked, jumping to her feet.

'No, no, stay please, you must meet Sidney. Everyone needs to meet Sidney.'

'Benedict,' she started, appearing rather flustered, 'I'm sorry for probing about Nell, it's just my nature and I've done it for so long it's ...'

'It's fine, really,' I butted in because she looked so contrite and concerned and I felt ungrateful and ridiculously guilty for being a little short with her. 'I'm very pleased you popped round, honestly.'

She bit her lip. 'If you're sure ...'

Before I could say any more, Sidney burst in, full of life. 'What ho, Benedict, and all that posh rubbish you speak.'

I turned to Thea. 'I assure you I have never spoken like that or used that particular phrase or anything similar in my entire life.'

She looked highly amused, especially when Sidney caught sight of her and realised I had company – female company at that. His eyes lit up like Blackpool Tower on a winter's night. 'I beg your pardon. I didn't know there was someone here.'

'That's OK, Sidney. This is Dorothea, Thea for short.'

'Thank goodness for that,' he muttered.

'Yes, daft name, but there you are, it's the only one I've got,' she told him, shaking his hand and pumping it up and down heartily.

'Did I interrupt anything?' he asked, his question loaded with hidden meaning and I rolled my eyes in exasperation at him without her seeing.

'I was just going,' Thea said, no doubt tuning into my discomfort.

'Not on my account I hope.'

'No, no, not at all, I have to go anyway.'

'I'll see you out.' I followed her to the front door.

'Thanks for the breakfast, Benedict; do call me, when you get a minute.'

'I will, I promise.'

She kissed my cheek, took hold of my face in her hands and looked deep into my eyes. 'I hope you do. Bye then.'

'Goodbye and thank you for coming to see me.'

'Pleasure,' she said, letting go of me and literally bouncing down the road, her hips and hair swaying in the mild spring breeze.

I was smiling to myself as I rejoined Sidney, anticipating the expression on his face. He was sitting with his arms folded across his belly and he had a self-satisfied grin. 'Sidney, why are you looking like that?'

He was innocence personified. 'Like what?'

'You know precisely how you are looking!'

'I don't know what you mean,' he replied, in a voice that exuded hurt, when in reality he was anything but.

'Would you like a coffee?'

He shook his head slowly. 'I don't how you do it, I honestly don't.'

'To what exactly are you referring?'

'Speak normally for Christ's sake, Benedict. You aren't in one of your plays now, you're talking to me.'

'But as I've told you before, this is me speaking normally.'

He was grinning. 'Fuck me! She's pretty damn hot, isn't she?'

'Damn hot?' I queried. 'Since when did you start using terms like that?'

'That's what my boys say,' he shrugged. 'But she is, isn't she? Where on earth do you find them?'

'I don't, they find me!'

'What did she want so early on a Saturday morning?'

'I don't know really, we were just having some breakfast and ...'

'Oh yeah...'

'Sidney!'

'Breakfast with Dorothea, eh? How delightful!' he said, trying to imitate my voice. 'Was she here all night?'

'Don't be ridiculous,' I retorted.

'What would Nell think?'

'Why would Nell think anything?' I snapped feeling unreasonably irritated.

Sidney's face fell a mile. 'Sorry, mate, I didn't mean anything by that. I was just having a laugh.'

'I know, I know, I apologise, it's just she threw me a bit the other night because she was strangely upset with me.'

'Who was upset with you? Thea? Why would she be?' he asked, perplexed.

'No, Nell!'

'I can't keep up with this,' he remarked. 'Why was Nell upset with you?'

I sat down wearily. 'I'm really not sure. She said she was jealous of me having lunch with Thea ...'

'Jealous! Jealous!' he gasped. 'She told you she was *jealous*?'

'Yes, Sidney, she said she was jealous. That's precisely what she told me. I have no idea why she should be. But there you are.'

His face was a picture of bemusement. 'Did she mean jealous in a *sexual* way?'

I laughed out loud. 'Well, hardly! There isn't one bit of me that still retains any of those feelings, as I've told you before.'

'No, but *they* obviously have,' he declared.

'No, no, you don't understand. Nell was jealous of me having another close friend, someone to chat with, go to lunch with, that sort of thing. A bit like you were. I think she feels that when she's in New York I'll forget her. Ridiculous I know, but that's what she feels.'

'Bless her,' he muttered.

I sighed deeply. 'I know, and she clung to me like a limpet when she left. It was awful!'

'And what about this one, what's her name again?'

'Her name is Thea.'

'That's a bloody silly name if you ask me.'

'I didn't ask you.'

'Well, it is.'

'That's hardly her fault.'

'She's quite ...' he frowned, searching for the words, 'quite you know, full on, isn't she? That tight sweater, a jumper with bumps in!'

'Say that again.'

'Lovely figure for a woman of her years,' he murmured, quickly changing the slant of his words.

'You aren't supposed to notice things like that, you're happily married.'

'Just because you're on a diet, it doesn't mean you can't look at the menu!'

'Quite!' I smiled appreciatively, "You know, you do cheer me up. I hope I die before you do.'

He frowned, 'Why do you say that?'

'I say that because I really couldn't live my life without you, Sidney.'

He looked astonished at my admission. 'Do you mean that?'

'I'm afraid I do.'

'Nobody's ever said anything like that to me before,' he mumbled. 'I don't know what to say.'

'You don't have to say anything, just believe it.'

His dear face broke into an enormous grin. But the grin softened into a curious smile and he said quietly, 'Cheers matey; that means a lot.' Clearing his throat noisily he abruptly grabbed for the cards in his pocket. 'Now, what shall we play?'

'You choose.'

'OK; poker then.' As he dealt the cards, he turned the conversation back to Nell and Thea, 'But why would Nell particularly care about you having lunch with Thea? She must be surrounded by adoring men.'

'I think it was the fact that she kissed me,' I replied, waiting in eager anticipation for his response.

His jaw dropped. 'Kissed you? Hang on, who kissed you?'

'Thea kissed me.'

'Where did she kiss you?'

'In the hall…'

'You know what I mean,' he said, succinctly.

'I told you all this, didn't I? I'm sure I did. She kissed me on the lips.'

'Fuck me!'

'No, she won't be doing anything of the kind.'

'She's only known you five minutes!'

'True.'

'Actually you did tell me that. I just wanted to hear you say it again,' he grinned. 'No wonder Nell was jealous,' he gasped. 'If Thea can be that forward after knowing you a day, then what's going to happen in a week, a month, a year?' His voice was growing higher with every word uttered. 'Watch yourself, matey.'

'Nothing is going to happen,' I told him, 'that's just what she's like. She doesn't hold back. She reminds me of a cart horse, charging through fields, felling everything in her path and leaving devastation in her wake.'

He opened his eyes wide. 'Well, you'll have to be on your guard, Benedict. She'll have no trouble in chewing you up and spitting you out! Mark my words.'

'You know, you're like an old woman who stands at the garden fence and loves gossip.'

'Ah, but I don't stand at the garden fence, I stand in my window; much better view.'

'Well, are we going to gossip or play poker, Sidney?'

We played until lunch time when Sheila knocked for him in no uncertain terms. He glanced across at me raising an eyebrow, 'Blimey, what's up with the wife?'

'Will you stop calling her *the* wife? You can say *the* chair, *the* table, Sidney, but it's *my* wife, *my* wife! She's probably fed up with you being in here all morning when you should have been helping her with housework and the like. Now, bugger off.'

He gathered up the cards and moved toward the door, 'I'm going, see you later maybe.'

'No, you will not!' I called after him, 'Stay in and spend some time with your lovely wife.'

'Cheers mate,' he yelled back as his head disappeared behind his fence.

I made myself some lunch, not that I had much appetite, but I forced down some pasta and sat gazing at my garden with a cup of tea. The grass was such a rich green and the trees had sprouted leaves almost overnight. The weather was gentle and a creamy sun was shining down on the conservatory roof making me rather warm, so I moved into the lounge where it was cooler and darker. My eyes felt a little heavy and I sank into the sofa and stretched my long, bony legs out, with my feet up on the coffee table opposite me. I had some aching across my shoulders and in the small of my back and I could feel tiny tremors almost under my skin. It was a weird sensation, unusual and unsettling because I had no control over them. But I had to look on the bright side because my thoughts had been less obsessive and introspective in the last couple of weeks, which was an enormous relief. I leant back and tried to relax my shoulders and neck, but they were so tense they almost throbbed.

Attempting to ignore the discomfort I once again allowed my thoughts to be dominated by Nell as they were every day and even at night in my dreams. I had met her in winter when unexpected snow had been thick and sparkling like diamonds on the ground and it was now well into spring and nature had woken up after a long sleep and was bursting with life and colour. I tried to fall into a light doze, but the thoughts of Nell prevented me from doing so. I therefore reached for the phone and dialled her number, which now was inscribed on my heart. The answer phone clicked on and her voice, light and airy and full of energy told me to leave a message.

'Hello, Nell, it's me. I'm not good with these answer phone things so, um, wanted to know how you are, how the rehearsals are coming along and, well, that's all. If you could call me back when you get a spare minute that would be great, so, um, hopefully speak to you soon. Bye, Nell. Bye.'

I sank back into the sofa feeling a little less tense now I had left her a message and sleep washed over me instantly. I must have slept for an hour or two, which was rather longer than the doze I had anticipated, because the sun had moved round considerably and a thin strip of sunlight was shining across my face and in my eyes.

Someone was calling me. It was a faint voice, but well known to me and I struggled to wake up. 'Benedict. Benedict; wake up, darling. It's time to go.'

'Go where?' I asked.

'We're all going for a walk in the bluebell wood, are you coming?'

'Yes, yes, I'm coming. Is that you Mother?'

My dream was shattered by a ringing sound and for a few seconds I couldn't work out where the hell I was or even *who* I was. The bell rang again and, realising it was the doorbell, I stumbled to my feet and down the hall, hanging on to the wall as I went. I groped for the handle and, as I pulled the door open, heard another voice that was very dear to me.

'Hello, Mr Marshall.'

Nell was smiling up at me with her hair pulled back in a pony tail, which always made her look younger than she was. Her face was pale, no make-up, and she was dressed casually in tracksuit bottoms and a sweat shirt. 'Dear girl,' I replied, my voice hoarse with relief, 'what are you doing here when you're so very busy?'

'I missed you so I've bought you a present.'

'You missed me?' I asked and I heard my voice breaking. 'Come in, please.'

She rushed by me reaching into her pocket as I followed like a little lamb. 'Here you go,' she declared, placing something small and wrapped in bright red paper covered with silver stars on the table between us.

'This is a present for me?'

'Yeah, of course for you,' she laughed, looking excited and even more beautiful than usual.

I was speechless. 'Why have you ... what is it?'

'Open it and find out.'

'Nell, this is so kind of you.'

'For God's sake open it,' she urged.

My hands were trembling, not with the illness, but with the sudden nearness of her. I was struggling to rip the paper so she helped me, her hands brushing mine. With the wrapping paper torn off a small box was uncovered and I looked intently at it. Nell sighed as if I were a hopeless being and took out a tiny mobile phone.

'Oh my goodness, it's a mobile! You expect me to use this with my shaking hands? I'll never do it.'

'Oh yes you will,' she declared. 'It will be good for your dexterity and I'll be able to get hold of you wherever you are. You need to get with it, Mr Marshall. What do you think of it?'

'I'm amazed at your faith in me,' I remarked. 'But it's very kind of you and thoughtful too. Thank you.' I bent down and kissed the top of her cheek. 'It must have cost you quite a bit.'

She ignored my comment regarding the cost. 'It's all charged up and ready to go. Are you sure you like it?'

'I'm sure, but you'll have to teach me how to use it.'

'That will be easy.'

'Not as easy as you think, my girl.'

'You took ages to answer the door.'

'I was having a sleep.'

She appeared crestfallen. 'Oh no, I'm sorry.'

'Not at all, I needed to wake up. I'd started to dream about my mother ...'

'That's lovely.'

I smiled at her simplicity. 'Yes, Nell, it was. Sit down, please. I left you a message.'

'I know. I heard it!'

'I hate leaving messages; I wonder what on earth my voice sounds like.'

'It sounds fantastic,' she told me, brimming with life.

'Thank you, but I think you're slightly biased. How are things with you?'

'Rehearsals are going very well for the revue and Matt and I both have our flights booked for America, so we're getting rather excited.'

I caught my breath. 'I can only imagine.'

'You know ...' she started, appearing a little troubled, 'I was well out of order the other day.'

'I don't think so.'

'No, I was, so I apologise.'

'No need, Nell.'

Her grey eyes were large and sombre suddenly. 'You forgive my behaviour then?'

'There's nothing to forgive.'

We looked at each other for a moment in silence and I thought she was going to elaborate, but she didn't. She merely put her head on one side and gave me a reassuring smile, finally asking, 'Still the best of friends then?'

'Always,' I replied.

'Let's have fun!'

'Fun would be wonderful.'

'Let's dance, shall we?'

'I think not.'

'You're a great dancer.'

'Let's not go into the realms of fantasy now.'

'Put some music on,' she demanded.

I looked at her over my glasses as if she was a schoolgirl suggesting something daft and I her stern teacher. 'I'm not dancing today, Nell.'

She looked resolute. 'You are! You *have* to improve your balance and dancing is the best way.'

I attempted to match her determined expression, but with my ever rigid facial muscles, I'm not sure what I looked like to her. 'I tell you I'm not.'

She went over to my stereo system and went through some of my CDs again as she had on other days, turning her nose up at nearly all of them. 'We can't dance to Wagner!'

'That's hard luck then, if that's all you can find.'

She turned on the radio and skipped through the channels until she found some awful, ear-splitting cacophony with a heavy beat. She began to sing along and move with such panache, I stood spellbound.

'*I said I love you baby, love you so, I said I love you baby oh oh oh oh oh ...*'

I sat down to watch her display. 'What wonderful, inspiring words.'

'Don't take the piss.'

'What's her name?'

'What?'

'The singer, what's her name, if you could call her a singer,' I laughed.

'It's a bloke, you idiot,' she laughed back. 'He's got a brilliant voice.'

'Sounds like a wailing cat!'

'Yeah, OK grand-dad.'

'I know, I know.'

'Come on, throw a few shapes,' she urged, 'like I've showed you before.'

'Say that again.'

'Get up you old duffer,' she cried, grabbing hold of my hands and pulling me up gently. 'Look, follow me. This is a routine in the revue. You step, step, circle, step. Take your hat off.'

I tried copying her. 'I may be mistaken, but I don't believe I'm wearing one.'

'You have to *pretend* you have a hat on.'

'Aha, I see.'

She grinned at me. 'You're taking the piss again, Mr Marshall.'

'I'm afraid I am.'

She continued to dance and I copied her as best I could, feeling suddenly carefree and ecstatic at having her company again.

'You're a great dancer!' she yelled over the music. 'You always seem to pick up whatever I show you and you have a fabulous sense of rhythm, you know.'

'I can't help being a natural,' I declared and I knew I looked anything but. Nell was twirling and moving like a leopard walking through long grass with its eyes on its prey. Her whole body was at one with whatever music she chose. 'I wish I looked just a little like you do when you dance,' I told her.

'You do! You do!

'Hardly,' I said puffing wildly and, laughing again, I collapsed onto the sofa. 'That's enough for me.'

'OK, you win." She turned the radio off and urged, 'Come and play the piano then; for me.'

'For you, anything,' I replied, getting up slowly and going over to my piano with her. I had just sat heavily on the piano stool when I received her next command.

'Shove over then so I can sit with you.'

'Hold on, I can't do anything quickly.'

'That's obvious,' she smiled and I smiled back at her, our easy intimacy a delight after the unease of our last conversation together. 'What shall I play for you?'

'Sooty!' she cried.

'Sooty it is.'

As my fingers ran lightly over the keys she threw her head back and let out a blast of laughter that Sidney and Sheila and the whole of Greenwich must have heard. A couple of times my left hand stumbled on a note, but I didn't particularly care. It was almost a part of me now, like my voice or the phrases I used that Sydney and Nell found so quaint and hilarious. Nell sang along to the tune and jigged about in her chair like a little child.

'That's brilliant, I love that tune, it's so full of fun and reminds me of my childhood. Now play ...' Nell didn't finish her sentence because the door bell rang.

'Who the devil is that?' I sighed.

'Expecting anyone?'

'No.'

'Shall I go?'

'Would you?'

She jumped up and scampered out like a young puppy and I played Sooty again because it made me smile until she came back in with Thea behind her. 'I'm so sorry, Benedict, I left my scarf here,' she told me, breathless and a little red in the face.

Nell was standing beside me waiting to be introduced and I got up in such a hurry I staggered and grabbed hold of the piano. 'Whoops, be careful, Mr Marshall,' Nell laughed, holding me steady, 'drunk again!'

After nearly falling over, I sat down again before addressing Thea, 'Hello again, this is ...'

'Nell, obviously,' Thea interrupted, 'I'm very pleased to meet you, Nell.'

Nell gave her the most beautiful warm smile. 'Hello there, where did you leave your scarf?'

'I think it may be on the chair I was sitting on earlier, in the conservatory,' she replied, looking straight at me, with a half smile.

'Ah, yes,' I spluttered, 'could you get it, Nell?' Nell went into the conservatory and picked it up off the floor where it had fallen. The atmosphere in the room felt suddenly tight and tense and awkward although both Thea and Nell seemed to be completely relaxed. I wondered momentarily if the tension was coming from me. 'We were just playing the piano,' I added, mumbling hideously.

Thea raised her eyebrows. 'I didn't know you could play. How lovely. Don't let me stop you. What were you playing?'

I shrugged. 'Sooty.'

Nell burst out laughing. 'It's my favourite. One day he was playing some Chopin for me and went straight into Sooty. I fell about, it was so funny.'

Thea was looking at me intently. 'I'd love to hear that.'

I sniffed imperiously. 'I never give repeat performances.'

'Oh go on, Mr Marshall,' Nell urged me.

'No, I definitely don't give repeat performances.'

'Just once more, please.'

She looked so appealing I simply didn't have the heart to say no, but I really did not want to play it in front of Thea because it was *our* tune, mine and Nell's and *our* bit of fun. But I really could not deny her any request. I began to play Chopin and my left hand misbehaved a couple of times, but I continued and ran swiftly into Sooty anticipating that Nell's usual blast of laughter might be muted because of a stranger's presence. But when it came it was gloriously unabashed and at full throttle and I glanced at Thea to see her reaction. She was watching Nell, a little astonished at the uninhibited way she reacted and possibly a little envious too.

'What do you think?' Nell asked her.

Thea clapped in appreciation. 'That was quite brilliant, Benedict.'

'Thank you, now no more performances. Drink anyone?'

My words were almost drowned out by Sidney banging on the wall so loudly it almost moved. Nell sprang over and knocked back as if she had lived in my house all her life. 'Thirty seconds,' she said, looking at her watch.

'This should be fun,' I muttered, knowing that Sidney had been at his usual place in the window with his nose pressed against it and had seen Nell arrive followed a little later by Thea.

It didn't even take thirty seconds for him to appear jauntily at my door, eager and excited. 'So, what's occurring then, Benedict?' he called, sauntering in.

'As you can see, there is nothing much going on, Sidney, as usual.'

He grinned at me. 'I wouldn't say that.'

Nell came and sat next to me on the piano stool once more, linking her arm through mine in an affectionate gesture. Thea was standing with her scarf in her hands unusually silent.

'Hello, Sidney, how are things with you?' Nell asked him.

'Very well, thank you.'

With an exaggerated sigh, I quietly asked, 'Did you want something, Sidney?'

'No, not really...'

'Then why are you standing in my living room?'

'Don't be rotten,' Nell told me. 'He's come to see you.'

'Oh I doubt that,' I muttered.

'I'd better be off,' Thea suddenly said.

'You don't have to go, does she, Mr Marshall?' Nell said kindly.

'No, of course not, I'm forgetting my manners. Thea, do stay and have a drink. Let's all have a drink.'

'Yes let's,' Sidney agreed, his eyes twinkling.

Nell turned to me, her eyes questioning. 'This is Thea?'

'Yes, sorry, I didn't introduce you properly. Thea, Nell, Nell, Thea.'

My Nell, the light of my ridiculous and absurd life, who had opened my heart for the first time, didn't let me down. If she felt jealous in any way of this mature, quietly sophisticated woman who she knew was strangely attracted to me, she did not show it in any way. The actress in her surfaced and she beamed at Thea with sincerity and delight.

'Oh Thea,' she gasped, springing forward and grabbing her hand, 'I'm so pleased to meet you, I've heard so much about you.'

Thea appeared dumbfounded for a split second, but recovered quickly and gave Nell a little kiss on the cheek. 'Likewise,' she said.

There was a moment's awkwardness which I attempted to fill with something banal, but my mouth would not behave. Luckily Sidney, whose eyes were glinting like a cat's, jumped into the silence.

'Isn't this fun? I love coming round here, Benedict.'

'And why is that, Sidney?'

'There's always something going on,' he grinned. 'It's never dull or boring, not even on a Sunday afternoon.'

'I assure you, it is,' I said to the assembled company.

'Shall we all have a cup of tea?' Nell asked, jumping up.

'Great,' Sidney muttered to himself, taking his place on my sofa and crossing his arms as if waiting for the show to begin.

Thea waved her hand in the air. 'No, thank you, I have to go. It was lovely to meet you, Nell. Bye Sidney.'

'I'll see you out,' I offered and followed her into the hall.

Once in the hall she wound her scarf round her neck. 'Well, goodbye again.' She appeared a little embarrassed and hesitant, but I knew she wanted to pass comment on Nell before she left. I could sense it bubbling up in her, even though I hardly knew her. 'It's so funny hearing her call you by your surname.'

'Yes, it's just something she likes to do – a bit of a joke between us.'

'She's undeniably lovely.'

'Yes, she is.'

'I had no idea ...'

I was perplexed. 'Why would you? You had never met her.'

She rolled her eyes as if I was hopeless. 'No, you idiot,' she sighed, 'I had no idea how much she loved you.' She turned on her heel and glancing over her shoulder, she gave a little wave and said, 'See you soon, Benedict.'

I was so shocked by her words I couldn't form any sort of reply before she walked away. How much she loved me? She had got it the wrong way round in her hurry to get away. She meant she had no idea how much I loved Nell. Yes, that was it. I'd put her right next time I saw her.

Sidney and Nell were chatting together on my sofa and when I saw them I felt a large lump form in my throat because it looked so right and so heartening to have the both of them there. 'Lovely lady,' Nell said in her usual generous way.

'Yes, she seems to be,' I replied. 'I don't really know her that well. I've spent a few hours in her company, that's all.'

'She's very attractive for her age; well, *any* age,' Nell added.

'I suppose she is.'

'Shame she had to leave,' Sidney chipped in, 'things were really getting steamy in here.'

'What does steamy mean, Sidney?'

'Two beautiful women in your front room,' he cried, as if I was completely daft and rubbing his hands in glee. 'How often does that happen?'

'Ah thanks, Sidney,' Nell said, leaning over and kissing him on the cheek, at which point he flushed like a schoolboy. 'Shall I make us all some tea?'

Sidney grinned. 'I'd rather have a whisky.'

Nell looked at me. 'Can he have a whisky?'

'Sidney, you are incorrigible, but I don't see why not. I might even join you.'

Nell gasped. 'It's too early for you, Mr Marshall. What about your tablets?'

'Yes, yes, of course, sorry; tea it is.' I saw the disappointment on Sidney's face and added, 'You can have a tot in your tea, Sidney.'

'That's big of you,' he sneered.

Nell stayed another half hour, in which time she tried to explain to me how to use my new mobile. Her patience was so endearing that half the time she was showing me the buttons I was staring at her beautiful face instead. But I did eventually get the hang of it and she left me and Sidney there to our own devices promising to drop two tickets in for the revue very soon.

Sidney was sitting with a self-satisfied smile on his face when I rejoined him after seeing Nell off; a smile that transformed into a smirk when he stated, 'Well, you old reprobate ...'

'I have no idea what you mean.'

'Or is it roué?'

'I am neither, as well you know.'

'Thea didn't like it.'

'Sidney, what are you implying with all these comments?'

'That Nell looked so comfortable here and the two of you ... the way you are together.'

'How are we together?' I asked him, bemused. He put his head on one side, deep in thought and I pushed him for an answer, 'Sidney! I asked you, how are we together?'

'Right somehow,' he replied. 'And Thea could see that too.'

'I think you've been drinking.'

'How dare you! No such bloody luck, but as the sun is over the yardarm ...'

Later that evening when I'd finally shipped Sidney home and was on my own, I sat in the low light of my conservatory and picked up the mobile phone, turning it over lovingly in my hand. Nell's kindness continued to overwhelm me and I knew I was slipping deeper and deeper into a bottomless, dark well of emotions that I would never recover from. This would be my life from now on. Loving her from afar, especially when she was in New York and being grateful for any contact I might have with her. Her friendship was like a brilliant light of positivity showering me with darting sparks that settled like snowflakes. I would welcome time with Thea because she was lively, good company and funny and we had much in common, but I could not deny my love for Nell to anyone, least of all myself.

I placed the mobile on my chest, near to my heart and dozed lightly. The *presence* was hovering as I slipped in and out of sleep and I could hear my father's voice in the distance somewhere. I glanced over towards the piano, but he wasn't there and I closed my eyes and sank into a deeper sleep only waking at around four in the morning, stiff and aching. The stillness and silence of the dawn was wonderful and although I longed for my bed I didn't want the spell to be broken by struggling to get up and so I stayed there and slept again until seven when the startling early sunshine flooded into the room.

Eating breakfast alone in the conservatory watching the blue tits flying on and off the bird table, I suddenly and inexplicably felt guilty about how uncomfortable Thea had looked when she was confronted by Nell and me together. I had caught a fleeting look of wistfulness in her eyes when she watched Nell call me 'Mr Marshall' and urge me to play Sooty again for them both. I immediately picked up the phone and called her, even though it was before eight-thirty.

'Hello, Thea speaking,' she said, in her usual breathless way.

'Good morning, it's Benedict. I'm sorry to call so early but ...'

'Oh Benedict, it's lovely to hear your voice. I was just thinking about you. Would you like to take a walk this morning in the park? It's such a bright morning, just right for a stroll.'

I felt a sudden rush of spring madness and mixed with my nagging guilt, I found myself saying, 'Why not? But it has to be a stroll and not a marathon.'

I heard a small gasp. 'Fantastic! I'll be round for you in an hour.'

'Fine,' I replied, but the line was already dead and I stood looking at the receiver, wondering what I was actually getting myself in to because of my hopeless, complex feelings.

She was on time, resplendent in a pair of jeans and a bright yellow jumper that fitted quite snugly and I almost laughed recollecting Sidney's comment about a jumper with bumps in. She was flicking her hair behind her ears? 'Are you ready?'

'I am, I think.'

'Don't look so scared,' she laughed.

'I'm not scared, just terrified.'

She looked perplexed. 'Are you terrified of me?'

'Yes, of you.'

'What on earth are you afraid of?'

I frowned. 'Not really sure.'

She had a glint in her eye. 'I'll be gentle with you.'

'Thank you.'

'Gentler than a younger woman would be,' she added, winking.

I didn't answer her comment because there was no answer except to tell her no-one could be gentler than my Nell, but that would have been unnecessary and so I simply smiled. Thea took hold of my arm boldly and steered me towards the park gates firmly. I glanced up at Sidney's window, but he wasn't there unfortunately because I would have loved to have given him a wry smile.

Thea chatted quite freely making a comment on all the various flowers that were springing to life in the flower garden and I enjoyed seeing them through her eyes. She was obviously a keen gardener and even offered to do some work in my garden over the summer months. I would like to say I was fully there, with her, making the most of the mild wind in my face and the warm sun on my back. But part of me was remembering all my walks with Nell through February, March and April and the joy of getting to know her through our long and easy conversations. And Thea of course, being tuned in to my every emotion and expression, must have felt my discomfort and reticence when she mentioned sitting for a while by the duck pond.

'I'd rather keep walking; my legs get a bit stiff.'

'Does the duck pond hold special memories for you?' she asked.

'Yes, it does...lovely memories.'

'Did you bring your daughter here?'

'I did, all the time. She used to think the ducks were hers.'

'But they must be wonderful memories.'

'Yes, wonderful.'

'Then why don't you like sitting here?'

'Oh, I don't know ...'

I heard her sigh. 'Benedict, you are such a deep man,' she declared. 'I find you hard to read sometimes.'

'Not so deep and I think you read me quite well actually.'

She was probing me with that intense look of hers. 'Aha, you've come here with Little Nell.

I was going to admit to anything, but I found myself saying, 'This is where we met.'

'I'm sorry, I should have thought.'

'Why should you?'

'Let's go and have a coffee then, shall we?'

I couldn't possibly then add I did not want to go in the café either because of Nell; she would have thought me a fool and perhaps I was a fool. My sister thought so and so did my daughter if truth be known, although she loved me too much to actually call me by that name, but I was past caring. If I was a fool to love Nell then I was a happy fool. Pushing these thoughts to the back of my mind, I simply uttered, 'A coffee would be great,' and the smile she gave me in return made me feel as if I was bestowing on her some great favour, which made me feel guilty yet again.

The muscle-bound man behind the counter who Nell always spoke to glanced briefly at me as I sat down. Thea ordered the drinks and brought them over looking excited. 'Isn't this lovely?' she beamed. 'It's so fabulous to have your company, Benedict. It's better than doing housework!'

'I have to agree and it's fabulous to have your company too.'

'My daughter rang last night and I was telling her about you. She said, oh Mum, he sounds a nice man and I said, *nice*? I wouldn't use the word *nice*! He's much more than *nice*! He's cultured, attractive, funny ...'

'Stop please,' I laughed, feeling slightly uncomfortable at her gushing description. 'You should have told her I'm sixty-two and have Parkinson's; that I stumble over my words, stagger and dribble. That would have been a much better description.'

'Don't be ridiculous, you do none of those things,' she said dismissively.

'I assure you I do, all the time. I'm surprised you hadn't noticed.'

'All I see is a man worth getting to know.'

'Well, thank you, but the Parkinson's can only get worse.'

'You can't think like that.'

'I try not to, but I live with it. However, I have to say that in the last couple of weeks I think my tablets are actually kicking in. The physical symptoms are a little better, but my mental ones are much improved. I had quite distressing thoughts all the time, distressing and obsessive, but my mind seems to be clearer now.'

'That's great, really great,' she said sincerely. There was a few seconds silence before she started speaking again and when she did, her words came out quickly, breathlessly and uninhibited. 'Benedict, I'm aware how much you feel for Nell. I can see it every time you say her name and to be honest I was shocked when I saw you together because she is *so* young ...'

'Not *so* young ...'

'No, let me finish. I need to get this out in the open. Emotions should always be expressed otherwise a person can have regrets.'

'I know about regrets,' I said wistfully.

'I had no idea how she felt about you and now I do, but there really can't be any future in it and if you think there can be you will be dreadfully disappointed. I mean, how much have you really got in common? Women only just get into their stride in their forties; believe me I know. We are at the peak of our sexual powers just as men start declining. All very disheartening I can tell you. We just begin to come into our own as men get out their pipe and slippers.'

'And start imagining they are masturbating in their rocking chairs,' I added, attempting to interrupt her flow.

She laughed loudly. 'Don't remind me I told you that after knowing you half an hour, it's so embarrassing. Anyway, where was I?'

'You were at the height of your sexual powers.'

'Oh yes,' she said, not really tuning in to my sarcasm. 'Nell will be working hard at her career as she approaches forty, maybe wanting kids and ...'

'Where is all this leading, Thea? I seem to remember a few days ago you were telling me to think positively and that age didn't matter? For the last time, we are friends! That is all. I love her, yes, but I am not expecting her to sacrifice her life and freedom to look after me. I'd rather die if you want to know.'

She looked quite shocked at my quietly spoken outburst. 'So, where does that leave us then?'

I was flummoxed and had no idea how to answer her. 'I'm sorry, I ...'

'I believe in being forthright and upfront about these matters.'

'So I gather.'

'I find you fascinating and irresistible if you must know.'

I was dumbfounded. 'You find me irresistible? Dribbling is hardly irresistible, Thea.'

'Will you shut up about dribbling, Benedict? I would like to have a relationship with you: you and I going out, spending time together, being together; that sort of thing.' She shrugged and appeared rather sorrowful suddenly. 'I just had to say that and I know how you feel about Nell, but please believe me when I tell you there is no future in it for you. Even to love her from afar, silently, is no life. You need a partner, someone to help you, someone more like you. Someone more mature who wouldn't mind so much about the physical side of things being off the agenda. Sorry, but that's the truth.'

I put my hand over my eyes in embarrassment. 'Thea, I'm not very comfortable with you discussing my non-existent sex life with me. If you want me to be upfront and forthright with you, then it's really none of your business.'

She looked crestfallen. 'Oh I'm sorry, I didn't know you felt like that.'

'Well, I do.'

'Benedict, I apologise. Nothing is off limits as far as I'm concerned, but I tend to forget not everyone is the same.'

'Apology accepted,' I replied, beginning to feel exhausted already by her forthright manner.

'Thank you,' she said, with a small smile. 'But you haven't answered me. Can we have any kind of relationship?'

I felt bemused by her insistent questions and a little shell-shocked, considering she knew how I loved Nell. She was an extremely attractive woman with a blatant, aggressive sexual power that I had a feeling she knew was hard to resist. She had a beguiling way of flicking her hair behind her shoulders and sticking her chest out at the same time. I imagined her poor husband had probably found her a little too outspoken, especially at the time of the masturbating incident. For me, she was fun, interesting and intelligent and I found her obvious attraction to me quite good for my battered ego. I knew that if I had been the same age as her, without my disease and ignorant of Nell's existence, Thea and I would probably get on like a house on fire. And yet, as I was now, I knew she would be too overpowering for me, in every way. Timing, of course, was everything and it was too late for the type of relationship with me she craved. But I knew I had to answer her question, and as candidly as I could: 'I doubt it, Thea and I'm sorry. It's been wonderful to meet you and spend time with you and I would welcome doing this again, but if you're looking for a long-term partner, it's not me.'

She appeared immediately deflated and yet resigned. 'Thank you for being honest, I appreciate that. It's a shame though because I feel we have so much in common, but I suppose the shadow of a certain young actress would always be hanging over us.'

'Yes.'

'You're not supposed to agree.'

'I'm sorry.'

She sighed. 'My God, what on earth are you going to do, Benedict?'

'Do? I'm not going to do anything,' I replied.

'But how can you bear to love someone so much and not tell them how you feel? How can you adore her silently and not want to touch her or be physically close to her? What is your game plan?'

'I haven't got one. I don't need one. And as for wanting to be physically close to her ... all of that is too personal to discuss. You think you would have to speak of your love if you were me, but that's *you*, Thea. You have to get everything out in the open and upfront, but I have a quieter soul and I would never, will never, do or say anything that I think will embarrass or upset Nell. So, I can easily bear loving her and not declaring it. I can easily bear adoring her silently and keep my hands to myself when I'm near her. Easily! When I think of ...' I gave a little shudder and Thea took hold of my hand.

'You are the antithesis of a dirty old man,' she remarked.

'Sidney would love that long word – but thank you. I have to say it's the last thing in the world I would want to be or have anyone think I am, especially Nell. But let's talk of other things, shall we?'

She gave me a wan smile. 'What else is there to talk about when your mind is constantly on her? Being with you is a little like being with someone who is only half here. All subjects will ultimately lead back to her.'

'Is that how you see me?'

'Yes.'

'I'm sorry, Thea. Part of that may be the Parkinson's too. My brain is being invaded don't forget. I'm not nearly as sharp as I used to be.'

She gave a little shrug. 'Not to worry.'

We had both finished our coffee and I sensed she was a little downhearted, but I had no idea how to change the situation we found ourselves in because I did not want to change it. I suddenly longed to be on my own with my thoughts. I needed some time for reflection.

'Shall we go?' I asked her.

'Yes, maybe it's best. You look a little tired. We can always do this on another day when – well, whenever.'

I placed my hand over hers and voiced my earlier thought, 'Timing, Thea, is everything and the timing is all wrong.'

She nodded. 'I know, but if ... look, I wish you well, Benedict and I hope we can continue to be friends and if anything changes ...'

Her voice trailed off and she glanced out of the window. I still had my hand over hers and I gave it a little squeeze. She grabbed hold of it and, even though she still had her eyes averted, I saw a huge tear roll down her cheek and my stomach churned. I wasn't very adept at consoling women who were crying, especially if I had caused the tears.

'Thea, I'm truly sorry you're so upset because of me.'

She linked her fingers with mine. 'I can't blame you. I know I come over as being confident and full of myself and normally I am but, to be honest, Benedict, I'm lonely. I've been lonely since my separation and my daughter moving away. I miss her dreadfully. I just recognised in you a kindred spirit and someone in the same situation as me who I could spend time with. But I obviously over-egged the whole situation and when I saw you and Nell together at your house – well,' she shrugged, wiping the tears from her face, 'I had no idea there was such a closeness between you. I thought, mistakenly, that the deep feelings were all from your side. But,' she added, shaking her hair from her face, 'that's for me to deal with and no fault of yours. I'm sorry for these tears. I really should get a grip and I will, I promise.'

'I'm sorry you are lonely and I understand completely how you miss your daughter. I'll always be just around the corner. Drop in any time you feel you need company, I mean it. Will you do that?'

'Yes.'

'Good.'

'And the same goes for you when Nell is away. I know you're going to suffer, Benedict.'

'The suffering is of my own making so it's just hard luck. Now, shall we stroll back?' She nodded and let go of my hand at last. She had been holding it in such an intimate manner I had felt quietly embarrassed and was relieved to get it back. We ambled back to my house, mostly in silence except for her pointing out some stunning, deep purple rhododendrons on the way. It was a slightly awkward silence and when we parted she reached up and gave me a hasty peck on the cheek, which I knew Sidney would enjoy if he was at his window.

'I'll see you soon,' she said.

'I do hope so,' I replied.

As she walked away I noticed her wiping another tear from her face and I was sorry for that because I knew I couldn't ease her loneliness without giving her any false hope. And I could not give her any hope because even if I had not loved Nell, Thea would have been too much of a woman for me now with my wretched disease and that realisation gave me an ache of sadness somewhere in my chest that left me slightly breathless.

Chapter 15

Nell's big night was fast approaching and every time I thought about it my stomach fluttered with nerves for her. I did not see her during the week leading up to the two performances on the Friday and Saturday evenings, but she telephoned occasionally to update me and I could tell by her voice that she was brimming with excitement and anticipation. On the Wednesday before Sidney and I were going on the Saturday, I woke at five in the morning with a hot sweat creeping over my entire body. My face was burning like a raging fire, my head felt as if it was going to explode and my chest was tight. I flung my quilt away and dozed on and off for another hour, but then I woke ice cold and began coughing hard and by the time the sun came filtering through my blinds I had to acknowledge I was in the throes of full-blown flu. I struggled to get up, but didn't have the strength and so I stayed where I was, occasionally sipping from the glass of water by the side of my bed. I knew Sidney would be knocking just after breakfast because we had arranged to have coffee together in my garden if it was warm, so I picked up the phone and dialled his number at about eight-thirty knowing he would be up.

His eternally optimistic voice answered straight away. 'Hello, Sidney Walpole speaking.'

'Sidney, it's me.'

'What's up with you? You never phone me.'

'I'm ill in bed, with flu. I can't get up.'

'Give me a minute, I'll find your key and come up.'

'Thank you.'

I heard my front door being opened and closed almost immediately and felt instantly relieved that the reliable, solid Sidney was in my house. He even knocked at my bedroom door before coming in, gentleman that he was and when I saw his face at the side of my bed I gave him a wan smile. I knew what his first words would be and I was right.

'Fuck me, Benedict! You look bloody terrible. What can I do for you?'

'It's just flu so there's nothing to be done but to stay here, but I'll need more water. There's a jug in the kitchen in the cupboard by the fridge. Fill it up and I need my Parkinson's tablets too.'

'Where are they?'

'In the drawer in my bureau, bring them all up, please.'

'Will do,' he said, disappearing.

While he was downstairs my thoughts were for Nell: Nell, who would be so looking forward to me seeing her in her show; Nell, who would soon be in America and out of my life for over six months and possibly longer; Nell, who had altered my view of the world so vastly, I would never be the same again.

Sidney reappeared and his concerned face was peering over me. 'You all right, mate? Here's your water and the pills. Look, I've put them here for you.'

'Thank you.'

'Do you need to sleep?'

'Yes, yes I do, sorry. Sidney, you and Sheila must go to Nell's show. Don't waste the tickets. Promise me you'll go and she said to go backstage afterwards so make sure you do.'

'Don't worry about that ...'

I made a grab for his hand. 'Promise me you'll both go.'

'OK, I promise.'

I had to close my eyes because the whole of my head felt about to split open and every single joint in my body ached so much it was unbearable. I didn't even see or hear Sidney leave and the next few days passed in a haze of perspiration and coughing. The phone rang a few times, but I was only just aware of it and did not have the strength to reach over and answer it. Taking my pills on an empty stomach made them stick somewhere between my throat and chest, as if I could feel them making their tortuous way down to my stomach. I knew Sidney was coming in to check on me regularly and leaving biscuits and cakes and at one point hot buttered toast from Sheila, but it all felt like chalk in my mouth. Eventually Sheila herself arrived and made me sit up and eat some of her home-made chicken soup, warning me that if I did not eat every mouthful the doctor was being called. Her firm voice was at odds with her round, homely face, but she was having no nonsense from me and watched over me as I ate it slowly. I did however remember them both telling me they were off to see Nell's show and they would have to tell her I was ill because they knew she would ask where I was.

That Saturday evening I watched a huge moon with dark clouds flying across it from my bed and listened to a strong wind gusting around my house, moaning as it flew down the fireplace and shook the windows. Days passed by with me alternating between sleep and restlessness; totally unaware of the early-morning light flooding my room or the sudden blackness of the night. I imagined Nell in full flow, singing as if her life depended on it, raising the roof with the power of her extraordinary voice and I longed to be there to watch other people's reactions to her immense talent.

The *presence* had been absent since my illness, but on that night it came back with full force, hovering by the fireplace, just out of reach and taunting me. It had such a powerful effect on me I thrashed about, trying to disturb it, move it on and rid myself of the unsettling feeling it caused throughout my entire body. I closed my eyes tightly hoping when I opened them it would be gone and it was and my father was sitting on the end of my bed.

'Papa, what are you doing here?'

'I'm watching over you, my boy. You must eat and get strong, people need you.'

'No, Papa, nobody actually needs me. I need them.'

He shook his head. 'You're very wrong, Benedict, very wrong.'

'What have you been doing, Papa?'

'I've been walking in the bluebell wood near our home, on a lovely spring day with the wind in my hair and the sun on my back.'

'That sounds lovely. I'd like to do that with Nell. You would love Nell, Papa.'

His eyes twinkled in the darkness of my room. 'You must let her go and she'll come back to you.'

'Nell? I wouldn't stop her going – I couldn't.'

There was no answer: he had gone, leaving a huge, empty and lonely space where he had been sitting. Seeing him there, so real, so lifelike, so *him*, was hard to bear and I leant back on my pillow exhausted and limp. Hours seemed to pass, silent and intense and I was slipping in and out of a deep sleep when I felt something move next to my bed. I imagined the *presence* there and kept my eyes firmly closed until I heard a soft voice by my ear.

'Mr Marshall, it's me, are you OK?'

The gentle tone of her voice when saying my name made my heart flip over with pleasure and I opened my eyes to her lovely face very near mine. 'Dear girl, what are you doing here? Am I dreaming?'

'Don't be a silly arse, of course you aren't.'

'How did you get in?'

'Sidney gave me the key. How are you feeling? Have you eaten?'

I shook my head, smiling at her freshness. 'Not much, except for some Sheila soup.'

She put her hand on my forehead. 'What would you like?'

'Toast and strawberry jam,' I said, taking her small, warm hand and holding it in mine. 'I'm so glad you're here, Nell.'

She smiled at me, but it was a hesitant smile. 'And I'm glad I'm here too. When I saw Sheila next to Sidney I knew something was very wrong.'

'I wouldn't have missed it for the world.'

She gave a tiny shrug as if she didn't particularly care. 'It's only a show. You're more important. I'll get your toast and some tea.'

She disappeared and a few minutes later I heard her light footsteps on the stairs and she came in with a tray of tea and toast, ordering me to sit up; a typical Nell order with which I was happy to comply immediately. She placed the plate on my lap and watched me closely, perching on the edge of my bed like a fairy. The taste of the butter and jam swimming together was very welcome and I ate it ravenously.

'I called you loads of times before the show,' she said, her soulful grey eyes betraying her obvious concern, 'but you didn't answer and the answer phone wasn't on. I presumed you were just out and about, maybe with Thea, so I wasn't particularly worried, but when Sidney and Sheila came backstage and said you'd been in bed for days, I was so upset. You look so thin.'

'I'm always thin. It's only flu, just flu,' I told her. 'Pass me my glasses. I look more distinguished with them on.'

Handing them to me, she gave a little laugh. 'You always look distinguished. Have you been taking your pills?'

'I have, Nell.'

'Good! And remember, flu plus an underlying health problem is not *just* flu,' she told me firmly.

'I promise to remember; but I'm fine now you're here. Now, tell me, how did it all go? The show; how was it?'

'Oh fine,' she replied, rather dismissively, 'a few problems backstage, but there always are.'

'What type of problem?'

'Silly things like someone's tap shoes disappearing just before their solo and one of the ensemble feeling ill in the wings and the sound check was a complete pig's ear, but all in all it went smoothly.'

'It all sounds rather haphazard to me.'

'No, it was quite normal,' she said airily as she poured us both some tea.

'And were you happy with your performance, Nell?'

She beamed at me. 'Yes, I was happy with it, thank you.'

I rested my head against the wall behind me and wondered what the hell I looked like in her eyes. Rake thin, grey-white skin like old parchment, hair limp and dishevelled and hollow-eyed probably, but for some reason it did not matter to me because through knowing her, I felt more at peace with myself than I ever had before.

'It's late, you must be very tired. Go home and rest, please.'

'I'm not going anywhere with you like this,' she declared, 'I'm staying here until I know you're on your feet again. So there!' she grinned.

'Oh, well, that's telling me!'

'It is! So shut your face and relax, Mr Marshall.'

I was so relieved and thankful she was there that I did as commanded and snuggled down under my duvet. 'I will shut my face, Nell. My face is now definitely shut! I'm still feeling very weak and I just can't keep awake, but the toast was stupendous, thank you.'

'Close your eyes and shove over,' she whispered.

'Say that again.'

'You heard me, shove over.' I was suddenly dumbstruck as she crawled under the duvet and stretched out beside me. Amused by my muteness, she reached for my hand and squeezing it very gently said, 'I can see the moon over there, look. Isn't it lovely? And you can see all the lights of the aeroplanes stacking up for Heathrow, or is it Gatwick?'

Finding my voice I uttered, 'Both. But never mind the aeroplanes; more importantly, what, madam, are you doing under my duvet?'

She smiled with the devil in her eyes. 'I'm looking after you.'

We lay there in a comfortable silence gazing out of the window until my thoughts wandered back to what she'd said some minutes before, 'Out and about with Thea?'

'Oh, you did hear me then! Yes, out and about with Thea. She's very attractive. Full of life and great tits!'

'Oh God,' I groaned, 'too much woman for this old man.'

Our heads were touching and I felt her shudder with silent laughter. 'I could tell that actually, Mr Marshall.'

'I thought you might, Nell.'

'Listen to the wind howling outside, isn't it wonderful? We could be on the Yorkshire moors in a tent, couldn't we?'

'God forbid!'

'You're funny,' she whispered.

'So I believe, dear girl.'

'Go to sleep.'

'Yes, Nell,' I replied and I drifted off easily with her still holding my hand.

Throughout the night I woke up and heard her soft breathing next to me. A couple of times I thought it must all be a dream caused by my high temperature, but feeling her hand still resting lightly in mine was a reality too strong too ignore and I would drift off again. When the blue-tinged dawn broke I was suddenly more refreshed and awake than I had been in days and I knew the worst was over. I turned my head to find Nell in a deep sleep with her mouth slightly open and her breathing low. I spent the next hour simply watching her, wondering how on earth this had happened to me at this late stage in my life and whether it had eluded me because I had never before been ready for such a kindred spirit, a rare spirit, to cross my path. How I was going to bear her absence after such closeness was a complete mystery to me and the thought of her departure made my heart beat rapidly.

When she eventually opened her eyes Nell was instantly awake and alert. 'Good morning, Mr Marshall. How are you feeling?'

'Better,' I replied, 'thanks to you, Nell.'

'Can you hear that rain beating against the roof?' she asked, her eyes shining.

'I can and it's just like being in a tent.'

'Stop taking the piss,' she laughed. 'No, really, listen to it.'

It was drumming hard above us and the wind was still high and rattling around the chimneys, yet we were dry and warm and cosy and I felt the happiest I had ever been. I wanted to stay there, my tremors half asleep, yet my senses on full alert, for hours and I hoped to God I would be able to recreate the feeling of complete and intense happiness, long after Nell had left for America.

'It is a wonderful sound, I have to agree.'

'Do you think you are well enough to get up and have breakfast?'

'I think so, yes.'

'I'll leave you to have a hot shower and I'll use one of your other showers – if that's OK with you.'

'Everything is OK with me.'

'And what exactly are you wearing?' she asked.

I had to look because I couldn't remember what I had on. 'It's just an old T shirt circa 1970. This tie-dye thing was once very fashionable I'll have you know.'

'If you say so, Mr Marshall,' she grinned.

Standing with the hot water running over me was blissful, although looking down at my bone-thin legs was not quite such a blissful experience. I had lost weight, which I couldn't afford to lose, through days of hardly eating and my weakness bore that out too.

Having negotiated the stairs a little shakily, the sight of Nell in my kitchen making breakfast was heart-warming and I sat on the sofa in the conservatory watching the spring rain hammering down on the glass roof. The tall silver birches were swaying in the high winds at the end of my garden, revealing more of Thea's house than usual and being so warmly contented with Nell so near and fussing over me, I felt Thea's loneliness sharply and I was sorry for it. We ate toast and drank coffee together, sometimes in a comfortable silence and sometimes chatting easily. She appeared totally relaxed with her legs curled up under her and her dark hair falling over her shoulders and across her face. And that face, animated at all times and endlessly fascinating to me, would soon be far away and being adored by others.

Sidney knocked at about nine and Nell jumped up to knock back and waited to greet him. I had great pleasure in anticipating the expression on his face when he saw me sitting there obviously eating breakfast with her and he didn't disappoint me.

'So, what's occurring then, Benedict?' he called out.

'Not much, Sidney, as you can see. Even less than normal I'd say,' I replied.

He opened his eyes wide and gave me a knowing look. 'I wouldn't say that!'

I stared at him over my glasses. 'Sidney!'

Nell looked seriously unabashed and unembarrassed. 'Would you like some coffee, Sidney? We were just having breakfast. He looks better don't you think?'

Sidney sniffed. 'I'll say – but then he would, wouldn't he?'

'I stayed last night to keep an eye on him and although I'm no expert, I'd say he's over the worst now,' Nell continued, either missing the meaning in, or ignoring, Sidney's words completely.

His face was a picture. 'I bet he is,' he muttered. 'Yes, I'd love a coffee, thank you.'

As Nell went to fetch another mug, he sat opposite me, a small smile on his face and I simply shook my head at him. 'What did you think of Nell's performance last night then?' I asked, hoping to divert his attention from the racy thoughts that were galloping through his mind at my imaginary sex life.

'Absolutely fantastic,' he said. Then raising his voice he called out to Nell in the kitchen, 'You were the best one on stage last night, I can tell you, Nell. By far the best and I'm not just saying that.'

Nell returned to the conservatory and putting the mug on the table, flung her arms around him and kissed his face, 'Ah, thank you so much, Sidney.' When Sidney flushed and grinned inanely at her, she winked at him, but simply added, 'It was just such a shame Mr Marshall couldn't make it.'

'One day,' I told her, 'one day.'

She poured the still speechless Sidney's coffee and handed it to him before perching on the sofa next to me. 'Now Sidney is here I'll make a move. Is that OK with you?'

'My dear girl, you have done enough for me. Go and live your life,' I replied. 'I feel so much better believe me, and thank you for staying last night.'

'Pleasure,' she whispered, leaning forward and kissing my forehead and in doing so she missed the look of humorous astonishment on Sidney's face.

'And Nell, you don't need to check on me later. I'll behave myself.'

'Do you promise?'

'Scout's honour.'

'Now the revue is over Matt and I have so little time to sort stuff for America. I'm glad actually that the revue was only a few performances because if it had been longer, we would never have enough time to get sorted.'

'When do you go?' Sidney asked her.

'Next Friday,' she told him, without looking at me. 'And the rehearsals start on the following Monday so I have to go over music and the script and ...'

'Go, go,' I told her, my heart doing somersaults, because her departure had become a stark reality now, 'do what you need to.'

'Thanks,' she said, avoiding my eyes yet again and I imagined she did not want me to see the obvious excitement on her face as she spoke about America. 'Speak soon, Mr Marshall. Bye, Sidney, glad you loved the show.'

Once the front door had closed, Sidney gave an enormous hoot of pretend laughter and clapped his hands in obvious delight. 'I don't believe you, you old rascal! You said you didn't have it in you, but you obviously have! Fuck me.'

'Sidney, have some decorum, please.'

'Bollocks to decorum!'

'That's quite obvious.'

'At your age – and *her* age – I don't know how you do it.'

'You don't know how I do it because I don't.'

'Bollocks!'

'I assure you I never touched her.'

'Double bollocks!'

'On Beth's life nothing happened. Good God man, I have Parkinson's *and* I've been in bed for days with flu! What do you think I am? I've told you before, I have none of those feelings any more unfortunately – or is it fortunately? And why the hell am I explaining myself to you?'

'You're still a man, Benedict,' he declared. 'A beautiful, thirty-five-year-old woman like that and you're telling me that ...'

'Yes, I'm telling you; nothing happened.'

'Where did she sleep then?' he asked suspiciously.

I began to laugh at his indignant face. 'Sidney, you aren't my wife you know.'

'Come on, where did she sleep?'

'In my bed, but ...'

'*What?*' he bellowed.

'In my bed,' I repeated, also rather loudly.

'She slept in your bed? And nothing happened? You're close enough to sleep in the same bed, but not to ...'

'It's not like that, it's different from anything else I've ever known, but then *I'm* different.'

'What did you do then?'

'We slept and listened to the wind and rain.'

'Bloody hell, you must be ill,' he remarked.

'Let's leave my love life nestling securely in your imagination, shall we? I have more pressing things on my mind now.'

'I know you have: Nell going away and I can tell you I'm not looking forward to it.'

'Oh, is that right? And why is that, Sidney?' I asked, knowing full well what he meant.

'Seeing your miserable face every day is going to be tough,' he replied, crossing his arms over his chest, in his characteristic stance of an old gossip at the garden fence.

'Don't be so brutal,' I mumbled, my mouth suddenly doing its own thing at the thought of Nell being so far away. 'And you don't *have* to come in every day and look at my miserable face,' I added succinctly.

His face fell. 'You don't mean that?'

I felt ashamed of being as brutal as I'd accused him of being. 'No, I don't, I'm truly sorry.'

'The time will fly, you'll see.'

'And she'll Skype.'

'That's science fiction to me.'

'And me.'

Sidney nodded slowly before pointing at my face, 'But you look so much better, mate. Christ, you looked bloody awful.'

'Thanks so much. Shall we play...'

'But, fuck me, you can still get a woman to sleep in your bed!'

'... *cards*, Sidney?'

Each day I felt stronger and each day I dreaded Nell going more and more. She flew in one day like a warm summer breeze, full of smiles and laughter and excitement. She appeared restless and nervous and I simply listened to her chatter, trying to store up every memory for when she was gone. Since our night together I felt even closer to her and she treated me with such kindness and gentleness, it often rendered me speechless. She encouraged me to dance with her once more, rifling through my music collection and choosing some Strauss again. A waltz was just what I needed, holding her close, feeling her hand on my back and looking down at her incomparable face as she gave me gentle directions. However, she had to change the music to some ballet when my legs began to misbehave.

'Stand up straight,' she told me, 'arms extended, now bend your legs...'

'You mean my long, spindly, stick insect legs,' I replied.

She merely laughed. 'Balance, Mr Marshall, balance,' she cried.

'Impossible, Nell, impossible...'

'It most certainly is not! It's merely practice and by the time I get back from New York I want you to be perfect at this.'

'Fantasy, mere fantasy,' I muttered, but she heard me and shook her head as if I was a hopeless being.

Then three days before her departure she made me sit with her at the computer as she installed Skype for us to communicate through and as she was describing what I had to do, I went into a dream of remembrance where we were dancing together by the statue in the park in the ice cold of winter. I could recall that moment instantly because it was the first time in my life I had lived in the moment completely and utterly, instead of constantly chasing the next passing thrill. I watched her profile as she was speaking, my face almost touching hers and I thought of what Thea had asked me: 'How can you bear not to touch her when you love her so much?' And I had declared, in my defence, that it was easy not to touch her because I wasn't sure she wanted me to and I could never embarrass her or make myself look foolish or seedy in any way. But at that moment the deeply buried feelings and longing surfaced like a crashing wave and I lifted my shaking hand. The trembling was obvious, whether it was the tremors or mere nerves and it revolted me. In my eyes suddenly, I was simply an old, infirm man who was about to touch a young, energetic and lovely woman and I couldn't go through with it. I withdrew my hand and swallowed hard.

'So, did you get all that, Mr Marshall?' she asked, turning to me.

'Oh, I think I'll manage and if I don't one of Sidney's boys will show me.'

'Are you sure? I don't want to try and speak to you and find a blank screen. It would be terrible to hear your fabulous voice and not be able to see your gorgeous face,' she told me, her almond-shaped eyes troubled.

'My fabulous voice and my gorgeous face, eh? Nell, you flatter me with your kind words.'

She frowned suddenly. 'It most certainly is not flattery, it's the truth.'

'Well, that's not how I see myself, but if you see me like that then I am sincerely flattered, believe me.'

'How do you see yourself then?' she asked.

I thought for a moment. 'I see myself as old and infirm, past my sell-by date and a man of many regrets.'

She shook her head slowly. 'Firstly, age is all in the mind and therefore you'll never be old. Secondly, you are not yet infirm and if you try and look after yourself you may never be. Thirdly, I don't understand why you think you're past your sell-by date because you still have a fine intellect, a wonderful way with words and a great sense of humour which means you could still write if you put your mind to it and don't tell me you can't. And lastly, everyone has regrets, everyone! You promised me you wouldn't look back, so you can't break your promise otherwise you'll be letting me down and I know you won't do that, Mr Marshall. I know you won't.'

As she spoke the last few words her eyes filled with tears and one spilled over onto her cheek and rolled down slowly towards her mouth. I wiped it away with my shaking fingers. 'No, I won't ever break a promise to you, Nell. And I give you my word that I *will* look forward, especially now you're going away because I can look forward to you coming home.'

'Mr Marshall, I need to tell you ...'

When she paused I prompted, 'What do you need to tell me?'

She took a deep breath before continuing. 'I need to tell you what knowing you has done for me.'

'Go ahead, but I think it's more pertinent the other way round.'

'I don't think so,' she said, with a faint smile. 'Knowing you has put to rest so many demons in my head about what Parkinson's is and what it does to a person. You are brave, funny, kind and ... and *always* emotionally present. Do you know what that means?'

'Not sure that I do.'

'So many men are not in the room when you speak to them. By that I mean, their eyes are flicking about in every direction, they aren't listening, they are only interested in what *they* say or what *they* want – that kind of thing. Emotionally present means eye contact at all times, being there and wanting to listen, wanting to help, wanting to connect and you do that all the time. Didn't you know that?'

'I have to say I didn't and my wife wouldn't have agreed.'

'Did she ever say you didn't listen to her?'

I thought for a moment. 'No, she didn't.'

'Did you look her in the eye when she was speaking?'

'Unfortunately, yes!'

She laughed. 'That's very funny, Mr Marshall. No, you've given me hope that I can be all I want to be, that I have the talent; that I can fly.'

'Thank you, Nell, but I'm not sure I have. I simply ...' I almost blurted out that I loved her, but luckily for me my misbehaving mouth wouldn't allow it. 'I simply want the best for you and that's all.'

She draped an arm carelessly round my shoulders. 'Will you play Sooty for me, one last time?'

I shuddered. 'Don't call it the last time.'

'The last time for now,' she added quickly.

'Your wish is my command.'

I played and she laughed, loud and hard and I played it again and she laughed some more and then she asked me to play her favourite Ray Charles song, which she had sung to me all those months ago when I first heard her powerful voice. She began to sing again and her voice sounded even more powerful and pure than before, but as she finished singing, her voice broke and she jumped up and picked up her bag from the coffee table.

'Right, I'm off, Mr Marshall.'

'See you soon, Nell,' I called, but she was out of the door before I had finished speaking.

The next day started bright, but windy with huge billowing white clouds like mountain tops slowly floating past my conservatory windows. I had been deep in thought all morning, wondering how and when I would be able to say farewell to Nell. She called me just before lunchtime to ask whether I would go with her to Victoria station where she would meet Matt to get a train to the airport.

'You want me to come with you?' I asked her, bemused.

'Yes, please,' she replied. 'Would you?'

'What about your mum or Frankie or ...'

'My mum doesn't want to come, too emotional for her and why would I ask Frankie?'

'I really don't know.'

'So you will?'

'It will be my pleasure and we'll go by cab, paid for by me.'

She had never accepted anything of that kind throughout the months I had known her, but this time was different. 'If that's what you want, Mr Marshall...'

'It most certainly is, Nell.'

'Then I accept.'

'What time shall I book it for?'

'Eight-thirty would be fine and send it to me first, OK? That's eighty-three Victoria Road.

'I will.'

'See you in the morning then?'

'I'll be ready.'

For the rest of the day I was in a complete dream. Sidney tried to engage me in conversation and to entice me to play cards, but I was having none of it. My mind was firmly on how I would bear watching the back of Nell's head with her hair swinging from side to side as she walked away from me. That thought caused my tremors to worsen considerably and the *presence* appeared to be hovering just to the left of Sidney's head.

'I wish you would just go away,' I sighed, sick to death of the feeling of never being alone in a room.

'*What?*' Sidney screeched.

'Not you, Sidney.'

He looked perplexed, as well he might and asked, 'Who then? I'm the only one here.'

'You aren't actually, but ignore me.'

He looked behind him. 'Fuck me, Benedict! You aren't losing it, are you?'

I had to smile. 'Probably, but I really couldn't care less at the moment. No, look … I'm sorry, it's just that the tablets or maybe the illness cause this kind of *presence* that hovers about near me and it's just out of reach, more a feeling than anything concrete. It's like never being alone. Sidney, I can't describe it to you. Just trust me, it's there.'

His most wonderfully horrified face tickled me because it was a face I hadn't ever seen him pull before and he pulled many. Swallowing hard, he murmured, 'Something hovering near you? Where exactly is it now?'

'Just to your right if you must know.'

He jumped out of his skin and out of his chair and gave a little high-pitched cry which sounded more like a woman than a man and I had to laugh, despite my precarious mood. 'Ah, Sidney Walpole, I do love you, you know? Life will never be dull or uninspiring with you as my friend.'

His terrified expression turned to one of undisguised delight and he sat back down again. 'Cheers, Benedict, I happen to feel the same about you.'

'What a pair of silly old fools we are,' I remarked, wondering how many men of our age would declare their feelings for each other as we had just done.

'Speak for yourself,' he sniffed.

'Drink, Sidney?'

He beamed at me. 'I don't mind if I do. The sun is well and truly over the yardarm.'

'It most certainly is, I agree, and even if it wasn't I need a drink today.'

We sank a few that afternoon and we continued to sink a few more into the early evening until Sheila knocked in a way that let us both know she expected her husband indoors within the minute. Sidney's hangdog expression denoted he was in trouble.

'The wife I believe.'

'I believe so,' I replied and for once I couldn't be bothered to correct him.

'Euphemistically!' he stated in a superior manner.

'What, Sidney?'

'Euphemistically – another long word I know.'

'How long ago did we have this conversation about the meaning of long words?'

He shrugged. 'About five months ago.'

'Talk about delayed reaction. So, what does it mean?'

'I haven't got a fucking clue. Goodnight.'

After the ray of sunshine that was my dear friend Sidney had gone home to his long-suffering, saintly wife, I succumbed to my dreary thoughts again until I slipped into a light, restless sleep due to way too much alcohol. When I woke it was raining softly and my parents were sitting together by the piano. They had their arms around each other in a close embrace. I had seen them so often like that as a child, but in the intervening years I had forgotten how tactile they always were. It made me ache with longing to have someone with me at all times who would hug me as they had hugged each other.

'Come here, Benedict,' my mother said. 'You need us tonight.'

'I always need you, but I'd forgotten how much. You forget you see. You have to otherwise you couldn't survive the pain of the grief. I still need you both. Nell is going away. You don't know her, but if you had you would know she is the simply the most lovely person I have ever known.'

'You have to let her go,' my father said solemnly.

'I know that and I am. I want her to go because it's what she wants, but I'm not sure how I'm going to stand my life without her.'

'Let her go and she'll come back to you.'

'Is that what you meant? Did you always mean her? It's so, so hard, Papa.'

'I know,' he whispered, 'I know. Come here to us.'

I struggled to my feet, my back and shoulders aching terribly and joined them by the piano. I thought they would turn to dust as I moved closer, but they didn't and I sat between them and felt their arms around me.

'You're still our boy,' my mother said, 'however old you are; so rest now.'

I closed my eyes and rested my head on my father's shoulder and the last sound I heard was my mother saying my name. A little while later I opened my eyes tentatively to find my head resting forward on the piano keys and I knew I was drunk. I was seeing double and I couldn't think straight. I knew I had to get to bed and be alert in the morning for our journey to the station. But what was I going there for? I shook my head and concentrated hard until Nell's face sprang into my mind.

'Oh Christ,' I muttered to myself, 'you bloody silly old fool.'

I made it up the stairs, laughing at something and collapsed onto my bed on my front, fully clothed and there I stayed all night.

The grey, unwelcome dawn filtered through the open blinds and I blinked hard to find my face buried in the duvet. Gradually I realised I was still dressed and that I hadn't moved all night. My head was throbbing and I cursed Sidney and his love of all things alcoholic. I narrowed my eyes at the clock and was appalled to see it was seven-thirty; only an hour before Nell would be here in the taxi and I was still prostrate on my bed. There was no time to shave or even shower so I staggered to the bathroom and stuck my head under the cold tap. Memories of my past came rushing towards me and I recalled so many mornings of my married life trying to sober up pretty sharp before Mary was aware of the extent of my drunkenness. I now knew that I had been trying to blot out my loneliness by being so drunk I couldn't even remember my own name let alone my unhappy existence and I had attempted to do the same the night before, as if I could forget Nell was going.

I changed my clothes after picking out a sparkling white shirt to wear in her honour. My hair was misbehaving quite badly so I simply ran my hand through it roughly and hastily forced down some toast. I stood by the window drinking my tea, watching for Nell, my heart beating furiously. Sidney knocked, but I ignored it knowing he would see me get into the taxi anyway. I was muttering to myself with nerves, something I had done long ago whenever Beth had a high temperature.

'You have to stand this – no tears in front of her; that would be unforgivable.'

The dreaded cab came into view just after eight-thirty and I went out immediately, my open-necked shirt and messy hair making me appear casual and carefree instead of wound up like a coiled spring. She was sitting in the back of the cab looking radiant and I took my place beside her.

'Mr Marshall,' she cried, her eyes wide open in surprise and looking quite alarmed, 'have you been on the lash?'

I gave her a sheepish smile. 'I'm afraid to say I have, Nell.'

She ran her hand across my chin. 'What do you call this, designer stubble?'

'Hardly...'

'Should you be drinking on your tablets and so soon after flu?'

'I only had a couple with Sidney, honestly. I look worse than I actually am.'

'If you're sure...'

'Forget me, how are you feeling this morning? You must be so excited.'

Her eyes were dancing. 'I am and my stomach has butterflies flying around it. I only hope Matt is there on time. I don't trust him, he's very unreliable.'

'He'll be there,' I told her.

We sped out of a leafy Greenwich towards the dusty city. I wanted the time to crawl, but it was rushing by like a high-speed train through sleepy countryside. Nell was chatting away, rather nervously I thought, full of pent up energy, her eyes darting around. I felt as if I was in a tunnel where all sound seemed far away and I was alone and watching everything from a distance. It was almost as if this moment wasn't a part of my life at all, but somebody else's and the last few months of meeting, getting to know and loving Nell had all been a wonderful, waking dream.

'I'm sharing an apartment with two other girls in the show,' she was saying.

I heard myself reply. 'Is it near the theatre?'

'Yeah, just around the corner, walking distance. I can't wait to see it.'

'Make sure you walk home with someone at night, never on your own.'

'I will,' she replied, smiling.

'Do you promise?'

'I promise.'

'Good.'

'And you,' she countered, 'you'll take care of yourself while I'm away? Take your pills, go walking and stay off the booze, even if Sidney's drinking.'

'Yes, Nell.'

'And dance! You must practice your dancing; it's so good for balance.

Remember that, won't you?'

'I will.'

'You can teach Sidney,' she declared.

'Good grief!'

'I'm only kidding,' she said, slipping her arm through mine. 'I'm kidding about the Sidney bit.'

'Thank God for that.'

The traffic began to build as we neared the centre of London and the time was dashing by us towards the moment when Nell would be gone. My heart was racing and my tremors were noticeably worse. I could feel them coursing through my body, under my skin, like insects crawling and a couple of times I jerked violently. Nell didn't seem to notice, despite being so close to me.

'Will you call or email Beth and tell her where the theatre is?' she asked.

'Of course and she'll come to see the show, I've no doubt.'

'That would be great, I could get her tickets I'm sure. Do you really think she'll come?'

'Yes, of course she will,' I assured her, knowing that if I asked Beth to go as a favour to me, she would, albeit begrudgingly.

We were moving at a snail's pace, nose to tail through Rotherhithe and Bermondsey and there was an atmosphere of light tension between us that Nell was probably unaware of because her mind was elsewhere, but I noticed the cabbie flick his eyes in the mirror towards me a couple of times and I guessed he had become receptive to atmospheres in his taxi over the years.

'I'm going to Skype tomorrow if I possibly can,' Nell said, interrupting my thoughts.

'Don't forget the time difference.'

'And I can text when I get there if you like.'

'Does that mean I have to text back?'

She laughed. 'Yeah, of course, that's what normally happens.'

'You want me to text with these fingers?' I asked, holding up my trembling hands.

'It will be good for them.'

'Oh, will it really?' I asked, as if I didn't believe a word of it.

'Well, you can have a go.'

I smiled at her; she was always so optimistic and sunny. 'Of course

I'll have a go.'

'What you can do is put an x for a kiss to let me know you've got it.'

'I certainly will, Nell.'

Victoria station came into view and I cursed it under my breath. We were now minutes away from being parted and my throat felt impossibly tight.

'I'll let you out here, sir,' the driver told me. 'You just need to go through there, OK?'

'Thank you.'

'And I'm to wait for you, aren't I?'

'Please.'

'OK, but if for any reason I've been moved on, just wait here and I'll be back.'

'Thank you.'

Nell had only one suitcase. 'You don't seem to have much,' I said.

'I don't need much and I can always buy some new clothes when I'm there. Perhaps Beth can point me towards some great department stores.'

'I'm sure she will,' I replied, walking beside her as she pulled her case and watching her excited face.

We made our way to the concourse and time was now galloping away and she was slipping away from me slowly, inch by brutal inch. The noise in the station was deafening and I kept my eyes on her, making the most of every second, as she searched for her platform.

'Blimey, I haven't got long.'

'Sorry, the traffic was heavy.'

She suddenly looked on edge. 'Yes; not your fault.'

I gave a careless shrug as if she was simply going away for the weekend. 'Go then, find Matt.'

She now appeared incredibly nervous. 'Yes, I think that's probably a good idea.' She turned to face me and that face, undeniably lovely, unforgettable and ever changing was inches from mine and about to disappear in the crowd. 'Well ...

I stood limp and shaky, hiding the fact that someone was reaching inside my chest and squeezing my heart hard. 'Well ...'

'This is it, Mr Marshall. It's time to go. Will you be OK?'

This was the time when I needed to make my rigid features as pliable as possible and to smile my most genuine smile. 'I'll be absolutely OK,' I told her, 'because I have you as my friend.'

'Your close friend,' she added.

'My close friend...'

'And I have you.'

'You most certainly do, Nell.'

Her eyes were flickering, almost twitching. I had never seen her look like that before and it unnerved me. 'I can't quite believe I'm going,' she whispered.

'Nor me, but you are and you're going to have the most wonderful experience over there.'

She sprang forward impulsively and hugged me hard and then leant her head against my chest. My arms were hanging loosely by my sides because I didn't have the physical or emotional strength to lift them.

'I can hear your heart,' she said. I was struck dumb by my wretched, trembling, ridiculous frayed-at-the-edges mouth. 'Say something,' she urged, stepping back to look at me and taking hold of my shaking hands. And I said the most selfless words I had ever uttered because she deserved it.

'Fly, Nell,' I whispered. '*Fly.*'

Her face lit up at last and she looked as happy as I had imagined her to be on this day, for the first time since I joined her in the taxi. 'I will, Mr Marshall. Thank you.'

For a tense split second we simply stared at each other, two friends parting, taking in the other one. 'Go, go,' I told her. 'You'll miss your train. Matt will be watching for you.'

She stared at me with the most forlorn look. 'Don't you forget about me.'

I could only shake my head, unable to speak as she turned and walked quickly away. I watched the back of her head, her hair flowing down past her shoulders, until she was lost in the crowd. Instantly the world turned dark grey and uninteresting, full of isolating shadows. It felt as if someone had flicked a switch and I was back in my former life, before I knew her. As I turned to retrace my steps, my father was standing a few feet away. His face was solemn.

'Go, son,' he called. 'Let her go.'

I tried to reply, but my frozen mouth would not move at all. I staggered out as if hit by lightening, stiff with shock. Someone was calling me.

'Over here, sir.' The driver was waving frantically to catch my attention. I waved back and walked over as quickly as was possible for my wayward legs. 'Get off OK, did she?' he asked kindly once I was settled in the back of the cab and had negotiated the difficult seat belt.

'Yes, thank you. Well, I left her in the middle of the station, couldn't watch the train pull away.'

He was watching me in his mirror. 'All this gap-year rubbish, we just went to work, didn't we?'

'Yes,' I mumbled.

'She loves you though.'

I thought I had misheard him. 'Sorry?'

'She loves you, I could tell that.'

'Could you?' I asked rather too desperately.

'Oh yeah, but girls and their dads, you know?'

If his comment hadn't been so funny, it would have been like a slap in the face. The momentary joy of knowing someone thought Nell loved me turned immediately to an aching dejection at realising he thought I was her father.

'Yes,' I muttered, staring aimlessly out of the window, 'girls and their dads.'

Chapter 16

'For crying out loud, Benedict!'

'What now, Sidney?'

'Have I got to put up with your face looking like a flipping bloodhound's every day? How long is it now, three weeks? It's doing my head in!'

'I didn't know I resembled a bloodhound? Ah yes, but then they do dribble constantly, don't they?'

'It's not the dribbling it's ...'

'Thank God for that.'

'It's the mournful expression in the eyes.'

'You don't *have* to sit opposite me for much of the day,' I remarked.

'Well, who else is going to?'

'Thea,' I offered.

He sneered a little. 'Oh yeah...'

'She left me a message yesterday telling me to pop in for one,' I told him, anticipating the look on his face.

'I bet she did,' he laughed. 'I bet she did. And will you? Pop in for one?'

'Sidney, I don't know why you find my uneventful life so interesting and full of supposed sexual tension when there isn't any.'

'You really have lost the plot if you can't feel the sexual tension coming from Thea, mate.'

'What about Nell?'

He frowned. 'No, funnily enough there's none from Nell.'

'Well, if you must know I am not popping in for one – coffee that is – because I don't wish to inflict this so-called mournful expression on anyone but you.'

He looked delighted. 'Cheers, Benedict, I take that as a compliment – I think.'

'It was a compliment, Sidney.'

'So, have you heard from Nell?'

'One text, to say she was there safely and that it was very warm and the apartment was lovely; that sort of thing. Then another to say rehearsals are going well, but they are long, tiring days and another two saying she will be Skyping me soon, so I'm waiting to be Skyped.'

He turned up his nose, almost in distaste. 'That sounds delightful.'

'At least I'll be able to see her face.'

He sighed heavily. 'What are you going to do for six months?'

'Bleed internally!'

'For fuck's sake talk normally!'

'I *am* talking normally. That is me talking normally. No, I'll have to keep myself busy, distracted, get out and about and meet people ...'

'But obviously not Thea,' he muttered.

'I would spend time with Thea, but she wants more from me than I can give her.'

'Oh yeah, I bet.'

'For once you are right, Sidney, that's exactly what she wants I believe.'

'Let's sit in the garden this afternoon, shall we? It's such a lovely day. June is busting out all over as they say.'

I laughed at him. 'Really, who says that?'

'I do and I reckon we're going to have a hot summer this year, barbecue weather. Why don't I get Sheila to do us a barbecue this teatime? Do you fancy that?'

I knew he was trying his best to chivvy me along so I smiled gratefully at him. 'The thought of Sheila barbecuing has cheered me up enormously, thank you. Although if past summers are anything to go by, your saint of a wife will prepare everything and then you will do your best to burn it.'

'Great, I'll go tell her.' He simply ignored my comment, as he often did. 'See you about five, eh? Bring a bottle of your old plonk,' he suggested, his eyes sparkling.

'I will do.'

I wandered around in my own garden that afternoon, inspecting the early summer flowers I didn't even know I had planted. The sun was high and strong and a bright white colour with a thin yellow line around it. The feel of it on my face invigorated me and later that afternoon I sat on my patio with a pot of tea on the table beside me thinking of Nell. I must have dozed because when I opened my eyes the *presence* was just in front of my face, an indefinable shape, but its outline seemed to shine like a star. It was inexplicable in its form and I beat it away with my hands, swearing loudly as I did so. Sidney's head appeared over the fence.

'Barbecue just going on, Benedict.'

'Fabulous, thank you, Sidney, I'll be there in a while.'

'Don't forget the wine, will you?'

'I'll get it now.'

Half an hour later we were sitting in Sidney's garden and he was being head cook and bottle washer and definitely in charge at his enormous, over-the-top barbecue. It smelt wonderful and Sheila had gone overboard with the chicken and steak as she normally did, which was exactly why Sidney had such a protruding stomach. I glanced over towards Thea's garden and imagined her sitting on her own, eating a lonely evening meal and my stomach lurched with guilt and a little sadness.

'Sheila,' I said impulsively, 'could I possibly call a friend who lives in that house over there and ask her to join us?'

'Of course,' she cried and her voice was high with delight. 'We can't eat all this. I always over-cater, don't I?'

'Just a bit, yes. Thank you.'

I took my mobile out of my pocket and dialled her number. Sidney was watching me intently beneath his eyebrows. She answered immediately. 'Thea speaking...'

'Thea, it's Benedict here. If you come round now you'll be just in time for some barbecued steak and a bottle or two of wine. How does that sound?'

There was a pause and I thought at first she hadn't heard me, but then I heard a slight gasp. 'I'd love to, Benedict.'

'I'll leave the front door on the latch, come through to the conservatory and then through Sidney's gate.'

'Just give me ten minutes to freshen up and I'll be there.'

'She's just freshening up,' I told them both.

'I bet she is,' Sidney remarked.

'Sidney, behave for once,' Sheila told him sharply.

He looked highly indignant. 'What, in my own garden? No chance.'

'How's Nell getting on?' Sheila suddenly asked, handing me a plate with some crusty bread on it.

'I'm not too sure, she's been too busy to Skype me, but I suspect she's having the time of her life, Sheila.'

Sheila had known me for quite a few years and wasn't fooled. She gave me an affectionate smile. 'I expect she is, but you're not are you, love?'

'I will be,' I replied. 'I need to see her face and then I'll be fine. I just miss her face.'

'Oh Christ,' Sidney muttered, 'don't start him off, Sheila.'

'Sidney, have some sensitivity,' his wife ordered.

'I'm always sensitive,' he declared, looking suitably hurt. 'Fuck me, the ship in full sail is here,' he whispered loudly.

'Sidney!' I whispered loudly back, getting up and shaking my knife at him. 'If you say anything out of place I'll ...'

'Hello, one and all.'

'Thea, how lovely to see you,' Sidney called jauntily from behind the barbecue. 'This is the wife, Sheila...'

'*My* wife, *my* wife,' I interrupted.

Thea was wearing a floating summer dress with no sleeves that appeared to be held up by willpower and her dark chestnut hair had grown a little. She shook Sheila's hand with her usual gusto. 'It is so nice of you to invite me, Sheila. Benedict, you look rather dashing tonight,' she gushed, kissing my cheek softly. 'I love your blue shirt. It brings out your eyes beautifully.'

'Dashing, eh?' Sidney almost sneered, but he stopped short of uttering anything more because I gave him such a straight look it silenced him instantly.

'I'm afraid I am anything but, but thank you,' I smiled.

'Have a seat, Thea,' Sheila said, 'Sidney is just about to dish up. Would you like a glass of wine?'

'Love one, thank you. Isn't this weather fantastic? I just spent a week in Greece with my daughter and we were so miserable at the thought of coming back to English drizzle, but it's just as hot here.'

'How is your girl?' I asked her.

She turned towards me and looked me in the eye for the first time since she had arrived. 'She's very well, thank you. How is yours and ... and Nell?' she asked, rather pointedly I thought, as if asking about my daughter and Nell in the same breath was a natural thing.

I gave Sidney, who I knew was enjoying every single moment of the discussion, another stern look to allay any comment he might be brewing, before replying 'Well, Beth's having too much of a good time to call her dear old dad very often, but she emails and I'm thankful for that, and Nell is fine; busy rehearsing.'

'I bet she loves it there,' Thea declared, adding pointedly, 'who wouldn't at her age?'

'Quite,' I muttered.

We ate the delicious, juicy steak and the darkly grilled chicken and sat chatting as a deep, tangerine sun went down behind the trees. Sidney lit some candles and remarked that it reminded him of camping and eating outside in the south of France. My mind wandered onto how Nell would have loved doing just that, in fact my thoughts were so dominated by her, the whole pleasant ambience of the balmy evening almost passed me by. I did notice however that Thea was drinking too much wine and professed to feeling as if she was still on holiday.

'Mind you, I only work part time now, so I'm constantly on holiday really,' she told us, flicking her hair behind her shoulders.

'Same here,' Sidney replied, 'only I do bugger all now, don't I, dear?'

'You can say that again,' Sheila laughed.

I struggled to my feet and made my way inside to the bathroom with Sidney inexplicably hot on my heels. 'Are you following me?' I asked him.

'Fuck me, Benedict,' he whispered, in the darkness of his hallway, 'she's flirting with you big time. How the fuck do you do it?'

I turned to face him. 'I don't! And she isn't!'

'If you can't see it you really are past it.'

'I can't see it because I don't *want* to see it and I have none of those feelings any more anyway, so will you allow me to go to the bathroom, please?'

He put on a serious expression which looked ludicrous because of the amount he had drunk. 'She's an extremely attractive woman.'

'I know but ...'

'But obviously not attractive enough for you!'

'I'm not interested,' I hissed at him, our faces inches apart, 'now can I use your bathroom?'

Sidney lowered his voice. 'I'd get in there if I were you. Nell is probably having the time of her life and you're always saying you're only friends anyway, so what's the problem?'

I whispered back. 'Well, you aren't me, are you?'

'Sometimes I wish I was you.'

'Oh, Sidney, we've had this conversation so often. *Why* do you wish you had lived my life? I wish I had lived *yours*. I'd trade all my soulless, vacuous, humourless encounters for just one year of your blissful marriage,' I sighed, peering at him in the half light of his hallway.

'I wouldn't swap Sheila,' he cried, as if I had lost my senses. 'But I'd like to have lived one year of your life *before* I met Sheila and I was just saying if I was you ...'

'Talk about having your cake and eating it,' I interrupted hurriedly, 'and why are we standing in your back passage discussing this?' I asked him, using the ambiguous words to amuse him and put him off his incessant quest to ignite my dormant love life.

'My *fully tiled* back passage, if you don't mind!'

'Yes, your fully tiled back passage with this very tasteful dado rail half way up it. Now, I'm going to use your bathroom and when I come out I don't want to see you standing there pulling any of your faces.'

He looked quite bemused. 'What faces?'

'Those under your eyebrows, knowing looks that are adding fuel to Thea's fire,' I replied.

He scoffed. 'She doesn't need any fuel on her fire, matey. But if you don't want me to look at you, I won't,' he told me, once again pretending to be hurt.

'Is that a promise?'

He didn't reply and I made for the sanctuary of his bathroom. When I rejoined the party Sidney was sitting next to Thea with a pious expression on his face that stated butter wouldn't melt in his mouth. It was a look that protested his innocence before he was accused of doing anything else, which of course he would be. Thea appeared to be enjoying the evening immensely and was glowing in the light given off by the candles.

'This is lovely sitting out here and great food, Sheila. Have some more wine, Benedict,' she urged, turning to me.

'Not for me.'

She grinned at me. 'Oh go on.'

'Madam, are you trying to get me drunk?'

'As if,' she winked. 'You can walk me home in a little while if you play your cards right.'

There was silence for a moment and in that silence I struggled for an answer until Sidney jumped in to fill it. 'Why not climb over the wall? It would be quicker, the speed Benedict walks these days.'

'Thank you, Sidney,' I retorted.

'Oh I could climb over the wall I assure you,' Thea said, running her hand through her hair.

'Not in that dress,' I mumbled.

'Easy,' she declared, giving me a sideways look.

'I'm sure it would be, but not a great idea.'

She looked me in the eye. 'Benedict, I'm still as fit as I was at thirty.'

'I don't doubt that,' I replied.

'What did you do on holiday, Thea?' Sheila asked, polite as ever, steering the conversation quite deftly in another direction.

'Drank quite a bit, swam in the pool, ate out every night, that sort of thing. It was very relaxing and I could have stayed another week to be honest. But it was too hot really, too hot to do much sightseeing.'

'Sounds lovely, we should go, Sidney.'

Sidney was busy emptying a glass of red wine down his throat and nearly choked on it. 'I'd be bored silly,' he remarked. 'So would you, wouldn't you, Benedict?'

'I have to say I probably would.'

'No you wouldn't,' Thea cried, 'all that lounging around in the warmth of the sun, plenty of alcohol, great restaurants, big comfortable beds, being totally relaxed, good company ...' There was a pause in which she fixed her eyes on me with such a look of longing, it made me feel decidedly uncomfortable. 'We should go some time, Benedict,' she eventually added.

'Yeah, great idea,' Sidney chipped in, highly amused at my discomfort as always. 'It would do you good, matey.'

'I thought you just said I'd be bored.'

He was grinning. 'Not with Thea for company you wouldn't.'

'I'm not going anywhere any time soon,' I muttered, my lips freezing as I finished my sentence.

'Not even New York?' Thea asked, her eyes glinting through the semi-darkness.

I knew what she meant, but I decided to ignore it. 'I don't think Beth wants her old dad out there and I really don't think I could stand the flight, too tiring now.'

'Hark at the silly old git,' Sidney laughed. 'But I agree and all that checking your luggage and over-the-top security and the queues. No thanks, Margate will do for me.'

'Or Window Sill Bay,' I added, 'which is where you spend all your time anyway.'

'Where on earth is Window Sill Bay?' Thea asked.

'Or skulking in your back passage in the darkness,' I added.

'My *fully tiled* back passage,' Sidney sneered.

'With a dado rail half way up it.'

Thea appeared totally perplexed. 'I wish I knew what you two were talking about.'

'Don't take any notice of them,' Sheila told her, 'they're both bonkers.'

'*And* Sidney's had quite a bit to drink,' I said.

'And you haven't?' he asked.

'No, I'm quite lucid, need to keep my wits about me at all times. My walking is so unsteady I have no desire to make it even worse.'

'Or your slurring,' Sidney added. 'Don't forget the slurring.'

'Why, thank you, Sidney.'

He beamed. 'It's my pleasure.'

The evening wore on, warm and still and the candles flickered occasionally. The conversation was easy and amusing and I was aware that Thea was watching me carefully whenever I spoke. At about half nine my mobile bleeped in my pocket and made us all jump. My heart leapt when I read the message from Nell that told me she would Skype me at ten, but because Thea's eyes were burning into me at that point, I simply put it back in my pocket without comment. A heavy silence hung between us like a dense November fog above the river and I avoided looking at her. Luckily, Sidney saved the tense moment by going to get up out of his chair and staggering before falling over. It looked so comical I laughed out loud. Sheila then told him off sharply for being so clumsy and drunk and the expression on his face, which was a mixture of bemusement and a devil-may-care attitude, made me laugh even harder.

'I've never heard you laugh like that before, Benedict,' Thea commented, appearing surprised at my reaction when Sidney was flailing around on the grass, 'and at Sidney's misfortune too.'

'I find my neighbour the most unwittingly hilarious and oddly amusing person I've ever come across and it's my great fortune to know him and have him as my closest friend. His misfortunes and extraordinary capacity to make me laugh are a constant source of joy to me and I feel enormously lucky to have him in my life. Sidney is,' I added, glancing over at him, 'a rare and wonderful man and he is the best medicine anyone can ever have.'

'And he's as silly as a sheep,' his wife added, her face completely serious, 'but he means well.'

'I'm having that put on my gravestone,' Sidney declared.

'What, that you were as silly as a sheep?' I asked.

'No! "He meant well."'

'Ah, yes and Sheila needs to have "saint" on hers,' I said.

We chatted for a while longer and I glanced at my watch now and again, aware that Nell's face would be appearing for the first time on my computer screen in less than half an hour and I began to feel unsettled and on edge. I knew immediately that Thea had picked up on my mood because I felt her watchful eyes on me constantly and eventually she gulped her drink down and stood up with a certain flourish and determination.

'I think I'll make a move, work tomorrow albeit only half a day in the bookshop, but I think I've drunk enough. Thank you, Sidney and Sheila, for a really lovely evening.'

'You're very welcome, love,' Sheila said, smiling warmly at her.

'Benedict will see you home,' Sidney offered pointedly.

'No, that's okay ...'

'No, please,' I butted in, aware of the time flying and wanting to be back just before ten, 'I insist. No climbing over the wall.'

Her face lit up. 'If you insist then I'll accept.'

'Come back after for a nightcap, Benedict,' Sidney suggested.

'I know what your nightcaps are like, Sidney,' I replied, 'and with my pills it might just be lethal.'

We walked together round the corner and Thea had her arm casually linked through mine. It seemed quite natural and easy to walk like that in the balmy evening air and yet my nerves were jangling with concern that I would miss Nell.

'You and Sidney are a funny pair,' Thea was saying.

'I don't doubt it.'

'You are *so* very different.'

'Not so much.'

'Oh you are,' she declared.

'Well, I suppose he is uncomplicated, kind and caring ...'

'And you don't think you are any of those things?' she asked, quite perplexed.

'I'm not uncomplicated, believe me.'

She did not comment and I was aware that she was possibly implying that Sidney was not as educated as I was and I had no intention of having any conversation of that kind.

'I really shouldn't drink, it makes me reckless,' she laughed, flicking her hair back from her face.

We had been through all this before and so I could only nod and mutter softly, 'I know.'

Thea looked a trifle ill at ease, but hurriedly regained her composure. 'Thanks for inviting me.'

'It has been my pleasure.'

'It's been lovely, really lovely to see you, Benedict,' she said, looking up into my face as we arrived at her front door. 'I was feeling quite down, after coming home from Greece, you know what it's like after a holiday.'

My mouth began to misbehave and I slurred badly. 'Yes, I know.'

'Is that slurring the drink?' she asked.

'No, it's the disease!'

She looked at me with such sympathy, I gave her a warm smile, which she returned, and for a few moments there was yet another moment of awkwardness between us. The awkwardness on my part was because I wanted purely friendship, but it produced in her a rush of emotion that made her grab hold of my shoulders hard. She pulled me closer and her strength shocked me; it was like being grabbed by a rugby full-back and she aimed a kiss somewhere near my mouth. She smelt of wine and a mild perfume and the kiss wasn't unwelcome, just unexpected. I froze, like an inexperienced schoolboy and my arms hung heavily by my side limply. Her face was so close to mine I could feel her warm breath.

'Do you want to come in?' she asked, her eyes swimming with a longing so deep it unnerved me.

'Thea ...'

'Please, Benedict, please come in, just for a chat.'

'Well ...'

'Please,' she said again, more urgently, 'you must be lonely with your little friend so far away. I can see it in your eyes and I understand.'

I knew the minutes were ticking away. 'Thank you for the invitation and the understanding ...'

'So, will you come in, Mr Marshall?' she asked, her head on one side.

Her unfortunate choice of words, calling me by my surname, sent a jolt through me like an electric shock. Her nearness, her sensuality, her neediness were a beguiling mix even for a man who had none of those urges any more, but her thoughtless decision to call me by the name Nell always used made me feel suddenly utterly listless. And I suspected it was said with a hint of sarcasm too. She realised as soon as she had spoken that it was the wrong choice of words and her face fell.

'I have to go, Thea. I'm quite tired now.'

'I'm sorry, I was only ...'

'Making fun of her?' I asked, coolly.

'No, Benedict, it was only said in jest, really. You know what I'm like, blunt and outspoken.'

'That's fine,' I shrugged, 'I admire that in a woman. I have no problem with outspoken.'

'You have no problem with it, except when it's in relation to Nell.'

I was now eager to get home. 'Goodnight, Thea.'

She put her hand on my shoulder. 'Please, don't go, not like this. I know you and I could make a go of it.'

'I can't, I'm sorry.'

Her eyes filled with huge tears suddenly. 'I just want to feel a man's arms around me again.'

'Not these shaking arms.'

'Yes, *your* shaking arms.'

'Look, there are plenty of men out there who would give their right arm to have a woman as lovely as you – sorry about the pun, but ...'

She shook her head. 'I don't want plenty of men, I want *you.*'

'I don't know what to say,' I muttered, my words slurring so badly at the end of my sentence I sounded sloshed. She shrugged almost carelessly and let go of my shoulder. She had been gripping me so hard I could still feel the imprint of her fingers on my bony body.

'It's just my luck to fall for a man who loves another woman. You know drink loosens my tongue and I'm sorry, I misread the situation and with the hot evening air I ... I was simply carried away, I apologise if I embarrassed you.'

'There is no need to apologise, honestly. I'm not embarrassed, I'm only sorry that I can't ... look, Thea, it's not only because of Nell, it's ...'

'But you do adore her, I know that and I must be the worst kind of masochist to want you when I can see it written all over your face that she's in your thoughts constantly.'

'I can't deny that,' I replied, now wishing myself away from there, but I did feel guilty and sorry that I had this attractive and interesting woman standing inches from me, declaring such strong feelings and not being able to reciprocate. 'But it's not only Nell; it's many other things too. It's much too complicated to go into.'

'If it's the Parkinson's, I don't care about that.'

'You *would*; you *will*. Honesty is the best policy. It's affected me in so many ways, too many and too intimate to go into here.'

'I don't mind about sex ...'

'You would,' I told her, 'believe me, you would. And I would for you.'

'You can have a sex life with Parkinson's, can't you?'

'Yes, I'm sure many people do, but for some reason I can't quite fathom, all of those feelings have fled to the hills for me.'

'But Nell is younger than me and would mind even more,' she declared rather thoughtlessly.

I put my finger to her lips to silence her. 'Don't say any more, please. You'll only regret it. Goodnight, Thea.'

I left her there standing in her doorway and walked quickly away without looking back aware that my unsteady legs were causing me to appear a little drunk when I was anything but. I felt I had begun to resemble a floppy puppet and it was more apparent when I tried to quicken my step. I hoped that perhaps it would make Thea think twice about her hasty declaration of not caring about my disease.

Sidney and Sheila were still in their garden when I returned and Sidney was grinning sheepishly. 'Everything OK then?' he asked.

'It is. Thank you. Now I must get to my computer. I have only...six minutes.'

'Invite you in, did she?'

'She did,' I replied.

'Oh yeah...'

'Sidney,' Sheila snapped, 'pack that in.'

'Pack what in?' he said indignantly, innocence personified.

'I declined her invitation. She's too much for me.'

'I agree,' Sheila declared. 'She's looking for someone lusty and vigorous, isn't she?'

'Yes, Sheila, she is.'

'Not someone like a piece of limp lettuce,' Sidney added.

'Quite.'

'Do you fancy another drink, mate?'

'No, thank you, I'm going in to be Skyped.'

'Ah, I thought you looked on edge when your mobile went off; it was Nell then.'

'It was indeed. I am now going inside to get a much needed glimpse of her face, so goodnight and thank you, Sheila.'

I bent down to kiss her and she put her rough, hard-working hands either side of my face. 'Goodnight, love. See you tomorrow maybe.'

'Coffee about eleven, Benedict?' Sidney asked.

'And why not, Sidney?'

I left them there and rushed to my computer, waiting impatiently for the first sight of Nell's face. I glanced at the clock and it was one minute past ten. I began to feel on edge, twitchy and slightly breathless. It occurred to me that someone may have distracted her and that perhaps she would forget she had promised to Skype me, but my tortuous thoughts fled immediately when the dialling tone started and the screen flickered to life.

&

'Hi, Mr Marshall,' I called, bubbling over with excitement at the sight of him peering at the screen with his distinctive dark-rimmed glasses.

'Nell,' he said gently, 'I can't believe that's you in front of me thanks to the wonders of modern technology!'

I laughed at his old-fashioned ways. 'Great, isn't it? You could be in the next room.'

'I only wish I was.'

'How are you?'

'I'm ... not too bad.'

I jumped on his hesitation. 'Hold up your hands to the camera.'

He looked astonished. 'I most certainly will not!'

'Hold them up,' I demanded.

He did as I asked and they trembled visibly. My heart lurched with compassion and he must have seen something of those feelings on my face because he appeared choked.

'Please don't worry about me; I'm not too bad at all, truly, Nell. In fact I can honestly say that my obsessive and inward-looking thoughts have improved considerably recently.'

'Do you reckon?'

He smiled at last. 'I reckon.'

'Do you think the pills are working then?'

'I think they just might be and if I had to choose between my physical symptoms improving and my mental and emotional symptoms improving, I would choose the latter.'

'That's brilliant, Mr Marshall.'

'But enough of me; how are things with you? How are rehearsals going?'

'Full on,' I told him, 'but the cast are fantastic and most of us get on very well. I'm not that keen on the company manager, she can be very difficult, one of those with a mouth like a duck's arse with the cramp. You know the type.'

He looked bemused. 'Say that again.'

'She's got a face like four pence.'

'Well, I think I can imagine that; and what news of Matt?'

'I don't know,' I sighed, 'I really don't know if he'll make the whole run.'

He was visibly shocked. 'Why wouldn't he? This is his big chance.'

I was so relieved to be talking to him about Matt because I hadn't mentioned my concerns to anyone else. 'It's as if he can't sustain anything. He's brilliant in flashes and then totally off the wall and unreliable.'

'Is he drinking?'

'I don't know, I haven't seen that much of him to be honest. Not as much as I thought I would. We see each other on stage and occasionally in breaks, but then he goes to his apartment and I go to mine. Well, I go to mine because I'm knackered, but I reckon he goes out for a few drinks with some of the other musicians. That's their life, you know? I miss chatting to him, but we're so short of time now and I think he prefers to be with them.'

I was watching him as I spoke and he was listening intently to every word. His eyes never left my face for a second and I remembered that rare feeling of talking to someone who was fully present when you spoke and not pretending to listen or flicking their eyes around the room, like so many people in my business. It made me ache with wanting to sit next to him on the piano stool in his classy lounge and to be able to just about smell his unusual, subtle aftershave. I imagined asking him to play Chopin and then Sooty and watch his eyes twinkle with mischief as he waited for a blast of my raucous laugh. There was nothing quite like witnessing the delight on his face when he had made me laugh like that and it all seemed so long ago, in another world and another time. Since being in New York I had been living my life at such a fast pace, England and Mr Marshall appeared to be very far away.

'But you are enjoying it, Nell?' he suddenly asked, as if he could read something in my face that told him I might not be.

'Oh yes, I'm enjoying the performing bit,' I assured him.

'But you're not enjoying New York?'

'I haven't seen that much of it to be honest. Hard to believe I know, but on our days off we sleep in and then perhaps go to a diner to eat and do a little shopping and that's it. We have gone out to breakfast a few times on our way to the theatre. There's a café bar thing just below us on the opposite corner and they do fabulous coffee and pancakes and it saves us cooking. Ed, the owner, says he can't understand one word of what I say, it's hilarious. Bloody big meals they serve out here. I can only eat half of it.'

'Yes, Beth says that. Talking of Beth, has she contacted you yet?'

'Not yet, but I'm sure she will. I'll get her tickets for opening night if she wants them.'

'Thank you, Nell.'

'How's Sidney?'

He gave one of his wry smiles that made the corner of his mouth turn up. 'He's ... Sidney.'

'And have you seen Thea?'

He paused for a moment and looked a little uncomfortable. 'Yes, we all had a barbecue in Sidney's garden this evening. It was such lovely hot weather today and they asked me in and I thought ...'

'You thought poor her, all on her own,' I added for him.

'Yes, something like that, Nell.'

'That was nice of you, Mr Marshall.'

'*I* thought so,' he replied.

'And?'

His face appeared rather rigid. 'And?' he repeated.

'How is she?'

'Oh, she's ...'

He didn't continue and appeared at a loss for words so I waved my hand in front of the screen. 'Hello, come in, Mr Marshall.'

'Sorry.'

I have no idea why I said what I did then, except to say that it just came out of my mouth without me thinking. 'She loves you, I reckon.'

'I don't think so, Nell,' he replied, a little wearily. 'She thinks I am someone or something I'm not. Whatever she wants, I'm not it. *Whoever* she wants, I'm not he. I might have been once, but not now. The man I was, before the disease was probably the right man for her, but I'm not that man any more, as you know, and I don't particularly want to be.'

'But she doesn't agree?'

He gave me a sweet smile. 'No, she doesn't agree.'

'And you're so kind you're finding it hard to convince her of that?' I suggested.

His face softened considerably. 'As usual you are right.'

Wanting to lighten his mood, I changed tack and asked, 'What shall we talk about now?' knowing what he would say.

His eyes twinkled. 'How I got to be so devastatingly attractive?'

'Shut your face you!'

'Delightful.'

'It's so good to see you.'

'Ditto, Nell.'

'And it's lovely to hear your voice.'

There was silence for a moment in which he stared unblinking at me and then he went to speak but slurred so badly nothing came out. I put my hand up to the screen as if I was adjusting his hair.

'What are you doing?' he managed to splutter eventually.

'Putting your syrup on straight,' I declared.

He played along with me. 'Is it a mess?'

'It is and it must be a syrup because no-one in their right mind would choose hair like yours, I reckon you've had a curler in it all night.' I laughed and his pale face broke into the broadest grin I had ever seen. 'That's better; I love to see you smile.'

'You do me good, Nell,' he muttered.

'I'd better go.'

His face became rigid again. 'Must you?'

'I'm afraid I have to see the company manager. I'll Skype again, I promise.'

He adjusted his glasses. 'It wasn't as painful as I thought.'

'You're funny.'

'So I believe.'

'See you soon, Mr Marshall and take good care of yourself, won't you?'

His eyes became unbearably sad. 'I will, Nell. Goodbye.'

I waved frantically. 'Bye, bye, bye. I'm switching off now, OK?'

He nodded slowly and I reached over to switch off and the screen went blank. One second there, the next gone and I pictured him sitting there elegantly in his beautifully furnished, classy house, his legs loosely crossed and his glasses slipping down his nose. I missed everything about him so much: his company, the wonderful tone of his perfect voice, his humour, his friendship, the very essence of him. Every day in New York had me wishing I was back in London, except when I was on stage and then I was reminded daily why I was there and what I lived for: the rehearsing, over and over again, constantly trying to improve, striving for that moment where everything else around me faded away into nothingness and I was elevated to a place of happiness so rare, it almost didn't exist except in my imagination; that place where you touch perfection momentarily and experience a rush of endorphins and ecstasy that surpasses everything else. But mostly it was hard slog, repetition, standing around in the wings, drinking coffee with some of the cast, worrying about Matt and going back to the apartment to sleep.

The sounds of New York were so very different from Greenwich. There was the constant, steady hum of traffic, a variety of hooters sounding off at all times of the day and night, and the constant drawl of the radio and television presenters who seemed to be always talking about the weather and the various fronts approaching as if they were of national importance and when I mentioned that to one of the native musicians he assured me they were.

'If you've ever been in New York during a snowstorm or thunderstorm or even a heat wave, you'd understand,' he told me. 'If you think we're hot now, give it a few weeks and you'll be watching the weather forecast as if your life depended on it.'

I had tried to see as much of Matt as I possibly could and we were in the same rehearsal room daily to begin with, urging each other on and having the occasional coffee together, but there was so little time to chat with him once we had joined the whole cast and I was immediately aware that in my absence he had made friends with a few of the band. They were the few I would have wanted him to avoid, however, and I had picked them out in the first few days we had been in the theatre as the wayward, alcohol-dependent musicians Matt should have given a wide berth. But I wasn't his keeper or his girlfriend and I had to let him be himself and live his life, whatever path he might choose to take. Birds of a feather always flocked together, especially where heavy drinkers were concerned. My sadness came from an intense fear that he would waste his immense talent and yet I knew from experience it was often the most talented people who found normal life the hardest.

We had been rehearsing in the theatre for a week and backstage the heat was stifling and dry. Matt had arrived on time most days, unshaven and wild eyed and his playing had been superb. He only ever had to be given any instruction once and it was in his head for good and yet he never seemed to be fully present unless he was in full flow. In the breaks he would twitch and buzz, anxious to be back on stage and playing again. But as the days raced on towards opening night, he began to dash in at the last minute looking dishevelled and grey. I tried to engage him in conversation in the breaks, but he avoided me and I felt he was quickly slipping away. The inevitable day came when I was standing alone at the front of the stage and Matt was nowhere to be seen.

I could hear a voice in the darkness at the back of the stalls talking quietly and then they called out to me. 'Helen, can you see your spot, darling?'

'Yes, I'm on it,' I called back, realising the director had arrived.

'OK, hold it there a moment. Have you got her OK?'

Another voice, who I recognised as one of the lighting technicians, answered. 'Yep, I've got her.'

'OK, great, waiting for Matt now. Is he backstage?' There was a whispering behind the curtain and one of the dancers appeared and shook her head at me. 'Can someone find Matt *please*?' I could hear the impatience in the director's voice. 'Where the hell is he?'

'I'm sure he'll be here in a minute,' I offered, glancing behind me where the lonely piano stood. 'Maybe he's not well,' I added as an afterthought and I knew it sounded weak.

'Well, he could *call*,' the director replied, with more than a hint of sarcasm. 'Jesus Christ, it's not much to ask and aren't you supposed to call in sick if you can't go to work?'

There was a sudden scrabbling sound behind me and Matt slid from behind the curtain at the back of the stage and onto his stool, his hair matted like an overgrown, tangled hedge and two days growth of stubble on his chin. His clothes looked crumpled and creased as if he'd slept in them and he was bleary eyed. His appearance reminded me of when I had first met him, when he was desperate, broke and lacking in confidence. I found it hard to believe that he would want to go back to living his life in that way and yet I could instinctively tell he was in danger of doing just that. He nodded in my direction without looking directly at me and began running his fingers over the keys. As was usual for him, he was able to play perfectly whatever state he was in and the director began to slow hand clap.

'Good of you to join us, Matthew! Now, can we get on?'

'Sure, sorry Louis,' Matt replied and he didn't utter another word all morning.

I sought him out in the lunch break and found him sitting in the small bar just up from the stalls, perched on a stool, drinking iced water and mumbling to Ben who was serving. Ben and I had spent many breaks chatting together about how he longed to visit England and wander around the West End. He was young and full of energy and loved the theatre so much he would have even cleaned the floors just to work in one. Most people who had heard Matt play were shocked at how he seemed to be hell bent on throwing away his chance to do something with his talent, and Ben was one of them. He rolled his eyes heavenward as I sat beside Matt and asked, 'Drink, Helen?'

'Just one of your brilliant cups of coffee thanks, Ben.'

Matt was staring at his glass of water intently as Ben poured me some strong, steaming coffee. 'Here you go. I heard you just now singing that song about making the most of your life. What's it called?'

'The Life You Were Meant To Live".'

'Yeah, that's the one. Wow! I don't have to come into the auditorium; I can hear you from here-great job!'

'Thank you.'

'You too, Matt,' he said generously.

The dishevelled pianist looked up at the young barman's enthusiastic face and nodded, 'Cheers.'

I tapped Matt on the arm, 'Where were you?' He still didn't look at me, but simply mumbled something. 'Where *were* you?' I repeated.

'Asleep, I was asleep.' He sounded irritated, but I wasn't going to be put off.

'Don't you put your alarm on?'

'Yeah, but I slept through it.'

'Did you have a skin full last night?'

He put his head in his hands. 'Don't have a go at me, Helen.'

'I'm not, I just think you're mad, that's all.'

'We found this great bar and it had a piano ...'

'So has the stage!'

He finally flicked his eyes my way. 'That's very funny, Helen.'

'I mean it. Why would you want to play a piano in a bar all night when you can play all day and get paid bloody good money for it? We're in New York, Matt. This is your dream, for God's sake!'

He visibly winced at my words. 'I know, I know but I just can't seem to ...'

'Sustain your interest?' I offered.

'It's my Achilles heel, my drinking and my lack of ...'

'Staying power?' I chipped in. 'I don't understand you. All you have to do is turn up and play, the rest comes naturally to you. You can be pissed one night and then play brilliantly the next day, so just turn up, *please*. Otherwise on opening night you won't be here, you'll be on your way home and your lucky first cover will be on stage instead of you.'

He then turned to look at me and his face was grey. 'But... I can't *not* drink.'

'What about your burst ulcer?'

'Oh I won't have another one of those,' he declared, as if it was of little importance. 'I took a load of pills for it and the doctor said it had gone.'

My concern was turning to impatience and he knew it. 'You're a fool, do you know that?'

He nodded and then flashed one of his playful smiles at me, while Ben, who had been listening to every word of our conversation because it made his job so much more interesting, laughed at us.

'Talk about tortured genius and his conscience,' he remarked.

'I won't let him throw it all away. I won't let him give up.'

Ben leaned over the bar towards Matt, 'You know, you're lucky to have a friend like her.'

Matt shrugged. 'It's what Helen does: saves people from themselves.'

Ben gave a short laugh. 'Maybe, but don't take it for granted, pal.'

I thought of Benedict then and his face came so vividly into my mind I took a long, deep breath. I thought of the man I had first met in the snowy depths of winter who had appeared lost and haunted and how I had taken his hand and urged him not to give up. Now I was thousands of miles from the person whose friendship I treasured above all others, living the life I thought I had wanted. And I did want it. I *still* wanted it, but the loneliness was becoming increasingly hard to bear and I had envisioned Matt helping me to get through the months away from home with his enthusiasm and love of life. I hadn't imagined that he was only enthusiastic and happy in short bursts and the rest of the time he simply lived to drink. I finished my coffee and kissed his rough cheek.

'I'll see you in a bit, OK?'

He gave me a small, sheepish smile. 'Yeah, see you in a bit.'

'Thanks for the coffee, Ben.'

'You're welcome, honey.'

As I made my way out of the bar I turned to see Ben flicking the cloth he had been drying glasses with around Matt's head playfully. All the theatre staff liked Matt and admired his playing and yet I felt my throat tighten with fear for his future.

I walked back onto the deserted, dark stage and sat on Matt's stool. The atmosphere was warm and dusty and smelt of stale stage make-up. I loved being on a deserted stage, looking out at empty seats. A theatre without people in it always appeared haunted to me, as if the ghosts of the past were still there, waiting in the wings. I relished the silence, the echoes of the footsteps and laughter of the performers who had been treading the boards over the years. I leant on Matt's piano with my head in my hands and pictured Benedict playing for me. The memory made me smile and I opened my eyes. Looking at Matt's music that was open on the stand, my attention was caught by notes he had scribbled at the side of the pages. They seemed to be instructions to himself, such as, 'Pause for Helen to turn', and 'Wait for the ensemble to be lit by blue light', but the one that caught my eye at the bottom of the score made my heart flip over.

In almost intelligible writing was scrawled the words, 'Find a reason to live'.

Chapter 17

'Beth, you will go and see Nell's show, won't you?'

I heard her sigh. 'OK, Dad.'

'Well, it's so kind of her to get you two free tickets. You can take the not-so-special boyfriend of yours.'

'Oh he's not around any more,' she replied, sounding a little hard, like her mother.

'Isn't he?'

'I told you, he wasn't a serious thing.'

'Is there anyone else on the scene?'

'No, not yet, but I could take a friend or work colleague I suppose.'

'And you'll go and see her backstage?'

I heard her sigh again, but her voice had the softness about it that she usually reserved for her dear old dad. 'Yeah OK, for you.'

'Thank you, Beth.'

'Will she leave the tickets at the box office?'

'I think so, yes. But I'll check with her. She's going to Skype me before opening night.'

I heard her gasp down the phone. 'You've got Skype now? I was always asking you to install that for me.'

'Were you, darling? I don't remember that.'

'Honestly, Dad! I could have Skyped you now.'

'I didn't think ...'

'Honestly, Dad!' she said again as if she was so disappointed in me she didn't know what else to say.

'I'm sorry, Beth,' I muttered, my voice dying away. 'I often forget things now. I'm not getting dementia or anything. I'm just preoccupied with all the other symptoms.'

'It's fine,' she said, a little brusquely.

Very aware that she was slightly miffed and probably a little jealous, I asked, 'Is it really fine?'

'Yes,' she replied wearily, her voice a little less harsh.

'Thank you, darling.'

Drawing a deep breath she then queried, 'You'll let me know then, about where the tickets will be?'

'I will.'

'Right, see you then.'

'See you.'

'Oh, and you're well?' she said hastily, probably feeling guilty for not having asked before.

'I'm very well, darling, and now that I've spoken to you I'm even better.'

'Good; that's good Dad, I'm pleased, bye Dad.' she said, finally sounding more like the daughter I knew who adored her wayward father.

I put the phone down and sat heavily on the sofa, reading more into Beth's voice than was probably there. She had sounded uninterested and distracted as soon as I started talking about Nell and it hurt me that her opinion of Nell had not changed, although it didn't surprise me that it hadn't. I leant my head back because of the heavy aching in my neck and the deep tension across my shoulders. The *presence* was everywhere and had been since the early hours and however hard I tried I could not rid myself of its constant floating inches from my eyes.

The day had started warm and bright with large, billowing clouds racing past my conservatory windows, but the sky was darkening quickly and a strong westerly wind was rushing through the silver birches between my garden and Thea's. It sounded like waves crashing on rocks and I closed my eyes and tried to imagine sitting with Nell on a Cornish beach somewhere watching a glorious sunset stretch before us. I pictured her face, full of excitement and wonder and her luxurious hair falling across her eyes and down her back. Missing her was becoming a part of me now, like my disease and my slurring and trembling. It flattened every emotion, filled my waking moments with a dull aching somewhere in my chest and disturbed my thoughts. Whoever I was having a conversation with, I was distracted constantly by images of her living her dream with other people by her side. The weeks were dragging by and I was so often living in my imagination, a whole day would pass without me remembering much of it at all.

It was early June and the weather had been pleasantly warm, not heavy or humid, and so I was taken by surprise by the strength of a sudden storm that threw rain hammering down on the glass roof. But the rhythm of the raindrops lulled me into a light and fitful sleep. Waking up slowly, I was confronted by the image of Nell sitting on my piano stool, smiling fondly at me. I shook my head in disbelief and wonder at the sight of her dear face, but she was replaced instantly by my father.

'Papa, where have you been?' I asked him, sleep still clinging to me.

'What do you mean?' he replied.

'Where have you been since you left us?'

He appeared perplexed by the question. 'I've been here all the time, you just can't see me.'

'I wish it were true,' I stuttered. 'I sincerely wish it were true.'

'Let her go, Benedict and she will come back to you.'

'Who do you mean? If you mean Beth it has never been a problem, but perhaps you mean Nell? I'm confused, Papa. I have let her go. I wouldn't have stopped her, I couldn't have. It's her life and nothing to do with me, but I just miss her ...'

'Benedict, look after Sidney ...'

I had struggled to move my head forward from the sofa, but his words made me wake up instantly. 'Why look after Sidney?'

'He needs you, Benedict.'

'What do you mean?'

He was gone and the space by the piano was full of the *presence*. I felt moved to throw something solid at it in the vain hope that it would flee for good. It was still raining hard and I felt bewildered, lost and alone. The mention of Sidney's name unsettled me greatly because there was no reason for it and I glanced instinctively towards his garden. The rain was lashing against my windows and it was hard to see anything clearly, but I had a feeling of unease, of something not being quite right and it would not leave me. I staggered to my feet with my bone-thin legs as heavy as two felled tree trunks and opened the conservatory doors. The gusting wind blew me backwards, but I clung on to the left-hand door and stepped into the garden without knowing why. Sidney and Sheila's fence was only four feet high so I grasped the top of it to balance myself and peered into their garden. My stomach lurched into my throat in a wave of panic. Sidney was flat on his back on the grass, soaked to the skin, his legs splayed.

'Jesus Christ! Sidney! Sidney!'

I stumbled through their gate, the rain pounding against my face and clothes and dropped down to my knees by his side. His eyes were closed, his mouth slightly open and his skin grey. It didn't look like him at all without his usual cheeky expression. I shook his shoulders roughly.

'Sidney! Sidney! Answer me, for Christ's sake!'

There was no flicker of recognition, no movement. I fumbled for my mobile and cursed my trembling hands and stiff fingers. It was difficult to get it out of my pocket and I swore loudly again, still fumbling. My fingers felt like ice as I pressed the buttons. The woman's voice on the other end was calm yet efficient.

'Emergency, which service?'

'Ambulance, quickly, my friend has collapsed. Hurry, please!' I broke off to try to rouse Sidney again, 'Sidney, for God's sake answer me.' After mumbling my address with my facial muscles freezing halfway through and hearing the operator assure me the ambulance was on its way, I half ran, half staggered through my house to open my door for when they arrived. I stopped in the conservatory, my mind racing, unsure whether to rush upstairs for a blanket to keep Sidney warm, but knowing how long that would take me with my unreliable legs, I dismissed the thought. With the inside of my mouth parched with panic and shock I then made my way back into the garden. This time, with the rain teeming down on his upturned face, I put my head on his chest. I hoped it wasn't my imagination, but I thought I could hear his heart beating and euphoria swept over me.

'Sidney, listen to me, the ambulance is coming so don't you do anything bloody stupid and go and die on me. I'm warning you, *I* have to go first. I mean it, Sidney. I wouldn't want my life without you here to get on my nerves every day. I mean it, Sidney, don't you bloody well die on me.'

There was no response and I leant forward and put my face by his mouth and nose to feel for his breath. There was so much rain and wind, it was impossible to feel anything, so I lifted his shoulders carefully and sat behind him, placing his head gently on my lap. And there we stayed, together with me stroking his blank face. He opened his eyes and mumbled just as I heard the ambulance crew arrive through the gate.

'Right, sir, how long has he been unconscious?'

I looked up at the young man's face, too young and pleasant for all that responsibility and shook my head in despair. 'I have no idea, I found him like this. He's just coming round, I think.'

His colleague, who resembled an East End gangster, quickly and expertly fitted an oxygen mask over Sidney's face and then felt his pulse. Sidney began thrashing his arms about and tried to rip the mask from his face.

'OK, mate, keep calm. His pulse is erratic, David. Has he had heart trouble before, sir?'

'No, I don't believe so.'

'Is he diabetic?'

'No.'

'Any other condition you know of?'

'No.'

'Does he live on his own or with you?'

Even in the midst of my sense of panic, I found the idea of Sidney and myself being two ageing, gay men highly amusing because I could picture his face if he ever found out.

'No, he's married, his wife must be out shopping and I'm surprised he hasn't risen from his coma to defend himself.'

The East End gangster smiled and it transformed his face. 'Right, let's be having him, you just move away so we can get him in the vehicle quickly.' He must have been a sensitive type, despite his rough appearance because he cottoned on immediately that I wasn't in complete control of my legs and helped me to my feet. 'You OK there, sir? There you go, let us take care of him. The doctors will sort him out, don't worry.'

His more easy-on-the-eye colleague put his hand gently on my shoulder before they lifted a confused, now swearing Sidney carefully and deftly onto the stretcher. 'He'll be in the Queen Elizabeth. You'll have to stay here and tell his wife,' he told me quite firmly.

'Is it a heart attack?' I asked, my voice slurring badly.

'Hard to tell, but they'll sort him out at the hospital. Do you know if he's on any medication?'

'I ... I don't know, I don't think so.'

'It's probably better if you drive his wife if possible. Don't let her drive, will you?'

'No ... he has three sons ... she'll probably ...'

My voice slurred so badly I saw him raise his eyebrows. 'Well, maybe let one of them drive her, if you've had a drink.'

'All I've had today is tea, the slurring is Parkinson's.'

He had the grace to look a little embarrassed, but then an expression of recognition crossed his face. 'Ah right ... sorry, but had to check. No offence, sir.'

'None taken, I assure you.'

'Right, let's go, Rich. Have you got him? One, two, three, lift.'

They were both calm, oddly reassuring without saying very much and not even old enough to shave in my eyes, but they carried my friend away and put him in the back of the ambulance with strength, expertise and ease and a detachment I could only envy. Sidney by now was telling them in no uncertain terms what they could do with their oxygen mask and attempting to get up off the stretcher. I watched from my front door, numb with delayed shock as they drove him away.

I was drenched and wanted to change my clothes, but I couldn't think clearly and I knew I had to wait by the window for Sheila to come home. What would I say to her? How would I break it? Should I call one of his sons before telling her? What would she do if he died? What would *I* do if he died? How long had he been out there, flat on his back in the rain? The thought of it made me feel physically sick. I felt as if a huge weight was crushing my chest and I took in gulps of air to try and relieve it. My hands were trembling and jerking so violently they were causing me intense pain and the *presence* tried desperately to distract me. I wouldn't be distracted though and simply kept my eyes fixed on the road outside, remembering Sidney's ashen face and splayed legs. By the time Sheila's car appeared, I was weak with the anticipation of breaking the dreaded news and shivering with the cold.

As she got out of her car, reaching inside for her shopping bags, she caught sight of me standing on my doorstep and gave me a little wave. Her ever-smiling, kindly face made me feel wretched and breathless and I took a shaky step forward. One glance at me and my sodden clothes made her stop and look again.

'Benedict?'

'Sheila ...now try not to worry ...'

&

The first sounds I heard every morning when I opened my eyes, were the shower and the far-away constant rumble of traffic from the main road. My flat mate, Georgia was usually up before me and would spend up to fifteen noisy minutes in the bathroom while I struggled to wake up after the show the night before. The first few performances had been a blast of press nights and previews and on the whole the reviews had been exactly what we had hoped for after all our hard work. Matt had been singled out for unanimous praise, which wasn't a surprise to anyone and two pieces written about my performance had given me a deep sense of satisfaction and an inner glow of happiness that I had been chasing all my working life. There had been no spare tickets until the second week and I had emailed Benedict to tell him which show Beth could see. His email back had been short yet sweet, thanking me and saying he had read my reviews on the internet, but nothing more about how he was feeling or any news of any kind, which troubled me. But I was distracted from my thoughts about what might or might not be happening in his life by my all-consuming passion for the show and my increasing concern for Matt.

After a few troubled mornings where he turned up late for rehearsals, he had pulled himself together after a sincere dressing down by the director and company manager and appeared to be behaving. Everyone was fooled except me because I recognised the signs. His erratic moods, drawn, pale face and his quick departure after the show with some of the band, all told me he was drinking heavily. Just before opening night I had cornered him in the bar again, under the concerned and watchful eye of Ben. Ben and I had become friends and I now knew he was an aspiring actor and dancer who worked in the theatre just to be a part of the whole experience while between jobs. That day, as I pounced on Matt, Ben shook his head sadly at me as if he had given up on Matt and his behaviour and seen it all before.

'Have you been avoiding me?' I asked him, joining him on a bar stool.

He glanced at me and gave me a small, forced smile. His eyes were unfocused and bloodshot. 'Yes, because you go on at me.'

'Ask yourself why, Matt.'

'Is it because I disappoint you?'

I put my arm around his shoulders. Often he appeared to be as vulnerable and lost as a young child on his first day at primary school. 'It's not a case of you disappointing me,' I insisted. 'It's about a waste of an incredible talent and that breaks my heart.'

'I don't want to break your heart, Helen, but I haven't got your staying power or sense of self. I have *no* sense of self, that's the problem.'

'Can't you do it for me then?' I asked, tears of frustration burning the back of my eyes.

'I *am* doing it for you,' he replied, his eyes trouble and glazed. 'I've only come here for you. If I hadn't had you urging me on I wouldn't even have auditioned for the part. I wanted to spend time with you, but it hasn't happened.'

'You need to stop drinking, Matt.'

'He can't,' Ben said flatly. 'I've seen it before so many times. Don't

440

waste your emotional energy on him, Helen.'

I thought Matt would rear up and protest, but he didn't and that was when my hopes for him fled. 'He could if he wanted to,' I protested, not understanding. 'I just have no idea how you can waste this opportunity and you will waste it. I can see it on everyone's faces. They're losing patience and the understudy is good, *bloody* good.'

'I agree,' Ben said. 'Then you'll be on your way back to England with your tail between your legs.'

'I could get a job in the bar just down the road here,' Matt argued.

I was mortified. 'What do you mean a job in the bar? A job in the bar is the one thing you don't need! You're a top-flight pianist in a show off Broadway and that's exactly where you should be. A job in the bar will be the finish of you. How can you say that, Matt?'

'Because there's no pressure there,' he muttered.

Ben and I glanced at each other with sadness and then replacing that sadness came a wave of anger that blew me sideways. I jumped off the stool and cried, 'So many people would sell their soul for your gift and for this chance. You're just a fool to be throwing it away; do you know that?'

He turned towards me, his face dull with alcohol. 'Yeah, I know that, but thanks for reminding me, Helen.'

I ran out of the bar and up the dark, narrow back stairs to my dressing room, which fortunately was empty for a change. The rising sense of indignation and fear for Matt's future welled up in me in and I sat down at my mirror and cried a torrent of tears. Black smudges of mascara appeared under my eyes and I looked a wreck. My first thought was for Benedict and I wished with all my heart I could talk with him. A sense of loneliness and separation from everyone I knew and loved engulfed me and I put my head in my hands and sobbed openly. Tears poured into my mouth and my nose began to run. A quiet, almost timid knock at my door made me grab a tissue and I hurriedly smeared my face with it. It was no use though. Anyone with any sense could see I had been crying, so I gave in to it without a care for what I looked like.

'Come in.'

Beth gingerly opened the door. Her hair was longer and curling round her face and she was dressed casually with a chiffon scarf hanging loosely around her shoulders despite the heat. She looked pretty and elegant and her face was so like her father's my heart jumped into my throat.

'Can I come in?' she asked, which well she might after taking a look at my dishevelled and tear-stained appearance.

I leapt to my feet, 'Oh my God, Beth, please come in. How lovely to see you. Sit down, please,' I told her, picking up some dirty clothes from the tattered old sofa that belonged to one of the ensemble and throwing them on the floor.

She looked a little apprehensive. 'Dad said you would leave tickets at the box office, but I've taken a few days holiday so I thought I'd pick them up from you, if that's OK?'

I was surprised, but hid it. 'Of course ... how nice of you ...'

'I'm usually running late wherever I go so I thought queuing at the box office would be a bit silly ...'

'That's fine, I'm really pleased you came up,' I replied, quite flustered by her sudden appearance. 'Would you like a drink? We can go to the bar. My friend Ben will get us a coffee.'

'No, I'm fine.'

'Well ... it's so strange to see you. How is your dad?'

'Quite well, the last time we spoke,' she said, not giving much away and she looked nervous, unsure of herself.

'That's good. I have spoken to him once on Skype, but I think he was a bit bemused by it all.' I too was still a little bemused by Beth being there but suddenly remembered *why* she was there, 'Now, I have your tickets here in an envelope somewhere ... where are they? Please excuse the mess, but it's not all mine. I share this room with three others so it's a little crowded. Dancers are rarely tidy.'

She was studying the room carefully. 'I've never been in a dressing room before. Big mirrors! It's interesting ...'

'This is one of the older theatres so these rooms aren't very big, but it's a bit better than some in the West End that I've seen. Here you go,' I said, handing her the tickets in a white envelope with her name on it.

'Thank you.'

'I hope you enjoy it and do let me know, won't you?'

'Yes, Dad gave me your email.'

'Or come backstage after?' I suggested, trying to get through her carefully constructed defences.

She looked a little shy and restless, so different from the self-possessed daughter of an adoring father, in her old home. 'Thanks. Well, I wish you the best of luck, you must be nervous. A show off Broadway is quite something.'

'I am a little, but it's a positive nervousness, if you know what I mean. It's quite exhilarating stepping out on stage on a press night – exhilarating and a tiny bit terrifying. No, it's a *lot* terrifying.'

'I can only imagine,' she said and she gave me a genuine smile, the first ever.

'We put so much of ourselves into our performances, it's an intensely personal thing, and criticism can tear you apart. Some people in this business have never read a review because it can have such a detrimental effect. I don't want to read them, but I can't help myself. We all want to be accepted and valued in our chosen profession after all, don't we?'

She gave another warmer smile than she usually did which changed her face instantly and I felt the tiniest hint of a softening in her opinion of me. Or perhaps it was the fact that I was there, all those miles away from her beloved father, getting on with my life and not a threat to their close relationship any more. There was an awkward silence for a moment and she tucked her soft, wavy fair hair behind her ears as if preparing to leave.

'Well, thanks for these. I'm looking forward to seeing it.'

I wanted to keep her there in front of me for a little longer. She was his darling daughter after all. 'You'll have to report back to your dad because he won't get the chance to see it and he missed my previous show because he had flu.'

'Yes, I heard about that. I was really worried about him. He's not as strong as he used to be, what with the Parkinson's and stuff ...'

'I know.'

'But yeah, I know he'll be on the phone immediately asking me all about it, so I'll have to take notes,' she said, giving a wry smile and for the first time I recognised his dry sense of humour in her voice.

I laughed out loud. 'Oh dear, be kind about me, won't you?'

She didn't reply, but I had the impression she wanted to ask me something but was plucking up the courage. I could sense the tension in her. 'Look,' she started, suddenly appearing hesitant and nervous, 'I'm sorry if I was less than welcoming at my birthday party, but I ...'

'Beth, you don't have to explain.'

'No, I do, because where he's concerned I have to be kind and behave in a courteous manner because of how much I love him and how proud he is of me and I want to be worthy of that pride ... and ...' She tripped over her words in her desperation to explain and at once I could see her vulnerability shining brightly from her like a beacon of light. 'And, it's just that ...'

'Beth ... honestly ...'

She put her hand up to silence me. 'Please, let me say it.'

'Sorry.'

'Apart from my mum, there's only ever been me and him. I've never had to share him with siblings and he always kept me apart from any women he knew, which was why I was so surprised ... no, *shocked*, when you suddenly appeared at my party.'

'But those other women, he was probably in a relationship with them and we aren't,' I interrupted, eager to help her in her apology.

'But the problem was – because I know him so well – I could see ... I could tell by the way he looked at you that you mean the world to him. It just knocked me sideways. Aunty Bethan saw it too. We both know him inside out. I had never seen him like that before, not even with my mum. Well,' she laughed hollowly, 'especially with my mum. And then my aunt started to have a go and I just went along with it because I was dumbstruck at how young you are and I was struggling to understand how someone like you could be interested in an older man with Parkinson's and ... and I began to wonder why ...'

'I just like him. We get on ...'

'And on the phone yesterday,' she went on, as if she hadn't heard me, 'I was off with him again because he was so insistent I call on you and come see the show and I thought, oh Dad, for God's sake, leave off about her and then when I put the phone down I imagined him being disappointed in me and I want to please him and it's such a little thing to do for him and I thought, what if he died tomorrow ...'

'Don't say that,' I gasped.

'But you understand, don't you? If he did, what would I feel like? He's never asked anything of me in my whole life. All he does is love me so ...' she paused, her face pinched with tension and sorrow, 'here I am and I hope you'll forgive my rudeness at home. I just can't share him you see. I just can't.'

I thought for a moment before I replied because her words, although heartfelt in her affection for him, were ultimately all about herself. But her upbringing and the way she had been the centre of his life for all her thirty years, was absolutely nothing to do with me and couldn't be undone. He had loved her completely and there wasn't anything wrong in that, but he had also spoilt her and consequently she would find it hard to ever accept me or any other woman fully.

'To be honest, Beth, I understood your reaction completely. It makes no difference to me. It didn't upset me. All I want is what is best for your dad and I'm pretty sure I can be a source of comfort in his life just through being his friend. If you think he'll ever put me before you, you're wrong. You'll *always* come first and rightly so, but we can both be a comfort to him in future years.'

Her face was serious. 'Do you love him?'

'Who wouldn't love him?'

She looked frustrated. 'No, I mean ... are you going to marry him?'

'Marry him? Why on earth would you think that?'

'It's just ...'

'You can't share him' I muttered, knowing Benedict would find our conversation very difficult to listen to. 'I know, you said.'

She suddenly realised how selfish she must have sounded and her eyes swam with tears. 'I know you must think I'm spoilt and immature, but that's how I feel.'

The conversation was not what I needed at that point. 'Look, Beth, I have no intention of ever coming between you and, as I just said, I only want what's best for him anyway. As long as he's happy ...' I shrugged my shoulders and didn't finish my sentence, but my pause was meant to imply, why don't you want what's best for him? 'You don't have to say any more, really you don't. I won't be seeing your dad for a very long time, so ... but enjoy the show.'

She wiped a tear from her pale cheek and I could tell by her demeanour that she was regretting even starting the conversation. 'Well, good luck with the reviews.'

'Thank you,' I replied. 'And hopefully see you again.'

'Yes,' she muttered, now hugely uncomfortable and embarrassed and desperate to be gone.

'Shall I see you downstairs?'

'No, I'm fine.'

'Right.'

She turned to go, but then paused. 'Had you been crying when I came in?'

'Yes, but it's not important. I'm just worried about a friend of mine here who seems to be throwing all he ever worked for away because of his drinking. Well, it is important, but I can't help him, he's beyond my help.'

'That's a shame. What part is he in the show?'

'He's the pianist on stage and he has a rare talent. I hope he's on when you come because he's fantastic. It's very sad. But I just have to accept it. Bye, Beth.'

She bit her lip and attempted a smile that didn't really work. 'Bye.'

I stood very still once she had gone, still and deep in thought. Seeing her, so like him facially, but so very different in character, sent my precarious mood plummeting. Her out-of-the-blue appearance coupled with Matt's ridiculous and depressing attitude to his talent caused a sudden and violent headache that felt as if someone with strong, muscular hands and arms was pressing hard on my temples. I sat at my mirror again and stared at the white, drawn face looking back at me with sad and wide grey eyes. I longed to be sitting opposite Benedict and having the pleasure of listening to his low, gentle and distinctive voice.

'What shall we talk about, Mr Marshall?' I would ask.

His eyes would twinkle. 'How I got to be so devastatingly attractive?'

I would laugh loudly. 'Shut your face you!'

'Delightful,' he would mutter.

I put my head in my hands, wondering why on earth I was thousands of miles away from the man who made me feel I was the loveliest person he had ever come across.

&

Without Sydney pestering me and making me laugh, my days seemed interminably long and I felt surprisingly isolated. A couple of times I had fallen asleep in my chair with the hot June sun blasting through the glass roof of my conservatory straight onto my upturned face and I woke with a start because I thought I heard his knock. The crashing sense of loneliness and disappointment when I realised I had imagined it caused a quickening of my tremors and a darkening of my mood. Nell was sparkling thousands of miles away and being her effervescent, dynamic self with strangers and

Sydney, who inadvertently brightened up every day with his nonsensical chatter and unintentionally hilarious expressions, was not just next door, within calling and knocking distance. The silence was blaring out around me, almost unbearably and time hung heavily on my aching shoulders. I even took to gazing over his fence in the hope it had all been a mistake, thinking that I might possibly catch him doing a bit of weeding or standing with a cup of tea looking out over his acres proudly, his stomach protruding like a suet pudding.

Sheila kept me posted almost hourly because I had telephoned her so many times on that first day and left messages on their answer phone. I had begun to allow my sombre mood and shock about what had happened to affect my rational mind and although I had heard him swearing as he was put into the ambulance, I had convinced myself he was in mortal danger and had actually been dead on arrival. Every time I imagined he had died, I had rung his number and left a ridiculous, rambling message until Sheila had arrived home and told me off in no uncertain terms.

'Benedict,' she had said, when I picked up the phone, 'how many messages have you left?'

'I'm sorry...I've been so concerned...'

'I know, but I've only just got back...'

'Is he...is he...'

'He's had a heart attack and they think he's diabetic...'

'Oh Sheila...'

'But he's stable now and we'll know more tomorrow,' she told me wearily.

'Is there anything I can do?'

'Come and visit him if need be.'

'Of course, of course...any time.'

'For now, I'm exhausted and going to bed, but I'll keep you up to date, don't worry.'

'Thank you, Sheila.'

'And Benedict, thank you for calling the ambulance and keeping calm.'

'I wasn't calm, not in the least.'

'I'm sure you were. Now, I must go.'

The next day I woke to more silence without my friend knocking on the wall early to share a coffee and get on my nerves, while Sheila was out shopping. I was inexplicably on edge, despite knowing he was being cared for and when I sat on my own, looking out on my garden, I tried to rationalise my feelings. Clear thoughts were beyond me, but it quickly dawned on me that life would be unquestionably dull without my funny, kind and terminally loyal friend to brighten my many dark, introspective moods. Nobody could be depressed for long with Sidney Walpole sitting opposite them with his array of ridiculous facial expressions and undeniably humorous, rambling conversations that I often pretended I didn't understand, when in reality I knew exactly what he was trying to say. But what I missed most was his obvious love and respect for me. I knew Sidney was a better man than I was in so many ways, but he didn't believe it and never would. So, when Sheila called that afternoon and invited me to visit him with her later that evening I jumped at the chance. I wouldn't be able to rest until I had seen him for myself.

Sheila drove us both to the hospital and I knew I was being mono-syllabic and taciturn, but she nattered away, as if she wasn't concerned at all. I wondered how on earth she could stay so calm and act so normally when she must have been sick with worry underneath and as she parked the car I turned to her and asked her as much.

'Oh I'm so used to keeping any worries I have from Sydney, it's become second nature,' she said.

'Is *he* a worrier then?' I asked.

'Dreadful,' she replied, 'absolutely dreadful. If the kids were ever sick he used to creep into their rooms and put a mirror up to their noses to make sure they were breathing and God help us if one of them had a temperature!'

'I never knew that,' I muttered.

Sheila put her hand on top of mine. 'When you told him you had Parkinson's he didn't sleep a wink for days, silly idiot, as if that was going to help you.'

'Good grief...'

'I told him the best way he could help you was to stop worrying and treat you exactly the same as he always had.'

'And he has,' I told her, 'he has, bless him.'

Sheila leant across and gave me a quick peck on the cheek. 'And now you have to do the same for him. Come on, let's go and see the silly old devil. This afternoon he was quite sleepy so I hope he'll be a bit more with it this evening.'

Sidney had been dozing and when Sheila squeezed his hand to let him know we were there, he opened his eyes and appeared quite cross.

'What the fuck am I doing here?'

'Sidney, don't swear! Honestly!'

'I'm not in a church, Sheila.'

'You're here because I rang for an ambulance you ungrateful bastard,' I muttered in his ear, so relieved to be having any kind of conversation with him.

His face was ashen still and he was connected to various monitors that bleeped intermittently. 'Trust you to be bloody dramatic,' he commented, giving me a Sidney look. 'Ringing for an ambulance, I don't know.'

'He probably saved your life,' Sheila told him.

'What's wrong with me anyway? Do we know yet?'

'Diabetes apparently,' she said gently. 'And apart from that something went wrong with your heart.'

He looked horrified. 'Fuck me!'

'Sidney, shush!'

'Let him swear away, at least we know he's getting better,' I remarked.

He looked at me. 'Am I in charge of all my bits?'

'How the hell would I know?'

'It's very common, dear,' Sheila said soothingly, taking his hand.

'Common! It didn't feel common at the time!'

'No, I'd agree with that,' I added.

'Who are you anyway?' he asked, smiling at last.

'That's very funny.'

'Don't joke about it,' Sheila scolded. 'Do you remember much about it?'

He frowned. 'I remember going into the garden for some reason, I think for a bit of air because I felt odd and it had just started to rain ... then I kind of fell about ... couldn't keep my balance, a bit like you are sometimes, Benedict.'

'I knew I wouldn't be able to be ill on my own,' I chipped in.

'I tried to stand up straight, but my legs wouldn't do what I wanted them to and I knew I was going to go ... pass out.'

I nodded, 'I know the feeling of having your legs doing their own thing.'

'That's all I remember really. When can I come home?' he asked Sheila forlornly.

'I'm not sure yet; they haven't told me, dear.'

'The foods fucking awful …'

Sheila spat out, 'Sidney, will you please keep your voice down? Not everyone in here wants to hear your bad language!'

He looked a little contrite. 'Sorry, love.'

'How are you actually feeling now?' I asked him.

'Very tired and my head is fuzzy, but I could murder a cup of tea.'

'Shall I get you one, my liege?' I asked, bowing slightly from the waist.

The elderly man in the bed beside Sidney must have been following our conversation closely. 'They bring one round in half an hour,' he told us.

'What's it like?' Sidney asked.

'Lovely … but the food's bloody horrible.'

'Oh Christ,' Sidney muttered. 'Get them to sort out my tablets and let's get home.'

'You'll stay here until the doctors tell you otherwise,' Sheila told him, in her no-nonsense, firmest voice.

'It will give me a bit of peace at home,' I mumbled.

He looked at me pitifully. 'If I have to stay in a few days, will you come and play cards with me?'

'I will,' I replied, 'but whisky is out of the question.'

His face fell a mile. 'Will I have to stop drinking?'

I laughed at his horrified expression. 'Perhaps you'll stop encouraging me now.'

'We'll cross that bridge when we come to it and Benedict will have to support your change of regime,' Sheila said, frowning hard at me. 'Your diet will have to be looked at and the drinking and you'll need to lose weight.'

His horrified face was a picture. 'Fuck me! Is it worth living?'

'They think you passed out because your blood sugar was all over the place. Or it might be something to do with the electrics in your heart, they aren't sure yet. We can't have you passing out again, dear. It was just lucky Benedict found you when he did.'

'I'll have a wander, let you two have a chat,' I said, 'I'll be back in a bit.'

'Don't get lost,' Sidney said, 'all the bays look the same.'

I strolled about, allowing Sidney and Sheila some time on their own, but I wished I hadn't when at every turn I encountered extremely ill men, some with oxygen masks on, some calling out in obvious pain and some hooked up to monitors that bleeped incessantly. My mood instantly began to plummet as I imagined myself becoming increasingly immobile, mute and without any longing to live. I scuttled back to my friends, hoping it was time to go home.

'Visiting time is over,' the elderly man called over to me as I arrived back at Sidney's bedside.

'Thank God,' I muttered.

'He's going to get on my nerves, I can tell,' Sidney whispered loudly to me. 'He's a know-all.'

'Tolerance, Sidney,' I whispered back.

'I haven't got any.'

'Bye, darling,' Sheila said, ignoring his moaning and kissing him on the forehead tenderly. 'See you tomorrow and behave yourself and do what you're told.'

He clutched at Sheila's hand. 'Ask at the desk when I can come home.'

'Leave off,' she sighed. 'They need to check you haven't got anything else wrong with you. But they'll chuck you out as soon as they can.'

I put my hand on his arm. 'Bye, Sidney.'

He then clutched at *my* hand like a drowning man. 'Benedict, bring some cards tomorrow, eh?' I hesitated because the thought of spending any time surrounded by such sickness made me want to wretch. Sidney picked up on my hesitation. 'Benedict, will you bring your cards in?'

'I will.'

He appeared so relieved I immediately felt like I had let him down, just by hesitating. 'I'm going to be bored witless in here,' he added.

'I know.'

'Don't forget, will you?'

'I won't, Sidney.'

'Sydney, leave off,' Sheila scolded. 'We're going now, get some sleep.'

I followed Sheila out of the small ward and turned to find Sidney watching us like a young child watching his parents leaving him on his first day at school. A lump formed in my throat as he waved and I felt so relieved that he was still with us I could have dissolved into useless tears. Sheila, who was so much stronger than either Sidney or me in every imaginable way, and eternally more sensible, was talking to a young, attractive woman. I assumed she was a doctor because the stethoscope hanging loosely around her neck was a giveaway but, to me, she looked young enough to still be at school.

'He's probably been diabetic for quite a while,' she was saying to Sheila. 'I'm guessing he doesn't like going to the doctor, which might explain why he isn't on blood-pressure tablets.'

'He won't *ever* go to see a doctor,' Sheila answered and her voice was now strained and weary.

'Well, his BP was very high and he's going to have to be on tablets now, I'm afraid, for the rest of his life for that and for diabetes and possibly blood thinners too.'

'That's fine,' Sheila said, 'I'll make sure he takes them.'

'Did he appear unwell in any way? Was he very tired or thirsty?'

'He's often tired.'

'And always thirsty, but mostly for alcohol,' I added.

The doctor looked askance at me. 'He'll need to moderate his alcohol intake.' 'We'll make sure he does, won't we, Benedict?' Sheila squeezed my arm.

'I ... yes, of course, Sheila.'

Sheila turned to the young doctor once more, 'What about his heart?'

'We will be monitoring his heart through the night, so we'll know more by tomorrow. But his heart beat was irregular and quite fast.'

'How long will he be in here doctor?' I asked, because I knew Sidney would want me to.

'We'll keep an eye on him tonight and tomorrow morning, that's all.'

'He'll be relieved about that. Be firm with him,' I told her.

She smiled. 'We will.'

Sidney came out the following evening, armed with sheets of information about a healthy lifestyle and various tablets. I thought he might be a little chastened by his brush with mortality, but he was still the same old Sidney. I was almost as delighted as his wife to have him back. Sitting on my own at home had been desolate. I had missed his knock dreadfully and having both him and Nell away I had felt bereft. On his arrival home he rang me immediately. I could have cheered when I heard his voice.

'Are you coming in to see me then?'

'Do you feel well enough?'

'Don't be an arse, of course I do, nothing wrong with me.'

I heard Sheila in the background. 'He's going straight to bed, Benedict.'

'Oh Christ, the wife's spoken!'

I didn't correct him. I was so overjoyed to know he was safely ensconced next door, I was happy to let him speak in his usual, vernacular language. 'I'd better not come round, Sidney.'

'I'll be round in the morning then,' he told me.

'Fine, but only if Sheila says it's OK.'

I put the phone down and smiled to myself. All was right with the world now he was back. Having him in hospital had been an odd experience as it didn't feel quite right knowing he wasn't just a knock away. The following morning he appeared at my conservatory door at nine-thirty, a little pale at the edges and dark under the eyes, but he was still Sidney.

'Welcome home,' I cried. 'How are you feeling?'

'I feel fine. I think they were glad to get rid of me,' he declared quite proudly. 'I was probably getting on their nerves.'

'No! Do you really think so?'

'The food was bloody awful.'

'Well, you are used to Sheila's wonderful cooking, aren't you?'

He sat in his favourite chair and looked over the rim of his glasses at me. 'Did you miss me then?'

'I did visit you, Sidney, or don't you remember that?'

'I know, but ...'

'Of course I missed you, who wouldn't? You're like the proverbial bad penny.'

'Cheers, Benedict. So, what's occurring then?'

'Very little, Sidney as you can see. Would you like a coffee?'

'Yes please and put a bit of whiskey in it, matey.'

'I most certainly will not!'

He looked mortified. 'I'm allowed whiskey,' he cried. 'Don't you start on at me!'

'Who said you could have whiskey?'

'The quack ... she said in moderation, honestly.'

'I'll ask Sheila!'

'Go on then, phone her now. Bloody marvellous, isn't it? My best friend and you don't believe me.'

I laughed out loud at his indignant face. 'I believe you. I'll put a dash in it and no more.'

'Lovely.'

I made the coffee while he read my newspaper, but as I picked the tray up my left hand trembled and jerked so violently I almost dropped the whole lot. 'Sidney, come and carry this in for me,' I called.

'Talk about the sick, lame and lazy,' he laughed. 'What a pair of old crocks we are.'

'You speak for yourself.'

'Has it got worse?' he asked, eyeing my hands, which appeared to have a life of their own, independent of the rest of my body.

'Not worse, but kind of more intermittent.'

'Speak normally.'

'This is normal for me! I mean, instead of being bad all the time, when it's bad it's bad, if that makes sense.'

He sniffed. 'Not really, but I never could understand half of what you say, which is just as well I reckon.'

'How very kind of you...'

'I'm in competition with you now anyway,' he remarked.

'And why is that, pray?'

'Talk like normal people,' he demanded, exasperated as ever.

'As I've said before, I'm not normal people.'

'Anyway, as I was saying...I've got this diabetes now, so there! *And* something wrong with my heart, so you're not the only one who needs sympathy.'

'Sidney, may I just say, Parkinson's was not my fault. Your diabetes was partly caused by your inability to partake in anything even remotely beneficial to your health.'

He was frowning. 'Do they know what causes Parkinson's then?'

'No, I don't believe they do. Well, they might do, but I haven't actually asked.'

'I bet you're worried that being pissed for most of your life contributed to it?' he said.

'Sidney, I do believe you have a point. As you say, my love affair with alcohol has made me wonder many times if it has played any part.'

'Blimey,' he laughed, 'you say it much better than I do. A love affair with alcohol,' he repeated, mimicking me perfectly.

'Or,' I added, 'as you say, being pissed! But we aren't in competition for sympathy. I'll moan to you and you can reciprocate.'

'Does that mean I can moan back?' he asked.

'It does.'

'Then I agree.'

We sipped our coffee and Sidney gazed out into my garden with a look of someone who knew they were lucky to be doing simple things and slightly chastened by his experience. Our mutual silence was comfortable and I felt deliriously happy he was sitting there with me again.

'Your garden is looking lovely, Benedict,' he remarked.

'Why, thank you. I can take no plaudits for that, I'm afraid.'

'You can still do some gardening, can't you?'

'What, with these hands, Sidney? I think not. Mind you, I never was much good at it. Mary used to be out there all the time, probably to get away from me.'

He looked a little reflective for a moment. 'It was lucky you saw me flat on my back in the garden, wasn't it? I wonder how long I'd been out there.'

'Not very long, I'm sure. Don't think about it.'

'What made you come out? It was pissing down, wasn't it?'

'It certainly was. I can't really tell you why I ...' I hesitated and he jumped on it.

'Go on, why can't you tell me?'

'Well, because you wouldn't believe me.'

He looked bemused. 'Of course I will, you dope.'

'You won't, Sidney.'

'Tell me.'

'My father told me to look after you.'

'Fuck off!'

'I knew you wouldn't believe me.'

'How did he tell you? Was it through a medium?'

'No, he was here, by the piano and he told me to take care of you and I felt restless and ill at ease and I wandered into the garden to find you and there you were.'

'Stop taking the piss.'

'That is exactly what happened and, although it sounds like a fairy story, I promise you that's how it was. My tablets, I believe, make me see things that obviously aren't there and although it was disconcerting at first to see my long-departed parents, oddly it is quite comforting sometimes.'

Sidney was staring at me with his mouth open. 'But if your father wasn't really there, how would he know I had collapsed in my garden? I mean, if you were just imagining something that wasn't real, why ... I mean, it doesn't make any sense.'

I gave him a warm smile. 'You are so right. But if I hadn't seen him and he hadn't said that, I wouldn't have come looking for you in the pouring rain. So, believe what you will.'

'Flipping heck, it's never dull in here, is it?'

'I assure you it is.'

'What with your parents and that thing that hovers about in the room and women ...'

'There aren't many women, Sidney. Not nearly as many as you think, I promise you.'

'Huh! In one day, just in one day, there was Nell and ...'

'Thea?'

'Yeah, bloody silly name! Thea, with the jumper with bumps in who was all over you that evening,' he remarked, winking.

'She was not all over me.'

'She most certainly was and I tell you, if I wasn't married and a bit younger ...'

'Well, you are and you aren't, so there's no point in making those observations.'

'Oh I do beg your pardon! Do you know what I reckon?'

'No, but I have an idea you're going to tell me what you reckon, Sidney.'

'I reckon you like Thea much more than you let on.'

'I assure you ...'

'No, I'll change that. I reckon you like her much more than you realise.'

'Ah, yes that's slightly different. But alas, you have the wrong end of the stick, as is quite usual for you.'

'I'm not so sure.'

'I'm not denying she is am extremely attractive woman ...'

'There you go!'

'Let me finish, Sidney. But, as your incredibly instinctive wife remarked, she is too much for me and although the lady in question doesn't think so, she needs a lusty, red-blooded man with all his faculties and all his bits in working order and that most certainly is not me.'

'That's true enough,' he muttered.

'In my life, Nell is all I want and all I need – as a friend. Anything else is beyond me now.'

'But doesn't Nell need a red-blooded, lusty man with all his faculties?' he asked.

'No, Nell doesn't want that.'

He looked aghast. 'Why on earth not at her age?'

'Nell wants someone to love the pilgrim soul in her.'

He rolled his eyes heavenward. 'Oh God, speak bloody English.'

'I believe I was.'

'What does it mean?'

'Someone who understands and loves her and supports her in everything she does and everything she aspires to be. She would forego all else for that.'

Sidney frowned and appeared at a bit of a loss. 'Right, I see, I think.'

'You must see that Thea and I would never fit.'

'If you say so, Benedict, but...'

'I do say so.'

'Well, I suppose that's an end to it then.'

'I think so.'

He grinned impishly. 'Sexy woman though.'

'She may well be,' I shrugged. 'So she needs a sexy man, doesn't she?'

'I suppose you're right, as usual,' he said begrudgingly.

'I don't always want to be right.'

'It's just a knack you have.'

I smiled at him, sitting there with his arms defiantly across his chest and resting on his belly. I could never tell him, in a way that would eloquently describe my feelings, how wonderful it was to have him sitting opposite me, with his dear, indignant face full of fun and various other expressions that were typical of him. I wanted to tell him that I loved him, but wasn't sure his manly emotions could deal with it right then. Instead I asked, 'So, when are you starting your diet then?' and waited for his reaction.

'What diet?' he screeched.

'Quite.'

'Anyone can have diabetes, not just overweight people,' he declared.

'Aha, you're an expert already on your condition.'

'I'll be fine with the wife looking after me, you know that.'

'*My* wife, Sidney...'

'Yeah, whatever you say.'

'I'm sure Sheila will look after you, but I seem to remember being in on a conversation between Sheila and that doctor who looked fifteen, to do with weight loss and high blood pressure and doing what you are told?'

'I don't really remember anything like that ...'

'That's extremely convenient. The doctor recommended ...'

'Oh I don't give a flying fuck! You can't live forever, can you? I'd much rather enjoy myself and have the occasional drink and eat what I fancy. Can you imagine being on a diet with Sheila cooking for me?'

'No, I can't,' I replied, with my firm face on, 'but what does Sheila think?'

He looked a little uncomfortable. 'She said something about cutting down on portions and alcohol, but I really didn't take much notice. You know me, Benedict I'll just eat what the wife gives me.'

'*My* wife, Sidney, *my* wife; will you *ever* get it right?'

'Yeah, yeah, I know, but I can't speak like you.'

'And anyway, what did they say about your heart? What happened with the twenty-four hour ECG thing?'

'Fuck knows, something called ... oh, I can't remember ... ask Sheila. They think it was the heart thing that made me pass out. The quack said something about my heart rate slowing down so much I went flying.'

'It's not serious, is it?'

'Nah, tablets will sort it out. Let's talk about something other than me being in hospital, can we? I want to forget it.'

'Of course we can.'

We sat in silence for a moment while he looked out at my garden. Then he peered intently at me over his glasses, which usually meant a personal question was about to surface. 'So,' he said, 'how's Nell getting on?'

'Wonderfully I believe and Beth is going to see her show, so she'll give me the lowdown on what it was like, as I can't be there. Time seems to be passing so slowly with her away. Do you remember when you were young, how the years dragged until you were twenty-one? And then once you reached adulthood and had the key of the door so to speak, the years passed with ever increasing rapidity.'

'I wish you'd speak like the rest of us mere mortals,' he quipped. 'But yeah, I know what you mean. I can't believe I'm this age. I don't really want to get older, but the alternative isn't much better.'

'That's very true, Sidney and very profound.'

'She'll soon be back, matey. It's summer already.'

'But we have the dark, wet autumn days to get through and then winter's icy hand will be upon us with all its fury ...'

'God help us!' Sidney cried. 'We aren't in one of your bloody plays! If you mean it will be fucking freezing then say so.'

'It will be fucking freezing,' I said.

458

'But once it's fucking freezing, she'll be back.'

'Yes.'

He sighed. 'What shall we chat about now?'

'How the ambulance crew thought we were a couple of ageing queens?'

'You *what*?'

After Sidney had left a little later in response to a resounding knock from Sheila, I felt restless and bored and I could no longer sit and look at my four walls, however much I knew Nell loved them. Describing to him how long it was before I saw her again had sent my mood heading downwards at speed and I longed for nature and beauty. It was a bright, cloudless day and the mass of trees in the park with their fresh and pure green leaves looked highly inviting. I locked up quickly and despite my shaky legs and aching back and shoulders, I made my way gingerly across the road and through the gate. On such a beautiful day the park was teeming with people. There were the perennial tourists studying maps, runners, bikers, students with rucksacks slung on their backs, little children running around and dogs playing together as their owners chatted. All human life gathered there and it lifted my spirits. I had often taken refuge there with Beth in the days when my marriage was floundering and in its death throes. I had walked her little legs off simply to stay out of the house as long as I could, pushed her on the swings and taken her on the boating pond and inevitably to the ducks where I would watch as she threw chunks of bread at them with all her might. Now, when walking on my own my thoughts were mostly for Nell, who had opened my eyes to so much in life when I had been deep in reflection about my diagnosis.

Summer was in full bloom and the searing hot sun was high in the sky. I struggled up the hill where Nell had encouraged me to walk and dance and then past the tennis courts where fit young people were throwing their able limbs around in pursuit of flying tennis balls and I envied them their grace and athleticism and their health. Our café came into view and I felt a sharp pang of missing her that manifested itself in my having to take a few deep breaths. My legs were trembling, unsure and heavy and my upper back and shoulders ached like hell, but I hoped the warm sun might melt into me and make them easier in some way.

I rested under General Wolfe and watched the gaggle of tourists queuing outside the Observatory. The city spread before me and the strong sunlight was kissing the grey river and making it sparkle. There was the usual buzz of laughter and conversation from the crowds, but without Nell to share any experience it all felt hollow. I knew summer would soon fly and the autumn months would be upon us with its hazy sunshine, falling leaves and cooling winds and I wondered what Nell would look like in autumn with a golden glow shining across her face. She wouldn't be back until winter and it seemed an interminable time until then. I knew I couldn't afford to wish my life away, but I was. I couldn't bear my feelings of isolation for one more second, so I stood up and without thinking clearly I ambled slowly towards the spot where Nell had made me dance in the snow. It didn't occur to me that people would think me insane. I just needed to feel near to her. I needed to recreate the feeling of intense happiness and freedom I had experienced in those few moments.

I fixed my eyes on the Queen's House below and the sweep of the grass before it, to enable me to keep my balance and I spread my arms wide. I then moved my disobedient legs as Nell had shown me, tapping my feet and swaying gently from side to side. I attempted a slight, theatrical flourish and some airy fairy arm waving that reminded me of washing hanging on a line on a windy day, but I didn't care. Nell had taught me to dance and I would dance! To my relief, it did indeed bring back the feelings I was chasing, of being completely in the moment and free from my turbulent thoughts for just a couple of minutes.

I heard some laughter from a group of Japanese tourists, but it wasn't unkind laughter because they were clapping and cheering and urging me on. There were no derisory comments either from others close by, although a couple of faces appeared to be rather surprised and perplexed and they obviously wondered about my sanity. I even heard, 'Go for it, man,' from a cheerful American who was snapping away with his expensive camera. I gave a little bow and the small crowd dispersed instantly, as if I had given them a few seconds of entertainment that didn't last, not only in that moment, but in their memories also. I then wandered back to my seat under the statue, feeling elated that I had managed, not only to stay upright, but also because I had been taught by Nell and I had done her proud. I imagined telling her, watching a smile slowly spread across her face and hearing her unmistakeable laugh.

As I was deep in thought something to my right caught my eye. I'm not sure why I looked up; I just had the oddest feeling that someone was still watching me and I suspected it might be the dreaded *presence* hovering nearby. But Thea was standing near the fence in a tight-fitting flowery dress that skimmed her knees and she looked years younger. Her dark red hair was longer and tucked behind her ears and she had huge sunglasses on. She waved tentatively and I instinctively beckoned to her. It seemed ridiculous not to. She came bounding over with the enthusiasm of an excited young girl.

'Hello, Benedict,' she gasped, 'I didn't know whether to come over when I saw you.'

I patted the bench beside me. 'Sit down, please. I'm delighted to see you, Thea.'

She impulsively leant towards me, planted a firm kiss on my cheek and sat back to study me. 'How have you been? If that display was anything to go by, I'd say you were feeling much more yourself. I couldn't quite believe it when I saw it was you. I didn't have dancing in public down as your kind of thing.'

'I was taught by a natural,' I replied, 'and I just felt like doing it, so I did. It's very good for my balance. I'm fine, thank you. And you?'

'Very well, thank you,' she gushed. 'What a glorious day! I'm not surprised you felt like dancing. I love this time of year. I come alive in this weather.'

'You seem to be pretty much alive in all weathers to me,' I remarked.

'Do I? I'm surprised, as this is my favourite time when everything is blooming with colour. It all seems to energise me.'

'I like the snow,' I told her, thinking of my first meeting with Nell.

She opened her eyes wide. 'You don't! I'm surprised at that. Normally anyone who has problems with walking and balance hates the snow and ice.'

'I know,' I replied, 'but I love the silence, the clear air, the pureness of the biting wind that makes your face sting.'

'Yes, it is pretty.'

'It's magical.'

She laughed suddenly. 'That's very poetic of you, Benedict.'

I put my nose in the air. 'I thought so.'

'So, what's been happening in your life, apart from learning to dance, that is?'

'I've been helping Sidney rehabilitate by playing cards with him and treating him normally.'

'Why, what's been wrong?'

'He has diabetes and high blood pressure and something wrong with his heart that nobody can remember the name of.'

She appeared concerned. 'That's awful.'

'He passed out cold in his garden for quite a while and gave me and his saintly wife a fright.'

'Poor Sidney,' she said, dropping her voice to a reverential whisper. 'He must be on tablets then.'

'Yes, so he's just like me now; we compare notes and try to outdo each other. What a pair of silly old sods we are.'

She placed a reassuring hand on my arm. 'Neither of you will ever be old.'

'Thank you for that, but we both feel it.'

She fidgeted beside me ever so slightly. 'And how is Nell getting on in America?'

'I suspect she's a triumph,' I replied. 'I looked up her reviews on the internet – took me a while to find them, but find them I did and they were pretty spectacular, as were Matt's, her friend.'

'How exciting, I'm quite envious.'

'Yes, she's waited a long time for this, a very long time. It's a difficult business to be in: competitive and sometimes cruel.'

Thea looked into my face intently. 'And how ...'

'How am I getting on without her?' I cut in.

She put her hand gently on my arm again. 'Sorry, I shouldn't stray onto that tricky subject. We always seem to end up bad friends when I ...'

'Don't worry, I don't mind. To be perfectly honest, I feel empty. There's always something missing and that part is a vital part. But she will be back and then what larks!'

'Do you think ... no, sorry, I won't ask that,' she gabbled, turning her face away.

'Go ahead.'

She studied me, waiting for my reply. 'Do you think you will retain your closeness?'

'I sincerely hope so, but who knows what life will bring. For me, time and distance can't change my feelings. But I can't speak for Nell.'

'I hope you do – retain your closeness, I mean,' she said.

I must have looked surprised. 'You do?'

'Yes, I do. I'm done with masochism. You love her – end of story. But I would still like to be mates and spend time with you, have fun. I think we'd have great fun together.'

'I need fun,' I muttered.

She jumped on my words. 'Does that mean we can see a bit of each other?'

I suddenly felt a great compassion for her and despite recalling Sidney's words about how I felt more for her than I realised, I acted on my compassion.

'I don't see why not.'

Her eyes lit up. 'Fantastic!'

'Well, I'm getting a little slower and more shaky by the month, so what we do will be limited, but tea in my garden tomorrow afternoon would be in order,' I told her.

She gave me a lovely, sincere smile. 'I'd love to.'

'Thea ...' I began, but my voice slurred so badly I had to wait for a few seconds before continuing, 'I can promise you nothing, you know that.'

'I have no expectations,' she said, but her shining eyes belied her words.

I pressed her on it. 'Are you sure?'

She hesitated. 'I'm sure.'

She gave me cause to doubt her sincerity because of the hesitation and her face held a look of deep-seated longing that could not be disguised. Her face and especially her eyes always gave her away.

'Look,' I started, 'I expect you think I'm a fool. I expect you think I'm an ageing man who has been given a diagnosis that makes him want to relive his youth. Perhaps you think it is a cliché for someone like me to adore the youth and vigour of a younger woman. But I assure you it is anything but. It is simply love, that's all.'

'I don't think any of those things now actually,' she said, placing her hand over mine. 'I don't doubt your love for her, but I do doubt her... sorry, I don't doubt she loves you but...'

'Please go on.'

'Look, you are gorgeous and clever and humorous and kind, but I think she is probably attracted to...' She paused and shook her head, adding, 'however, enough of my opinions,' she continued, raising her voice slightly to silence any indignation from me, 'our friendship can still flourish. I think you could probably do with all the support and friendship you can get. What time shall I come?'

'About four, if that's OK,' I replied, deciding against an argument at that time because she appeared so delighted at the mention of having tea together, I felt it would have been churlish.

'See you at four,' she replied, jumping up. 'And now I must dash.' She leant down and planted another firm kiss on my cheek. 'Enjoy the sunshine, Benedict. Oh, shall I bring something? I make a fabulous Victoria sponge cake and you don't need to watch your weight, do you?'

'That would be lovely, if you're sure.'

'Great. I hope I don't drop it on the way round,' she laughed.

'That's my trick. Till then,' I said.

'Till then,' she repeated and I watched her as she walked away, her legs tanned and enviably sturdy.

She left me with so many thoughts racing around in my head. Had I been right to invite her? Could she accept me as a friend without hoping for more? And, more to the point was Sidney right? If I hadn't met Nell, would I be feeling a deeper affection for Thea? But that question was a pretty useless one. I *had* met Nell and she occupied all my heart, no space for any other woman. But what was I thinking? I was infirm, with a chronic illness. Why on earth did I think I had two younger women to choose from? Nell would only ever be a close friend and she would ultimately fall for a younger, more vibrant man. And Thea, although she imagined she wanted a close relationship with me, she would pretty soon get to the point where she would realise what taking on a man with a long term medical condition was like in reality.

'Dream on, Benedict,' I whispered to myself. 'Get a grip and dream on.'

Chapter 18

The next day was a scorcher with burning sunshine and a warm, balmy breeze that felt more like Spain than England. Sidney and I had played cards all morning until he lost so many times he began to complain vociferously.

'What the fuck has happened to my luck today?' he cried.

'It ran out, as luck always does,' I smiled benignly.

'I reckon you're dealing me some dodgy hands,' he declared, eyeing me suspiciously over his glasses.

'How dare you!' I said, trying not to laugh at his continually indignant face.

'Maybe it's the diabetes – done something to my memory.'

'I doubt that, but you never know.'

'Maybe passing out for that long has left me slightly barmy.'

'You seem exactly the same to me, Sidney.' I glanced over at him, but he appeared to completely miss my irony, or chose to ignore it.

'Ah well, I'll get me own back tomorrow. It's so bloody hot,' he sighed, leaning back in his chair.

'I agree. Are you feeling OK? Would you like a cold drink?'

'Not unless you put some Scotch in it,' he muttered, as if Sheila might hear, when in reality she would have needed ears like an elephant to pick up any of our conversation.

'I most certainly will not! You had some Scotch in your coffee and that's enough for today.'

He frowned hard at me before remarking, 'You're getting boring. Don't do that to me. Life wouldn't be worth living if you got boring, Benedict.'

'I have no intention of becoming boring, but your doctor said ...'

'I don't give a flying fuck!' he bellowed.

'Well, you should!' I bellowed back.

He caved in immediately. 'I know, I know; save me the lectures, please.'

'So, would you like a cold drink, without alcohol?'

'No,' he answered, somewhat sulkily.

'That's fine.'

'What's occurring later then?' he asked, changing the subject because he knew he had come up against my stubborn side.

'Very little is happening later, Sidney, as usual.'

'Do you want to come to tea then? Sheila wants me to grill some fish on the barbecue, says it's good for me. I've had so much bloody fish I could swim the channel,' he moaned. 'I'll never drown at this rate, with fish and bloody rabbit food all the time. I'm having salad, salad and more salad.'

'I would, but ...'

'But what?' he asked, sensing I was holding something back.

'Thea is coming round.'

'Oh yeah...'

'Sidney!'

'What's she coming round for then? Or shouldn't I ask?'

'She's coming for tea.'

'I bet she is!'

I had to laugh at his face. It was so superior. 'Will you stop that?'

'She wants more than tea, matey,' he muttered. 'You watch yourself; she'll have you up those stairs in a jiffy.'

I laughed out loud. 'I won't be going up any stairs in a jiffy, as well you know, not with these legs. In fact, I won't be going *anywhere* in a jiffy.'

'I'm telling you, Benedict, it's written all over her face.'

'If that were true, she'd be picking someone hale and hearty, whose blood is coursing round his veins and other parts without any problem. So, we will be having tea on the lawn and that will be all.'

'Oh swipe me, tea on the lawn,' he sniffed, trying to mimic my voice.

'Yes, tea on the lawn and *only* tea on the lawn...'

'Well, I'll be nosing over the fence, I promise you.'

'Sidney, I don't doubt it and I'm deliriously happy that you will be. I really missed you nosing over the fence when you were in hospital.'

'And if you disappear inside with her hot on your heels, am I to come in and rescue you?'

'Yes, please.'

He grinned, 'Will do.'

Thea arrived dead on four in a low-cut, peasant-style top and a long cotton skirt. She looked quite Bohemian, but it suited her. In her hands she held a tin and presented it to me as I opened the door.

'I hope the cake's OK,' she said, her face glowing with health.

'I'm sure it will be, come through.'

'Your walking is changing a bit,' she observed as she followed me into the garden. 'Do you mind me saying that?'

'Not at all, I'd rather everyone was honest with me. I know I now walk like a puppet whose master is permanently drunk.'

'Oh no, you don't.'

'I'm afraid I do.'

'I just thought your legs looked a little stiff.'

'Everything is stiff,' I replied.

'Not everything,' Sidney called over the fence.

Before I could say anything, Thea burst out laughing. She laughed so hard and so infectiously I had to join in, finally managing to say, 'I do apologise for my neighbour.'

'Don't apologise for him, he's a hoot.'

'Sidney, will you please stop ear-wigging behind that fence?'

'No! I find your life so much more interesting than mine,' he declared, looking over at us. 'And you missed me when I wasn't here.'

'It really isn't,' I assured Thea.

'Hello, Thea, nice to see you.'

'Hi, Sidney,' she called, 'how are you now? Benedict said you'd been in hospital.'

Sidney beamed at her. 'I'm absolutely fine, back to normal and getting on Benedict's nerves.'

'His role in life,' I announced cynically.

Thea smiled at him. 'You must have given everyone a fright though.'

'I gave myself a fright too. Mind you, I don't remember much about it except for falling all over the place like a bloody idiot and I couldn't stop myself however hard I tried.'

'That must have been terrifying for you.'

'Weird more like,' he replied. 'But anyway, I'll leave you in peace, shall I?'

'You can join us if you like, Sidney,' I told him.

'Nah, I'm okay, mate. I've got to do our barbecue in a bit.'

'If you're sure...'

'You'll both get our meal wafting over later on.'

Thea smiled. 'I don't mind that.'

'And may I say you are looking particularly lovely today?' Sidney conjured up his most ingratiating smile.

'Why, thank you, Sidney,' she gushed.

'Isn't she looking particularly lovely, Benedict?' he repeated, looking pointedly at me.

'She is,' I slurred, avoiding Thea's eyes. 'Now, I'll bring the tea out, if I can manage it.'

She jumped to her feet. 'I'll help you ...'

'No, no, stay here and enjoy the sun. I like to try and stay independent if I can, but if I find it too hard I'll call you.'

I made a large pot of tea, using the old brown teapot I used on special occasions that my mother had once given me, and cut a slice of her cake for us both. When I picked it all up my hands were shaking hard, but I gritted my teeth, determined to carry it through without any assistance. I gingerly walked out into the garden and placed the tray with great precision on the table between us.

'I have to say, Thea, your cake looks delicious.'

'I hope so.'

'Nell would love it,' I muttered and then I blanched. 'Sorry, did I say that out loud?'

She smiled. 'Yes, you did.'

'I'm sorry, I seem to be doing that lately. It might be the disease. Mind you, I tend to blame everything on Parkinson's. Most of it is probably old age creeping up on me.'

'Does she like cake then?'

'Yes.'

'Well, I suppose at her age and with all the dancing she does, she doesn't have to worry too much about her figure. I only eat something as yummy as this on special occasions.'

'Is this a special occasion then?' I queried as I poured the tea; a little of it spilt in the saucers because of my hands, but neither of us mentioned it.

'Of course,' she declared, her eyes shining with enthusiasm. 'How often do I get to have tea with a distinguished gentleman?'

'I don't know and who is the distinguished gentleman again?'

'You must be aware that you're different from most men,' she said, running her hand through her hair and moving it away from her face in a decidedly flirty manner. 'Very different I'd say.'

'Oh, I wouldn't say that. Although I am *very* different from Sidney,' I laughed, raising my voice so he could hear because I knew he had his ear stuck to the other side of the fence.

'I heard that,' he called out.

'You were meant to.'

Thea gave a throaty laugh. 'You two are like a double act.'

'I don't know if I'm pleased about that or not.'

'You couldn't live without each other,' she added, with a warm smile.

'That's right,' Sidney called, 'he'd be lost without me, wouldn't you, mate?'

'I dare say.'

'You know it's true.'

'Sidney, are you going to be listening to us all afternoon? Thea might not like you eavesdropping.'

'I don't mind – really.'

Sidney's face appeared again and he pretended to look contrite, but it didn't work because he had a twinkle in his eye. 'I'm sorry, Thea. I'm going in now and I won't be back out for a while, so feel free to chat away.'

She laughed, giving him a little wave and he disappeared.

I gave a huge and deliberate sigh, 'Thank God for that.'

'He's delightful, really delightful.'

'He's not so bad,' I said and we were both suddenly aware that we were now alone and an awkward silence replaced the cheerful conversation. I felt my shoulders stiffen a little with embarrassment. I looked across at her, all long, athletic legs and thick, deep-red hair and I knew she had made an effort with her appearance because she had lip gloss on and smelt strongly of perfume.

'Benedict,' she suddenly said, 'I know so little about you really. Tell me a bit about your life.'

'What would you like to know?'

'Well, start with your childhood.'

'Madam, you sound as if you are in your consulting room again.'

'Oh I won't try to analyse you.'

'Is that a promise?'

'Are you afraid of giving too much away?'

'No, I have nothing to hide at this time in my life; much to be sorry for, but nothing to hide.'

She sat forward a little in her chair. 'Where did you live when you were a child?'

'In Sussex, it was idyllic: country lanes, meadows, climbing trees, picnics in endless sunshine. We were, *are*, a happy family. I have one brother and two sisters and our parents were kind and loved each other, that sort of thing. I have no complaints at all about my upbringing. It's just a shame I made such a hash of my so-called grown-up years.'

She frowned slightly and looked hard at me as if she didn't quite believe me. 'You think you made a hash of them then?'

'On the whole, yes.'

'But you have a daughter who no doubt adores you.'

'Yes, luckily for me.'

Thea looked thoughtful and continued, "You know, it's interesting that many people who had parents who were very happily married, feel their own relationships didn't ever quite come up to their parents' relationship; but chasing an ideal is futile because there would have been some difficulties in their marriage, as in all marriages, but you won't have been aware of them.'

'But it does help if you love each other,' I remarked.

'Yes, that's a good starting point,' she said. 'Why did you marry your wife?'

I was surprised by her question, but felt no embarrassment at answering it. I had asked myself the same thing endlessly. 'I don't know is probably the best answer.'

'No, you do know,' she told me. 'You just don't want to admit it.'

'Well, I...'

I felt she was putting me on the spot and I squirmed a little under her intense look. In truth, I felt far more uncomfortable opening up to Thea than I had to Nell and my reluctance to respond, and perhaps a rare facial expression, must have made it plain to Thea that she was being personal.

She put her hand up. 'Sorry, sorry, that's me being too pushy again, but old habits die hard I'm afraid.'

'No, no ... it's ... Well, the honest answer is, it seemed to be the right thing to do at the time. With hindsight, I know I was wrong to marry her, but hindsight is a wonderful thing. We did have strong feelings for each other and she wanted to get married, but we were young and I was shallow and foolish.' I looked down and the hand holding my tea cup was shaking noticeably. 'I suspect if she knew about my Parkinson's then she ... I have no doubt she would consider she had a lucky escape.'

'I'm sure you weren't shallow and foolish. It's just as you've grown older your emotions and actions have matured with you.'

'Yes,' I muttered, grateful for her kind comments, 'you're probably right and then when you find someone who you love without reservation, you realise what you felt before was anything *but* love.'

Thea drank her tea and fiddled with her hair. 'But there are different kinds of love,' she said eventually.

'I'm sure,' I replied, recalling a similar conversation with Nell, 'but an unselfish love is the most meaningful. There is something quite pure and wholly satisfying about forgetting your own needs and putting the other person's feelings first. Unselfish, gentle and kind is what it needs to be for me now. Any other kind of love is not worth having in my situation.'

Thea was unusually silent. I wondered whether I had said too much or been too outspoken. The hot, late afternoon sun was shining on her face and she was squinting slightly, which made her look as if she was watching me with extreme interest.

'You were a teacher weren't you?' she continued, 'English literature wasn't it?'

Before I could reply, Sidney's grinning face suddenly appeared over the fence yet again. 'He was a Professor of English, not just your common-or-garden teacher.'

'Sidney, did I ask you to butt in?'

'*And* he wrote some plays that he got awards for,' he added, rather proudly.

'Sidney!'

'You wrote plays?' she gasped.

'I did, yes,' I admitted reluctantly. 'However, it was a long time ago.'

She looked intrigued. 'And they were performed?'

'Yes.'

'I saw those awards in your living room, but I didn't like to ask ...'

'Clever bugger, isn't he?' Sidney chipped in. 'Mind you, you'd never know sometimes when you have to listen the rubbish he comes out with.'

'Very clever,' she agreed, 'how fascinating.'

I felt a little hot and flustered. 'Well ... I ... not very ...'

'So you were very successful.'

'How do you gauge success?'

'By awards I'd say,' Sidney remarked, still peering over the fence.

'Perhaps,' I muttered.

'Only someone who'd had success could be so blasé about winning awards,' Thea declared. 'You kept all this pretty quiet.'

'He never tells anyone,' Sidney told her.

Suddenly Sheila's voice came ringing out from their house and Sidney duly jumped out of his skin. 'Sidney! Stop nosing over the fence and leave Benedict alone.'

He smiled at Thea. 'That's the wife; always on at me for pestering my long suffering friend.'

'*My* wife, Sidney, *my* wife...

'She's not your wife, she's my wife. Better go. See you in a bit.'

His head disappeared and I shrugged at Thea, in a kind of apologetic way. 'That's my friend Sidney.'

'Back to you hiding your talents,' she said. 'I'd be telling everyone if I had won awards. What a dark horse you are.'

'Am I?'

She crossed her long legs. 'The more I get to know you the more interesting you become.'

I felt strangely uncomfortable. I did not want, in even the smallest way, to add fuel to her fire of desire and admiration for me. 'It was over twenty years ago, Thea. In another life it seems. I don't talk about it because I'm not that man who wrote those plays any more. That man was always out socialising, drinking too much, flirting and being flattered by many unsuitable women and floundering in a sea of loneliness.' At the end of my little speech my voice died away and slurred so much, the last few words sounded unintelligible to my ears. I paused and took a deep breath to gather my thoughts and words. 'I was lonely and unhappy then,' I added, 'so I have no wish to remember those times.'

'So, you're happier now?' she asked, almost as if she was surprised.

'Yes, inside I'm happier.'

She frowned as if she couldn't comprehend how I could be. 'You're happier now, even with the dreaded Parkinson's?'

'Yes, I'd say so.'

'Why?'

A soft, warm breeze blew up from nowhere and trembled through the silver birches at the end of my garden. It made a sound like gentle waves breaking onto the beach. My feelings about my illness were hard to explain to anyone because learning of it on that dismal winter's day led me to sitting alone by the duck pond and chancing upon a wonderful, vibrant young woman who had changed the way I thought about life. The two were interwoven, almost as one and couldn't be separated. To talk of my life with Parkinson's was to talk of my life since meeting Nell, and I wasn't entirely sure it was appropriate to speak like that to Thea. Gathering my thoughts I said simply, 'I'm more at peace with myself; I prefer the man I am now.'

'I'm intrigued,' Thea replied. 'Did you ever think you would say that when you first had your diagnosis?'

'No, that was a low point.'

She gave me a genuine smile. 'I can only imagine.'

'I had suspected something was very wrong though. You do, don't you?'

'Yes, I'd agree with that. It still must have been hard, finding out I mean.'

'It was very isolating. I felt isolated in my own body, like it had let me down. I had abused it for so long as a young man, I really felt indestructible. And of course, I dreaded telling my daughter.'

'Yes, of course.'

'But all of that is behind me and I have to look forward and not dwell on things. It's a glorious day and I still have most of my mental capabilities so hurrah for that!'

She looked crestfallen for a moment. 'It doesn't affect the brain in that way does it?'

'My brain seems fine at the moment. Beth scoured the internet for information, but I'd rather not know. Do you know what the worst symptom is, for me?'

'I'd say the tremors?'

'No, at the moment I can stand them and the tablets are helping. It's the introspection, the obsession with guilt and the obsessive thoughts, the searching for peace.'

She gave a wry smile. 'What guilt? What terrible secrets do you have?'

'There don't have to be any in reality, that's the problem. Some days, I felt guilty about everything I'd ever said or done. But that has improved, maybe because of the pills. But this disease is an integral part of me now. I have it and it is here to stay, so I have to live with it. End of story. The doctors know so little about it and I suspect there isn't much money for research. I feel sometimes as if it's a forgotten illness. There must be so many people out there fighting this and you never get to hear about any of them, except the famous ones. If it had a higher profile with the public then the charities might receive more money.'

Thea brushed something from her cheek that may have been a tear, but I wasn't entirely sure. 'Hearing you speak about it like this, it makes me realise how deeply it affects your life. I think you are all heroes, living with the problems every day. I can see why you call it the forgotten illness,' she whispered, 'and you are all the forgotten heroes.'

I hadn't planned to talk so openly about my Parkinson's, but subconsciously I may have been trying to let her know quite honestly the bare truth about what she believed she wanted to take on. The unintended ploy seemed to have worked because the playful flicking of her hair and crossing and uncrossing of her legs had stopped; she appeared to be genuinely interested in the grisly details of my day-to-day life. Having her close attention I continued in the same vein.

'And I haven't even started on the physical symptoms. They are so varied; apart from the slight tremors there is the occasional staggering, shaking, twitching like a sleeping dog, sudden jerking, fatigue like I've never experienced before, heavy limbs, rigid facial muscles, slurring and the dreaded dribbling. I won't even go into the more personal and intimate problems that strip you of your manhood and all the usual feelings that a man likes to think are part of his nature. But the most incredible part of it all is that you don't even mind about *that* any more. There's too much else to worry about.'

'Perhaps acceptance helps.' Thea said, so quietly I almost didn't hear.

'You may well be right.'

'I'm so sorry, Benedict.'

'Why are you sorry?'

'Because I had no idea ...' she stopped and corrected herself, 'because I had the arrogance to think I knew what having Parkinson's meant and of course I didn't. I really didn't have a clue. It was stupid of me.'

I automatically thought of Nell who did know in every detail because of her life with Joshua. 'Not at all ...'

'No, it was stupid of me. But that's me, jumping in with both feet, like a ship in full sail and blunt as old Harry.'

'Who on earth is old Harry?'

'No idea, but he must have been blunt.'

We both laughed and the atmosphere was easier and more comfortable than it had ever been with her. 'You have no need to be sorry about anything, Thea. Really, you don't. There are many people who live with much worse than this, so I'll shut up. Now, let's have another cup of tea. The sun is going behind those trees which means it must be nearly five and if I'm not very much mistaken, Sidney is behind that fence cooking his fish and listening to every word...'

'Yes, I am,' he called. 'Lovely smell, don't you think?'

'It certainly is,' Thea called back.

His head popped up again. 'Do you both want some? There'll be loads over. You know what the wife is like with food, Benedict.'

'Sidney, it is *my* wife; the chair, the table, the fridge, but *my* wife!'

'Talk about nag,' he laughed. 'I'll have to call you Pegasus.'

Thea looked bemused. 'Pegasus?'

'Yeah, the eternal nag,' Sidney replied. 'Benedict told me that.'

She laughed out loud. 'I haven't a clue what you're talking about, but it sounds funny.'

'So, are you coming in for some tea?' he asked, obviously desperately wanting us to.

Thea looked at me and nodded with a mischievous grin on her face as if she was enjoying herself immensely. I sighed, 'OK, Sidney.'

'Great, break out the old Riesling then, matey. You know the one I like.'

'Are you allowed?'

'Bollocks to being allowed!' he declared. 'The sun is over the yardarm.'

'Sidney, are you swearing again?' Sheila scolded as she appeared carrying two bowls of salad.

'No, love,' he replied, 'as if!'

I motioned for Thea to walk before me through the gate to Sidney's and she turned and smiled. 'I love it here, Benedict. It's such fun.'

'I'm glad,' I answered and I *was* glad to have her there, very glad.

She had to leave just before eight because she had a friend visiting. I offered to see her out, but Sidney suggested she climb over the wall between our two gardens because she had threatened to do it before.

'As I've had three glasses of white wine and I feel quite reckless, I'm going to do just that!' she told us.

'Sidney's only kidding you,' Sheila said, 'don't do it to amuse him.'

'I'm not. I'm doing it to amuse myself,' she replied. 'Stay where you are, Benedict, and don't get up. Thanks for a wonderful few hours all of you. I've so enjoyed it. Please ask me again.'

I felt rather concerned about her climbing the wall. 'Thea, be careful.'

'I'm fit as a fiddle, don't worry. See you all soon.'

We all watched silently as she swayed down the garden. She had drunk a few large glasses of wine and appeared a little unsteady on her feet. She hitched her skirt up, revealing her long, firm legs and clambered over the red brick wall. At the top, sitting astride it, she waved and threw her head back and laughed, like a naughty schoolgirl. She then dropped over the other side into her own garden and was gone. We were all speechless for a few seconds until Sidney whistled through his teeth.

'What a woman!'

'Quite,' I muttered.

The long, light summer's evening was so sticky and close that we stayed outside until ten, when a flame-red sky stretched away from us into the distance. We were sitting in the glow of the candles Sheila had lit earlier and I felt relaxed and comfortable sipping my wine slowly. Sheila took everything inside to clear up while Sidney leant back in his chair.

'Well, it's been nice,' he sighed, 'very nice.'

'It has, Sidney.'

'I can't quite believe I was in a hospital, I feel so well now.'

'I'm glad to hear you say that. But you must do as the doctors tell you.'

'You're a fine one to talk. You kicked against all advice at first.'

'Well, yes but only in a small, pathetic way. I know now I was trying to pretend I didn't have Parkinson's. I was in denial.'

'An evening like this makes you feel lucky to be alive, don't you reckon?'

'I do.'

'I tell you what ...'

I interrupted him quickly, 'If you're going to sing Thea's praises I ...'

He looked bemused. 'How did you know?'

'Because I can tell what you're going to say before you say it.'

'Am I that easy to read?'

'You most certainly are.'

'I was only going to say, she's quite a woman, that's all.'

'I agree.'

He looked surprised. 'You do?'

'I do, yes. Aha, that took the wind out of your sails, didn't it?'

'A bit...'

'But so is Nell, wouldn't *you* agree?'

'Nell's bloody lovely!'

'Well then.'

'What's that got to do with the price of fish? Nell's in America and most probably going to stay there a long time.'

I shook my head at him. 'What of it?'

'Look, matey, see sense. You say yourself she's too young for you and she has never given you any reason to hope for anything more than friendship. You wouldn't want her looking after you either.'

'I'd rather die.'

'And at the bottom of your garden – literally at the bottom of your garden – is an attractive, intelligent woman nearer your age who bloody well wants you, warts and all, or should I say Parkinson's and all? What's the problem?'

'The problem is my heart.'

'Go on,' he urged, frowning.

'When I'm with Thea, my heart is in another place.'

'In America!' he declared. 'And that's a bloody long way!'

'Mileage has nothing to do with it, Sidney.'

He sighed. 'You bloody silly old sod.'

'Yes, Sidney, I agree. And who made you my psychotherapist?'

The long, stifling summer days passed slowly. I would sit in my conservatory with the door and all the windows flung open, dozing in the early afternoon heat, listening to the bees humming and the distant sound of lawnmowers. Sidney would come in most mornings to play cards, or just to annoy me, while Sheila was out shopping and often Thea would call round at about four for tea. Occasionally we would take a stroll in the park across the wide sweep of grass in front of the Queen's House, avoiding the tennis courts, General Wolfe, the café or the duck pond. I have to admit, she grew on me. I didn't realise it was happening at first, it was such a slow, almost invisible thing, but day by day she grew on me. We never spoke of Nell. Many times I went to say her name, but stopped myself in time and eventually it became second nature to speak of everything except her.

Without being reminded of Nell constantly, Thea seemed to blossom in my presence. She appeared relaxed, even more articulate, deep-thinking and extremely caring. She didn't have Nell's sense of living in the moment and her sense of wanting to have fun, but she was great company and funny in different ways. She recounted so many stories about how and when she had embarrassed her stuffed shirt of a husband that I came to appreciate her sense of humour and innate sense of timing enormously. We spent most of our walks together laughing and I felt she was doing me good. I imagined the laughter seeping down into my cells and restoring them slowly. Whenever Thea left after one of our walks, Sidney would appear instantly at my conservatory door with a self-satisfied grin on his face.

'And that look on your face is because?' I would ask.

'I don't know what you mean.'

'It was just a walk, Sidney; just a walk.'

'Like you used to walk with Nell,' he remarked one day.

I felt a sharp stab of pain in my chest and reacted badly. 'What does that mean?'

'It means nothing at all.'

'Sidney,' I exclaimed tersely, 'as you told me very succinctly one day, Thea is a lovely woman of around the same age ...'

'I know! I know! Don't jump out of your pram!'

'She's very good company ...'

'I agree.'

'Chatty ...'

'I agree.'

'Great sense of humour ...'

'I agree.'

'Attractive ...'

'Oh yeah...'

'Sidney!'

'What's your problem then?'

'I haven't got a problem, you have!'

He looked bemused. 'What's my problem?'

'Nell.'

He was at a loss. 'She's not *my* problem, she's *your* problem.'

'She is not my problem,' I declared. 'You said to me, after I've just come in from a walk with Thea, that I used to walk with Nell.'

'Well, you did.'

'And what exactly are you implying?'

'What am I implying?' he asked, wrinkling his nose. 'I'm not sure what I'm implying.'

I gave a big sigh. 'I'm definitely going to be having this conversation till I die.'

'Do you mean, what did I mean?'

'Yes, Sidney, that is exactly what I mean.'

'Well, why can't you talk like normal people?' he cried, raising his voice considerably.

'I'm not normal people,' I yelled back, raising mine even more in frustration.

'You're bloody right there!'

'I like her; I just like her, that's all. She isn't Nell, but she's a good woman, a nice woman.'

'Oh dear,' he sighed.

'What do you mean by "Oh dear"?'

He crossed his arms defiantly across his chest. 'Look, what are you going to do?'

'Sidney, I have no idea. I never expected to feel so much for her.'

'Oh Christ...'

'But it shouldn't be a problem to like someone. How did we get into this? I never get a straight answer out of you.'

'That's because I don't understand a flipping word you say half the time.'

'Let's talk about something else, shall we?'

'Fine, fine,' he muttered. 'But she's a lovely woman, Benedict.'

I gazed out of my conservatory towards Thea's house. The tall trees were swaying gently and as they moved, her upstairs windows could just be seen. 'But, Nell ... my sweet girl,' I whispered.

'Think on this,' Sidney continued, obviously unaware of my last comments, 'you have a wonderful lady who is nearer your age who adores you, shakes and all. You have no idea how Nell feels.'

'Sidney, I seem to remember you telling me that you thought she felt the same. That Sheila said there was this incredible electricity between us, do you remember all that?'

'Yeah, course I do and I stand by that, but is she ever going to take you on?' he asked. 'Sorry to be harsh, mate.'

'I don't know why I'm discussing this because I don't want her to take me on as you so succinctly put it.'

'Well, there's no problem with you and Thea then, is there?' he announced, looking pleased with himself. 'Don't reject someone who could make you happy.'

'Sidney ...'

'Do you really love Nell, or is it a bit of a geriatric infatuation?'

'Geriatric! Look, I know what everyone must think, older man after a young bit of skirt, age-old story, pathetic and unsavoury, but it isn't like that, never has been.'

Sidney looked suitably hurt. 'I've never thought that. I'd never call you a dirty old man or anything of the sort like a lecherous old git or an old reprobate or roué or...'

'Yes, thank you Sidney, enough. I believe you did call me a roué once.'

'What is a roué anyway?'

'I'm not entirely sure of the correct definition, but suffice to say it is someone of dubious character in many ways.'

He laughed. 'Sounds more like me.'

'My feelings for Nell are love in the purest sense,' I continued, desperate to clear my thoughts. 'They have to be pure, I have no other feelings. Everything was clear I ... I just didn't expect to have such strong feelings for Thea and I don't want to hurt her.'

'Why do you have to hurt her?' he asked, frowning.

'Because, I suspect she wants more from me than I can give and I love Nell and it wouldn't be right, be fair, to lead her on when I love another woman.'

He smiled fondly at me. 'Benedict, you think too much!'

'Yes, perhaps I do, but I've made so many mistakes with women and at this stage in my life I don't want to get anything else wrong.'

'Fair enough,' he sighed, 'what a to-do, eh? Who'd have thought it? Parkinson's and all that, but two women coming round and all that sexual tension...'

'Not from me.'

'I can't tell you what to do and Nell is adorable, it's just that ...' he paused, obviously wondering whether to continue or not.

'Go on.'

'Well, she *is* young and chances are she'll go for a younger bloke and ...'

'Why wouldn't she?' I declared. 'As you say, she's adorable and could have anyone she wants. No doubt about that.'

'So, what are you going to say to Thea then?'

'I don't know is the honest answer.'

'Silly old sod,' he muttered.

'Yes, Sidney, I'm a silly old sod; I agree.'

We left the conversation at that because we seemed to be going round and round in circles and I thought it hopeless anyway because it was all immaterial. Nell was my dear friend who would find a young, fit, dynamic man to love and I would stand aside and adore her from afar, hoping that the man she would ultimately choose would allow our friendship to remain close.

Later that week Nell's face appeared on the screen before me. She looked tired and out of sorts, not her usual sparkling self.

'Hi, Mr Marshall, how are you?' she asked, waving.

'I'm fine; and you?'

'Knackered to be honest,' she said. 'Mind you, I've been burning the candle at both ends. There have been quite a few parties recently.'

'Well, you're young,' I started to say, but my face stiffened and nothing more would come out.

'I'm not that young any more. Parties aren't really my scene now. But how are you?' She moved nearer to the screen. 'It's hard to tell with those glasses that keep slipping down your nose, but you look a bit down.'

'No, not down, just tired. It's just the wretched disease.'

She frowned and stared hard at me, as if trying to discern the truth by scrutinising my face. 'Are you sure?'

I hesitated. 'Yes, I'm sure.'

'What have you been doing? Tell me all.'

'I've been doing very little, Nell, just the usual.' My voice was flat and falling away at the end of the sentence with nerves because I wasn't being entirely honest with her and that made my heart bleed. 'Time seems to trudge on.'

She was still watching me closely and there was a sudden barrier between us, invisible but distinctly touchable. 'How's Sidney?'

'He's Sidney,' I replied, avoiding the truth and I wondered what on earth had happened to me, to us. Before she left I would have poured out my heart to her about Sidney being unwell. 'But let's talk about you, Nell. Is it all you thought it would be?'

'What, being in the show or in New York?'

'I mean being a success.'

'Oh that,' she said airily, as if she hadn't given it a moment's thought, 'I don't know. If you mean do I feel any different? No, I don't. It's great to be appreciated and we get standing ovations every night, so that's lovely.'

'It must be; and what of Matt?'

Her face fell. 'He's hanging on in there, but only just. I've never known anyone drink so much and still perform so well.'

I felt some sympathy for the brilliant, vulnerable Matt. 'Perhaps he needs to drink to perform like that every night.'

She gave a small smile. 'You know, you could be right. Real life, the day-to-day monotony of it is death to him.'

'Then that's why he drinks, or one of the reasons he drinks, to escape normal life. Normal life, for him, is unbearable for whatever reason. I drank to escape when I was younger.'

'But it's so frustrating to watch.'

'I know, Nell. I do understand.'

'But he's got such an awe-inspiring talent.'

'It's difficult.'

'But hey,' she shrugged, 'maybe he'll last the whole run. He's full of surprises.'

'I hope he does.'

There was a moment's silence as she stared into space, but then she gave an unexpected smile. 'Have you been out at all?'

'Out,' I repeated, in an airy-fairy way. 'Yes, a few walks in the park ...'

'On your own?' she cried. 'I am surprised.'

I slurred badly as I went to answer. 'No. Well, actually, I sometimes walked on my own, but a couple of times with Thea.'

She looked surprised. 'You've been out walking with Thea? Oh, that's ... great.'

'Do you think so, Nell? Yes, it was pleasant, she's good company, if a little full on.'

Nell was scrutinising my face again. 'But she's nice.'

'She is, yes and quite funny too, but ...'

She was staring into the camera and when I broke off urged, 'But what, Mr Marshall?'

I was trying to say that I would always rather walk, laugh and dance with the free spirit that was Nell, but somehow that seemed unfair and unkind to Thea after all her trouble, so I said nothing and just felt my hands trembling violently and my heart thumping hard. Nell was tilting her head as if trying to get inside my head to work out what I wanted to say.

'It's so good to see you, Nell,' I slurred, at last.

'I think you like her more than you realise,' she murmured.

'I ... well ...'

She gave a hesitant smile. 'It's fine to like her, Mr Marshall.'

'Yes and I do like her, she's a lovely person, but ...'

'That's good.'

We stared blankly at each other, both seemingly lost for words. I hadn't wanted the conversation to take this turn, but Nell had obviously read something in my face, despite its rigidity. I suddenly jerked violently, completely out of control and then jerked again even harder. So hard I almost fell backwards off my chair and my glasses shot forward down my nose. I heard her gasp.

'Are you OK?'

'Yes, I'm fine, just a tremor.'

She looked horrified. 'But I've never seen you jerk like that.'

'No, just a huge one, I fear.'

'It looked awful, did it hurt?' As I nodded, my stiff mouth unable to form any words, she whispered, 'Dear God, are you getting worse?'

'No, no, it just happens occasionally,' I replied, pushing my glasses back. 'The symptoms are actually much better, more controlled.'

'I'll let you go, you look shattered.'

I nodded again and spluttered. 'OK, Nell.'

Her face was ashen. 'Take care of yourself, won't you?'

'I will and you, Nell, you take care of you.'

She smiled, but it wasn't a full-on, dazzling Nell smile which lit up a room, the world and my humdrum life like a flashlight. But for a moment we were back on track with that warm, loving feeling between us and I wished she was in the same room with me for real and not just on a screen.

'Speak soon, Mr Marshall.'

'I hope so, Nell.'

She waved. 'Bye then.'

'Goodbye.'

She reached forward and turned off the connection and I was left with my drawn, stiff reflection staring back at me from the black screen. I whispered, 'Goodbye, my darling,' and then berated myself harshly. 'Jesus Christ,' I muttered savagely, spitting it through my gritted teeth. 'You bloody idiot! What the hell is wrong with you?'

I put my head in my trembling hands and felt the tremors coursing through my body like ripples of water on a flat, calm sea. Nell, my dear, dear girl has appeared slightly withdrawn, not herself at all, a little down and I could have sparkled and pretended for her to lift her spirits. But no, what did I do? I had to mention Thea! Why hadn't I asked more about what was going on in her life and how she was feeling? I could have asked so many questions, made her laugh, been more like my old self, but no! I had to mention my walks with Thea for God's sake. What was wrong with me? Had I stayed mentally and emotionally at sixteen? Had I learnt nothing in all those years of silly mistakes? Where was her life-affirming smile? And the canon-fire blast of laughter that could silence a room? I had to Skype her back. What time was it there? Was she just about to go on stage? I hadn't even asked. My hands jerked again, causing a sudden surge of anger and I stumbled to the sofa and collapsed. The *presence* was very near, haunting me and I glared at it, wherever it was, whatever it was and threw a cushion vaguely in its direction. I just aimed blindly because I could never quite place the cursed thing and knocked over my favourite lamp that Beth had once bought me. I wanted to move to pick it up, but my legs felt like jelly and so I stayed where I was and the lamp stayed where *it* was on the floor, on its side, mocking me.

What had Nell meant about it being OK for me to like Thea? Was she carefully and subtly guiding me into Thea's arms? Is that what she wanted? My eyes were heavy and sore and my head full of cotton wool. I slipped into a light doze where pictures of Nell, with her hand firmly in the small of my back pushing me gently towards a smiling woman with red hair, swarmed around in bright colours. I was stumbling forward and fell into Thea's open arms. I felt safe and cared for and not unhappy, but when I turned to look at Nell she was crying silently and I started to shake uncontrollably and fought to get back to her. Three times the same dream haunted me until I woke with such a start I almost fell off the sofa and my whole body was bathed in a hot sweat. The *presence* was gone, but in its place was a beautiful, hazel-eyed cat sitting on top of my piano staring unblinking at me.

Chapter 19

'Sidney, I'm now seeing cats!'

His face was suitably perplexed. 'Seeing cats? What cats?'

'I don't know what cats; I mean cat. There was just one large, fluffy-haired, hazel-eyed cat, sitting over there. Bit of a wild looking thing.'

'Perhaps you let it in by mistake.'

'I did not!'

'Is this one of your...you know ...'

He was looking at me with such a doubtful expression on his face I almost laughed out loud but I simply nodded, 'Hallucinations? I think so, yes.'

'Fuck me, Benedict, whatever next?'

'I don't know.'

'But why did you see a cat? I can understand you wanting to see your old Pa, but a cat?'

'I'm as perplexed as you.'

'Go and see the quack again, eh?'

'What's the point? To be told I'm having more hallucinations? I know it wasn't real, I'm just trying to work out *why* I saw a cat.'

'Do you hate cats?' he asked, eager to help.

'No, I like animals of all kinds, especially ducks,' I replied, thinking of Beth and Nell.

Sydney looked blank. 'Ducks?'

'It doesn't matter, Sidney.'

'Well, I suppose seeing a cat is harmless enough. If ever you see an angel, then you need to worry.'

I laughed. 'Sidney, you do me good, do you know that?'

He preened. 'Thanks, matey, how about a drop of the hard stuff?'

'No.'

'Oh come on, Benedict, don't get boring at this stage in your life. I couldn't bear that.'

'You shouldn't be drinking and I have enough on my plate seeing dead relatives and cats without adding to the problem,' I remarked, trying not to be swayed by his forlorn face. 'And I hope never to become boring, as boring is unforgivable in my book, as you well know.

'And mine!'

'I can't just give you alcohol willy-nilly because of your blood sugars.'

'Fuck the blood sugars!'

'Right, now that's out the way, what shall we discuss on this fine morning?'

'Magnanimosity!' he declared loudly.

'What, Sidney?'

'Another long word I heard on Radio Four, so I thought I'd share it with you.'

'How very kind; what does it mean?'

'I thought you'd know.'

'It's absolutely no good spouting off these various words if you have no idea what they mean because one day you'll be in company and hold forth and some bright spark will challenge you.'

He laughed. 'I don't give a flying fuck.'

'That's eloquent as usual and actually I think you mean magnanimously, my dear friend.'

'Well, it was something similar,' he said, his voice trailing off at the end of the sentence, as if his thoughts had run on to some other topic. He stood by my window and looked out over my garden. I had the feeling he wanted to talk about something because he always fidgeted when worried and he was fidgeting now. 'Lovely day for it,' he commented.

'It is,' I replied, 'whatever *it* is. Would you like coffee or tea?'

He appeared preoccupied. 'Oh I don't mind, whatever you want, matey.'

'Sidney, is there something on your mind?'

'Why do you say that?'

'I can sense something in you bursting to come out. I have known you a long time now. Your face and your demeanour are like an open book to me.'

He turned to look at me. 'Are they?'

'Yes.'

'Well ...'

'Go on, spit it out.'

He sat down opposite me on his favourite chair. 'I don't think I'm right,' he muttered.

'You don't think you're right about what?'

He frowned. 'What?'

'You don't think you're right about what?' I repeated.

'What are you on about?'

'I don't know what I'm on about because I don't know what *you're* on about,' I smiled benignly.

'You're a silly bugger!'

'I don't doubt it, but you aren't making much sense. Please rephrase what you said in a way that I can decipher.'

'There's something wrong with me. I'm not right.'

The penny dropped. 'Aha, I see what you mean. OK, so what's not right with you exactly?'

He looked bemused. 'How the fuck would I know, I'm not a doctor.'

'But what makes you think something is wrong? Give me a clue.'

He looked troubled, not himself. 'Lots of things; I don't know ...'

'Do you mean to do with the diabetes or the heart problem?'

'I don't know,' he repeated and shrugged. 'I just don't feel right.'

I scrutinised his dear, flushed face. He did appear older suddenly and more drawn around his eyes, but other than that he seemed to be the same old Sidney I had always loved and admired.

'Well,' I said firmly, 'we have to do something about this.'

'Don't say anything to the wife ...'

'*My* wife,' I cried. Concerned by his admission I suddenly felt unreasonably rattled with him. 'For once in your life say *my* wife, not *the* wife.'

He looked exasperated with me. 'Oh what the fuck does it matter?'

'Because it sounds like you're lumping her in with the furniture. That's how you refer to furniture, Sidney, not your dearly beloved, saintly wife.'

He frowned at me because he didn't understand where *my* exasperation had sprung from. 'Don't get on your high horse about it, Benedict. It's only a way of speaking.'

'I'm sorry, forgive me, please. I'm just worried about you. You haven't ever said you don't feel right in all the years I've known you, not even before your collapse ...'

'Passing out, not collapse,' he interrupted.

'Yes, of course, passing out. But back to how you feel. Describe it to me, your symptoms.'

'Oh they're quite vague really. My memory isn't what it was, but that could be age.'

'Yes, that's true.'

'My balance is naff sometimes.'

'Naff? Be more explicit please.'

'My balance is poor, like yours is.'

'Oh dear, we can't have two of us falling about the place, it wouldn't look good, would it?'

He laughed. 'And that's without a few glasses of your finest.'

'Should your face be flushed like it is all the time?'

'I've always looked like this,' he remarked. 'I can't help looking like this any more than you can help looking like that!'

'Like what?'

'Like that,' he stabbed a finger at me in the air, 'all bony and white.'

'I didn't know I looked all bony and white. I thought I was devastatingly attractive.'

'Ha bloody ha! No, my face just has a high colour, that's all.'

'That might be the high blood pressure, but the tablets will alter all that. Tell Sheila,' I urged. 'That's the best advice I can give you; tell Sheila and leave it in her capable hands.'

'Oh she'll panic and get me to the quack so sharp my feet won't touch the ground.'

'Of course she will and you should thank God for her, Sidney.'

'The thing is ...'

'Yes?'

He looked down at his hands resting in his lap. 'Well, the thing is, I'm scared, Benedict. I've never been ill in my life and I'm scared.'

I was going to say something flippant, something sarcastic, something crass, but his craggy, lived-in, honest face had changed and he appeared intensely vulnerable and childlike.

'I understand, my friend,' I said.

He gave a small smile. 'I knew you would.'

I held out my hand. 'I'm scared too. Let's be scared together, shall we?'

He took my hand in his and squeezed it hard. 'I'd like that,' he murmured.

'Then we will.'

He opened his mouth to answer me, but my door bell rang and we looked at each other blankly. 'Who the fuck's that?' he asked, instantly back to his normal self.

'I haven't got X-ray vision, Sidney, so I have no idea and do you have to use the word *fuck* as a noun, a verb, an adverb, an adjective ...'

'Shut the fuck up.'

'I rest my case and I'll answer the door, shall I?'

His eyes were glinting with mischief. 'I bet it's the lovely Thea with a low cut top on!'

'Sidney, shut the fuck up!'

He burst out laughing and his belly wobbled up and down alarmingly as I struggled to the front door. When I opened it, Thea stood before me in a tight, bright yellow summer dress that didn't even reach her knees and displayed a large expanse of chest and I almost lost control as I anticipated Sidney's face and had to subdue the laughter storming up my throat. It crossed my mind that we were no better than school boys sniggering together over something titillating, but I suddenly didn't care. We both needed, occasionally, to act the fool in order to lighten our lives a little. I would never have let Thea know though.

'You OK, Benedict?' she asked, bemused.

I shrugged. 'It's just Sidney.'

'Making you laugh again?' she offered, 'what a great friend to have.'

I pulled myself together, immediately feeling a little guilty. 'He certainly is and I wouldn't swap him for all the tea in China. Please come in.'

I stood aside and she placed her hands on my shoulders, reached up and planted a kiss on my cheek as she passed by me, 'Thanks. Shall I go through?'

'Please do.'

Sidney's face was quite the picture of self-satisfied amusement and delight when he caught sight of my guest walking casually through to the conservatory in her tight-fitting dress. 'Aha, I said it was you,' he cried, grinning.

'And you were right. How are you, Sidney?'

'Desperate for a drink, but Benedict is becoming boring in his old age, aren't you, mate?'

'Guilty as charged,' I said. 'Thea, do sit down, I'll get us all some coffee. Chat to Sidney, if you can bear it.'

'I'd love to talk to Sidney.'

'Thanks, *I'm* not getting boring, I can promise you that.'

'I'm pleased to hear it.'

Just as she finished speaking the doorbell rang again. 'It can't be Nell,' Sidney remarked.

'Why would it be?' I asked, so exasperated with him for the comment and for not making the effort to get up and open the door, I said a little brusquely, 'I'll get it, shall I, Sidney?'

'It is your front door, matey,' he retorted.

I made my painful way through the hall and flung the door open. My sister was standing there with her briefcase in her hand. I stared blankly at her and she arched her eyebrows at me.

'Hello, Benedict. I have half an hour to spare before making my way to a meeting in town so I thought I'd pay my favourite brother a visit.'

'Bethan, how lovely ...'

'Is it convenient? Well, it doesn't matter because I'm coming in anyway,' she said, her mouth twisting in its usual, unusual way.

'Well, I do have company ...'

She swept by me. 'Not the young actress!'

My heart began thumping with indignation. 'The young actress, whose name is Nell, as you well know, is in New York being the wonderful success I always knew she would be.'

Bethan eyed me coolly. 'And you're heartbroken no doubt.'

'I most certainly am not! I couldn't be more proud of her.'

She reached up and took hold of my face in her hand. Her fingers held on tightly to my cheeks and I felt my muscles twitch. 'You can't fool me, Benedict. You always were an emotional wreck where the female form is concerned. But I love you, dear brother, none the less.'

'I'm honoured.'

'Don't be sarcastic. So,' she said loudly as she strode through my house and into the conservatory, 'who have we here?'

On Bethan's determined entrance, Thea jumped up and wriggled her dress down. When she'd sat down to chat to Sidney, the dress's extremely tight fit had ensured that the skirt had ridden halfway up her thighs, to his obvious delight. Bethan was silent for a few seconds while she surveyed the scene before her and Sidney sat with arms folded, enjoying the occasion enormously. I hovered behind my sister, my mouth stuck and my hands shaking furiously.

I finally found my voice, 'Thea, this is my sister, Bethan; Bethan, this is a friend of mine: Dorothea.'

'Thea will do, Benedict. Dorothea is such a bloody mouthful, don't you think so?'

'I do think so,' my sister replied curtly.

'Would you like coffee, dear sister?' I asked, feeling absurdly uncomfortable.

'Please. How are things with you, Sidney?'

He beamed. 'I couldn't be better at this moment actually. I love it here, it's never dull.'

'I assure you it is,' I corrected him, retreating to the safety of the kitchen.

I made a pot of coffee for all of us and I could hear Sidney holding forth. Good old, reliable, solid, ever-faithful Sidney who could fill the most awkward silences with his nonsensical chatter. My hands were trembling so violently I could hardly pick up the boiling kettle and I swayed noticeably as if I was drunk. My brain felt scrambled suddenly and I tried to centre my thoughts on Nell's unforgettable face, and in my mind heard her say, 'Lean on me, Mr Marshall.'

'I will, Nell,' I muttered to myself.

A harsh voice cut through my daydreaming instantly. 'What are you doing, Benedict?' Bethan was standing in the doorway, frowning so hard there were two deep lines between her eyebrows that looked as if they had been carved with a knife.

Startled, I staggered forward, losing my balance and hanging on to the fridge, 'Sorry ... I was just ...'

'Jesus Christ! Is that how bad it is now?'

'No, it's fine, well ... sometimes. I was in a dream. You made me jump.'

'I'm sorry, steady yourself on me.'

She stood next to me and put her arm around my waist. She felt strong, unflinching and steady as a rock. Her lined face, heavily made up and normally as hard as flint, was softer suddenly and she looked entirely different. I leant on her gently. 'You looked like you did when you were twelve then.'

'You don't!' she retorted. 'You look ninety.'

'You're too kind.'

'Are you OK now?'

'Yes, yes – fine.'

She let me go and I held on to one of my kitchen cupboards, but she was scrutinising my face so intently I almost squirmed. 'So, who is the sexy redhead in your conservatory?'

'I, well, it's ... she's...' I gabbled hopelessly.

'Honestly, Benedict!' she said in a stage whisper. 'Where do you find them?'

'I don't,' I whispered back. 'They find me. She's just a neighbour.'

She arched her eyebrows again. 'Just a neighbour coming round dressed like that?'

I feigned ignorance. 'Dressed like what?'

'That dress is so tight she must have poured herself into it. Don't pretend you haven't noticed. I mean, who goes around tarted up like that in the daytime?'

'What an awful expression. That's hardly fair, is it?'

'Well, she's not trying to impress Sidney, is she?'

'She's not trying to impress anyone, she always dresses like that.'

'You *are* kidding!'

'I assure you I'm not.'

'Mind you, she's nearer your age,' she remarked pointedly.

'How did I know you were going to say that?' I sighed.

'Does she know about ...?'

'Nell?'

'No, I meant the Parkinson's, you idiot!'

'Of course, why wouldn't she? Christ, she'd have to be blind not to notice my symptoms now.'

Bethan's eyes softened a little. 'That's true, poor brother. Your walking has deteriorated a little bit if I'm honest ...'

'Try not to be honest. I don't feel up to your brutal honesty at the moment.'

'It hasn't deteriorated much, just a little and it's not the stagger, it's the floppiness of it,' she added, oblivious to how her words might be affecting me. 'But your face doesn't look quite as rigid as it did at your party.'

'I'm grateful for small mercies.'

She took another glance into the conservatory where Sidney and Thea were happily chatting and then turned to look at me again. 'Nearer your age but ...'

'Do go on, dear sister,' I told her, '*please* don't hold back.'

She shook her head. 'No, I'm not sure I ought to say this.'

'Probably not, but I'm sure you will.'

'A bit ... lusty is probably the word.'

'Yes, it probably is the word.'

'So why is she after you, for God's sake?' she asked. 'It's quite absurd

492

and why are you smiling like that?'

'Ah, Bethan,' I sighed. 'You never change, do you?'

'What's that supposed to mean? And you haven't answered the question, Benedict.'

'No, Your Honour, I'm sorry. I have absolutely no idea why she's after me because as you imply, there would be no lustiness from this quarter.'

'She'd be all over you like a rash I've no doubt. Mind you, if she lives round here she's not short of money so you don't have to worry that she's ...'

'After my house...'

'Quite!'

'Like Nell is...'

'Quite!'

'Carry the coffee in for me if you will and you can decide for yourself what type of person my guest is.'

'Oh now you've got the hump with me just because the actress has been mentioned. You silly old bugger,' she scolded, taking the tray and walking purposefully through to the conservatory.

'About time too,' Sidney cried. 'I thought you'd gone to Brazil for the coffee.'

'Benedict and I were just having a little chat.'

Sidney chuckled. 'I can imagine.'

'So, Thea, what do you do?' Bethan asked immediately, as I knew she would.

'Not much really,' Thea replied, unaware that she was about to be interrogated. 'I do a bit of part-time work in the local book shop; more for the social aspect than for any other reason. The money's crap, but hey ho! I'm semi-retired I suppose.'

'Aren't you a bit young for retirement?' my sister commented. 'You must be a similar age to me. I couldn't possibly retire.'

Thea nodded. 'But everyone's different, aren't they? I'd had enough of my chosen profession.'

There was a moment's silence where I thought Bethan would ask what her chosen profession was, but she didn't. Sidney was grinning foolishly, savouring every second of my discomfort and Thea suddenly gave me an almost conspiratorial wink which Bethan missed as she poured the coffee. I sat back and relaxed, knowing that my flame-haired friend was going to be a match for my sister in a quiet, polite, psychologist way.

'Bethan, have you heard from William?' I asked, steering the conversation in another direction, 'or from Sarah?'

'No, not for a few weeks, but then I don't call them. I'm just too busy. I spoke to Beth the other day though.'

The mention of my daughter's name perked me up somewhat. 'How lovely for you, how was she?'

'Fine,' she replied. 'She'd been to pick up the tickets from your little friend at the theatre.'

'Oh yes, of course.'

Bethan leant back with her coffee cup near her mouth. 'She said she'd been crying.'

My stomach lurched. 'Beth had been crying?'

'No, Beth wasn't crying, don't be daft,' she laughed.

My heart was now beating furiously. 'Nell had been crying?'

'That's what she said.'

'Why was Nell crying?'

Bethan gave me one of her imperious courtroom looks. 'How the hell would I know?'

The room was unexpectedly silent except for a lone song thrush singing its heart out nearby. The hot sunlight was shining across Bethan's face, highlighting the deep lines around her mouth and making her appear cruel. I felt a slight tension coming from Thea on my left and I knew she was looking at me, as was Sidney.

'She never cries,' I muttered, my voice sliding away into nothing.

I felt Thea's hand on my arm. 'Perhaps she's exhausted, Benedict. I'm sure being on Broadway is glamorous and exciting and all that, but it must be pretty tiring when you have to give your best performance every single night.'

'Yes, maybe ...'

'And I expect it's quite competitive too,' she added. 'We all have our down days, don't we?'

I turned to look at her and her eyes were full of concern and kindness for me. I was suddenly grateful she was there as an antidote to my sister's brittle nature and also immensely thankful she was my friend.

'She's probably a bit homesick too,' Sidney suggested, 'who wouldn't be? All those miles away from your family and friends, I'd bloody hate it.'

'Yes but that's what they do, isn't it?' Bethan insisted. 'They have to go where the work is. No point longing for a part and then being upset it's in

New York. She's lucky to be working and New York is a fabulous place.'

'It's not luck,' I mumbled, my mouth not moving properly. 'It is talent and hard work and sweat and tears and an endless round of soulless auditions and rejections. That's the reality of it. You couldn't be in that business unless you had to be.'

Silence again until Bethan sighed. 'Well, sorry to have mentioned it, but I thought you would want to know, knowing how you feel about her. I thought you might like to give her a ring, check up on her.'

'He'll Skype her, won't you, mate?' Sidney declared as if he knew what he was talking about and trying to lighten the atmosphere. 'It's dead clever stuff all that Skype business and science fiction to boot.'

'Yes, I'll Skype.'

'Oh God,' Bethan sighed again. 'You've got a face like ... I don't know what now.'

'Like a slapped arse,' Sidney laughed.

'I can hardly help my face.'

'It's a lovely face,' Thea said, squeezing my hand.

Bethan put her cup down and turned to me. 'I'm sorry, brother. I never think, do I?'

'Why change the habits of a lifetime?' I replied, jerking so hard suddenly I spilt most of my coffee in the saucer.

Sidney choked and coughed hard as he had just taken a mouthful of his own coffee, but then spluttered, 'Fuck me!' You nearly jumped out of your chair then.'

'Let me take that, Benedict,' Thea offered, placing my cup and saucer on the table. 'Did it spill on you?'

'No, no, it's fine, sorry.'

'Silly sod,' Sidney remarked. 'Imagine what would happen if someone really made you jump.'

'Thank you, Sidney.'

'Why can Sidney get away with a comment like that? If I'd said that you would tell me off for being blunt,' Bethan declared.

'Sidney doesn't have your acid tongue,' I told her, 'he just speaks without thinking, but has no malice in him.'

She appeared suitably hurt. 'And I do?'

'If the cap fits ...'

'Thea, did you know my brother could be this hurtful?'

'I think most of what comes out of his mouth is said tongue in cheek,'

Thea said.

'Good job I love you,' Bethan told me.

'All I'll say is ditto, dear sister.'

'And on that note, I'll be on my way.'

'Must you go so soon?' I asked, definitely with my tongue firmly in my cheek.

'Sarcasm is the lowest form of wit, Benedict.'

'So I believe; but seriously, stay for just a while longer, please. We so rarely see each other.'

'You're a soft bugger! Ten minutes,' she said, glancing at her watch.

'Well, what shall we talk about now?' Sidney asked, sitting back and grinning like the proverbial Cheshire cat. 'I'm enjoying myself immensely.'

I raised my eyebrows at him. 'I can tell.'

Bethan fixed her eyes on Thea. 'How long have you two known each other?'

'Only a few months, I nearly knocked him over in the park, didn't I, Benedict?'

'You certainly did.'

'We've actually been neighbours for years,' Thea continued, 'but had never met. I live in that house at the bottom of this garden. You can just about see the chimneys, although I suspect in winter when the trees are bare you could probably see much more of my house.'

'Do you live there alone?'

Before Thea could answer I butted in. 'My sister is a barrister, can't you tell by the direct questioning?'

Thea gave a warm smile. 'I have nothing to hide and therefore I don't have a problem with direct questioning. I'm a little forthright too, Bethan, as Benedict will testify.'

'She certainly is.'

'Honesty and being direct is always the best policy,' Bethan added.

'Not always,' Sidney muttered. 'It depends whether you mean to be hurtful or not. If something is said to be helpful that's fine, but if it's said to be hurtful, that's a different matter entirely.'

'Thank you, Carl Jung,' I smiled.

Bethan gave a derisory laugh. 'Not in my book.'

Sidney look alarmed. 'I wouldn't like to be in your book then, I mean in your world.'

'I have to agree,' I murmured.

'You're a couple of silly old fools, aren't you?' Bethan sighed, but she had the grace to say it with a little fondness in her normally harsh voice.

'You know what? I have no idea how you and Benedict come from the same parents,' Sidney remarked. 'He's as soft as old sh...'

'Yes, thank you, Sidney,' I interrupted hurriedly, 'that'll be enough.'

'Daft as a brush,' Bethan added, 'always has been, especially where women are concerned. No, I'll qualify that, especially a *certain* young woman.'

I put my shaking hand over my eyes in despair. 'You aren't in court now you know. I apologise for my sister, Thea, she likes to be outspoken on purpose. I fear it has something to do with being the youngest as a child and needing to shock to be noticed by our parents.'

Thea didn't appear the least embarrassed. 'It's fine, really ...'

'Rubbish, Benedict!' Bethan spat out. 'I didn't try to shock when I was a child.'

'I'm afraid to say that's exactly what you did and it became a life-long habit because mostly it worked.'

'You have a selective memory. I was always the quiet one.'

'Huh! *I* was the quiet one.'

Sidney suddenly laughed out loud. 'I bloody love it here.'

'So do I,' Thea agreed, beaming. 'And what's more, Bethan, I love your brother too. Is that honest enough for you? And if I'm going to be forthright, I love him to bits despite knowing he worships a certain young woman, who, I might add, deserves to be worshipped by him and not because she's beautiful, highly talented and young, but because she's understanding, kind and warm-hearted. And there I rest my case.'

At the end of Thea's declaration, the tense atmosphere was so crushing it seemed to hang in the air inches from my face, just like the *presence,* and all I could do was stare like an idiot at my sister's face. Nobody had ever got the better of her in any way, shape or form and yet she was utterly speechless. But what *could* she say? A prolonged silence met Thea's pointed speech and in the end it was my dear friend Sidney who shattered that silence in his own inimitable way.

'Fuck me! I'd rather be in your house than anywhere else in the world, matey.'

'Sidney, don't swear in front of the ladies.'

'I'm no lady,' Thea laughed, tossing her thick and shiny red hair from in front of her face with a flourish. 'Sidney, one day I'll have to tell you the story about my husband, my *ex*-husband, in the rocking chair.'

'That sounds like a great story,' Sidney replied. 'Have you heard it, Benedict?'

'I certainly have and it won't disappoint.'

'Can't you tell me now?' Sidney asked.

Thea smiled. 'It's a little rude.'

'I really must go,' Bethan suddenly said, picking up her briefcase and standing up with a certain flounce. 'It's been ... interesting.'

'Let me see you out.'

'No, stay here, save your shaky legs.'

'I want to see you out.'

She gave a deep sigh. 'OK, if you insist. Bye, Sidney, bye, Thea. Please don't get up either of you.'

Sidney stayed in his chair and gave her a little wave, but Thea stood up and wrestled her dress down once again. 'It was lovely to meet you, Bethan. I'd love to meet all Benedict's family at some point.'

Bethan gave a hollow laugh. 'Well, the rest of them are a push over – like this one is,' she added, looking at me. When we reached the front door, my younger sister kissed me roughly and looked up at me as if I was a hopeless case. But then she often had that expression on her face when she was with me. 'Well, she's an interesting one I must say.'

'I thought you might think that.'

'I think a little too much for you.'

'In what sense is she too much for me?'

She gave a wry laugh. 'You know what sense.'

'Well, it's a good job we're just friends then, isn't it?'

Her mouth curled up. 'Just friends, yes, like you and Nell.'

'Not like Nell and me actually, very different, but just friends none the less. I have nothing other than friendship to give.'

'What do you mean?'

'What I just said. All sexual feelings fled to the hills about two years ago – part of my disease I fear and possibly age. I'm half the man I was, so I have very little to offer any red-blooded woman.'

Bethan's normally stern features that had been honed over years of fighting her corner in court, changed altogether in an instant and my young sister, who had always idolised me, was standing before me again, her eyes swimming with sudden, inexplicable tears.

'My poor brother,' she whispered. 'That was such a huge part of you and your life; my poor, dear brother.'

I was astonished by her sudden change. 'Bethan, don't get upset; that's not like you.'

'Maybe not, but you are the one person I've always loved unconditionally. I may not always act like it. You're so like Dad, Benedict, it's quite uncanny.'

I took her cold hand in mine. 'I know and the older I get the more like him I become I believe.'

'Yes, even with these shakes,' she murmured, lifting my hand and looking at its obvious tremors. 'I'm sorry it had to be you.'

'Had to be me? I don't understand what you mean.'

'Out of all of us, why did it have to be you with this God-forsaken illness? You were the most beautiful, the one with the loveliest nature, the most naturally gifted, the kindest.'

I was completely perplexed by her words. 'I've never seen myself like that at all. I felt you were all much cleverer than me. Papa used to worry about what would become of me. He didn't worry about the rest of you.'

'No, but you were his favourite after all. I wish it had been me.' She wiped a stray tear and shook her head and immediately her stony courtroom face was back in place. 'Bye now. Take care and don't tell anyone about … this.'

'You mean your tears?'

'They weren't exactly tears, more an emotional blip. I'll be in touch.'

'See you soon, I hope,' I slurred, wishing she had more emotional blips so she could join the human race more often.

'Possibly, yes, and in the meantime, keep yourself safe from the overtly sexy redhead and the poor, young actress. Neither will do you any good at all in the long run, believe me. Falling in love at our age is … well, it's the quickest route to madness.'

'Who *will* do me some good then?' I asked her, a little forlornly.

'In my eyes no woman has ever been worthy of you, Benedict. They all want something from you, ultimately.'

I wanted to assure her that Nell was worthy of me, sincerely worthy, but she kissed me once more and turned on her heel and was gone. I could hear her heels clicking on the pavement long after she had turned the corner out of sight and yet I stayed rooted to the spot. I was our father's favourite? She was mistaken of course because our father didn't have favourites, at least not in my opinion. But perhaps her childhood memories were very different.

Sidney was regaling Thea with stories about his time in the navy as a young lad and she was sitting forward, listening eagerly. When he glanced over at me, he let out a loud peel of laughter. 'You look like you've been trampled on. Your face is all crumpled, mate.'

'Are you OK, Benedict?' Thea asked kindly.

I sat down heavily, 'Yes, yes, all is fine. I normally look like this when my younger sister has paid me a visit.'

'What a ball-breaker she is.'

'Sidney, try not to speak like that in front of Thea.'

Thea scoffed. 'Don't be daft, Benedict. I've heard most things before. I probably swear more than Sidney.'

'I doubt that,' I mumbled. 'But I have to apologise for my sister's probing questions and comments about Nell. She does it on purpose, God knows why.'

'You don't have to apologise for her,' Thea said. 'She's very easy to analyse.'

'She is?'

'Absolutely and you had it partly right when you said she liked to shock for attention. But she's also jealous, envious even.'

'Well, I don't know what she has to feel jealous or envious about, but she's certainly too ferocious for most people.'

Thea's eyes were sparkling. 'I bet she's riveting to watch in court though.'

'Yes and if you had to go into battle you would want Bethan by your side.'

Thea gave me a wry smile. 'She needs a lover. That would knock the hard edges off her.'

'Fuck me, who would be brave enough for that?' Sidney remarked.

'Yes, I agree. I pity any man involved with my sister.'

'It's all a front, I tell you,' Thea insisted.

I gave her a small smile. 'Perhaps a tiny part is.'

'You'd be surprised, Benedict.'

'Yes, I'm sure I would.'

Sidney was grinning. 'I fucking love it here.'

'Sidney, haven't you got a home to go to and a saintly wife who loves you?'

He winked at Thea. 'Want to be alone, do we?'

'You need to be with your long-suffering wife.'

'Maybe, but it's much more interesting in here. There's always something going on.'

Shaking my head, I turned to Thea, 'I assure you there is not.'

She quickly changed the subject, 'Benedict, you didn't mind my speaking up for myself, did you?'

'No, I didn't mind. I was astonished! It was inspiring and eloquent and I ought to thank you for saying what you did about Nell.'

'Well, your sister was making a futile attempt to shock me and I wanted her to know she couldn't. It's all quite easy to interpret. Plus of course she's the tiniest bit jealous too, as I said.'

I was frowning hard because I wasn't quite sure what she meant. 'But jealous of what, or who?'

'It's quite easy to understand; a little jealous of me, of Nell.'

'Why would she be?'

Thea sighed. 'She idolises you.'

'She used to when we were little. I was always her pal, her protector.'

'You still are. Look, the envy comes from being aware she can't quite engage with people as you do. She would love to be like you, but she knows she can't. She has a hard, tough side that you certainly don't have and she finds it increasingly difficult to let her gentler side come to the fore. It is there though – somewhere.'

'You reckon?' Sidney laughed.

'I do see it occasionally,' I said, thinking of the sudden tears, 'rarely though.'

'That's a shame,' Thea added. 'She'd be much happier if she could relax more.'

'Yes.'

'You'd be amazed at how jealousy and envy mould people and how they act.'

'I'm sure.'

'And she's hiding something too, not sure what, but I'd hazard a guess she has her own emotional problems and she's merely putting on a front to get through it.'

I was astonished. 'You could see all that?'

'Oh yes!'

'You can't think much of human nature after doing your job for all those years,' I commented.

'It's all just part of being human.'

'Bloody hell,' Sidney muttered. 'I wonder what you make of me.'

We all laughed and then Thea put her hand on my arm. 'Benedict, I actually came round to ask you to lunch tomorrow.'

'Oh, yes, thank you, I'd like that.' My voice slid away to nothing so alarmingly I sounded drunk.

'Good, see you about half-twelve then. I'd better go; I'm in the shop later. Bye, Sidney.'

Making the effort to stand I said, 'I'll see you out.'

'No, please stay here. I'll let myself out.'

She swept out, swaying her hips and flicking her hair behind her shoulders and Sidney and I sat staring at each other. 'Did the last half hour actually happen?' I asked him. 'I feel like I've been run over by a truck.'

'What a woman!' Sidney cried, clapping his hands in glee. 'I've never seen your sister so surprised and dumb.'

'I have a feeling she could have put up more of a fight, but for some reason she didn't.'

'It's all good fun here, matey!'

'Glad to be of assistance, Sidney.'

'Thea sticking up for Nell didn't sound kosher.'

'It did rather flummox me too,' I admitted, 'but perhaps that's what she really feels. I do hope so anyway. I am at a time in my life when I want everyone to be friends not enemies. Having enemies is exhausting.'

'Well, after such a morning I think a little tipple will be in order this evening about seven. What do you say?'

'Sidney ...'

His face fell. 'Oh don't be boring, please.'

'If you'd let me finish, Sidney, I was going to say that I think you may be right.'

The expression of pure delight spreading across his dear features made my heart sing. 'Brilliant! See you later then.'

'I've no doubt I'll be here.'

I tottered down to the local supermarket and delicatessen after lunch and then sat in the sunshine reading for the rest of the afternoon. My sister's sudden appearance, her brittle outer casing and then her astonishing tears had worn me out. I thought about us all as children and tried to envisage my parents singling me out for praise and attention over and above the others, but my memory was becoming increasingly unreliable and I couldn't recall one instance of them favouring me. In fact, I was sure our father had given

Bethan the most affection because she was his youngest.

I rested my head back in my lounger and closed my eyes to the startling sun. Birdsong, mowers and bees were the only sounds and I dozed effortlessly. I had a vivid dream of running with my two sisters through a meadow of colourful wild flowers and Bethan, who was only a toddler, climbed on my back and clung to me for dear life as I raced home for afternoon tea. Then the dream changed to her crying because I was going off to school happily without kissing her goodbye. Her face crumpled as I walked away from her; I wanted to run back, but my friends called me and I was more concerned about them going without me than worrying about her.

I woke with a start, but my eyes were so heavy I went back to sleep instantly and into another dream: William and Sarah were clambering on our father's lap and pulling his moustache gently. Our mother was reading to me and Bethan was sitting by the fire with her doll, sucking her thumb and watching us. Then she began to cry silently, huge tears rolling down her cheeks. 'Papa, Bethan is crying,' I said.

'Oh darling, why are you crying? Come here to me.' Papa pushed William and Sarah gently off his lap and picked her up in his capable arms. 'Don't be upset. Shush now. Shush now. Look, Benedict is here to cuddle you too.'

Then the dream moved on; Bethan was older, we all were. We were huddled together at our old childhood home, desperate and stunned with grief because our beloved father had died. I had been worried about Bethan because she hadn't cried at his funeral service and now she was grey and silent and shivering from head to toe.

I held her close and said, 'I don't know what I can say to you to make this feel better.'

'Just always be here and don't die before me,' she whispered.

I promised her she could always rely on me, that I would always be there. I jerked awake once more to find Bethan was still on my mind. I remembered how from that moment after the funeral she had hardened visibly and how, since that time I only ever saw the gentler side of my younger sister in very rare flashes.

The following day the weather changed dramatically. The wind shifted to the north and brought with it a sharp wind and intermittent showers. I pottered about doing very little of consequence until lunchtime and then made my tortuous way to Thea's house. She opened the door with a flourish, dressed in tight trousers and a loose flowery blouse that was ever so slightly see-through.

'Hello, come in,' she gushed, 'what a turn in the weather.'

'Yes, but I came prepared,' I replied, shaking out my large black umbrella on her doorstep. 'I can smell something delightful cooking.'

'Beef muck-up,' she declared, 'exactly the same as chicken muck-up – only with beef!'

'Well, if it's as delicious as the chicken muck-up it'll be wonderful.' I followed her through to her sitting room.

'Good! The only thing is I slurped a load of red wine in it before thinking that you might not be allowed that with your pills?'

'Well, I'm sure a little won't hurt.'

She grinned. 'Actually my hand slipped as I poured it in.'

'Did it slip accidentally on purpose?'

'I never measure anything when I'm cooking. It's a dollop of this and a slurp of that. I can't be doing with measuring everything.'

'I'm with you there.'

'Sit down, Benedict and relax. Would you like a coffee? Lunch will be half an hour.'

'Coffee would be lovely, thank you.'

I made myself comfortable on her large, squashy sofa and crossed my arms to hide the fact that my hands were shaking slightly. I could hear her banging and crashing about in the kitchen and I pondered on how someone could make so much noise by simply making a coffee. I had no doubt that her loud and sometimes outspoken personality that I liked and admired could become irritating in a marriage if you no longer loved her. That thought made me wince with guilt because she had shown me only kindness and generosity and yet I felt a stab of longing for Nell's gentle, searching intelligence and loving nature, which made me feel even guiltier. Almost as if it were feeding on my guilt, the *presence* appeared and began to hover inches from my face in a kind of shimmering form, just out of reach and indefinable. I shifted my position and gazed out of the window where the long windows of my home were just visible. The small panes of glass were reflecting the dull, rainy light and for a split second I imagined I saw Nell's face looking out of one of them. Her normally dazzling smile was absent and she appeared lonely and forlorn. I started and jerked violently just as Thea walked in with two cups of coffee.

She gasped. 'Bloody hell, are you OK?'

'Yes, yes, just a tremor; I'm fine.'

She placed the cups just in front of me. 'Does that hurt when you do that?'

'A little, yes.'

'You poor old thing...'

'Thea, if I were you I'd move those cups because I could jerk my leg and kick them over.'

'Yes, yes of course.' She pulled the table towards her and looked at me with pity in her eyes. 'There, that's better. Do you want to hang on before you drink this, in case you jerk again?'

'No, I'm fine. I never know when they're coming so I could wait all day.'

'If you're sure,' she said, appearing concerned and a little nervous at the same time.

'Are you worried about the furniture?' I asked, meaning it to be tongue in cheek.

'No, I couldn't care less about the furniture.'

I gave her a warm smile. 'That was a joke, Thea.'

She relaxed a little. 'Oh sorry, silly me, I can be a bit thick sometimes.'

'You most certainly are not thick.'

She handed me the coffee. 'Here,' she said grinning, 'throw it all over the place if you like.'

'Don't tempt me.'

'Are the jerks getting worse?'

'Not worse, but often unpredictable. I shake mostly, but the jerking is only every now and again. It would be better if I could predict it, but I can't.'

'It's awful for you.'

I gave a little shrug. 'It could be a lot worse.'

She looked doubtful. 'Could it?'

'Yes. The tablets are actually improving things considerably.'

'OK, if you say so. Now, what was I going to ask you when I was making the coffee? Oh yes, I was going to ask about your sister.'

'Oh dear, must you ask about her?'

'No, not if you don't want me to.'

'I don't mind talking about Bethan because I love her dearly, but I seem to spend much of my time explaining her to people and that's difficult as I don't really understand her myself. And I've known her all her life obviously.'

'She has an unfortunate manner, that's all. I suspect much of that is a front, as I said before.'

'Some of it, but she is tough. She has to be. But she has the same human emotions underneath that we all have, they're just well hidden.'

'You two are chalk and cheese, aren't you?'

'Yes.'

She was silent for a moment, but looked intently at me. 'Let's talk about something else then. I can see by your face you'd prefer not to have me analysing her any more than I did yesterday. That's extremely loyal of you, Benedict.'

'Perhaps, but she would defend me too.'

'I'm sure.'

I drank my coffee gingerly, hoping to God I wouldn't jerk and chuck it all over the room. My shoulders were so tense they were almost throbbing and I tried hard to relax them, but they felt like concrete. Thea crossed her legs, flicked her hair behind her ears and sat back.

'Do you know what I did last night?' she said.

'I have no idea. Something exciting I hope. You need excitement, I think.'

She laughed at me. 'You think so?'

'I know so.'

'Well, I joined a Salsa class. It's such fun.'

'It sounds it.'

Her eyes looked playful suddenly. 'Some of the men can really move.'

I looked aghast, just to make her laugh. 'Men do it?'

She duly threw her head back and laughed out loud. 'Yes, of course.'

'It sounds as if it might be painful.'

'That's very funny, Benedict.'

'It would suit you down to the ground,' I remarked.

'It does. It's lovely to be able to dance with a man again.'

'I can only imagine.'

'Benedict, stop taking the piss.'

'Sorry.'

'I'd like to be able to say that you could do it, but ...'

'I fear not.'

'But you can dance, I saw you.'

'That was shuffling about, not dancing.'

'You would find Salsa difficult. It is a bit fast and there are so many twists and turns and you have to move your hips about.'

'God forbid!'

'No, really it's great fun and the music is wonderful. I loved it.'

'I can only tap dance.'

'Tap dancing is difficult.'

'And I've done some ballet.'

'You're having me on.'

'I assure you I'm not. The first time I tap danced was in the snow.'

She narrowed her eyes at me. 'You were tap dancing in the snow?'

'Madam, you doubt me?'

'Yes, just a bit.'

'I tap danced in the snow with Nell. She wouldn't take no for an answer.'

'Could you do it now for me? Like you did in the park?'

'Oh I never give repeat performances,' I told her, smiling.

'Just have a go for me, Benedict. I'd love to see you tap dance again.'

I suddenly felt bold and carefree and I dearly wanted, once again, to recreate that feeling of freedom and living in the moment I had experienced with Nell on that day. And I hoped it would bring me closer to her even if only for a split second. I slowly struggled to my feet and tried to focus on my balance. I remembered a few of the steps and pictured Nell holding my hand, but as I stuck out one foot I staggered immediately and almost fell, only just saving myself at the last minute. Thea jumped up and held on to me.

'Oh, I'm sorry,' I gasped.

'Not bad,' she laughed, 'one step wasn't bad.'

'It was pathetic, but I need Nell to follow.'

She looked up at me. 'Yes,' she said almost sadly, 'you need Nell to follow.'

My body then jerked again involuntarily and it was lucky for me she was still holding onto me otherwise I would have flown across the room in a most unfortunate and embarrassing manner. 'Sorry, I'm fine, please don't worry.'

'Benedict, are you really? Perhaps the doctor should take another look at you.'

'There's nothing to be done but live with it and be grateful for small mercies and keep taking the blessed tablets.'

'But it won't get any better, will it?'

'No, unfortunately it won't, unless some clever doctor finds the cure.

But you can stay the same for a long time without deteriorating, so I'm banking on that.'

We both sat down. 'Are you bitter?' she asked.

'Bitter? No, I'm not bitter at all. Why would I be?'

'That it landed on you and not someone else.'

'No, I don't think like that.'

'But it always seems to be the lovely people who get hit by these things; the kind people, those who do no harm.'

'Well, firstly, thank you for that, but I think possibly some of us don't have a brittle coating that protects us from life's hard knocks and we are possibly more vulnerable. It's just a theory I have.'

'You may have a point.'

'But let's not dwell on my Parkinson's, let's talk about you. Are you having another holiday this year?'

'Maybe,' she shrugged, 'I might go on a walking holiday in Scotland with some old friends.'

'Fabulous.'

'Hopefully it will be, if we get the right weather.'

I gave a rueful smile. 'I don't think I'll be going on a walking holiday any time soon.'

Thea frowned and looked down at her feet. No ...'

'But I can tap dance.'

She laughed, 'and in the snow no less.

'Yes, in the snow.'

Her face changed then and her eyes, which constantly betrayed her feelings, looked impossibly sad. 'You really do miss her dreadfully, don't you?'

What could I say but, 'Yes, I do.'

'And yet you hadn't known her long.'

'No, but let's just say she made a great and lasting impression in a short space of time.'

'One of those people you can never forget.'

'You could say that. Thea, I'm glad we can talk like this now, it helps me.'

'I'm glad we can too.'

'You have a way of getting to my innermost secrets.'

She smiled. 'It was my job, after all.'

'Yes and you must have been a brilliant psychologist.'

'Thank you, Benedict and now, beef muck-up is in order,' she declared.

'Beef muck-up smells wonderful, but I'll keep away from the rocking chair in case you accuse me of doing something unmentionable.'

She clapped her hands in delight and grinned. 'You may sit in the rocking chair and do exactly as you please.'

'Well, maybe I will then,' I replied, feeling more relaxed in her company than I ever had before, but my mobile bleeped loudly and made us both jump. 'Sorry, I'd better check this.'

'That's fine.'

I knew it was Nell and I fumbled with my useless fingers to get it out of my pocket and open the text. My heart began to thump wildly as I read her message: *Matt on final warning, don't know what to do to help him. I need your help! Will Skype later.*

Chapter 20

After Nell had sent her plaintive message I could not settle. I thought it best to explain to Thea because I knew she would pick up on my swift change of mood.

'How incredibly sad,' she remarked as we ate lunch.

'Yes, it is. Apparently he has the most enviable talent, completely natural and Nell had such high hopes for him in this show. But I fear he will blow it.'

'Genius often has a price to pay,' she added.

'Yes, my father used to say that. He had this saying about nature giving and nature taking away or something like that. But I don't know Matt so I can't honestly comment on his life, but I worry about the effect it will have on Nell. She likes him, she befriended him and this will upset her greatly.'

Thea put her hand gently on my arm. 'So she turns to you for advice and comfort.'

'Well, I used to drink quite a bit so ...'

She shook her head. 'No, it's not that. That's not why she's calling you.'

'Are we being a psychologist again?'

'No, *we* aren't! It doesn't need a psychologist to understand why she is turning to you.'

I wasn't at all sure what she meant and I couldn't read her face because she had her head down and was eating her beef muck-up heartily. So I let it go and ate my lunch, even though my appetite had fled to the hills since Nell's text. The summer rain was lashing against the windows and yet there was bright sunshine flooding into the room.

'There must be a rainbow,' I commented quietly.

'There should be somewhere. Is summer over I wonder?'

'Not yet surely,' I replied, secretly longing for autumn because that brought us nearer to winter and Nell's return.

'Well, September is here at the end of the week. My God hasn't it flown? It seems ages since my holiday.'

'Yes, flown,' I muttered, when in reality the long, scorching and airless high summer days had dragged endlessly for me, not only because of Nell, but because more gentle, temperate weather suited me much better.

'But then not for you, Benedict,' she added, smiling fondly at me as if reading my thoughts.

'No, but then I have done so little. I seem to have settled quite easily into spending all my time at home, in the garden, shopping locally, playing cards with Sidney ...'

'Sounds quite wonderful to me,' she interrupted, laughing. 'But you are retired so you can do as you please.'

'Yes, but I've become a little anti-social. I'm quite happy with my own company and Sidney's and yours.'

Her eyes shone. 'Thank you, what a compliment!'

'I mean it. I spent so many futile hours at parties when I was much younger. Not that I remember much about them. Now when I look back I was merely trying to escape my life. What a bloody waste of time it all was.' I went to speak again, but no sound came out so I simply pretended I had finished my sentence when in reality I was going to add that I preferred my life as it was now, except for the Parkinson's.

'Maybe you can understand Matt then. What made you stop?'

I paused for a moment and swallowed, not only to think about her question, but I was also hoping a few intelligible words would come out. 'Separating and divorcing my wife. After that I was no longer lonely. In the marriage I was terribly lonely. Mind you, I must have abused my body so badly, maybe ...'

'The Parkinson's is a result of that?'

'I do wonder.'

She frowned. 'There hasn't been any proof of that, I don't think. But then often people need to blame themselves instead of accepting things are pretty random. Believing in random is difficult.'

I had cleared my plate and although I had struggled to eat it, it was tasty and filling and I was grateful to her for having cooked for me. 'Thank you, the beef muck-up was delicious.'

'You're very welcome. Did you taste the red wine in it?'

'Yes and I can feel its effects too. My head is swimming slightly. You must have jerked uncontrollably like me when you had the bottle hovering over the casserole.'

'I can't feel its effects,' she sighed, adding, 'unfortunately.'

'Ah, but you're not on heavy-duty pills, are you?'

'Will you be OK? Red wine and pills aren't a lethal combination are they?' she asked, biting her lip with concern.

'I doubt it. I've drunk wine and whiskey with Sidney while on my tablets, so it *should* be fine.'

'Good, I'll put the kettle on for some tea.'

She went into the kitchen again and I sat watching the showers tapping the window like a wanderer wanting to be let in. What was Nell feeling? What had been going on over there? She should have been having the time of her life, revelling in her undoubted success, meeting new people and making friends. I glanced at my watch and fidgeted in my chair, anxious for the time to race by until her dear face would appear in front of me on the screen. And I wanted to sit quietly on my own till then just thinking, but I needed to hide my wish to be gone from Thea, as it was unfair and ungrateful, not to mention downright rude.

'Here we go, Benedict,' she said cheerfully, placing a bone china cup and saucer in front of me.

I knew my distraction must have been obvious to her as I murmured, 'Thank you.'

She was watching me carefully as I picked up the tea in my trembling hands and put it slowly to my lips. 'When you've drunk that you had better go,' she said flatly.

'Had I?'

'Well, the spell has been broken by that text.'

Her words perplexed me. 'How do you mean, the spell?'

'You know when there's a relaxed, amiable mood between two friends where the conversation is flowing and the silences don't matter? And then something happens and the spell is shattered, either by someone's thoughtless words or badly timed laughter … or a text?'

'I'm so sorry.'

She smiled warmly at me. 'I understand, honestly.'

I looked at her appealing face, so close to mine and her bouncing red hair falling across her forehead so she was constantly having to run her hand through it and I felt moved to lean towards her and kiss her cheek. As I moved back she took hold of my chin in her fingers and then laughed softly.

'Do I look that ridiculous?' I asked.

'No, you don't and you never would!'

'I don't believe a word of it. Madam, you were laughing.'

'I just suddenly found the whole situation quite ludicrous.'

'Parkinson's *is* ludicrous!'

'Not the Parkinson's, that's never funny. No, just you and me and…

never mind.'

'No, please explain; you can tell me anything. I won't be upset, Thea. I find myself quite hilarious most of the time,' I remarked and as I finished speaking I felt the saliva gathering at the corner of my mouth. 'You see what I mean? Dribbling is pretty ludicrous, ridiculous and pathetic, don't you agree? I mean, you have to laugh otherwise...' I didn't feel the need to finish the sentence.

She said nothing as I reached for a tissue and wiped it away, but when I glanced at her she was frowning hard and looking down at her cup. The silence spoke volumes to me and I struggled to find words to fill the aching gap in the conversation that had opened up like a vast crack in a wall.

'You weren't dribbling! Many people get saliva there, nothing to do with Parkinson's.'

'Perhaps...'

'I think you're a pretty spectacular man,' she continued, her voice shaking with emotion, 'who needs a pretty spectacular woman.'

I gave her a small smile. It could only be a small one as my features had become quite rigid. 'Thank you for the spectacular,' I muttered. 'But you're right, I had better go. I apologise for the dribbling, it's most unpleasant for whoever is watching.'

She waved her hand in the air. 'Don't be silly, you *weren't* dribbling.'

I struggled to my feet, my legs aching and the tremors in my hands noticeably worse and she fetched my umbrella from the kitchen. 'Do you want me to walk you home, Benedict? You look a little unsteady.'

'No, I'm fine, honestly. My legs are normally like this when I've been sitting for a while. It's just a kind of cramp.'

She kissed my face softly. 'Let me know about Nell and her friend, will you?'

'I will; thank you.'

'And you didn't ask,' she added.

'I didn't ask about what?'

'Who the spectacular woman is...'

'I wouldn't presume...'

'Well, let's just say this. I would never call myself spectacular, so you can work the rest out for yourself.'

'Thea, I'm sorry...'

She put her hand on my back and pushed me gently forward, saying quietly, 'Go, Benedict.'

She stood on her doorstep as I almost pranced like a puppet away from her house and when I reached the corner we waved to each other. A heavy downpour splashed about my feet, but the sound of the raindrops hard against the pavement made me smile because I imagined Nell standing on her own by the statue with her face turned up to the dark sky. I thought the memory of her would lift my spirits, but it only compounded the fact that she had looked supremely happy at that time and not once since she had been in New York had she looked like that on Skype.

The rest of that day I whittled away the time by emailing Beth, Sarah and William, listening to the radio and sitting on my own watching the changing sky. Sidney knocked but I didn't reply because I couldn't have concentrated at all and I didn't want to be distracted with him because he didn't deserve it either. The light faded quickly at about four because of the storm clouds and I ate some toast and jam and drank a few cups of tea. Eventually my mobile bleeped loudly and I shot to my computer without even reading the text, almost falling flat on my face in my haste to reach it. It made the usual sound and I held my breath waiting for Nell to appear. Then there she was her face pale and devoid of make-up, her hair pulled back in a pony tail and a sleeveless, summer vest on that made her look thin. But it was still Nell, with the unusual almond-shaped, grey eyes, the perfect cheekbones and the constantly changing face. I wondered what on earth I must have looked like to her with my greying hair and dark rimmed glasses half way down my nose as usual, peering at the screen.

She gave a tiny wave. 'Hi, Mr Marshall, how are you?'

'Hello, Nell. It's so good to see you.'

'It's so good to see you too,' she replied smiling, but it was a half smile, a weary smile. I had to comment on it.

'Where is that dazzling smile that could light up a stadium? Since you've been in New York I've hardly seen it.'

'It's gone up the pictures.'

'Say that again.'

She shrugged. 'I don't know, I'm just so knackered. It's such a demanding schedule and the worrying over Matt is getting me down to be honest.'

'I can see that. Tell me about it.'

'It's so frustrating,' she cried, 'I can't believe he's being so stupid, I really can't. He's been drunk on stage twice and missed a couple of cues. Why is he doing it? This is what we live for, you know? Landing a show like this in

America, with regular money, and it's sold out, totally. We are both being interviewed on the radio, television, interviews for magazines, meeting so many famous people backstage who are tripping over themselves for a ticket ...'

'I can only imagine.' I interrupted in order to slow her down a little.

She rubbed her eyes and it was hard to tell whether she was wiping away a tear or simply weary. 'Parties, cocktails, nightclubs, you name it, we're doing it. Not that I'm interested in all that, but *he* is. My God, you should see him drink! I don't know where he puts it. No wonder he was coughing up blood in the last show he was in.'

'He's a silly boy!'

Her face came alive for a moment. 'Silly boy is just about right! I knew you'd understand, Mr Marshall.'

'Nell, I understand only too well and he's just running away, that's all. I'm not sure what from because I don't know him well enough, but he's numbing his senses with drink so he doesn't have to feel what he doesn't want to feel.'

'But what can I do to help? I've tried getting angry, nagging him, checking up on him – nothing works,' she sighed, putting her head in her hands. 'He says I'm constantly on his back, but I just want him to succeed and hang on to the job. If he gets fired he'll never live it down. Word goes round so quickly in our game. If he blows it it's over for him.'

'Nell ...'

'The company manager had him in the office yesterday and gave him a final warning,' she continued, her face so strained it didn't look like the happy-go-lucky, vibrant, vital girl I knew. 'And do you know what he said to me when he came out?'

'That he didn't care?'

She looked perplexed. 'How did you know?'

'I know because he cares more about the drink than he does the show.'

She shook her head in disbelief. 'How could he?'

'I know it's difficult for someone as dedicated as you to understand, but he's just running away. I suspect he has a default mechanism that kicks in when things are going smoothly and it sabotages everything great in his life. I should imagine Thea could analyse him perfectly if she met him and perhaps that's what he needs. Nell,' I urged her, 'you can only be his friend and support him as much as he will let you. But perhaps you need to let him live his life as he wants to, mistakes included.'

'Why would Thea be able to help him?' she asked.

'Oh, sorry, she's a clinical psychologist, or was.'

Nell's face dropped even more. 'Did I know that? She's very bright then.'

'Yes, I would say so.'

'Like you,' she whispered.

'Brighter than me I would say.'

'But ...'

'What is it?' I asked, sensing I had worried her even more.

'Well, she's probably a good match for you, Mr Marshall.'

I went to speak but slurred badly and I had to swallow and wait for a few seconds before trying again. 'I don't know about a good match. I think she'd prefer a man who doesn't dribble, Nell.'

She visibly brightened. 'Remember, get the tissue and swipe it!'

'Hang on,' I told her, fumbling for my tissue and pretending to do exactly that.

'There you go,' she said.

'You do me good, Nell. Do you know that?'

Her pale face softened. 'I hope so.'

'So, apart from your wayward friend, how is it all going for you?'

'It's going ...'

'It's going?' I prompted.

'The time is going.'

I was bemused by her words. 'Is that all you want to say about life in New York?'

He face instantly became like a mask. 'Tell me something to remind me of home, Mr Marshall.'

'Oh ... well ...' I hesitated, surprised by the longing in her voice, 'we're nearly in September and I can sense the light changing ever so slowly. It's been showery today and there was a rainbow spreading right across the sky from near my house and ending over the other side of the river.'

She was sitting with her chin in her hands staring at me. 'On the Isle of Dogs,' she added. 'That sounds lovely. It's so hot here, stifling, especially backstage. There's something wrong with the air con and we've asked for it to be fixed because it's so draining. I'd love to be walking in a summer shower through the park.'

'Yes,' I said, 'I know you would.'

'Isn't it funny when you look back to childhood summer holidays from school, that it's always hot and sunny with bright blue sky?'

'Endlessly sunny,' I remarked, 'except, of course, when you were in that tent.'

She gave a faint smile. 'Yes, except for then.' She stayed with her chin in her hands and she appeared a little more relaxed. 'What did you do in your holidays in Sussex?'

'When I was a child?'

'Yeah, all those years ago, back in the dark ages,' she laughed and she was suddenly more like the Nell I knew.

'We played in the meadows near our home: William, Sarah, myself and sometimes Bethan, although she was a bit younger so we often left her behind because she slowed us down.'

She frowned. 'Ah, that's a shame, poor Bethan.'

I thought, yes how like you Nell, to have pity for my hard-faced sister who had been so cool towards you. 'I did carry her on my back quite a bit though. We would play in the woods too and hide from each other behind the tall trees. Our father told us the tallest tree in the world was just beyond a clearing and of course we believed him. And that's exactly what it looked like. It seemed to reach right up and skim the clouds. The best time in the wood was when the little bluebells were out in force, spreading for as far as the eye could see like a fairy blanket. And the daffodils nodding their cheerful heads and the delicate purple and white crocuses everywhere; it was wonderful.'

'Go on,' Nell urged. 'I can see it all.'

'My favourite time was when it snowed,' I continued, 'heavy snow where everything is hushed. You can't replicate the silence that heavy snow brings or the special kind of light that floods into your bedroom in the morning after it's been snowing all night. I still find it magical even as an older man.'

'That's because you'll never be old, Mr Marshall.'

'Thank you, Nell you do me a power of good.'

'One day,' she started, sudden tears welling up and spilling over onto her cheeks, 'when I come home, will you take me to Sussex and show me the tallest tree in the world?'

My rigid face must have been smiling because I know it moved ever so slightly. 'It would be my pleasure. But ...'

She wiped her face with the back of her hand, 'But what?'

'But only if you don't cry, Nell. I can't stand to see you cry.'

She tried to smile through the tears. 'Oh, is that all? I'm not really crying, I'm just a bit emotional at the moment. I thought you were going to say, but Thea wouldn't like it.'

My hands jerked forward suddenly, but they were out of shot, so Nell was completely unaware of it. 'I don't understand. Why would Thea mind?'

'It doesn't matter.'

'It matters to me.'

Her eyes became playful and she sat up a little. 'Let's have fun, shall we?'

'Fun would be wonderful, but I'm not sure how we are going to achieve it when we are on different sides of the ocean.'

'Move the camera so I can see the piano, can you?'

'Oh, right ... I'll try.'

'That's it, a bit more, to the right a bit, whoa, that's fine. I can see it now.'

'And what do you want me to do now, pray?'

'You sound as if you're in a Shakespearian play,' she laughed.

'Sidney says I don't talk like normal people.'

'You don't! But then you aren't normal people! Now play Sooty for me, please.'

'Your wish is my command, Cinderella.'

I sat on my piano stool and began to play Chopin, quickly running into the Sooty theme tune that Nell loved. Her laughter, loud and glorious at last echoed all the way from America, through the computer and bounced off my walls. It was the sound I had missed the most since her departure and only then, hearing it again after so long did I realise just how deeply I had missed it.

'That's brilliant, Mr Marshall, thank you,' she called. 'I have to go now, thanks for cheering me up, I needed it.'

'Nell, wait,' I called back, making my tortuous way back to the computer. 'Remember, Matt is the master of his own fate. Let him take his own path, wherever that may take him. You must concentrate on yourself and your own career. You must fly remember. Promise me, Nell.'

She blew me a kiss and gave me her dazzling smile. 'I promise.'

'Thank you.'

'Mr Marshall ... I need to tell you something ... I ...'

The screen went blank, the signal gone in an instant and I was left with my own reflection staring back at me with my ridiculously wayward hair and blank features. I closed my eyes with embarrassment at knowing that was what Nell had been looking at. In my head I often forgot how old I was and imagined myself the twenty-one year old with his whole life ahead of him. But what had she been going to say? She needed to tell me something? It sounded important, very important. Perhaps it had been about Matt. Maybe, just maybe, she was intending to tell me they were … yes, that was why she was so terribly upset about his behaviour. She was falling for him. Of course, why wouldn't she? They were birds of a feather, in the same profession, both highly talented and with creative personalities. He already loved her, I knew that because I had seen them in the pub together and he couldn't take his eyes off her. He had a manic, pent-up energy that drew people to him and Nell's kind and loving nature would be drawn into rescuing him from himself. That's where her heartache came from and I had urged her to distance herself from him and let him go. What would she think of me being so hard? That I had more in common with Bethan than she realised?

I collapsed onto my sofa and watched the soft early evening rain splatter against my conservatory roof. The *presence* hung just out of reach, hovering nearby like a glittering light that shone directly in your eyes and couldn't be avoided or ignored. I suddenly felt as if all my blood had drained out of my body and left me limp and deflated. Nell was still months from coming home and when she did, the stunningly, enviably talented, but inevitably doomed Matt would be by her side.

'Benedict.'

Sheila's hesitant voice made me jump out of my skin. She was standing in the conservatory doorway, obviously on edge.

'Sheila, come in, please.'

'Sorry, were you having a sleep?'

'No, not at all, just thinking and that does me no good at all. Is his Lordship OK?'

'Yes, yes, he's fine. Well, he's at the doctor's so I thought I'd come and have a chat before he gets back.'

'Sit down, please. Would you like a cup of tea?'

'No, thank you. I'd better be quick, he'll be back soon and I don't want him to know I've spoken to you.'

'How can I help?'

'He's driving me nuts to be honest,' she started. 'He's in complete denial about all this. He keeps saying the doctors have got it wrong, there's never been any diabetes in his family and he's never felt better in his life.'

'Well, that's obviously not true because he passed out and you don't feel well if you pass out,' I remarked.

Sheila's homely, kind face was pinched with concern and frustration and she looked weary. 'It's only because he's scared out of his wits,' she went on, knowing her husband only too well. 'The boys have been nagging him and I'm completely changing his diet.'

'Oh dear, he won't like that.'

'He doesn't, but he's got to lump it.'

'I agree with you.'

'But look, I need your help with this, Benedict.'

'I'll do anything, Sheila.'

'Talk to him for me, he'll listen to you. He thinks you are the cleverest person on this earth.'

I smiled. 'Then he is greatly mistaken.'

'Oh you know what I mean. Everything you say is gospel and he wants to be like you, talk like you, have your charisma, all of that,' she declared.

I was bemused. 'I have no idea why on earth he would want to be like me when he has everything I would sell my soul for, Sheila. You two have the happy, mutually supportive relationship I can only dream about and Sidney has more common sense in his little finger than …'

Her laughter interrupted my flow and the laughter lines either side of her eyes creased up like pieces of paper. 'Well, *I* know that, but he's always looked up to you and you are great pals after all. I sometimes think he'd miss you more than he'd miss me.'

'I doubt that,' I told her. 'I can only pray for his sake that he shuffles off this mortal coil first because Sidney without you would be a lost soul, you know that.'

'Just talk to him for me, would you? He hasn't grasped the fact that diabetes can affect your eyes, your kidney function *and* your feet, practically everything.'

'Of course I'll talk to him, but I can assure you he does believe he has diabetes because we had a short conversation on the topic of his health recently and he's simply trying to escape his diagnosis. I understand where he's coming from, believe me.'

She gave a relieved smile and stood up. 'Thank you, I'd better go. If he finds me in here on my own he'll know we're up to something. I feel guilty enough already saying these things about him behind his back, but he's a bloody pain in the backside.'

I struggled to my feet and she threw her arms around me in a spontaneous gesture of affection. I was surprised at her strength and I put my trembling arms around her and attempted a gentle hug. 'You can always come in here and sound off about him, Sheila, and you're not betraying his confidence because I don't think there is much you could tell me about your dear husband that I don't already know.'

She kissed my cheek and looked at me fondly. 'He really needs you, Benedict.'

'And I need him.'

'I know, you're a pair of silly old fools,' she remarked, but it was said with such love and affection it moved me.

'I know we are and long may we reign.'

'One other thing before I go ...'

I squeezed her arms. 'I know what you're going to say. Don't encourage him to drink when he's here.'

'How did you know?'

'Just a guess,' I shrugged. 'And I'll be strict with him, never fear.'

She hugged me again. 'I can feel all these tiny tremors in your body. Do you have them all the time?'

'I'm afraid so, but I'm getting quite used to them actually. It could be worse.'

'Yes, you could be married to Sidney Walpole.'

'Sheila, you should be canonised.'

'Bye, Benedict and thanks. Come to dinner tomorrow evening. I'm cooking something ultra healthy and if you're there he's more likely to eat it without complaining too much.'

'I'll be there, thank you.'

'Come in about six.'

'Lovely.'

She left me there standing by the open conservatory door and a soft, cool, showery wind blew on my face. I looked at the darkening sky and realised summer was almost over as the nights were already drawing in and signalling autumn was on its way at last. At first that thought made my heart thump with excitement because the weeks were passing and Nell would be home, but then I remembered her tears and obvious anxiety for the poor, brilliant Matt and I realised she was slipping away from me as quickly and as certainly as the long summer evenings.

&

He had looked so different, sounded so different, it was unsettling. But I guessed it was because of Thea. Every time I had called him on Skype he had mentioned her. She was an attractive, bright woman nearer his age, sophisticated probably and full of sex appeal. She was experienced, intelligent and more his class too. I had no doubt she was whittling away his defences because those defences weren't very strong; they were shaky and prone to a slow, gentle prodding. If they were together would she allow me to be a big part of his life? I doubted it and that worried me so much I felt a rising sense of panic shooting up from my chest into my throat like acid. Glancing at my watch I felt an even more urgent sense of panic because I needed to get to the theatre.

New York continued to be the boiling cauldron it had been all summer. It was a humid, blistering heat, airless and uncomfortable. The steam continually hurtling up from below the pavements reminded me of hundreds of boiling kettles and simply compounded the feeling of airlessness. I was an avid watcher of the weather reports now, like a regular New Yorker and I longed for some cooler days with heavy rain hammering on the roof. The heat coming up from the pavements was unrelenting and I grabbed a coffee and pastry from the diner on the corner and raced to the stage door. Some of the dancers were limbering up backstage and in the corridors, full of their usual energy and smelling faintly of make up and sweat. Some of them called to me, some were in a world of their own. Hoofers, as they were known, were a law unto themselves, stuck together, understood each other and had a coded language only they understood; a kind of shorthand often indecipherable to the rest of us. They were supremely and enviably fit with figures to die for, but often hideously injured and on restricted diets.

I had a feeling Matt might be in the upstairs bar talking to Ben, so I raced up there hoping to make some peace with him. When he had missed his cue on stage I had stormed out of the theatre in despair without talking to him and I wanted to apologise. My anger wouldn't help his situation, I knew that now. He was there, perched on a bar stool, staring at his tonic water with his head down, his shoulders hunched and his hair matted and tangled at the back. Ben was wiping glasses at the other end of the bar and gave me his usual friendly wave when he saw me.

I sat next to Matt, but he barely looked up. 'Hello, Matt,' I whispered.

His eyes were bloodshot and his complexion grey. He gave me a conciliatory smile and I put my arm around his shoulders. Ben raised his eyebrows at me and shook his head.

'Are you talking to me then?' he asked sulkily.

'Depends,' I replied.

'Ah depends on whether I've had a drink?'

'Yes.'

'I haven't, Helen, on my mother's life.'

'Did you have much after the show last night?'

'A bit,' he admitted, but when Ben cleared his throat to catch my eye and raised his eyebrows again, he added, 'Are you dobbing me in, Ben?'

Ben laughed. 'Am I *what*?'

'Judas!'

'Man, you need to get a grip on yourself.'

'You leave Ben out of this. I don't need anyone to tell me what's going on with you, Matt. I can always tell by your complexion how much you've been drinking. But let's not argue any more about that. If you don't care about your career I can't care for you and I won't.'

He turned to me. 'I do care.'

'Then show it! Or get yourself some help.'

'I can stop like that,' he told me, clicking his fingers.

Ben let out a loud derisory laugh. 'If I had a dollar for every time I heard one of the musicians say that.'

'Shut your noise you,' Matt said, but it was said without any meaning malice and Ben flicked a tea towel at his head playfully.

'We have half an hour before the show, so let's have a chat together, shall we? We've spent hardly any time with each other.'

'Not my fault.'

'Yes it is,' I declared. 'You're in bed nearly all day and then after the show you go to the bars.'

He looked a little ashamed. 'I know ... sorry.'

'Are you finding the monotony of being on stage too hard to handle?'

He put his head in his hands. 'It's not the show; it's just *me*. It's always been me. But ...' he stopped and glanced at Ben who was chatting to one of the band at the other end of the bar. He took my hand and looked intently at me.

'What were you going to say?' I asked him.

'If I had you, I could be different.'

I snatched my hand away. 'I can't ...'

'No, no,' he gasped, 'I'm so sorry, Helen. I didn't mean to embarrass you.'

'You haven't embarrassed me. I just can't be responsible for you. It's too much. You need to do it for yourself.'

'Me?' he sneered, 'I'm the last person I'd do it for. I'm such a stupid, useless, piece of shit.'

I was appalled at his remarks. 'But you aren't, Matt. You are the opposite of all that. I've never heard anyone play like you and you've got this innate sense of timing, musicality, feeling, everything.'

He shrugged. 'But that's all easy. It's life that's hard.'

'But if the playing on stage is easy why can't you just stick with it and finish the run?'

'Because life gets in the way, Helen,' he sighed. 'Don't you understand that?' I couldn't pretend I did understand, when in reality I thought it a downright crime he could waste his incomparable talent by dulling his wits with alcohol, so I didn't answer. He pounced on my silence. 'You don't, obviously. But that's okay because I wouldn't if I was you. But hey,' he cried, shaking his wild hair and sitting upright suddenly instead of slouching, 'what's new with you? It's immensely boring talking about me all the time, don't you reckon?'

I smiled forbearingly, 'I do as a matter of fact. Well, no, I'll qualify that. *You* are never boring, but alcohol is. But before we change the subject, will you promise to try for me? Just try to finish the run? If you're sacked word will go round like wildfire and you'll find it hard to ever get another job.'

He gave a little smirk. 'Well, for you I'll try, Helen. But sometimes I reckon I'd be happier just playing in a bar with no pressure to be endlessly brilliant every single fucking time.' And there it was: the bare truth of the matter. If he didn't think that would be an unbearable waste of his talent, what hope did I have of convincing him? He broke into my thoughts, 'Do you remember, the night we stood in that doorway in the rain?'

'Of course I do. It seems such a long time ago.'

'We were both full of hope and excited?'

I nodded. 'Yes.'

His eyes were troubled. 'Has it been all you thought it would be, Helen? Really, has it?'

'I love the performing, the whole being on stage thing, the applause; all of that. I love doing what I was born to do, using my talent every night and being successful at what I love but ...'

'Go on.'

'If I'm honest I miss home. I miss London, my family and my friends, and I could do without the constant backbiting and the anxiety that your understudy is hovering behind you, waiting for you to trip up or go off sick so she can step into your shoes and show the world she's much better than you.'

'What would you do if they asked you to stay on?'

'If they want to extend my contract, you mean? Logan would kill me if I turned it down.'

'You'd better decide because Ben heard a whisper.'

'No! Has he really?'

'What would you do?' he asked again.

My heart was fluttering with excitement and nerves. 'I don't know. I might stay, I *should* stay. I'd be mad not to if they wanted me, but ... I don't know. I want to work in London, the West End or maybe get some television work, that sort of thing. I shouldn't really turn money down though.'

He looked a little hurt. 'I hoped you'd say you'd want to come home with me. They won't ask me to stay on.'

'They might if you'd behave.'

He was silent for a moment, but then he looked directly at me and smiled. 'Do you miss your soul mate?'

The mere thought of Benedict made my stomach lurch. 'Yes, I do, very much.'

'More than you thought you would?'

'No, I knew I would. I'm not good at separations, especially when ...'

'You should tell him,' he urged, his wild eyes searching mine. 'People can be here one minute and gone the next, like my Dad. No time for goodbye or I love you or thank you, nothing. Just goodnight, forever and then it's too bloody late.'

'I know,' I muttered, thinking of Joshua.

'Helen, it's brilliant to talk like this. I've missed you since I've been here. I thought we'd spend all our days off together and have a laugh and see the sights and stuff.'

His neediness surprised me and he wasn't attempting to hide it at all, it was just there, blatant and desperate for the entire world to see. I ruffled his hair. 'So did I, but you're always in bed because you've been playing in the clubs till three in the morning. You can't be in a show off Broadway every night and be out till the early hours drinking. It's just not on, Matt. Don't blame me if we haven't spent time doing all that.'

He gave me a sheepish smile, but I did feel enormously guilty that I hadn't tried harder to drag him away from the guys who were so obviously a bad influence on him.

'I'm not really blaming you,' he said, 'I only ever blame myself. Or fate or timing! I know I'm easily led, pathetic really.'

I gave him a spontaneous, affectionate hug. 'You aren't pathetic and if you want me to tell you how I feel about you just in case one of us pops our clogs in the middle of the show or in bed tonight, I think you are the most naturally gifted person it has ever been my good fortune to meet. You're intensely lovable and appealing. You have charisma in spades, especially when you're on stage and lost in your music and I am very, very fond of you.'

He grew visibly brighter and less hunched with every word I spoke and his eyes grew larger and more of a vivid hazel colour, like a startled cat with a bright light shining in its eyes. 'Is that honestly how you see me?'

'Yes, honestly,' I replied, '*but* – and it's a big but – I don't like you at all when you drink.'

He blinked hard in his usual nervy way. 'Neither do I,' he muttered.

Ben flicked a tea towel at Matt's head again. 'If you two sit there thirty seconds more, you'll both get the sack!'

We both jumped off our stools like lightning. 'I'll see you on stage, Matt, and we'll have breakfast tomorrow morning at eleven at the diner on the corner, so you'll have to go straight home to bed tonight and sleep.'

'If you'll have breakfast every morning with me I'll stay off the booze,' he called as we parted backstage on our way to our dressing rooms, his neediness shining like a halo around his wild hair.

'You're on,' I told him and he was grinning as his face disappeared.

&

'Are you there, Dad?'

Beth had good reason to ask because as I had picked up the phone and gone to speak no actual sound came out of my mouth, just a low, hideous, mumbling slur and I had to concentrate hard to bring my speech to heal.

'Yes, darling, sorry, not had a drink – before you ask.'

'Is that the Parkinson's?' she asked forlornly.

'I'm afraid to say it is, but hey, my voice is back now, how lovely to hear from you.'

'How are you feeling generally? And don't fib to me, Dad, because I'll know.'

'Beth, as if I'd be anything but honest with you. Generally I am feeling very well with just a few annoying tremors, some fatigue and a little stumbling now and again, but that's it, honestly.'

'Are you sure?'

'Yes, I'm sure. Now, how is New York? Stifling as ever?'

'It's been a scorcher, but the last two days we've had really heavy thunderstorms.'

'And work, darling? Did you go for the promotion?'

'No, I decided against it.'

'Oh? I thought you were dead set on it.'

I heard her sigh. 'I feel too young for the role, Dad. I like my life as it is and there would have been enormous pressure to do longer hours, you know? It's pretty relentless as it is.'

'Of course, darling; there's always another ...'

'Dad, I've rung because I saw the show last night.'

'Fabulous, what did you think?'

'It's amazing, really amazing, shame you can't see it. The staging is spectacular and the dancers are out of this world ...'

'How wonderful and what about Nell?' I interjected, only wanting to hear about her and not some faceless people prancing about.

There was a slight pause. 'Well, I have to admit she's brilliant. I'll be completely honest and say I was surprised, really surprised. She can't half belt a song out and she's got great stage presence.'

'Yes, I can only imagine. She's got great stage presence when she isn't on stage,' I remarked.

Beth laughed. 'Oh Dad, don't be daft. Trust you to say something like that. But I tell you what, it was the pianist who stole it.'

'Matt ...'

'He has this long piece to play and when the spotlight goes on him he starts off by playing gently and then, my God, you should hear him thump out this piece of classical music. I'm surprised he isn't a concert pianist, he's incredible. Anyway, I went backstage after, like she asked me to, and he was in her dressing room and she introduced me.'

'How lovely for you, Beth,' I said, longing for a vivid description of Nell and how she looked and did she appear happy and relaxed and all those questions I couldn't ask my daughter.

'I reckon they're pretty close,' she went on, 'he was lounging about on this sofa thing she has in the dressing room and she had hardly anything on, well, a pair of leggings and a cropped vest. But I liked him, he was ever so friendly, but a bit manic looking.'

'Yes.'

'They invited me for a quick coffee, but they both looked knackered and I was a bit knackered too, so I made my excuses.'

As I tried to ask whether Nell had mentioned me, my voice slurred badly again and so it all came out garbled, but Beth obviously deciphered my question. 'She said to say hello and sent her love and said she'd Skype soon. I told her I'd been asking you to Skype me for ages and she laughed and said you were hopeless, which I agree with.'

'Well, thank you for that vote of confidence, Beth, and thank you for giving me her message.'

'She was good, Dad.'

'Thank you, darling.'

'They should keep her on and Matt. They were the best in the whole show.'

'I don't doubt it.'

'Do you know what he reminds me of?'

'No, darling...'

'He's like a wild cat, with all this hair standing up on end and bright hazel eyes and he kind of stares at you like a cat does when it's trying to make you out, you know?'

'Yes, well, he's quite an intense person by all accounts.'

'He's attractive though, in a manic kind of way. They would suit each other.'

'I'm sure,' I mumbled, hearing in her voice that she hoped they would suit each other and then perhaps I would come to my senses. 'They would understand each other...'

'I think they kind of spark off each other on stage; great chemistry.'

My heart was sinking with every word she uttered. Not because I expected Nell to come home and throw herself into my tremulous arms, but because he would be a difficult person to love. I wouldn't want that life for her.

'Great chemistry is a bonus, darling.'

'I'd better go; I'll speak soon, OK?'

'Lovely! Speak soon, Beth and thank you for telling me about the show. I'm so glad you enjoyed it and that you went back to talk to Nell. I've no doubt she'll tell me all about it too. Take care, sweetheart.'

'And take care of you, Dad. Bye then.'

As the line went dead Sidney knocked. I wanted to sit for a while with my thoughts because Nell's name had been mentioned, but I knew he would want to talk about his trip to the doctor's so I took pity on him and knocked back. It took him less than a minute to appear, all protruding stomach and indignant expression.

'What's occurring, Benedict?' he asked, sitting down heavily opposite me.

'Well, not much in here, but I can tell by your face that ...'

'I'm not happy!' he declared, crossing his arms.

'Obviously.'

'Don't eat this, don't eat that, take regular exercise – *exercise* for fuck's sake, at my time of life? Don't drink too much.'

'Aha, therein lies the origin of your indignation, Sidney.'

'When did a drop of splosh ever hurt you?' he continued, ignoring my comment completely. 'My aunt Sally used to drink Mother's ruin and brown ale and Guinness and she ate steak and kidney puddings, dripping on toast *and* cream *and* chips...deep fried chips I'll have you know and all those things that are supposed to be bad for you now and she lived until she was ninety-eight for fuck's sake!'

'There is always the exception to the rule, Sidney.'

'*And* she smoked!'

'But did she have a huge gut?'

He looked perplexed. 'I can't remember, but I don't think so.'

'That might be significant, especially with diabetes.'

He appeared suitably hurt. 'It's not that huge, is it?'

'Well ...'

'I might as well go and join the bleeding vegetarian brigade!'

'I can't quite see that happening in your house.'

'I'm fed up to the back teeth with being told what I can and can't do, just to add three years to my life. I'd rather die happy with a drink in my hand than live till eighty and be depressed.'

'Sidney, that isn't very fair on your saintly wife and three children, now is it?'

My remark appeared to deflate him immediately because he screwed his nose up and sighed. 'I suppose not, but honestly, you must know how I feel, mate.'

'I most certainly do and it's a strange and unearthly business to realise you feel out of control, because that's what it is. But you have more control over your disease than I do, Sidney.'

'Have I?'

'I believe so.'

'Oh, I suppose I'd better shut up then.'

'Not at all, feel free to sound off as much as you like, but let me warn you, in the end you'll end up doing exactly what Sheila tells you because you always do and you always will. And the reason for that is, she's more sensible than you and, secondly, she loves you and only wants what's in your best interests.'

He had the grace to look a little guilty. 'I know, I know.'

'Now, would you like a cup of tea?'

'I'd prefer a drink,' he muttered.

'So would I, but tea it will be for now.'

He suddenly brightened. 'Obsequious!'

'What, Sidney?'

'Obsequious! I heard it on Radio Four earlier.'

'And it means?'

'How the fuck would I know?'

'Well, do you want to know what it means?'

'Not really. How's Thea?'

'She's fine.'

He grinned. 'I bet she is.'

'Sidney, stop it.'

'I don't know what you mean.'

'And before you ask, Nell is fine too.'

'I think the sexy red head is the more pressing problem.'

'Neither of them are a problem.'

Sidney's eyes were now twinkling. 'Well, Thea might be if she doesn't get the message.'

'And what message is that?'

'You know what message.'

I tried my best not to smile. 'I assure you I don't.'

'The message that it's not only your walk that's floppy these days, matey.'

'How very unsavoury, Sidney.'

'She obviously doesn't think so.'

'She's starting Salsa classes.'

'Oh yeah...'

'It's a type of dancing.'

'Well, you won't be joining her, will you?'

'I think not.'

'She might meet a nice, healthy bloke.'

'She might, yes. I'm making the tea.' I stumbled into the kitchen.

'Fuck me, what's happening to your legs?' he gasped.

'Not much, as you can see,' I replied. 'Picture me at the Salsa class if you will.'

'I'd rather not,' Sidney declared. 'Mind you, Thea could probably steer you round the floor.'

'Heaven forbid!'

He was quiet while I made the tea and I carried the tray in carefully. Placing it on the low table between us was more luck that skill and Sidney felt moved to applaud. 'Well held, sir! Blimey, that was dicey, mate.'

'I know.'

He sat back and grinned. 'What a pair of twats we are!'

I pushed my glasses back up my nose as they had slipped during the difficult tray manoeuvre. 'Sidney, speak for yourself. I would call myself more ... ridiculous, comical, or ludicrous - something like that.'

'I prefer twat! It's much more descriptive. But then I talk normally and you don't.'

'Yes,' I sighed for effect, 'you're right, of course.'

'You know what I reckon?'

'I have no idea what you reckon and I'm flinching in anticipation.'

'I reckon you should still be writing your plays.'

I raised my eyebrows at him. 'Why on earth do you think that?'

'Because it's like you live inside one of them anyway.'

'Sidney, what are you talking about?'

'Sitting talking to you is like watching someone reading a script, Benedict. People, ordinary people, normal people, don't talk like you. If you wrote it down maybe we could have a conversation that doesn't have all those silly words in it.'

'Those silly words, Sidney are spoken by other people too. You just don't know any.'

'No, I only know you now. Well, you're the person I spend most of my time with, let's say that.'

'Ditto and I think if I started using *fuck* as a verb, a noun and an adjective you would go into another diabetic coma with shock.'

'Oh I think it sounds great when someone with a posh accent swears. It has more ...'

'Gravitas is probably the word you're looking for.'

'Yeah, something like that.'

As he sipped his tea, something moving to my right made me turn my head. The hazel eyed, scruffy cat was perched elegantly on my open bureau. It was staring at me intently. 'Sidney, can you see that cat sitting over there?' He glanced over towards the piano. 'No, not by the piano, that's where my father sits. Over there!'

'No, I can't see anything. If I saw your father sitting there I'd freak. No cat either.'

'Just me then,' I sighed, but I was slightly disturbed by the cat because I had the strangest notion it represented the wild eyed, scruffy haired, doomed Matt. However, I couldn't admit that to Sidney who was already eyeing me suspiciously under his thick eyebrows.

'Aha,' he cried, 'maybe *I'm* not real, matey.'

'No, you're real enough. I doubt even Parkinson's could conjure up a vision like you.'

He shook his head and sighed deeply. 'I don't know.'

'You don't know what?'

'I don't know about...well, life eh?'

'Yes, Sidney, I agree.'

'I suppose I'll have to do what the wife says.'

I didn't correct him this time. My mind was preoccupied with the cat and what it represented. I simply said, 'Twas ever thus.'

He laughed out loud. 'Thus! You see what I mean? Just speak

normally, for fuck's sake, Benedict.'

I laughed back at him because his face was so impossibly indignant and of course he was right. But I couldn't change my way of speaking any more than he could change his.

'Sorry, Sidney,' I muttered. 'I'm just a twat after all.'

Chapter 21

Autumn dragged on for me like a dreary Sunday afternoon and the startling sunlight of summer slowly began to change. It became muted, hazy and golden and there were early-morning mists hovering in the park like strands of silver silk. In early to mid-September we did have some glorious days, but I could almost taste the difference in the atmosphere on my occasional walks. The air smelt musty, like damp leaves covered in heavy dew and by the beginning of October the wind had shifted round to the east and the first winter frosts were deep, hard and crisp like a faint dusting of snow. By November there were moody skies and dismal, dark days where the slanting rain swept in across London. Throughout those months, Thea became someone I relied on for companionship and endlessly interesting conversation, and it soon became apparent that she was extremely good company once she relaxed and forgot to flirt with me. She recounted numerous stories to me about her 'extremely odd family,' as she called them, although they simply sounded eccentric to me rather than odd, but I kept that to myself, wondering whether some of them resembled me. I laughed at all the various stories, but also at her telling of them because her face would become animated and her eyes sparkled and she would giggle like a naughty schoolgirl at the back of a class, which was endearing. In fact, many times we had both giggled liked naughty children. In fact we spent much of our time giggling like school children, but it was such a relief to behave like that when the rest of the time I was an ageing man with a disease and haunted by the relentless *presence*.

Nell was on Skype regularly and seemed more settled, but often said how she had disliked the searing August heat in New York. She also mentioned Matt in every conversation. He was being his usual wild self except that he had stopped drinking so much, but only because they were spending every available spare minute together, and he leant on her like a heavy blanket apparently. But Nell was the kind of person you could lean on for support and as she had spent so many years doing exactly that for Joshua, it must have come as second nature to her. While she related how much Matt leant on her, I had made a solemn promise to myself that I would never do that to her: be a heavy blanket draped around her capable shoulders, weighing her down. She could lean on *me*. I would be *her* support system, not the other way round. And so, I listened and advised and in an effort to prove to myself I wouldn't be a burden to her, I kept my shaking hands in my lap when she appeared on the screen and I resolutely informed her, I was determined to stay as strong as I possibly could for many years to come, even though I knew I had little say in the matter.

Sometimes she would sit with her chin in her hands and ask me to speak about my childhood. 'What did you do in the evenings, in the old days?' she asked cheekily once, her eyes clear and mischievous.

'Well, there wasn't much to do then,' I had told her. 'Not like there is now. We had no computers or computer games, or any technology really. We would roam outside in the fields and the wood ...'

'Looking at the tallest tree in the world?'

'Yes or we usually just played together indoors or read books and listened to the radio.'

'There was radio in those days?' she asked, wide-eyed with pretend wonder.

'That's very funny, Nell. There was television too I'll have you know, but we were probably one of the last families to get a set because my father thought it would stultify our imaginations.'

'He was probably right. What else did you do? What about in the winter when you couldn't play outside?'

'We would play board games around the fire,' I told her, 'and my parents would place chestnuts in the flames to roast for us to eat. If I eat chestnuts now the smell of them just transports me back there instantly and my brain is flooded with nostalgia. We would eat them with the wind howling outside and the rain drumming against the windows and you felt safe, completely safe.'

'How lovely,' she murmured, listening intently, 'like in a tent.'

'Yes, Nell, just like that. And I would watch the flames flickering across my parents' faces and I remember how they would glance at each other and smile and he would reach across and take her hand in his ...' my voice faltered and slurred. Nell said nothing, but her eyes had grown large and solemn, and I finally continued, 'I remember knowing ... I knew they loved each other ...'

'And it was *real* love, Mr Marshall,' she added.

'Yes, Nell, it was real love, the best kind of love and we, their children, were bathed in its light.'

'You paint it so perfectly; I can see it all in my mind.'

'But you see,' I went on, 'that's what *I* wanted. That's what I was constantly searching for, in so many varied and unsuitable places I might add, but I was searching none the less. I used to dream sometimes that I was married to someone and in the dream I couldn't ever see her face, but I knew when she kissed me that I had found her: the one who would make me intensely happy, like my parents were. Sorry, I'm rambling, Nell.'

'No,' she said, 'you aren't at all. It all makes perfect sense to me. When I come home will you show me some photos of when you were little, all of you – and some of your parents? I'd love to see them, Mr Marshall.'

Her request was so touching I almost couldn't answer her. 'Of course, dear girl,' I muttered. 'Of course I will.'

'Mr Marshall,' she almost whispered, her expression changing, 'do you ever think you can halt your symptoms by wanting it enough?'

'I don't know what you mean, Nell.'

'Well, do you believe in the power of the mind?' she asked earnestly, moving nearer to the screen.

'I don't know…I haven't really ever thought about it…'

'Ask me if I do.'

'Do you, Nell?'

She appeared excited. 'Yes, I do.'

'I'm sure your mind is pretty powerful and that whatever you want you can have.'

She frowned. 'But maybe, just maybe, if Parkinson's originates in the brain and something going wrong in the brain, then the brain can put it right.'

I had to smile at her sweet simplicity. 'Interesting theory, Nell…'

'What if…you could heal yourself by the power of thought?'

'If only it were so,' I sighed.

'What if it was, I mean were, I mean what if simply believing you could do it would make it happen?'

'I think,' I replied, 'that would be something akin to a miracle.'

'But miracles have happened and I believe in magic.'

'Do you, Nell?'

She grinned suddenly. 'What have you got to lose?'

I shrugged. 'Nothing I suppose.

'Then let's pretend to hold hands and concentrate…'

'Is there anybody there?' I said, in a spooky voice.

'Stop taking the piss,' she scolded, playfully.

'I'm sorry, Nell.'

'Close your eyes, Mr Marshall. Now imagine as hard as you can that you are slowly healing. Imagine new cells, vibrant cells forming in your body and your brain. Imagine your symptoms getting less and less and ask out loud for what you want,' she urged.

'Heal me,' I whispered, 'that's all, heal me.' I waited for the words I had heard on that February night, but there were none this time. 'Heal my body, heal my life.' I opened my eyes and Nell was staring at me, her eyes large and solemn. The screen was startlingly bright, as if Nell was under a spotlight. I felt calm, content and at peace.

'If you had the choice,' she began, 'what would you do? Would you sit there in your conservatory and look out at your beautiful garden? Would you walk through the avenue of ancient oak trees in the park and sit by the duck pond? Would you...'

'I'd dance,' I replied, without hesitation, 'I'd do all those things, but I'd prefer to dance, with you, Nell.'

Tears appeared in her eyes instantly and she placed her right hand by the camera and instinctively I mirrored her. She then pretended to curl her fingers around mine, as if all our fingers were interlocking. Imagining her hand in mine caused a surge of deep love welling inside me like the enormous swell of the ocean.

'I can't feel any tremors,' she whispered, her face alive with excitement and lighting up my life. 'You see,' she continued, 'miracles can happen, even if only for one magical moment.'

'I'll take one magical moment,' I whispered back, '*this* one magical moment.'

'Let's dance then, Mr Marshall,' she said, 'dance for your life!'

We both moved slowly, swaying from side to side, in silence, as if we were the same branches of one of those old oaks, moving gently in an imperceptible summer breeze. I had never dared hold her closely before when we had danced together for fear of embarrassing her and myself. But for some reason this moment, when we were in different rooms, different times and different countries held the greatest intimacy. I felt no embarrassment, only gratitude, contentment, gentleness, kindness and love. If real love could move mountains, survive death and heal all grief and wounds then it could heal my disparate longing and the isolation I had been feeling in my own body. The moment was suddenly over though as the signal failed and the screen went dark. I sat silently for a long time, trying to hold onto the wonderful feelings flooding through my body. I didn't want to break the spell we had conjured up together and I felt quite light headed as if I was experiencing an out of body moment.

Often, after speaking to Nell on Skype I would sit quietly and replay our conversation in my head and I always wondered why we were constantly talking about anything and everything other than her life in New York. Was it because she was growing ever closer to Matt and didn't want me to ask about him? Was she deflecting those questions because her deep feelings for him were too personal to share with me? Before she had travelled to America I imagined us speaking only about the show, her new-found friends, the parties, the interviews, the audiences, the rapturous applause, the exhilarating feeling just before she stepped on the stage. I had expected her to be excited, fulfilled, literally sparkling like a jewel with the knowledge that she was at last using her talent and getting the recognition that talent deserved. But no, we spoke about me and the minutiae of my life past and present and about my Parkinson's and I was constantly bewildered by that. One misty evening in late November when I was playing cards with Sidney and he had been making me laugh by complaining that his journey to my conservatory, from his garden to mine, had been hampered by fog, my mobile bleeped.

'Nell,' he cried.

'And only Nell,' I replied.

'What does she say?'

'I'll turn on Skype.'

'Oh good, I'll say hello to her,' he grinned.

I pointed my finger at him. 'Behave or else!'

'Benedict,' he said, appearing shocked, 'as if I'd be anything but on my best behaviour! Don't you trust me?'

'No.'

I waited, with Sidney looking over my shoulder, but the connection was misbehaving and I could hear her voice, but the screen was dark for what seemed like an eternity. 'Can you hear me OK, Mr Marshall?' she asked.

'We can hear you,' I replied.

'Is there someone with you?'

'I'm afraid so.'

There was a pause. 'Is it Thea?'

'No, it's my ever-present near-neighbour, Sidney. Say something, Sidney.'

'Hello, Nell, it's Sidney here. This science fiction isn't very reliable, is it?'

'Hello, Sidney, lovely to hear your voice ... hang on ... I'll just ...'

Suddenly her face appeared, as lovely and as luminous as ever like a harvest moon in a black sky and it took my breath away. I had a feeling it did the same for Sidney because he clapped his hands in delight.

'There she is,' he cried, 'this is seriously weird.'

'Ah, Sidney,' she cried, with her mega-wattage smile lighting up our dismal, dreary November night. 'It's so nice to see you again. Are you keeping Benedict company?'

'No, I'm losing money to him, as usual.'

'Ha!' I snorted, 'Don't believe a word of it, Nell. But, is everything OK with you?' I was wondering why she had called. 'Nothing wrong I hope.'

'Yes, fine,' she started, but the connection was lost again and I swore loudly with frustration. 'I heard that,' she laughed.

'It was Sidney.'

'Fuck off,' Sidney said.

'No, *that* was Sidney,' she added.

Her face appeared again and my heart began to beat furiously because I had the strangest notion she needed to tell me something and I was fearful of what it was going to do to me. 'I have a feeling this connection is going to play silly buggers tonight,' I remarked.

'It's the weather,' Sidney declared, as if he knew what he was talking about.

'Don't talk daft, Sidney.'

She leant on her hand and stared into the screen. 'What's it like there?'

'Foggy,' we replied in unison.

'Yeah, I had trouble getting here tonight,' Sidney said. 'I nearly went headlong in the garden, no bloody moon and the fog is very low.'

'Very low fog, eh?' she replied. 'I'm not sure how fog can be low, but it sounds wonderful; a misty night in old London town –heaven!'

I was perplexed by her words, but I didn't comment on them. 'Well, I suppose it is December tomorrow, Nell. However, what's going on with you?' I asked, desperate to know why she was looking so refreshed, excited and dare I say it, happy at last?

She was watching my face intently. 'Nothing much, except that the company manager has asked me to stay on for another six months.'

My stomach sunk to my knees like a rock through water and my pulse raced, but I managed a Bafta-winning performance for her sake. 'That's wonderful news. I'm thrilled for you.'

Sidney poked me hard in the back which made me jump and gasp and Nell looked concerned. 'Are you OK, Mr Marshall?'

'Yes, dear girl, I'm fine. Sidney accidentally kicked me. Sidney, will you please be careful with this frail body of mine?'

'Sorry, mate, I just kind of ...'

'Nell, carry on and pretend he's not here, will you?'

'That's bloody nice!'

'Ah, poor you, Sidney,' she said and there was something in her expression and in her light voice that had changed dramatically from the last few times I had spoken to her.

'This news has obviously delighted you, Nell.'

She looked a little embarrassed. 'Well, I wouldn't tell anyone else this, but I'm the only one out of the whole company who has been asked to stay on for an extended run.'

Tears pricked at the back of my eyes like hot needles. 'I'm so proud of you, I can't tell you.'

'Thank you, Mr Marshall.'

'Well done, Nell,' Sidney added, sticking his thumb up right in front of my face.

'Thanks, Sidney.'

'After all your hard work, you now have the recognition you deserve. It's fantastic news. I knew you would fly. I told you, didn't I, that it was your time?'

She stared into my eyes and it was as if she was trying to communicate with me without Sidney hearing. 'Yes,' she whispered, 'you did, Mr Marshall. But there's something else ...'

'Do you want me to go?' Sidney asked, unusually receptive to the atmosphere for him because when he wanted to be he was as dense as the low fog outside.

She smiled fondly at him. 'No, don't be daft, you're fine. I'm interrupting your cards anyway. No, I just wanted to tell you ... I just wanted to let you know ...' Her eyes were dancing wildly now and she looked excited and carefree like the Nell I had known before she went away. It was heart warming. 'Mr Marshall, I don't know whether to tell you this ... I was going to keep it a secret ... I just wanted to tell you that Matt and I are ...'

The screen went blank. Sidney peered into the darkness. 'What's happened now?'

'Nell, can you hear me?' There was silence. 'Nell, are you still there?'

'Fuck me, it's so bloody annoying this Skype business. What was she going to say?'

'I don't know,' I cried.

'It was obviously important, Benedict.'

'Yes, Sidney, it obviously was.' I began to feel irritated and my heart was banging against my ribs like a bass drum. 'I'll try to call her back.'

'Her and Matt are what?' he asked me.

'How the hell would I know?' I screeched and my voice high enough to shatter glass.

'She was bursting to tell you.'

'I know, Sidney. Try not to state the obvious, please.'

'Can you get the signal back?'

'Fuck it! No, I can't.'

Sidney laughed out loud. 'You sound like me, matey.'

'I obviously spend too much time with you.'

'Leave it,' he sighed. 'Come back and play cards. That thing is bloody irritating. I'd rather talk on a phone.' I left the computer reluctantly and joined him in the conservatory. But I couldn't settle and he knew it. 'Oh Christ,' he moaned, 'that's finished you off for the night.'

I couldn't stop tapping my fingers on my knees. 'What did she want to tell me?'

'It's bleeding obvious, isn't it?' I went to say, yes it was bleeding obvious that she wanted to tell me she was in love with Matt and that they were together and didn't she look ecstatic and wasn't it wonderful for her she had been the only performer asked to stay on, but that meant she wouldn't be home for months and my heart was sinking into my boots at the thought of that. But I merely slurred and my mouth got stuck and I stared at him forlornly. 'Fucking hell,' he muttered. It seemed that the effect Nell's words were having on me were only just dawning on him as he continued, 'I'm sorry, matey. What are you going to do?'

'Bleed,' I replied.

Sidney stayed for another half an hour, but I was so preoccupied by Nell's sparkling, lively, effervescent face, he knew I was longing to be on my own with my bad mood and scrambled thoughts.

'I'll leave you to it, mate,' he told me, frowning with concern. 'Now don't dwell on it. It was always going to happen. I did tell you.'

'You don't understand. I'm delighted for her, honestly. I only want her happiness, that's all. I just thought she'd be home soon.'

Sidney shook his head. 'You're such a silly old sod.'

'I agree, Sidney, sorry.'

He leant forward and patted me on the shoulder. 'Don't worry. See you in the morning, bright and cheerful.'

'I'll be neither.'

'Silly old sod,' he muttered again as he left.

The *presence* hovered just to my left, unreachable, but there none the less and it taunted me. I poured myself a large scotch and drank it quickly. I leant my head back and the room moved backwards and made me giddy. I poured myself another drink, hoping for that longed-for feeling of relaxation to swim through me and sat motionless with my head in my hands. Nell was slipping away from me and I could hardly breathe, the pain in my chest was so intense.

'Benedict.'

My father was sitting by the piano, one leg crossed casually over the other, just like me, uncannily like me in every sense. 'Papa,' I gasped, 'I've lost her.'

He gave me a loving smile. I had forgotten that smile since his death. It was a smile that told you everything would be fine, he was there, he loved us and would take care of us and he always would. 'Benedict, she needs you. She will always need you.'

'No, Papa just listen to me. I've lost her I tell you.'

'Let her go and ...'

'She won't be coming back!' I yelled at him. 'You've got it all wrong.'

He didn't flinch, he remained calm and steady as he had in life and the tiny laughter lines around his eyes that had always fascinated me were clearly visible as he smiled. 'You have to see the bigger picture.'

I struggled to my feet. 'There is no bigger picture,' I declared. 'Not from where I am.'

'There is from where I am.'

I felt angry suddenly, frustrated and lost. 'And where exactly *are* you?'

'I'm here with you. Always here with you.'

'But you aren't really, are you? It's just the disease. *That's* what's here; this fucking awful, soul-destroying, life-sapping, insidious, bastard disease creeping through my body. And I'll tell you what else is here: a *presence,* the relentless, fucking ridiculous *presence* and the endless fucking horse tablets, but not *you.* Not really you, Papa. You are long gone ... long gone ... long gone ...' I staggered forward and then fell back onto the sofa, my legs splayed and my head bursting and all I could think about was Nell spending the rest of her precious, golden life with a drunk.

I must have fallen into a deep sleep because when I woke the clock was striking midnight. I attempted to move, but my neck, back and shoulders were rigid and ached and my head felt as if it was going to explode into a million pieces and splatter all over my living room walls.

All I could think was: 'I've lost her ... I've lost her ... I've lost her. Without ever really having her, I've lost her. Her life will be taken up with looking after a drunk.'

I slept again until four when I was woken by the shrill sound of foxes prowling around my garden calling to each other. The two lamps that had been on when I had been playing cards with Sidney were still on and the fire was giving off a low, orange glow. I attempted to move again and this time I was able to curl up into a ball on the sofa and go back to sleep. When I woke once more at about seven, a metal-grey dawn was breaking just outside my windows, but in the distance was the most remarkable sunrise seeping through what was left of the fog. The burning red rays of the new day's sun were reaching across the sky like flames and for some unfathomable reason I felt a warm happiness flooding through me. It made no sense because Nell was not coming home for at least another six months and the missing of her was becoming like a chronic illness; unforgettable, often painful and constantly at the back of my mind. Because I'd been sleeping all night on the sofa in a ridiculous position for someone of my years and infirmity, my bones creaked like a door in a haunted house, and tremors were sweeping through my body. And yet I felt a strange calmness, a deep sense of ease and an almost heightened sense of life needing to be lived that I couldn't fathom.

I remembered shouting at my father, yelling at him, with an unstoppable anger spilling over like boiling milk. I found it rather humorous that in life I had never spoken to him like that and yet I raged at him when he was no longer alive and appearing to me in a hallucination. Thinking how bizarre it all was, I had to laugh and that laughter in my large old house when only I was there to hear it sounded odd and hollow to my ears, which made me laugh some more. I laughed for so long I began to wonder if my tablets had reacted in some peculiar way to the alcohol I had thrown down my throat the night before.

I tried to get a grip. Nell wasn't coming home for a long time it was true and yet I had her in my life, she was my friend, my dear, sweet girl who had transformed an isolated existence with a disease into a life worth living. She had only ever wanted and longed for her talent to be recognised and now it had been. I had to be magnanimous and delighted for her because any other emotion would be churlish. All I could hope for was that if she and Matt loved each other, I could continue to be an important part of her life and that having her love would enable him to give up his hard drinking. And with that thought, I rubbed my eyes and decided to face the new day.

I staggered upstairs and had a hot shower which refreshed me instantly and then I changed into some clothes that weren't crumpled like yesterday's newspaper. I felt surprisingly alert, but then I had slept like a log despite being curled up in the foetal position on the sofa. I made myself some strong coffee and toast and sat with it on my lap in the conservatory, gazing out at a clearing sky. There had been no knock from Sidney, which was alarming as it was a daily ritual for him to annoy me early every morning, but I comforted myself by thinking if anything was wrong Sheila would have called me instantly.

I watched a few wagtails and blue tits landing effortlessly on my bird table and I wondered momentarily where the sparrows had all gone. Beth had always loved the little brown, rounded sparrows and robins the best and the memory of the robin frantically pecking for food in the snow last winter reminded me yet again of meeting and getting to know Nell. Not even a year had passed and yet my world had altered so dramatically in that short space of time, I hardly recognised myself. My deep shock, unhappiness and isolation at hearing of my Parkinson's seemed like a long-forgotten nightmare because it had been followed closely by a unique young actress making her appearance on the stage of my life.

With that thought I decided to take a walk in the park to clear my head for an hour. I needed to feel close to her and I knew the best places for that: the duck pond, the café and under the statue. I put on my overcoat and scarf but because my mind was so preoccupied, I didn't pick up my gloves and hat. I hadn't gone far before the surprisingly cold air struck me and the remaining icy fog seeped into my bones, making them rattle like castanets. I almost turned back, but I thought of Nell and could almost feel her hand in the small of my back giving me a gentle push. 'Lean on me, Mr Marshall,' I heard her say, so clearly she could have been beside me.

I made my faltering way across the large expanse of grass sloping down towards the river in front of the Queen's House and the Maritime Museum. It had been such a dense fog the night before, the heavy dew resembled a sheet of clear water. I stuffed my white hands into my pockets because they were stiffening rapidly. The words: 'Here, have my gloves, Mr Marshall,' made me swing round. Again, her voice seemed so near, I expected, hoped to see her, but there was only a black Labrador sniffing around my ankles as if I was a lamp post, and I felt a fool.

Visibility was quite poor and shadowy figures in the distance loomed out of the fog like ghosts. My legs were cramping up alarmingly and I realised I had been rather foolhardy to come out on such a morning. In the circumstances, there was only one place to be: the café, with its circular shape and small windows overlooking the rose garden. I had avoided it so far, for obvious reasons, but now I suddenly longed to be there and I walked purposefully yet puppet-like towards it. I remembered the smell of strong coffee and toasted sandwiches and I was transported back to the beginning of the year to the heavy snow and unearthly silence when Nell and I had visited the café for the first time. The same young, muscle-bound man was serving behind the counter in his white, short-sleeved shirt that showed off his biceps perfectly as I approached, fumbling in my pocket for some change.

'Yes, sir?' he asked, without making eye contact.

'I'd like a coffee, please.'

He turned his back to pick up a mug, 'Anything else?'

'No, thank you ... um yes, chocolate cake I think.'

'Sure.' He placed the coffee and cake in front of me. 'Three pounds seventy please, sir.'

I handed over the money, my hands shaking noticeably and I saw him flick his eyes towards them momentarily. 'Do you remember my friend, Nell?' I asked.

His face lit up instantly. 'Helen, you mean?'

'Yes, sorry, Helen, of course.'

'I thought I recognised you. Aren't you related you two?'

I wanted to laugh out loud for some reason. Probably because in his memory I was her grandfather and always would be. 'No, we aren't, but that's an easy mistake to make.'

'I haven't seen her for ages.'

'She's in New York, in a show off Broadway, doing brilliantly.'

'Good for her,' he said, looking past me at the next customer as if he couldn't have cared less.

'Yes, it's wonderful for her,' I persisted.

'Fame at last, eh?' he added.

'Well, it isn't the fame; it's the recognition of her talent that's so heart warming ...' my voice tailed off, sensing his shallow disinterest and recalling how Nell had said he was only ever interested in himself and the gym and wondering how I could ever have believed she would be attracted to a man like him.

'When is she back?' he asked, presumably because he felt he ought to.

'Not for a while.'

'Well, if you speak to her, tell her Wayne sends his best then. Sorry, can I just serve the bloke behind you,' he said, looking past me. 'Yes, what can I get you?'

I shuffled off to a table nearby, carrying my coffee and plate precariously. Yes, I thought, watching him, your name would be 'Wayne'. Wayne with the bulging muscles and washboard abdominals; Wayne with the attention span of a gnat; Wayne with the charisma bypass! And I felt a warm glow of contentment knowing Nell would rather sit with someone as old and infirm as me who looked like her grandfather than with the boring, self-absorbed Wayne. I had tried to speak of her success. I wanted to boast to someone about it. I wanted to tell the whole world and his wife and anyone else who would listen. I wondered if Beth would be pleased for her – I hoped so.

My legs were still cramping with the cold and I was twitching badly. Getting the cake from the plate to my mouth was rather haphazard and I took hold of the paper serviette and swiped my mouth in case I was dribbling. Gazing out of the window at the leggy, spindly roses with pearls of clear water resting on their leaves, I still had an uncanny sense of calm that I couldn't understand or decipher. Sitting in our café I expected to feel lost, lonely and ill at ease without her constantly changing expressions opposite me, but I just couldn't shake the feeling that she was somewhere near. I certainly felt she was and I wondered whether it was my pills again, making me sense those longed-for faces I missed so terribly.

Having finished my coffee and half the gooey chocolate cake, I made my way gingerly through the tables and outside again, pulling my scarf tighter and putting my overcoat collar up. Instead of going to the duck pond or the statue and risking turning into a chilled piece of marble, I made the sensible decision to visit Thea instead and I walked, with a few stumbles, towards St George's gate.

I knocked a little shakily on Thea's door and after a few seconds she flung the door open and beamed at me, which was a heartening sight on such a miserable day. 'Benedict, what a lovely surprise, come in, come in, it's freezing.'

'Yes, freezing fog,' I said.

'What on earth are you doing out on a morning like this? Come through, please.'

She was dressed in a black, tight, figure-hugging woollen dress which accentuated her curves and I thought of my sister's comment that nobody dressed like that during the day and I had to quash an unwanted smile because Thea always did and I rather admired her for it.

'I just needed to get out ...'

'Sit down; I'll put the kettle on. Make yourself comfortable. It's so nice of you to pop in.'

'Not at all, I felt like some company.'

She disappeared into the kitchen and was banging about in her usual slapdash, noisy, endearing way. 'Would you like a biscuit or some toast or anything?' she called.

'No, I've just had a piece of cake, thank you.'

She laughed as she came back in. 'Ah yes, you people with slim builds don't have to worry about extra calories, do you?'

'No, we don't.'

'It makes me sick,' she said. 'I normally have to deny myself practically everything.'

'Thea, you have a lovely figure,' I found myself saying.

Her eyes sparkled. 'Do you really think so? Thanks, Benedict, but that's because I starve myself much of the time. Hang on, I'll make the coffee. Or would you prefer tea?'

'I'll have whatever you would have at this time,' I replied.

'We'll have tea then, shall we?'

'Splendid.'

I sat back and felt the warmth flooding back into my legs but, with the cramping, was uncertain how they'd managed to get me to Thea's living room. I felt quite relaxed though and humbled by her obvious delight. I should have been sitting chatting with Sidney, as I did most days, and I wondered if he had been hammering on the wall for me.

'So, what's new?' she asked, placing a pot of tea on the table between us and leaning towards me. 'How's Sidney?'

'Sidney is ... Sidney.'

'He's such a character, isn't he?'

'That's an understatement.'

'You two need each other,' she said, looking at me and smiling.

'I need him. I wouldn't deny that. He has Sheila, so he doesn't need me as much as he thinks he does.'

'It's pretty unusual for a man to admit that. Normally a man will only admit he needs his partner and not many even admit that.'

'Maybe I admit it because I don't have a partner. Sidney takes the place of a partner for me.'

'There's more truth in that than you know. He needs you too though, more than you probably realise.'

'No, I know he does.'

'And what of Nell?' she asked, pouring the tea.

I paused while I attempted to wrap my useless, unpredictable mouth around some sensible words. 'Nell is staying in America for quite a while longer.'

Thea pushed the mug nearer to me. 'I see,' she muttered, her normally sunny face suddenly serious. 'I'm sorry, Benedict, really sorry. I know you probably won't believe that, but I am.'

'Oh I believe you,' I told her. 'It's not your words, it's your eyes. Your feelings are completely given away by your eyes and I can tell you mean it.'

She sat back and crossed her legs, but not in her usual flirty way. She sipped at the scalding tea and pushed her thick chestnut hair back behind her ears. 'Well, if I'm honest, I know I shouldn't be, but how can anyone who loves you deny you her companionship?'

Her words hung between us like the *presence* often did just in front of my eyes, but out of reach and not quite clear. 'Are you someone who loves me then?'

'If we're going to talk openly, then – yes, I am, but I hope that doesn't embarrass you.'

I hardly knew what to say to her. 'I really don't know how to respond to you, except to say thank you. But, I don't feel I deserve your affection.'

She looked surprised. 'Why wouldn't you deserve it?'

'Because of my ...' I was at a loss as to how I could express adequately what I wanted to say. 'Because of my...'

'Because of your preoccupation with a certain young actress...'

'Not preoccupation – I wouldn't call it that.'

'As you've always told me, it was bad timing.'

'Yes.'

'What will you do then?'

'Do?'

'I mean with Nell staying away.'

'I have no idea. Live my life, play cards with dear old Sidney, manage my Parkinson's, stay positive, be happy for her, be proud of her, talk to her on Skype and love her from afar.'

She leant forward and grabbed my stiff hand. 'And me?'

'I'm sorry?'

'What do you feel about me?'

I thought I would feel uncomfortable with her probing, but I was relaxed and content to be there. 'I do have strong feelings for you.'

Her eyebrows shot up in surprise. 'You have?'

'Yes, of course.'

She squeezed my hand. 'Then I'll take that gladly, Benedict.'

'You make me feel terrible by your acceptance of the situation.'

'Oh do shut up man!' she laughed. 'It's my life; I can love and care for whomever I choose.'

I smiled. 'Yes, of course.' I withdrew my hand slowly because her strong grip was cutting of my blood supply. 'Thea, will you be completely honest with me if I ask you a direct question?'

'I always am, well I try to be.'

'How can I ask this? Was there ever a moment when you thought it wrong, no ... I'll put it another way...a little unsavoury of me to love someone so much younger than myself?'

'That's so typical of you, Benedict, but unsavoury in what sense?'

'Not unsavoury then, just foolish.'

She thought for a moment. 'Foolish? No.'

'Is it dirty old man-ish then?'

'No,' she replied succinctly.

'Are you sure? Why didn't you think that?'

'That's easy, because you love her. If you'd been after a quick fling, an affair, a fleeting physical thrill with a younger woman to recapture your youth, you know, all that kind of stuff that men often do, then that would be different. But you can't choose who you fall for and you fell for her, end of story.'

Hearing her describe my feelings in those terms heartened me somewhat and I went to reply, but my mouth got stuck around the words and for a second I thought I was dribbling and I wiped my hand across my mouth. I finally managed to splutter, 'Yes.'

'I have to say though,' she added, 'that I think you were ready for love.'

'Do you? That's interesting.'

She frowned and finished her tea. 'Well, subconsciously I think you were looking for someone to love and that was compounded by the fact that you'd suddenly been given a life-changing diagnosis. Who wouldn't be looking for love and comfort and affection? Then, almost at the same moment, into your life steps this incredible young woman with a life force so strong and powerful ...'

'Timing again...'

'Yes and she's so beautiful, loving and ...'

'But I would have loved her had she not been beautiful. It isn't her beauty.'

My constant interruptions didn't seem to faze Thea; she smiled, but voiced her doubts, 'Would you have, Benedict? Would you really? Men are normally visual.'

I did not hesitate. 'Absolutely I would have.'

She gave a little laugh. 'What if she'd looked like the back end of a bus?'

'Well, I'm no oil painting myself. Especially with the staggering and dribbling and slurring ...'

'OK, I get the picture. But would you even have noticed her if she hadn't been stunning?'

I thought for a moment, recalling Nell's vibrancy, direct manner, humour and kindness. The way she had put her gloves on my frozen hands, her playful eyes, her words: 'Lean on me, Mr Marshall.' I held Thea's gaze and spoke deliberately, 'I can honestly say, hand on my heart, it was the person inside I noticed first. It's hard to define exactly what it was that shone out from her.'

'Kindness?' she suggested.

'Yes, you're right, kindness and compassion.'

Thea took my cup and, pouring me another one, took the conversation off at a slight tangent, 'I hope she enjoys her success in America. It must suck you in all that adulation every night.'

I nodded, 'Perhaps, for some, but Nell would pass on the adulation, it doesn't seem to touch her. She simply craved the recognition of her talent, that's all. And I want that for her too, so much. I'll just watch quietly from the wings.'

'Very noble of you,' Thea commented, 'but hard. She must be having the most fantastic time over there.'

'You'd think so, wouldn't you? But last night was the first time I've actually seen her looking happy in a very long time.'

'She might be exhausted.'

'Yes, probably, I don't know ...'

Thea leant across the table and stroked my hand. The comforting gesture was welcome and my stiff shoulders began to relax. 'You're a good man, Benedict, a very good man.'

'Thank you, but ...'

'No buts!' she cried, halting any more of my self-depreciating nonsense in a flash. 'What crimes have you committed in your life? None! Cut yourself some slack, for goodness sake.'

I had to laugh at her. She was so forthright it was refreshing. 'OK, OK, I will.'

'Concentrate on your strengths for a change. You are kind, considerate, a good friend to Sidney, a loving and supportive father, your manners and way of speaking are exquisite ...'

'I do try to be as courteous as I can. I probably get that from my father. He was courteous and well-mannered to a fault. I'll never forget how proud I was of him when he used to doff his trilby hat when he passed a lady.'

'How quaint...'

'Yes and when my brother William and I were very young and in primary school, he taught us to doff our school caps when a lady approached us. Looking back it must have appeared very old-fashioned, but everyone looked so impressed when we did it.'

'I bet.'

There was a moment's silence where I was lost in my crystal clear memories. I knew Thea was watching me closely. She then stood up and leant over me, her perfume tickling my nose and making me want to sneeze. As she bent forward she put her chest right in my face and I tried not to think of how Sidney would have reacted if he had been in the room because I knew he would have relished the whole scene immensely. She kissed my forehead tenderly and it felt like a kiss you would reserve for a fond uncle or a young wayward child.

'What was that kiss for?' I asked.

She shrugged her shoulders. 'I just felt you needed it and I felt like doing it. So there!'

'I'm not complaining.'

'So you shouldn't. Think yourself lucky.'

'I most certainly do.'

She suddenly changed tack by saying, 'I'm guessing that you probably worry about losing that wonderful voice of yours.'

'Not of losing it. I don't know if I'll actually lose my voice with Parkinson's, but slurring and spluttering while I speak will no doubt turn the listener's attention from the actual sound of it to what is happening to my mouth, wouldn't you say?'

She gave a wry smile. 'Do you care about what other people think? Do you really care? Those of us who love you will just accept it as part of you.'

Her warm words touched me greatly and I could not answer because I was moved to sudden unwanted, hot tears. If she noticed, she didn't comment but suddenly glanced at her watch. 'I don't want to rush you, Benedict but ...'

'I'm so sorry, are you going out?'

'I'm only covering a shift in the book shop, but it is bad form to be late.'

I struggled to my feet. 'Oh dear, I've acted selfishly, turning up here like this and expecting to be entertained. I'm so sorry.'

She waved her hand dismissively. 'Don't be silly. I'd much rather sit here and chat with you all day.'

'How is the ... what was the dance class called?'

'Salsa,' she laughed.

'Yes, how's it going?'

Her eyes shone with an undisguised enthusiasm. 'It's fantastic! I wish I'd done it years ago. You have to swing your hips and sway about and it's fabulously sexy.'

'I can think of nothing worse,' I remarked, with my nose firmly in the air. 'Ballet and tap dancing are hard enough.'

'You're so old-fashioned!'

'I know, but it sounds right up your street. Thanks for the tea. See you soon.'

She saw me to the door. 'Mind how you go, Benedict.'

'I think I can find my way home.'

'What are you doing tomorrow?'

'Playing cards and listening to Sidney moaning about not being able to drink, no doubt.'

'Shall I pop in?' she asked.

'That would be lovely.'

'OK, I'll do that. I'll be in the book shop in the morning, then I'm going shopping, so what, about four?'

I smiled at her energy. 'Four it is then.'

I sauntered home despite the air still being thick with icy fog, but a lukewarm sun was trying to force itself through the low clouds without much luck. I caught sight of Sidney with his nose pressed against the window pane and gave him a wave. His face disappeared and I knew without a shadow of a doubt that he would appear at my back door before I could make it in through my front door.

'Where the hell have you been?' he demanded as I unlocked the conservatory.

'I've been walking, Sidney.'

'Walking in this weather, with your legs?'

'How dare you! What exactly are you implying?'

'That you'll go fucking headlong with the pavements this damp if you're not careful.'

'That was very eloquent of you.'

'I know, I just can't help it,' he replied, sitting down heavily on my sofa in his usual place. 'Where have you been? I knocked earlier.'

'You didn't knock first thing ...'

'No, I didn't. The wife was nagging me.'

'*My* wife, *my* wife...'

'Yeah, yeah, whatever you say.'

'If your wife was nagging you then you deserve it.'

'I thought you'd be on my side ... that's bloody charming,' he grumbled.

'Sheila gets my vote every time because she has so much common sense and wants only the very best for you at all times. So, you'll get no sympathy from me.'

'This fucking diet is getting on my fucking nerves,' he sighed.

'I had a feeling it would. Look, it will do you the world of good ...'

'I don't give a flying fuck how much good it will do me!'

'Again, you command of the English language is staggering.'

'We can't all speak like we live in a stately home, Benedict.'

'That's true.'

He peered at me over his glasses. 'I've been here five minutes and not been offered a drink yet.'

I peered back at him over mine. 'If you mean an alcoholic drink you're going to be sorely disappointed.'

He appeared hurt. 'No, I meant a cup of tea.'

'Just give me a minute to rest my legs and I'll make you one.'

'Sorry, mate. I'll make it, you sit there.'

'Thank you, Sidney.'

'What a miserable day, eh?' he called from the kitchen.

'It is December,' I remarked.

'I'd prefer snow to this.'

I thought of sitting by the frozen duck pond and being shaken out of my terminal doldrums by a lovely young woman with a life-changing, blast of a laugh. 'Yes, so would I,' I muttered.

Sidney's head appeared round the door. 'What cups shall I use, matey?'

'Take your pick.'

'I fancy a mug.'

'They're in the cupboard to the right of the sink.'

He appeared with the tea, announcing, 'There you go.'

'Cheers, Sidney. So, without mentioning the diet, how are you feeling?'

'I feel as rough as old bollocks.'

I had taken a sip of my tea and I almost spat it out. 'How very delightful I must say.'

He laughed back at me. 'Well, you did ask.'

'Do you really feel rough? Perhaps you ought to talk to your nurse.'

'That's what Sheila says, but I'm all right. The quack did say it might take a while to stabilise my sugars.'

'Well, if you're sure.'

'Yeah, I'm sure. I just like to make a fuss.'

I smiled at him fondly. I loved the man, simple as that. 'Sidney, you can always come in here and moan about your health as much as you like. I'll understand, I promise you.'

He appeared moved. 'Cheers, matey. I'll hold you to that.'

'I don't doubt it.'

'So,' he sighed, 'what's occurring then?'

'There is very little occurring, as usual.'

'You just went for a walk then? On your own?' he asked, pulling a face that meant he knew very well that I was withholding something.

'Yes, on my own and then I called round at Thea's for a bit.'

'Oh yeah...'

'Sidney!'

'Called round for a *bit*, did we? I bet she loved that.'

'We just chatted, as we always do.'

'Was she wearing a super-tight jumper with bumps in?'

'No, she was wearing a super-tight woollen dress with bumps in,' I replied.

'Lovely.'

'It did suit her, I have to admit it.'

'Oh yeah...'

'She was different,' I muttered, more to myself than Sidney, as the thought that she was different had only just entered my mind.

Sidney frowned. 'What do you mean?'

'I'm not sure what I mean.'

'Come on, man with all the words; explain to me.'

'I'm trying to work out why,' I told him. 'She kissed me ...'

'She's done that before, so that's not different.'

'No, it wasn't the kissing, it was – well, she was just different from how she normally is. I don't know, less ...'

'Sexual tension,' Sidney offered, his eyes twinkling like night stars.

I laughed out loud. 'There never has been or will be any sexual tension coming from me.'

'But there has been from her,' he remarked, 'loads of it.'

I snapped my fingers. 'Yes, that was it. There wasn't any coming from her either and there always has been and she was just her normal self, as she would be with you. Well done, Sidney.'

He preened. 'Thanks, Benedict. You see, I'm not such an idiot as I thought. I mean as you thought.'

'My friend, you know I've never thought that.'

'I was only kidding.'

'It *was* very strange though.'

'Oh, she's gone off you. Someone else is floating her boat so you've lost your chance there.'

I shrugged. 'We both know that Thea needs a healthy, energetic man with strong, steady arms to support her. She may have found just that at Salsa.'

Sidney turned up his nose. 'Isn't that a type of sauce you put on chicken or something?'

I felt a warm, broad smile creeping across my stiff features. 'Sidney Walpole, you make life worth living.'

He beamed back at me. 'Nobody's ever said that to me before. Do you mean it?'

'I do and actually *I* have said that to you before. I wouldn't want to live my life without you.'

His eyes glistened. 'I'm touched, matey, really touched. Now break out the whiskey, eh?' he grinned.

'I most certainly will not!'

'Bollocks.'

'That was as eloquent as ever! You can have another cup of tea and lump it.'

'Double bollocks.'

We heard a loud thump against the wall and I raised an eyebrow knowingly, 'Sheila, I believe.'

'It must be almost lunch time. I wonder what delights she'll be serving up today. I've had so much salad and green vegetables I'll be growing long ears and buck teeth,' he moaned, his droopy, mournful expression making him look more like a bloodhound than a rabbit.

'Bye, Sidney.'

'See you later, about seven, for cards?'

'You will.'

I emailed Beth after watching the birds flying on and off my bird table, pecking at the nuts and shaking their feathers furiously as if to rid themselves of the icy fog. I told her all my news, so it was a short, but sweet email, but I did tell her about Nell being asked to stay on in New York, just in case she wanted to go and see the show again and take her friends. I was so proud of her success I wanted to shout it from the rooftops and inform anyone and everyone who might listen that only she out of the whole cast had been asked to stay on. But apart from Beth there was only really Sidney and Thea to tell and I had already told them.

My thoughts rambled over the last few months: my diagnosis, living with my symptoms, my hallucinations, the *presence,* loving Nell, losing Nell, meeting Thea. It had been quite a year, the most challenging and yet rewarding of my life. For some unknown reason I wanted to laugh again and I felt relaxed and content, despite knowing I wouldn't be seeing Nell on this side of the ocean for many more months. I leant my head back and smiled foolishly, at nothing in particular.

'Benedict...'

I sat up like a shot and my father was sitting a few feet away. 'Hello, Papa.'

'Look after Bethan for me, won't you?' he urged.

'What do you mean? Bethan doesn't need my help. She's the last person who needs my help.'

He smiled, one of his rare smiles that my mother loved. 'Don't be fooled.'

'But you aren't really here, are you? It's just the drugs. I know it's the drugs.'

'I'm always here. I always have been.'

'Have you, Papa?'

'And Benedict ... she loves you.'

'Oh I'm sure Bethan does, she just doesn't show it.'

The doorbell suddenly rang and I jumped out of my skin. In that split second my father disappeared and the *presence* hung in front of my eyes like the fog outside. I tried to touch it, but it ran through my fingers.

'Just go away, for heaven's sake!' I yelled.

The doorbell rang again and I flopped towards the front door feeling like a rag doll. As I pulled it open my sister's face crumpled and she fell into my arms.

Chapter 22

'Bethan, what on earth is wrong?' I asked, shocked as I led her into the conservatory. She was like a lost child, sobbing quietly and trying to catch her breath.

'I'm losing my way,' she gasped, her words almost unintelligible.

I was bewildered. 'Losing your way in what sense? Look, please don't cry, I can't bear to see you like this.'

'I'm sorry, but I need to get it all out and you're the only one I can ...'

I sat next to her and put my arms around her shoulders. She was shuddering with emotion and when she looked at me her mascara was running down her cheeks in two thick, smeared, black lines. 'Then get it all out,' I told her gently, 'you can say what you want to me. Are you ill?'

'No, not ill ... I ...not in that sense...I don't know,' she replied, her voice quaking between sobs. 'I don't know anything any more. I used to, but not now.'

'Explain to me, right from the start.'

'I don't know how to. I don't know who I am any more, Benedict. I feel distanced from everyone and everything, as if I'm in another world.'

'I understand that very well. I've often felt the same, but that must be hard at work,' I commented.

'It's bloody impossible, but quite frankly I wish I cared.'

I could hardly believe my ears. 'That really isn't like you. Your work has always been your life. Have you seen a doctor about this? It sounds like depression to me. Not that I know much about it of course.'

'No, I've told nobody, only you now,' she muttered, wiping her eyes with the back of her hand. 'Oh God, look at this mess. All this bloody make-up I have to wear.' She turned to look at me. 'It feels like a mask some days.'

'What do you think is the root cause of all this? What's brought it all to the surface? I want to try and help, Bethan.'

She gave a pitiful smile. 'The root cause is ... I don't know, everything, anything ... my life ... childhood,' she added somewhat flippantly I felt.

'We all had an idyllic childhood, didn't we?'

'Yes, but, oh I don't know,' she said flatly. 'You were always Dad's favourite.'

I was completely perplexed by her words. And as she was speaking, I saw all her toughness, her often bitter tongue, her hard, brittle exterior fall away and she was instantly transformed into my five-year-old sister again who I carried on my back.

'Well, I think you're wrong about that. I was there don't forget. In my eyes you were doted on.'

'No, *you* were,' she told me, her eyes filling up again. 'For me there was something missing, something I can't explain in words. It was as if I was an afterthought and of course Mum and Dad were so completely wrapped up in each other ...'

'This is extraordinary. My memories are so completely different; it's as if we are talking about a different home.'

'Don't you believe me then?' she asked accusingly.

I hugged her tightly. 'Of course I believe you. And I'm so very sorry you feel like this.'

'I do,' she declared, 'and I'm sorry to have to say it. I know Dad was your idol.'

'He still is ...'

She jumped up as if I'd hit her and sat down heavily opposite me. 'Then keep your idol,' she snapped at me, almost bitterly. 'I thought you would understand, but ...'

'I do. If your memories are different from mine then so be it. I can't remember the last time I saw you cry, not like this, so I can see how upset you are. But it can't all be about Mum and Dad, surely.'

'No, it isn't. I'm fifty-seven, divorced and I had my life completely sorted out, but now I'm ...' She bit her lip and shook her head. 'I'm ...'

'Menopausal?' I suggested, smiling.

'Don't be ridiculous, Benedict!' she snapped again, in her usual way and I was almost glad I had the old Bethan back because her tears had been extremely difficult to stomach as they were so rare. 'I'm well past all that and I sailed through it.'

'Yes, you would,' I remarked. 'So, what's wrong? Come on, spill the beans.'

'No, I can't ... I feel so foolish ... especially as I ridiculed you ...'

'Go on,' I urged, playfully, 'I'm a silly old fool, as you are constantly telling me, so let's be silly fools together.'

She sighed and attempted a smile, but it got stuck halfway and ended up almost like a sneer. 'That's the whole point,' she declared.

'I'm sorry, I don't understand. Am I missing something here?'

'I called you all the silly old fools under the sun when really ...'

'For goodness sake, just tell me.'

She almost spat the words out as if she had been poisoned. 'I'm in love with a younger man. There, now you can gloat and laugh and mock all you like.'

I stared at her like the village idiot, unblinking and blank. 'Say that again.'

'You heard me.'

'I did and I'm stunned.'

She looked a little hurt. 'Why? I'm a normal woman after all.'

'But you don't act like one.'

'That's not very gallant of you.'

'Sorry, I didn't mean it like that. I simply meant you always seemed to be so single-minded about your work. How on earth did you get the time to meet someone?'

She shrugged, 'At work.'

'Of course, yes.'

'Well, say something then, Benedict.'

'I don't know what you want me to say. If you're in love and you're happy then I'll be happy, but I'm guessing by your tears that all is not straightforward.'

'You guess right,' she mumbled.

'How young is he?'

She looked suitably embarrassed. 'Never mind how young he is.'

'Come on, you can tell me. I won't mock, I promise you. Is he younger than Nell?'

'Yes, a little, so now you can gloat if you must.'

Now it was my turn to be hurt. 'Why would I gloat? Does he feel the same?' Her face crumpled again and she shook her head. 'Ah,' I murmured, 'unrequited love; the worst possible situation to be in.'

'It is,' she cried.

'Does he know?'

'How I feel about him?'

'Yes.'

'I think he suspects and I have no doubt he thinks I'm a ridiculous, middle-aged woman with a crush, but I'm not and I have this longing that I don't know what to do with. I can't even begin to tell you ... well, I expect you feel like that with Nell.'

I thought for a moment before I answered her because I doubted whether what I felt for Nell was in any way similar to her situation. 'He might be secretly flattered. And no, I don't feel like that with Nell. My feelings are incredibly complicated and unusual I suspect.'

'Why?' she asked and for the first time I felt she actually was interested, instead of berating me for being a fool.

'I've just been told by Nell that she's staying in New York for much longer.'

'Then you must be heartbroken.'

'You would think so, wouldn't you?' I said. 'But after the initial shock, where I felt as if I was slowly suffocating, I was so immensely proud and delighted for her and those selfless emotions overcame every selfish one. Missing her has become like part of my disease, constant and with me in every waking moment, but how can I be churlish and wish her home when she is such a success? And don't forget, I have absolutely no right to be unhappy or disappointed. We aren't in a relationship and are unlikely to ever be in one. I love her from afar and will for the rest of my life.'

'Then we're in a similar position.'

'Yes and no. Bethan, is it love or is it a sexual thing with this young man?'

'It's love,' she declared. '*And* desire.'

'Is it *real* love?'

She frowned hard. 'Of course, what other type is there?'

'There are many types, too many to describe.'

'Oh you're just splitting hairs.'

'I'm not, honestly. Someone unavailable is often very attractive because he or she is just that.'

'All I know is I've never felt like this. I don't care about my work any more, my friends, my social life, all I think about is why can't I be younger and then he might be attracted to me? It's driving me insane. I can't concentrate on anything,' she almost wailed, 'I feel as if I've been hit by a truck!'

'I'm sorry,' I said. 'I know it must be hard. Does he feel anything for you?'

'I don't know,' she replied, tears spurting out of her eyes again. 'I doubt it. He isn't seeing anyone at the moment, I know that much.'

'Do you want advice from me or not?'

'Yes, I want some advice,' she replied, almost angrily.

'Let it be, let it evolve. Be his friend and get on with your life. If need be, when the time comes, let him go to whoever he wants to go to. You can do it, I know you can.'

'I can't,' she gasped, 'I can't.'

'You can,' I urged her. 'You have always been able to do anything you want to in life; you're the strongest person I know.'

'I'm not though, not with him. I can't let go of the longing. I don't know what to do with it.'

'You can, I promise you.'

Her face was strained and stained with tears. 'I don't always want to be the strong one.'

'I know,' I told her, 'I understand. You always have to be strong because of your career and sometimes you must feel like being supported and cared for. Now please, wipe your eyes and try to look on the bright side.'

'Huh!' she cried. 'What bloody bright side? There isn't one!'

'I assure you there is. Did you love Jeremy like this?'

'No, nothing near,' she remarked.

'Then thank God for it.'

'What do you mean?' she asked, looking at me as if I was insane.

'One day, maybe not soon, but one day, you'll be pleased you feel love like this. Imagine going to your grave and never having experienced it. Wouldn't that be awful?'

She shook her head as if trying to clear her thoughts. 'I suppose you're right, but at the moment...'

'You don't feel like that.'

'No.'

'Fine, but remember I said that.'

She looked suitably contrite. 'And now you can have a go at me for ridiculing you over Nell.'

'I wouldn't ever have a go at you, Bethan. You're my sister and I love you and I know you were only saying it through concern. Often in life our greatest critics have secrets of their own.'

She gave a wry smile. 'You're so bloody perfect, be careful, your halo will slip.'

I preened a little. 'I always have been.'

'Mum and Dad thought so,' she added.

'Let's get this settled, shall we? Dad told me to take care of you.'

She visibly brightened. 'When did he say that?'

'Always ... before he died ... all the time ...' I slurred, stretching the truth a little for her sake. I couldn't tell her I had seen him moments before she arrived in a drug-induced dream.

'Did he really?' she whispered, her vulnerability almost too painful to witness.

'Hand on my heart,' I told her, 'he didn't say it about the others, only ever you.'

She looked perplexed and unsure. 'Why did he say it about me?'

'He said it, obviously because he loved you so much. You were his baby, for goodness sake. Look, I'm no expert and perhaps I'm wrong about this, but I think the feeling of not being loved is partly coming from you. You are vulnerable at the moment, extremely vulnerable. Your emotions are raw and you're longing for some love and affection from this man. Don't confuse that with being unloved as a child. You weren't unloved, you *aren't* unloved.'

She frowned at me. 'Benedict, did Papa really say that about me?'

I held her intense gaze. 'Do you doubt me?'

'No, of course I don't.'

'Then believe it and remember it, please. And Bethan, don't let your love for this man be a negative thing.'

'I'll try,' she said, her face pale and drawn.

'Strange, isn't it?' I added, 'I wonder if our parents' intense and deep love for each other has made us how we are?'

'How do you mean?' she asked, dabbing at her eyes.

'Well, we have both been searching, probably all our lives, for what they had together. Is this young man incredibly kind and caring?' She nodded, unable to speak. 'So is Nell. And that's why we love them. Now, why don't we have some lunch together?'

She shook her head and wiped her face with the back of her hand to remove the still drying tears. 'I can't, I'm late already, sorry.'

'You can't possibly go out looking like that. Go and wash your face and put some more make-up on.'

'Yes, you're right. Do I look as if I've been crying then?'

'Just a little.'

'I won't be a minute.'

I sat quite still and waited for her. In truth I felt drained myself. I was still reeling from the shock of her tears and her declaration of love for this unknown young man. What did a man who Bethan adored look like? I had no picture in my mind at all, just a blank canvas. She appeared again and looked a little refreshed.

'That's better,' I told her, 'almost perfect.'

She looked a little morose. 'I don't feel it.'

'What does he look like? What's his name, your young man? And what does he do?'

'He works in our offices. His name is James and he looks like ...'

'Go on,' I urged.

Her eyes softened considerably and she shrugged. 'I can't really describe him. He's quite small, slim and has a mass of curls and he's sweet.'

'Sweet, eh,' I said, 'not your usual type then.'

'He's the sweetest person I've ever met, except for you of course. He makes me softer, you know? I never thought somebody like him would change me, but just being near him...it makes me want to be kinder to everyone around me and his softness kind of rubs off on me. And I need that, Benedict.'

'You aren't so bad.'

'You would say that. Now, I'm going. Stay here, I'll let myself out.'

I put my arms around her. 'You can always come to me, remember.'

'If you're still around,' she muttered, looking up at me. 'Don't ever die, will you?'

'I don't intend going anywhere any time soon, I'll have you know.'

She smiled warmly. 'Good. Bye, dear brother, keep taking the tablets and thanks.'

'There is nothing to thank me for.'

'And I'm sorry ... that your young actress is staying in New York, but it was always going to happen with someone so young and talented. She obviously has a wonderful career ahead of her. She needs to grab it with both hands, especially in her business.'

'I couldn't agree more and you can see now how someone like her was never after my money when she has such a future ahead of her.'

She looked decidedly guilty. 'I suppose I can,' she replied, begrudgingly, despite her outburst, 'but you're still a good catch you know.'

'You're forgetting the *disease*, dear sister.'

She took hold of my trembling hand and studied it. 'This would mean nothing to someone who loves you.' She kissed my cheek quickly. 'See you soon.'

I stood on the doorstep and watched her stride away, her heels clicking on the pavement, until she was out of sight. Yes, I thought, she did have deep feelings for the unknown young man in her office because before falling for him she wouldn't have made the understanding remark about my shaking.

I prepared a sandwich for my lunch and sat reflecting on the morning. It was hard to believe my hard-headed sister had fallen so hopelessly in love. Life, with all its sudden twists and turns was certainly unfolding in a surprising way. I had never been aware that she felt unloved as a child compared to the rest of us and I found it unsettling and unbelievable, knowing as I did how adored and doted on she was. My mind immediately wandered onto how Thea would probably understand all of it and I felt relieved she was coming to tea.

The fog didn't lift all day and was sitting heavy and low across my garden and Thea's house was completely obliterated by it. But I felt cosy and content sitting on my own knowing she and Sidney would be visiting later. I had no idea where my contentment came from because Nell was still miles away and would be for much longer than I'd hoped. However, I couldn't shake the feeling that she was near me and it was perplexing and downright odd and I convinced myself that it was to do with my pills and my Parkinson's. If I could see my father and my mother and a bright-eyed cat sitting on the piano and bureau, then sensing Nell nearby wasn't exactly a surprise, but it continued to bewilder me and I eventually admitted to myself that perhaps it was a subconscious longing manifesting itself as an actual feeling. As I stared out into my garden, the *presence* distracted me constantly and I waved it away a few times, but it was belligerent and stubborn and would not leave me. My usual answer to its never-ending haranguing was to close my eyes and slip into a fitful sleep and I leant my head back and dozed easily.

&

My mobile was ringing and Logan's name was flashing on it. My stomach lurched because I knew I would have to tell him the bad news. He was going to blow his top, that was for sure and I braced myself. 'Hi, Logan, how are you?'

'Helen, tell me it isn't true,' he said, his voice devoid of emotion, but cold and distant.

'Who told you?'

'The company manager who, I might tell you, is spitting blood.'

'I know ...'

'What the fuck is wrong with you?' he demanded, his Glaswegian accent making his words almost unintelligible.

'Look, just calm down and listen without shouting at me, OK?'

'This had better be good.'

'It's good for me.'

'What does that mean?'

'I want to go home, Logan.'

He gave an audible groan. 'Is that all? For fuck's sake, Helen! It's only another six months. Think of the money, can't you? Not to mention the kudos and experience.'

'I want to go home, Logan,' I told him again, more firmly this time.

'I suppose you're going to be stubborn about this,' he remarked.

'It's not a question of being stubborn. It's my life and it's what I want.'

'But have you any idea how rare it is for them to single one person out? Normally the whole fucking cast goes, but your reviews have been spectacular.'

'I know and I've worked hard and I'm very grateful for having been here and I've learnt so much...'

'I can't believe you, I honestly can't,' he muttered.

'I'm sorry, Logan.'

'What about the money? You're giving up a bloody brilliant salary.'

'You know me well enough to know it's never been my motivator.'

'God knows how long you'll be out of work when you get back here,' he declared.

'That's down to you to get me the auditions.'

'I beg your pardon, you cheeky mare.'

'Sorry, forgive me, please?'

'It's not a question of forgiveness. I'm just so disappointed in you, after all your hard work and all the auditions that you loathe...'

'You do forgive me then?' I insisted.

'Shut up!'

'Say you forgive me.'

I heard him swear under his breath before uttering, 'I forgive you, but you'd better go for every damn thing I send you for when you get home and no moaning about them.'

'I will, I promise, but make them in London, OK?'

'Ah,' he cried, 'there's a bloody man involved here. That makes sense. Bloody men always get in the way. I thought you were different, Helen. I thought you were a feminist!'

'I am, but being a feminist doesn't mean you can't choose what you want to do, and I want to come home. Feminism has given us the choice to live our lives as we want.'

'You're not bloody pregnant, are you?'

I started laughing at his indignant voice. No, I'm most certainly not. Bye then, Logan.

'You call me as soon as you land.'

'I will do.'

'Bye, Helen. And I hope you don't live to regret this decision.'

I won't,' I told him and he put the phone down.

I had said my farewells to the theatre staff. Ben had taken down my number, promising to look me up when he came to London. 'Helen,' he said, 'don't waste your life on Matt, will you?'

'Why would I?'

He shrugged. 'I get the feeling you're very fond of him.'

'I am.'

'But that's not why you're going home? I thought maybe because he wasn't staying you had decided...'

'It's nothing to do with Matt,' I said. 'I care about him, I really do, but he drains me and I don't understand him. I've tried, honestly I've tried, but I can't get my head round his drinking and ruining his health. I know he can't help it, but I know people who have become unwell through no fault of their own and Matt just...doesn't care. He loves the alcohol more than he loves anything or anyone and I just don't get it.'

He nodded slowly. 'I see quite a bit of it here, but Matt is in a league of his own. His addiction controls everything he does. You need someone who will support *you*. Your talent will take you far if you want it to, but Matt couldn't ever be that support. Drinkers just can't support anyone else. It takes all their energy to get through the day.'

'I could cry for him,' I said, giving Ben a tight hug. 'I really could.'

'Your tears would be wasted,' he replied, hugging me back.

I collected my belongings from my dressing room and took a few moments to sit in front of the mirror and look at my face. All I could feel was a deep sense of ease and contentment. I would be back in London, out of work. I wouldn't be stepping out on stage every night under a spotlight and doing what I loved best. I would be returning to a day-to-day life of endless, soul-destroying, energy-sapping auditions. I would be back to worrying about how much money I had to last until the end of the month and having to tell lies to my mum about how hard up I was. I picked up my bag and stepped out into the corridor, closing the dressing room door behind me. I felt such a sense of relief – mixed with a little sadness – because I was going home. My sadness came from knowing I might never get the chance again to hear such applause and the relief sprung from knowing I would soon be with Benedict.

Back at my apartment I quickly packed my suitcase and checked my plane ticket. The doorbell rang and I was relieved to know Matt was actually on time for a change. I opened the door to his unshaven face and birds-nest hair. 'You could have brushed your hair,' I told him exasperatedly.

He had his hands stuffed in his pockets and his shoulders were hunched. 'Why change the habits of a lifetime?'

I'm almost ready. Where are your bags?'

He was twitching and fidgeting and his eyes resembled a cat, unexpectedly caught in headlights. 'Helen, I need to tell you something.'

'What's up?'

'I'm staying.'

'What?'

'I'm staying – just for six months.'

'What, in the show?'

He let out a derisory laugh. 'Don't be daft. They've had enough of me I reckon. No, I'm going to bum about a bit, play in bars ...'

My heart sank. 'Oh God, you're not! It's the worst thing you could do, Matt.'

He shrugged. 'It's what I want to do. No pressure, playing for the love of it, with my mates. It's me, you know?'

'But you're too talented for that,' I insisted.

'But you need *more* than talent to succeed in this business, Helen. You know that. You need grit and strength and clarity of thought. I haven't got any of that, have I? I haven't got your determination or your staying power.' He smiled almost apologetically. 'I haven't got any of your qualities really.'

'Yes you have,' I sighed, 'stop putting yourself down. I haven't got much staying power either, have I? Logan is furious with me.'

'But you'll get something else, I know you will.

'That's not a definite, is it? You never can tell in this business. This could be the pinnacle of my career.' I took hold of his hands. 'Oh Matt, I worry about you. Playing in a bar will probably kill you. If you don't stop drinking it will kill you.'

He shook his head and his eyes were laughing. 'You actresses are so dramatic.'

I felt deflated. 'You're probably right and it is your life, but I'll miss you.'

His face fell. 'But you won't miss me enough,' he said, squeezing my hands and there was silence for a moment until he smiled and ran his fingers down my cheek. 'And I'll miss you more than you can ever imagine. I'd never have come here if it wasn't for you and I wouldn't have stuck it either. What will I do without you?'

'I honestly don't know, but call me, keep in touch and when you come home look me up, won't you?'

He nodded and his eyes swam with sudden tears. 'See you around.'

I flung my arms around him and he hugged me so hard I thought he would break my back. 'Take care of yourself, Matt,' I whispered, 'really, I mean it, take care of yourself.'

'I'll try,' he whispered back, 'and thanks.'

He pulled away from me and just before he closed the door he glanced back. In that one glance I could see the regret in his eyes, on his face and by his posture; regret that he couldn't be the man I wanted him to be and that I didn't love him. The last I saw of him was the back of his head with his hair sticking straight up as if he'd had a shock. I was fearful for him, fearful yet relieved. Being his support system in New York had been a burden and taken its toll on me. It had felt leaden, difficult and I was weary. I thought of Joshua and how, despite his illness, loving him had been effortless. I had wanted to take on his Parkinson's, meet it head on, battle against it and take the heartache of living with it from him. But the difference was that I had loved Joshua blindly. I wasn't in love with Matt and I could not wage war against his drinking. Now I was free to go home and wage war on Parkinson's for Benedict.

Thea arrived dead on four wrapped up in a deep-purple winter coat and a long matching scarf wound round her neck and over her mouth countless times.

'My God, it's cold,' she declared. 'I hope it's warm in here.'

'Very warm,' I assured her. 'Come in, I'll make a pot of tea. What would you like to eat? Crumpets or toasted tea cakes or scones?'

'Toasted tea cakes sound wonderful, thank you.'

'Make yourself comfortable.'

I made the tea and put some tea cakes under the grill. I made a hash of buttering them because of the tremors and took the tray in. My hands felt so numb I couldn't feel very much and the cups rattled in the saucers, but Thea didn't comment on it. She had taken her coat off and was wearing the tight woollen dress again. I hoped her visit would overlap with Sidney's because I couldn't wait to see his face.

'They smell wonderful,' she said, rubbing her hands together in delight.

'They do and they look pretty good too. Here, take two.'

'Thank you. It's so cosy in here with that fire on. It almost looks real, doesn't it? I love open fires, but they aren't practical so that's the next best thing.'

'It reminds me of when I was a child,' I told her, immediately thinking of Bethan.

'The problem with open fires is they heat your legs and not much else,' she laughed.

'Yes, that's true. What did we do before central heating? It's almost dark already out there. What a day.'

'Typical December though.'

'Thea, I need to pick your brains.'

'What brains?'

'Your clinical psychologist brains,' I added.

'OK, that sounds interesting.'

'I had a surprise visit from my sister earlier. It was a surprise, fleeting and emotional visit to say the least.'

She raised her eyebrows. 'I thought you looked a little drained when you opened the door. From the look on your face all was not well.'

'To say it was bizarre is an understatement.'

She leant forward eagerly. 'In what way was it bizarre? Tell me more.'

'Well, I wouldn't tell anyone else this because it's kind of confidential and I don't like repeating...'

'Benedict,' she said, smiling, 'I know you wouldn't, but if it's worrying you and it obviously is, telling a psychologist is different from simply gossiping, so just tell me, OK? I'll be able to help, I'm sure.'

'Yes, of course, I'm sorry.'

'Is it anything to do with Nell?' she asked.

'No, it's nothing to do with Nell. She's on top of the world. No, it's just the things Bethan came out with earlier.'

'Aha, the brittle one who isn't half as tough as she makes out,' Thea remarked.

'Quite.'

'I did sense, when I met her on her recent visit, that all is not well in her life. I have no idea what it is, but it's obviously something emotional.'

'Isn't everything?'

'Very astute, Benedict, but I mean personal, deeply personal.'

'Yes. She's intensely vulnerable at the moment, which isn't like her one bit.'

'To be honest that shone out from her like a beacon.'

I was astonished. 'I'm amazed, Thea. I don't normally see that in her, I never have.'

She laughed at me. 'Well you wouldn't, you're too close to her; but all that behaviour.'

'What behaviour? Explain, please.'

'The brisk way of speaking, the aloof manner, the nervous energy, it's all a front.'

'But she's been like that for so long now I've forgotten she can be any other way.'

'I'm sorry, I've side-tracked you. What did you want to ask me?'

'She says she feels she wasn't as loved by our parents as much as the rest of us were, especially me. She said this morning that she always felt as if she was an afterthought and it simply isn't true.'

She gave me a fond smile. 'It may have been true.'

I was shocked by her reply. 'I assure you it isn't.'

She put down her plate, crossed her long legs and sat back in her chair, making herself comfortable, as if she thought it was going to be a long night convincing me of my parents' failings. 'You can't say what is true for her and what isn't; that's up to her. Having met her, I would imagine that she is extremely bright and complex and truthful and knows her own mind.'

'You could say that.'

'OK, so why don't you believe what she says?'

'It isn't that I don't believe her,' I replied, rather defensively, 'but I was there, in that childhood and believe me she was doted on. My father especially spoilt her. She was constantly on his lap being cuddled and she was quite demanding I can tell you.' I smiled ruefully and added, 'She still is.'

Thea narrowed her eyes. 'What about your mother?'

'She loved her, of course she loved her,' I insisted, knowing I sounded slightly irritated.

'I wonder if she was an accident, a mistake. How much younger is she than you?'

'Five years but ...'

'Perhaps, just perhaps, either your mother or your father wanted to stop at three kids and Bethan was an afterthought. Had you ever thought of that?'

I sighed. 'Even if she had been and I will never know that now, they would never have shown it. Honestly, they were the most loving, doting couple. And they didn't favour any of us.'

She looked thoughtful. 'Well, there will be reason for her feeling as she does. The most complex relationship can be between mother and daughter and I've seen so many people fucked up by poor relationships with their mothers. Excuse my French.'

I gave a small smile. 'I've never heard you use that word before.'

'Fuckity fuck, fuck, fuck!' she cried, laughing loudly. 'There, what do you think of that?'

'You should live with Sidney,' I told her.

Her eyes softened. 'Look, Benedict, it's so hard for people who have great memories of their childhood to know one of their siblings doesn't feel the same – however old you are.'

'Yes and especially if you feel it's unjustified. I feel disloyal to them to even contemplate that it may be true. She was greatly loved, I know she was,' I muttered. 'No, it's just the way her life is panning out that has made her overly critical, I'm sure.'

'Well, something made her as she is. All that bristling and ...'

'She was sobbing today, really sobbing.'

'About your parents?' she asked. 'What brought that on now after all this time? Something must have.'

'She's in love with a younger man, a much younger man.'

Thea's eyebrows shot up. 'No! That is quite bizarre! That it should happen to the both of you. No wonder she came to cry on your shoulder, Benedict. She knew she'd have a sympathetic hearing. Poor Bethan! And I suppose he isn't interested in a post-menopausal woman, even an attractive, intelligent one. Not many men go for older women. Fools!' she remarked. 'We have so much to give.'

'Are you including me in that?'

'Maybe,' she replied. 'Although knowing you as I do now, I reckon if Nell had been any other age you would still have fallen for her. Hang on, why exactly was Bethan sobbing?'

'She was sobbing because she's unhappy, lost her way, that kind of thing. I don't think she ever thought this would happen to her, not now. She likes to be in control and she's totally out of control with this young man. I've never seen her like she was this morning. I've never seen such longing on her face. It was astonishing and it upset me.' I poured some more tea for us both and glanced over at Thea. Talking with her had never seemed so easy or natural. 'Life continues to surprise me.' I smiled, knowing her eagle eyes would have picked up what I was thinking as it crossed my face. 'You just can't ever tell, can you?'

'You really can't,' she replied, smiling back at me. 'And she may eventually find that her intense feeling for this man isn't actually love at all.'

I was surprised by her words. 'But surely she knows what love is at her age.'

'Yes, of course. But there are so many different types of love and so many different layers to it too. I'm not saying she doesn't love him, but it may be fuelled by desire, longing, loneliness, his unavailability because of his age – all of that.'

'Yes, perhaps; in fact *I* wondered that.'

'A need to recapture her youth before it's too late,' she added.

'Yes ...'

'I wouldn't mind betting that if he suddenly showed an interest, they would have a short, intense, lust-driven affair and then it would burn out and she'd go on to find someone more her age and more her type.'

'I hope she does. I want her to be happy, so much.'

'And that would be the more satisfying relationship, one that would last.'

'Who knows?' I said, wondering if she felt the same about me and my love for Nell.

'But this unsettling period, her longing for this young guy, it has probably stirred up all these long-hidden feelings about her past and she needs to work through them because she's been hiding behind them all her life. At least she's shared them with you now.'

'Yes, even if I don't recall any of it as she does.'

'That often happens,' she said.

'It might be real love though, what she feels for this young man.'

Thea laughed. 'You want it to be, don't you? What a romantic fool.'

'Anything else won't last,' I mumbled, my mouth freezing all of a sudden.

'It could just be a love for the moment.'

'I wouldn't want anything like that. Not now at this stage in my life.'

'No,' she replied, 'I know, but back to your sister. Her life has been turned upside down by this sudden, totally unexpected, all-consuming passion for someone she knows she probably hasn't got a realistic chance with. All of that has made her question absolutely everything in her life, especially her past. Nothing seems quite as it was. She's going through all her past relationships with a fine-tooth comb and examining them, including her close family. Honestly, Benedict, I wouldn't mind betting, when she's over this and more settled she will see it all differently.'

I had a sudden and overpowering urge to put my weak, shaking arms around Thea. Her explanations made complete sense and put my mind at rest about my parents' obvious devotion or what Bethan thought of as their lack of it. I had first-hand knowledge of putting your life and your past under close scrutiny. I had spent the last year doing just that.

'You are a rare woman, Thea,' I told her.

She smiled knowingly. 'However...'

I wasn't quite sure what she meant. 'I'm sorry, I don't understand.'

'However...there's always a tone in your voice that indicates a *however* is coming next.'

'Is there?'

'Yes and the *however* means there is something or someone in the way of your feelings for me and her name is Nell.'

'This has nothing to do with Nell. I am immensely grateful to have you as my friend.'

She shrugged. 'But you love Nell.'

We stared at each other. She looked the most lovely I had ever seen her: strong, intelligent, kind and a rare breed of no-nonsense honesty and down-to-earth sensuality.

'Yes, I love Nell. I can't and won't deny that.'

She looked at me fondly. 'What are we to do about you?'

'I'm a hopeless case.'

'You certainly are. But I'm going to stay your friend come what may. At times I've wanted to be more, but I'm well aware that's not possible and if I'm honest ...' She bit her lip and ran her eyes down to my hands. 'I didn't realise that ... I mean, I thought I could take on your illness, but I now know I can't.'

I was quite shocked by her unexpected words. 'What brought you to that conclusion?'

'Do you want the brutal truth?'

'I'll have the truth, but try not to be brutal. I need gentle, not brutal, at this stage in my life.'

'No, you don't deserve brutal. OK, how can I explain it? I was so attracted to you from the first moment I heard you speak. I made quite a play for you and looking back I must have been an absolute pain in the arse.'

'No, you weren't.'

'But you see, I thought I knew what having Parkinson's meant, but that was ludicrous of me. Being with you, seeing it at close quarters, watching you deal with it day to day, hour by hour, the problems associated with it, I realised how little I really understood. I was just being foolish and hard-headed and stubborn. You are such a unique man, Benedict ...'

'I'm really not.'

'Just shut up a minute, will you?' she laughed.

'Sorry.'

'You are a unique man and a unique man needs a unique woman and I'm not she ...'

'Thea ...'

'Hang on, let me finish,' she said, as if she wanted, needed to get something out in the open. 'I hate to admit that, but I'm quite aware of my limitations. You were right; I need a man who can hold me in his arms ...'

'His strong arms ...'

'Yes, his *strong* arms. He won't be like you.'

'Perhaps that's just as well,' I muttered.

'I need someone I can lean on physically as well as mentally. I'm a red-blooded woman and I miss ...'

'I understand.'

'I'm probably making the biggest mistake of my life, Benedict, but I'll let you go to her gladly.'

'Well, that's extremely noble of you,' I chuckled, thinking that the conversation was becoming almost as bizarre as the one I'd had with my sister earlier, 'but the lovely young woman in question I suspect has found a younger, more able-bodied, less disease-ridden model.'

She looked at me in disbelief. 'What?'

'However,' I continued, 'that aside, I hope you meet the man worthy of you, Thea.'

She had been staring at me open-mouthed, but rallied herself to ask softly, 'Nell has someone else?'

'I believe so, although that term can't really be applied to us because we were never together. She was never mine to lose. But you get my drift.'

'Benedict, you must be heartbroken.'

'No, I'm not heartbroken. It's what I want for her, honestly,' I insisted, knowing that she probably wouldn't quite believe me. 'All I want is her happiness. If another man makes her heart sing then my heart will sing too.'

'But you hoped ...'

'I only ever hoped she would be in my life and *stay* in my life.'

'I can't believe you're being so magnanimous about it,' Thea remarked.

'Look at me, how can I be anything else?'

'So,' she said, 'was it all a dream?'

'Was it a dream to have her? Yes, it was just a dream, as seeing my father is.'

'Seeing your father?'

'And the cat that sometimes sits on my piano and sometimes on my bureau.'

'I beg your pardon?'

'And, of course, the shining, see-through, untouchable *presence...*'

'Benedict, are you going mad?'

'I don't doubt it.'

She let out a throaty laugh. 'Sounds like it. I take it it's the medication.'

'Either the medication or the Parkinson's itself. Now my dream is to stay in her life, as her friend, her support system, her guardian angel and hope that the man of her choice will be secure enough to allow that.'

'I can picture you watching her from afar, being Godfather to her kids, that sort of thing.'

'Yes,' I said, my voice falling away, 'that sort of thing sounds wonderful to me.'

'We all have to have dreams, Benedict. I'd quite like to marry again.'

'No! I'm shocked.'

'Well, sometimes I want to and sometimes I don't. I don't actually need a *man*. But, if the right man came along ...'

'One with strong arms,' I added for her.

Her cheerful face fell. 'I'm sorry.'

'Don't be,' I told her. 'You've been a good friend to me this summer and I'll never forget it and thank you for being honest about my Parkinson's. Not many people would have been so honest and I appreciate it.'

'It's my pleasure.'

We smiled at each other and there was an intense, fleeting intimacy that I think surprised both of us. But I then shattered the atmosphere by jerking uncontrollably and my tea sloshed around in its cup and ended up in my lap. It wasn't too hot, but the wet patch down the front of my trousers looked extremely unappealing. Thea was trying not to smile.

'I now look like an old man who has wet himself,' I remarked.

'I knew you'd say that,' she laughed. 'I'll get some kitchen roll.'

She jumped up and fetched a tea towel instead. I took it from her and dabbed at my trousers. 'Thank you. What a disgusting sight.'

'Oh do shut up! Anyone can spill their tea.'

'Not regularly.'

'That jerking looks positively painful.'

'It's not exactly painful, just a strange sensation. I don't mind it now and again, but I'd prefer not to do it in front of an attractive woman.'

'It's just a part of you,' she shrugged.

'Thank you.'

'Benedict, there's something else I want to talk to you about.'

'Talk away, I'm all ears.'

She looked down at her hands and appeared a little on edge. Then she glanced over at me and gave what I can only describe as a nervous smile.

'You know this Salsa class I've joined?'

'Oh my God, you're not going to ask me to go with you, are you?'

'Very funny I must say. No, it's just that ...'

'Go on, don't be shy.'

'It's just that ... I've met this man.'

I tried to hide my surprise, which was wholly unfounded because why wouldn't she meet a man? She was so sexy and bright; I was constantly astonished they weren't all beating a path to her front door.

'Aha,' I cried, 'a man with strong arms.'

Her face flushed a little. 'Well, they seem to be when we are dancing the Salsa together.'

'Is he worthy of you?' I asked.

'I have no idea yet, but he's pretty damned hot!'

We both laughed and I felt a great weight lift from my shoulders, although I had no idea what that weight was. 'I'm glad for you, Thea.'

'Are you, Benedict? Are you really?' she asked, her face a little strained.

'Yes, very. Both you and Nell deserve all the happiness in the world.'

'Thanks, but what about *you*?'

I gave a little careless shrug. 'I'm happy enough. I have Sidney after all.'

'Dear old Sidney. He needs you.'

'We need each other.'

'Well, what a day!' she remarked.

'Yes, you're right there, what a day. I am still reeling from my sister's visit.'

'It's so often the case that those who criticise us the most are secretly doing something similar. Did you know that? It's a part of human nature to be harder on someone when you are guilty of the same thing. So, she let rip at you for falling for a much younger woman, knowing she was doing exactly the same. Interesting, eh?'

'Yes, very interesting and thank you for your insights. It makes me feel less of a fool in her eyes,' I admitted. 'I hope it doesn't end in more tears for her,' I added, more to myself.

She looked doubtful. 'I'm afraid it probably will. But, if she has a fling and enjoys the attention for a while, maybe it will do her the world of good. Intelligent, strong middle aged women have a lot to offer the world. The world just has to wake up to that fact.'

'I couldn't agree more!'

We chattered on as the darkness fell and the freezing fog settled around us. We drank more tea and ate a hastily prepared bowl of pasta together and enjoyed each other's company. She was in no hurry to leave and I was in no hurry for her to leave and we were sitting on the sofa side by side with a glass of wine, looking at a photograph album of when Beth was little when Sidney knocked at dead on seven. I had been relishing her nearness because she felt warm and huggable in the woollen dress and because her sensuality was no threat to me now she wanted another man. I had never felt so close to her, emotionally as well as physically, and for a split second I almost envied the man at her Salsa class with his strong, capable arms. I felt rather sorry for him too as he wouldn't know what had hit him if Thea turned the full weight of her personality and sexual desire his way.

She jumped slightly when Sidney knocked at dead on seven. 'Thea, would you be kind enough to knock back three times, please? My legs are a little stiff.'

'Sure,' she replied, jumping up and doing as I asked.

'Give it thirty seconds.'

'He's a creature of habit then?'

'We both are if truth be told. Come and sit by me again and watch his face as he spots us.'

'Shall we cuddle up, just for his sake?' she asked, her eyes glinting.

'What a wonderful idea,' I replied, enjoying the conspiratorial nature of our conversation.

She sat as close as she could to me and linked her arm through mine in a gesture of intimacy. 'Why haven't we done this before, Benedict? You feel lovely to hug you know.'

'What, with this impossibly thin frame? There is very little to hug. Here he is now.'

Sidney appeared within seconds at the conservatory door with a scarf over his mouth and gloves on. 'Fuck me, it's freezing,' he declared, concentrating on ensuring the door was closed securely.

'You are as eloquent as ever, Sidney. There's a lady present you know.'

'Hello, Sidney,' Thea said huskily, in an overtly sexy way.

He stopped fiddling with the door handle and stared blankly at us with his mouth slightly open. I was so amused by his dumbfounded expression, but asked simply, 'Sidney, why are you wearing a scarf and gloves when you've only walked ten yards?'

'It's so bloody cold, that's why!' He peered over the top of his glasses and began to grin as he took in the homely scene. 'Hello there, nice to see you again.'

'Hello, Sidney, lovely to see you too.'

'What are you grinning at?' I asked him.

'This is all very cosy. Shall I go home again?'

'Don't be ridiculous. Thea has been here hours.'

'Oh yeah...'

'We were just having a cuddle, weren't we, Benedict?' she said, enjoying the fun immensely.

'So I see.'

'Sit down, Sidney and stop grinning like the proverbial Cheshire cat. Would you like a small glass of my best white wine?'

He looked perplexed, as well he might. 'You're offering me alcohol? Are we celebrating something then?'

Thea turned to look at me and we gave each other an intimate, knowing smile. 'You know, I think we are,' she said.

'Oh yeah...'

'Sidney, sit down. Do you want a small glass of wine or not?'

'What do you think, matey?'

'I take it you do.'

'Let your hand jerk a bit when you pour it,' he laughed.

'Cruel, Sidney, cruel.'

'So, what's occurring then?'

Thea smiled. 'We've been chatting and looking at photos of Beth when she was little. That's about it really. It's been lovely in here, warm and cosy.'

Sidney was looking at me with mischief plastered across his face, like a young child plotting something. 'I bet,' he murmured before raising his voice to give us a weather forecast, 'Snow's expected tomorrow morning, so we might have to have a day in annoying each other, matey.'

'How delightful, I'll look forward to it.'

'Well,' Thea said, 'I'm going to let you two play your cards long into the night. I have some phone calls to make.'

Sidney looked a little embarrassed, but only a little as he rarely felt embarrassed about anything very much. 'Don't go on my account, Thea.'

'I'm not,' she assured him. 'I've taken up too much of Benedict's time anyway.'

'You most certainly have not!' I declared, handing Sidney his glass of wine.

'What the fuck is this, the widow's mite? There are only two mouthfuls in here!'

'Sidney! Watch your language!'

'I'm sorry, I won't swear again,' he insisted, pretending to be contrite when in reality he was anything but, 'but really Benedict ... you tight bastard.'

'I'm not being tight; I'm looking after your health – something you don't appear to be doing, so I have to.'

'I don't give a flying fuck!'

'Sidney, will you please stop swearing?'

Thea was laughing fit to bust. 'I'm old enough to swear in front of, don't worry. I'll leave you two to it.'

'I apologise for my friend,' I said.

Sidney grinned. 'We can't all speak like Shakespeare, thank God!'

Thea bent over Sidney and gave him a kiss. 'It's lovely to see you. Enjoy your cards.'

'Bye, love. Sorry to have butted in. I didn't know you were here otherwise I wouldn't have knocked.'

'No problem. I was getting a little too comfortable actually. See you soon.'

'I'll see you to the door, Thea; and Sidney, I know how much is in that bottle so don't even think about it.'

'For fuck's sake,' he muttered.

At my front door Thea put her arms around me. It was an embrace you would reserve for an old friend. 'Thanks for a lovely afternoon. Let's do it again soon.'

'Pop in tomorrow afternoon if you like,' I suggested. 'Sidney will be here getting on my nerves, I have no doubt. You would be a welcome relief. We can all have tea together in the warm and watch the snow falling.'

'You romantic,' she laughed. 'If it will take your mind off Nell and this new guy then I will.'

I took her hand in mine. 'Thank you, Thea.'

She gave me a fond smile and put her coat and scarf on. 'See you tomorrow.'

'Be careful in the fog,' I called as she walked away and she turned and waved before disappearing in the gloom.

'You should have seen your face,' I told Sidney, who was shuffling his playing cards.

'You should have seen yours!'

'I don't know what you mean.'

'You were enjoying every minute of her sitting so near you in that dress with bumps in. We looked very intimate together I must say!'

'Did we now?'

'Now tell me there's nothing going on between you.'

'There's nothing going on between us.'

'Bollocks!'

'She has someone else in her sights.'

'Double bollocks!'

'I'm telling you, Sidney. We were talking about it before you came in. Some man at Salsa, with strong arms.'

He laughed out loud and spluttered, 'with strong what?'

'Strong arms,' I repeated, 'unlike these.'

'Are you jealous?' he asked, peering over his glasses.

'Don't be silly.'

'Are you upset then?'

'Do I look it?'

'So they've both forsaken you.'

'Alas.'

Sidney raised his eyes to the ceiling. 'Why the fucking hell don't you speak like normal people?'

'I don't speak like normal people because I'm *not* normal people.'

His face was suitably expressionless for a moment, but then he beamed at me. 'My God, when she leant over me to kiss me she almost put her chest right in my face. A man could suffocate like that, but what a way to go, eh?'

'Quite!'

'Anyway, speaking of ways to go, how about another drink? I believe the sun is just about over the ...'

'No!'

'You're such a boring old git.'

'The sun isn't anywhere to be seen in this fog.'

'Stop being a clever git and pour me another...'

'Aha, five seconds ago I was a boring git, now I'm a clever git, so which one is it?'

'Both!'

'Coffee, Sidney?'

'Fuck me! Is this what it's going to be like from now on?'

'I'm afraid it is. As I said a little earlier, if you won't look after yourself, I will, with the help of the saintly Sheila.'

'Talking of the wife, she's going out to see the old girl tomorrow afternoon, so I'll be round about three.'

'*My* wife, Sidney; for once in your life don't refer to her as a piece of furniture.'

'Yeah, yeah, whatever you say, matey. Get the kettle on then and I'll deal.'

We drank our coffee, chatted about inconsequential matters and played a few games, which I won, as I normally did.

'You know what?' Sidney said at one point.

'No, Sidney, I don't know what.'

'Neither do I because I've forgotten what I was going to say ...'

'What a relief!'

'Oh no, I remember. What harm can the odd drink do? I don't think the quack knows what he's talking about.'

I rolled my eyes. 'Of course he does. He did about seven years' training and has years of experience, especially in treating idiots like you, so I'd be a little more respectful if I was you.'

'You can talk!' he cried.

'I have done everything my doctor told me to do and more!'

'Huh! That's what you say, but ...'

'You'd do well to tackle your problems with as much respect and diligence as I have mine,' I told him, in my best superior manner.

'Fuck me, Benedict. Good job you've got big ears otherwise your halo would fall right off.'

I laughed. 'That's the second time today someone has accused me of having a halo. I can't help being perfect any more than you can help being an idiot, Sidney.'

'This is true,' he replied. 'If you don't mind me saying, your shakes are quite bad today.'

'Yes, well, that's not going to go away any time soon.'

'Neither is the Ministry of Silly Walks, is it?'

'You're only envious. Not many people can walk like I do.'

'Thank fuck! Oh, and I forgot...procrastination!'

'Radio 4 again?'

We played cards until ten when Sheila gave a resounding knock and Sidney shuffled off for his cocoa. I sat back and put my feet up on the sofa. It had been a long, emotionally draining day and my eyes felt heavy and sore. A couple of times, when playing cards with Sidney, I had jerked and at one point I had thrown my hand on the floor, much to his delight because he had been losing and we had to start the game again. I turned one of the lamps off and sat in the half darkness. The *presence* was somewhere in the room, but I had trouble locating it, so I closed my eyes and tried to doze.

'Benedict.'

My father was standing at the other end of the room by the front window. 'What is it, Papa?' I asked him.

'It's snowing. Shall we roast chestnuts in the fire again? You loved that, all of you.'

'Yes, we did. Papa, why does Bethan think ...?'

'She's a little lost, my boy. We all feel a little lost at some point in our lives. Don't worry, she will find herself again. She needs you, they all need you.'

'Can I really see you or is it my pills?'

'What do you think?'

'Unfortunately, I think it's the pills.'

'The snow will be heavy tonight. Love her – all you need to do is love her.'

'Who must I love?'

'Don't turn her away, Benedict. Whatever you do, don't turn her away.'

'Papa, who are you talking about?'

He had gone and I was staring at the empty space. 'Bloody tablets,' I spat out, my voice slipping away into nothingness, 'bloody tablets and *bastard* disease!'

I crawled up to my bedroom, pulled off my clothes wearily and sank my head into the pillows. The last thing I saw before I closed my eyes was the street light with snowflakes floating by it in flurries.

Chapter 23

I knew immediately it had been snowing all night because of the white light flooding in through the window. It gave everything a slightly bleached look and I snuggled down under my duvet, not in a hurry to go anywhere. There was also the silence, unearthly and almost unnerving because it was so rare and deeply calming. On waking, I often forgot I had Parkinson's. My body was more or less still and at peace with itself. I had no idea whether I shook or trembled in my sleep at all, but my immediate waking moments were relaxed and uneventful.

I closed my eyes again and thought of Nell curling up beside me all those months ago when I had been floored by the flu. I blindly reached out for her hand, but felt only the cool sheet against my fingers. It all seemed so long ago, in another world where I had felt isolated and been struggling to come to terms with the man I would be for the rest of my life. Since then, we had been separated for so many months and living our very different lives. She had been on stage, applauded and adored, a success, surrounded by young, energetic, athletic dancers and good-looking, talented musicians. I had been gritting my teeth, trying to cope with my illness and being more or less my anti-social self. I had grown close to Thea and delighted in her earthy personality, but apart from that, Sidney had continued to be my constant companion and I did not feel the need for anyone else. Dear, kindly, unintentionally funny Sidney, who livened up any dark, miserable winter's day with his sunny chit chat and endless swearing. I decided to give him a treat later on that day and allow him one, very small whisky, for being such a remarkable selfless friend and I smiled to myself imagining his cheerful, rosy face as I placed the glass in his hand. I knew I had promised Sheila to keep him on the wagon, but I also knew that if he had one small one in my company, it would stop him drinking more, on his own, whenever Sheila was out.

For some unknown and unfathomable reason I suddenly felt deliriously happy, even when I moved and instantly felt the tremors coursing through my body. Why I felt like that I had no idea. At odd times, in the previous few days, I had sensed Nell near me and even glanced around in the hope I might just catch a glimpse of her in one of my hallucinations, as I had once before. The feeling didn't make any sense, none of it did, but she was there, almost like the *presence,* shimmering just out of reach.

The snowfall had muffled any traffic noise and consequently I could just hear early-morning bird song outside my window. The life-enhancing twittering of birds had my mind rushing back to childhood when the dawn chorus was so deafening it often woke me. I remembered Bethan had been given a book on English birds by our father and she had studied it religiously as she had all books and could name any by sight. Thinking of her as a toddler sitting on his lap in the garden with her arms tightly around his neck made my eyes swim with tears. She had often pulled on his moustache mercilessly just to keep his attention, but he merely took her hands and kissed them to divert her attention. Her recent sudden, violent outburst about not being as loved as the rest of us made me feel restless with frustration on our father's behalf because I had been a day-to-day witness to his deeply loving and caring nature and his devotion to all of us, including her. We had all been given the very best start in life and now, for whatever reason, Bethan found herself floundering in a sea of unrequited feelings and I could never have imagined that happening to her. But then I was not one to talk.

Coming from that loving, stable home I should have repeated my parents close relationship, but I had made a complete hash of my marriage and most of my emotional life and even now, at sixty-two I was in the grip of an all-consuming love for a woman who merely saw me as her friend. I would have thought Bethan and I were two of the last people to lose our hearts as we had and it left me feeling powerless and reflective about life's bewildering, surprising and unbelievable events.

Reflecting on my sister's emotional roller coaster again made me think of my first meeting with Nell. I had been wallowing in an oasis of self-pity about my diagnosis, alone and full of regrets and obsessive thoughts when I'd stumbled towards the duck pond simply to feel nearer to Beth. The temperature had plummeted and the air had been like ice when I'd brushed the thick powdery snow from the bench and sat down to watch the sleeping ducks. I had always loved the way they tucked their heads in their feathers and on that morning they had been silent and still with the cold. I had had no idea how I was going to live with Parkinson's and its battery of unrelenting symptoms and yet the diagnosis had also come as a relief because I had known something was terribly wrong with me. I had felt justified in being a miserable recluse who had gradually and inexplicably changed from being the life and soul of the party, an incorrigible flirt, a shallow man and a poor excuse for a husband, to someone who had no more libido or social skills than a dead pigeon.

Then onto that stage of my pathetic existence had stepped a beautiful, vibrant and giving young actress who had turned my world upside down and changed the way I viewed my life forever. Nell knew how to live in the moment because she had been traumatised by her partner's sudden death. She knew instinctively that everything could change in an instant, be taken from you, as quickly as clicking your fingers and so when she felt like dancing in the snow, that's exactly what she did. If she had the urge to turn her face to the sky and allow a sudden thunderstorm and torrential rain squall to cover her, then she would. I could merely be a bystander in her show and admire from the wings and I would for the rest of my life.

Those reflective thoughts spurred me into action and I struggled out of bed, stood under the hot shower for a few minutes while my body caught up with my brain, dressed carefully and shuffled downstairs to make some toast and tea.

My garden looked ravishing, covered in a pure white blanket under a pale sun and the branches of the trees were heavy and bent under the weight of the snow. The stillness refreshed and invigorated me, made my heart swell with gratitude for being alive and witnessing nature at its most breathtaking. I sat on the sofa, enjoying every second of the profound silence, sipping my morning tea and relishing each mouthful of the hot buttered toast. Everything I saw, everything I tasted, everything I felt had a kind of newness to it, a clarity and a depth. I had no idea why and I glanced around for the *presence,* but it was strangely absent.

Having finished my breakfast I emailed Beth and asked her when she was next coming home. I then looked in my mobile at where Bethan had inserted her number. I felt an overpowering need to call her and hear her voice. She answered immediately and not knowing my number she put on her very best, articulate and business-like voice.

'Bethan Marshall speaking...'

'Hello, dear sister, it's me.'

'Benedict?'

'Yes and I didn't know you still used your maiden name.'

'When did you get a mobile?' she asked, almost accusingly as if in court questioning the accused.

'I bought it a few months ago. Why are you so surprised?'

'I'm surprised because you're such a dinosaur!'

'Thank you so much.'

'I have always used my maiden name professionally, once a Marshall always a Marshall.'

'I don't know why, but I'm strangely pleased you do.'

'What's wrong?'

'There is absolutely nothing wrong.'

'Are you sure?'

'I'm very sure. I'm just checking on you. How are you feeling now?'

'Just a minute, I'm going out into the corridor.' I heard her heels clicking as she walked and there were other telephones ringing and loud voices. 'Right, that's better; people ear wigging in there.'

I lowered my voice a little, 'Sorry, I didn't think.'

'It's fine.'

'So, how are you?'

'If you mean am I over my funny five minutes, yes I am.' Her voice was brusque and curt. 'I'm very pleased to say.'

'Your funny five minutes being?'

'My outburst,' she whispered. 'It just all built up like a volcano. I'm sorry you had to deal with it.'

'Don't be silly. How are things?'

'Do you mean has the young man in question suddenly realised the error of his ways and flung himself at me?'

'Something like that.'

'No, not yet, but ...' she paused when somebody walked by and said a few words to her, responding quite tersely before returning her attention to me, 'I'm sorry, Benedict, but it's hard to talk here ...'

When she hesitated again I said, 'For God's sake Bethan, I'm hanging on your every word here, don't leave me in suspense!'

'Well, we went to the pub round the corner for a drink and had a long talk ...'

Another pause was too much for me, '*And*?'

'What?"

'I said "*And*?"!'

'Oh, did you? I couldn't hear because you're whispering; Why *are* you whispering when there is nobody listening at your end?' she asked, in her regal, brisk, dry manner.

'I'm not.'

'You're *still* doing it!'

'Sorry,' I said, in what I hoped was my normal voice. 'Don't forget, with this disease, your brain tells the rest of your body to do something and it does, but when it feels like it.'

'Poor brother – OK, we had a long talk and I summoned up all my courage and spilled my guts and told him how I felt and he was terribly flattered, a little embarrassed, although he said he had felt a strong vibe coming from me ...'

'A vibe?' I interrupted. 'What a useless, nonsensical word that is.'

She sighed. 'Do shut up, Benedict, not everyone talks like they've swallowed the Oxford dictionary for breakfast. Anyway, the long and short of it is, he isn't seeing anyone at the moment, I have no idea why because he's so gorgeous and we're going to see how it goes and have a brilliant, torrid affair.'

'You're going to have a torrid affair! How very unsavoury...'

She laughed loudly down the phone. 'Yes, I hope it is.'

'My God, have you the energy for all that?' I asked, wondering why I wasn't in the least bit envious as I would have been a few years earlier.

'We haven't all got Parkinson's you know,' she replied.

'Oh how cruel!' I cried, but she hadn't really offended me and I retorted, 'from anyone else that would have cut me to the quick. But from you ...'

'You expected it. Look, I've got to go.'

I suddenly felt concerned for her. 'Bethan, what if it goes horribly wrong?'

'That's a chance I'm willing to take for him. It was you who said I should be delighted I feel like this. Do you remember?'

'Yes, of course I do and I still think that.'

'Well then.'

'And what about love?' I added.

She gave a hollow laugh. 'What about it?'

'Well, I don't know ... isn't that what you want from him?'

'For now I'll take this. I just want to be near him. If he doesn't ever fall in love with me then so be it, but I'm going to make the most of every second. Look, I must go, I'm due in court.'

'Before you go ... what about Papa?'

She didn't answer for a moment and I was going to press her on the point, but then she sighed heavily. 'I know he loved me. I know mother loved me too, but I suppose it was just me, it was never enough. I'm demanding of everyone I love, very demanding. You know that, Benedict. You've always been the opposite, just like Dad. There, keep your idol, he's intact.'

'Good luck.'

'I need it. And you keep taking those wretched tablets otherwise you'll end up speaking like someone half pissed all the time. Got to go; bye.'

The phone went dead and I pictured her with her pencil skirt, white blouse and high heels making her way to court to fire off her wonderfully clever and sarcastic questions to some poor soul standing in the dock who wouldn't know what had hit them. I thanked God I was loved by her and not her enemy and it occurred to me that the young man of her dreams, if the affair ended badly, might have to remove himself from anywhere near her acid tongue otherwise he would get badly burnt.

While I had been talking to Bethan it had begun to snow again softly and the sky was leaden and slate grey. The flakes were floating gently past the conservatory windows and I found them mesmerising. A robin was perched on the bird table, pecking at the nuts I had placed there days before. His little head bobbed up and down and he continually looked around him, alert and on edge. I remembered seeing the lone robin in my front garden the last time it snowed, when I had first known of Nell's existence and in a flurry of excitement and unusual nervous energy, I stumbled into the hall, hurriedly put on my coat and scarf, checked my keys were in the pocket and purposefully walked out of my front door. Immediately the crisp morning air hit me full in the face and I blanched and held onto my garden fence for dear life. The ground was like a skating rink with clear, pure ice leading all the way up my front path. I laughed at my stupidity because I could hardly keep upright at the best of times and it was fairly obvious I was in danger of ending up flat on my back if I wasn't careful. That thought should have deterred me, but I simply *had* to sit by the duck pond. I wouldn't be able to settle if I didn't see it in all its frozen, silent glory.

Cautiously I stepped out of my garden, holding tightly onto the railings and tried to keep my balance. I chose where I trod very carefully and attempted to avoid the obvious slippery bits on the pavement. I had an idea Sidney might be in his usual place, with his nose firmly against the window pane and I was proved right when he called out to me.

'Benedict ...'

It took all my concentration to turn round without falling backwards and I knew I must have looked ridiculous. 'Did you want something, Sidney?'

He was leaning out of the window. 'Where the fuck are you going in this weather?'

'I need to take a walk, *if* that's OK with you?'

He appeared suitably indignant. 'You'll go bloody flying you silly old fool.'

'Thank you so much for reminding me of what I'm already well aware.'

'What are you on about?'

'I have no idea what I'm on about.'

'Stay there, I'll come with you.'

'You will not! I want some peace to think.'

He pulled a face that was pure Sidney. 'To think about what?' he called.

'Never you mind to think about what.'

'Oh yeah...'

'Sidney!'

He looked worried and I could see he was frowning. 'Be careful then, mate.'

I had to smile at his concern. 'I will, don't worry.'

'Don't fall over, Benedict.'

'I'll try my very best not to.'

'Christ Almighty, you look as if you've been on the sauce all night. You look like a puppet. What's up with your legs?'

'I always walk like this now – it's called Parkinson's.'

'Christ!'

'Quite.'

His head disappeared suddenly as he looked into his living room. 'What was that, love?' Sheila must have said something because when he turned to me again he was smiling sheepishly. 'The wife says I'm to stop pestering you.'

'*My* wife, Sidney,' I called back, still clinging to the railings. 'The wife, the table, the chair ...'

'Yeah, yeah, whatever you say.'

'I don't know why I bother. I'm going for my walk, I'll see you later.'

'Benedict ...'

'What is it now?'

'It's nearly Christmas so I thought I'd hang some pretty lights in the tree there. What do you reckon?'

'Good grief! Why does my heart sink when you start going on about putting lights up?'

He grinned, 'Because every year something goes disastrously wrong?'
'That could be why.'

'So, shall I? I could also put some up in your front window if you like, flashing on and off, what do you think?'

'Sidney, I believe you're winding me up.'

'Cards at about four?' he asked, grinning. I looked up at his face, his dear, vulnerable, caring face. What had Thea said? That we needed each other, Sidney and I? She was right, of course, but I needed him just as much as he needed me, maybe even more so. 'Benedict, did you hear me? Christ, you don't go deaf with Parkinson's as well, do you?'

I started to laugh, 'I can hear perfectly well … unfortunately.'

Sidney was laughing too now and repeated his question, 'I said, do you want to play cards at about four?'

'Sidney, I heard you the first time and I'd love to play cards at four.'

He put his thumb up. 'I'll give you a knock.'

'I'll see you then and as long as I don't go flying I'll get back by four.'

'You are a silly old fool.'

'Takes one to know one, Sidney, see you later.'

&

When I started out I intended to go straight to his house, watch the astonishment on his face as he opened the door, but I found I was making my way towards the duck pond instead. The silence of the snow felt exhilarating after the long, arduous flight and thankfully it seemed to clear my head. I had gone straight to bed and slept soundly despite the difference in time, before surprising my mum by tapping on her front window. We had eaten breakfast together and she had proudly shown me all my reviews that my brother and sister had found on the internet and printed off for her to keep. Reading them instantly transported me back there to the heat and the steam, the deafening applause each night, the smell of stale stage make-up and the constant worry over Matt. Now I was back, in a soft, white and strangely silent London and all I could think of was seeing Benedict again. The snow was dry and like soap flakes and the park deserted except for a couple of gardeners clearing paths and someone walking their two terriers who were sticking their noses in the snow drifts and shaking their heads manically. More snow was falling and by the look of the sky it was going to continue to fall for most of the day. It reminded me of the first time I had seen the lonely, hunched figure sitting on the bench by the duck pond, with one long, slim leg crossed carelessly over the other and a cigarette between his fingers. I made my way past the bandstand. I thought he would be drinking coffee in his conservatory, watching the birds and I just wanted to stand and remember our first meeting for a few minutes before surprising him at home. But when I walked by the bed of heather, normally a mass of soft mauve and pink and now covered in a sparkling blanket of snow, he was there. My heart leapt in my chest and began to pound furiously and I felt as if I had been given a shot of adrenaline.

He was staring at the sleeping ducks with their heads tucked deep in their feathers, his scarf wound tightly round his neck and his hair, against the dark wool of the scarf looked even more silvery and golden. I thought of the first time I had heard him speak and how his remarkable, unique voice had me hooked from the first word he had uttered. As an actress I was mesmerised by distinct voices and it was the first thing I noticed about someone. His had stopped me dead in my tracks. He had turned to glance at me when I shook the stone from my trainer and his face with the square jaw and deep lines of age and experience had matched that voice. While in New York I had missed so desperately his clear, blue, mischievous eyes that always looked directly at you when you spoke and never wavered from that directness, and the missing became a constant ache somewhere inside me that I couldn't shake off.

My first instinct was to rush over and fling my arms around him and feel the tiny tremors under his skin, but I was rooted to the spot, unable to move closer because I doubted his reaction to seeing me after such a long time. How would he feel about my unexpected presence in his life again when in my absence he had grown so close to Thea? She was everything I was not: highly intelligent, intellectual, mature and experienced and she was bursting with sex appeal that simply flowed from her like a gushing waterfall. I had occasionally been told I was pretty by casting agents and often by Joshua, but nobody had ever spoken about me in terms of being sexy and I didn't feel it was part of my nature to flirt or be overtly sexual in any way. But Thea was naturally flirty and had masses of charisma oozing out of every pore. I had no doubt she had overpowered him with all her warm, easy, tactile ways and he would now find me vacuous and immature and dramatic with my often over-animated facial expressions and futile conversation.

I put my hand out to touch his hair, but Thea's face came so strongly into my mind, I pulled back. I pictured them sitting together, their arms entwined and her head resting on his shoulder with her red hair cascading down and across his chest. I imagined them talking about highbrow things like psychology, literature, his plays. He would find his old scripts in a drawer somewhere and show them to her and she would encourage him to write again. And I would look on with envy.

I saw him turn his head slightly as if aware someone was nearby and the movement was stiff and unnatural, but he turned back again almost immediately and fidgeted, kicking one leg out and jerking suddenly. My longing overtook my reticence and I moved forward and rested my hand on his shoulder. He didn't look up or move at all, but I could see he was smiling, as if he had been expecting me. I brushed the snow off the bench and sat down next to him. Neither of us spoke for a few moments and I held my breath, waiting for his first words. His hands were trembling and his legs twitching and some saliva formed in the corner of his mouth which I knew would horrify him, so I quickly delved for a tissue in my pocket and gently wiped it away. We were both now smiling from ear to ear like fools and to me he looked no different from when we parted at the station.

'My God,' he said at last, 'I can't believe you're here. No, this must be one of my hallucinations.'

'No, Mr Marshall, it's not one of your dreams.' I took his cold, white hand and put it to my face. 'I'm quite real I promise.'

'You are real and yet not real because I can't trust my senses any more. The last few days I've felt you near me constantly, but so is the *presence.*'

'But you can't touch the presence, can you?'

'No, I can't touch the *presence*,' he said. 'It haunts me almost constantly but then so do you...'

&

I was aware of someone behind me even though their footsteps were silent. But that silence spoke volumes because the ducks and pigeons didn't scatter, they simply continued to float and peck and go about their business of hunting for scraps of food under the snow or sleeping with their heads tucked down under their feathers. They instinctively knew, as all creatures do, that this was a gentle person approaching; someone who would do them no harm. I went to turn, but my neck was stuck and painful, so I changed my mind and gazed at the beauty of the clear, frozen water and the reflection of the branches hanging low over the pond with inches of snow weighing them down. Without seeing her I knew it was Nell. I will never be able to explain how I knew it was her when I believed she was staying in New York; it was just a magical, intense emotion of knowing I was not alone any more.

I felt her touch my shoulder, but even before that light touch I had begun smiling. She brushed the snow from beside me and sat down. To see her face at such close quarters, the dazzling smile, the laughing grey eyes, the beautiful bone structure, made me feel more alive in that moment than at any time in the last few months. We took each other in for a few moments, grinning like fools without speaking. I couldn't have spoken anyway because my thoughts were racing. What must I look like to her? Had I aged in her eyes? Did my symptoms appear worse? Did I look old and careworn to her after being with so many vibrant and talented young men with muscles bulging out in all directions? Had she changed in any way? She must have; travel changes everyone. Success and adulation must have altered her because they were teasing and addictive and perhaps that adulation would mean we were two very different people now. I was certainly different: shakier, less flexible and walking like a man without a skeleton to support him. She was even lovelier than I remembered. I went to speak, but no sound came out and I felt the saliva begin to run out of the corner of my mouth. She put her hand in her pocket, produced a tissue and reached over and wiped it away. I thought I would cringe with embarrassment, but for some unearthly reason it did not matter to me one jot.

'My God,' I said, my mouth forming the words at last, 'I can't believe you're here. No, this must be one of my hallucinations.'

'No, Mr Marshall, it's not one of your dreams.' She took my trembling hand and put it to her chilled face. 'I'm quite real I promise.'

'You are real and yet not real. I can't trust my senses any more. I'm constantly seeing and hearing things that aren't really there. The last few days I've felt you near me constantly, but so is the *presence*.'

'You can't touch the presence, can you?'

'No, I can't touch the *presence*, it haunts me almost constantly. But then so do you ...'

She looked surprised. 'Why do I haunt you?'

I couldn't answer her question because my mind was racing in so many different directions. 'You're home then, Nell.' That was all I could manage, my voice was slurring with emotion. 'I can't believe it.'

'Yes, I'm home.'

'Sorry to state the obvious, but you said you were staying much longer. *Only* you ...'

'No,' she corrected me, 'I said they had *asked* me to stay longer.'

'You and only you,' I added. She nodded shyly and I asked tentatively, 'How long are you home for?'

She gave a little laugh. 'For good, you silly arse.'

'Say that again.'

'For ... good!' she repeated slowly. 'Did you get that?'

I gave a single nod, 'Promise?'

'I promise.'

'I can't believe you're here.'

'Well, I am.'

I scanned her whole face. 'Nell, it's so wonderful to see you. Skype is all very well, but it isn't like being near the real person.'

She frowned slightly. 'Are you sure? Are you sure it's wonderful to see me?'

I was astonished and there was a moment of awkwardness between us that concerned me. 'How could you doubt it?' She looked down at her hands, then back at me and I urged, 'Tell me.'

She shrugged and I thought she was going to mention Matt and her exciting life in New York and how she imagined us being close friends for the rest of our lives, but that she had grown so fond of him and his wayward, manic, lovable ways. Her eyes grew large and tearful.

'Your friend, Thea,' she whispered, saying her name in a hushed, almost fearful way.

I was completely bemused. 'Thea? Dear God, did I really give you cause to think ...'

'I know you've grown close to her and I'm really happy for you because she's bright and classy and ...'

'Yes, she's a lovely person and I've grown extremely fond of her, but ...'

She put her hand on mine. 'Do you love her, Mr Marshall?' My mouth misbehaved so badly I couldn't form my lips round any articulate words, so I said nothing. Tears flooded her eyes. 'You love her, don't you?'

'I do, as you would a dear friend, but it's not *real* love, Nell.'

Her hands flew to her mouth. 'I really thought ...'

I was bewildered. 'What did you think?'

'You are *so* suited.'

I laughed. 'Are we? In what way are we suited?'

'Similar age and ...'

I started to tease her now, knowing what she meant, 'I'm actually quite a bit older than her, but what do you mean, *and*?'

'Class,' she muttered.

'What class am I then? What class is she? That's all irrelevant to me, as is age and looks. All I care about, all I want is to love someone who loves me.'

She looked into my eyes for some kind of truth. 'But she loves you, surely.'

'In her way, but she doesn't love my Parkinson's.'

'Does that hurt?' she asked, her face a picture of concern.

'Not one bit. Nell, Thea needs, wants, a strong, fit man who has all his bits in working order. But enough of all that. How are you, dear girl?'

She beamed at me, her full-on and headlight beam. 'I'm happy now.'

'But weren't you happy in New York?'

'I wasn't unhappy.'

'That's not the same thing. I have to say, you weren't sparkling on Skype like I imagined you would. You were a success though.'

'Yes.'

'I knew you would be. I'm so proud.'

'Thank you, Mr Marshall. That means the world to me.'

'Will it lead to other parts?'

'Let's hope it does.' She leant forward and carefully wiped some snowflakes from my hair. 'Yes, I know it will. My agent already has some auditions lined up for me – in London I hasten to add.'

'But why weren't you happy? It was what you had always wanted, your dream.'

She gave a small, shy smile. '*You* weren't there.'

'Nell, you flatter me.'

'It's so good to see you, in the flesh as it were.'

'And it's good to see you, in the flesh as it were.'

Her eyes homed in on my shaking legs. 'Are the pills working?'

'Yes, they are. I've had them tweaked a bit and they may need tweaking again apparently, but on the whole I can't complain.' Again we simply stared at each other and again I wondered whether I had aged in her eyes. 'So, how are things with you and Matt?'

She looked perplexed. 'I don't know ... we parted on good terms, I think. That's what I was going to say on Skype when we lost the connection. And the secret I mentioned, well, it was still a secret that I'd decided to leave the show.'

As she was speaking all I could think about was Matt. 'You parted on good terms?'

'Yeah, he's staying in New York for a while. He just wants to bum about, play in bars, that kind of stuff. Hideous waste of his talent, but he's hopeless with pressure and stress and can't be reliable. It makes him turn to drink, so what's the point? It's *his* life.'

'But why on earth would he stay there when you are here?'

She gave a blast of her wondrous laugh. 'Oh I reckon he's had enough of me nagging him to be someone he isn't. I can't take on his problems. I don't love him, so why would I?'

'You don't love him?'

She shook her head. 'I'd have to be some kind of masochist to love a man like Matt.'

'But sometimes it just happens whether we want it to or not,' I remarked.

'That's true, but he couldn't ever love the pilgrim soul in me. He wouldn't even know it exists.' She crept closer to me and rested her head on my shoulder. The nearness of her made me catch my breath and her hair smelt of summer roses. 'I don't ever want to go away from you again.'

I had to swallow hard before I answered. 'I won't ask you to.'

Her face was turned away from me and she took a deep breath, as if summoning up courage. 'You do know I love you, don't you?'

My heart was thumping hard in my chest and I felt breathless. I slurred, but I paused to regain control of myself and tried again, desperate to speak clearly. 'You love me, Nell? Do you? Do you really? What kind of love?'

She sat up and looked into my eyes. 'It's *real* love, Mr Marshall. Didn't you suspect?'

'No, I dared not.'

'Why?'

I loved her most then. The dark spectre of my Parkinson's didn't even enter her mind. 'My *disease*,' I stuttered.

She took my hand and gazed at the tremors lovingly. 'But I want to look after you.'

I withdrew my hand in fear. Fear for her and her future. The idea of her being my carer appalled me. 'I won't let you, Nell.'

Her face fell and she looked bewildered. 'Why won't you let me? I thought perhaps you loved me. Don't you love me then?'

'It's because I love you.'

She smiled and looked determined. 'It's not your decision to make. Parkinson's is a part of you and it's a part I love, the same as any other part.'

'But, Nell ...I...' My mouth stuck and my facial muscles felt rigid with the cold. 'There are very good reasons, sensible reasons for me wanting to spare you the job of caring for me. You are young, energetic ...'

'I don't care!'

I felt I was floundering in the face of her devotion. 'No, listen ... you *should* care!'

'I don't give a toss about all that stuff, you being older and infirm as you call it. It's *you* I love, the very essence of you. The Parkinson's is all about the outer shell.'

'But you don't understand,' I insisted. 'It may diminish me.'

'It will *never* diminish you. I do understand what's involved, of course I do.'

'Do you? Do you really? There are so many barriers to cross...'

'Love knows no barriers. Don't forget I've done it before with Joshua.'

'That's my point exactly!' I declared. 'Look, Nell ... there would be no ... I have no ...' I couldn't finish my sentence for fear of slurring and dribbling. 'There will be no ...'

She put her fingers to my cheek. 'I don't mind.'

'Nell, you *should* mind.'

Her eyes became playful suddenly. 'You could always hang it out the window and pray for a frost.'

I had to laugh at her wonderful sayings. 'Say that again.'

She looked defiant. 'I'm trying to make you see I don't care. I've thought about all of this and I won't change my mind, Mr Marshall.'

I thought I must be in one of my dreams. 'You mean you really find this ageing, shaking body attractive?'

She shook her head as if I was a hopeless case who understood very little about anything much. 'It's not the body; it's the *man* I love. I love and care about the man who loves the pilgrim soul in me. I want to sit in the mornings with a man I can talk to, who looks in my eyes and finds me fascinating. I want to sit in the evenings with someone who makes me laugh out loud. On a long, winter afternoon I want to be with a man I find endlessly interesting and amusing. Through your eyes I feel I can conquer the world. We are right, you and I. We are just *right*.'

I was dumbfounded. 'Nell, I don't know what to say to you. This is all so unexpected. In my wildest dreams I never ... I had made up my mind I would be your friend for life and adore you from afar while you chose someone ... But, you can't ... I won't let you ...'

Tears streamed out of her eyes. 'Don't turn me down because of some misguided honour on your part. It isn't honourable to walk away from the woman who loves you because you think she should be leading a life she doesn't want or need. She wants *you* – she needs *you*.'

'Nell, you need to ask yourself so many questions.'

'Do you love me, Mr Marshall? That's the only question I need to ask.'

'How can you doubt it?'

'And do you believe I love you?' she asked, wiping her eyes.

'I can hardly believe it ...'

'Believe it,' she urged.

It was my turn to let tears stream down my face. 'I don't want you to end up as my carer. I'd rather die. You were born for greater things. You need to fly.'

'I *can* do great things and I *can* fly if I have you by my side,' she cried and then her expression changed from one of defiance to one of amusement. 'And anyway, who says I'll be doing things for you? I'll make you do it yourself and when you lapse into feeling sorry for yourself, I won't let you!'

She looked so determined, so strident, so strong, so sure. I raised my eyebrows. 'I see, it's like that, is it?'

'I'm afraid it is,' she declared.

'You've made up your mind then.'

She crossed her arms. 'I have.'

'I see.'

Then she grabbed both my hands. 'It isn't about me caring for you; it's about us caring for each other.'

I felt my whole body relax in an instant. 'I could handle that.'

She gave me one of her brilliant, life-affirming smiles. 'So, you'll have me?'

I stuck my nose in the air. 'I might.'

She let out a blast of her laugh and flung her arms around my thin frame in a tight embrace. I clung to her with all the strength my shaking muscles could muster.

'I'm so lucky to have met you,' she told me, putting her hands either side of my face.

'Ditto, Nell.'

'I can feel you shaking.'

'That's not my *disease*.'

'Don't call it that any more. Call it by its proper name. Confront it, admit you have it, embrace it, it's a part of you I love.'

'Then if you love it, I will too,' I told her.

'Kiss me, Mr Marshall.'

I kissed her gently and I imagined a thousand stars exploding over our heads in celebration, but in reality there were snowflakes floating around us. This was what I had longed for from the first moment I heard her speak. I would take my Parkinson's now as part of the life that had her loving me and I would take it gladly.

'You'll have to tell Beth,' she said, looking concerned.

'You leave Beth to me.'

'And your sister...'

'She will understand.'

She kissed my trembling hands. 'Let's take a walk. You look freezing.'

We joined hands and she helped me to my feet. Life could throw what it liked at me now. I had Nell to help me fight every battle and Nell to stand bravely between me and the relentless symptoms like a beautiful warrior. She put her arm through mine and we made our way slowly up the path past the frozen heather garden, away from the duck pond towards my house. She looked up at me, smiling cheekily.

'Have you got any cake at home?'

'As a matter of fact I have.'

'What type of cake?'

'Oh it matters does it?'

'Of course it does.'

'Banana cake, I believe.'

'I'll have two pieces, please.'

'Will you indeed?'

'Have you been practising your dancing?'

'I have,' I replied. 'I'll show you later if you play your cards right.' She threw her head back and laughed again and I felt that laughter shoot directly into my veins and restore me. 'Nell, your laughter will heal me.'

'Well, that's my long term plan,' she said and squeezing my arm she added, 'as we're now in December, can we put up some Christmas lights in your conservatory? We can make it look like a fairy grotto. Your house was born to have lights twinkling in the windows.'

'Have you been plotting with Sidney?'

'And can my family come on Christmas day? Ever since I was little I've imagined having Christmas in that house. And we could have your family and Sidney and Sheila and Thea ...'

'You might see Sidney and Thea earlier than that,' I said. 'Invite who you like,' I added, happiness surging through me at such a rate I stumbled slightly, 'and I'll cook for them all in a silly hat and pinafore and happily make an utter fool of myself.'

She held my arm tightly, giving me her support and looked up at me. 'You really do love me then?'

I bent down and kissed the top of her head. 'I have to say I do.'

She stopped suddenly and faced me. Her grey eyes were dancing with excitement and snowflakes were falling on her head. She had never looked so lovely. 'Is it *real* love, Mr Marshall?' she asked, confident about the answer.

I touched her face with my white, trembling fingers and I hoped that my mouth would behave for the most important declaration of my life. 'It is, Nell. I seem to have been waiting for you all my life and I have to tell you, it was worth the wait. Ask me if I'd rather have Parkinson's and you or not have it and forfeit having this.'

'I know the answer.'

'I'd live my whole life again with all its sorrows and absurdities because it led to meeting and loving you.'

'Nobody talks like you,' she remarked.

'Thank God for that!'

'You have snowflakes splattered against your glasses,' she laughed, wiping them away. I bent down to kiss her face and it seemed easy, natural, destiny. The *presence* hovered just behind her, but it couldn't haunt me now. Nell was standing between its ghostly form and myself like Boadicea in all her wild glory. 'You know,' she said, looking up at me, 'one day, very soon, they'll find a cure and when they do you'll be restored to the man you were.'

'I'll take a cure willingly,' I replied, hugging her close, 'but I want to stay the man I am now.'

'What shall we talk about when we get back?' she asked, like a playful child.

'How about how I got to be so devastatingly attractive?'

'Shut your face you!'

'Delightful.'

She squeezed my hand gently and we walked towards my house together. 'Lean on me...'

'I will, thank you, Nell.'

'Let's go home, Mr Marshall.'

'Say that again.'

'Benedict, let's go home.'

Something to my right caught my eye. It was a cat, sitting in the snow, elegant and completely still, staring at us with huge, bright eyes and long, messy hair. It then turned and walked away slowly towards the cafe. I watched it until it disappeared. Nell was holding my arm firmly, knowing I needed her support.

'I love that guy's hat,' she was saying as I was pondering on the young, brilliant musician who would no doubt squander his talent and would later regret doing just that.

'Yes,' I replied absentmindedly, looking over to where she had pointed.

It was my father standing by the bandstand, the trilby hat he always wore in winter pulled low over his forehead in that distinguished way my mother had loved. I could just see his unforgettable face and he was smiling.

'I have her,' I whispered and I watched as my words floated towards him through the falling snow. 'Now at last I'm happy, like you were.'

'I'm so pleased for you, my boy,' he said. 'I told you she would come back to you, Benedict.'

'And I am healed, Papa. Now I have her, I am healed.'

He raised his hat slowly. 'Yes, my boy, you are.'